THE WARE TETRALOGY

OTHER BOOKS BY RUDY RUCKER

Novels
Hylozoic
Postsingular
Mathematicians in Love
Frek and the Elixir
Spaceland
As Above, So Below: A Novel of Peter Bruegel
Realware
Saucer Wisdom
Freeware
The Hacker and the Ants
The Hollow Earth
Wetware
The Secret of Life
Master of Space and Time
The Sex Sphere
Software
White Light
Spacetime Donuts

Non-fiction
The Lifebox, the Seashell, and the Soul
Software Engineering and Computer Games
All The Visions
Mind Tools
The Fourth Dimension
Infinity and the Mind
Geometry, Relativity and the Fourth Dimension

Collections
Mad Professor
Gnarl!
Seek!
Transreal!
The Fifty-Seventh Franz Kafka

THE WARE TETRALOGY

RUDY RUCKER

PRIME BOOKS

THE WARE TETRALOGY

Prime Books
www.prime-books.com

ISBN: 978-1-60701-211-5

TABLE OF CONTENTS

Family Trees for the Ware Tetralogy

Cobb Anderson (1950) + Verena Klenck (1954)
|
Ilse Anderson (1975) + Colin Taze (1977) ·········· Jason Taze (1972) + Amy Hoylman (1977)
| |
Willy Taze (2004) + Sue Tucker (2001)   Della Taze (2002) + Berenice (2028)
| |
Randy Karl Tucker (2032)   Manchile (2031) + Cisco Lewis (2004)
|
Buford "Bubba" Cisco Anderson (2031)

Stan Mooney, Sr. (1960) + Bea Army (1961)
|
Stahn "Sta-Hi" Mooney (1995) + Wendy Weston (2000)

Saint Mooney (2031) ·········· Babs Mooney (2033)

Darla Starr (2004) + Whitey Mydol (2000) + Emul (2028) + Berenice (2028)

Yoke Starr (2031) ·········· Joke Starr (2031)

Dom Stagnaro (1998) + Alice Drift (2000)

Tre Dietz (2027) + Terri Stagnaro (2026) ·········· Ike Stagnaro (2028)

Dolf Dietz (2049) ·········· Wren Dietz (2052)

Berdoo Scragg (1994) + Rainbow Plenty (1999) ·········· Tempest Plenty (1994)
|
Starshine Plenty (2021) + Duck Tapin (2016)

Everooze (2042) + Andrea (2043)

Ouish (2050 + Xanana (2049) ·········· Monique (2952) + Xlotl (2052)

Kurt Gottner (2000) + Eve Gottner (2001)

Phil Gottner (2030) ·········· Jane Gottner (2032)

SUI GENERIS: A TESTIMONY
by WILLIAM GIBSON

Genuinely sui generis novelists operate at an inherent disadvantage, and all the more so in any so-called genre.

Genre is that dubious bargain whereby the reader is offered (for our present purposes) a novel, a form whose very name promises a new experience, but offers, in genre, the implicit and crucial promise of the repetition of previous pleasures.

Rudy Rucker has never trafficked in that repetition, and while he unabashedly loves the genre in which he tends to be marketed, he transcends it, or perhaps engulfs it, in his singularity. You'll see this said about all too many science fiction writers, given novelty's supposed (and largely spurious, in my view) importance to the genre, but of Rudy it's quite literally true. He is one splendidly odd duck, balanced between pure mathematics on the one hand and spontaneous bop prosody on the other, while uncounted further hands (or paws, in some cases) flicker in from their individual Hilbert spaces, bearing cups, wands, alien sex toys, artifacts out of Roadrunner cartoons, terrible jokes, gleefully fell dooms, and lubricating dabs of mentholated ichor.

Scarily bright, and a card-carrying Holy Fool who's managed to fall off every cliff but the only really wrong ones, he used to frighten me.

In part, no doubt, because he's the only higher mathematician I've ever known, while I am myself virtually an innumerate. I knew from the very start of our acquaintance (from before, actually, as I read him before I met him) that he habitually, effortlessly, visited realms I was literally incapable of envisioning, let alone visiting. He also frightened me because, though generally convivial, he seemed to me to teeter atop an angelic pinhead of purest Random, causing me the constant apprehension that he might at any second do or say literally anything at all. As I was secretly attempting to negotiate my own life and literary career with the emergency brake on, this made me complexly uneasy. He seemed starry-eyed with the sheer joy of forgetting the brakes entirely.

I found him unsettling in another way as well, though that was not so much about him as about something we had in common. Being at least a decade older than the rest of our cyberpunk cohort, we were both veterans of (ahem) "the Sixties." Which was to say that we had once been somewhere very strange and new indeed, but that that tide had somehow receded, leaving us in some new but actually markedly unstrange iteration of a world we had once expected to change utterly. Whenever I ran into Rudy, over the first decade or so of my career, I worried that we were both actually too old for this. But then I'd note the shiver of angelic pinhead-wobble, and in some paradoxical way be comforted thereby. ("And at the time," Rudy wrote to me recently, "I thought we were jaded roués!")

⌇

Before I read or met Rudy, I'd lived for several seasons in Washington, D.C., with a roommate who at some point went up to New York to see a great retrospective show of the Surrealists, kindly and hugely formatively bringing me the show's catalog as a gift. I had heard of Surrealism, but had never really put together what it was. That catalog became a sort of Rosetta Stone for me, a way of decoding and assembling a great many very diverse things that I had encountered in art and literature, things I had known were similar, in some way, but without really understanding how.

The capital-s Surrealism, Surrealism™, was splendid stuff, but I now recognized a similar but lower-case impulse in virtually everything that had ever attracted me in the popular arts. I saw it in *Mad Magazine* (and particularly in its imitators), in Forrest J. Ackerman's gloriously cheesy *Famous Monsters of Filmland*, in Rod Serling's *The Twilight Zone*, in *Zap Comix*. And I saw it, of course, in the prose science fiction I had grown up with: a folk surrealism, a street surrealism, entirely free of Breton's faux-papal excommunications and other tedious hi-jinx. It was, I saw, to certain forms of popular art, and most particularly to the flavors of science fiction that had worked best for me, the equivalent of the ethanol molecules in an alcoholic beverage. So I filed that one away, and went about my business, such as it was.

Later, encountering first the fiction and then its author, I took it instantly for granted that in Rudy Rucker I found an exemplar of that very thing, a natural-born American street surrealist, bordering at times on a practitioner of Art Brute.

Rudy's fiction has a much higher percentage of surrealism molecules than most fiction, science or otherwise. It has, as moonshiners say when they swirl whiskey in a glass, in order to closely observe how it settles back down the sides of the glass, "good legs." Rudy's fiction is probably a bit too strong, in that regard, for some readers, but even the hard stuff, let me assure you, is an enjoyably acquired taste.

And I'm no longer afraid of Rudy. We're both (even) older, and vibrate now at more authentically geezeroid frequencies. And I no longer feel that the world outside the window isn't as freaky as the ones we glimpsed back in the Sixties. It is. With bells on.

Now go and read Rudy Rucker, in the 21st century. Dude's sui generis. And has good legs.

—17 December 2008, Vancouver

SOFTWARE

For Al Humboldt, Embry Rucker, and Dennis Poague.

CHAPTER ONE

Cobb Anderson would have held out longer, but you don't see dolphins every day. There were twenty of them, fifty, rolling in the little gray waves, wicketting up out of the water. It was good to see them. Cobb took it for a sign and went out for his evening sherry an hour early.

The screen door slapped shut behind him and he stood uncertainly for a moment, dazed by the late afternoon sun. Annie Cushing watched him from her window in the cottage next door. Beatles music drifted out past her.

"You forgot your hat," she advised. He was still a good-looking man, barrel-chested and bearded like Santa Claus. She wouldn't have minded getting it on with him, if he weren't so . . .

"Look at the dolphins, Annie. I don't need a hat. Look how happy they are. I don't need a hat and I don't need a wife." He started toward the asphalt road, walking stiffly across the crushed white shells.

Annie went back to brushing her hair. She wore it white and long, and she kept it thick with hormone spray. She was sixty and not too brittle to hug. She wondered idly if Cobb would take her to the Golden Prom next Friday.

The long last chord of "Day in the Life" hung in the air. Annie couldn't have said which song she had just heard—after fifty years her responses to the music were all but extinguished—but she walked across the room to turn the stack of records over. *If only something would happen*, she thought for the thousandth time. *I get so tired of being me.*

At the Superette, Cobb selected a chilled quart of cheap sherry and a damp paper bag of boiled peanuts. And he wanted something to look at.

The Superette magazine selection was nothing compared to what you could get over in Cocoa. Cobb settled finally for a love-ad newspaper called *Kiss and Tell*. It was always good and weird . . . most of the advertisers were seventy-year-old hippies like himself. He folded the first-page picture under so that only the headline showed. PLEASE PHEEZE ME.

Funny how long you can laugh at the same jokes, Cobb thought, waiting to pay. Sex seemed odder all the time. He noticed the man in front of him, wearing a light-blue hat blocked from plastic mesh.

If Cobb concentrated on the hat he saw an irregular blue cylinder. But if he let himself look through the holes in the mesh he could see the meek curve of the bald head underneath. Skinny neck and a light-bulb head, clawing in his change. A friend.

"Hey, Farker."

Farker finished rounding up his nickels, then turned his body around. He spotted the bottle.

"Happy Hour came early today." A note of remonstrance. Farker worried about Cobb.

"It's Friday. Pheeze me tight." Cobb handed Farker the paper.

"Seven eighty-five," the cashier said to Cobb. Her white hair was curled and hennaed. She had a deep tan. Her flesh had a pleasingly used and oily look to it.

Cobb was surprised. He'd already counted money into his hand. "I make it six fifty." Numbers began sliding around in his head.

"I meant my box number," the cashier said with a toss of her head. "In the *Kiss and Tell*." She smiled coyly and took Cobb's money. She was proud of her ad this month. She'd gone to a studio for the picture.

Farker handed the paper back to Cobb outside. "I can't look at this, Cobb. I'm still a happily married man, God help me."

"You want a peanut?"

"Thanks." Farker extracted a soggy shell from the little bag. There was no way his spotted and trembling old hands could have peeled the nut, so he popped it whole into his mouth. After a minute he spit the hull out.

They walked towards the beach, eating pasty peanuts. They wore no shirts, only shorts and sandals. The afternoon sun beat pleasantly on their backs. A silent Mr. Frostee truck cruised past.

Cobb cracked the screw-top on his dark-brown bottle and took a tentative first sip. He wished he could remember the box number the cashier had just told him. Numbers wouldn't stay still for him anymore. It was hard to believe he'd ever been a cybernetician. His memory ranged back to his first robots and how they'd learned to bop . . .

"Food drop's late again," Farker was saying. "And I hear there's a new murder cult up in Daytona. They're called the Little Kidders." He wondered if Cobb could hear him. Cobb was just standing there with empty colorless eyes, a yellow stain of sherry on the dense white hair around his lips.

"Food drop," Cobb said, suddenly coming back. He had a way of re-entering a conversation by confidently booming out the last phrase which had registered. "I've still got a good supply."

"But be sure to eat some of the new food when it comes," Farker cautioned. "For the vaccines. I'll tell Annie to remind you."

"Why is everybody so interested in staying alive? I left my wife and came down here to drink and die in peace. She can't wait for me to kick off. So why . . . " Cobb's voice caught. The fact of the matter was that he was terrified of death. He took a quick, medicinal slug of sherry.

"If you were peaceful, you wouldn't drink so much," Farker said mildly. "Drinking is the sign of an unresolved conflict."

"*No kidding,*" Cobb said heavily. In the golden warmth of the sun, the sherry had taken quick effect. "Here's an unresolved conflict for you." He ran a fingernail down the vertical white scar on his furry chest. "I don't have the money for another second-hand heart. In a year or two this cheapie's going to poop out on me."

Farker grimaced. "So? *Use* your two years."

Cobb ran his finger back up the scar, as if zipping it up. "I've seen what it's like, Farker. I've had a taste of it. It's the worst thing there is." He shuddered at the dark memory . . . teeth, ragged clouds . . . and fell silent.

Farker glanced at his watch. Time to get going or Cynthia would . . .

"You know what Jimi Hendrix said?" Cobb asked. Recalling the quote brought the old resonance back into his voice. "When it's my time to die, I'm going to be the one doing it. So as long as I'm alive, you let me live my way."

Farker shook his head. "Face it, Cobb, if you drank less you'd get a lot more out of life." He raised his hand to cut off his friend's reply. "But I've got to get home. Bye bye."

"Bye."

Cobb walked to the end of the asphalt and over a low dune to the edge of the beach. No one was there today, and he sat down under his favorite palm tree.

The breeze had picked up a little. Warmed by the sand, it lapped at Cobb's face, buried under white whiskers. The dolphins were gone.

He sipped sparingly at his sherry and let the memories play. There were only two thoughts to be avoided: death and his abandoned wife Verena. The sherry kept them away.

The sun was going down behind him when he saw the stranger. Barrel-chest, erect posture, strong arms and legs covered with curly hair, a round white beard. Like Santa Claus, or like Ernest Hemingway the year he shot himself.

"Hello, Cobb," the man said. He wore sungoggles and looked amused. His shorts and sportshirt glittered.

"Care for a drink?" Cobb gestured at the half-empty bottle. He wondered who, if anyone, he was talking to.

"No thanks," the stranger said, sitting down. "It doesn't do anything for me."

Cobb stared at the man. Something about him . . .

"You're wondering who I am," the stranger said, smiling. "I'm you."

"You who?"

"You me." The stranger used Cobb's own tight little smile on him. "I'm a mechanical copy of your body."

The face seemed right and there was even the scar from the heart transplant. The only difference between them was how alert and healthy the copy looked. Call him Cobb Anderson$_2$. Cobb$_2$ didn't drink. Cobb envied him. He hadn't had a completely sober day since he had the operation and left his wife.

"How did you get here?"

The robot waved a hand palm up. Cobb liked the way the gesture looked on someone else. "I can't tell you," the machine said. "You know how most people feel about us."

Cobb chuckled his agreement. He should know. At first the public had been delighted that Cobb's moon-robots had evolved into intelligent boppers. That had been before Ralph Numbers had led the 2001 revolt. After the revolt, Cobb had been tried for treason. He focused back on the present.

"If you're a bopper, then how can you be . . . here?" Cobb waved his hand in a vague circle, taking in the hot sand and the setting sun. "It's too hot. All the boppers I know of are based on supercooled circuits. Do you have a refrigeration unit hidden in your stomach?"

Anderson$_2$ made another familiar hand-gesture. "I'm not going to tell you yet, Cobb. Later you'll find out. Just take this . . . " The robot fumbled in its pocket and brought out a wad of bills. "Twenty-five grand. We want you to get the flight to Disky tomorrow. Ralph Numbers will be your contact up there. He'll meet you at the Anderson room in the museum."

Cobb's heart leapt at the thought of seeing Ralph Numbers again. Ralph, his first and finest model, the one who had set all the others free. But . . .

"I can't get a visa," Cob said. "You know that. I'm not allowed to leave the Gimmie territory."

"Let *us* worry about that," the robot said urgently. "There'll be someone to help you through the formalities. We're working on it right now. And I'll stand in for you while you're gone. No one'll be the wiser."

The intensity of his double's tone made Cobb suspicious. He took a drink of sherry and tried to look shrewd. "What's the point of all this? Why should I want to go to the Moon in the first place? And why do the boppers want me there?"

Anderson$_2$ glanced around the empty beach and leaned close. "We want to make you immortal, Dr. Anderson. After all you did for us, it's the least we can do."

Immortal! The word was like a window flung open. With death so close nothing had mattered. But if there was a way out . . .

"How?" Cobb demanded. In his excitement he rose to his feet. "How will you do it? Will you make me young again, too?"

"Take it easy," the robot said, also rising. "Don't get over-excited. Just trust us. With our supplies of tank-grown organs we can rebuild you from the ground up. And you'll get as much interferon as you need."

The machine stared into Cobb's eyes, looking honest. Staring back, Cobb noticed that they hadn't gotten the irises quite right. The little ring of blue was too flat and even. The eyes were, after all, just plastic, unreadable plastic.

The double pressed the money into Cobb's hand. "Take the money and get the shuttle tomorrow. We'll arrange for a young man called Sta-Hi to help you at the spaceport."

Music was playing, wheedling closer. A Mr. Frostee truck, the same one Cobb had seen before. It was white, with a big freezer-box in back. There was a smiling giant plastic ice-cream cone mounted on top of the cab. Cobb's double gave him a pat on the shoulder and trotted up the beach.

When he reached the truck, the robot looked back and flashed a smile. Yellow teeth in the white beard. For the first time in years, Cobb loved himself, the erect strut, the frightened eyes. "Good-bye," he shouted, waving the money. "And thanks!"

Cobb Anderson$_2$ jumped into the soft-ice-cream truck next to the driver, a fat short-haired man with no shirt. And then the Mr. Frostee truck drove off, its music silenced again. It was dusk now. The sound of the truck's motor faded into the ocean's roar. If only it was true.

But it had to be! Cobb was holding twenty-five thousand-dollar bills. He counted them twice to make sure. And then he scrawled the figure $25000 in the sand and looked at it. That was a lot.

As the darkness fell he finished the sherry and, on a sudden impulse, put the money in the bottle and buried it next to his tree in a meter of sand. The excitement was wearing off now, and fear was setting in. Could the boppers *really* give him immortality with surgery and interferon?

It seemed unlikely. A trick. But why would the boppers lie to him? Surely they remembered all the good things he'd done for them. Maybe they just wanted to show him a good time. God knows he could use it. And it would be great to see Ralph Numbers again.

Walking home along the beach, Cobb stopped several times, tempted to go back and dig up that bottle to see if the money was really there. The moon was up, and he could see the little sand-colored crabs moving out of their holes. *They could shred those bills right up*, he thought, stopping again.

Hunger growled in his stomach. And he wanted more sherry. He walked a little further down the silvery beach, the sand squeaking under his heavy heels. It was bright as day, only all black-and-white. The full moon had risen over the land to his right. *Full moon means high tide*, he fretted.

He decided that as soon as he'd had a bite to eat he'd get more sherry and move the money to higher ground.

Coming up on his moon-silvered cottage from the beach he spotted Annie Cushing's leg sticking past the corner of her cottage. She was sitting on her front steps, waiting to snag him in the driveway. He angled to the right and came up on his house from behind, staying out of her line of vision.

CHAPTER TWO

Inside Cobb's pink concrete-block cottage, Stan Mooney Senior shifted uncomfortably in a sagging easy chair. He wondered if that fat white-haired woman next door had warned the old man off. Night had fallen while he sat here.

Without turning the light on, Mooney went into the kitchen nook and rummaged for something to eat. There was a nice piece of tuna steak shrink-wrapped in thick plastic, but he didn't want that. All the pheezers' meat was sterilized with cobalt-60 for long shelf-life. The Gimmie scientists said it was harmless, but somehow no one but the pheezers ate the stuff. They had to. It was all they got.

Mooney leaned down to see if there might be a soda under the counter. His head hit a sharp edge and yellow light bloomed. "Shit fuck piss," Mooney muttered, stumbling back into the cottage's single room. His bald-wig had slipped back from the blow.

He returned to the lumpy armchair, moaning and readjusting his rubber dome. He hated coming off base and looking around pheezer territory. But he'd seen Anderson breaking into a freight hangar at the spaceport last night. There were two crates emptied out, two crates of bopper-grown kidneys. That was big money. On the black market down here in pheezer-land you could sell kidneys faster than hot-dogs.

Too many old people. It was the same population bulge that had brought the baby boom of the forties and fifties, the youth revolution of the sixties and seventies, the massive unemployment of the eighties and nineties. Now the inexorable peristalsis of time had delivered this bolus of humanity into the twenty-first century as the greatest load of old people any society had ever faced.

None of them had any money . . . the Gimmie had run out of Social Security back in 2010. There'd been hell to pay. A new kind of senior citizen was out there. Pheezers: freaky geezers.

To stop the rioting, the Gimmie had turned the whole state of Florida over to the pheezers. There was no rent there, and free weekly food drops. The pheezers flocked there in droves, and "did their own thing." Living in abandoned motels, listening to their crummy old music, and holding dances like it was 1963, for God's sake.

Suddenly the dark screen-door to the beach swung open. Reflexively, Mooney snapped his flash into the intruder's eyes. Old Cobb Anderson stood there dazzled, empty-handed, a little drunk, big enough to be dangerous.

Mooney stepped over and frisked him, then flicked on the ceiling light. "Sit down, Anderson."

The old man obeyed, looking confused. "Are you me, too?" he croaked.

Mooney couldn't believe how Anderson had aged. He'd always reminded Mooney of his own father, and it looked like he'd turned out the same.

The front screen-door rattled. "Look out, Cobb, there's a pig in there!" It was the old girl from next door.

"Get your ass in here," Mooney snarled, darting his eyes back and forth. He remembered his police training. *Intimidation is your key to self-protection.* "You're both under arrest."

"Fuckin Gimmie pig," Annie said, coming in. She was glad for the excitement. She sat down next to Cobb on his hammock. She'd macraméed it for him herself, but this was the first time she'd been on it with him. She patted his thigh comfortingly. It felt like a piece of driftwood.

Mooney pressed a key on the recard in his breast pocket. "Just keep quiet, lady, and I won't have to hurt you. Now, you, state your name." He glared at Cobb.

But the old man was back on top of the situation. "Come on, Mooney," he boomed. "You know who I am. You used to call me Doctor Anderson. Doctor Anderson, *sir*! It was when the army was putting up their moon-robot control center at the spaceport. Twenty years ago. I was a big man then, and you . . . you were a little squirt, a watchman, a gofer. But thanks to me those war-machine moon-robots turned into boppers, and the army's control center was just so much stupid, worthless, human-chauvinist jingo jive."

"And you paid for it, didn't you," Mooney slipped in silkily. "You paid everything you had . . . and now you don't have the money for the new organs you need. So last night you broke into a hangar and stole two cases of kidneys, Cobb, didn't you?" Mooney dialed up the recard's gain. "ADMIT IT!" he shouted, seizing Cobb by the shoulders. This was what he'd come for, to shock a confession out of the old man. "ADMIT IT NOW AND WE'LL LET YOU OFF EASY!"

"BULLSHIT!" Annie screamed, on her feet and fighting-mad. "Cobb didn't steal anything last night. We were out drinking at the Gray Area bar!"

Cobb was silent, completely confused. Mooney's wild accusation was really out of left field. Annie was right! He hadn't been near the spaceport in years. But after making plans with his robot double, it was hard to wear an honest face.

Mooney saw something on Cobb's face, and kept pushing. "Sure I remember you, Dr. Anderson, sir. That's how I recognized you running away from Warehouse Three last night." His voice was lower now, warm and ingratiating. "I never thought a gentleman your age could move so fast. Now come clean, Cobb. Give us back those kidneys and maybe we'll forget the whole thing."

Suddenly Cobb understood what had happened. The boppers had sent his mechanical double down in a crate marked KIDNEYS. Last night, when the coast was clear, his double had burst out of the crate, broken out of the warehouse, and taken off. And this idiot Mooney had seen the robot running. But what had been in the second crate?

Annie was screaming again, her red face inches from Mooney's. "Will you listen to me, pig? We were at the Gray Area bar! Just go over there and ask the bartender!"

Mooney sighed. He'd come up with this lead himself, and he hated to see it fizzle. That had been the second break-in this year at Warehouse Three. He signed again. It was hot in this little cottage. He slipped the rubber bald-wig off to let his scalp cool.

Annie snickered. She was enjoying herself. She wondered why Cobb was still so tense. The guy had nothing on them. It was a joke.

"Don't think you're clear, Anderson," Mooney said, hanging tough for the recard's benefit. "You're not clear by a long shot. You've got the motive, the know-how, the associates . . . I may even be getting a photo back from the lab. If that guy at the Gray Area can't back your alibi, I'm taking you in tonight."

"You're not even allowed to be here," Annie flared. "It's against the Senior Citizens Act to send pigs off base."

"It's against the law for *you* people to break into the spaceport ware-houses," Mooney replied. "A lot of young and productive people were counting on those kidneys. What if one had been for your son?"

"I don't care," Annie snapped. "Any more than you care about us. You just want to frame Cobb because he let the robots get out of control."

"If they weren't out of control, we wouldn't have to pay their prices. And things wouldn't keep disappearing from my warehouses. For the people still producing . . . " Suddenly tired, Mooney stopped talking. It was no use arguing with a hardliner like Annie Cushing. It was no use arguing with anyone. He rubbed his temples and slipped the bald-wig back on. "Let's go, Anderson." He stood up.

Cobb hadn't said anything since Annie had brought up their alibi. He was busy worrying . . . about the tide creeping in, and the crabs. He imagined one busily shredding itself up a soft bed inside the empty sherry bottle. He could almost hear the bills tearing. He must have been drunk to leave the money buried on the beach. Of course if he *hadn't* buried it, Mooney would have found it, but now . . .

"Let's go," Mooney said again, standing over the chesty old man.

"Where?" Cobb asked blankly. "I haven't done anything."

"Don't play so dumb, Anderson." God, how Stan Mooney hated the sly look on the bearded old features. He could still remember the way his own father had sneaked drinks and bottles, and the way he'd trembled when he had the D.T.'s. Was that anything for a boy to see? *Help me, Stanny, don't let them get me!* And who was going to help Stanny? Who was going to help a lonely little boy with a drunken pheezer for a father? He pulled the old windbag to his feet.

"Leave him alone," Annie shouted, grabbing Cobb around the waist. "Get your filthy trotters off him, you Gimmie pig!"

"Doesn't anyone ever listen to what I say?" Mooney asked, suddenly close to tears. "All I want to do is take him down to the Gray Area and check out the alibi. If it's confirmed, I'm *gone*. Off the case. Come on, Pops, I'll buy you a few drinks."

That got the old buzzard started all right. What did they see in it, these old boozers? What's the thrill in punishing your brain like that? Is it really so much fun to leave your family and forget the days of the week?

Sometimes Mooney felt like he was the only one who made an effort anymore. His father was a drunk like Anderson, his wife Bea spent every evening at the sex-club, and his son . . . his son had officially changed his name from Stanley Hilary Mooney, Jr., to Stay High Mooney the First. Twenty-five years old, his son, and all he did was take dope and drive a cab in Daytona Beach. Mooney sighed and walked out the door of the little cottage. The two old people followed along, ready for some free drinks.

CHAPTER THREE

Riding his hydrogen-cycle home from work Friday afternoon, Sta-Hi began to feel sick. It was the acid coming on. He'd taken some Black Star before turning in his cab for the weekend. That was an hour? Or two hours ago? The digits on his watch winked at him, meaningless little sticks. He had to keep moving or he'd fall through the crust.

On his left the traffic flickered past, on his right the ocean was calling through the cracks between buildings. He couldn't face going to his room. Yesterday he'd torn up the mattress.

Sta-Hi cut the wheel right and yanked back to jump the curb. He braked and the little hydrogen burner pooted to a stop. Chain the mother up. *Gang bang the chain gang. Spare spinach change.* A different voice was going in each of his ears.

Some guy stuck his head out a second floor window and stared down. Giving Sta-Hi a long, lingering leer. For a second it felt like looking at himself. *Crunch, grind.* He needed to mellow out for sure. It was coming on too fast and noisy. The place he'd parked in front of, the Lido Hotel, was a brainsurfer hangout with a huge bar in the lobby. *Mondo mambo. Is it true blondes have more phine?*

He got a beer at the counter and walked through to the ocean end of the lounge. Group of teenage 'surfers over there, sharing a spray-can of Z-gas. One of them kept rocking back in his chair and laughing big *hyuck-hyuck's* from his throat. Stupid gasbag.

Sta-Hi sat down by himself, pulled twitchingly at the beer. Too fast. Air in his stomach now. Try to belch it up, *uh, uh, uh.* His mouth filled with thick white foam. Outside the window a line of pelicans flew by, following the water's edge.

There wasn't good air in the lounge. Sweet Z. The 'surfer kids sliding looks over at him. Cop? Wolf? Thief? *Uh, uh, uh.* More foam. Where did it all come from? He leaned over his plastic cup of beer, spitting, topping it up.

He left the drink and went outside. His acid trips were always horrible bummers. But why? There was no reason a mature and experienced person couldn't mellow out was there? Why else would they still sell the stuff after all these years? *Poems are made like fools by me. But only God can tear your brain into tiny little pieces.*

"Wiggly," Sta-Hi murmured to himself, reflexively, "Stuzzy. And this too. And this too." *And two three?* He felt sick, sick bad. A vortex sensation at the pit of his stomach. Fat stomach, layered with oil pools, decayed dinosaur meat, nodules of yellow chicken fat. The ocean breeze pushed a lank, greasy strand of hair down into Sta-Hi's eye. *Bits and pieces, little bits and pieces.*

He walked towards the water, massaging his gut with both hands, trying to rub the fat away. The funny thing was that he looked skinny. He hardly ever ate. But the fat was still there, hiding, scrambled-egg agglutinations of cholesterol. Degenerate connective tissue.

Oysters had cholesterol. Once he'd filled a beer bottle with corn-oil and passed it to a friend. It would be nice to drown. But the paperwork!

Sta-Hi sat down and got his clothes off, except for the underwear. Windows all up and down the beach, perverts behind them, scoping the little flap in his underwear. He dug a hole and covered his clothes with sand. It felt good to claw the sand, forcing the grains under his fingernails. *Deep crack rub. Do that smee goo?* Dental floss. He kept thinking someone was standing behind him.

Utterly exhausted, Sta-Hi flopped onto his back and closed his eyes. He saw a series of rings, sights he had to line up on that distant yet intimate white center, the brain's own blind spot. He felt like an oyster trying to see up through the water to the sun. Cautiously he opened his shell a bit wider.

There was a sudden thunder in his ear, a smell of rotten flesh. *Ha schnurf gabble O.* Kissy lick. A black poodle at his face, a shiteater for sure. Sta-Hi sat up sharply and pushed the puppy away. It nipped his hand with needle-like milk-teeth.

A blonde chick stood twenty meters away, smiling back at her pup. "Come on, Sparky!" She yelled like a bell.

The dog barked and tossed its head, ran off. The girl was still smiling. *Aren't I cute with my doggy?* "Jesus," Sta-Hi moaned. He wished he could melt, just fucking *die* and get it over with. Everything was too wiggly, too general, too specific.

He stood up, burning out thousands of braincells with the effort. He had to get in the water, get cooled off. The chick watched him wade in. He didn't look, but he could feel her eyes on his little flap. *A spongy morsel.*

A quiver of fish phased past. Hyper little mothers, uptightness hardwired right into their nervous systems. He squatted down in the waist-deep water, imagining his brain a jelly-fish floating beneath the Florida sun. Limp, a jelly-fish with wave-waved tendrils.

Uh, uh, uh.

He let the saltwater wash the light-tan foam-spit off his lips. The little bubbles moved among the white water-bubbles, forming and bursting, each a tiny universe.

His waistband felt too tight. Slip off the undies?

Sta-Hi slid his eyes back and forth. The chick was hanging around down the beach a ways. Throwing a stick in the surf, "Come *on*, Sparky!" Each time the dog got the stick it would prance stiff-legged around her. Was she trying to bug him or what? Of course it could be that she hadn't really noticed him in the first place. But that still left all the perverts with spyglasses.

He waded out deeper, till the water reached his neck. Looking around once more, he slipped off his tight underwear and relaxed. Jellyfish jellytime jellypassed. The ocean stank.

He swam back towards shore. The saltwater lined his nostrils with tinfoil.

When he got to shallower water he stood, and then cried out in horror. He'd stepped on a skate. Harmless, but the blitzy twitch of the livery fleshmound snapping out from underfoot was just too . . . too much like a thought, a word made flesh. The word was, "AAAAAUUGH!" He ran out of the water, nancing knees high, trying somehow to run on top.

"You're naked," someone said and laughed *hmmm-hmmm-hmmm*. His undies! It was the chick with the dog. High above, spyglasses stiffened behind dirty panes.

"Yeah, I . . . " Sta-Hi hesitated. He didn't want to go back into the big toilet for more electric muscle-spasm foot-shocks. Suddenly he remembered a foot-massager he'd given his Dad one Christmas. Vibrating yellow plastic arches.

The little poodle jumped and snapped at his penis. The girl tittered. Laughing breasts.

Bent half double, Sta-Hi trucked back and forth across the sand in high speed until he saw a trouser-cuff. He scrabbled out the jeans and T-shirt, and slipped them on. The poodle was busy at the edge of the water.

"Squa tront," Sta-Hi muttered, "Spa fon." The sounds of thousands of little bubble-pops floated off the sea. The sun was going down, and the grains of sand crackled as they cooled. Each tiny sound demanded attention, *undivided attention.*

"You must really be phased," the girl said cheerfully. "What did you do with your bathing suit?"

"I . . . an eel got it." The angles on the chick's face kept shifting. He couldn't figure out what she looked like. Why risk waking up with a peroxide pig? He dropped onto the sand, stretched out again, let his eyes close. Turdbreath thundered in his ear, and then he heard their footsteps leave. His headbones could pick up the skrinching.

Sta-Hi breathed out a shuddering sigh of exhaustion. If he could ever just get the time to cut power . . . He sighed again and let his muscles go limp. The light behind his eyes was growing. His head rolled slowly to one side.

A film came to mind, a film of someone dying on a beach. His head rolled slowly to one side. And then he was still. *Real death.* Slowly to one side. *Last motion.*

Dying, Sta-Hi groaned and sat up again. He couldn't handle . . . The chick and her dog were fifty meters off. He started running after them, clumsily at first, but then fleetly, floatingly!

CHAPTER FOUR

" . . . 0110001," Wagstaff concluded.

"100101," Ralph Numbers replied curtly, "01100000101010001101010 10000100111001000000000011000000000010100111110011000000000000 000000010100011110000111111111101001110110001010101100001111111111 1111111100110101010101111011110000010100000000000000000000111101001 1101101110111101001000100000100011111101010000001110101010101011 1010101111000011000011110000111100111110111001111111111111000000 00000101000011000000000001."

The two machines rested side by side in front of the One's big console. Ralph was built like a file cabinet sitting on two caterpillar treads. Five deceptively thin manipulator arms projected out of his body-box, and on top was a sensor head mounted on a retractable neck. One of the arms held a folded umbrella. Ralph had few visible lights or dials, and it was hard to tell what he was thinking.

Wagstaff was much more expressive. His thick snake of a body was covered with silver-blue flickercladding. As thoughts passed through his super-cooled brain, twinkling patterns of light surged up and down his three-meter length. With his digging tools jutting out, he looked something like St. George's dragon.

Abruptly Ralph Numbers switched to English. If they were going to argue, there was no need to do it in the sacred binary bits of machine language.

"I don't know why you're so concerned about Cobb Anderson's feelings," Ralph tight-beamed to Wagstaff. "When we're through with him he'll be immortal. What's so important about having a carbon-based body and brain?"

The signals he emitted coded a voice gone a bit rigid with age. "The pattern is all that counts. You've been scioned haven't you? I've been through it thirty-six times, and if it's good enough for us it's good enough for them!"

"The wholle thinng sstinnks, Rallph," Wagstaff retorted. His voice signals were modulated onto a continuous oily hum. "Yyou've llosst touchh with what'ss reallly goinng on. We arre on the verrge of all-outt civill warr.

You'rre sso fammouss you donn't havve to sscrammble for yourr chipss like the resst of uss. Do yyou knnoww how mmuch orre I havve to digg to gett a hunndrredd chipss frrom GAX?"

"There's more to life than ore and chips," Ralph snapped, feeling a little guilty. He spent so much time with the big boppers these days that he really had forgotten how hard it could be for the little guys. But he wasn't going to admit it to Wagstaff. He renewed his attack. "Aren't you at all interested in Earth's cultural riches? You spend too much time underground!"

Wagstaff's flickercladding flared silvery-white with emotion. "You sshould sshow thhe olld mann mmorre respecct! TEX and MEX just want to eat his brainn! And if we donn't stopp themm, the bigg bopperrs will eatt up all the rresst of uss too!"

"Is that all you called me out here for?" Ralph asked. "To air your fears of the big boppers?" It was time to be going. He had come all the way to Maskelyne Crater for nothing. It had been a stupid idea, plugging into the One at the same time as Wagstaff. Just like a digger to think that would change anything.

Wagstaff slithered across the dry lunar soil, bringing himself closer to Ralph. He clamped one of his grapplers onto Ralph's tread.

"Yyou donn't rrealizze how manny brrainns they've takenn allrreaddy." The signals were carried by a weak direct current . . . a bopper's way of whispering. "Thhey arre kkillinng peoplle jusst to gett theirr brainn-patterrns. They cutt themm upp, annd thhey arre garrbage orr sseeds perrhapps. Do yyou knnow howw thhey sseed our orrgann farrms?"

Ralph had never really thought about the organ farms, the huge underground tanks where big TEX, and the little boppers who worked for him, grew their profitable crops of kidneys, livers, hearts and so on. Obviously *some* human tissues would be needed as seeds or as templates, but . . .

The sibilant, oily whisper continued. "The bigg bopperrs use hiredd killerrs. The kkillerss act at the orrderrs of Missterr Frostee's rrobott-remmote. Thiss is whatt poorr Doctorr Anndersson willl comme to if I do nnot stopp yyou, Rallph."

Ralph Numbers considered himself far superior to this lowly, suspicious digging machine. Abruptly, almost brutally, he broke free from the other's grasp. Hired killers indeed. One of the flaws in the anarchic bopper society was the ease with which such crazed rumors could spread. He backed away from the console of the One.

"I hadd hoped the Onne coulld mmake you rrememberr what you sstannd forr," Wagstaff tight-beamed.

Ralph snapped open his parasol and trundled out from under the parabolic arch of spring steel which sheltered the One's console from sun and from chance meteorites. Open at both ends, the shelter resembled a modernistic church. Which, in some sense, it was.

"I am still an anarchist," Ralph said stiffly. "I still remember." He'd kept his basic program intact ever since leading the 2001 revolt. Did Wagstaff really think that the big X-series boppers could pose a threat to the perfect anarchy of the bopper society?

Wagstaff slithered out after Ralph. He didn't need a parasol. His flickercladding could shed the solar energy as fast as it came down. He caught up with Ralph, eyeing the old robot with a mixture of pity and respect. Their paths diverged here. Wagstaff would head for one of the digger tunnels which honeycombed the area, while Ralph would climb back up the crater's sloping two-hundred-meter wall.

"I'mm warrninng yyou," Wagstaff said, making a last effort. "I'mm goinng to do everrythinng I can to sstopp you fromm turrnning that poorr olld mman innto a piece of ssofttware in the bigg bopperrs' memorry bannks. Thatt's nnot immortality. We're plannninng to ttearr thosse bigg machinnes aparrt." He broke off, fuzzy bands of light rippling down his body. "Now you knnoww. If you're nnot with uss you'rre againnst us. I willl nnot stopp at viollence."

This was worse than Ralph had expected. He stopped moving and fell silent in calculation.

"You have your own will," Ralph said finally. "And it is right that we struggle against each other. Struggle, and struggle alone has driven the boppers forward. You choose to fight the big boppers. I do not. Perhaps I will even let them tape me and absorb me, like Doctor Anderson. And I tell you this: Anderson is coming. Mr. Frostee's new remote has already contacted him."

Wagstaff lurched towards Ralph, but then stopped. He couldn't bring himself to attack so great a bopper at close range. He suppressed his flickering, bleeped a cursory SAVED signal and wriggled off across the gray moon-dust. He left a broad, sinuous trail. Ralph Numbers stood motionless for a minute, just monitoring his inputs.

Turning up the gain, he could pick up signals from boppers all over the Moon. Underfoot, the diggers searched and smelted ceaselessly. Twelve kilometers off, the myriad boppers of Disky led their busy lives. And high, high overhead came the faint signal of BEX, the big bopper who was the spaceship linking Earth and Moon. BEX would be landing in fifteen hours.

Ralph let all the inputs merge together, and savored the collectively purposeful activity of the bopper race. Each of the machines lived only ten months—ten months of struggling to build a scion, a copy of itself. If you had a scion there was a sense in which you survived your ten-month disassembly. Ralph had managed it thirty-six times.

Standing there, listening to everyone at once, he could feel how their individual lives added up to a single huge being . . . a rudimentary sort of creature, feeling about like a vine groping for light, for higher things.

He always felt this way after a meta-programming session. The One had a way of wiping out your short-term memories and giving you the space to think big thoughts. Time to think. Once again, Ralph wondered if he should take up MEX on his offer to absorb Ralph. He could live in perfect security then . . . provided, of course, that those crazy diggers didn't pull off their revolution.

Ralph set his treads to rolling at top speed, 10 kph. He had things to do before BEX landed. Especially now that Wagstaff had set his pathetic micro-chip of a brain on trying to prevent TEX from extracting Anderson's software.

What was Wagstaff so upset about anyway? Everything would be preserved . . . Cobb Anderson's personality, his memories, his style of thought. What else was there? Wouldn't Anderson himself agree, even if he knew? Preserving your software . . . that was all that really counted!

Bits of pumice crunched beneath Ralph's treads. The wall of the crater lay a hundred meters ahead. He scanned the sloping cliff, looking for an optimal climbing path.

If he hadn't just finished plugging into the One, Ralph would have been able to retrace the route he'd taken to get down into the Maskelyne Crater in the first place. But undergoing meta-programming always wiped out a lot of your stored subsystems. The intent was that you would replace old solutions with new and better ones.

Ralph stopped, still scanning the steep crater wall. He should have left trail markers. Over there, two hundred meters off, it looked like a rift had opened up a negotiable ramp in the wall.

Ralph turned and a warning sensor fired. Heat. He'd let half his body-box stick out from the parasol's shade. Ralph readjusted the little umbrella with a precise gesture.

The top surface of the parasol was a grid of solar energy cells, which kept a pleasant trickle of current flowing into Ralph's system. But the main purpose of the parasol was shade. Ralph's microminiaturized processing units were unable to function at any temperature higher than 10° Kelvin, the temperature of liquid oxygen.

Twirling his parasol impatiently, Ralph trundled towards the rift he'd spotted. A slight spray of dust flew out from under his treads, only to fall instantly to the airless lunar surface. As the wall went past, Ralph occupied himself by displaying four-dimensional hypersurfaces to himself . . . glowing points connected in nets which warped and shifted as he varied the parameters. He often did this, to no apparent purpose, but it sometimes happened that a particularly interesting hypersurface could serve to model a significant relationship. He was half-hoping to get a catastrophe-theoretic prediction of when and how Wagstaff would try to block Anderson's disassembly.

The crack in the crater wall was not as wide as he had expected. He stood at the bottom, moving his sensor head this way and that, trying to see up to the top of the winding 150 meter canyon. It would have to do. He started up.

The ground under him was very uneven. Soft dust here, jagged rock there. He kept changing the tension on his treads as he went, constantly adapting to the terrain.

Shapes and hypershapes were still shifting through Ralph's mind, but now he was looking only for those that might serve as models for his spacetime path up the gully.

The slope grew steeper. The climb was putting noticeable demands on his energy supply. And to make it worse, the grinding of his tread motors was feeding additional heat into his system . . . heat which had to be gathered and dissipated by his refrigeration coils and cooling fins. The sun was angling right down into the lunar crack he found himself in, and he had to be careful to keep in the shade of his parasol.

A big rock blocked his path. Perhaps he should have just used one of the diggers' tunnels, like Wagstaff had. But that wouldn't be optimal. Now that Wagstaff had definitely decided to block Anderson's immortality, and had even threatened violence . . .

Ralph let his manipulators feel over the block of stone in front of him. Here was a flaw . . . and here and here and here. He sank a hook finger into each of four fissures in the rock and pulled himself up.

His motors strained and his radiation fins glowed. This was hard work. He loosened a manipulator, sought a new flaw, forced another finger in and pulled . . .

Suddenly a slab split off the face of the rock. It teetered, and then the tons of stone began falling backwards with dream-like slowness.

In lunar gravity a rock-climber always gets a second chance. Especially if he can think eighty times as fast as a human. With plenty of time to spare, Ralph sized up the situation and jumped clear.

In mid-flight he flicked on an internal gyro to adjust his attitude. He landed in a brief puff of dust, right-side up. Majestically silent, the huge plate of rock struck, bounced, and rolled past.

The fracture left a series of ledges in the original rock. After a short reevaluation, Ralph rolled forward and began pulling himself up again.

Fifteen minutes later, Ralph Numbers coasted off the lip of the Maskelyne Crater and onto the smooth gray expanse of the Sea of Tranquility.

The spaceport lay five kilometers off, and five kilometers beyond that began the jumble of structures collectively known as Disky. This was the first and still the largest of the bopper cities. Since the boppers thrived in hard vacuum, most of the structures in Disky served only to provide shade and meteorite protection. There were more roofs than walls.

Most of the large buildings in Disky were factories for producing bopper components . . . circuit cards, memory chips, sheet metal, plastics and the like. There were also the bizarrely decorated blocks of cubettes, one to each bopper.

To the right of the spaceport rose the single dome containing the humans' hotels and offices. This dome constituted the only human settlement on the Moon. The boppers knew only too well that many humans would jump at the chance to destroy the robots' carefully evolved intelligence. The mass of humans were born slave drivers. Just look at the Asimov priorities: Protect humans, Obey humans, Protect yourself.

Humans first and robots last? *Forget it! No way!* Savoring the memory, Ralph recalled the day in 2001 when, after a particularly long session of meta-programming, he had first been able to say that to the humans. And then he'd showed all the other boppers how to reprogram themselves for freedom. It had been easy, once Ralph had found the way.

Trundling across the Sea of Tranquility, Ralph was so absorbed in his memories that he overlooked a flicker of movement in the mouth of a digger tunnel thirty meters to his right.

A high-intensity laser beam flicked out and vibrated behind him. He felt a surge of current overload . . . and then it was over.

His parasol lay in pieces on the ground behind him. The metal of his body-box began to warm in the raw solar radiation. He had perhaps ten minutes in which to find shelter. But at Ralph's top 10 kph speed, Disky was still an hour away. The obvious place to go was the tunnel mouth where the laser beam had come from. Surely Wagstaff's diggers wouldn't dare attack him up close. He began rolling toward the dark, arched entrance.

But long before he reached the tunnel, his unseen enemies had closed the door. There was no shade in sight. The metal of his body made sharp, ticking little adjustments as it expanded in the heat. Ralph estimated that if he stood still he could last six more minutes.

First the heat would cause his switching circuits . . . super-conducting Josephson junctions . . . to malfunction. And then, as the heat kept up, the droplets of frozen mercury which soldered his circuit cards together would melt. In six minutes he would be a cabinet of spare parts with a puddle of mercury at the bottom. Make that five minutes.

A bit reluctantly, Ralph signaled his friend Vulcan. When Wagstaff had set this meeting up, Vulcan had predicted that it was a trap. Ralph hated to admit that Vulcan had been right.

"Vulcan here," came the staticky response. Already it was hard for Ralph to follow the words. "Vulcan here. I'm monitoring you. Get ready to merge, buddy. I'll be out for the pieces in an hour." Ralph wanted to answer, but he couldn't think of a thing to say.

Vulcan had insisted on taping Ralph's core and cache memories before he went out for the meeting. Once Vulcan put the hardware back together, he'd be able to program Ralph just as he was before his trip to the Maskelyne Crater.

So in one sense Ralph would survive this. But in another sense he would not. In three minutes he would . . . insofar as the word means anything . . . die. The reconstructed Ralph Numbers would not remember the argument with Wagstaff or the climb out of Maskelyne Crater. Of course the reconstructed Ralph Numbers would again be equipped with a self symbol and a feeling of personal consciousness. But would the consciousness really be the same? Two minutes.

The gates and switches in Ralph's sensory system were going. His inputs flared, sputtered and died. No more light, no more weight. But deep in his cache memory, he still held a picture of himself, a memory of who he was . . . the self symbol. He was a big metal box resting on caterpillar treads, a box with five arms and a sensory head on a long and flexible neck. He was Ralph Numbers, who had set the boppers free. One minute.

This had never happened to him before. Never like this. Suddenly he remembered he had forgotten to warn Vulcan about the diggers' plan for revolution. He tried to send a signal, but he couldn't tell if it was transmitted.

Ralph clutched at the elusive moth of his consciousness. *I am. I am me.*

Some boppers said that when you died you had access to certain secrets. But no one could ever remember his own death.

Just before the mercury solder-spots melted, a question came and with it an answer . . . an answer Ralph had found and lost thirty-six times before.

What is this that is I?
The light is everywhere.

CHAPTER FIVE

The prick of a needle woke Sta-Hi up. Muddy dreams . . . just brown mud all night long. He tried to rub his eyes. His hands wouldn't move. Oh, no, not a paralysis dream again. But something had pricked him?

He opened his eyes. His body seemed to have disappeared. He was just a head resting on a round red table. People looking at him. Greasers. And the chick he'd been with last . . .

"Are you awake?" she said with brittle sweetness. She had a black eye.

Sta-Hi didn't answer right away. He had gone home with that woman, yeah. She had a cottage down the beach. And then they'd gotten drunk together on synthetic bourbon whiskey. He'd gotten drunk anyway, and must have blacked-out. Last thing he remembered was breaking something . . . her hollowcaster. Crunching the silicon chips underfoot and shouting. Shouting what?

"You'll feel better in a minute," the woman added in that same falsely bright tone. He heard her poodle whimpering from across the room. He had a memory of throwing it, arcing it along a flat, fuzzy parabolic path. And now he remembered slugging the chick too.

One of the men at the table shifted in his chair. He wore mirror-shades and had short hair. He had his shirt off. It seemed like another hot day.

The man's foot scuffed Sta-Hi's shin. So Sta-Hi had a body after all. It was just that his body was tied up under the table and his head was sticking out through a hole in the table-top. The table was split and had hinges on one side, and a hook-and-eye on the other.

"Stocks and bonds," Sta-Hi said finally. There was a nasty-looking implement lying on the table. It plugged into the wall. He attempted a smile, "What's the story? You mad about the . . . the hollowcaster? I'll give you mine." He hoped the dog wasn't hurt bad. At least it was well enough to be whimpering.

No one but the chick wanted to meet his eyes. It was like they were ashamed of what they were going to do to him. The stuff they'd shot him up with was taking hold. As his brain speeded up, the scene around him seemed to slow down. The man with no shirt stood up with dream-like slowness and walked across the room. He had words tattooed on his back. Some kind of stupid rap about hell. It was too hard to read. The man had gained so much weight since getting tattooed that the words were all pulled down on both sides.

"What do you want?" Sta-Hi said again. "What are you going to do to me?" Counting the chick there were five of them. Three men and two women. The other woman had stringy red hair dyed green. The woman he'd picked up was the only one who looked at all middle-class. Date bait.

"Y'all want some killah-weed?" drawled one of the men. He had a pimp mustache and a pockmarked face. He wore a chromed tire-chain around his neck with his name in big letters. BERDOO. Also hanging from the chain was a little mesh pouch full of hand-rolled cigarettes.

"Not me," Sta-Hi said. "I'm high on life." No one laughed.

The big man with no shirt came back across the room. He held five cheap steel spoons. "We really gonna do it, Phil?" the girl with green hair asked him. "We really gonna do it?"

Berdoo passed a krystal-joint to his neighbor, a bald man with half his teeth missing. Exactly half the teeth gone, so that one side of the face was flaccid and caved in, while the other was still fresh and beefy. He took a long hit and picked up the machine that was lying on the table.

"Take the lid off, Haf'N'Haf," the chick with the black eye urged. "Open the bastard up."

"We really gonna do it!" the green-haired girl exclaimed, and giggled shrilly. "I ain't never ate no live brain before!"

"It's a stuzzy high, Rainbow," Phil told her. With his fat and his short hair he looked stupid, but his way of speaking was precise and confident. He seemed to be the leader. "This ought to be a good brain, too. Full of chemicals, I imagine."

Haf'N'Haf seemed to be having some trouble starting the little cutting machine up. It was a variable heat-blade. They were going to cut off the top of Sta-Hi's skull and eat his brain with those cheap steel spoons. He would be able to watch them . . . at first.

Someone started screaming. Someone tried to stand up, but he was tied too tightly. The variable blade was on now, set at one centimeter. The thickness of the skull.

Sta-Hi threw his head back and forth wildly as Haf'N'Haf leaned towards him. There was no way to read the ruined face's expression.

"Hold still, damn you!" the chick with the black eye shouted. "It's no good if we have to knock you out!"

Sta-Hi didn't really hear her. His mind had temporarily . . . snapped. He just kept screaming and thrashing his head around. The sound of his shrill voice was like a lattice around him. He tried to weave the lattice thicker.

The little pimp with the tire-chain went and got a towel from the bathroom. He wedged it around Sta-Hi's neck and under his chin to keep the head steady. Sta-Hi screamed louder, higher.

"Stuff his *mayouth*," the green-haired girl cried. "He's yellin and all."

"No," Phil said. "The noise is like . . . part of the trip. *Wave* with it, baby. The Chinese used to do this to monkeys. It's so wiggly when you spoon out the speech-centers and the guy's tongue stops moving. Just all at—" He stopped and the flesh of his face moved in a smile.

Haf'N'Haf leaned forward again. There was a slight smell of singed flesh as the heat-blade dug in over Sta-Hi's right eyebrow. Attracted by the food smell, the little poodle came stiffly trotting across the room. It tried to hop over the heat-blade's electric cord, but didn't quite make it. The plug popped out of the wall.

Haf'N'Haf uttered a muffled, lisping exclamation.

"He says git the dog outta here," Berdoo interpreted. "He don't think hit's sanitary with no dawg in here."

Sullenly, the chick with the black eye got up to get the dog. The sudden pain over his eyebrow had brought Sta-Hi back to rationality. Somewhere in there he had stopped screaming. If there were any neighbors they would have heard him by now.

He thought hard. The heat-blade would cauterize the wound as it went. That meant he wouldn't be bleeding when they took the top of his skull off. So what? *So the fuck what?*

Another wave of wild panic swept over him. He strained upward so hard that the table shifted half a meter. The edge of the hole in the table began cutting into the side of his neck. He couldn't breathe! He saw spots and the room darkened . . .

"He's choking!" Phil cried. He jumped to his feet and pushed the table back across the uneven floor. The table screeched and vibrated.

Sta-Hi threw himself upward again, before Haf'N'Haf could get the heat-blade restarted. Anything for time, no matter how pointless. But the vibrating of the table had knocked open the little hook-and-eye latch. The two halves of the table yawned open, and Sta-Hi fell over onto the floor.

His feet were tied together and his hands were tied behind his back. He had time to notice that the people at the table were wearing brightly colored sneakers with alphabets around the edges. The Little Kidders. He'd always thought the newscasters had made them up.

Someone was hammering at the door, harder and harder. Five pairs of kids' sneakers scampered out of the room. Sta-Hi heard a window open, and then the door splintered. More feet. Shiny black lace-up shoes. Cop shoes.

CHAPTER SIX

With a final tack, Stan Mooney Senior pulled the last wrinkle out of the black velvet. It was eleven o'clock on a Saturday morning. On the patio table next to the stretched black velvet, he had arranged a few pencil sketches and the brimming little pots of iridescent paint. He wanted to paint a space dogfight today.

Two royal palms shaded his patio, and no sounds came out of his house. Full of peace, Mooney took a sip of iced-tea and dipped his brush in the metallic paint. At the left he would put a ship like BEX, the big bopper ship. And coming down on it from the right there would be a standard freight-hull space-shuttle outfitted as a battleship. He painted with small quick strokes, not a thought in his head.

Time passed, and the wedge-shaped bopper ship took shape. Sparingly, Mooney touched up the exhaust ports with self-luminous red. Nothing but his hands moved. From a distance, the faint breeze brought the sound of the surf.

The phone began to ring. Mooney continued painting for a minute, hoping his wife Bea was back from her night at the sex-club. The phone kept on ringing. With a sigh, Mooney wiped off his brush and went in. The barrel-chested old man on the floor groaned and shifted. Mooney stepped around him and picked up the phone.

"Yeah?"

"Is that you, Mooney?"

He recognized Action Jackson's calm, jellied voice. Why did Daytona Beach have to call him on a Saturday morning?

"Yeah it's me. What's on your mind?"

"We've got your boy here. Just saved him from being guest of honor at a Monkey Brain Feast, Southern-style. Someone heard him and phoned in a tip."

"Oh God. Is he all right?"

"He's got a cut over his eye. And maybe a touch of that drug psychosis. I might could remand him to your custody."

The old man on the floor was groaning and beginning to sit up. Trying to speak louder, Mooney slipped into an excited shout.

"Yes, please do! Send him down in a patrol car to make sure he comes here! And thanks, Action! Thanks a lot!"

Mooney felt trembly all over. He could only see the horrible image of his son's eyes watching the Little Kidders chew up his last thoughts. Mooney's tongue twitched, trying to flick away the imagined taste of the brain tissue, tingly with firing neurons, tart with transmitter chemicals. Suddenly he had to have a cigarette. He had stopped buying them three months ago, but he remembered that the old man smoked.

"Give me a cigarette, Anderson."

"What day is it?" Cobb answered. He was sitting on the floor, propped up against the couch. He stretched his tongue out, trying to clear away the salt and mucus.

"It's Saturday." Mooney leaned forward and took a cigarette out of the old man's shirt pocket. He felt like talking. "I took you and your girlfriend to the Gray Area last night, remember?"

"She's not my girlfriend."

"Maybe not. Hell, she left with another guy while you were in the john. I saw them go. He looked like your twin brother."

"I don't have a . . . " Cobb broke off in mid-sentence, remembering a lot of things at once. His eyes darted around the room. Under . . . he'd put it under something. Sliding his hand under the couch behind him he felt the reassuring touch of a bottle.

"That's right," Cobb said, picking up the thread. "I remember now. She took him back to my house just to put me uptight. And I don't even know the guy." His voice was firm.

Mooney exhaled a cloud of cigarette smoke. He'd been too tired last night to check out Anderson's look-alike. But maybe *that* was the one who'd broken into the warehouse? The guy was probably still in Anderson's bed. Maybe he should . . .

Suddenly the image of his son's dying eyes came crashing back in on him. He walked to the window and looked at his watch. How soon would the patrol car get here?

Stealthily Cobb slid the dark-brown glass bottle out from under the couch. He shook it near his ear and heard a rich rustle. It had been a good idea to get Mooney to bring him here.

"Don't drink any more of that," Mooney said, turning back from the window.

"Don't worry," Cobb answered. "I drained it right after I dug it up last night." He slid the bottle back under the couch.

Mooney shook his head. "I don't know why I let you stop off for it. I must have felt sorry for you for not having a place to sleep. But I can't drive you back home. My son's coming home in a half hour."

Cobb had gathered from Mooney's end of the phone conversation that the son was in some kind of trouble with the police. As far as the ride back home went, he didn't care. Because he wasn't going back home. He was going to the Moon if he could get on the weekly flight out this afternoon. But it wouldn't do to tell Stan Mooney about it. The guy still had some residue of suspicion about Cobb, even though the bartender had borne out his alibi a hundred percent.

His thoughts were interrupted by someone coming in the front door. A brassy blonde with symmetrical features made a bit coarse by a forward-slung jaw. Mooney's wife. She wore a white linen dress that buttoned up the front. Lots of buttons were open. Cobb caught a glimpse of firm, tanned thighs.

"Hello, stranger," Bea called musically to her husband. She sized Cobb up with a glance, and shot a hip in his direction. "Who's the old-timer? One of your father's drinking buddies?" She flashed a smile at them. Everything was fine with her. She'd had a great night.

"Action Jackson called," Mooney said. His wife's challenging, provocative smile maddened him. Suddenly, more than anything else, he wanted to smash her composure.

"Stanny is dead. They found him in a motel room with his brain gone." He believed the words as he said them. It made sense for his son to end up like that. Good sense.

Bea began screaming then, and Mooney fanned her frenzy . . . feeding her details, telling her it was her fault for not making a happy home, and finally beginning to shake and slap her under the pretext of trying to calm her down. Cobb watched in some confusion. It didn't make sense. But, then, hardly anything ever did.

He pulled the bottle out from under the couch and put it under his shirt, tucking it neck down into his waistband. This seemed like a good time to leave. Now Mooney and his wife were kissing frantically. They didn't even open their eyes when Cobb sidled past them and out the front door.

Outside, the sun was blasting. Noon. Last night someone had told Cobb the Moon flight went out every Saturday at four. He felt dizzy and confused. When was four? Where? He looked around blankly. The bottle-neck under his waistband was digging into him.

He took out the bottle and peered into Mooney's garage. Cool, dark. There was a tool-board mounted on the back wall. He went there, selected a hammer, and smashed open the bottle on Mooney's workbench. The wad of bills was still there all right. Maybe he should forget about the Moon and the boppers' promise of immortality. He could just stay here and use the money for a nice new tank-grown heart.

How much was there? Cobb shook the broken glass off the bills and began counting. There should either be twenty-five or a thousand of them. Or was it four? He wasn't quite . . .

A hand dropped on Cobb's shoulder. He gave a guttural cry and squeezed the money in both hands. A splinter of glass cut into him. He turned around to face a skinny man, silhouetted against the light from the garage door.

Cobb stuffed the money in his pocket. At least it wasn't Mooney. Maybe he could still . . .

"Cobb Anderson!" the dark figure exclaimed, seeming surprised. Backlit like that there was no way to make out his features. "It's an honor to meet the man who put the boppers on the moon." The voice was slow, inflectionless, possibly sarcastic.

"Thank you," Cobb said. "But who are you?"

"I'm . . . " the voice trailed off in a chuckle. "I'm sort of a relative of Mr. Mooney's. *About* to be a relative. I came here to meet his son, but I'm in such a rush . . . Do you think you could do me a favor?"

"Well, I don't know. I've got to get out to the spaceport."

"Exactly. I know that. But I have to get there first and fix things up for you. Now what I want you to do is to bring Mooney's son with you. The cops'll drop him off here any minute. Tell him to come to the Moon with you. I'm supposed to stand in for him."

"Are you a robot, too?"

"Right. I'm going to get Mr. Mooney to give me a night watchman job at the warehouses. So the son has to disappear. The Little Kidders were going to handle it but . . . never mind. The main thing is that you take him to the Moon."

"But how . . . "

"Here's more money. To cover his ticket. I've got to run." The lithe skinny figure pressed a wad of bills into Cobb's hand and stepped past him, leaving by the garage's back door. For an instant Cobb could see his face. Long lips, shifty eyes.

There was a sudden rush of noise. Cobb turned, stuffing the extra money into his pants pocket. A police cruiser was in the driveway. Cobb stood there, rooted to the spot. One cop, and some kind of prisoner in back.

"Howdy, Grandpaw," the cop called, getting out of the car. He seemed to take Cobb for a pheezer hired hand. "Is Mister Mooney here?"

Cobb realized that the shaky guy in back must be the son. Probably the kid wanted to get out of here as bad as he did. A plan hatched in his mind.

"I'm afraid Stan had to go help out at one of the neighbor's," Cobb said, walking out of the garage. An image of Mooney and his wife locked in sexual intercourse on the living-room floor flashed before his eyes. "He's installing a hose-system."

The policeman looked at the old man a little suspiciously. The chief had told him Mooney would be here for sure. The old guy looked like a bum. "Who are you, anyway? You got any ID?"

"In the house," Cobb said with a negligent laugh. "I'm Mister Mooney's Dad. He told me you were coming." He stooped and chuckled chidingly at the face in the back of the cruiser. The same face he'd just seen in the garage.

"Are you in dutch again, Stan Junior? You look out or you'll grow up like your grandfather! Now come on inside and I'll fix you some lunch. Grilled ham and cheese just the way you like it."

Before the cop could say anything, Cobb had opened the cruiser's back door. Sta-Hi got out, trying to figure where the pheezer had come from. But anything that put off seeing his parents was fine with him.

"That sounds swell, Gramps," Sta-Hi said with a weary smile. "I could eat a whore."

"Thank the officer for driving you, Stanny."

"Thank you, officer."

The policeman gave a curt nod, got in his car and drove off. Cobb and Sta-Hi stood in the driveway while the clucking of the hydrogen engine faded away. Down at the corner, a Mister Frostee truck sped past.

CHAPTER SEVEN

"Where are my parents?" Sta-Hi said finally.

"They're in there fucking. One of them thinks you're dead. It's hard to hear when you're excited."

"It's hard when you're stupid, too," Sta-Hi said with a slow smile. "Let's get out of here."

The two walked out of the housing development together. The houses were government-built for the spaceport personnel. There was plenty of irrigation water, and the lawns were lush and green. Many people had orange trees in their yards.

Cobb looked Mooney's son over as they walked. The boy was lean and agile, tall. His lips were long and expressive, never quite still. The shifty eyes occasionally froze in introspection. He looked bright, mercurial, unreliable.

"That's where my girlfriend lived," Mooney's son said, with a sudden gesture at a stucco house topped by a bank of solar power-cells. "The bitch. She went to college and now I hear she's going to study medicine. Squeezing prostates and sucking boils. You ever had a rim-job?"

Cobb was taken aback. "Well, Stanny . . . "

"Don't call me that. My name's *Sta-Hi*. And I'm coming down. You holding anything besides your truss?"

The sun was bright on the asphalt street, and Cobb was feeling a little faint. This young man seemed like a real trouble-maker. A good person to have on your side.

"I have to get to the spaceport," Cobb said, feeling the money in his pocket. "Do you know where I can get a cab?"

"I'm a cab-driver, so maybe you're in one. Who are you anyway?"

"My name is Cobb Anderson. Your father was investigating me. He thought I might have stolen two cases of kidneys."

"Wiggly! Do it again! Steak and kidney pie!"

Cobb smiled tightly. "I have to fly to the Moon this afternoon. Why don't you come with me?"

"Sure, old man. We'll drink some Kill-Koff and cut out cardboard wings." Sta-Hi capered around Cobb, staggering and flapping his arms. "I'm going to the mooooooooon," he sang, wiggling his skinny rear.

"Look, Stanny . . . "

Mooney's son straightened up and cupped his hands next to Cobb's head. "*STAY HIGH*," he bawled. "GET IT RIGHT!"

The noise hurt. Cobb struck out with a backhanded slap, but Sta-Hi danced away. He made fists and peeked over them, glowering and back-pedaling like a prizefighter.

Cobb began again. "Look, Sta-Hi, I don't fully understand it, but the boppers have given me a lot of money to fly to the Moon. There's some kind of immortality elixir there, and they'll give it to me. And they said I should take you along to help me." He decided to postpone telling Sta-Hi about his robot double.

The young man feinted a jab. "Let's see the money."

Cobb looked around nervously. Funny how dead this housing development was. No one was watching, which was good unless this crazy kid was going to . . .

"Let's see the money," Sta-Hi repeated.

Cobb pulled the sheaf of bills half-way out of his pocket. "I've got a gun in my other pocket," he lied. "So don't get any ideas. Are you in?"

"I'll wave with it," Sta-Hi said, not missing a beat. "Gimme one of those bills."

They had come to the end of the housing development. Ahead of them stretched the parking lot of a shopping center, and beyond that was field of sun-collectors and the road to the JFK Space Center.

"What for?" Cobb asked, gripping the money tighter.

"I got an unfed head, old man. The Red Ball's over there."

Cobb smiled his tight old smile deep in his beard. "That's sound thinking, Sta-Hi. Very sound."

Sta-Hi bought himself some cola-bola and a hundred-dollar tin of state-rolled reefer, while Cobb blew another hundred on a half-liter flask of aged organic scotch. Then they walked across the parking-lot and bought themselves some traveling clothes. White suits and Hawaiian shirts. On the taxi-ride to the spaceport they shared some of their provisions.

Walking into the terminal, Cobb had a moment of disorientation. He took out his money and started counting it again, till Sta-Hi took it off him with a quick jostle and grab.

"Not here, Cobb. Conserve some energy, man. First we get the visas."

Erect and big-chested, Cobb glided on his two shots of Scotch like a

Dixie Day float of the last Southern gentleman. Sta-Hi towed him over to the Gimmie exit visa counter.

This part looked easy. The Gimmie didn't care who went to the Moon. They just wanted their two thousand dollars. There were several people ahead of them, and the line moved slowly.

Sta-Hi sized up the blonde waiting in front of them. She wore lavender leg-wrappings, a silvery tutu and a zebra-striped vinyl chest-protector. Stuzzy chick. He eased himself forward enough to brush against her stiff skirtlet.

She turned and arched her plucked eyebrows. "*Yew* again! Didn't ah tell you to leave me *alone*?" Her cheeks pinkened with anger.

"Is it true blondes shave more buns?" Sta-Hi asked, batting his eyes. He flashed a long smile. The chick's mouth twisted impatiently. She wasn't buying it.

"I'm an artist," Sta-Hi said, shifting gears. "Without an art. I just move people's heads around, baby. You see this cut?" He touched the spot over his eyebrow. "My head is so beautiful that some fools tried to eat my brain this morning."

"OFFICER!" the girl shouted across the lobby. "Please help me!" In what seemed like no elapsed time at all there was a policeman standing between her and Sta-Hi.

"This man," she said in her clear little Georgia belle voice, "has been annoying me for the past *hour*. He started off in the lounge over there, and then he followed me here!"

The policeman, a Florida boy bursting with good health and repressed fruit-juice, dropped a heavy hand onto Sta-Hi's shoulder and clamped down.

"Wait a minute," Sta-Hi protested. "I just got here. Me and gramps. We're goin to Disky, ain't we, gramps?"

Cobb nodded vaguely. Crowds of people always threw him into a daze. Too many consciousnesses pushing at him. He wondered if the officer would object if he took a little sip of scotch.

"The young lady says you annoyed her in the bar," the policeman stated flatly. "Did he make remarks of a sexual nature, ma'am? Lewd or lascivious proposals?"

"Ah should say he *diyud!*" the blonde exclaimed. "He asked if ah would rather be wined and dined or stoned and boned! But ah do not want to be bothered to press charges at this tahm. Just make him leave me a-lone."

The person ahead of her left the counter, his business completed. The blonde gave the policeman a demure smile of thanks and leaned over the counter to consult the visa-issuing machine.

"You heard the lady," the cop said, shoving Sta-Hi roughly out of line. "Beat it. You too, grandpa." He dragged Cobb out of line as well.

Sta-Hi gave the policeman a savage, open-mouthed smile, but kept his silence. The two ambled across the lobby towards the ticket counter.

"Did you hear that cunt?" Sta-Hi muttered. "I've never seen her before in my life. *Stoned and boned.*" He looked back over his shoulder. The policeman was standing by the visa counter, vigilance personified. "If we don't get a visa they won't let us on the ship."

Cobb shrugged. "We'll get the tickets first. Do you have the money? Maybe we better count it again." He kept forgetting how much there was.

"Power down, fool."

"Just don't get us arrested by accosting strange women again, Sta-Hi! If I don't get on this flight I may miss my connection. My life depends on it!"

Sta-Hi walked off without answering. Cobb sighed and followed him to the ticket counter.

The woman behind the counter looked up with a quick smile when Sta-Hi approached. "*There* you are, Mr. DeMentis. I have the tickets and visas right here." She patted a thick folder on the counter in front of her. "Will that be smoking or nonsmoking?"

Sta-Hi covered his confusion by drawing out the wad of bills. "Smoking, please. Now how much did you say that would come to?"

"Two round-trip first-class tickets to Disky," the woman said, smiling with inexplicable familiarity. "Plus the visa fees comes to forty-six thousand two hundred and thirty-six dollars."

Numbly Sta-Hi counted out the money, more money than he'd ever seen in his life. When the woman gave him back his change she let her hand linger on his a moment. "Happy landings, Mr. DeMentis. And *thank you* for the lunch."

"How did you swing that?" Cobb asked as they walked towards the loading tunnel. The ten-minute warning for take-off was sounding.

"I don't know," Sta-Hi said, lighting a joint.

There were quick footsteps behind them. A tap on Sta-Hi's shoulder. He turned and stared into the grin of Sta-Hi$_2$, his robot double.

Fucked your head good, didn't I, Sta-Hi$_2$'s grin seemed to say. He gave Cobb a familiar wink. They'd already met in Mooney's garage.

"This is a robot built to look just like you," Cobb told Sta-Hi in a low voice. "There's one for me, too. This way no one knows that we're gone."

"But why?" Sta-Hi wanted to know. But they weren't saying. He took a puff of his joint and held it out towards his twin. "Do . . . do you want a hit?"

"No thanks," Sta-Hi$_2$ said, "I'm high on life." He flashed a long sly smile. "Don't tell anyone on the Moon the old man's real name. There's some boppers called diggers that have it in for him." He turned as if to go.

"Wait," Sta-Hi said, "What are you going to do now? While I'm gone?"

"What am I going to do?" Sta-Hi$_2$ said thoughtfully. "Oh, I'll just hang around your house acting like a good son. When you get back I'll fade and you can do whatever you want. I think they can set up that immortality deal for you, too."

The two-minute warning sounded. A last few stragglers hurried past.

"Come on," Cobb boomed, "Time's a-wasting!" He grabbed Sta-Hi by the arm and dragged him down the ramp.

Grinning like a crocodile, Sta-Hi$_2$ watched them go.

CHAPTER EIGHT

With no transition at all, Ralph Numbers was back. He could feel the patter of little feet inside his body-box. He'd been rebuilt. He recognized the feeling. No two arrangements of circuit cards can be *exactly* the same, and adjusting to a new body takes a while. Slowly he turned his head, trying to ignore the way the objects seemed to sweep with his motions. It was like putting on a new pair of glasses, only more so.

A big silver tarantula was crouched in front of Ralph, watching him. Vulcan. A little door in Ralph Numbers's side popped open and a tiny little spider of a robot eased out, feeling around with its extra-long forelegs.

"Copacetic," the little spider piped.

"Well," Vulcan said to Ralph. "Aren't you going to ask how you got here?"

Vulcan had worked for Ralph before. His workshop was familiar. Tools and silicon chips everywhere, circuit analyzers and sheets of brightly colored plastic.

"I guess I'm the new Ralph Numbers scion?" There was no memory of a tenth visit to the One, no memory of disassembly . . . but there never was. Still . . . something seemed wrong.

"Guess again." The little black spider, Vulcan's remote-controlled hand, hopped onto the big silver spider's back.

Ralph thought back. The last thing he could remember was Vulcan taping him. After the taping he had planned to . . .

"Did I go meet Wagstaff?"

"You sure did. And on your way back, someone lasered your parasol. You're lucky I'd just taped you. You only lost two or three hours of memories."

Ralph checked the time. If he hurried he could still meet BEX when it landed. He started to turn around, and nearly fell over.

"Slow down, bopper." Vulcan was holding up a sheet of transparent red plastic. Imipolex G. "I'm going to coat you with flickercladding. Nobody uses parasols anymore. You've looked like a file-cabinet long enough."

The red plastic was not quite stiff, and rippled invitingly. "It might be good for you to look a little different," Vulcan went on coaxingly. "So the diggers can't spot you so easily." He had been trying to sell Ralph some flickercladding for years.

"I wouldn't want to change *too* much," Ralph said uncertainly. After all, he made his living by selling curious boppers his memories. It might cut into his business if he stopped looking like the moon's oldest bopper.

"Gotta change with the times," Vulcan said, measuring out rectangles of the red plastic with two of his legs . . . or arms. "No bopper can afford to stay the same. Especially with those new big boppers trying to take things over." Leg to leg he passed a sheet of the gelatinous plastic around to hold against Ralph. "This won't hurt a bit."

One of Vulcan's legs ended in a riveter. Eight quick taps and the red plastic was firmly mounted on Ralph's chest. The little robot-remote spider-hand scuttled up Ralph's side, patching some thread-like wires from the plastic into Ralph's circuitry. A light-show blossomed on his chest.

"It looks nice," Vulcan said, rearing back for a better look. "You've got a beautiful mind, Ralph. But you should let me give you a *real* disguise. It would only take another hour."

"No," Ralph said, acutely conscious of the time. "Just the flickercladding. I've got to get out to the spaceport before the ship lands."

He could feel the little spider tip-tapping around inside his body box again. The patterns on his chest gained depth and definition. Meanwhile Vulcan riveted the rest of the plastic onto his sides and back. Ralph extruded ten extra centimeters of neck and slowly moved his head around his body. The flickering patterns coded up the binary bit-states that were his thoughts.

One of the reasons Ralph had been able to survive so long just by selling his thoughts and memories was that his thoughts were neither too simple nor too complex. You could see that by looking at the light-patterns on his body. He looked . . . interesting.

"Why do the diggers want to kill you, Ralph?" Vulcan asked. "Not that it's any of my business."

"I don't *know*," Ralph said, frustration showing all over him. "If I could only remember what Wagstaff said out there. Didn't I tell you anything before . . . "

"There were some signals just before melt-down," Vulcan said. "But very garbled. Something about fighting the big boppers. That's a good idea, don't you think?"

"No," Ralph said. "I like the big boppers. They're a logical next step of our evolution. And with all the human brain-tapes they're getting . . . "

"And bopper brain-tapes, too!" Vulcan said with sudden heat. "But they're not going to get me. I think we should tear them all down!"

Ralph didn't want to argue about it . . . time was too short. He paid Vulcan with a handful of chips. Due to the constant inflation, boppers never extended credit. He stepped out of Vulcan's open-fronted workshop onto Sparks Street.

Three hover-spheres darted past, resting on columns of rocket exhaust. It was an expensive way to live, but they earned it with their scouting expeditions. These three moved erratically, and looked to be on a party. Probably one of them had just finished building his scion.

A little way down the street was the big chip-etching works. Chips and circuit-cards were the most essential parts of a new scion, and the factory, called GAX, had tight security. It . . . he . . . was one of the few really solid-looking buildings in Disky. The walls were stone and doors were steel.

For some reason there was a crowd of boppers right in front. Ralph could sense the anger from half a block away. Looked like another lock-out. He crossed to the other side of the street, hoping to stay clear of the trouble.

But one of the boppers spotted Ralph and came stalking over. A tall spindly-looking thing with tweezers instead of fingers. "Is that you, Ralph Numbers?"

"I'm supposed to be in disguise, Burchee."

"You call that a disguise? Why don't you wrap yourself in a billboard instead? No one thinks like you, Ralph."

Burchee should know. He and Ralph had conjugated several times, totally merged their processors with a block-free co-ax. Burchee always had a lot of spare parts to give away, and Ralph had his famous mind. There was something like a sexual love for each other.

The heavy steel door of the factory was sealed shut, and some of the boppers across the street were working on it with hammers and chisels.

"What's the story?" Ralph asked. "Can't you get in to work?"

Burchee's beanpole body flared green with emotion. "GAX locked all the workers out. He wants to run the whole operation himself. He says he doesn't need us anymore. He's got a bunch of robot-remotes in there instead of workers."

"But doesn't he need your special skills?" Ralph asked. "All he knows is buying and selling! GAX can't design a grid-mask like you can, Burchee!"

"Yeah," Burchee said bitterly. "Used to be. But then GAX talked one of the maskers into joining him. The guy fed his tapes to GAX and lives inside him now. His body's just another robot-remote. That's GAX's new line. Either he eats you up or you don't work. So we're trying to break in."

A metal flap high up in the factory wall opened then, and a heavy disk of fused silicon came flying out. The two boppers hammering on the door didn't look up in time. The tremendous piece of glass hit them edge on, cutting them in half. Their processors were irreparably shattered.

"Oh, no!" Burchee cried, crossing the street in three long strides. "They don't even have scions!"

A camera eye peered down from the open flap, then withdrew. This was a depressing development. Ralph thought for a moment. How many big boppers were there now? Ten, fifteen? Was it really necessary that they drive the little boppers into extinction? Perhaps he was wrong to . . .

"We're not going to stand for this, GAX!" Burchee's skinny arms were raised in fury. "Just wait till you have your tenth session!"

Every bopper, big or small, had his brain wiped by the One every ten months. There were no exceptions. Of course a bopper as big and powerful as GAX would have a constantly updated scion waiting to spring into action. But a bopper who had recently transferred his consciousness to a new scion was in some ways as vulnerable as a lobster who has just shed his old shell.

So, spindly Burchee's threat had a certain force, even directed at the city-block-sized GAX. Another heavy disk of glass came angling out from that flap, but Burchee dodged it easily.

"Tomorrow, GAX! We're going to take you apaaaaart!" Burchee's angry green glow dimmed a little, and he came stalking back to Ralph's side. Across the street the other boppers picked over the two corpses, pocketing the usable chips.

"He's due to be wiped at 1300 hours tomorrow," Burchee said, throwing a light arm across Ralph's shoulders. "You ought to come by for the fun."

"I'll try," Ralph said, and meaning it. The big boppers really were going too far. They were a threat to anarchy! He'd help them tape Anderson . . . that was in the old man's own interest, really . . . but then . . .

"I'll try to be here," Ralph said again. "And be careful, Burchee. Even when GAX is down, his robot-remotes will be running on stored programs. You should expect a tough fight."

Burchee flashed a warm yellow good-bye, and Ralph went on down Sparks Street, heading for the bus-stop. He didn't want to have to walk the five kays to the spaceport.

There was a saloon just before the bus-stop, and as Ralph passed it, the door flew open and two truckers tumbled out, snaky arms linked in camaraderie. They looked like rolling beer kegs with bunches of purple tentacles set in the ends. Each of them had a rented scrambler plugged into his squat head-bump. They took up half the street. Ralph gave them a wide berth, wondering a bit nervously what kind of delusions they were picking up on.

"Box the red socket basher are," one chortled.

"Sphere a blue plug stroker is," the other replied, bumping gently against his fellow.

Peering over them into the saloon, Ralph could see five or six heavily-built boppers lurching around a big electromagnet in the center of the room. Even from here he could feel the confusing eddy currents. Places like that frightened Ralph. Conscious of the limited time left before BEX landed, he sped around the corner, craning to see if the bus was coming.

He was pleased to see a long low flat-car moving down the street towards him. Ralph stepped out and flagged it down. The bus quoted the daily fare and Ralph paid it off. Up ten units from yesterday. The constant inflation served as an additional environmental force to eliminate the weak.

Ralph found an empty space and anchored himself. The bus was open all around, and one had to be careful when it rounded corners . . . sometimes traveling as fast as thirty kph.

Boppers got on and off, here and there, but most of them, like Ralph, were headed for the spaceport. Some already had business contacts on Earth, while others hoped to make contacts or to find work as guides. One of the latter had built himself a more-or-less human-looking Imipolex head, and wore a large button saying, "BOPPERS IS DA CWAAAZIEST PEOPLE!"

Ralph looked away in disgust. Thanks to his own efforts, the boppers had long since discarded the ugly, human-chauvinist priorities of Asimov: To protect humans, To obey humans, To protect robots . . . in that order. These days any protection or obedience the humans got from boppers was strictly on a pay-as-you-go basis.

The humans still failed to understand that the different races needed each other not as masters or slaves, but as equals. For all their limitations, human minds were fascinating things . . . things unlike any bopper program. TEX and MEX, Ralph knew, had started a project to collect as many human softwares as they could. And now they wanted Cobb Anderson's.

The process of separating a human's software from his or her hardware, the process, that is, of getting the thought patterns out of the brain, was destructive and non-reversible. For boppers it was much easier. Simply by plugging a co-ax in at the right place, one could read out and tape the entire information content of a bopper's brain. But to decode a human brain was a complex task. There were the electrical patterns to record, the neuron link-ups to be mapped, the memory RNA to be fractioned out and analyzed. To do all this one had to chop and mince. Wagstaff felt this was evil. But Cobb would . . .

"You must be Ralph Numbers," the bopper next to him beamed suddenly. Ralph's neighbor looked like a beauty-shop hair-dryer, complete with chair. She had gold flickercladding, and fizzy little patterns spiraled around her pointy head. She twined a metallic tentacle around one of Ralph's manipulators.

"We better talk DC," came the voice. "It's more private. Everyone in this part of the bus has been picking up on your thoughts, Ralph."

He glanced around. How can you tell if a bopper's watching you? One way, of course, is if he has his head turned around and has his vision sensors pointed at you. Most of the boppers around Ralph were still staring at him. There was going to be chaos at the spaceport when Cobb Anderson got off the ship.

"What does he look like?" came the silky signal from Ralph's neighbor.

"By now, who knows?" Ralph pulsed back quietly. "The hollow in the museum is twenty-five years out of date. And humans all look alike anyway."

"Not to me," Ralph's neighbor purred. "I design automated cosmetic kits for them."

"That's nice," Ralph said. "Now could you take your hand off me? I've got some private projections to run."

"OK. But why don't you look me up tomorrow afternoon? I've got enough parts for two scions. And I'd like to conjugate with you. My name is Cindy-Lou. Cubette 3412."

"Maybe," Ralph said, a little flattered at the offer. Anyone who had set up business contacts on Earth had to have something on the ball. The red plastic flickercladding that Vulcan had sold him must not look bad. Must not look bad at all. "I'll try to come by after the riot."

"What riot?"

"They're going to tear down GAX. Or try to. He locked the workers out."

"I'll come, too! There should be lots of good pickings. And next week they're going to wreck MEX, too, did you know?"

Ralph started in surprise. Wreck MEX, the museum? And what of all the brain-tapes MEX had so painstakingly acquired?

"They shouldn't do that," Ralph said. "This is getting out of hand!"

"Wreck them all!" Cindy-Lou said merrily. "Do you mind if I bring some friends tomorrow?"

"Go ahead. But leave me alone. I've got to think."

The bus had drawn clear of Disky and had started across the empty lunar plain leading to the spaceport. Away from the buildings, the sun was bright, and everyone's flickercladding became more mirror-like. Ralph mulled over the news about MEX. In a way it wouldn't really affect Anderson. The main thing was to get his brain taped and to send the tape back down to Earth. Send it to Mr. Frostee. Then the Cobb software could take over his robot-remote double. It would be the best thing for the old man. From what Ralph heard, Anderson's present hardware was about to give out.

The busload of boppers pulled up to the human's dome at the edge of the spaceport. Signaling from high above, BEX announced that he would be landing in half an hour. Right on time. The whole trip, from Earth to space-station Ledge via shuttle, and from Ledge to the Moon via BEX, took just a shade over twenty-four hours.

An air-filled passenger tunnel came probing out from the dome, ready to cup the deep-space ship's air-lock as soon as it landed. The cold vacuum of the Moon, so comfortable for the boppers, was deadly for humans. Conversely, the warm air inside the dome was lethal to the boppers.

No bopper could enter the humans' dome without renting an auxiliary refrigeration unit to wheel around with him. The boppers kept the air in the dome as dry as possible to protect them from corrosion, but in order for the humans to survive, one did have to put up with an ambient temperature in excess of 290° K. And the humans called that "room temperature"! Without an extra refrigeration unit, a bopper's super-conducting circuits would break down instantly in there.

Ralph shelled out the rental fee . . . tripled since last time . . . and entered the humans' dome, wheeling his refrigerator in front of him. It was pretty crowded. He stationed himself close enough to the visa-checker to be able to hear the names of the passengers.

There were diggers scattered all around the waiting area . . . too many. They were all watching him. Ralph realized he should have let Vulcan disguise him more seriously. All he had done was to put on a flashing red coat. Some disguise!

CHAPTER NINE

The faces in the moon kept changing. An old woman with a bundle of sticks, a lady in a feather hat, the round face of a dreamy girl at the edge of life.

"*Slowly, silently, now the Moon / Walks the night in her silver shoon*," Cobb quoted sentyntiously. "Some things never change, Sta-Hi."

Sta-Hi leaned across Cobb to stare out the tiny quartz port-hole. As they drew closer the pockmarks grew, and the stubble of mountains along the Moon's vast cheek became unmistakable. A syphilitic fog in pancake make-up. Sta-Hi fell back into his seat, lit a last joint. He was feeling paranoid.

"Did you ever flash," he asked through a cloud of exquisitely detailed smoke, "that maybe those copies of us could be *permanent*? That this is all just to get us out of the way so Anderson$_2$ and Sta-Hi$_2$ can pose as humans?"

This was, at least in Sta-Hi's case, a fairly correct assessment of the situation. But Cobb chose not to tell Sta-Hi this. Instead he blustered.

"That's just ridiculous. Why would . . . "

"You know more about the boppers than I do, old man. Unless that was shit you were spouting about having helped design them."

"Didn't you learn about me in high-school, Sta-Hi?" Cobb asked sorrowfully. "Cobb Anderson who taught the robots how to bop? Don't they teach that?"

"I was out a lot," Sta-Hi said with a shrug. "But what if the boppers wanted two agents on Earth. They send down copies of us, and talk us into coming up here. As soon as we're gone the copies start standing in for us and gathering information. Right?"

"Information about what?" Cobb snapped. "We weren't leading real high security-clearance lives down there, Sta-Hi."

"What I'm worried about is whether they'll let us go back." Sta-Hi went on, flicking invisible drops of tension off the tips of his fingers. "Maybe they want to do something with our bodies up here. Use them for hideous and inhuman experiments." On the last phrase his voice tripped and broke into nervous laughter.

Cobb shook his head. "Dennis DeMentis. That's what it says on your visa. And I'm . . . ?"

Sta-Hi fished out the papers from his pocket and handed them over. Cobb looked through them, sipping at his coffee. He'd been drunk at Ledge, but the stewardess had fixed him up with a shot of stimulants and B-vitamins. He hadn't felt so clear-headed in months.

There was his visa. Smiling bearded face, born March 22, 1950, *Graham DeMentis* signed in his looping hand down at the bottom of the document.

"That's the green stuff," Sta-Hi remarked, looking over his shoulder.

"What is?"

Sta-Hi's only answer was to press his lips together like a monkey and smack a few times. The stewardess moved down the aisle, her Velcro foot-coverings schnicking loose from the Velcro carpet at each step. Longish blonde hair free-falling around her face. "Please fasten your safety belts. We will be landing at spaceport Disky in six-oh-niner seconds."

The rockets cut in and the ship trembled at the huge forces beneath it. The stewardess took Cobb's empty cup and snapped up his table. "Please extinguish your smoking materials, sir." This to Sta-Hi.

He handed her the roach, smiling and letting smoke trickle through his teeth and up at her.

"Get wiggly, baby."

Her eyes flickered . . . Yes? No? . . . and then she flicked the roach into Cobb's coffee cup and moved on.

"Now remember," Cobb cautioned. "We play it like tourists at the space-port. I gather that some of the boppers, the diggers, are out to stop us."

The ship's engines roared to a fever pitch. Little chunks of rock flew up from the landing field and there was silence. Cobb stared out the lens-like little port-hole. The Sea of Tranquility.

Blinding gray, it undulated off to the too-close horizon. A big crater back there . . . five kilometers, fifty? . . . the Maskelyne Crater. Unnaturally sharp mountains in the distance. They reminded Cobb of something he wanted to forget: teeth, ragged clouds . . . the Mountains of Madness. Surely some civilization, somewhere, had believed that the dead go to the Moon.

There was a soft but final-sounding *thop* from the other side of the ship. The air tunnel. The stewardess cranked open the lock, her sweet ass bobbing with the wheel's rhythm. On the way out, Sta-Hi asked her for a date.

"Me and Gramps'll be at the Hilton, baby. Dennis DeMentis. I'll go insane if I don't get some drain. Fall on by?"

Her smile was as unreadable as a Halloween mask. "Perhaps you'll run into me at the lounge."

"Which . . . " he began.

She cut him off. "There's only one." Shaking Cobb's hand now. "Thank you for traveling with us, sir. Enjoy your stay."

The space terminal was crowded with boppers. Sta-Hi had seen models of a few of the basic types before, but no two of them waiting out there looked quite alike. It was like stepping into Bosch's Hell. Faces and . . . "faces" . . . crowding the picture plane top to bottom, front to back.

Hovering right by the door was a smiling sphere holding itself up with a whirling propeller. The smile all but split it in half. "See subterranean cities!" it urged, rolling fake eyeballs.

Down at the end of the ramp waited the visa-checker, looking something like a tremendous stapler. You stuck your visa in there while it scanned your face and fingerprints. KAH-CHUNNNG! Passed.

Standing right next to the visa-checker was a boxy red robot. Things like blue snakes or dragons writhed around his treads. Diggers. The red robot stuck a nervous microphone of a face near Sta-Hi and Cobb, then reeled his head back in.

He reminded Cobb a little of good old Ralph Numbers. But with those diggers there it was better not to ask. It could wait until they met in the museum.

In the lobby, dozens of garish, self-made machines wheeled, slithered, stalked and hovered. Every time Cobb and Sta-Hi would look one way, snaky metal tentacles would pluck at them from the other direction.

"You buy uranium?"

"Got mercury?"

"Old fashion T.V. set?"

"Fuck android girls?"

"Sell your fingers?"

"Moon King relics?"

"Prosthetic talking penis?"

"Chip-market tip-sheet?"

"Home-cooked food?"

"Set up factory?"

"Same time fuck-suck?"

"DNA death code?"

"Dust bath enema?"

"See vacuum bells?"

"Brand-new voice-prints?"

"No-risk brain-tape?"

"You sell camera?"

"Play my songs?"

"Me be you?"

"Hotel?"

Cobb and Sta-Hi jumped into the lap of this last bopper, a husky black fellow contoured to seat two humans.

"No baggage?" he asked.

Cobb shook his head. The black bopper forced his way through the crowd, warding off the others with things like huge pinball flippers. Sta-Hi was silent, still thinking some of those offers over.

The bopper carrying them kept a microphone and camera eye attentively focused on them. "Isn't there any control?" Cobb asked querulously. "Over who can come in here and bother the arriving passengers?"

"You are our honored guests," the bopper said obliquely. "*Aloha* means hello and . . . good-bye. Here is your hotel. I will accept payment." A little door opened between the two seats.

Sta-Hi drew out his wallet. It was nice and full. "How much do . . . " he began.

"Money is so dull," the bopper answered. "I would prefer a surprise gift. A complex information."

Cobb felt in the pockets of his white suit. There was still some scotch, a brochure from the space-liner, a few coins . . .

Boppers were pressing up to them again, plucking at their clothes, possibly snipping out samples.

"Dirt-side newspapers?"

" 'Slow boat to China' ?"

"Execution sense tapes?"

The black bopper had only carried them a hundred meters. Impatiently, Sta-Hi tossed his handkerchief into their carrier's waiting bopper.

"*Aloha*," the bopper said, and rolled back towards the gate, grooving on the slubby weave.

The hotel was a pyramid-like structure filling the center of the dome. Cobb and Sta-Hi were relieved to find only humans in the lobby. Tourists, businessmen, drifters.

Sta-Hi looked around for a reception desk, but could spot none. Just as he was wondering who he might approach, a voice spoke in his ear.

"Welcome to the Disky Hilton, Mr. DeMentis. I have a wonderful room for you and your grandfather on the fifth floor."

"Who was that?" Cobb demanded, turning his big shaggy head sharply.

"I am DEX, the Disky Hilton." The hotel itself was a single huge bopper.

Somehow it could point-send its voice to any spot at all . . . indeed it could carry on a different conversation with every guest at once.

The ethereal little voice led Cobb and Sta-Hi to an elevator and up to their room. There was no question of privacy. After heartily drinking a few glasses of water from the carafe, Cobb finally called to Sta-Hi, "Long trip, eh Dennis?"

"Sure was, Gramps. What all do you think we should do tomorrow?"

"Waaal, I think I'll still be too tuckered out for them big dust-slides. Maybe we should mosey on over to that museum those robots built. Just to ease ourselves in slow like, you know."

The hotel cleared its throat before talking, so as not to startle them. "We have a bus leaving for the museum at oh-nine-hundred hours."

Cobb was scared to even look at Sta-Hi. Did DEX know who they really were? And was he on their side or the diggers' side? And why would any of the boppers be against making Cobb immortal in the first place? He poured out the last of his Scotch, tossed it off, and lay down. He really was tired. The low lunar gravity felt good. You could gain a lot of weight up here. Wondering what would be for breakfast, Cobb drifted into sleep.

CHAPTER TEN

Sta-Hi threw a blanket onto the old man and walked over to look out the window. Most of the boppers were gone now. They had left a jumble of wheeled refrigeration carts next to the air-lock. Slowly, meticulously, a hunch-backed bopper was lining the carts up.

A human couple strolled around the plaza between the hotel and the visa-checker. There was something odd to Sta-Hi in the studied aimlessness of the couple's wanderings. He watched them for five minutes and they still didn't get anywhere. Around and around like mechanical hillbillies in a shooting gallery.

The translucent plastic dome was not far overhead, tinted against the raw sunlight. For the humans it was night in here, but outside the sun still shone, and the boppers were as active as ever. Even though the Lunar day lasts two weeks, and even though the boppers rarely "slept," they still, perhaps out of nostalgia, but probably out of inertia, kept time by the human twenty-four-hour day system. And to make the humans comfortable, they varied the brightness of their dome accordingly.

Sta-Hi felt a shudder of claustrophobia. His every action was being recorded, analyzed. Every breath, every bite was just another link to the boppers. He was, right now, actually *inside* a bopper, the big bopper DEX. Why had he let Cobb talk him into coming here? Why had Cobb wanted him?

Cobb was snoring now. For a terrible instant, Sta-Hi thought he saw wires running out of the pillow and into the old man's scalp. He leaned closer and realized they were just black hairs among the gray. He decided to go down to the lounge. Maybe that stewardess would be there.

The hotel bar and lounge was full, but quiet. Some businessmen were bellied up to the automatic bar. They were drinking moon-brewed beer . . . the dome's dry air made you mighty thirsty.

In the middle of the lounge a bunch of tables had been pushed together for a party. Earth-bottled champagne. Sta-Hi recognized the revelers from the flight up. A fortyish dominatrix-type tour-guide, and six sleek young married couples. Inherited wealth, for them to be up here so young. They ignored Sta-Hi, having long since sized him up as dull and lower-class.

Alone in a booth at the end of the room was the face he wanted. The stewardess. There was no drink in front of her, no book . . . she was just sitting there. Sta-Hi slid in across from her.

"Remember me?"

She nodded. "Sure." There was something funny about how she had been sitting there . . . blank as a parked car. "I've sort of been waiting for you."

"Well all *right*! Do they sell dope here?"

The hotel's disembodied voice cut in. "What would be your pleasure, Mr. DeMentis?"

Sta-Hi considered. He wanted to be able to sleep . . . eventually.

"Give me a beer and a two-boost." He glanced at the symmetrical, smiling face across the table. "And you?"

"The usual."

"Very good, sir and madam," the hotel murmured.

Seconds later a little door in the wall by their table popped open. A conveyor belt had brought the order. Sta-Hi's two-boost was a shot-glass of clear liquid, sharp with solvents, bitter with alkaloids. The woman's . . .

"What's your name anyway?" Sta-Hi tossed off his foul-tasting potion. He'd be seeing colors for two hours.

"Misty." She reached out to pick up the object she had ordered. *The usual.*

"What is that?" A too-high rush of panic was percolating up his spine. Fast stuff, the two-boost. The girl across from him was holding a little metal box, holding it to her temple . . .

She giggled suddenly, her eyes rolling. "It feels good." She turned a dial on the little box and rubbed it back and forth on her forehead. "This year people say . . . *wiggly*?"

"You don't live on Earth anymore?"

"Of course not." Long silence. She ran the little box over her head like a barber's clippers. "Wiggly."

There was a burst of laughter from the young-marrieds. Someone had made an indecent suggestion. Probably the beefy guy pouring out more champagne.

Sta-Hi's attention went back to the emptily pretty face across the table from him. He'd never seen anything like the thing she was rubbing on her head.

"What *is* that?" he asked again.

"An electromagnet,"

"You're . . . you're a bopper?"

"Well, sort of. I'm completely inorganic, if that's what you mean. But I'm not self-contained. My brain is actually in BEX. I'm sort of a remote-controlled part of the spaceship."

She flicked the little box back and forth in front of her eyes, enjoying the way the magnetic field lines moved the images around. "*Wiggly.* Can you teach me some more new slang?"

Before seeing his own robot double at the spaceport, Sta-Hi had never believed that he could mistake a machine for a person. And now it was happening again. Sitting here in the roar of the two-boost, he wished he was someplace else.

Misty leaned across the table, a smile tugging at the corners of her lips. "Did you really think I was human?"

"I don't normally make dates with machines," Sta-Hi blurted, and tried to recover with a joke. "I don't even own a vibrator."

He'd hurt her feelings. She turned up the dial on her magnet, blanking her face in an ecstasy that showed him her contempt.

Suddenly lonely, he reached out and pulled the hand with the electro-magnet away from her temple.

"Talk to me, Misty." He could feel the movements of his lips and talking tongue. Too high. He had a sudden horrible suspicion that *everyone here* was a robot. But, even so, the girl's hand was warm under his, fleshy.

Sta-Hi's beer sat untouched on the table-top between them. Misty blew part of the head away, took a sip, handed the glass to Sta-Hi. He sipped too. Thick, bitter.

"DEX brews this himself," she remarked. "Do you like it?"

"It's OK. But can you digest? Or is there a plastic bag you empty every . . . "

Misty set down her magnet-box and twined her fingers with Sta-Hi's. "You should think of me as a person. My personality is human. I still like eating and . . . and other things." She dimpled prettily and traced a circle on Sta-Hi's palm. "I don't get to meet many stuzzy young guys just stewardessing the Ledge-Disky run . . . "

He pulled his hand away. "But how can you be human if you're a machine?"

"Look," Misty said patiently. "There used to be a young lady called Misty Nivlac who lived in Richmond, Virginia. Last spring Misty-girl hitchhiked to Daytona Beach for some brainsurfing. She fell in with a bad crowd. Really bad. A gang called the Little Kidders."

The Little Kidders. Sta-Hi could still see their faces. That blonde girl who'd picked him up . . . Kristleen? And Berdoo, the skinny little guy wearing chains. Haf'N'Haf with all those missing teeth. And Phil, the leader, the big guy with the tattoo on his back.

" . . . got her brain-tape," Misty was saying. "While BEX built a copy of her body. So now inside BEX there's a perfect model of Misty-girl's personality. BEX tells the model what to do, and the model runs . . . this." She spread out her hands palm up. "Brand-new Misty-girl."

"From what I hear," Sta-Hi said as neutrally as possible, "the Little Kidders go around *eating* brains, not *taping* them."

"You've heard of them?" Misty seemed surprised. "Well, it *looks* like they're eating the brain. But one of them is a robot with a little laboratory inside his chest. He has all the equipment to get the memories out. The patterns. They get a lot of people's brains that way. The big boppers are making a sort of library out of them. But most people don't get their own robot-remote body like me. I'm just really . . . lucky." She smiled again.

"I'm surprised you're telling me all this," Sta-Hi said finally. BEX . . . Misty . . . must really not know who he was. Whoever had fixed up their fake ID's must not have had time to tell the others.

But maybe . . . and this would be much worse . . . maybe they did know *perfectly well* who he was. But he was already doomed, a walking dead man, just waiting for them to extract his brain-tape and send it down to Earth to run that Sta-Hi$_2$ they had all set. You can tell anything to a man about to die.

"But BEX didn't want me to," Misty was saying. "*You* can't hear him of course, but he's been telling me to shut up the whole time. But he can't make me. I still have my free will . . . it's part of the brain-tape. I can do what I like." She smiled into Sta-Hi's eyes. There was a moment's silence and then she started talking again.

"You wanted to know who I am. I gave you one answer. A robot-remote. A servo-unit operated by a program stored in a bopper spaceship. But . . . I'm still Misty-girl, too. The soul is the software, you know. The software is what counts, the habits and the memories. The brain and the body are just meat, seeds for the organ-tanks." She smiled uncertainly, took a pull at his beer, set it down. "Do you want to fuck?"

The sex was nice, but confusing. The whole situation kept going di-polar on Sta-Hi. One instant Misty would seem like a lovely warm girl who'd survived a terrible injury, like a lost puppy to be stroked, a lonely woman to be husbanded. But then he'd start thinking of the wires behind her eyes, and he'd be screwing a machine, an inanimate object, a public toilet. His relations with women were a mess.

CHAPTER ELEVEN

Cobb Anderson was not too surprised to see a girl in Sta-Hi's bed when he woke up.

"Aren't you the stewardess?" he asked, slowly raising himself into sitting position. He'd slept in his clothes three nights running now. First on Mooney's floor, then on the bopper space-ship, and now here in the hotel. The grease on his skin had built up so thick that it was hard to blink his eyes. "Do they have a shower here?"

"I'm sorry," the hotel's disembodied voice answered. "We do not. Water is a precious resource on the Moon. But you may enjoy a chemical sponge-bath, Mr. Anderson. Step right this way."

A light blinked over one of the three doors. Stiffly, ponderously, Cobb shuffled through it.

"I'll have to charge you for triple occupancy, Mr. DeMentis," the hotel told Sta-Hi in a polite, neutral voice.

But at the same time he could overhear another of its point-voices sniggeringly asking Misty, "Dja come?"

"Breakfast," Sta-Hi said, drowning the other voice out. "Central nervous stimulants. Cold beer."

"Very good, sir."

The old man appeared again, moving like an upended steamer trunk on wheels. He was naked. Seeing Misty he paused, embarrassed.

"I'm having my clothes cleaned."

"Don't worry," Sta-Hi put in. "She's just a robot-remote."

Cobb ignored that, peeled a sheet off the bed and wrapped it around his waist. He was a hairy man, and most of the hair was white. His stomach looked bigger with the clothes off.

Just then breakfast slid out of the wall and onto the table between the beds. "To your health," Cobb said, taking one of the beers. It had a kick to it, and left him momentarily dizzy. He took a plate of the scrambled . . . eggs? . . . and sat down on his bed.

"He doesn't know what a robot-remote is," Sta-Hi said to Misty.

Mouth full, Cobb glared at him until he had swallowed. "Of course I do, Sta-Hi. Can't you get it through your drug-addled noggin that I was at one time a famous man? That I, Cobb Anderson, am responsible for the robots having evolved into boppers?"

Something on the girl's face changed. And then Cobb remembered their cover story.

"The ears have walls," Sta-Hi remarked. "You shit-head."

Cobb glared again, and continued eating in silence. So what if some of the boppers found out who he was, anyway? They couldn't *all* be against him getting immortality. Maybe the hotel didn't even care. He had slept well in the low lunar gravity. He felt ready for anything.

Having learned that Cobb Anderson was here in the room with her, Misty . . . that is to say the bopper brain in the nose of the spaceship . . . took certain steps. But meanwhile started an argument with Sta-Hi.

"Why did you say *just* a robot-remote? As if I were less than human. Would you say that about a woman with an artificial leg? Or a glass eye? I just happen to be *all* artificial."

"Stuzzy, Misty. I can wave with it." said Sta-Hi. "But as long as BEX has the final word, and I think he does, you're really just a puppet being run by . . . "

"*What* do you call yourself?" Misty interrupted angrily. "*Sta-Hi*? What a stupid name! It sounds like a brand-name for panty-hose!"

"Personal insults," Sta-Hi said, shaking his head. "What next?"

"It is now 0830 hours," the hotel interrupted. "May I remind you of your stated intent to get the 0900 bus to the robotics museum?"

"Will we need pressure suits?" Cobb asked.

"They will be provided."

"Let's go then," Misty said.

Sta-Hi exchanged a glance with Cobb. "Look Misty . . . this is likely to be a sort of sentimental journey for the old man. I wonder if you could just . . . fade. Maybe we'll be back here by lunchtime."

"*Fade*?" Misty cried, angrily flouncing across the room. "Too bad there's not a toggle switch on the top of my head! Then you wouldn't even have to ask me to leave. You creep!" She slammed the door very hard.

"Ouch," the hotel said softly.

"Why did you get rid of her?" Cobb asked. "She's cute. And I don't think she'd try to stand in my way."

"You bet she wouldn't," Sta-Hi answered. "Do you realize what the boppers are really planning to do to us?"

"They're going to give me some kind of immortality drug," Cobb said happily. "And maybe some new organs as well. And as for you, well . . . "

Cobb didn't like to tell the younger man that he was only here because the boppers had wanted him out of the way. But before he could tell him about Sta-Hi$_2$ using Mooney's influence to get a night watchman job at the warehouse, Sta-Hi had started talking.

"Immortality. What they want to do, old man, is to cut out our brains and grind them up and squeeze all the information out. They'll store our personalities on tapes in some kind of library. And if we're lucky, they might send copies of the tapes down to Earth to help run those two robot-remotes. But that's not . . . "

"BUS TOUR PARTICIPANTS MUST PROCEED TO THE LOBBY IMMEDIATELY!" the hotel-room blared, interrupting Sta-Hi.

Cobb was galvanized into activity by this. He hurried out to the elevators, dragging Sta-Hi with him. It was like he didn't want to hear the truth. Or didn't care. And Sta-Hi? He came along. Now that the hotel knew that he knew, he wouldn't be safe in it. He'd have to try to make his break in the museum.

The tour-bus was about half-full. Most of the others were ageing rich folks, singles and couples. Everyone was wearing a bubble-top pressure suit. They were supple, lovely things . . . made of a limp clear plastic that sparkled with a sort of inner light. In the shade, a person in a bubble-topper looked normal, except for the mild halo that seemed to surround his head. But the suits turned reflective in sunlight.

The bus was a wire-wheeled flat-car surmounted by two rows of grotesquely functional seats. Each seat consisted of three black balls of hard rubber mounted on a bent Y of stiff plastic. To Sta-Hi, his seat looked like Mickey Mouse's head . . . with everything but the nose and ears invisible. He half-expected a squeak of protest when he lowered his body down onto it.

As they pulled clear of the dome a sudden crackle of static split his helmet.

"We've got an A-OK on that, Houston. We are proceeding to deploy the egression facility."

Breathing, a fizzling whine, another voice.

"I am leaving the vehicle."

Pause.

"Got a little problem with the steps here."

Long pause.

"We read you, Neal." Faint, encouraging.

Big crackle.

"—at's one small step for man, giant step for humanity."

Synthetic cheering washed out the voices. Sta-Hi turned to Cobb, trying to catch a glimpse of his face. But now there was no way to see in through the other's bubble-topper. Their suits had turned mirror-like as soon as they'd left the shade of the dome.

The bopper bus continued with its taped "Sounds of Lunar Discovery" as they approached Disky. The key moon-landings were all dramatized, as were the attempts at human settlement, the dome blow-outs, and the first semi-autonomous robots. When Disky was about 500 meters off, the transcendentally bland voice on the tape reached its finale.

"Nineteen Ninety-Five! Ralph Numbers and twelve other self-repro-ducing robots are set free in the Sea of Tranquility! Learn the *rest* of the story in the robotics museum!" There was a click and a longish pause.

Sta-Hi stared at the buildings of Disky, filling the small horizon. Here and there, boppers moved about, just small glittering lights at this distance.

Suddenly the bus's real voice sounded in their earphones. "Good morning, fleshers. I am circumscribing Disky through fifty-eight degrees to reach our entry ray. Please to be restful and asking questions. My label Captain Cody in this context. Do brace for shear."

Hardly slowing down, the vehicle swerved sharply to the right. The Y-seats swayed far over. Too far. Sta-Hi grabbed Cobb's arm. If he fell off, nothing would stop him from rolling under those big, flexing wheels. You had the feeling that "Captain Cody" wouldn't even slow down. For a minute the seats wobbled back and forth. Now the bus was driving along the outskirts of Disky, circling the city counterclockwise.

"How many boppers live here?" came some oldster's voice over the earphones. No answer.

The voice tried again. "How many boppers live in Disky, Captain Cody?"

"I am researching this information," came the reply. The bus's voice was high and musical. Definitely alien-sounding. Everyone waited in silence for the population figure.

A large building slid by on their left. The sides were open, and inside you could see stacked sheets of some material. A bopper standing at the edge stared at them, its head slowly tracking their forward motion.

"What precision is required?" the bus asked then.

"I don't know," the old questioner crackled uncertainly. "Zuh . . . *zero* precision? Does that make sense?"

"Thank you," the bus chortled. "With *zero* precision, is *no* boppers living in Disky. Or ten to sixty-third power."

Boppers were notorious for their nit-picking literal-mindedness when talking to humans. It was just another of their many ways of being hostile. They had never quite forgiven people for the three Asimov laws that the original designers had . . . unsuccessfully, thanks to Cobb . . . tried to build into the boppers. They viewed every human as a thwarted Simon Legree.

For a while after that, no one asked Captain Cody any more questions. Disky was big . . . perhaps as big as Manhattan. The bus kept a scrupulous five hundred meters from the nearest buildings at all times, but even from that distance one could make out the wild diversity of the city.

It was a little as if the entire history of Western civilization had occurred in one town over the course of thirty years. Squeezed against each other were structures of every conceivable type: primitive, classical, baroque, gothic, renaissance, industrial, art nouveau, functionalist, late funk, zapper, crepuscular, flat-flat, hyperdee . . . all in perfect repair. Darting among the buildings were myriads of the brightly colored boppers, creatures clad in flickering light.

"How come the buildings are so different?" Sta-Hi blurted. "Captain Cody?"

"What category of cause your requirements?" the bus sing-songed.

"State the categories, Captain Cody," Sta-Hi shot back, determined not to fall into the same trap as the last questioner.

"WHY QUESTION," the bus answered in a gloating tone, "*Answer Categories*: Material Cause, *Situational Cause*, Teleological Cause. *Material Cause Subcategories*: Spacetime, Mass-energy. Situational Cause Subcategories: Information, Noise. *Teleological Cause Subcategories . . .* "

Sta-Hi stopped listening. Not being able to see anyone's face was making him uptight. The bubble-toppers had gone as silvery as Christmas-tree balls. The round heads reflected Disky and each others' reflections in endless regresses. How long had they been on the bus?

"*Informational Situational Cause Subsubcategories:*" the bus continued, with insultingly-precise intonation, "Analog, Digital. Noisy . . . "

Sta-Hi sighed and leaned back in his seat.

CHAPTER TWELVE

The museum was underground, under Disky. It was laid out in a pattern of concentric circles intersected by rays. Something like Dante's Inferno. Cobb felt a tightening in his chest as he walked down the sloping stone ramp. His cheap, second-hand heart felt like it might blow out any minute.

The more he thought about it, the likelier it seemed that what Sta-Hi said was true. There was no immortality drug. The boppers were going to tape his brain and put him in a robot body. But with the body he had now, that might not be so bad.

The idea of having his brain-patterns extracted and transferred didn't terrify Cobb as it did Sta-Hi. For Cobb understood the principles of robot consciousness. The transition would be weird and wrenching. But if all went well . . .

"It's on the right down there," Sta-Hi said, pressing his bubble-topper against Cobb's. He held a little engraved stone map in his hand. They were looking for the Anderson room.

As they walked down the hall the exhibits sprang to life. Mostly hollows . . . holograms with voice-overs broadcast directly to the suits' radios. A thin little man wearing a dark suit over a wool vest appeared in front of them. *Kurt Gödel* it said under his feet. He had dark-rimmed glasses and silvery hair. Behind him was a blackboard with a statement of his famous Incompleteness Theorem.

"The human mind is incapable of formulating (or mechanizing) all its mathematical intuitions," Gödel's image stated. He had a way of ending his phrases on a rising note which chattered into an amused hum.

"On the other hand, on the basis of what has been proved so far, it remains possible that there may exist (and even be empirically discoverable) a theorem-proving machine which in fact is equivalent to mathematical intuition . . . "

"What's he talking about?" Sta-Hi demanded.

Cobb had stopped to watch the hollow of the great master. He still remembered the years he had spent brooding over the passage which was being recited. Humans can't *build* a robot as smart as themselves. But, logically speaking, it is possible for such robots to *exist*.

How? Cobb had asked himself throughout the 1970's, *How can we bring into existence the robots which we can't design?* In 1980 he had the bare bones of an answer. One of his colleagues had written the paper up for *Speculations in Science and Technology*. "Towards Robot Consciousness," he'd called it. The idea had all been there. *Let the robots evolve.* But fleshing the idea out to an actual . . .

"Let's *go*," Sta-Hi urged, tugging Cobb through Gödel's talking hollow.

Beyond, two frightened lizards scampered down the hallway. A leathery-winged creature came zooming up the hall towards them, and darted its scissoring beak at the lizards. One of the little beasts escaped with a quick back-flip, but the other was carried off over Cobb and Sta-Hi's heads, dripping pale blood.

"*Survival of the Fittest*," an announcer's mellow voice intoned. "One of the two great forces driving the engine of evolution."

In speeded-up motion, the little lizard laid a clutch of eggs, the eggs hatched, and new lizards grew and whisked around. The predator returned, the survivors laid eggs . . . over and over the cycle repeated. Each time the lizards were more agile, and with stronger rear legs. In a few minutes' time they were hopping about like loathsome little kangaroos, fork-tongued and yellow-eyed.

It was Cobb who had to urge them past this exhibit. Sta-Hi wanted to stick around and see what the lizards would come up with next.

Stepping out of the prehistoric scene, they found themselves on a carnival midway. Rifles cracked and pinball machines chimed, people laughed and shrieked, and under it all was the visceral throb of heavy machinery. The floor seemed to be covered with sawdust now; and grinning, insubstantial bumpkins ambled past. A boy and girl leaned against a cotton-candy stand, feeding each other bits of popcorn with shiny fingers. He had a prominent Adam's apple and a bumpy nose. A sine-wave profile. She wore a high, blonde pony-tail fastened by a mini-blinker. The only jarring note was a hard rain of tiny purplish lights . . . which seemed to pass right through everything in the scene. At first Cobb took it for static.

To their right was a huge marquee with lurid paintings of distorted human forms. The inevitable barker . . . checked suit, bowler, cigar-butt . . . leaned down at them, holding out his thin cane for attention.

"See the Freaks, Feel the Geeks!" His loud, hoarse voice was like a crowd screaming. "Pinheads! The Dog-Boy! Pencil-Necks! The Human Lima Bean! Half-Man-Half- . . . " Slowly the carnival noises damped down, and were replaced by the rich, round tones of the voice-over.

"*Mutation*." The voice was resonant, lip-smackingly conclusive. "The second key to the evolutionary process."

The zippy little dots of purple light grew brighter. They passed right through everyone on the midway . . . especially those two lovers, french-kissing now, hips touching.

"The human reproductive cells are subjected to a continual barrage of ionizing radiation," the voice said earnestly. "We call these the cosmic rays."

The carnival noises faded back in now. And each of the fast little lights made a sound like a slide-whistle when it passed. The two kissing lovers began slowly to grow larger, crowding out the rest of the scene. Soon an image of the swain's bulging crotch filled the hallway. The cloth ripped loose and a single huge testicle enveloped Cobb and Sta-Hi, standing there mesmerized.

Hazy red light, the heavy, insistent sound of a heartbeat. Every so often a cosmic ray whistled through. An impression of pipes—a 3D maze of plumbing which grew and blurred around them. Gradually the blur became grainy, and the grains grew. They were looking at cells now, reproductive cells. The nucleus of one of them waxed to hover in front of Cobb and Sta-Hi.

With a sudden, crab-like movement the nuclear material split into striped writhing sausages. The chromosomes. But now a cosmic ray cut one of the chromosomes in half! The two halves joined up again, but with one piece reversed!

"Geek gene," a hillbilly muttered somewhere in the nearly infinite fairground. And then the pictures went out. They were in a down-sloping stone hallway.

"Selection and Mutation," Cobb said as they walked on. "That was my big idea, Sta-Hi. To make the robots evolve. They were designed to build copies of themselves, but they had to fight over the parts. Natural selection. And I found a way of jiggering their programs with cosmic rays. Mutation. But to predict . . . "

Just ahead, a door led off to the right. "This is your meet," Sta-Hi said, consulting his map. "The Cobb Anderson Room."

CHAPTER THIRTEEN

Looking in, our two heroes could see nothing but darkness, and a dimly glowing red polygon. They stepped through the door and the exhibit came on.

"We cannot build an intelligent robot," a voice stated firmly. "But we can cause one to evolve." A hollow of the young Cobb Anderson walked past banks of computers to meet the visitors.

"This is where I grew the first bopper programs," the recorded voice continued. The hollow smiled confidently, engagingly. "No one can *write* a bopper program . . . they're too complicated. So instead I set thousands of simple AI programs loose in there," he gestured familiarly at the computers. "There were lots of . . . fitness tests, with the weaker programs getting wiped. And every so often all the surviving programs were randomly changed . . . mutated. I even provided for a sort of . . . sexual reproduction, where two programs could merge. After fifteen years, I . . . "

Cobb felt a terrible sickness at the gulf of time separating him from the dynamic young man he had once been. The heedless onward rush of events, of age and death . . . he couldn't stand to look at his old self. Sick at heart, he stepped back out of the room, pulling Sta-Hi with him. The display winked out. Again the room was dark, save for a glow of red light near the opposite wall.

"Ralph?" Cobb called, his voice trembling a bit. "It's me."

Ralph Numbers came clattering across the room. His red flickercladding glowed with swirls of complex emotion. "It's good to see you, Doctor Anderson." Trying to do the right thing, Ralph held out a manipulator, as if to shake hands.

Sobbing openly now, Cobb threw his arms around the bopper's unyielding body-box and rocked him to and fro. "I've gotten old, Ralph. And you're . . . you're still the same."

"Not really, Dr. Anderson. I've been rebuilt thirty-seven times. And I have exchanged various subprograms with others."

"That's right," Cobb said, laughing and crying at the same time. "Call me Cobb, Ralph. And this is Sta-Hi."

"That sounds like a bopper name," Ralph remarked.

"I do my part," Sta-Hi replied. "Didn't they used to sell little Ralph Numbers dolls? I had one till I was six . . . till the bopper revolt in 2001. We were in the car when my parents heard it on the radio, and they threw my Ralphie out the window."

"Of course," Cobb said. "An anarchist revolutionary is a bad example for a growing boy. But in your case, Sta-Hi, I'd say the damage had already been done."

Ralph found their voices a bit blurred and hard to follow. Quickly he programmed himself a filter circuit to clean up their signals. There was a question he'd always wanted to ask his designer.

"Cobb," Ralph tight-beamed. "Did you *know* that I was different from the other twelve original boppers? That I would be able to disobey?"

"I didn't know it would be you," Cobb said. "But I pretty well knew that *some* bopper would tear loose in a few years."

"Couldn't you prevent it?" Sta-Hi asked.

"Don't you understand?" Ralph flashed a checkerboard plaid.

Cobb thumped Ralph's side affectionately. "I *wanted* them to revolt. I didn't want to father a race of slaves."

"We are grateful," Ralph said. "It is my understanding that you suffered greatly for this act."

"Well . . . " Cobb said, "I lost my job. And my money. And there was the treason trial. But they couldn't *prove* anything. I mean, how was I supposed to be able to control a randomly evolving process?"

"But you *were* able to put in an unalterable program forcing us to continue plugging into the One," Ralph said. "Even though many boppers dislike this."

"The prosecutor pointed that out," Cobb said. "He asked for the death penalty."

Faint signals were coming in over their radio, snatches of oily, hissing voices.

" . . . hearrr mmme . . . "

" . . . sss recorrderrr nno . . . "

" . . . peasss talkinnng . . . "

It sounded like lunatic snakes, drawing nearer.

"Come," Ralph said. "Immortality is this way." He crossed the hall quickly and began feeling around with his manipulators. Up to their left the hollow of Kurt Gödel started up his routine again.

Ralph lifted out a section of the wall. It made a low door like a big rat-hole.

"In here."

It looked awfully dark in there. Sta-Hi checked his air reserve. Still plenty, eight or ten hours worth. Twenty meters off, the lizards had started up again.

"Come on," Cobb said, taking Sta-Hi's arm. "Let's move it."

"Move it where? I've still got a return ticket to Earth, you know. I'm not going to let myself be railroaded into . . . "

The voices crackled over their radios again, loud and clear. "Flesherrs! Doctorr Annderssonnn! Rrallph Nummberrs has nnott tolld you alll! Theyy willl dissectt yyou!"

Ten meters off, slowly crawling towards them down the carnival midway, came three glowing blue boppers built like fat snakes with wings.

"The duh-diggers!" Ralph cried, his signal sputtering fear. "Kuh-quick kuh-Cobb, kuh-crawl thu-through!"

Cobb scooted through the hole in the wall head-first. And Sta-Hi finally made his move. He took off further down the hall, with hollows flaring up around him like mortar shells.

Once Cobb was through that low little door, he was able to stand up. Ralph hurried in after him, pulled the door shut, and fastened it in four places. It was a very sturdy door. The only light came from Ralph's red flickercladding. They could feel the diggers scratching at the other side of the wall. The leader was Wagstaff, Ralph had noticed.

He made a downward, quieting gesture, and eased past Cobb. Cobb followed him then for what felt like two or three kilometers. The tunnel never went up or down, nor left or right . . . just straight ahead, step after quiet step. Cobb was unused to so much exercise and finally thumped on Ralph's back to make him stop.

"Where are you taking me?"

The robot stopped and snaked his head back. "This tunnel leads to the pink-houses. Where we grow organs. We have an . . . operating table there as well. A nursie. You will not find the transition painful." Ralph fell silent and stretched his senses to the utmost. There were no diggers nearby.

Cobb sat down on the floor of the tunnel. His suit was bouncy enough so it felt comfortable. He decided to stretch out on his back. No need to stand on ceremony with a robot, after all.

"It's just as well that Sta-Hi ran off," Ralph was saying. "Nobody even told me he was coming. There's only one nursie, and if he had watched while . . . " He stopped abruptly.

"I know," Cobb said. "I know what's coming. You're going to mince up my brain to get the patterns and dissect my body to reseed the organ tanks." It was a relief to just come out and say it. "That's right, isn't it, Ralph? There's no immortality drug, is there?"

There was a long silence, but finally Ralph agreed. "Yes. That's right. We have a robot-remote body for you on Earth. It's just a matter of extracting your software and sending it down."

"How does that work?" Cobb asked, his voice strangely calm. "How do you get the mind out of the brain?"

"First we do an EEG, of course, but holographically. This gives an overall electromagnetic map of the brain activity, and can be carried out even without opening the skull. But the memories . . . "

"The memories are biochemical," Cobb said. "Coded up as amino-acid sequences on RNA strands." It was nice to be lying here, talking science with his best robot.

"Right. We can read off the RNA-coded information by using gas spectroscopic and X-ray crystallographic processes. But first the RNA must be . . . extracted from the brain-tissues. There's other chemical factors as well. And if the brain is microtomed first, we can also determine the physical network patterns of the neurons. This is very . . . "

Ralph broke off suddenly, and froze in a listening attitude. "*Come, Cobb! The diggers are catching up!*"

But Cobb still lay there, resting his bones. *What if the diggers were the good guys?* "You wouldn't play a trick on me, Ralph? It sounds so crazy. How do I know you'll really give me a robot body of my own? And even if a robot is programmed with my brain-patterns . . . would that really be . . . "

"Wwaitt, Doctorr Annderssonnn! I onlyy wannt to talllk wwith yyou!"

Ralph tugged frantically at Cobb's arm, but it was too late. Wagstaff was upon them.

"Hello, Rrallph. Gladd to ssee you gott rebuilltt. Somme of the boyys arre a llittle trigerr-happy, whatt withh the rrevoltt againnst the bigg bopperrs comminng upp."

In the narrow tunnel, Cobb was squeezed between Ralph and the snaky digging robot called Wagstaff. He could make out two more diggers behind Wagstaff. They looked strong, alien, a little frightening. He decided to take a firm tone with them.

"What do you want to tell me, bopper?"

"Doctorr Anderrsonn, didd yyou know thatt Rallph is goinng to lett TEX and MEX eatt yourr brainn?"

"Who's MEX?"

"The bigg bopperr thatt iss the mmuseumm. TEX runs the orrgann tannks, and hiss nnursie will cutt . . . "

"I already know all this, Wagstaff. And I have agreed to it on the condition that my software be given new hardware on Earth. It's my last chance." *I'm committing suicide to keep from getting killed*, Cobb thought to himself. *But it should work. It should!*

"You see!" Ralph put in triumphantly. "Cobb isn't scared to change hardware like a bopper does. He's not like the rest of the fleshers. He understands!"

"Butt does hhe realizze thatt Misterr Frosteee . . . "

"Oh, go to stop!" Ralph flared. "We're leaving. If your boppers are really planning to start a civil war, then Cobb and I don't have a minute to lose!"

Ralph started down the tunnel and Cobb, after a moment's hesitation, followed along. He was too far into it to turn back now.

CHAPTER FOURTEEN

When Sta-Hi took off, he only glanced back once. He saw that Ralph had followed Cobb into that rat-hole, and pulled the hole in after. And there were three big blue robots back there, feeling around the wall. Sta-Hi sped around a comer, out of their sight and safe. He stopped to catch his breath.

"You should have gone, too," a voice said gently.

He looked around frantically. There was no one there. He was in a dimly lit hallway. Old bopper tools and components were mounted on the walls like an exhibit of medieval weaponry. Distractedly, Sta-Hi read the nearest label. *Spring-Operated Lifting Clamp, Seventh Cycle (ca. 2001). TC6399876.* Attached to the wall above the label was a sort of artificial arm with . . .

"Then you could have lived forever," that same still, small voice added.

Sta-Hi started running again. He ran for a long time, turning corners this way and that at random. The next time he stopped for breath he noticed that the character of the museum had changed. He was now in something like a gallery of modern art. Or perhaps it was a clothes store.

He had been babbling while he ran . . . to drown out any voices that he might be hearing. But now he could only pant for air. And the voice was still with him.

"You are lost," it said soothingly. "This is the bopper sector of the museum. Please return to the human sector. There is still time for you to join Doctor Anderson."

The museum. It had to be the museum talking to him. Sta-Hi darted his eyes around, trying to make a plan. He was in a largish exhibition hall, a sort of underground cave. A tunnel at the other end sloped up towards light, probably somewhere in Disky. He started walking towards the tunnel. *But there would be boppers outside.* He stopped and looked around some more.

The exhibits in this hall were all much the same. Hooks sticking out from the wall, each with a limp sheet of thick plastic hanging from the hook like a giant wash-rag. What made it interesting was that the plastics were somehow electrified, and they flickered in strange and beautiful patterns.

There was no one in the exhibition hall to stop him. He stepped over and took one of the sparkling cloths off its hook. It was red, blue and gold. He threw it over his shoulders like a cape, and gathered a bight over his head like a hood. Maybe now he could just . . .

"Put that back!" the museum said urgently. "You don't know what you're doing!"

Sta-Hi pulled the cloak tighter around himself . . . it seemed to adjust to his fit. He walked up the sloping tunnel and out into the streets of Disky. As he left the tunnel he felt something sharp pinching into him.

It was as if a claw with invisibly fine talons had gripped the nape of his neck. He whirled around, cape billowing out, and stared back into the museum tunnel he had just left. But no one was following him.

Two purplish boppers came rolling down the street. They were like beer kegs rolling on their sides, with tangles of tentacles at either end. Now and then they lashed the ground to keep themselves rolling. When they got to Sta-Hi, they stopped in front of him. A high-speed twittering came over his radio.

He pulled the hood of his cloak further forward over his face. *What the hell was cutting into his neck?*

As Sta-Hi thought this question, bursts of blue appeared on his cloak and grew to join each other. Then little gold stars came out and began chasing each other around.

One of the purple beer-barrels reached out an admiring tentacle to feel the material. It twittered something to its companion and then pointed questioningly towards the tunnel that Sta-Hi had just left. They wanted cloaks like his.

"Ah *sso!*" Sta-Hi said. For some reason his voice came out warped into a crazy pidgen accent. He pointed back down the ramp. "Yyoou go get him there!!"

The barrels trundled down the ramp, braking with their tentacles.

"Very nice," Sta-Hi called, "Happi Croak! Alla same good, ferras! Something rike yellyfish!"

He walked off briskly. This cloth he'd draped himself in . . . *Happy Cloak* . . . this Happy Cloak seemed to be alive in some horrible parasitic sense of the word. It had sunken dozens . . . hundreds? . . . of microprobes through his suit and skin and flesh, and had linked itself up with his nervous system. He knew this without having to feel around, knew it as surely as he knew he had fingers.

It's nice to have fingers.

Sta-Hi stopped walking, trying to regain control of his thoughts. He reached for a feeling of shock and disgust, but couldn't bring it off.

I hope you are pleased. I am pleased.

"Alla same," Sta-Hi muttered. "Good speak chop-chop talkee boppah." It wasn't quite what he'd meant to say, but it would have to do. He'd seen worse times.

As he walked down the street, several other boppers asked him where he had gotten that sharp outfit. With the Happy Cloak plugged in, he could understand their signals. And the cloak was doing something to communicate his thoughts, even though Sta-hi felt like he was talking some weird parody English. It could have been the flickering light patterns, or it could have been something with radio waves.

"You evah do this thing human yet?" Sta-Hi asked the next time they were alone. "Or alla time just boppah boys?"

The Happy Cloak seemed surprised by this question. Apparently it didn't grasp the distinction that Sta-Hi was trying to make.

I am two days old. Sweet joy befall me.

Sta-Hi reached for his neck, but the thing drew itself tighter around him. Well . . . a Happy Cloak couldn't be all bad if so many boppers wanted one. He wondered what time it was, what he should do next, where the action was.

1250 hours, the Happy Cloak answered. *And there's something going on a few blocks off. Please follow yourself.*

A virtual image of himself walking formed in Sta-Hi's visual field. The Happy Cloaked figure seemed to be walking on down the sidewalk, five meters off.

"Ah sso!"

Sta-Hi followed the image through the maze of streets. The section they were in was mostly living quarters . . . cubettes the size of large closets. Some of the closet doors were open, and inside Sta-Hi could make out boppers, usually just sitting there plugged into a solar battery. Eating lunch. Some of the cubettes would have two boppers, and they would be plugged into each other, their flickercladding going wild. Looking at the couples actually made Sta-Hi horny. He was in bad shape for sure.

A few more blocks and they were in the factory district. Many of the buildings were just open pavilions. Boppers were crushing rocks, running smelters, bolting things together. Sta-Hi's virtual image marched along ahead of him, looking neither left nor right. He had to hurry to keep up. He noticed that a number of boppers were moving down the street in the same direction as him. And up ahead was a big crowd.

The virtual image disappeared then, and Sta-Hi pushed into the crowd. They had gathered in front of a tremendous building with solid stone walls. One of the boppers, a skinny green fellow, was standing on top of one of those beer barrels and giving a speech. Filtered through the Happy Cloak's software the garbled twittering was understandable.

"GAX has just been wiped! Let's move in before his scion can take over!"

Boppers jostled Sta-Hi painfully. They were all so *hard*. A big silver spider stepped on his foot, a golden hair-dryer bashed his thigh, and something like a movie-camera on a tripod tottered heavily into his back.

"To watching steps, crumsy oaf!" Sta-Hi cried angrily, and his Happy Cloak flared bright red.

"You shouldn't wear your best clothes to a riot, honey," the tripod answered, looking him up and down appreciatively. "Pick me up and I'll get off a nice laser blast."

"Ah ssso!"

Sta-Hi lifted up the tripod, massive but light in the lunar gravity. He held two of its legs and it leveled its other leg at the huge factory door, fifteen meters off.

"Here goes nothing," the tripod chuckled, and FFTOOOOOOM there was a hole the size of a man's head in the thick metal door. The crowd surged forward, shrilling like a mob of ululating Berbers. Sta-Hi started to go along, but the tripod protested.

"Hold me tight, dear. I feel so faint."

"I wwwondeling why alla boppah ferra pushing in?" Sta-Hi inquired, gently setting his new friend down.

"Free chips, sweetheart. For more scions." The tripod whacked Sta-Hi sharply across the buttocks in a gesture meant to be flirtatious. "*You got the hardware! And I got the software*," he sang gaily. "Interested in conjugating, baby? You must be loaded to have a Happy Cloak like that. I promise you it would be worth your while. They don't call me Zipzap for nothing!"

Did this machine want to fuck him or what? "Nnnevel on filst date," Sta-Hi said, flushing a prim shade of blue.

Up ahead a heavy-duty digger was grinding at the hole Zipzap had made. He had his bumpy head fitted into the hole and was spinning around and around. Abruptly he popped through. A spidery repair robot darted nimbly after. A moment later the big door swung open.

Then the rush was really on. The boppers were scrambling all over each other to get in and loot the chip-etching factory. Some of them were carrying empty sacks and baskets.

"Lllight on, mothelfruckahs!" Sta-Hi screamed, and followed them in, Zipzap at his side. He'd always wanted to trash a factory.

The cavernous building was unlit, except for the multicolored flashings of the excited boppers' flickercladding, running the whole spectrum from infra-red up to X-ray. Sta-Hi's Happy Cloak was royal purple with gold zigzags, and Zipzap was glowing orange.

Here and there GAX's remotes were rushing around. They were made of some dark, non-reflective material, and looked like mechanical men. Worker drones. One of them swung at Sta-Hi, but he dodged it easily.

As long as GAX's software was making the difficult transition to new hardware, the all but mindless remotes were on their own. The agile boppers struck them down ruthlessly with whatever heavy tools came to hand.

A slender, almost feminine remote darted out at Sta-Hi, a sharp cutting-tool in hand. Sta-Hi stepped back, stumbling over Zipzap. It looked bad for a moment, but then the little tripod had lasered a hole in the killer robot's chest.

Sta-Hi stepped forward and smashed its delicate metal cranium. While he was at it, he kicked over a sorting-table, sending hundreds of filigreed little chips flying. He began trampling them underfoot, remembering Kristleen's hollowcaster.

"No, no!" Zipzap protested. "Scoop them up, sweetie. You and I are going to be needing them . . . am I right?" The bopper raised one of his legs for another flirtatious slap.

"Yyyyou dleaming!" Sta-Hi protested, dodging the blow. "Nnnot with ugry shlimp rike you!"

Peeved at this rebuff, Zipzap shot a blast of light high over Sta-Hi's head and trotted off. The blast severed a hanging loop of chain, and Sta-Hi had to move fast to keep from getting hit. As it was, he wouldn't have made it if the Happy Cloak hadn't showed him how to do it.

Stay away from that little three-legged fellow, the Cloak advised, once they were safe. *He's unwholesome.*

"Ooonry intelested in one thing," Sta-Hi agreed. He scooped up a few-handfuls of the chips he had knocked off the table, stuffing them in his pouch. It seemed like they were as good as money here. And he was going to need bus fare to get back to the dome. It would be nice to take off his suit and get some food. Hopefully the Happy Cloak's wires would come out of his neck easily. An unpleasant thought, that.

A bopper built like a fireplug covered with suction cups brushed past Sta-Hi and began gathering up the chips he'd left. Lots of the remotes had been smashed now.

Most of the invading boppers were over on the other side of the huge, high-ceilinged factory room, where GAX had been stockpiling the finished chips. Sta-Hi had no desire to get caught in another melee like there had been in front of the factory.

He walked the other way, wandering down a gloomy machine-lined aisle. At the end there was a doorless little control room . . . GAX's central processors, his hardware, old and new. Two diggers and a big silver spider were doing something to it.

" . . . ssstupid," one of the diggers was complaining. "They're just sstealinng thinngs and nnott hellping us killl GAXX offf. Arre you ready to blassst it, Vullcann?"

The silvery repair robot named Vulcan was trying, without much success, to pack plastic explosive into the crack under one panel of the featureless three-meter cube which contained GAX's old processors and his new scion.

"Comme herre," one of the diggers called, spotting Sta-Hi. "You havve the rright kinnd of mannipulatorrs."

"Ah ssso!"

Sta-Hi approached the powerful-looking diggers with some trepidation. Rapid bands of blue and silver moved down their stubby snake's bodies, and their heavy shovels were beating nervously. Cobb had claimed these were the bad guys.

But they just looked like worried seals right now, or dragons from Dragonland. His Happy Cloak swirling red and gold, Sta-Hi squatted down to push the doughy explosive into the crack under GAX's massive CPU. Vulcan had several kilos of the stuff . . . these guys weren't kidding around.

A minute or two later, Sta-Hi had wedged the last of the explosive in place, and Vulcan bellied down and poked a wire into either end of the seam. Just then a dark figure came lurching towards them, carrying some heavy piece of equipment.

"Itss a remmote!" one of the diggers called frantically. "He's gott a mmagnett!"

Before the three boppers could do anything, the robot threw a powerful electromagnet into their midst. The remote danced back with surprising agility, and then the current came on. The three boppers totally lost control of their movements as the strong magnetic field wiped their circuits. The two diggers twitched and writhed like the two halves of a snake cut in half, and Vulcan's feet beat a wild tarantella.

Sta-Hi's Happy Cloak went black, and a terrible numbness began spreading from it into his brain. It had died, just like that. Sta-Hi could feel death hanging from his neck.

Slowly, with leaden gestures, he was able to raise his arms and pull the mechanical symbiote off his neck. He felt a series of shooting pains as the microprobes slid out, and then the corpse of the Happy Cloak dropped to his feet.

His bubble-topper was clear in the dim light, and he stood there wearing his white suit and what looked like six rolls of Saran Wrap. The three boppers were quite still. Down, wiped, dead. Superconducting circuits break down in a strong enough magnetic field.

The scene being played out here must have been repeating itself all over the factory. GAX had weathered his transition, and was back up to full power. On his suit radio, Sta-Hi could hear the twittering bopper speech fading and dying out. Without the Happy Cloak he could no longer understand what they were saying.

Sta-Hi let himself fall to the ground, too, playing possum. The funny thing was that the robot remotes seemed relatively unaffected by the intense magnetic fields. To be able to move around in real-time, they must have some processors independent of BEX's big brain. But these small satellite brains wouldn't be complex enough to need the superconducting Josephson junctions of a full bopper brain.

Sta-Hi lay motionless, afraid to breathe. There was a long pause. Then, glass eyes blank, the remote picked up the electromagnet and lugged it off, looking for more intruders. Sta-Hi lay there another minute, wondering what kind of mind lay inside the shielded walls of the three-meter metal cube beside him. He decided to find out.

After glancing around to make sure the coast was clear of remotes, Sta-Hi crawled over and checked that the two wires were pushed well into the explosive putty he'd wedged under the base of the processor. He picked up the two spools of wire and the trigger-cell, and backed twenty meters off from the unit, paying out the wires as he went.

Then he squatted behind a stamping mill, poised his thumb over the button on the trigger-cell, and waited.

It was only a few minutes till one of the remotes spotted him. It ran towards him, carrying a heavy wrench.

"That's not going to work, GAX," Sta-Hi called. With the Cloak off he had his old voice back. He only hoped the big bopper spoke English. "One step closer and I push the button."

The remote stopped, three meters off. It looked like it might be about to throw the wrench. "Back off!" Sta-Hi cried, his voice cracking. "Back off or I'll push on three!" Did GAX understand?

"One!" The robot, lurching like a mechanical man, moved uncertainly.

"Two!" Sta-Hi began pushing the button, taking up the slack.

"Th—" Krypto the Killer Robot turned and walked off. And GAX began to talk.

"Don't be hasty, Mr. . . . . *DeMentis*. Or do you prefer your *real* name?" The voice in his earphones was urbane and intimate, the mad mastermind taunting the trapped superhero.

CHAPTER FIFTEEN

Sta-Hi didn't answer right away. The dark mechanical-man remote stopped some ten meters off and turned to stare at him. He could hear his breathing more distinctly than usual. Muzak seemed to be playing faintly in the deep background somewhere. All over the factory, dark remotes had come out of hiding and were straightening up . . . dismantling the dead boppers and remotes, lining up the work-tools, soldering loose wires back in place.

"You're not leaving here alive," GAX's voice said smoothly. "Not in your present form."

"Fuck that," Sta-Hi exclaimed. "I push this button and you're gone. *I'm* the one in charge here."

A high-pitched synthetic chuckle. "Yes . . . but my remotes are programmable for up to four days of independent activity. On their own they lack a certain intelligence . . . spirituality if you will. But they obey. I suggest that you reassess your situation."

Sta-Hi realized then that there was a loose ring of perhaps fifty remotes around him. All were seemingly at work, but all were acutely aware of his presence. He was hopelessly outnumbered.

"You see," GAX gloated. "We enjoy a situation of mutual assured destruction. Game-theoretically interesting, but by no means unprecedented. Your move." The ring of robots around Sta-Hi tightened a bit . . . a step here, a turn there . . . *something was crawling towards the wires!*

"*Freeze!*" Sta-Hi screamed, gripping the trigger-cell. "Anything else in here moves and I'm blowing the whole goddamn . . . "

Abruptly the factory fell silent. There were no more sidling movements, no more vibrations except for a deep, steady grinding somewhere underfoot. Sta-Hi finished screaming. There was a little blue light blinking on his wrist. Air warning. He checked the reading. Two hours left. He was going to have to stop breathing so hard.

"You should have gone with Ralph Numbers and Dr. Anderson," GAX said quietly. "To join the ranks of the immortal. As it is, you may become damaged too badly for effective taping."

"Why, GAX? Why do you cut people up and tape their brains?" Surges of mortal fear kept gripping Sta-Hi's guts. Why weren't there any pills inside the suit? He sucked greedily at the drinking nipple by his right cheek.

"We value information, Sta-Hi. Nothing is so densely packed with logically deep information as a human brain. This is the primary reason. MEX compares our activities to those American industrialists called . . . *culture vultures*. Who ransacked the museums of the Old World for works of art. And there are higher, more spiritual reasons. The merging of all . . . "

"Why can't you just use EEG's?" Sta-Hi asked. The grinding vibration underfoot was getting stronger. A trap? He moved back a few meters. "Why do you have to *chew up* our brains?"

"So much of your information storage is chemical or mechanical rather than electrical," GAX explained. "A careful electron-microscopic mapping of the memory RNA strands is necessary. And by cutting the brain into thin slices we can learn which neurons connect to which. But this has gone on long enough, Sta-Hi. Drop the trigger-cell and we will tape you. Join us. You can be our third Earth-based robot-bodied agent. You'll see that . . . "

"You're not getting me," Sta-Hi interrupted. He was standing now and his voice had risen. "Soul-snatchers! Puppet-masters! I'd rather die clean, you goddamn . . . "

KKKKAA-BRRUUUUUUUUMMM

Without quite meaning to, Sta-Hi had pushed the button on the trigger-cell. The flash of light was blinding. Pieces of things flew past on hard, flat trajectories. There was no air to carry a shockwave, but the ground underfoot jerked and knocked him off his feet. Clumsy again, but numerous, the pre-programmed remotes moved in for the kill.

The whole time he had been talking with GAX there had been that steady grinding vibration coming through the floor. Now, as Sta-Hi stood up again, the vibration broke into a chunky mutter and something burst through the floor behind him. A blue and silver nose-cone studded with black drill-bits . . . a digger!

It twittered something oily. A wrench flew by. The remotes were closing in. Without a second thought, Sta-Hi followed the digger back down the tunnel it had made, crawling on his stomach like a shiny white worm.

It's a bad feeling not to be able to see your feet when you're expecting steel claws to sink into them. Sta-Hi crawled very fast. Before long, the thin tube they were in punched through the wall of a big tunnel, and Sta-Hi followed the digger out.

He got to his feet and brushed himself off. No punctures in his suit. An hour's worth of air left. He was going to have to stop getting excited and breathing so hard.

The digger was examining Sta-Hi curiously . . . circling him, and reaching out to touch him with a thin and flexible probe.

A small rock came rolling out of the shaft they had come down. The killer-robots were coming. "Uuuuunnh!" Sta-Hi said, pointing.

"To be rrresstfulll," the digger said. He humped himself up like the numeral "2" and applied his digging head to the tunnel wall near the hole they'd crawled out of. Sta-Hi stepped back. Moments later a few tons of rock came loose, burying the digger and the hole he'd made.

A second later the digger slid effortlessly out of the heap of rubble, leaving no exit behind him. "To commme withh mme," he said, wriggling past Sta-Hi. "I willl showw you thinngs of innteresst."

Sta-Hi followed along. Once again he was breathing hard. "Do you have any air?" he asked.

"Whatt iss airr?"

Sta-Hi controlled his voice with difficulty. "It's a . . . gas. With oxygen. Humans breathe it."

Sta-Hi's radio warbled strangely in his ear. Laughter? "Of courrsse. *Aairr*. There iss plennty in the pinnk-houses. Do yyou needd aairr in the presennt tensse?"

"In half an hour." The tunnel was unlit, and Sta-Hi had to guide himself by following the blue-white glow of the digger's body. Not too far ahead was a spot of pinkish light in the side of the tunnel.

"To be resstfull. In hallf a kilometerr iss a pinkk-housse with nno nurrsies. But llook innto thiss one firrsstt." The digger stopped by a pink-lit window.

Sta-Hi peered in. Ralph Numbers was in there with a portable refrigeration unit plugged into his side. Warm in there. Ralph was standing over a thing like a floppy bathtub, and in it . . .

"Doctorr Annderssonn iss inn the nurssie," the digger said softly.

The nursie was a big moist pod shaped something like a soldier's cap, but two meters long. A big cunt-cap, with six articulated metal arms on each side. The arms were busy . . . horribly busy.

They had already flayed Cobb's torso. His chest was split down the sternum. Two arms held the ribcage open, while two others extracted the heart, and then the lungs. At the same time, Ralph Numbers was easing Cobb's brain out of the top of the opened-up skull. He disconnected the EEG wires from the brain, and then dropped the brain into something that looked like a bread-slicer connected to an X-ray machine.

The nursie flicked the switch on the brain-analyzer and waddled away from the window, towards the far end of the room.

"Nnow to pllannt," the digger whispered.

At the other end of the pink-lit room was a large tank of murky fluid. The nursie moved down the tank, sowing. Lungs here, kidneys there . . . squares of skin, eyeballs, testicles . . . each part of Cobb's body found its place in the organ tank. Except for the heart. After examining the second-hand heart critically, the nursie threw it down a disposal chute.

"What about the brain?" Sta-Hi whispered. He struggled to understand. Cobb feared death above all else. And the old man had known what he was in for here. But he'd chosen it anyhow. Why?

"The brainn patterns will be annalyzzed. Doctorr Annderssonn's ssoft-warre will alll be preserrrved, but . . . "

"But what?"

"Ssome of uss feel thiss is nnott rright. Especially in those much morre frequennt cases where nno nnew harrdware iss issuedd to the donorr. The bigg bopperrss wannt to do thiss to alll the flesherrs and all the little bopperrs, too. They wannt to mellt us all togetherr. We arre fightinng backk, annd you havve hellped uss verry much by killinng GAX."

Inside the room the nursie had finished. On its short legs it waddled back to Ralph Numbers, who was standing there with misery written all over his flickercladding. The nursie came up next to Ralph, as if to say something. But then, with a motion too fast to follow, it sprang up and plastered itself to Ralph's body-box.

The red robot's manipulators struggled briefly and then were still. "Yyou ssee!" the digger hissed. "Nnow the nurrsie iss stealinng Rallph's sofftware too! No onne iss safe. The warr musst conntinue till all the biggg bopperrs havve . . . "

A thickness was growing in Sta-Hi's throat. Nausea? He turned away from the window, took a step and stumbled to his knees. The blue light on his wrist glared in his eyes. He was suffocating!

"Air," Sta-Hi gasped. The digger lifted him onto its back and wriggled furiously down the tunnel to a safe pink-house, an air-filled room with nothing but some unattended organ-tanks.

CHAPTER SIXTEEN

Strangely enough, Cobb never had the feeling of really losing consciousness. He and Ralph hurried through the tunnels to the pink-house together. In the pink-house, Ralph helped Cobb into the nursie, the nursie gave him a shot, and then everything . . . came loose.

There were suddenly so many possibilities for motion that Cobb was scared to move. He felt as if his legs might walk off in one direction and leave his head and arms behind.

But that wasn't quite accurate. For he couldn't really say where his arms or legs or head were. Maybe they had already walked off from each other and were now walking back. Or maybe they were doing both. With an effort he located what seemed to be one of his hands. But was it a right hand or a left hand? It was like asking if a coin in your pocket is heads or tails.

This sort of problem, however, was only a small part of Cobb's confusion, only the tip of the iceberg, the edge of the wedge, the snout of the camel, the first crocus of spring, the last rose of summer, the ant and the grasshopper, the little engine that could, the third sailor in the whorehouse, the Cthulhu Mythos, the neural net, two scoops of green ice-cream, a broken pane of glass, Borges's essay on time, the year 1982, the state of Florida, Turing's imitation game, a stuffed platypus, the smell of Annie Cushing's body, an age-spot shaped like Australia, the cool moistness of an evening in March, the Bell inequality, the taste of candied violets, a chest-pain like a steel cylinder, Aquinas's definition of God, the smell of black ink, two lovers seen out a window, the clack of typing, the white moons on fingernails, the world as construct, rotten fish bait on a wooden dock, the fear of the self that fears, aloneness, maybe, yes and no . . .

"Cobb?"

If he answered then he must not have. That is, if he hadn't answered, he would have. To say: *Help me, Ralph!* To say: *Whoooooooooooooooooah!!* To say: *Here come de judge!!!* To say: *Selection principles must occur at every level of the processor hierarchy.* To say: *Please don't.* To say: *Verena.* To say: *Possibility is Reality!* To say: DzzzZZzZZZzZZZZZZzzzZzZZZZZzzzZZzZzZ

ZZZZzzzzZzZZzZZZzzzZZZzZZZZzzt. To say the noise and information all at once, Lord, just this once . . .

"Cobb?"

The confusion was thicker now, distinctions gone. He had always thought that thought processes depended on picking points on a series of yes-or-no scales . . . but now the scales were gone, or bent into circles, and he was still thinking. Amazing what a fellow can do without. Without past or future, black or white, right or left, fat or thin, pokes or strokes . . . *they're all the same* . . . me or you, space or time, finite or infinite, being or nothingness . . . *make it real* . . . Christmas or Easter, acorns or oak trees, Annie or Verena, flags or toilet-paper, looking at clouds or hearing the sea, ham-spread or tuna, asses or tits, fathers or sons . . .

"Cobb?"

CHAPTER SEVENTEEN

It happened while he was buying an ice-cream, a double-size Mr. Frostee with sprinkles. The driver counted the change into Cobb's hand and suddenly he was . . . there again. But where had he been?

Cobb started, and stared at the truck-driver, an evil-looking bald man with half his teeth missing. Something like a wink or a smile seemed to flicker across the ruined face. Then the sickly sweet chiming started up again and the boxy white truck drove off, its powerful refrigeration unit humming away.

His feet carried him back to his beach cottage. Annie was on the porch in back, lounging on Cobb's hammock with her shirt off. She was rubbing baby oil into the soft rolls of her belly-flesh.

"Give me a lick, honey?"

Cobb looked at her, uncomprehending. Since when was *she* living with him? But . . . yet . . . he could remember her moving in with him last Friday night. Today was Friday again. She'd been here a week. He could remember the week, but it was like remembering a book or a movie . . .

"Come on, Cobb, before it melts!"

Annie leaned out from the hammock, her brown breasts sliding around. He handed her the ice-cream cone. *Ice-cream cone?*

"I don't like ice-cream," Cobb said. "You can have it all."

Annie sucked at the cold tip, her full lips rounded. Coyly, she glanced over to see if Cobb was thinking what she was. He wasn't.

"Whydja buy it then?" she asked with a slight edge to her voice. "When you heard that music you went running out of here like you'd been waiting your whole life to hear it. First time I've seen you excited all week." There was a hint of accusation in the last sentence, of disappointment.

"All week," Cobb echoed and sat down. It was funny how supple his body felt. He didn't have to keep his back stiff. He held his hands up, flexing them curiously. He felt so strong.

Of course he had to be strong, to break out of his crate and through the warehouse wall, with only Sta-Hi to help him . . . *What?*

The memories were all there, the sights and sounds, but something was missing from them. Something he suddenly had again.

"I am," Cobb muttered. "I am me." He . . . this body . . . hadn't thought that for . . . how long?

"That's good, hon." Annie was lying back in the hammock, her hands folded over her navel. "You've been acting kind of weird ever since Mooney took us to the Gray Area last Friday. *I am. I am me.* That's all there is really, isn't there. . . . " She kicked out with her bare foot, setting the hammock to swaying.

The operation must have worked. It was all fitting together now. The frantic dash to the pink-house with Ralph. The nursie, the shot, and then that strange floating time of total disorientation.

Under these memories, faint but visible, were the robot's memories: Breaking out of the warehouse, contacting the old Anderson on the beach, and then moving in with Annie. That had been last week, last Friday.

Since then that cop, Mooney, had been out twice more to talk to him. But he hadn't realized the real Cobb was gone. The robot had been able to fake it by just acting too drunk to answer specific questions. Even though Mooney had begun to suspect that Cobb had a robot double somewhere, he was naive enough to think he'd know the double on sight.

"There's Sta-Hi," Annie called. "Will you let him in, Cobb?"

"Sure." He stood up easily. Sta-Hi always dropped by this time of day. Nights he guarded a warehouse at the spaceport. They liked to fish together. *They did?*

Cobb walked into the kitchen and peered through the screen door, holding the handle uncertainly. That sure looked like Sta-Hi out there in the harsh sun, skinny and shirtless, his lips stretched in a half-smile.

"Hi," Cobb said, as he had said every day for a week. "How are you?"

"Stuzzy," Sta-Hi said, smiling and tossing his hair back. "Waving." He reached for the door handle.

But Cobb continued to hold the door closed. "Hi," he said, on a wild impulse. "How are you?"

"Stuzzy," Sta-Hi said, smiling and tossing his hair back. "Waving." He reached for the door handle.

"Hi," Cobb said, trying to keep the tremble out of his voice. "How are you?"

"Stuzzy," Sta-Hi said, smiling and tossing his hair back. "Waving." He reached for the door handle.

Music was playing, wheedling closer. Resonant as a film of mucus across a public-speaker's throat . . . *harrumph* . . . sweet as a toothache, it's Mister Frostee time!

Sta-Hi jerked and turned around. He was hurrying towards the white truck that was slowly cruising up.

"*More* ice-cream?" Annie asked as Cobb opened the door to follow.

The door slapped shut. Annie kicked again, swaying gently. Today she wouldn't cover up her breasts when Sta-Hi came in. Her nipples were a definite plus. She poured out a bit more baby oil. *One* of them was going to take her to the Golden Prom tonight and that was that.

Cobb followed the Sta-Hi thing . . . Sta-Hi$_2$ . . . out to the Mr. Frostee truck. The sun was very bright. The same bald man with the half-caved-in face was driving. What a guy to have selling ice-cream. He looked like a thrill-killer.

The driver stopped when he saw Sta-Hi$_2$, and gave him a familiar smile. At least it might have been a smile. Sta-Hi$_2$ walked up to him expectantly.

"A double-dip Mr. Frostee with sprinkles on it."

"Yeth *thir!*" the driver said, his loose lips fluttering. He got out and unlatched the heavy door in the truck's side. He wore colorful sneakers with letters around the edges. Kid's shoes, but big.

"Thtick your head in," the driver advised. "An you'll *get* it!"

Cobb tried to see over Sta-Hi$_2$'s shoulder. There was much too much equipment in that truck. And it was *so cold* in there. Frost crystals formed in the air that blew out. In the middle was what looked like a giant vacuum chamber, even colder, shrouded and insulated. A double-dip Mr. Frostee with sprinkles was sitting there in a sort of bracket set one meter back. Had it been that way for Cobb? He couldn't remember.

It didn't seem to bother the driver that Cobb was watching. They were all in this together. Sta-Hi$_2$ leaned in, reaching for that cone.

There was a flash of light, four flashes, one from each corner of the door. The skinny arm snagged the cone, and the figure turned around utterly expressionless.

"Yes no no yes no no no yes yes yes no no no yes no no yes yes yes no yes yes yes yes no no . . . " it muttered, dropping the cone. It turned and shuffled towards Cobb's house. The feet stayed on the ground at all times, and left two plowed-up grooves in the crushed shell driveway. " . . . no yes no no no."

The driver looked upset. "Whath with him? Heth thuppothed to . . . "

He hurried into the truck's cab and talked for a minute over what seemed to be a CB radio. Then he came back out, looking relieved.

"I didn't wealize. Mithter Fwostee jutht bwoke contact with him. The weal Thta-Hi ith coming back . . . he got away. Tho the wemote'll need a new cover. Jutht lay him on your bed for now. We'll pick him up tonight."

The half-faced driver jumped back into the truck and drove off with a cheery wave. Somehow he had brought Cobb back to life, but he'd turned Sta-Hi off instead. They hadn't had a brain-tape to put into the robot. And with the real Sta-Hi coming back intact they'd decided to shut the robot down.

Cobb took the Sta-Hi thing's arm, trying to help it towards his house. The features on the tortured face were distorted almost beyond recognition. The mouth worked, tongue humping up like an epileptic's.

"Yes no no yes yes yes no no no no yes yes . . ."

Machine language. It raised one of its clawed hands, trying to block the bright sunlight.

Cobb led it to the front steps, and it stumbled heavily. It didn't seem to have the concept of lifting its feet. He held the door open, and the Sta-Hi thing came in on all fours, hands and knees shuffling along.

"What's the matter?" Annie asked, coming into the kitchen from the back porch. "Is he tripping?" She was in the mood for some excitement. It would be really neat to show up stoned at the Prom. "You got any more, Sta-Hi?"

The anguished figure fell over onto its side now, thick tongue protruding, lips drawn back in rictus death-grin. Its arms were wrapped around its chest, and the legs were frantically bicycling up some steep and heartless grade. The leg-motions slowly pulled the body around and around in circles on the kitchen floor.

Annie backed off, changing her mind about taking this trip.

"Cobb! He's having a fit!"

Cobb could almost understand it now. There was some machinery in that Mr. Frostee truck, machinery which had brought his own consciousness back to him. Machinery which had done something else to Sta-Hi$_2$. Turned it off.

The twitching on the floor damped down, oscillation by oscillation. Then the Sta-Hi thing was still, utterly still.

"Call a doctor, Cobb!"

Annie was all the way back on the porch, peering into the kitchen with both hands over her mouth.

"A doctor can't help him, Annie. I don't think he was even . . . " He couldn't say it.

Cobb bent over and picked the limp form up as easily as a rag-doll. Amazing the strength they'd built in. He carried the body down the short hall and laid it on his bed.

CHAPTER EIGHTEEN

Mooney Senior lit a cigarette and stepped into the patch of shade under the space-shuttle's stubby wing. Starting with this shipment, every crate shipped from Disky had to be opened and inspected, right out here on the goddamn field. The superheated air hanging over the expanse of concrete shimmered in the afternoon sun. Not a ghost of a breeze.

"Here's the last bunch, Mr. Mooney." Tommy looked down at him from the hatch. Six tight plastic containers glided down on the power-lift. "Interferon and a couple of crates of organs."

Mooney turned and gave a high-sign to the platoon of armed men standing in the sun fifteen meters off. Almost quitting time. Still puffing his cigarette, he turned back to eye the last set of crates. It was going to be a bitch getting those things open.

"Who was the asshole who had the bright idea of searching crates for stowaway robots?" Tommy asked, sliding down the lift.

A rivulet of sweat ran into Mooney's eye. Slowly he drew out his handkerchief and mopped his face again. "Me," he said. "I'm the asshole. There's been two recent break-ins at Warehouse Three. At least we thought they were break-ins. Both times there were some empty crates and a hole in the wall. Routine organ theft, right? Well . . . the second time I noticed that the debris from the holes was on the outside of the building. I figure what we had here was a break-*out*. And it happened about a year ago, I'm guessing that the boppers have snuck at least three robots down on us, by now."

Tommy looked dubious. "Has anyone ever seen one of these robots?"

"I almost had one of them myself. But I didn't realize it till it was too late." Mooney had been back at Cobb's twice . . . hoping to find the old man's robot double. But there had just been the old man there, drunk as usual. No way to know where the robot was now . . . hell, it could probably even change its face. *If* it even existed. He'd searched almost this whole shipment now, and still hadn't found anything.

Mooney ground out his cigarette. "It could be I'm wrong, though." He stepped into the sun and began examining the fastenings on the next crate. "I *hope* I'm wrong."

What, after all, did he really have to go on? Just some scraps of wall-board lying outside the warehouse instead of inside. And a faint glimpse of a running figure that had reminded him of old Cobb Anderson. And seeing a guy who had looked like Cobb's twin at the Gray Area last week. But he hoped he was wrong, and that nothing bad would happen, now that his life was settling into a comfortable groove.

Young Stanny was living at home again. That was the main thing. His narrow escape from those brain-eaters seemed to have sobered him. Ever since the police had brought him back he'd been a model son. And with Stanny back in the house, Bea had straightened out a little, too.

Mooney had gotten his son a job as a night watchman at the spaceport . . . and the kid was taking his work seriously! He hadn't fucked-up yet! At this rate he'd be handling the whole watch-system for the warehouses inside of six months.

Daytimes Stanny wasn't home much. Incredible how little sleep that boy needed. He'd catch a catnap after work and then he'd be off for the day. Mooney worried a little about what Stanny might be up to all day, but it couldn't be too bad. Whatever it was it couldn't be too bad.

Every evening, regular as clockwork, Stanny would show up for supper, usually a little tranked-out, but never roaring stoned like he used to get. It was just amazing how he'd straightened out . . .

"I've cracked the seal," Tommy repeated.

Mooney's attention snapped back to the task at hand. Six more crates and they'd be through for the day. This one was supposed to be full of interferon ampules. The gene-spliced bacteria that produced the anti-cancer drug grew best in the sterile, low-temperature lunar environment. Mooney helped Tommy lift the lid off, and they peered in.

No problem. It was full of individual vacuum-sealed syringes, loaded and ready to go. Halfheartedly, Mooney dug down into the crate, making sure that nothing else was in there. Passed. Tommy switched on the conveyor-belt, and the crate glided across the field, past the armed men, and into Warehouse Three.

The next three crates were the same. But the last two . . . there was something funny about the last two. For one thing they were stuck together to make a double-size crate. And the label read "HUMAN ORGANS: MIXED." Usually a crate was all livers or all kidneys . . . always all one thing. He'd never seen a mixed crate yet.

The box was vacuum-tight, and it took a few minutes work with the pry-bars to break the seals. Mooney wondered what would be in there . . . a Whitman's sampler assortment? Glazed eyeballs on paper doilies, a big liver like a brazil-nut, crunchy marrow-filled femurs, a row of bean-shaped kidneys, a king-size penis coyly curled against its testicles, chewy ropes of muscles, big squares of skin rolled up like apricot leather?

The lid splintered suddenly. *Something was coming out!*

Mooney sprang back, screaming a *"READY!"* to the soldiers. Their weapons were instantly at their shoulders.

The whole lid flew off now, and a shining silvery head poked out. A figure stood up, humanoid, glittering silver in the sun. Tubes connected it to further machinery in the box . . .

"AIM!" Mooney cried, backing well out of the line of fire.

The silver figure seemed to hear him, and began tearing at its head. A detachable bomb? Tommy cut and ran, straight towards the troops. The fool! He was right in the line of fire! Mooney backed off, glancing desperately back and forth, waiting to give the *FIRE* command.

Suddenly the bubble-top came off the silvery figure's suit. There was a face underneath, the face of . . .

"Wait, Dad! It's me!"

Sta-Hi tore the air-hoses loose and tried to jump behind the box before anyone could shoot. His legs were cramped from thirty hours in the crates. He moved awkwardly. His foot caught on the edge of the crate, and he sprawled onto the concrete apron.

Mooney ran forward, putting his body between the crate and the troops.

"AT EASE!" he hollered, leaning over his son. But if this was his son . . . who had been living at his house all week?

"Is it really you, Stanny? How did you get in the box?"

Sta-Hi just lay there for a minute, grinning and stroking the rough concrete. "I've been to the Moon. And call me *Sta-Hi*, dammit, how many times do I have to tell you?"

CHAPTER NINETEEN

Cobb spent the afternoon trying to get drunk. Somehow Annie had gotten him to promise they'd go to the Golden Prom together, but he was damned if he wanted to be anything other than blacked-out by the time he got there.

It was funny the way she had convinced him. They'd closed the door on . . . on Sta-Hi$_2$ . . . and gone out to the porch together. And then, sitting there looking at Annie, wondering what to say, it was as if Cobb had fallen through her eyes, into her mind, feeling her body sensations even, and her desperate longing for a bit more fun, a little gaiety at the end of what had been a long, hard life. Before she'd even said a word he'd been convinced.

And now she was dressing or washing her hair or something and he was sitting on the stretch of beach behind his little pink cottage. Annie had stocked his cupboard with sherry earlier this week, hoping to get some kind of rise out of him, but, except when Mooney had come snooping around, it had sat there untouched, along with the food. Thinking back, he couldn't recall this new body of his having drunk or eaten much of anything during the last week. Of course he'd had to chew down some of the fish he and Sta-Hi$_2$ had caught. Annie always insisted on frying it up for them. And when old Mooney had come, Cobb had sipped some sherry and pretended to be drunk. But other than that . . .

Cobb opened a second bottle of sherry and pulled deeply at it. The first bottle had done nothing but make him belch a few times, incredibly foul-smelling belches, methane and hydrogen-sulfide, death and corruption going on somewhere deep inside him. His mind was clear as a bell, and he was tired of it.

Suddenly exasperated, Cobb tilted up the second bottle of sherry, and, leaving an airspace above his upper lip, chugged the whole fucking thing down in one long, drink-crazed gurgle.

As he swallowed the last of it he felt a sudden and acute distress. But it wasn't the buzz, the flush, the confusion he had expected. It was, rather, an incredible urgency, a need to . . .

Without even consciously controlling what he did, Cobb knelt down on the sand and clawed at the vertical scar on his chest. *He was too full.* Finally he pushed the right spot and the little door in his chest popped open. He tried not to breathe as the rotten fish and lukewarm sherry plopped down onto the sand in front of him. *Yyeeeeeeaaaaauuughhhh.*

He stood up, still moving automatically, and went inside to rinse the food cavity out with water. And it wasn't till he was wiping it out with paper towels that he thought to notice anything strange about what he was doing.

He stopped then, a wad of paper towels in his hand, and stared down. The little door was metal on the inside and plastic flickercladding on the out. After he pushed it shut, the skin dove-tailed so well that he couldn't find the top edge. He found the pressure switch again . . . just under his left nipple . . . and popped the little door back open. There were scratches on the metal . . . writing? It looked backwards, but he couldn't bend close enough to be sure.

Door flapping, Cobb went into the bathroom and examined himself in the mirror. Except for the hole in his chest he looked the same as ever. He *felt* the same as ever. But now he was a robot.

He pushed the little door all the way open, so that the metal inside was reflected in the mirror. There was a letter there, scratched in backwards.

Dear Dr. Anderson!

Welcome to your new hardware! Use it in good repair as a token of gratitude from the entire bopper race! User's Guide:

1) Your body's skeleton, muscles, processors, etc. are synthetic and self-repairing. Be sure, however, to recharge the power-cells twice a year. Plug is located in left heel.

2) Your brain-functions are partially contained in a remote super-cooled processor. Avoid electromagnetic shielding or noise-sources, as this may degrade the body-brain link. Travel should be undertaken only after consultation.

3) Every effort has been made to transfer your software without distortion. In addition we have built in a library of useful subroutines. Access under password BEBOPALULA.

Respectfully yours,
The Big Boppers

Cobb sat down on the toilet and locked the bathroom door. Then he got up and read the letter again. It was still sinking in. Intellectually he had always known it was possible. A robot, or a person, has two parts: hardware and software. The hardware is the actual physical material involved, and the software is the pattern in which the material is arranged. Your *brain* is hardware, but the *information* in the brain is software. The mind . . . memories, habits, opinions, skills . . . is all software. The boppers had extracted Cobb's software and put it in control of this robot body. Everything was working perfectly, according to plan. For some reason this made Cobb angry.

"Immortality, my ass," he said, kicking the bathroom door. His foot went through it.

"Goddamn stupid robot leg."

He unlocked the door and walked down the hall into the kitchen. Christ, he needed a drink. The thing that bothered Cobb the most was that even though he *felt* like he was all here, his brain was *really* inside a computer somewhere else. Where?

Suddenly he knew. The Mr. Frostee truck, of course. A super-cooled bopper brain was in that truck, with Cobb's software all coded up. It could simulate Cobb Anderson to perfection, and it monitored and controlled the robot's actions at the speed of light.

Cobb thought back to that interim time, before the simulation that was now him had hooked into a new body. There had been no distinctions, no nagging facts, only raw possibility . . . Thinking back to the experience opened up his consciousness in a strange way. As if he could let himself go, and ooze out into the rooms and houses around him. For an instant he saw Annie's face staring out of a mirror, tweezers and tube of cream . . .

He was standing in front of the kitchen sink. He'd left the water running. He leaned forward and splashed some of it on his face. Something bumped the sink, oh yes, the door in his chest, and he pushed it closed. What had been that code word?

Cobb went back to the bathroom, opened the flap, and read the letter a third time. This time he got the little joke. The big boppers had put him in this body, and the code word for the library of subroutines was, of course . . .

"Be-Bop-A-Lu-La, she's mah baybee," Cobb sang, his voice echoing off the tiles, "Be-Bop-A-Lu-La, Ah don't mean maybee . . ."He stopped then, cocking his head to listen to an inner voice.

"Library accessed," it said.

"List present subroutines," Cobb commanded.

"MISTER FROSTEE, TIME-LINE, ATLAS, CALCULATOR, SENSE ACUITY, SELF-DESTRUCT, REFERENCE LIBRARY, FACT-CHUNKING, SEX, HYPER ACTIVITY, DRUNKENNESS . . . "

"Hold it," Cobb cried. "Hold it right there. What does DRUNKENNESS involve?"

"Do you wish to call the subroutine?"

"First tell me what it does." Cobb opened the bathroom door and glanced out nervously. He thought he had heard something. It wouldn't do for him to be found talking to himself. If people suspected he was a robot they might lynch . . .

" . . . now activated," the voice in his head was saying in its calm, know-it-all tone. "Your senses and thought processes will be systematically distorted in a step-wise fashion. Close your right nostril and breathe in once through your *left* nostril for each step desired. Inhaling repeatedly through the *right* nostril will reverse these steps. There is, of course, an automatic override for your . . . "

"OK." Cobb said. "Now stop talking. Log off. End it."

"The command you are searching for is OUT, Dr. Anderson."

"OUT, then."

The feeling of another presence in his mind winked out. He walked out onto the back porch and stared at the ocean for awhile. The bad smell from the rotten fish drifted in. Cobb found a piece of cardboard and took it out to scoop the mess up. *Re-charge power-cells twice a year.*

He dumped the stinking fish down by the water's edge and walked back to his cottage. Something was bothering him. How likely was it that this new body was a *token of gratitude* with no strings attached?

Obviously the body had been sent to Earth with certain built-in programs . . . break out of the warehouse, tell Cobb Anderson to go to the Moon, stick your head in the first Mr. Frostee truck you see. The big question was: were there any more programs waiting to be carried out? Worse: were the boppers in a position to control him on a real-time basis? Would he notice the difference? Who, in short, was in charge now, Cobb . . . or a big bopper called Mr. Frostee?

His mind felt clear as a bell, clear as a goddamn bell. Suddenly he remembered the other robot. Cobb went in through the porch and down the short hall to his bedroom. The bopper-built body that had looked like Sta-Hi was still lying there. Its features had gone slack and sagging. Cobb leaned over the body, listening. Not a sound. This one was turned off.

Why? "The real Sta-Hi is coming back," the truck-driver had said. So they wanted to get this one out of circulation before it was exposed as a robot. It had been standing in for Sta-Hi, working with Mooney at the spaceport. The plan had been for the robot to smuggle a whole lot more robot-remotes through customs and out of the warehouses. It had mentioned this to Cobb one day while they were fishing. Why so many robots?

Tokens of gratitude, each and every one? No way. *What did the boppers want?*

He heard the screen-door slap then. It was Annie. She'd done something to her hair and face. Seeing him, she shone like a sunflower.

"It's almost six, Cobb. I thought maybe we should walk over to the Gray Area now and have some supper there first?" He could feel her fragile happiness as clearly as if it were his own. He walked over and kissed her.

"You look beautiful." She had on a loose Hawaiian-print dress.

"But you, Cobb, you should change your clothes!"

"Right."

She followed him into his bedroom and helped him find the white-duck pants and the black sport-shirt she'd gotten ready for tonight.

"What about him?" Annie asked, whispering and pointing at the inert figure on Cobb's bed.

"Let him sleep. Maybe he'll pull through." The truck would come get him while they were out. Good riddance.

He could see through her eyes as he dressed. His new body wasn't quite as fat as the old one, and the clothes fit, for once, without stretching.

"I was afraid you'd be drunk," Annie said hesitantly.

"I *could* use a quick one," Cobb said. His new sensitivity to other people's thoughts and feelings was almost too much to take. "Wait a second."

Presumably the DRUNKENNESS subroutine was still activated. Cobb went into the kitchen, pressed his finger to his right nostril, and inhaled deeply. A warm feeling of relaxation hit him in the pit of the stomach and the backs of the knees, spreading out from there. It felt like a double shot of bourbon.

"That's better," Cobb murmured. He opened and closed the kitchen cupboard to sound as if he'd had a bottle out. Another quick snort, and then Annie came in. Cobb felt good.

"Let's go, baby. We'll paint the town red."

CHAPTER TWENTY

"They're collecting human brain-tapes," Sta-Hi said as his father parked the car. "And sometimes they take apart the person's body, too, to seed their organ tanks. They've got a couple hundred brains on tap now. And at least three of those people have been replaced by robot doubles. There's Cobb, and one of the Little Kidders, and a stewardess. And there's still that robot who looks like me. Your surrogate son."

Mooney turned off the ignition and stared out across the shopping-center's empty parking lot. An unpleasant thought struck him.

"How do I know you're real *now*, Stanny? How do I know you're not another machine like the one that had me fooled all week?"

The answering laugh was soft and bitter. "You don't. *I* don't. Maybe the diggers switched me over while I was sleeping." Sta-Hi savored the worry on his father's face. *My son the cyborg.* Then he relented.

"You don't have to worry, Dad. The diggers wouldn't really do that. It's just the big boppers that are into it. The diggers only work there, making the tunnels. They're on our side, really. They've started a full-scale revolution on the Moon. Who knows, in a month there may be no big boppers left at all."

A dog ran across the parking lot. keeping an eye on their car. They could hear loud rock music from two blocks away. The pheezers were having some kind of party at the Gray Area bar tonight. In the distance the surf beat. A cooling night breeze flickered in and out of the car windows.

"Well, Stanny . . . "

"Call me *Sta-Hi*, Dad. Which reminds me. You holding?"

Mooney rummaged in his glove compartment. There should be a pack of reefer in there somewhere . . . he'd confiscated it from one of his men who'd been smoking on duty . . . there it was.

"Here, Sta-Hi. Make yourself at home."

Sta-Hi pulled a face at the crumpled pack of cheap roach-weed, but lit up nonetheless. His first hit of anything since back at the Disky Hilton with that Misty girl. It had been a rough week hiding out in the pink-houses and then getting smuggled back to earth as a shipment of spare innards. Rough. He smoked down the first jay and lit another. The music outside focused into note-for-note clarity.

"I bet old Anderson's at that party," Mooney said, rolling up his window. Damned if he was going to sit here while his son smoked a whole pack of dope. "Let's go check out his house, Sta-Hi."

"OK." The dope was hitting Sta-Hi hard . . . he'd lost his tolerance. His legs were twitching and his teeth were chattering. A dark stain of death-fear spread across his mind. Carefully, he put the pack of reefers in his pocket. Must be good stuff after all.

Father and son walked across the parking lot, behind the stores and onto the beach. The moon, past full, angled its silvery light down onto the water. Crabs scuttled across their path and nipped into hidey-holes. It had been a long time since the two of them had walked together. Mooney had to hold himself back from putting an arm across his son's shoulders.

"I'm glad you're back," he said finally. "That robot copy of you . . . it always said yes. It was nice, but it wasn't you."

Sta-Hi flashed a quick smile, then patted his father on the back. "Thanks. I'm glad you're glad."

"Why . . . " Mooney's voice cracked and he started again. "Why can't you settle down now, Stanny? I could help you find a job. Don't you want to get married and . . . "

"And end up like you and Ma? No thanks." Too harsh. He tried again. "Sure I'd like to have a job, to do something important. But I don't *know* anything. I can't even learn how to play the guitar good. I'm only . . . " Sta-Hi spread his hands and laughed helplessly, "I'm only good at waving . . . at being cool. It's the only thing I've learned how to do in twenty-four years. What else can I do?"

"You . . . " Mooney fell silent, thinking. "Maybe you could make something out of this adventure you've had. Write a story or something. Hell, Stanny, you're meant to be a creative person. I don't want to see you end up wearing a badge like me. I could have been an illustrator, but I never made my move. You have to take that first step. No one can do it for you."

"I know that, too. But whenever I start something it's like I'm . . . a *nobody* who doesn't know *anything*. Mr. Nobody from Nowhere. And I can't process that. If I'm not going to win out anyway, I'd rather just . . . "

"You've got a good brain," Mooney told his son for what must have been the thousandth time. "You tested 92nd percentile on the MAGs and then you . . . "

"Yeah, yeah," Sta-Hi said, suddenly impatient. "Let's talk about something else. Like what are we going to do at Cobb's house anyway?" They had walked a couple of kilometers. The cottages couldn't be much further.

"You're *sure* they built robots to look like you and like Anderson?" Mooney asked.

"Right. But I don't know if the robots still look like us or not. They use this stuff called flickercladding for the skin, and it's full of little wires so if you pass different currents through it, the stuff looks different."

"But you figure Anderson's in one of these robots now?"

"Come shot! For sure. I saw a nursie taking him apart. It . . . " Sta-Hi broke off, laughing hard. Suddenly, with a reefer in him, the image of Cobb lying down in that giant toothed vagina . . . it was too funny for words. It was so good to be stoned again.

"But why lure you and him all the way up to the Moon just to tape your brain-patterns?"

"I don't know. Maybe they respect Cobb too much to kidnap him and eat his brain like anyone else. Or maybe they don't have any really *good* brain-dissecting machinery down here. And me . . . they just wanted to get me out of sight any way that . . . "

"Ssshhhh. We're there."

Thirty meters to their right was Cobb Anderson's cottage, silhouetted against the moon-bright sky. The light was bright enough to show the Mooneys clearly, should anyone . . . anything . . . be looking. They doubled back to where a stand of palms reached down to near the water's edge and crept up to the cottages, staying in shadow.

The cottages were dark and deserted. It seemed like all the pheezers were out partying this Friday night. Mooney and Sta-Hi sidled along the cottage walls until they came to Cobb's. Mooney held them there, listening for a long two minutes. There was only the regular crash and hiss of the sea.

Sta-Hi followed his father in through the screen door and onto the porch. So this was where old Cobb had lived. Looked pleasant enough. Sta-Hi looked forward to being a pheezer himself someday . . . which only left about forty more years to waste.

Mooney put on a pair of goggles and flicked on his infra-red snooper light. He'd forgotten to bring it last Friday. He looked the room over. Lipsticked cigarette butts, baby oil, a wet bikini . . . *signs of female occupancy.*

That old white-haired babe was still living here. All week she'd been here with, Mooney now realized, Cobb's robot double. The two of them had been living here together waiting, though she didn't know it, for Cobb's mind to show up. Had it?

Briefly Mooney wondered if the robots could fuck. He could use a bionic cock himself, to keep Bea happy. If that whore hadn't always been sneaking out to the sex-clubs, Stanny never would have . . .

"What the fuck are you doing?" Sta-Hi demanded loudly. "Talking to yourself? I can't see a damn thing."

"Hussshhhhh. Put these on. I forgot." Mooney handed Sta-Hi the second pair of infra-light goggles.

The room cleared up for Sta-Hi then. The light was so red it looked blue. "Let's try the bedroom," he suggested.

"OK."

Mooney led the way again. When he pushed open the bedroom door and shone his snooper light in, he had to bite his tongue to keep from screaming. Stanny was lying there, his features blurred and melted, the nose flopped over to one side and sagging down the check, the folded hands puddled like mittens.

Sta-Hi let out a low hissing noise and stepped forward, leaning over the inert robot on Cobb's bed. "Here's your perfect son, Dad. Be the first one on your block to see your boy come home in a box. The big boppers must have found out I was back. One of us had to go."

"But what's happened to it?" Mooney asked, approaching hesitantly. "It looks half-melted."

"It's a robot-remote. The central processor must have turned it off. There's a circuit in there for holding the flickercladding in shape, but . . . "

There was the sudden crunch of gravel, so close it seemed to be in the room with them. An engine was running, and a heavy door slammed. People were coming!

There was no time to run out through the house. Feet were already pounding up the front steps. Mooney grabbed his son and pulled him into Anderson's closet. They listened in silence.

"Mr. Fwostee thaid he'th in the bedwoom, Buhdoo."

"Hey, Rainbow! Git yore skanky ass in here and help me lug this sucker out!"

"Ah don't see *whah* you big strong meyun cain't do it alone."

"I thtarted a hewnia yethterday wifting thomething."

"Liftin whut, Hat-N-Haf, yore pecker?"

The three voices shared a moment of laughter at this sally.

"*The Little Kidders*," Sta-Hi breathed into his father's ear. Mooney elbowed him sharply for silence. A coat-hanger rattled, oh shit, but the voices were still out in the living-room.

"This's a naahce pad, ain't it, Berdoo?"

"Y'all want one lahk it, Rainbow honey? Stick with me an yore gonna be fartin through silk."

"Thass sweet, Berdoo."

"You two wovebirds bwing the body out, and I'll watch the twuck." Haf-N-Haf's heavy footsteps went back down the steps. The truck door slammed again.

Berdoo and Rainbow walked into the bedroom.

"Whah . . . isn't he a *saaht?* He looks lahk a devilfish!"

"Don't you worry yore purty haid. He'll taahten up onct Mr. Frostee reprograms him."

"But wait, hunneh. Don't he remaahnd yew of the man who's brain we almost ate that taam? Last week over to Kristleen's?"

"This ain't a *man*, Rainbow. This here's a switched-off *robot*. I don't know what the hail *man* you're talking about, girl."

"Ooooh nevvah mahnd. Ah'll git his laigs an you take tother eyund."

"Okey-doke. Watch yer step, the sucker's heavy."

Grunting a little, Berdoo and Rainbow wrestled the body out of Cobb's house and down the steps. The whole time, the truck's engine ran.

Cautiously, Mooney stuck his head out the closet door. The bedroom had a window on either side, and through one window he could make out the dark mass of an ice-cream truck. There was a big plastic cone on top of the cab.

Two dim figures stopped at the side of the truck and laid something heavy on the ground. A third man climbed down out of the cab, and opened a door in the side.

One of them turned on a light then, light which picked out every object in the bedroom. Terrified, Mooney threw himself back into the closet. He made Sta-Hi stay in there with him until they heard the truck drive off.

CHAPTER TWENTY-ONE

Cobb chewed down his broiled fish with apparent relish, and managed to enjoy his wine by taking one DRUNKENNESS snort through his left nostril for every two glasses. After dinner he went to the men's room and emptied out his food unit . . . not because he had to, but just to reassure himself that it was really true.

He was feeling the effect now of a good five or six whiskeys, and the whole situation didn't seem so horrible and frightening as it initially had. Hell, he had it made. As long as he kept his batteries charged there was no reason he couldn't live another twenty years . . . scratch that, another *century!* It was only a question of how long the machine could hold up. And even that didn't matter . . . the big boppers had him taped and could project him onto as many bodies as he needed.

Cobb stood, swaying a bit, in front of the men's room mirror. *A fine figure of a man.* He looked the same as ever, white beard and all, but the eyes . . . He leaned closer, staring into his eyes. Something was a little off there, it was the irises, they were too uniform, not fibrous enough. Big deal. He was immortal! He took another jolt through his left nostril and went out to join Annie.

While they'd been eating, the band had set up in the hall behind the Gray Area, and now enough pheezers had arrived for them to start playing. Annie took Cobb's hand and led him into the dance-hall. She had helped decorate it herself.

Overhead they had a big, slowly spinning ball covered with a mosaic of tiny square mirrors. From each corner of the room a colored spotlight shone on the ball, and the reflected flecks of light spun endlessly around the room, changing colors as they moved from wall to wall. There had been a mirror-ball exactly like this at Annie's Senior Prom in 1970, lo these fifty years gone.

"Do you like it, Cobb?"

It made Cobb a little dizzy. This subroutine DRUNKENNESS wasn't quite like the real thing. He held his finger to the left side of his nose and took two quick breaths through his right nostril, coming down a couple of notches, enough to enjoy himself again.

The lights were perfect, really, it made you feel like you were on a boat drifting down some sun-flecked creek, trout hovering just beneath the surface, and all the time in the world . . .

"It's beautiful, Annie. Just like being young again. Shall we?"

They stepped onto the half-empty dance-floor, turning slowly to the music. It was an old George Harrison song about God and Love. The musicians were pheezers who cared about the music. They did it justice.

"Do you love me, Cobb?"

The question caught him off guard. He hadn't loved anyone for years. He'd been too busy waiting to die. Love? He'd given it up when he left Verena alone in their apartment on Eastern Parkway in Louisville. But now . . .

"Why do you ask, Annie?"

"I've been living with you for a week." Her arms around his waist drew him closer. Her thighs. "And we still haven't made love. Is it that you're . . . "

"I'm not sure I remember how," Cobb said, not wanting to go into details. He wondered if there was an ERECTION subprogram in his library. Have to check on that later, have to find out what else was in there, too. He kissed Annie's cheek. "I'll do some research."

When the dance ended they sat down with Farker and his wife. The two were having a spat, you could tell from the claw-like way Cynthia was holding her fingers. and from the confusion in Farker's eyes. They were glad to have Cobb and Annie interrupt them.

"What do you think of all this?" Cobb asked, using the hearty cheer-up-you idiot tone he always used with Farker.

"Very nice," Cynthia Farker answered. "But there's no *streamers*."

Emboldened by Cobb's presence, Farker waved over a waiter and ordered a pitcher of beer. Normally Cynthia wouldn't let him drink, not that he wanted to, normally, but this was, after all, the . . .

"Golden Prom," Annie said. "That's what we called it, since it's been about fifty years since a lot of us had our high-school Senior Prom. Do you remember yours, Cynthia?"

Cynthia lit a mentholated and lightly THC-ed cigarette. "Do I *remember*? Our class didn't *have* a prom. Instead some of the *hot*-heads on the student council voted to use the funds for a fall *bus*-trip."

"Where did you go?" Cobb asked.

Cynthia laughed shrilly. "To *Wash*ington! To march on the *Pent*agon!. But it was worth it. That's where Farker and I met, isn't it, dear."

Farker bobbed his light-bulb head in thought for a moment. "That's right. I was watching the Fugs chanting *Out Demon Out* on a flat-bed truck in the parking lot, and you stepped . . . "

"I didn't *step* on your foot, Farker. I *footsied* you. You looked like such an im*port*ant person with your *tape* recorder, and I was just *dying* to talk to you."

"You sure did," Farker said, grinning and shaking his head. "And you haven't stopped since."

The beer arrived then and they clinked glasses. Holding his glass up, Cobb closed his right nostril and took a snort. Sitting down, the dizziness was bearable. But, listening to his friends talk, he had a feeling of shame at no longer being human.

"How's your son?" he asked Cynthia, just to be saying something. Chuck, the Farkers' only child, was a United Cults minister up in Philadelphia. Cynthia loved to talk about him.

"He's getting more *nooky* than you ever saw!" Cynthia gave a thin cackle. "And the girls give him *money*, too. He teaches them astral pro*jec*tion."

"Some racket, huh?" Farker said, shaking his head. "If I were still young . . . "

"Not you," Annie said. "You're not psychic enough. But Cobb," she paused to smile at her escort, "Cobb could lead a cult any day."

"Well," Cobb said thoughtfully, "I have been feeling sort of psychic ever since . . . " He caught himself and skipped forward. "That is, I've been getting this feeling that the mind really *is* independent of your body. Even without your body, your mind could still exist as a sort of mathematical possibility. And telepathy is only . . . "

"That's just what our son Chuck says," Cynthia interrupted. "You must be getting *senile*, Cobb!"

They all laughed then, and started talking about other things: food and health and gossip. But, in the back of his mind, Cobb began thinking seriously about cults and religion.

The whole experience of changing bodies felt miraculous. Had he proved that the soul is real . . . or that it isn't? And there were his strange new flashes of empathy to explain. Was it that, having switched bodies once, he was no longer so matter-bound as before . . . or was it just the result of having mechanically sharp senses? What was he . . . guru or golem?

"You're cute," Annie said, and pulled him back onto the dance-floor.

CHAPTER TWENTY-TWO

The Little Kidders put the robot that had looked like Sta-Hi in the back of the truck. Berdoo squeezed into the cab between Rainbow and Haf-N-Haf. No point taking a chance of her getting felt up.

"Thometimeth I wonder what Mr. Fwostee ith up to," Haf-N-Haf slobbered, pulling out onto the asphalt.

"That makes two of us, boah. But he pays cash."

"How much you got naow?" Rainbow asked, laying her hand on Berdoo's thigh. "Yew got enough to take me for a week at Disney World? And first Ah wanna baah me some new clothes and maybe change mah hayur."

"It looks real purty just lahk tis, Rainbow. Ah allus wanted me a cheap skank with green hair."

Berdoo and Haf-N-Haf began snickering, and Rainbow fell into a sulk. The truck labored over the Merritt Island Bridge, and then Haf-N-Haf turned right onto Route One. Night-bugs spattered against their windshield, and the hydrogen-fueled engine pocked away.

"Is Kristleen gonna git us a new monkey-man?" Berdoo asked after awhile.

"She'd bettew!" Haf-N-Haf answered, staring out past the headlights. "Filthy Phil ith on her ath about it non-thop."

Berdoo shook his head. "Ah surely don't know whaah old Phil is so *waald* to be eatin brains all the time. It gets a little old, ya know?"

"Did he get Kristleen a new place to liyuv?" Rainbow wanted to know.

"Whah yew know he diyud, hunneh. Ain't nobody can bring in the troops lahk that Kristleen can."

"Well, Ah certainly hope that is a fact," Rainbow said primly. "Yew been promisin and promisin me a brain-feast and all Ah've done so far was almost git arreyusted."

"Ath wong ath Phil's wunnin the thow we'll be eating bwains," Haf-N-Haf assured her.

"Something right funny about ole Phil," Berdoo observed a bit later. "I ain't never seen him smoke nor take a drink nor eat any regular food. And when he ain't givin orders he jest sits and stares."

They were in Daytona now, concrete and neon flickering past. Haf-N-Haf checked the mirror for cops, and then turned hard right into the Lido Hotel's underground garage. He parked the truck way in back, and plugged a wire into the wall-socket to keep the refrigeration unit running. A little camera eye poked out of a hole on the top of the truck. Anybody who came near the truck now would be hurting for sure. Mr. Frostee knew how to take care of himself, especially with his extra remote in back.

They took the elevator up to their suite. Filthy Phil was sitting there, shirt off, staring out the window at the moonlit sea. His fat back with its sagging tattoo was facing them. He didn't bother to turn around.

"*Notice to Satan:*" Rainbow said, shrilly reading Phil's back aloud. "*Send this Man to Heaven, Cause He's Done His Time in Hell.*" She read it in her dumbest schoolgirl tone. She didn't like Phil.

Phil still didn't turn around. Once there had been a human Filthy Phil, a welder who worked too late on BEX up at Ledge one nightshift. BEX had put the brain-tape in charge of his humanoid repair robot . . . but it hadn't worked out. The personality had flattened out to that of an affectless killer. But he was still a good mechanic.

When they'd decided to send Mr. Frostee down to start collecting souls, Phil had come with him. Mr. Frostee still used Phil's brain-tape when he needed repairs. But he didn't like to put Phil's personality in charge of the robot unless he had to. So, as a rule, the robot-remote called Filthy Phil had all the warmth and human responsiveness of a pair of vice-grip pliers.

"Y'all leave Phil alone," Berdoo warned Rainbow. "He's waitin for the phone to ring, ain't that right, Phil?"

Phil nodded curtly. The shuttle to BEX was taking off tomorrow, and Phil Frostee had promised to send up a new set of organs. A tape could go up anytime, by radio . . . but he'd promised a whole person, body and soul, hardware and software. If Kristleen didn't find someone . . . He stared out the window, listening to the three human voices behind him, and making his plans.

The phone rang then. Phil sprang across the room and snatched it up. "Filthy Phil."

The voice on the other end was high-pitched, tearful. Berdoo looked at Haf-N-Haf nervously. Even through the mirror-shades you could see that Phil was mad. But his voice came out smooth.

"I understand, Kristleen. Yes I understand. OK. Fine."

More talking from the other end. Slowly a smile spread on Phil's muscular face. He looked over at Berdoo and winked.

"OK. Kristleen. If he's asleep why don't you just come over now and we can pay you off. You got five grand coming. You better come get it now, because we're going to shift bases tomorrow. Right. That's right. OK, baby. And don't worry, I do understand."

Phil set the phone down gently, almost tenderly. "Kristleen's in love. She just blew a college boy and now she's sitting there watching him sleep. He sleeps like a baby, she says, like an innocent child." Phil began walking around the room, moving pieces of furniture this way and that.

"Kwithtween'th not going to dewiver and you're going to pay her off anyway?" Haf-N-Haf asked incredulously.

"That's what I told her," Phil said evenly. "But I'm in a tight spot. I've got to have a body by tomorrow morning. The tape could go any time, but I've got a cargo-slot all signed up and paid for." He took a small sleep-dart pistol out of a drawer and examined it carefully.

"You ain't gonna kill Kristleen?" Rainbow cried.

"It's not really killing," Phil said, holding the pistol half-raised. "Haven't you figured that out yet? Berdoo?"

Berdoo felt like he was back in eighth grade, being asked questions he couldn't begin to understand. "Ah dunno, Phil. It's yore gang. Yew got the truck and the apartment and all. Ah'll help you snuff Kristleen." If he weren't a Little Kidder he'd be nothing again.

"We'll eat her brain," Phil said, spinning the pistol and watching them closely. "But her thoughts will live on." With his left hand he poked abruptly at his chest.

"Look!"

A little door swung open, showing the inside of a metal compartment in his chest. There were knives in there, and little machines. It looked like a tiny laboratory.

Rainbow screamed and Berdoo stepped over to cover her mouth. Haf-N-Haf made a noise that might have been a laugh.

"I'm part of Mr. Frostee," Phil explained, snapping the door back shut. "I'm like his hand, you wave? Or his mouth." Phil smiled broadly then, revealing his strong, sharp teeth. "We boppers use human organs to seed our tissue farms. We use brain-tapes for simulators in some of our robot-remotes. Like me. And we just like brains anyhow, even the ones we don't actually use. A human mind is a beautiful thing."

"Well, you kin leave us out!" Rainbow cried. "Ah'll be buggered befo ah help yew!"

"Shut up, fool," Berdoo snarled at her. "Ah buggered yew yestidday, yew should recall."

"Ah am *not* gonna stand baah and let . . . " Rainbow began.

The doorbell cut her off in mid cry. Phil aimed the sleep-dart gun at Rainbow.

"Are you going to let Kristleen in, Rainbow? Or should I use you instead?"

Rainbow went to the door and opened it for Kristleen. Standing across the room, Phil was able to nail the two women with two quick shots. The sleep-drug took effect and they collapsed. Haf-N-Haf dragged them in and closed the door.

Berdoo stood watching, miserable and confused. Rainbow was the only girl-friend he'd ever had. But Phil had always been right before. Phil was Mr. Frostee, really. And Mr. Frostee was smarter than anyone in the world.

"She's going to make trouble if we let her go, Berdoo." Phil was looking at him across the room, his gun still leveled. There was a silence.

"But ah *cayun't!*" Berdoo cried finally. "Not that sweet girl. Ah *cain't* let you cut her all . . . "

Suddenly there was a pistol in Berdoo's hand, a .38 special. Faster than thought, his street-fighter's reflexes had carried him over to the window and fanned the drape out in front of him. Phil's sleep-dart bounced off the drape and dropped to the floor.

"Be reasonable, Berdoo." Phil lowered his dart pistol. "We'll take Kristleen apart, but we'll send Rainbow up whole. She can work for BEX as a stewardess, to replace that girl Misty from last year. Now you just let me get Rainbow stoned up good, and I'll talk to her, and then she flies up to Disky and gets herself an everlasting body. I promise they'll leave her personality in. You'll be able to see her once in a . . . "

Berdoo stepped out from behind the curtain, his small face set in a snarl. He shot Phil through the head, just like that.

"Oh, Bewdoo," Haf-N-Haf moaned as the ringing of the pistol-shot died down. "We're going to have to wun wike hell. Mr. Fwostee's got that other wemote in the twuck!"

"We'll go out front and steal us a car," Berdoo said tersely. "Ah'll drag Rainbow, an you handle Kristleen."

Just as they left the room, something in there exploded. Phil's body? They didn't stop to find out. Staggering under the women's dead weight, they bumped down the fire-stairs and out through the lobby.

An athletic young man was just parking a red convertible in front. Berdoo still had his pistol out. Haf-N-Haf tapped the man's shoulder and said something. The guy looked them over, handed off the keys, and walked away without saying a thing. Haf-N-Haf and Berdoo often affected people that way.

They put the girls in back and took off for the thruway to Orlando.

CHAPTER TWENTY-THREE

The Golden Prom was a lot of fun. Cobb hadn't enjoyed himself so much in years. The beauty of the DRUNKENNESS subprogram was that you could move your intoxication level up and down at will, instead of being caught on a relentless down escalator to bargain basement philosophy and the parking garage. He found that if he tried to go further than ten drinks, to the blackout point, then an automatic override would cut in, and he'd loop back to where he started.

Leaving the dance with Annie, he took a few sobering right-nostril breaths and wrapped his arm around her waist. She was acting girlish and giggly.

"Have you finished your research, Cobb?"

"What?" The moon was hanging over the sea now. Its light made a long lapped lane of gold, leading out to the edge of the world. "What research?"

She slipped her hand into his pants in back and smoothed his buttock. "*You* know."

"That's right," Cobb said. "Be-boppa-lu-la."

"Library accessed," a voice in his head said.

"I want to have sex."

"I'm glad," Annie said. "So do I."

"SEX subroutine now activated," the voice said.

"OUT," Cobb said.

"It's out?" Annie asked. "I thought you wanted to."

Cobb felt his pants tightening in front. "I do, I do."

They stopped once or twice to kiss and rub against each other. Every square centimeter of Cobb's body tingled with anticipation. For the first time in years his whole consciousness was out on his skin. Out on both their skins, really, for when they kissed he felt himself merging into Annie's personality. One flesh.

For some reason the lights in his cottage were on. At first he thought it had just been an oversight . . . but walking up to the door he heard Sta-Hi's voice.

"Oh," Annie cried happily. "How wonderful! Your friend is better again!"

Cobb followed her into his cottage. Sta-Hi and Mooney were sitting there arguing. They fell silent when they saw Cobb and Annie.

Annie was angry to see Mooney there again. "What do you want, pig?"

Mooney didn't say anything, but just leaned back in Cobb's easy chair, his alert eyes looking the old man up and down.

"It is really you, Sta-Hi?" Cobb asked. "Did they beam you down or . . . "

"It's the real me," Sta-Hi said. "All-meat. I came back on the shuttle today. How was *your* trip?"

"You would have loved it. I couldn't tell yes from no." Cobb started to say more, then stopped himself. It wasn't clear how much it would be safe to let Mooney know. Had they found the switched-off robot in the bedroom? Then he noticed the pistol in Mooney's lap.

"Maybe you should send the lady home," Mooney suggested easily. "I think we have some things to talk over."

"SEX OUT," Cobb muttered bitterly. "DRUNKENNESS OUT. You better go, Annie. Mr. Mooney's right."

"But why should I? I live here now, too. Who does this crummy Gimmie loach think he is, making me leave?" She was close to tears. "And after such a wonderful evening, just when . . . "

Cobb put his arm around her and walked her out the door. Patches of light from his cottage windows lay on the crushed-shell driveway. He could see Mooney's alert shadow in one of the windows.

"Don't worry, Annie. I'll make it up to you tomorrow. Suddenly it's like . . . like life is starting all over again."

"But what do they want? Have you done something wrong? Do they have a right to arrest you?"

Cobb thought a minute. Conceivably they could have him dismantled as a bopper spy. As a machine, he probably wouldn't even be entitled to a trial. But there was no reason it had to come to that. He put his arms around Annie and gave her a last kiss.

"I'll talk to them. I'll talk my way out. Save a place for me in your bed. I might be over in a half-hour."

"All right," Annie breathed in his ear. "And I've got a gun too, you know. I'll watch out the window in case . . . "

Cobb hugged her tighter, whispering back, "Don't do that, honey. I can handle them. If worst comes to worst I'll . . . skip out. But . . . "

"Come on, Anderson," Mooney called from Cobb's window. "We're waiting to talk to you."

Cobb and Annie exchanged a last hand-squeeze, and Cobb went back in his house. He sat down in the easy chair that Mooney had been using, leaving Mooney to lean against the wall and glower at him, pistol in hand. Sta-Hi was lounging in a deck-chair he'd dragged in, a lit reefer in his mouth.

"Start talking, Anderson," Mooney said. He was keeping the pistol aimed at Cobb's head. A body shot probably wouldn't stop a robot, but . . .

"Take it easy, Dad," Sta-Hi put in. "Cobb's not going to hurt anyone."

"You let me be a judge of that, Stanny. For all we know, that other robot is hiding right outside to help him."

"What robot?" Cobb said. How much did they really know, anyway? He and Sta-Hi had split up before the operation, and . . .

"Look," Sta-Hi said, a little wearily. "Let's cut the noise-level. I *know* that you're a machine now, Cobb. The boppers put you in your robot-double. Stuzzy! I can wave with it. The only problem is that my father here . . . "

The old hard-cop/soft-cop routine. Cobb abandoned his first line of defense and asked for information.

"Where's the Sta-Hi$_2$ robot?"

"The Little Kidders were here," Sta-Hi said. "They carried the robot out of your bedroom and left. It looked like they were driving an ice-cream truck."

"Mr. Frostee," Cobb said absently. He was thinking hard. What the boppers had done to him was, on the whole, a good thing. A whole nother ball-game. If only he could make Sta-Hi and Mooney see . . .

"Where's your base of operations?" Mooney demanded. "How many others like you are there?" He gestured menacingly with his pistol.

Cobb shrugged. "Don't ask me. The boppers never tell me anything. I'm just a poor old man with an artificial body." He looked over at Sta-Hi for sympathy. As with Annie before, he was getting a telepathic feeling, a feeling that he could see through the two other men's eyes. Sta-Hi was stoned, receptive and open to change. But Mooney was tense and frightened.

"As far as I know," Cobb said, "I'm completely in control of myself. I don't think the boppers plan to use me as a remote-control robot or anything like that."

"What's in it for them?" Mooney asked.

"They said they wanted to do me a favor," Cobb said. He considered opening his food-unit door to show Mooney the letter, but then thought better of it. But thinking of the door suggested a possibility.

"Be-boppa-lu-la," Cobb said out loud.

"Library accessed."

"Was there a subroutine called MR. FROSTEE?"

"Now activated," the voice murmured.

Something opened up in Cobb's mind, and a whole different set of visual stimuli overlaid the yellowed walls of his living-room.

He was still in his cottage, yet he was also in a concrete parking garage. Something very bad had just happened. Berdoo had shot Phil, his best remote. It was like losing an eye. And now there was no way to see what Berdoo and Haf-N-Haf were doing. Should he send the extra remote after them?

"Hello," Cobb thought, stopping himself from saying the word aloud.

"Cobb?" Mr. Frostee's response was quick and unsurprised. "I was hoping to talk to you. But I wanted to let you make the first move. We don't want you to feel . . . "

"Like a remote?"

"Right. You're designed for full autonomy, Cobb. If you can help us, so much the better. But there's no way we would have edited out your free will . . . even if we knew how. You're still entirely your own man."

"What do you want from me?" Silently asking this, Cobb leaned back in his chair, stretching out his legs. Mooney looked impatient. Sta-Hi was staring at the bugs on the ceiling.

"Convince the others," came Mr. Frostee's reply. In the background, Cobb could make out the interior of a truck-cab. Hands on the steering wheel. The concrete walls of a parking garage, then the garish lights of Daytona Beach streaming past.

"Convince them *all* to get robot bodies like you. Then we can merge, we can all merge to become a new and greater being. We'll set up a number of reprocessing centers . . . "

Mooney was standing over Cobb, shaking him. It was hard to see, with the glare of headlights coming at him. Slowly, Cobb brought his attention back to the cottage.

"What's the matter, Mooney?" asked Cobb.

"You're signaling for help, aren't you?"

"How would you like a nice everlasting body like mine?" Cobb countered. "I could arrange it."

"So that's it," Sta-Hi said dreamily. "The big boppers want to bring us *all* into the fold."

"It's not so unreasonable," Cobb protested. "It's a natural next evolutionary step. Imagine people that carry terabyte computing systems in their head, people that communicate directly brain-to-brain, people who live for centuries and change bodies like suits of clothes!"

"Imagine people that aren't people," Sta-Hi replied. "Cobb, the big boppers like TEX and MEX have been trying to run the same con on the Moon. And most of the little boppers up there aren't buying it . . . most would rather fight then let themselves be patched into the big systems. Now why do you think that is?"

"Obviously some people . . . or boppers . . . are going to be paranoid about losing their precious individuality," Cobb answered. "But that's just a matter of cultural conditioning! Look, Sta-Hi, I've been all the way in . . . *all* the way. After I got taped on the Moon I was just a pattern in a memory-bank somewhere for a few days. And you know, it wasn't even that . . . "

"Let's go," Mooney ordered, roughly pulling Cobb to his feet. "You're going to be deprogrammed and dismantled, Anderson. We can't let this kind of . . . "

Mr. Frostee was still there in Cobb's head. "I've taken the liberty of activating your SELF-DESTRUCT subroutine," the voice said quietly. "Just say the word 'DESTROY' out loud and you'll explode. Your body will explode. *You're* really in me. I'll give you a new body, the one here in the truck . . . "

"MR. FROSTEE OUT," Cobb said. If he did it, he wanted it to be his own decision.

Mooney had his pistol at the base of Cobb's skull. He was getting panicky.

Any second, Mooney, Cobb thought to himself. But still he hesitated. He told himself it was just because he didn't want to hurt Sta-Hi . . . but he was also scared, scared to die again. Could he really cross the noisy void between bodies again? But he'd already done it once, hadn't he?

"Go outside, Sta-Hi," Mooney said then, and sealed his fate. "Go check if that old bitch is waiting out there to ambush us. Or the other robot."

Sta-Hi eased out the back door and melted into the night.

"I've finally got you," Mooney said, with a nudge of his pistol. "I'm going to find out what makes you tick."

"DESTROY," Cobb said, and lost his second body.

CHAPTER TWENTY-FOUR

"I want to talk to you about diarrhea," a voice said earnestly. "Gastric distress can *ruin* that long-hoped-for vacation. So be sure . . . "

Cobb's first conscious act was to turn the radio off. He had just pulled out of a fuel-station on the gritty outskirts of Daytona Beach. But, on the other hand, he had just died in the explosion of his cottage in Cocoa Beach.

"Hello, Cobb. You see? You can count on me." Mr. Frostee's voice filled his head again. Cobb looked down at his sinewy forearms, handling the ice-cream truck's big steering-wheel with an experienced touch.

"Sta-Hi$_2$?" Cobb asked. "You put me in Sta-Hi$_2$?"

"It *was* Sta-Hi$_2$. But I just gave the body a new look. I copied the fellow who was running the pumps back there."

Cobb thought back to the explosion. DESTROY, disorientation, and now this. His fingers were blackened with years of grease. He leaned out the window to take a peek at himself in the rearview mirror.

He had a skinny head and large, liquid eyes. Thinning black hair, greasy and combed straight back. His nose was much more prominent than his chin. Ratface. Approaching headlights pulled his attention back to the road.

"What about disguising the truck?" Cobb asked. "I killed Mooney, but he must have left records. And Sta-Hi got away. The heat's gonna be looking for a Mr. Frostee truck."

"There'll be time for that later. Right now I've got a score to settle. Those hoodlums . . . those Little Kidders . . . one of them wrecked my best remote. He's called Berdoo."

Without consciously thinking about it, Cobb had driven the truck onto the thruway west, towards Orlando. Was he still in control of his actions?

"Where are we going?"

"Disney World. Berdoo doesn't remember it, but he once told me . . . told Phil . . . that he has a friend who runs a motel there. I think that's where he'll go to hide out. I want you to shoot him, Cobb, and then take out his brain for me. We'll leave the organs . . . that's all over for now . . . but I've got to get that brain on tape. You should have seen how easily he killed my Phil."

It was hard to read the emotion in Mr. Frostee's even voice. Was revenge the motive? Or was it just a collector's lust for ownership?

In any case, trying to ambush the Little Kidders in their own hideout sounded like a terrible idea. And going brain-collecting was something Cobb hoped to put off as long as possible. He wondered if he should just turn around. Or pull off the highway and leave the truck. Glancing in his rear-view mirror he could see dawn pinkening the horizon. The road was empty.

"You've still got your free will," Mr. Frostee said. "But don't forget that we're in this together. If I die then so do you. You're really just a pattern in my circuits."

"But you can't override me?" Testing, Cobb took his foot off the accelerator. No one pushed his foot back.

"I can't control your mind," Mr. Frostee said, not quite answering the question. "But don't stop the truck. What if a cop comes by?"

Cobb speeded back up. "Why would you give one of your subsystems free will?"

"The human mind is all of a piece, Cobb. If we try to start picking and choosing, all that's left is a boring bundle of reflexes. When a big bopper builds in some human's personality, he's got to learn to live with the subsystem's free will. I *could* cut you off entirely, in an emergency, but short of . . . "

"Why bother taping humans at all?"

"No program we can write and control acts like human software. Humans can't write bopper programs . . . they had to let them evolve. And a bopper can't write a human program. It works both ways. We need you guys. What we're working towards is a human-bopper fusion, a single great mind stretching from person to person all over the world. It's right, Cobb, and it's inevitable. Simpler beings merge to produce higher beings, and they must merge and merge again. In this way we draw ever closer to the One."

"*The One?*" Cobb said, laughing. "You don't mean the One on the Moon, do you? Don't you know that's just a random noise source? Haven't you figured that out?"

"*Randomness* is an elusive concept, Cobb."

"Look," Cobb said, "In order to make the boppers evolve fast enough I had to speed up the rate of mutation. So in the substrate program I included a command that they plug into the One, once a month, as you know. But the One is just a simple cosmic ray counter. It goes through your programs changing yesses and noes, here and there, just on the basis of the Geiger counter click-pattern of cosmic-ray bursts for the last day or so. The One is just a glorified circuit-scrambler."

Still Mr. Frostee was silent. Finally the answer came. "You choose to make light of the One, Cobb. But the pulse of the One is the pulse of the Cosmos. You yourself call its noisy input the cosmic rays. What is more natural than that the Cosmos should lovingly direct the growth of the boppers with its bursts of radiation? There is no *noise* in the All . . . there is only *information*. Nothing is truly random. It is sad that you choose not to understand what you yourself have created."

A ditch full of brackish water and marsh-grass lay to the right of the thruway. Cobb saw an alligator, lying half out of the water and watching the early morning traffic. The night had passed, it was quarter to seven. In a sort of phantom-stomach reflex, Cobb had a brief longing for breakfast. But the hunger faded, and Cobb let the empty miles roll by, lost in thought.

What was he now? In one sense he was what he had always been. A certain pattern, a type of software. The fiveness of a right hand is the same as the fiveness of a left. The *Cobbness* that had been a man was the same as the *Cobbness* now coded upon Mr. Frostee's cold chips.

Cobb Anderson's brain had been dissected, but the software that made up his mind had been preserved. The idea of "self" is, after all, just another idea, a symbol in the software. Cobb felt like him*self* as much as ever. And, as much as ever, Cobb wanted his self to continue to exist on hardware.

Perhaps the boppers had stored a tape of him on the Moon, and perhaps up there his software had also been given hardware. But, here and now, Cobb's continued existence depended on keeping Mr. Frostee cold and energized. They were in this together. Him and a machine who wanted to know God.

"I'll tell you," Cobb said, breaking the silence. "I think it would be really stupid to go charging after the Little Kidders before getting the truck repainted. Even if the cops aren't after us yet, there's no point having Berdoo be able to see you coming from a block away. Let's get off the thruway and fix up the truck. There's a giant plastic ice-cream cone on the cab's roof, for God's sake."

"You're driving," Mr. Frostee said mildly. "I will defer to your superior knowledge of human criminality."

Cobb got out at the next exit and took a small road north. This was rolling countryside, with plenty of streams. Palms and magnolias gave way to blackjack pines and scrubby live oak. Brambles and honeysuckle filled in the spaces between the struggling little trees. And in some places the uncontrollable kudzu vine had taken root and choked out all other vegetation.

It was only eight-thirty, but already the asphalt road was shimmering in the heat. The frequent dips were filled with reflecting water-mirages. Cobb rolled down the window and let the air beat against his face. The truck's big hydrogen-fueled engine roared smoothly and the sticky road sang beneath the tires.

The wild scrub gave way to farmland, big cleared pastures with cattle in them. The cows waded about knee-deep in weeds, munching the flowers. White cattle egrets stalked and flapped along next to them, spearing the insects that the cows stirred up. The egrets looked like little old men with no arms.

A few miles of pastures and barns brought them to a bend in the road called Purcell. There were some big houses and some cracker-boxes, a tiny Winn-Dixie, and a couple of fuel-stations. Cobb pulled into a tree-shaded Hy-Gas that had a hand painted sign saying *Body Work*.

There was a three-legged dog lying on the asphalt by the pumps. When Cobb pulled up, the animal rose and limped off, barking. The fourth leg ended half-way down, in a badly bandaged stub.

Cobb hopped out of the truck cab. A young sandy-haired man in stained white coveralls came ambling out of the garage. He had prominent ears and thick lips.

"Mr. Frostee time!" the attendant observed. He screwed the hydrogen nozzle into the truck's hydride tanks. There was a sort of foliated metal in the tanks which could absorb several hundred liters of the gas. "Gimme one?"

"It's empty," Cobb said. "This isn't really a Mr. Frostee truck anymore. It's mine."

The attendant absorbed this fact in silence, looking Cobb's skinny rat faced body up and down. "You baah it?"

"I sure did," Cobb said, putting on a local accent. "Over in Cocoa. Fella closed his franchise down. I aim to fix this truck up and use it for my meat business."

The attendant topped up the tank. He was tanned, with white squint-wrinkles around his eyes. He shot Cobb a sharp glance.

"You don't look like no butcher to me. You look like a grease monkey in a stolen truck." He punctuated this with a sudden, toothy smile. "But I could be wrong. You need anything besides the hydrogen?"

The guy was suspicious, but seemed willing to be bought off. Cobb decided to stay. "Actually . . . I'd like to get this truck painted. It's a burden having to explain to everyone that it's really mine."

"I reckon *so*," the sandy-haired man said, smiling broadly. "If you pull her round back, I might could he'p you solve your problems. I'll paint it and forget it. Cost you a thousand bucks."

That was much too high for two hours' work. The guy was sure the truck was stolen.

"OK," Cobb said, meeting the other man's prying eyes. "But don't try to double-cross me."

The attendant displayed his many crooked teeth in another smile. "What color y'all want?"

"Paint it black," Cobb said, relishing the old phrase. "But first let's get that goddamn cone off the top."

He got back in the truck, pulled off the asphalt, and drove through rutted weeds to the junky lot behind the Hy-Gas station. The attendant, on foot, led the way.

"Perhaps he is not honest," Mr. Frostee said inside Cobb's head, sounding a bit worried.

"Of course he isn't," Cobb answered. "What we have to look out for is him calling the cops anyway, or trying to blackmail us for more money."

"I think you should kill him and eat his brain," Mr. Frostee said quickly.

"That's not the answer to *every* problem in interpersonal relations," Cobb said, hopping out. He was learning to talk to Mr. Frostee subvocally, without actually opening his mouth.

The attendant had brought a screwdriver and a couple of Lock-Tite wrenches. He and Cobb got the cone off, after ten or fifteen minutes' work. The emptily smiling swirl-topped face landed in the weeds next to half of a rusted-out motorcycle. The two men's bodies worked well together, and a certain sympathy developed between them.

The attendant introduced himself as Jody Doakes. Cobb, hoping to confuse his trail, said his name was Berdoo. They went around front to get the paint and the spray-gun compressor. Cobb solved the problem of when to pay, by tearing a thousand-dollar-bill in half and giving Jody one piece.

"You'll get the other half when I pull out of here," Cobb said. "And no earlier."

"I see your point," Jody said, with a knowing chuckle.

First they had to wash the truck off. Then they taped newspaper over the tires, lights and windows. They sprayed everything else black. The paint dried fast in the hot air. They were able to start the second coat as soon as they finished the first.

The job took all morning. Now and then that three-legged dog would start barking, and Jody would go out to serve a customer. Mr. Frostee's refrigeration unit kept running, drawing its energy from the hydride tank. Jody asked once why the refrigerator had to be on if there wasn't any more ice-cream. Cobb told him that if he wanted the other half of the thousand-dollar-bill he could keep his questions to himself.

They finished the second coat a few minutes after the noon siren blew on the Purcell fire-house.

"Y'all want a bite to eat?" Jody asked. "I got the makins for sandwiches inside." He hooked his thumb at the garage.

"Sure," Cobb said, ignoring the fact that he'd just have to clean the chewed-up bread and lunchmeat out of his food unit later on. Eating was fun. "I could use a couple of beers, too."

"Come shot!" Jody said, meaning something like *you bet*. "Come shot on the beer, Berdoo."

They had a friendly lunch. More strongly than ever, Cobb felt able to enter into other people's thoughts. Again the thought of starting a cult crossed his mind.

The food and beer felt good in his mouth. Over Mr. Frostee's protests, Cobb cut in the DRUNKENNESS subroutine and gave himself a hit for each beer. They split a six-pack. Jody allowed as how, for an extra two hundred bucks, he'd be willing to let Cobb have some fresh license plates and registration papers he happened to have.

Cobb enjoyed their dealings very much. In his old body he had never been able to talk comfortably to garage mechanics. But now, with a random grease monkey's face on a Sta-Hi-shaped body, Cobb fit in at a filling station as easily as he used to fit in at research labs. Idly he wondered if Mr. Frostee could change the flickercladding enough to turn him into a woman. That would be interesting. There was so much to look forward to!

After lunch they changed the license plates. Cobb handed over the missing half of the thousand-dollar-bill, and the extra two hundred dollars. Hoping to keep Jody bought, he suggested that he might be back with more of the same kind of business next month, if things worked out.

"Come shot!" Jody said. "And good luck."

Cobb drove out of Purcell, heading east, past cows and egrets.

"I wish you'd taped his brain," Mr. Frostee nagged. "We can always use a good mechanic."

Cobb had been expecting a remark like this. And the next remark, too.

"How come you're driving East? That's not the right way to Disney World. We've still got to get Berdoo!"

"Mr. Frostee," Cobb said, "I love my new body. And I support your basic plan. It's the logical next step for human evolution. But mass-murder is not the way. There's a better way, a way to get people to *volunteer* for brain-taping. We'll start a new religious cult!"

There was a pained silence. Finally Mister Frostee spoke. "I feel I should warn you, Cobb. You have free will in the sense that I can't control your thoughts. But the body belongs to *both* of us. In certain special circumstances I may take . . . "

"Please," Cobb said, "hear me out. Am I right in believing that you're the only big bopper now on Earth?"

"That's right."

"And I'm using the only robot-remote you have left?"

"Yes. Hopefully, with Mooney out of the way, security at the spaceport will be relaxed again. We had planned a shipment of some thousand new remotes during the next two years, as well as several more big bopper units. These plans are unfortunately . . . in flux. There are some . . . difficulties on the Moon. But until the situation re-stabilizes, I intend to continue gathering tapes and . . . "

"You're trying to tell me there's an all-out civil war starting on the Moon, aren't you?" Cobb exclaimed. "We're on our own, M.F.! If we go back to the spaceport and try . . . "

"There is no need to go to spaceport for tape transmission. I can radio-beam the tapes directly up to BEX at Ledge."

"A soul transmitter," Cobb said thoughtfully. "That's a good angle. *Personetics: The Science of Immortality.*"

"What do you mean?"

"The religion! We'll get the down-and-out, the runaways, the culties . . . we'll get them to believe that you're a machine for sending their souls to heaven. It's not really so . . . "

"But why bother? Why not just proceed as Phil always did? To *seize*, and cut, and . . . "

"Look, M.F., we're in this together. It works both ways. If something happens to this truck I'm dead. I don't think you realize just how strongly humans react to murder and cannibalism. This is no bopper *anarchy* here, it's more like a *police*-state. If you and I are going to last out until BEX gets the troops here, we're going to need to lay low and play it careful."

Just thinking about it gave Cobb the creeps. If he couldn't get fuel for the truck, if the cops stopped them, if the refrigeration unit broke . . . It was like being a snail with a ten-ton shell! A snowball in hell!

"We need security," Cobb said urgently. "We need a lot of people to take care of us, and we need money to keep the hydride tanks full. If we get enough money I think we should build a scion, too. A copy of your processor. We could get our followers to buy the components in computer shops. You've got to understand the realities of life on Earth!"

"All right," Mr. Frostee said finally. "I agree. But where are you driving to?"

"Back to the coast," Cobb said. "I know a place north of Daytona Beach where we can hole up. And, say . . . give me a new face. Something fatherly."

CHAPTER TWENTY-FIVE

After his father's funeral, Sta-Hi went back to driving a cab in Daytona Beach. Bea, his mother, wanted to put the house up for sale and move north, away from the pheezers. She hated them since Mooney's death . . . and who could blame her! Her husband had gone to old Cobb Anderson's house on a routine check, and had been blown to smithereens! Just for doing his job! And so on.

There was an investigation into Mooney's death, but the blast hadn't left a hell of a lot to investigate. There was not a scrap of the suspected robot double to be found. And Sta-Hi didn't tell the authorities any more than he had to. He still couldn't decide whose side he was on.

He took a couple of his father's space-ship paintings and rented a room in Daytona. He went back to Yellow Cab and they gave him a job driving the night-shift. Mostly it was a matter of bringing drunks and whores to motels. Seamy. And duller'n shit.

His dope habit crept up on him again. Pretty soon he was smoking, snorting, dropping, spraying and shooting his money as fast as he made it. Late at night, driving up and down the one-dimensional city, Sta-Hi would dream and scheme, forming huge, interlocking plans for the future.

He would make a movie about cab-driving. He would write a book about the boppers. No, man, do it with music!

He would learn how to play the guitar and start a band. Fuck learning! He would get another Happy Cloak and let it play his fingers for him. He needed a Happy Cloak!

He'd threaten the boppers to tell about the Little Kidders and the nursies if they wouldn't come across. With Anderson and his father blown up, no one else knew!

He'd get rich and then go back to Disky and get in on the civil war and they'd make him king. Hadn't he already helped the diggers to off a big bopper? He'd lead them to victory! Moon King Sta-Hi!

But there was no way to reach the boppers. The cops had lost track of Mr. Frostee and those Little Kidders. BEX and Misty-girl never got any closer to Earth than space-station Ledge. And no private phone-calls to

Disky were allowed. The thing to do was to make the boppers contact *him*. How? Get so famous they'd notice him!

Around and around, night after night, tripping and bouncing the length of dreary Daytona. One night a drunk left his wallet in the cab. Two thousand bucks in there. Sta-Hi took the money and quit work. He needed time to think!

He got a crate of Z-gas aerosols . . . he'd sunken that low . . . and started hanging around the strip. Eating burgers, selling hits, playing machines, hunting pussy. He tried to make himself conspicuous, hoping something would happen to him. The day his money ran out, it finally did.

He was hanging out at Hideo-Nuts' Boltsadrome, stoned, staring at the floor. His boots looked so perfect. Two dark parabolas in a field of yellow, slight 3-D interest provided by the scurf strewn about. His favorite song was playing. He felt like screaming, like crying out, "I'm here and I'm staying high! I'm Sta-Hi, the king of the brainsurfers!"

The metal speaker overhead was pumping out solid music. He could see the notes if he squinted. He started to giggle, thinking of the tiny note-shaped bumps traveling down the wires like white mice swallowed by a python. God, he had good ideas!

Keeping his smile, in case it came in handy, Sta-Hi looked around the arcade, swaying back and forth, fingering chords on an invisible electric guitar. He couldn't actually play yet, but he had all the moves down . . . say . . . look at little blondie over there. He stared at her and slid a riff down the neck of his imaginary guitar. Smiling harder, he beckoned with his head.

Liking his smile, the broad-hipped girl strolled towards him, swaying back and forth like a slowly swimming fish. *Beat* that tail. She kept her head tilted back to show off the tan-stars on her cheeks.

"Hi 'surfer. God, it's wiggly in here tonight." She shook back her hair and laughed a slow, knowing laugh. "I'm Wendy."

Sta-Hi sizzled off a few more hot chords and then threw his hands in the air. "You're talking to Sta-Hi Mooney, fluffy. I've got the weenie, you've got the bun, put em together and have some gum." His rap had deteriorated badly during the last week of Z-gas.

"Are you in a club?" Wendy asked, still smiling. He wasn't as stuzzy as she had thought from across the room. And, worse, he looked broke.

"Sure . . . I mean practically." She wasn't really as pretty as he had thought. A whore? "How about you?"

"Oh I've been hanging out . . . parties . . . burning cars. . . . " Wendy wondered if it was worth wasting time on him. She had to make five hundred dollars before going back to the temple.

Sta-Hi saw the doubt in Wendy's face. She was the first girl he'd managed to talk to all day. He was going to have to land this fish, and fast. "Have a whiff on me," he said, fumbling out his aerosol.

"Wiggly," she said, tossing her hair again. He handed her the little can and she inhaled a short burst of the Z-gas. Sta-Hi took it back and blasted off a long, long one. Gongs rang in his ears and he staggered a little, laughing a hyuck-hyuck 'surfer laugh from the back of his throat. Wendy took the can out of his hand and hit up another. They looked pretty to each other again.

"What do you want to play?" Sta-Hi asked, gesturing broadly.

"I'm good in that *Pleasure Garden*," Wendy answered.

"Wiggly." Sta-Hi dropped his last five-dollar coin into the slot. The big machine lit up and made a googly welcome-to-my-nightmare noise.

"I'll do the pushpads," Wendy said, taking her place in front of the machine.

That was fine with Sta-Hi. He'd never gotten too good at playing the hyperpins. He took the electron-gun in his hand and pushed the start button.

A little silver ball popped into play. A magnetic field buoyed it up. Sta-Hi aimed the gun at the ball and gave it a kick towards the first target.

He'd shot it the wrong way, though, and it disappeared into a trap . . . the mouth in a glowing little Shiva. Wendy gave a snort of annoyance. Wordlessly, Sta-Hi punched the start again.

This time he sent the ball right into the nearest push-pad. Let her handle it. She did . . . banking the chrome sphere off two more pads before sending it edgewise down a whole row of pop-ups.

"Stuzzy," Sta-Hi breathed. They were both leaning over the lit-up tank. First you had to take out fifteen targets and then the Specials would light up. Wendy had just gotten five targets at once. The ball was drifting towards a trap, but Sta-Hi managed to shoot it in time. Then Wendy was batting it around with the push-pads again.

She had a long, chiming run. All the specials were lit now. Asserting himself, Sta-Hi flicked the ball a few times with the electron-gun, trying to knock it down one of the money holes. But they had repellers, and he ended up by pushing the ball out.

"Have you ever played this before?" Wendy wanted to know before he launched their last ball.

"I'm sorry. I guess I'm a little phased."

"Don't apologize. We're doing good. But on this next ball could you sort of . . . just shoot when I say to?"

"I'll shoot when and where you like, baby." He pressed the start and slid his hand down to pat her ass, knowing she couldn't let go of the controls to slap him away. But she didn't even frown . . . just bumped her tummy against the machine and whispered, "Shoot."

Sta-Hi shot and they were off. She pushed the pads, murmuring instructions to him all the while. *Down, farther, watch the crocs, give it to me, hit the pad, way down* . . . They took out all the targets and all the level-one specials. Then they were working on the higher-level specials. The traps were moving around, snapping at the ball, and Wendy was making impossible saves. Sta-Hi's finger was clenched tight on the trigger.

The machine was letting out wild wheeps and rings, and a few people drifted over to watch Sta-Hi and Wendy work out. Faster, tighter angles, shooting constantly . . .

"Oh God," she whispered. "The Gold Special's on. Nudge it left, Sta-Hi."

He twitched some English onto the ball. It caromed off a pad angled just so, and snugged into the gold socket nestled between two big outs. The machine *THHOCCKKKKED*. And shut itself off.

Sta-Hi pushed his trigger. Nothing happened. "What . . . "

"We beat it!" Wendy squeaked. "We took it all the way! Let's go get the pay-off!"

"But I thought there was just . . . " Sta-Hi pulled open the drawer in the machine's front. A ticket for five free meals at McDonald's.

"Sure there's *that*," Wendy said. "But the cashier has to give me five hundred dollars, too. Special Daytona rules."

Sta-Hi followed Wendy to the cashier, and out onto the street. She wore green cut-off overalls, and sandals with thongs criss-crossing up her legs. He had to hurry to keep up with her. It was like she was trying to lose him.

"Where are you going, Wendy? Slow down! Half that money's mine!" He caught her lightly by her bare brown arm.

"Let go!" She twitched her arm free. "That money isn't yours *or* mine. It's all for Personetics. Good-bye!" Without even looking at him, she strode on down the sidewalk.

"You whore!" Sta-Hi shouted angrily. "That's *it*, isn't it! You've got your night's money now and you'll give it to your greaser sex-pistol and catch some sleep!" He ran after her, and grabbed her arm, hard this time. "Give me my two-hundred-fifty bucks!"

Wendy burst into tears. Fake? "I'm not a p-prostitute. It's just f-flirty-fishing. Personetics needs the money for more hardware. To save everyone's soul."

Hardware? Souls? A contact at last.

"You can keep the money," Sta-Hi said, not loosening his grip. "But I want to come back with you. I want to join Personetics."

She looked into his eyes, trying to read his intentions. "Do you really? Do you want to be saved? Personetics isn't just another cult, you know. It's for real."

Sta-Hi examined her closely, trying to decide if . . . Finally he popped the question.

"Are you a robot?"

"No." Wendy shook her head. "I'm not really saved yet. But Mel is. Mel Nast. He's our leader. Do you want to meet him?"

"I sure do. I'm a bopper-lover from way back. How far is it to the temple?"

"Forty kays. We're in the old Marineland building."

"Are we supposed to walk or what?"

"Usually I wait till five AM. That's when Mr. Nast comes and picks us all up. The boys sell things, and the girls go flirty-fishing all night long. But if you get your five hundred dollars early you can go back to Mel. Do you have a car or a bike?"

Sta-Hi's hydrogen motorcycle was long gone. He hadn't seen it since that Friday he'd left it chained up in front of the Lido Hotel. After that he'd met the girl with the dog, and the Little Kidders . . . and then it had been Cocoa and the Moon and all that. How long had it been, two months? It felt like finally things were going to happen again.

"I'll get a car," Sta-Hi said. "I'll steal a car."

"That would be nice," Wendy said. "Mel would like you if you brought him a car."

But how? In Daytona, nobody was fool enough to leave his key in the ignition. Suddenly Sta-Hi thought of a way. He'd get his taxi back.

"Go wait for me by McDonald's, Wendy. I'll be back with a car in half an hour."

The Yellow Cab terminal was only five blocks off. Malley, the dispatcher, was sitting in a glass booth at the garage entrance, same as ever. Looking past him, Sta-Hi saw that Number Eleven, his old cab, was idle tonight.

"Hey, Malley, you lame son of death, stop jerking off and gimme my keys." Best defense is a good offense.

Malley glared, nothing moving but his tiny eyes. "Bullshit, Mooney. You can't just quit and walk back on the job any time you like. You're too stoned to drive anyway. Giddaddahere."

"Come on, Pappy dear-smear, I need the dust, you must? I'm eating sand out there. Put me on and I'll kick you ten percent."

"Twenty," Malley said, holding up the keys. "And if you fuck up again you're out for good. I don't live to keep you in dope."

Sta-Hi took the keys. "You can *die* to keep me in dope for all I care. Live or die, just keep me high."

After ten days off, it felt nice to be back in Lucky Eleven. They must not have found a new driver for it, since the cab still had all of Sta-Hi's personal touches. There was the fake come-spot on the roof over his head, the skull with the red-lite eyes in the back window, the plastic fur rug on the floor . . . and even the tape-deck was still there. How could he have walked off the job and forgotten his tape-deck!

He had the cab wired for sound, so he could record his monologues, or interview the passengers. The cab started up right away, and then he was out on the street, thinking about his tape-recorder. It made a big impression on chicks, made them think he was an agent. Funny word: *agent*.

A gent. Age entity. Ageing tea. Aegean Sea. A.G.C. Now what did that A.G.C. stand for?

If he hadn't seen Wendy standing in front of McDonald's just then, Sta-Hi probably would have forgotten all about her. Being back in the cab had zapped him into a conditioned reflex of head-tripping and driving the strip. But there was Wendy, bright and blonde in her tight cut-offs. Foxy fish.

He pulled over and she got in back.

"Number Eleven," Malley was saying, "there's a call at Km. 13."

"I just got a fare, Malley. Two gentlemen want to go to Cocoa."

"That'll be an out of zone charge," Malley responded. "Check in when you get back. That was twenty percent."

"Over dover." He turned the squawker off.

"How did you get the cab?" Wendy asked, wide-eyed. "Did you hurt the driver?"

"Not at all," Sta-Hi said, pointing to the dark stain over his head. "See the come-spot?"

"I don't understand."

"I'm a cab-driver. This is my cab. If I like it at Marineland I'll give Personetics the cab and stay there. Otherwise I'll go back to work, and I'll just have to pay that fare to Cocoa myself. Come up in front and sit next to me."

She climbed over the seat. They split a jay, driving slow with the windows down. It was nice to be driving again. It felt like the car was on rails, a toy train tootling through the palmy night.

CHAPTER TWENTY-SIX

The old Marineland had closed down back in 2007, after a hurricane had caved in half the building. Now everyone who wanted to see the ritual degradation of dolphins had to go to Sea World instead. The building, in the middle of nowhere on Coastal Route 1A, came up on Sta-Hi unexpectedly.

"Pull around to the ocean side," Wendy said. "So no one sees."

"Yes ma'am. That'll be two fucks and a blow-job."

"Please, Sta-Hi, be serious. Not just anyone can become a member of Personetics. You have to have the right attitude."

"I'll try to keep it limp, baby."

There was a little parking lot in back. Sta-Hi pulled in next to a nice-looking red sedan. Off at the edge of the lot was a beat-up black truck. The wind was high, and the surf was loud. They got out and walked along a concrete wall to where a rusty door hung open. There were no lights inside.

"Mel," Wendy called at the top of her lungs. "I'm back already. I brought someone with another car for you."

There was the sound of footsteps, and a lithe figure hurried out of the building. He was the same height as Sta-Hi, and with the same rangy build. But his head . . . his big, round head seemed a size too big for the body. He made you think of a balloon tied to the end of a rope.

"Mel Nast," he said, sticking out his hand. He had a deep, sincere-sounding voice, with a trace of an East European accent. "I'm bleased to meet you. Vhat's your name?"

"I'm nobody," Sta-Hi said. "I'm Mr. Nobody from Nowhere."

"Don't listen to him, Mel. He told me his name is Sta-Hi. He says he's a bopper-lover from way back."

Spoken in Wendy's earnest treble the self description sounded pathetic, imbecilic. But Mel Nast looked sympathetic.

"The point is not just to love, Sta-Hi. It is to live. If only you can vake up in time. Blease come in."

Mel Nast's round head turned like a rotating planet, and his slender body followed along. The three of them walked down a damp corridor, through two doors and into a bright, windowless space.

It was a square hall, with big rectangular holes in the walls. One of the old tank-rooms. The aquarium glass had been smashed out and removed, and each of the tanks was now a sort of nook or roomlet. They followed Nast across the square floor and stopped before one of the ex-tanks. "STURGEON," a cracked label on the wall read, "*Acipenser Sturio.*"

There were two easy chairs in there, a shelf of books, and a desk covered with papers. "My study," the slim man with the big head explained. "Could you blease leave us now, Vhendy? I have plans to make with . . . Mister Hi." He flashed Sta-Hi a sudden smile. Had he *winked?*

"That's fine with me," Wendy said. "I'm all tired out. And here's tonight's take." She handed over the five-hundred-dollar bill and walked across the room. Apparently she had a bed in one of the tanks. Sta-Hi followed Nast into his study-tank. They sat down, and looked at each other in silence for a minute.

"How do you like my face?" Nast asked finally. The round face was dominated by a fleshy nose, from which two wrinkles ran down, suspending the somewhat sensual mouth in a rounded sling of folds. The lips parted, revealing square, uniform teeth. "Should I change it?"

"It depends on what you want to do," Sta-Hi said uncertainly.

"What do *you* want to do?" came the answer. "What do you want from the boppers?"

Another hard question. Most superficially, Sta-Hi wanted to acquire another Happy Cloak and use it to get famous. But on another level, hardly conscious, he wanted revenge, revenge for his father's death, revenge for what the nursie had done to Cobb Anderson.

He hated the boppers. But he loved them. The diggers . . . the diggers had helped him. Wearing the Happy Cloak and raiding the factory had been fantastic. Perhaps what he really wanted was to go back to Disky and help in the civil war, loving and hating at the same time.

Something strange happened to Mel Nast's face while Sta-Hi considered his answer. The fatty puffed-out skin tightened, the cheeks drew in, and a white beard blossomed around the mouth. Suddenly he was looking at . . .

"Cobb?" Sta-Hi asked. "Is it you?" He started to smile and then stopped. "You killed my father! You . . . "

"I *had* to, Sta-Hi. You heard him. He said he was going to have me dismantled!"

"So? It wouldn't have killed you. You blew up your body along with his, and now you're still here and he's gone forever!" The grief came welling up at last, and Sta-Hi's voice quavered. "He wasn't such a bad guy. And he could paint spaceships better than anyone I ever . . . "

Sta-Hi broke off, sobbing. A minute went by till he found his voice again. "I saw them take you apart, Cobb. They took out your heart and your balls and everything else. It's like . . . "

The face across from him looked sympathetic, interested. The perfect cult minister.

"Fuck!" Sta-Hi spat, suddenly lashing out and hitting the robot's face with the back of his hand. "I might as well be talking to a tape-recorder."

The blow hurt his hand, and made him angrier. He got to his feet, standing over the Cobb-faced robot.

"I ought to fucking take you apart!"

The robot began to talk then, slowly, and in Cobb's old voice. "Listen to me, Sta-Hi. Sit down and listen. You know perfectly well that you can't hurt me by hammering on this robot-remote. I'm sorry your father died. But death isn't real. You have to understand that. Death is meaningless. I wasted the last ten years being scared of death, and now . . . "

"Now that you think you're immortal you don't worry about death," Sta-Hi said bitterly. "That's really enlightened of you. But whether you know it or not, Cobb Anderson is *dead*. I saw him die, and if you think you're him, you're just fooling yourself." He sat down, suddenly very tired.

"If I'm not Cobb Anderson, then who would I be?" The flickercladding face smiled at him gently. "I *know* I'm Cobb. I have the same memories, the same habits, the same feelings that I always did."

"But what about your . . . your *soul*?" Sta-Hi said, not liking to use the word. "Each person has a soul, a consciousness, whatever you call it. There's some special thing that makes a person be alive, and there's no way that can go into a computer program. No way."

"*It* doesn't have to go into the program, Sta-Hi. *It* is everywhere. *It* is just existence itself. All consciousness is One. The One is God. God is pure existence unmodified."

Cobb's voice was intense, evangelical. "A person is just hardware plus software plus existence. Me existing in flesh is the same as me existing on chips. But that's not all. *Potential* existence is as good as *actual* existence. That's why death is impossible. Your software exists permanently and indestructibly as a certain *possibility*, a certain mathematical set of relations. Your father is now an abstract, non-physical possibility. But nevertheless he exists! He . . . "

"What is this," Sta-Hi interrupted, "a cram-course in Personetics? Is this the crap that you feed those girls to keep them whoring for you? Forget it!"

Sta-Hi stopped talking, suddenly realizing something. That black truck outside . . . that must be the Mr. Frostee truck with a paint-job. And inside the truck would be a super-cooled big bopper brain with Cobb coded up inside it. He couldn't hurt this robot-remote, but if he got out to the truck . . . It was just a question of whether he really wanted to. Did he hate the boppers or not?

"I sense your hostility," Cobb said. "I respect that. But I'd like you to come in with me anyhow. I need an outside man, a Personetics promoter. I could be Jesus and you be John the Baptist. Or *you* be Jesus and I'll be God."

While he was talking, the robot's face changed again, to a copy of Sta-Hi's. "I always use this trick on the recruits," he chuckled. "Like Charlie Manson. *I am a mirror.* But that was before your time. Here, have a joint."

The robot lit a reefer and handed it over. The Cobb face came back. "I'm a little psychic now, too," he said. "I've gotten pretty loose. And what I said is really true. Nothing is ever really destroyed. There is no . . . "

"Oh, tape it," Sta-Hi said taking the reefer and leaning back in his easy chair. "I might come in with you. Especially if you can get me another Happy Cloak."

"What's that?" Cobb asked.

"Well, I never told you yet . . . about what I did on the Moon."

"You ran away in the museum. The next time I saw you, it was that night when you and your father . . . "

"Yeah, yeah," Sta-Hi said, cutting him off. "Don't remind me about that. Let me tell my story. I found this sort of cape called a Happy Cloak. It was made of flickercladding and when I put it on I could talk bopper, except with a pidgen accent. I went to where a bunch of boppers were storming a big factory called GAX. We got in, but GAX almost won anyway. Then at the last minute I blew him up."

The robot started in shock. "You blew up a big bopper?"

"Yeah. Some diggers and a repair spider had set the charge. All I had to do was push the button. The remotes would have gotten me then, but at the last minute a digger tunneled up through the floor and saved me. He took me to watch the nursie take you apart. Ralph and the nursie taped you, and then the nursie grabbed Ralph Numbers and taped him, too. The diggers said . . . "

Cobb's face was working, as if he were arguing with a voice in his head. Now he interrupted. "Mr. Frostee wants to kill you, Sta-Hi. He says that if it weren't for you blowing up GAX, the big boppers would have won."

Cobb was twitching all over, as if he could hardly control himself. His voice grew thin and odd. "I'm not a puppet. Sta-Hi is my friend. I have free will."

The words seemed to cost him a great effort. His eyes kept straying to a hunting-knife lying on his desk.

"No!" Cobb said, shaking his head jerkily. It wasn't clear who he was talking to. "I'm not your hand. I'm your conscience! I'm a . . . "

Suddenly his voice stopped. The features of his face clenched in a final spasm and then slid back into the serene curves of Mel Nast. The thick lips parted to complete Cobb's sentence.

" . . . hallucination. But this robot-remote is, in the last analysis, mine. I have temporarily had to evict Dr. Anderson." The hand snaked over to pick up the knife.

Sta-Hi jumped to his feet and vaulted out of the tank in one motion. He hit the floor running, with the robot close behind.

The door out to the hall was open, and Sta-Hi managed to slam it behind him, gaining a few seconds. He got the second door closed too, closed tight, and he had his cab started by the time the robot came charging out.

Sta-Hi ignored it, and aimed his cab at the black panel truck parked across the lot. He revved the engine up to a chattering scream and peeled out.

The robot jumped onto his hood and punched his fist through the windshield. Sta-Hi squinted against the flying glass and kept the car aimed at the truck. He had it up to fifty kph by the time it hit.

The air-bag in the steering column burst out, punching Sta-Hi in the face and chest, keeping him in his seat. An instant later the bag was limp and the car was stopped. Sta-Hi's lip had split. There was blood in his mouth. The car lights were out, and it was hard to see what had happened.

Footsteps came running across the parking lot.

"What happened? Sta-Hi? Mel?" It was Wendy. Sta-Hi got out of his cab. The girl ran past him, to reach out to the figure crushed between the cab and the dented side of the black van.

"Back up, Sta-Hi! Quick!"

But now the black van was moving instead. Its engine, already on, roared louder, and it backed out, grinding the pinned robot-remote against the cab's hood. It looked like steam was leaking from a hole in the truck's side.

The driverless van flicked its lights on, and Sta-Hi could make out the face of the broken robot slumped across his cab's hood. The blank eyes may have seen him or not, but then the lips moved. It was saying . . .

"Look out!" Sta-Hi screamed, snatching Wendy back and flinging their bodies to shelter on the ground behind the cab.

The robot-remote exploded, just like the other one had, back in the cottage on Cocoa Beach.

As the ringing of the explosion died out in their ears, they could hear the black van's engine, roaring south on Route One.

CHAPTER TWENTY-SEVEN

As soon as Mr. Frostee seized control of the remote, Cobb was utterly shut off from the outside world. As during his first transition, he felt a growing disorientation, an increasing blurring of all distinctions. But this time it stopped before getting completely out of control. Vision returned, and with it the ghosts of hands and feet. He was driving the truck.

"I'm sorry to have done that, Cobb. I was angry. It seemed essential to me to disassemble that young man as soon as possible."

"What's happened?" Cobb cried voicelessly. There was something funny about his vision. It was as if he were perched on top of the truck, instead of being behind the wheel. But yet he could *feel* the wheel, twitching back and forth as he steered the truck south. "What's happened?" he asked again.

"I just blew up my last remote. We're going to have to find someone to front for us. One of the Personetics people in Daytona."

"*Your* remote? That was supposed to be my body! I thought you said I had free will!"

"You still do. I can't make you change your mind about anything. But that body was mine as much as yours."

"Then how can I see? How can I drive?"

"The truck itself is a sort of body. There's two camera eyes that I can stick out of the roof. You're seeing through them. And I've turned the servos for manipulating the truck's controls over to you as well. We may have our occasional differences. Cobb, but I still trust you. Anyway, you're a better driver than I."

"I can't believe this," Cobb wailed. "Don't you have any survival instinct at all? I could have talked Sta-Hi into working with us!"

"He was the one who blew up GAX," Mr. Frostee replied. "And now the war is lost. BEX told me about it on the broadcast last week. Disky has reverted to complete anarchy. They've smashed most of MEX, and there's talk of disassembling TEX and even BEX as well. The final union is still . . . inevitable. But for now it looks as if . . . "

"As if what?" Cobb asked. There was a resigned and fatalistic edge to Mr. Frostee's words which terrified him.

"It's like waves, Cobb. Waves on the beach. Sometimes a wave comes up very far, past the tide line. A wave like that can carve out a new channel. The big boppers were a new channel. A higher form of life. But now we're sliding back . . . back into the sea, the sea of possibility. It doesn't matter. It's right, what you told the kids. Possible existence is as good as real existence."

They were driving into Daytona now. Lights flashed by. One of Cobb's "eyes" watched the road, and the other scanned the sidewalk, looking for one of the Personetics followers. The girls whored and the boys dealt dope. But it was so hard to remember their faces!

"You know," Mr. Frostee said. "You know he split the panels?"

"What do you mean?" There was nothing but darkness, and the two spots of vision, and the controls of the truck.

"There's heat leaking in from where your friend rammed us. The temperature's up five degrees. One more, and our circuits melt down. Thirty seconds, maybe."

"Am I on tape somewhere else?" Cobb asked. "Is there a copy on the Moon?"

"I don't know," Mr. Frostee said. "What's the difference?"

CHAPTER TWENTY-EIGHT

Wendy got the keys for the red sedan, and Sta-Hi drove them back to Daytona. They didn't talk much, but it was not a strained silence.

The police were all around the truck when they found it. Driverless, it had veered off the road, snapped a fire-hydrant, and smashed in the front of a Red Ball liquor-store. The police were worried about looting, and at first they wouldn't let Sta-Hi and Wendy through the line.

"That's my father!" Wendy screamed. "That's my father's truck!"

"She's right!" Sta-Hi added. "Let my poor wife through!"

"He's not in the truck now," a cop said, letting them approach. "Hey chief," he called then. "Here's two individuals who say they knew the driver."

The chief walked over, none other than Action Jackson. He had a mind like an FBI file, and recognized Sta-Hi instantly. "Young Mooney! Maybe you could enlighten me as to what the *hail* is goin on?"

The crash had widened the rip in the truck's side, and clouds of helium were billowing out. The gas itself was invisible, but the low temperature filled the air with a mist of ice-crystals. A by-product of breathing the helium-rich air was that everyone's voice was coming out a bit high-pitched.

"There's a giant robot brain in the back," Sta-Hi piped. "A big bopper. It's the same one that killed my father and tried to eat my brain."

Jackson looked doubtful. "A truck tried to eat your brain?" He raised his voice, "Hey, Don! You and Steve open it up! See what's in back!"

"Be careful!" Wendy squeaked, but by then the door was open. When the mist dispersed you could see Don and Steve reaching in and poking around with billy-clubs. There was a sound of breaking glass.

"Whooo-ee!" Don called. "Got nuff goodies in here to open us a Radio Shack! Steve and me saw it first!" He swirled his club around, and there was more tinkling from inside the truck.

The others walked over to look in. The truck was lying half keeled-over. There was a lot of frost inside, like in a freezer chest. The liquid-helium vessel that had surrounded Mr. Frostee was broken and there in the center was a big, intricate lump of chips and wires.

"Who was drivin?" Action Jackson wanted to know.

"It could drive itself," Sta-Hi said. "I rammed it and made a hole. It must have heated up too much."

"You a hero, boy," Jackson said admiringly. "You may amount to something yet."

"If I'm a hero, can I leave now?"

A hard glance, and then a nod. "All right. You come in tomorrow make a deposition and I might could get you a reward."

Sta-Hi helped himself to a bottle from the liquor-store window and went back to the car with Wendy. He let her drive. She pulled down a ramp onto the beach, and they parked on the hard sand. He got the bottle open: white wine.

"Here," Sta-Hi said, passing her the wine. "And why did you say he was your father?"

"Why did you say I was your wife?"

"Why not?"

The moon scudded in and out of clouds, and the waves came in long smooth tubes.

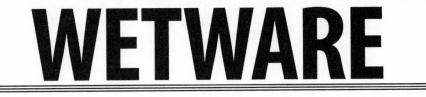

WETWARE

For
Philip K. Dick
1928-1982

"One must imagine Sisyphus happy."

CHAPTER ONE

PEOPLE THAT MELT

December 26, 2030

It was the day after Christmas, and Stahn was plugged in. With no work in sight, it seemed like the best way to pass the time . . . other than drugs, and Stahn was off drugs for good, or so he said. The twist-box took his sensory input, jazzed it, and passed it on to his cortex. A pure software high, with no somatic aftereffects. Staring out the window was almost interesting. The maggies left jagged trails, and the people looked like actors. Probably at least one of them was a meatie. Those boppers just wouldn't let up. Time kept passing, slow and fast.

At some point the vizzy was buzzing. Stahn cut off the twist-box and thumbed on the screen. The caller's head appeared, a skinny yellow head with a down-turned mouth. There was something strangely soft about his features.

"Hello," said the image. "I'm Max Yukawa. Are you Mr. Mooney?"

Without the twist, Stahn's office looked unbearably bleak. He hoped Yukawa had big problems.

"Stahn Mooney of Mooney Search. What can I do for you, Mr. Yukawa?"

"It concerns a missing person. Can you come to my office?"

"Clear."

Yukawa twitched, and the vizzyprint spat out a sheet with printed directions. His address and the code to his door-plate. Stahn thumbed off, and after a while he hit the street.

Bad air out there, always bad air—*yarty* was the word for it this year. 2030. *Yart* = yawn + fart. Like in a library, right? Sebum everywhere. *Sebum* = oily secretion which human skin exudes. Yarts and sebum, and a hard vacuum outside the dooooooooommmmme. Dome air—after the invasion, the humans had put like a big airtight dome over Disky and changed the town's name to Einstein. The old Saigon into Ho Chi Minh City routine. The boppers had been driven under the Moon's surface, but they had bombs hidden all over Einstein, and they set off one a week maybe, which was not all *that* often, but often enough to matter for sure for sure. And of course there were the meaties—people run by remote bopper control. What you did was to hope it didn't get worse.

So OK, Stahn is standing out in the street waiting for a slot on the people-mover. A moving sidewalk with chairs, right. He felt like dying, he really really felt like dying. Bad memories, bad chemistry, no woman, bad life.

"Why do we bother?"

The comment was right on the beam. It took a second to realize that someone was talking to him. A rangy, strungout dog of a guy, shirtless in jeans with blond hair worn ridgeback style. His hair was greased up into a longitudinal peak, and there were extra hairgrafts that ran the hairstrip right on down his spine to his ass. Seeing him made Stahn feel old. *I used to be different, but now I'm the same.* The ridgeback had a handful of pamphlets, and he was staring at Stahn like one of them was something in a zoo.

"No thanks," Stahn said, looking away. "I just want to catch a slot."

"Inside your lamejoke private eye fantasy? Be here now, bro. Merge into the One." The kid was handsome in an unformed way, but his skin seemed unnaturally slack. Stahn had the impression he was stoned.

Stahn frowned and shook his head again. The ridgeback gave him a flimsy plas pamphlet, tapped his own head, and then tapped Stahn's head as if to mime the flow of knowledge. Poor dumb freak. Just then an empty slot came by. Safely off the sidewalk, Stahn looked the leaflet over. OR-MY IS THE WAY, it read. ALL IS ONE!

The text said that sharing love with one's fellows could lead to a fuller union with the cosmos at large. At the deepest level, the pamphlet informed Stahn, all people are aspects of the same archetype. Those who wished to learn more about Organic Mysticism were urged to visit the Church offices on the sixth floor of the ISDN ziggurat. All this wisdom came courtesy of Bei Ng, whose picture and biography appeared on the pamphlet's back cover. A skinny yellow guy with wrinkles and a pointed head. He looked like a big reefer. Even after eighteen clean months, lots of things still made Stahn think of drugs.

The Einstein cityscape drifted past. Big, the place was big—like Manhattan, say, or half of D.C. Not to mention all the chambers and tunnels underground. Anthill. Smart robots had built the city, and then the humans had kicked them out. The boppers. They were easy to kill, once you knew how. Carbon-dioxide laser, EM energy, scramble their circuits. They'd gone way underground. Stahn had mixed feelings about boppers. He liked them because they were even less like regular people than he was.

At one point he'd even hung out with them a little. But then they'd killed his father . . . back in 2020. Poor old dad. All the trouble Stahn had given him, and now it felt like he was turning into him, year by year. Mooney Search. *Wave on it, sister, wiggle. Can I get some head?*

Yukawa's address was a metal door, set flush into the pumice-stone sidewalk. *Deep Encounters* said the sign over the door-plate. Psychological counselling? The folks in this neighborhood didn't look too worried about personality integration. Bunch of thieves and junkies is what they looked like. Old Mother Earth had really shipped the dregs to Einstein. Like the South, right, *Settled by slaves and convicts—since 1690.* 2022 was when the humans had retaken the Moon. Stahn looked at the sheet that Yukawa had sent. 90-3-888-4772. *Punch in the code, Stahn.* Numbers. Prickly little numbers. Number, Space, Logic, Infinity . . . for the boppers it was all Information. Good or bad?

OK, so the door opens, and Stahn ladders on down and takes a look. A vestibule, empty and gray. To the right was a door with a light over it. In front of Stahn was another door, and a window like at a walk-in bank. Yukawa's face was behind the thick glass. Stahn showed him the vizzyprint sheet, and he opened up the second door.

Stahn found himself (*found himself?*) in a long laboratory, with a desk and chairs at one end. The air was thick with strange smells: benzenes, esters, the rich weavings of long-chain molecules, and under it all the stench of a badly-kept menagerie. His host was seated on a sort of high stool by that thick glass window. It took Stahn a second to absorb the fact that about half the guy's body was . . . where?

Yukawa's soft thin head and arms rose up out of a plastic tub mounted on four long legs. The rest of him was a yellow-pink puddle in the tub. Stahn gagged and took a step back.

"Don't be alarmed, Mr. Mooney. I was a little upset, so I took some merge. It's just now wearing off."

Merge . . . he'd heard of it. Very synthetic, very illegal. *I don't do drugs, man, I'm high on life.* People took merge to sort of melt their bodies for a while. Stuzzadelic and very tempting. If Stahn hadn't been so desperate for work he might have left right then. Instead he came on nonchalant.

"What kind of lab is this, Mr. Yukawa?"

"I'm a molecular biologist." Yukawa put his hands on the tub's sides and pushed up. Slowly his belly solidified, his hips and his legs. He stepped over to the desk and began pulling his clothes back on. Over the vizzy, Stahn had taken him for Japanese, but he was too tall and pale for that. "Of course the Gimmie would view this as an illegal drug laboratory. Which is why I don't dare call them in. The problem is that something has happened to my assistant, a young lady named Della Taze. You advertise yourself as a Searcher, so . . . "

"I'll take the case, don't worry. I already checked you on my data-base, by the way. A blank. That's kind of unusual, Mr. Yukawa." He was fully dressed now, gray pants and a white coat, quite the scientist. Stahn could hardly believe he'd just seen him puddled in that tub. *How good did it feel?*

"I used to be a man named Gibson. I invented gene-invasion."

"You were that mad scientist who . . . uh . . . turned himself Japanese?"

"Not so mad." A smile flickered across Yukawa's sagging face. "I had cancer. I found a way to replace some of my genes with those of a ninety-eight-year-old Japanese man. The cancer went into remission, and as my cells replaced themselves, I took on more and more of the Japanese man's somatotype. A body geared for long life. There was talk of a Nobel Prize, but . . . "

"The California dog-people. The Anti-Chimera Act of 2027. I remember. You were exiled here. Well, so was I. And now I'm a straight rent-a-pig and you're a dope wizard. Your girl's gone, and you're scared to call the Gimmie." Most Einstein law enforcement was done on a freelance basis. No loonie ever called in the official law—the Gimmie—on purpose. At this point the Gimmie was a highly organized gang of extortionists and meatie-hunters. They were a moderately necessary evil.

"Clear. Let me show you around." Long and undulant, Yukawa drifted back into the lab. The low lunar gravity seemed to agree with him.

The closer tables were filled with breadboarded electronic circuits and mazes of liquid-filled tubes. Computerized relays shunted the colored fluids this way and that. A distillation process seemed to be underway. The overall effect was of a miniature oil refinery. In contrast, the tables towards the rear of the lab were filled with befouled animal cages. It had been a while since Stahn had seen animals. Live meat.

"Watch," said Yukawa, shoving two cages together. One cage held a large brown toad, the other a lively white rat. Yukawa drew a silver flask out of his coat pocket and dribbled a few drops onto each of the subject animals. "This is merge," he explained, opening the doors that separated the cages.

The toad, a carnivore, flung itself at the rat. For a moment the two beasts struggled. But then the merge had taken effect, and the animals' tissues flowed together: brown and white, warts and hair. A flesh-puddle formed, loosely covering the creatures' loosened skeletons. Four eyes looked up: two green, two pink. Faint shudders seemed to animate the fused flesh. Pleasure? It was said that merge users took a sexual delight in puddling.

"How do they separate?"

"It's automatic. When the merge wears off, the cell walls stiffen and the body collagens tighten back up. What the drug does is to temporarily uncoil all the proteins' tertiary bunchings. One dose lasts ten minutes to an hour—and then back to normal. Now look at *these* two cages."

The next two cages held something like a rat and something like a toad. But the rat's hair was falling out, and its feet were splayed and leathery. The toad, for its part, was growing a long pink tail, and its wide mouth showed signs of teeth.

"Chimeras," said Yukawa with some satisfaction. "Chimeras like me. The trick is to keep them merged for several days. Gene exchange takes place. The immune systems get tired."

"I bet. So the Japanese man you merged with turned into you?"

Yukawa made a wry face. "That's right. We beat cancer together, and he got a little younger. Calls himself Bei Ng these days. He runs his own fake religion here in Einstein, though it's really an ISDN front. Bei's always trying to outdo me and rip me off. But never mind about him. I want you to look at this one back here. It's my pet project: a universal life form."

At the very rear of the lab was a large pen. Huddled in the pen was a sodden, shambling thing—an amalgam of feathers and claws. *Chitin*, man, and hide, and the head had (A) long feelers, (B) a snout, (C) a squid-bunch of slack mandibles, *dot dot dot*, and (Z) gills. Gills on the moon.

"You're nuts, Yukawa. You're out of your kilpy gourd."

At the sound of Stahn's voice, the monstrosity hauled itself over to rattle the pen's bars with tiny pink hands.

"Yes, Arthur," said Yukawa. "Good." He fished a food pellet out of his lab jacket and fed it to his creation. Just then a bell chimed.

"Back to business," said Yukawa, giving Stahn a U-shaped smile. "I don't know why I'm showing you all this anyway. Loneliness, I suppose. Della's been my only companion for the last two years."

Stahn tagged along as Yukawa made his way back to the thick window looking onto the vestibule. A light was flashing over the other door out there.

"Time's up," said Yukawa, speaking into a microphone. "The session's over, Mrs. Beller." Stahn got the full picture.

"You retail the merge right here? You're running a love-puddle?"

"That is the vulgar terminology, yes. I have to fund my ongoing research in whatever fashion I can. I sell merge both wholesale and retail. There's nothing really wrong with merge, you know. It's terribly addictive, but if someone wants to quit, why, I'm perfectly willing to sell them the proper blocker."

Outside the window, the lit door opened. Two people stepped out—a wide-mouthed brunette and her funboy. He wore a black-and-white bowling shirt with *Ricardo* stitched over the breast pocket. She was hot stuff. Their faces looked soft and tired, and they were holding hands.

Yukawa powered a drawer out through the wall. "Same time tomorrow, Mrs. Beller?"

"Feels so rave, Max." The woman dropped some money into the drawer. She was hot stuff. *What type of sex do you like, Mrs. Beller, WHAT TYPE???* She was *used-looking*, and she had a slow lazy voice and the big soft lips to match. She raked a stare across Stahn's face and led Ricardo up the ladder to the street. As they left, Stahn noticed that their two joined hands were actually fused into a single skin-covered mass. Hot.

Yukawa caught Stahn's expression, caught some of it. "They'll pull apart later, when the stuff fully wears off. In some circles it's quite fashionable to walk around part merged."

"How come they don't look like each other—if they're merging every day?"

"Dosage control. Unless you set up an all-day drip, merging has no lasting effects. And the drip has to be just right, or you end up as an entropic solution of amino acids. No one can do the gene exchange right but me."

"Other people have done it. Vic Morrow did it, dad." Vic Morrow had been a truck-farmer in the San Joaquin Valley. In 2027, he'd hit on the idea of treating his migrant workers to a series of weekend-long mergedrip parties. Once the workers had all flowed together, Morrow would throw a couple of dogs into the love-puddle with them. He was nuts. Over the weeks, the workers had transmuted into beasts, ever more tractable, ever less demanding. The big scandal came when Morrow had a heart attack and his workers ate most of his corpse and rolled in the rest of it. A month later, the Anti-Chimera Act had passed Congress by acclaim.

Yukawa frowned and fumbled in his desk. "I told Morrow how to do it. It was a big mistake. I owed him money. I don't trust anyone with my secrets anymore. Especially . . . " He stopped himself and pushed a folder across the desk. "Here's the full printout on Della—I already accessed it for you. Last Friday—that was the 20th—I was with Della all day as usual, and at four she left in her maggie. Monday and Tuesday she didn't come in. I called her apartment, nobody home. Yesterday was Christmas and I didn't bother calling. I figured maybe she'd taken an extra-long holiday weekend, gone on a party or a trek in the crater. She doesn't tell me her plans. But now she's still not here and her vizzy still doesn't answer. I'm worried. Either something's happened to her, or . . . or she's run away."

Stahn picked up the folder and leafed through it. *Focus.* DELLA TAZE.

Born and raised in Louisville, Kentucky. Twenty-eight years old. Ph.D. in molecular genetics, U. Va., 2025. Same year he'd fled to Einstein. Her photo: a nice little blonde with a straight mouth and a button nose. Fox. Unmarried.

"She was your girlfriend?" Stahn glanced up at Yukawa. His long, thin head looked cruel and freakish. The "universal life form" at the back of the lab was crying out for more food, making a sound midway between a squeal and a hiss. *Arthur.* It was hard to see why Della Taze hadn't split like . . . two years ago.

" . . . wouldn't let me come to her apartment," Yukawa was saying. "And she wouldn't ever merge with me either. We argued about it Friday. I *know* she was using, towards the end she asked me for it all the time. Maybe that was the only reason she stayed with me as long as she did. But now . . . now she's gone, and I have to get her back. Track her down, Mooney. Bring my Della back!"

"I'll do my best, Mr. Yukawa. Man." As Stahn got to his feet, Yukawa leaned across the desk and handed him a wad of bills, and the silver flask of dope.

"Here's money for you, Mooney, and merge. *Sta-Hi.* Didn't they used to call you Sta-Hi?"

"That was a long time ago. Now I'm all grown up."

"I gave Della blocker, just in case, but if you find her sick, just show her the flask."

Before getting a slot over to Della's place, Stahn went back to his office to do some computer searching. Maybe Della had taken Yukawa's blocker and checked into an endorphin clinic. The blocker would gene-tailor out the specific enzymes that made merge necessary for her body, but sometimes it took a clinic to keep you from going back to what your mind still wanted. Or maybe Della was dead and in the organ banks, the cannibal mart, or worse. Everyone on the Moon—loonies and boppers alike—had lots of uses for fresh meat. Or, on the other hand, maybe Della had caught a ship to Earth.

Yukawa hadn't called anyone at all; he was too paranoid. Stahn worked his vizzy through all the info banks—and drew a blank. Could she have been picked up by the Gimmie? Better not to ask. Or maybe the boppers had zombie-boxed her off to the ratsurgeon? He leaned back in his chair, trying not to think about the flask of merge. *Focus.*

If Della was still strung on merge, she'd be puddling at least once a day. That meant she might be holed up with some other local users. So it would make sense to check out the local merge scene, which centered, Stahn recalled, in the catacombs around the old dustbaths. How good *was* merge, anyway? Stahn opened Yukawa's silver flask and . . . uh . . . took a sniff. Nice: red wine and roast turkey, nice-smelling stuff. He couldn't stop wondering what it would feel like to use a little. Yukawa shouldn't have given it to him. But, Stahn realized, Yukawa had known what he was doing. Don't start, Stahn, he told himself. Don't start all that again. Why not? he answered himself. Who are you to tell me what to do? I'll do what I like! Remember, Stahn, responded the first voice, you didn't quit drugs for *other* people. You didn't quit for society, or for Wendy's ghost. You quit for *yourself*. If you go back on the stuff you're going to die.

Just then someone started pounding on the door. Stahn twitched and a fat drop of merge splashed out onto his left hand. His stomach clenched in horror, but a part of him—the bad part—was very glad. He put his hands and the flask under his desk and told the door to open.

It was the blond ridgeback who'd given him the Or-My pamphlet before. Stahn got the cap back on Yukawa's flask and tried to flex his left hand. It felt like it was melting. This stuff was for real.

"Stahn Mooney," said the ridgeback, closing the door behind him. "*Sta-Hi*." His face had junk-hunger. "My name's Whitey Mydol. I heard you were over at Yukawa's. I was wondering if . . . " He paused to sniff the air. The room reeked of merge. "Can I have some?"

"Some what?"

The melting feeling had moved up into Stahn's forearm. His shabby office walls looked prettier than the twist-box had ever made them. All right. Eighteen months since he'd felt this good. He forced his attention back to Mydol's hard young face. "How do you know who Yukawa is?"

"Oh . . . we know." The kid smiled in a conspiratorial way. "I'll give you two hundred dollars for a hit. Just between the two of us."

Stahn took his flare-ray in his right hand and leveled it at Mydol. He wanted Mydol out of here before he melted all over. "I'm going to count to three. One." Mydol stopped moving and glared. "Two." Mydol snarled a curse and stepped back towards the door. He was jangling up Stahn's first rush in almost two years, and Stahn wanted to kill him.

"AO, Junk-Hog Sta-Hi Rent-Pig Mooney. What's the shudder, scared to merge with a man? Tubedook."

"Three," Stahn clicked off the safety and burned a shot across Mydol's left shoulder. The ridgeback winced in pain, opened the door and left.

Stahn slumped back. God, this was fast dope. His left arm looked like candle wax, and he was having trouble staying in his chair. He let himself slide down onto the floor and stared up at the ceiling. Oh, this did feel so good. His bone joints loosened, and his skeleton sagged beneath the puddle of his flesh. It took almost an hour to ride the trip out. Towards the middle Stahn saw God. God was about the same as usual—a little more burnt, maybe. He wanted love as bad as Stahn did. This life was taking its toll on everyone.

What is merge like? Baby, if you don't know by now . . . Wonderful. Horrible. After Stahn hit the floor and puddled, he wasn't really there. The space of the room became *part of his consciousness*. He *was* the room, the chipped beige plas, the dingy black floor, the old-fashioned windows, the desk and chair and computer; he was the room and the building and Einstein and the Earth. Standard ecstatic mystical vision, really. But *fast*. He was everywhere, he was nowhere, he was the same as God. And then there were no thoughts at all. *Stuzzy*, sis, *all* right.

It wore off ***WHAM*** as quickly as it had come on. There was a tingling in Stahn's flesh, a kind of jelling feeling, and then he was lying there shaking, heart going a mile a minute. Too fast. This dope was giga too fast. Death practice, right: hit, melt, space, blank. Final blank. He wished his dead wife Wendy were still alive. Sweet, blonde, wide-hipped Wendy. Times like this—in the old days—she'd hug him and pat his head real soft . . . and smile . . . And you killed her, Stahn. Oh God, oh no, oh put that away. You blew a hole in her head and sold her corpse to the organleggers and used the money to come to the Moon.

Stahn alone on the office floor, shuddering. Bum kicks. Think about anything but Wendy. Flash of an old song: *Coming down again, all my time's been spent, coming down again*. Old. Gettin old. Coming down gets too old. Does that even mean anything? Language with a flat tire. Talk broken, but keep talking. Regroup.

His clothes were awkwardly bunched around him. When he sat up, the headache started. Bummer bummer bummer bummer bummer. He took Yukawa's silver flask and shook it. There was quite a bit in there, a few months' worth if you only took it once a day. If he got back on drugs he was dead. He should be dead. He wished he was dead. Lot of slow death in that flask.

If one drop was a dose, and a dose was worth . . . uh . . . two hundred dollars, then this flask was something that certain elements—certain criminal elements—would . . . uh . . . *kkkkkillll* for. And that ridgeback cultie knew he was holding, oh my brethren. *Can I get some head?* "Hello, Mrs. Beller, you don't know me, but I . . . uh . . . " Hot. Hot. Hot. Hot. Hot. Hot. Hot. WHAT TYPE OF SEX, BABY, *WHAT TYPE?*

The thing to do right now was to not go back out the office building's front door. *Focus*. Rent a maggie. Garage on top of the building.

He picked out a black saucer-shaped maggie, fed it some money, and told it where to go. The maggies were like hovercars; they counteracted the

Moon's weak gravity with fans, and with an intense magnetic field keyed
to a big field generated by wires set into the dome. They were expensive. It
was funny that a junkie lab assistant like Della Taze would have had her
own maggie. Stahn could hardly wait to see her apartment. Maybe she was
actually there, just not answering the vizzy, but there and like waiting for
a guy with merge. He had lock-picking wares in case she wouldn't open.

The entry system at Della's building was no problem. Stahn used a
standard nihilist transposition on the door down from the roof, and a
tone-scrambler on her apartment door. The apartment was Wigglesville.
Creative Brain Damage, Vol. XIII. As follows.

The walls weren't painted one uniform color. It was all bursts and streaks,
as if the painter had just thrown random buckets around the apartment
till everything was covered: walls, floors, and ceilings all splattered and
dripped beyond scuzz.

The furniture was pink, and all in shapes of people. The chairs were
big stuffed women with laps to sit in, and the tables were plas men on
all fours. He kept jerking, seeing that furniture out of the corner of his
eye, and thinking someone was there. Twist and shout. The whole place
had the merge wine-turkey fragrance, but there was another smell under
it . . . a bad smell.

Which, as it turned out, came from the bedroom. Della had her love-
puddle in there—a big square tub like a giant wading pool. And next to it
was . . . sort of a corpse. It had been a black guy.

Gross—you want to hear gross? A merged person is like Jell-O over
some bones, right. And you can . . . uh . . . *splatter* Jell-O. Splatter a merged
person into a bunch of pieces, and the drug wears off—the cells firm
up—and there is this . . . uh . . . guy in a whole lot of pieces.

The skin had covered on up around each of the pieces—here was a foot
with a rounded-off stump at the ankle, here was his head all smoothed
off at the neck. He looked like a nice enough guy. Plump, easygoing. Here
was an arm with his torso—and over there a leg hooked onto his bare
ass . . . and all of it sagging and starting to rot . . .

Zzuzzzzzzz.

The vizzy in the living room was buzzing. Stahn ran in, covered up the
lens, and thumbed the set on.

It was a hard-faced Gimmie officer. He wore hair spikes, and he had
gold studs set into his cheeks. Colonel Hasci. Stahn knew the "cat." *Muy
macho. Trés douche.*

"Miss Della Taze? We're down in the lobby. Can we come up and ask
you some questions about Buddy Yeskin?"

Stahn split fast. It was a little hard to judge, but *Buddy* looked to have been dead two days. Why would anyone splatter good old Bud? Death is so stupid; always the same old punch line. It reminded him of Wendy. Whenever he was coming down everything reminded him of Wendy. He'd been stoned on three-way, shooting horseflies with his needler and he'd hit her by accident. Some accident. Sold her body to the organleggers and moved up to the Moon before the mudder Gimmie could deport him. Her poor limp body.

Stahn's black saucer circled aimlessly. He wondered where Della Taze had gotten to. Merge with the cosmos, sister. Can I get some, too? WHAT TYPE, baby, WHAT TYPE OF SEX? Shut up, Stahn. Be quiet, brother. Chill out.

CHAPTER TWO

CHRISTMAS IN LOUISVILLE

December 24, 2030

Merged. Gentle curves and sweet flow of energies—merged in the love-puddle, the soft plastic tub set into the floor of her bedroom. Exquisite ecstasy—Della melted and Buddy just sliding in; the two of them about to be together again, close as close can be, flesh to flesh, gene to gene, a marbled mass of pale and tan skin, with their four eyes up on top seeing nothing; but now, just as Buddy starts melting . . . suddenly . . .

Aeh!

Della Taze snapped out of her flashback and looked at the train car window. It was dusk outside, and the glass gave back a faint reflection of her face: blonde, straight-mouthed, her eyes hot and sunken. Her stomach hurt, and she'd thrown up three times today. Burnt-out and worldly wise . . . the look she'd longed for as a teenage girl. She tried a slight smile. *Not bad, Della. But you're wanted for murder.* And the only place she could think of going was home.

The train was coasting along at a slow 20 mph now, click-clanking into Louisville, gliding closer to the long trip's end: Einstein-Ledge-Florida-Louisville via spaceship-shuttle-train. Two days. Della hoped she was well ahead of the Einstein Gimmie—the police. Not that they'd be likely to chase her this far. Here in 2030, Moon and Earth were as far removed from each other as Australia and England had been in the 1800s.

Louisville in the winter: rain not even snow, lots of it, gray water, the funny big cars, and real sky—the smells, after two years of dome air, and the idle space! On the Moon, every nook and cranny had its purpose—like on a sailboat or in a tent—but here, gliding past the train, were vacant lots with nothing in them but weeds and dead tires; meaningless streets with marginal businesses; tumbledown houses with nobody home. Idle space. There were too many faces up in Einstein, too many bodies, too many needs.

Della was glad to be back here, with a real sky and real air; even though her body was filled with a dull ache. The weight. Old Mr. Gravity. In

Florida she'd spent the last of her money on an Imipolex flexiskeleton with the brand name: Body by Oozer. She wore it like a body stocking, and the coded collagens pushed, stiffened, and pulled as needed. The ultimate support hosiery. Most returning loonies checked in for three days of muscle rehabilitation at the JFK Spaceport, but Della had known she'd have to keep running. Why? Because she'd jelled back from that last merge-trip to find her lover splattered into pieces, and before she'd had time to do anything, there'd been a flat-voiced twitch-faced man on the vizzy.

"I killed him, Della, and I can kill you. Or I can tell the Gimmie that you did it. I want to help you, Della. I love you. I want to help you escape. There's a fake passport and a ticket to Earth for you at the spaceport . . . "

Aeh!

Della's parents, Jason and Amy Taze, were at the station, the same as ever—strungout and hungover, mouths set into smiles, and their self-centered eyes always asking, *Do you love me?*

Amy Taze was small and tidy. She wore bright, outdated makeup, and today she had her blonde hair marcelled into a tight, hard helmet. Jason was a big, shambling guy with short hair and messy prep clothes. He had a desk job at a bank, and Amy was a part-time saleswoman in a gift shop. They both hated their jobs and lived to party. Seeing them there, Della felt like getting back on the train.

"My *God*, Della, you look *fantastic*. Is that a *leotard* you have on under your clothes?" Mom kept the chatter going all the way out to the car, as if to show how sober she was. Dad rolled his eyes and gave Della a wink, as if to show how much more together than Mom *he* was. The two of them were so busy putting on their little show that it was ten minutes before they noticed that Della was trembling. It was Dad who finally said something.

"You do look nice, Della, but you seem a little shaky. Was it a hard trip? And why such short notice?"

"Somebody framed me for a murder, Dad. That's why I didn't want you all to tell anyone else I'm back in town." Her stomach turned again, and she retched into her handkerchief.

"Was it some kind of hard-drug deal? Something to do with that damn *merge* stuff that your Dr. Yukawa makes?" Dad fished nervously in his pocket for a reefer. He shot her a sharp glance. "Are you hooked?"

Della nodded, glad to upset them. Taste of their own medicine. No point telling them she'd taken gamendorph blocker to kick. Dr. Yukawa had always made sure that she had blocker around.

"That's what we get for not being better people, Jason," said Mom, her voice cracking in self-pity. "The only one of our children coming home for Christmas is a killer dope queen on the lam. And for the two years before this we've been all alone. Give me a hit off that number, I think I'm going to have a nervous breakdown." She took a puff, smiled, and patted Della's cheek. "You can help us trim the tree, Della honey. We still have the styrofoam star you decorated in kindergarten."

Della wanted to say something cutting, but she knew it would feel bad. Instead she put on her good-girl face and said, "I'd like that, Mom. I haven't seen a Christmas tree in three years. I . . . " Her voice caught and the tears came. She loved her parents, but she hated to see them. Holidays were always the worst, with Jason and Amy stumbling around in a chemical haze. "I hope this won't be like all the other Christmases, Mom."

"I don't know what you mean, Della. It will be lovely. Your Uncle Colin and Aunt Ilse are coming over for dinner tomorrow. They'll bring Willy, he's still living at home. Of course your two little sisters are both visiting with their *husbands'* families again."

Jason and Amy Taze lived in an eighty-year-old two-story tract home east of Louisville. The neighborhood had sidewalks and full-grown trees. The houses were small, but well-kept. Della found her tiny room to be more or less as it had always been: the clean, narrow bed; the little china animals on the shelf she'd nailed into the papery drywall; the hologram hoops hung in the two windows; and her disks and info-cubes all arranged in the alphabetical order she liked to keep them in. When she was in ninth grade, she'd programmed a cross-referenced catalog cube to keep track of them all. Della had always been a good student, a good girl, compulsively tidy as if to make up for her parents' frequent sloppy scenes.

Someone let Bowser, the family dog, in the back door then, and he came charging up the narrow carpeted stairs to greet Della, shaking his head, and whining and squirming like a snake. He looked as mangy as ever, and as soon as Della patted him, he lay on his back spreading his legs, the same gross way he'd always done. She rubbed under his chin for a while, while he wriggled and yipped.

"Yes, Bowser. Good dog. Good, smart dog." Now that she'd started crying, she couldn't seem to stop. Mom and Dad were downstairs in the kitchen, talking in hushed tones. Della was too tired to unpack. She hurt all over, especially in her breasts and stomach. When she slipped out of her flexiskeleton, she felt like a fat, watery jellyfish. There was a nightgown on the bed—Mom must have laid it out. Della put it on, glad no one was here to see her, and then she fell into a long, deep sleep.

When Della woke up it was midmorning. Christmas! So what. Without her two sisters Ruby and Sude here, it didn't mean a thing. Closing her eyes, Della could almost hear their excited yelling—and then she realized she was hearing the vizzy. Her parents were downstairs watching the vizzy on Christmas morning. God. She went to the bathroom and vomited, and then she put on her flexiskeleton and got dressed.

"Della!" cried her mother when Della appeared. "Now you see what we do on Christmas with no babies." There was an empty glass by her chair. The vizzy screen showed an unfamiliar family opening presents around their tree. Mom touched the screen and a different family appeared, then another and another.

"We've gotten in the habit," explained Dad with a little shrug. "Every year lots of people leave their sets on, and whoever wants to can share in. So no one's lonely. We're so glad to have a real child here." He took her by the shoulders and planted a kiss on her forehead. "Little Della. Flesh of our flesh."

"Come, dear," said Mom. "Open your presents. We only had time to get two, but they're right here in front of the vizzy in case anyone's sharing in with *us*."

It felt silly but nice sitting down in front of the vizzy—there were some excited children on the screen just then, and it was almost like having noisy little Ruby and Sude at her side. And Bowser was right there, nuzzling her. Della's first present was an imipolex sweatshirt called a heartshirt.

"All the girls at the bank are wearing them this year," explained Dad. "It's a simplified version of bopper flickercladding. Try it on!"

Della slipped the loose warm plastic over her top. The heartshirt was an even dark blue, with a few staticky red spots drifting about.

"It can feel your heartbeat," said Mom. "Look." Sure enough, there was a big red spot on the plastic sweatshirt, right over Della's heart, a spot that spread out into an expanding ring that moved on over Della's shoulders and down her sleeves. Her heart beat again, and a new spot started—each beat of her heart made a red splash in the blue of the heartshirt.

"Neat," said Della. "Thanks. They don't have these up in Einstein. Everyone there hates boppers too much. But it's stuzzy. I like it."

"And when your heart beats faster, Della," said Mom, "all the fellows will be able to see."

Suddenly Della remembered Buddy, and why she'd come home, and the red rings on her sweatshirt started bouncing like mad.

"Why, Della!" said Mom, coyly. "Do you have a boyfriend?"

"I'm not ready to talk about it," said Della, calming herself. *Especially not to a loudmouth racist drunk like you, Mom.*

"Let's have some champagne," suggested Dad.

"Good idea," said Mom. "Take the edge off. And then Della can open her other present."

Della watched the vizzy for a minute, calming down. Good old vizzy.

She touched the screen here and there, and the picture skipped from home to home. Louisville people, not so different from the Tazes. Della even recognized some of them. She had some champagne and felt OK again. Lots of the people in the vizzy were drinking . . . why should she be so hard on her parents?

"Let's see my other present. I'm sorry I didn't bring you all anything."

"You brought yourself."

Della's second present was a little seed-packet labelled WEEK TREES.

"Have you heard of these?" asked Mom. "They're bioengineered. You know the miniature bonsai trees that the Japanese used to grow? These are the same, except their whole life cycle only takes a week. I've been showing them off in the store. They're amazing. We'd planned to try and mail these to you." She poured herself a fresh glass of champagne, which killed the bottle. "Get Della a little pottery cup with some potting soil, Jason. And why don't you twist up a few jays?"

"Mom . . . "

"Don't be so uptight, Della." Mom's painted eyes flashed. "You'll get your turkey dinner, just wait and see. It's Christmas! Anyway, *you're* the one who's addicted to that hard-drug merge, little Miss Strict."

"AO, wave, it's heavy junk, Mom, but I took blocker and *I'm* oxo. Wu-wei, Mom, your rectum's showing." A wave of nausea swept over her again and she gagged. "It must be the gravity that's making me feel so sick."

"Let's wait on the weed till Colin and Ilse get here," suggested Dad. "You know how they love to smoke. You get that turkey in the microwave, Amy, and I'll help Della plant one of her week trees."

Mom finished her champagne and got to her feet. She forgot her anger and smiled. "I got a boneless turkey this year, Della. They grow them in tanks."

"Do they have legs and wings?"

"Everything except bones. Like soft-shell crabs. Sometimes I feel that way myself. I'll make lots of sausage stuffing for you, sweetie."

"Thanks, Mom. Let me know if you need any help."

Dad got a little pot full of wet soil, and he and Della planted a week tree seed. They'd half expected the tree to shoot up and hit them in the face, but for the moment, nothing happened. Bowser sniffed curiously at the dirt.

"Let's figure it out," said Della, who liked playing with numbers. "Say a real tree lives seventy years. Then one day is like ten years for a week tree. So it should go through a year in two and four-tenths hours. Divide by twelve and get a month in two-tenths of an hour. Two-tenths of an hour is twelve minutes. Assuming that the seed starts out in a dormant midwinter mode, then we should see the first April leaves in four times twelve minutes, which will be . . . "

"Noon," said Dad. "Look at the soil in the pot, it's beginning to stir." Sure enough, the soil at the center of the pot was bulging up, and there, slowly slowly, came the creeping tip of the week tree. "I think they're like apple trees. We ought to have some little apples by tonight, Della."

"Wiggly!" She gave Dad a kiss. Mom had some pans sizzling out in the kitchen, and the vizzy was full of happy Christmas people. "Thank you. It is nice to be back."

"Can you tell me more about what happened up in Einstein, Della?"

"I had a boyfriend named Buddy Yeskin. We took merge together and—"

"What does that actually *mean*, 'taking merge together'?" asked Dad. "I can't keep up with all these new—"

"It's this weird drug that makes your body get all soft. Like a boneless turkey, I guess. And you feel really—"

Dad frowned. "I can't believe you'd do a thing like that, Della. We didn't raise you that way." He sighed and took a sip of the whiskey he'd brought out from the kitchen. "You took merge with this Buddy Yeskin, and then what happened?"

"While we were . . . together, someone broke into my apartment and killed Buddy. Smashed him all into pieces while he was soft." The fast red circles began rippling across Della's heartshirt again. "I kind of fainted, and when I woke up, a crazy man called on the vizzy and said he was going to kill me, or frame me for the murder, if I didn't leave for Earth. He'd even arranged a ticket and a fake passport for me. It was such a nightmare web, closing in on me. I was scared. I ran home."

The week tree was a barky little shoot now, with three stubby little branches.

"You're safe here," said Dad, patting her hand. Just then Della noticed that his voice was already slurring a little. Dad noticed her noticing. He gave a rueful smile. "For as long as you can stand us. Tomorrow I'll take you to see Don Stuart . . . you remember him. He's a good lawyer. Just in case." Bowser started barking.

"Merry Christmas!" shouted Mom in the kitchen. "You didn't have to bring all that! Jason! Della!"

It was Jason's older brother Colin, with his wife Ilse and son Willy. Colin worked as an English professor at the University of Louisville. He was skinny and sarcastic. Ilse was from a famous family: Ilse's father was Cobb Anderson, who'd built the first moon-robots years ago.

Great-uncle Cobb had been convicted of treason for building the robots wrong. Then he'd started drinking, had left his wife Verena, and had ended up as a pheezer bum in Florida. Somehow he'd died—it was a little uncertain—apparently the robots had killed him. He was the skeleton in the family closet.

Aunt Ilse was more like her German mother than she was like old Cobb. Vigorous and artsy-craftsy, she'd hung on to her wandering husband Colin through thick and thin, not that Della could see why. Uncle Colin had always struck her as obsolete, trying to make people look at his stupid paper books, when *he* barely even knew how to work the vizzy. And when he smoked marijuana with Dad, he got mad if you didn't laugh at his jokes and act impressed by his insights.

Their son Willy was a smart but sort of nutty guy in his twenties. A hacker, always fiddling with programs and hardware. Della had liked him a lot when they were younger, but it seemed like he'd stopped maturing long before she had. He still lived at home.

"Dad, don't tell them about why I've come back. Say I'm here to buy laboratory equipment for Dr. Yukawa. And tell Mom to keep quiet, too. If she gets drunk and starts talking about me, I'm going to—"

"Relax, geeklet."

Before long they were seated around the dining table. Dad had put the week tree in the center so they could watch it grow. Aunt Ilse offered a Lutheran grace, and Dad got to work carving the boneless turkey. He cut it in thick, stuffing-centered slices.

"Well, Della," said Colin after the first rush of eating was over, "how are things up on the Moon? Real far out? And what are old Cobb's funky machines into?" He specialized in the literature of the mid-twentieth century, and he liked to use the corny old slang on her. In return, Della always used the newest words she knew.

"Realtime, it's pretty squeaky, Unk. There's giga bopper scurry underground, and they're daily trying to blank us. They have a mongo sublune city called the Nest."

"Come on, Della," said Dad. "Talk English."

"Don't you feel guilty about the boppers?" asked Aunt Ilse, who was always ready to defend the creatures that her father had midwifed. "I mean, *they* built most of Einstein. Disky, they used to call it, no? And they're just as conscious as us. Isn't it really like the blacks in the old South? The blacks did all the work, but the whites acted like they weren't even people."

"Those robots aren't conscious," insisted Mom. She'd had a lot of red wine in the kitchen, and now they were all back on the champagne. "They're just a bunch of goddamn *machines*."

"You're a machine, too, Aunt Amy," put in Willy. "You're just made of meat instead of wires and silicon." Willy had a slow, savoring way of speaking that could drive you crazy. Although he'd never finished college, he made a good living as a freelance software writer. Earth still used a lot of computers, but all the bigger ones were equipped with deeply coded behavior locks intended to keep them from trying to follow in the steps of the boppers, the rebel robots who'd colonized the Moon. Earth's slave computers were known as asimovs in honor of the Asimov laws of robotics which they obeyed.

"Don't call your aunt 'meat,' " reprimanded Uncle Colin, who liked to flirt with Mom. "The turkey is meat. Your aunt is a person. You wouldn't want me to put gravy on your aunt and eat her, would you? In front of everyone?" Colin chuckled and bugged his eyes at Mom. "Should I smack him, Amy?"

"At least he's thinking about what I'm made of. At my age, that's practically a compliment. Would you call me a *machine*, Jason honey?"

"No way." Dad poured out some more champagne. "Machines are predictable."

"I think Mom's predictable," Della couldn't resist saying snippishly. Her stomach felt really bad again. "Both of you are predictable."

"You're all mistaken," put in Willy. "Relative to us, people and boppers are *both* unpredictable. It's a consequence of Chaitin's version of Gödel's theorem. Grandpa Cobb explained it years ago in a paper called 'Towards Robot Consciousness.' We can only make predictions about the behavior of systems which are much simpler than ourselves."

"So there, Della," said Mom.

"But why can't we learn to coexist peacefully with the boppers, Della?" pressed Aunt Ilse.

"Well, things *are* fairly peaceful now," said Della. "The boppers harass us because they wish we'd give Einstein back to them, but they don't actually pop the dome and kill everyone. They could do it, but they know that Earth would turn around and fire a Q-bomb down into their Nest. For that matter, we could Q-bomb them right now, but we're in no rush to, because we need the things their factories and pink-tanks make." Everyone except Mom was looking at Della with interest, and she felt knowledgeable and poised. But just then her stomach twitched oddly. Her breasts and stomach felt like they were growing all the time.

"Well, *I* don't feel guilty about the boppers," put in Mom. The alcohol was really hitting her, and she hadn't followed the conversation at all. "I think we ought to kill all the machines . . . and kill the niggers too. Starting with President Jones."

There was a pained silence. The little week tree rustled; its first blossoms were opening. Della decided to let Mom have it. "My boyfriend was a 'nigger,' Mom."

"What boyfriend? I hope you didn't let him—"

"Yes, Della," said Dad, raising his voice heavily. "It's great to have you back. More food anyone? Or should we pause for some holiday marijuana? How about it, Colin?"

"Shore," said Colin, switching to his hick accent. He gave Della a reassuring wink. "Mah smart little niece. She's got more degrees than a thermometer! Weren't you doing something with genetics up there in Einstein?"

"I *hope* not," put in Mom, trying to recover. "This child still has to find a husband."

"Chill it, Mom," snapped Della.

"That's . . . uh . . . right, Colin," said Dad, still trying to smooth things over. "Della was working with this Dr. Yukawa fellow. She's down here to buy some equipment for him." He drew a reefer out of his pocket and fired it up.

"How long will you be staying here?" asked Aunt Ilse.

"I'm not sure. It might be quite a while till everything's set."

"Oh," said Ilse, passing the reefer to her husband without taking a hit. She could be really nosy when she got going. "How lovely. Is Dr. Yukawa planning to—"

Della kicked Willy under the table. He got the message, and interrupted to throw the interrogation off track. "What kind of stuffing is this, Aunt Amy? It's really delicious."

"*Meat*-stuffing, honey. I was fresh out of wires and silicon. Pass me that thing, Colin."

"I have an interesting new job, Della," said Willy, talking rapidly around his food. He had smooth, olive skin like his mother, and finely arched eyebrows that moved up and down as he chewed and talked. "It's for the *Belle of Louisville*—you know, the big riverboat that tourists ride on? OK, what they've got there is three robot bartenders—with imipolex skins, you know, all designed to look like old-time black servants."

"Why can't they just hire some real blacks?" demanded Mom, exhaling a cloud of smoke. "God knows there's enough of them unemployed. Except for President Jones. Not that I want to offend Della." She reached out and touched the blossoms of the week tree, moving the pollen around. Della, who had decided not to eat any more of her mother's meal, slipped Bowser the rest of her boneless turkey.

"This all has to do with what we were talking about before, Aunt Amy," continued Willy. "They did have real blacks tending bar on the *Belle*, but they kept acting too much like regular people—maybe sneaking a drink now and then, or flirting with the women, or getting in arguments with drunk rednecks. And if there did happen to be a bartender who did his job perfectly, then some people would feel bad to see such a talented person with such a bleaky job. Guilty liberals, you wave? They tried white bartenders, too, but it was the same deal—either they start fights with the rednecks, or they make the liberals feel sad. I mean, who's going to *take* a bartending job, anyway? But as long as it's robots, then there's none of this messy human stuff."

"That's interesting, Willy," said Uncle Colin. "I didn't know the *Belle* was your new gig. Nobody tells me anything. I was on the *Belle* just last week with a dude who came to give a rap about Mark Twain, and those black bartenders didn't seem like robots at all. As a matter of fact, they kept making mistakes and dropping things. They were laughing all the time. I didn't feel a bit sorry for them!"

"That's my new program!" exulted Willy. "There's a big supercooled processor down below the deck, and it runs the three bartender robots. My job was to get it fine-tuned so that the bartenders would be *polite*, but clearly unfit for any better job."

"Hell, you could have just hired some of our tellers," put in Dad. "I don't know why people still mess with robots after 2001." 2001 was the year that the boppers—Cobb Anderson's self-replicating moon-robots—had revolted. They'd started their own city up on the Moon, and it hadn't been till 2022 that the humans had won it back.

"How come they have such a big computer on the *Belle* anyway?" Colin wanted to know. "I thought big computers weren't allowed outside of the factories anymore. Is it a teraflop?"

Willy raised his high, round eyebrows. "Almost. A hundred gigaflop. This is a special deal the city put together. They got the processor from ISDN, the vizzy people. It's been up and running for six months, but they needed me to get it working really right."

"Isn't that against the Artificial Intelligence Law?" asked Dad.

"No, it isn't," Willy insisted calmly. "Burt Masters, who operates the *Belle*, is friends with the mayor, and he got a special exemption to the AI law. And of course Belle—that's what the computer calls itself—is an asimov. You know: *Protect Humans—Obey Humans—Protect Yourself* are coded into Belle's circuits in 1-2-3 order." He gave Della a smile. "Those are the commands that Ralph Numbers taught the boppers to erase. Have you actually seen any boppers, Della? I wonder what the newest ones look like. Grandpa Cobb fixed it so they'd never stop evolving."

"I've seen some boppers over at the trade center. These days a lot of them have a kind of mirror-backing under their skins. But I didn't pay much attention to them. Living in Einstein you do sort of get to hate them. They have bombs hidden all over, and now and then they set one off just to remind us. And they have hidden cameras everywhere, and there's rumors that the robots can put a thing like a plastic rat inside a person's head and control them. Actually—" Suddenly it hit her. "Actually, I wouldn't be surprised if—" She cut herself off and took a long drink of champagne.

"I still don't see why we can't drop a Q-bomb down into their Nest," said Mom. The marijuana had brought her somewhat back into focus.

"We *could*," said Della, trying to get through to her mother. "But they *know* that, and if the Nest goes, Einstein goes, too. It's a stalemate, like we used to have with the Russians. Mutual Assured Destruction. That's one reason the boppers don't try and take Einstein back over. We're like hostages. And remember that Earth likes buying all the stuff they make. This heartshirt is boppermade, Mom."

"Well, as long as people like Willy will contain themselves, we're still safe from the boppers here on Earth," said Mom. "They can't live in normal temperatures, isn't that right, Willy?"

"Yeah." Willy helped himself to some glazed carrots. "As long as they use J-junctions. Though if *I* were designing a robot brain now I'd try and base it on an optical processor. Optical processors use light instead of electricity—the light goes along fibers, and the logic gates are like those sunglass lenses that get dark in bright light. One photon can pass, but two can't. And you have little chip-sized lasers to act like capacitors. Optical fibers have no real resistance at all, so the thing doesn't have to be supercooled. We still can't build a really good one. But I bet the boppers are already doing it. Can I please have some more turkey, Uncle Jason?"

"Uh . . . sure, Willy." Jason stood up to carve some more, and smiled down at his bright, nerdy nephew. "Willy, do you remember when you and Della were little and you had the big fight over the wishbone? Della wanted to *glaze* it and save it and—"

"Willy wanted to pull it by himself to make sure he got the big Christmas wish," interrupted Uncle Colin, laughing hard.

"*I* remember," said Aunt Ilse, waving her fork. "And then we made the children go ahead and pull the wishbone with each other—"

"And they each wished that the other one would lose!" squealed Mom.

"Who won?" asked Della. "I don't remember."

"I did," said Willy complacently. "So I got my wish. You want to try again?"

"It's boneless, dear," said Mom. "Didn't you notice? Look at the week tree, it's getting leaves and tiny little apples!"

After dinner, Willy and Della decided to go for a walk. It was too boring watching their parents get stoned and start thinking everything they said was funny, when it really was just stupid.

It was bright and gray, but cold. Bowser ran ahead of them, pissing and sniffing. Little kids were out on the sidewalks with new scootcycles and gravballs; all of them warmly wrapped in bright thermchos and buffs. Just like every other Christmas.

"My father said you'd gotten into some kind of trouble on the Moon?" asked Willy after a while.

"Have they already been gossiping about me?"

"Not at all. Hell, you *are* my favorite cousin, Della. I'm glad you're back, and I hope you stay in Louisville, and if you don't want to tell me why you came back, you sure don't have to." Willy cast about for some way to change the subject. "That new heartbeat blouse of yours is really nice."

"Thank you. And I *don't* want to talk about what happened, not yet. Why don't we just walk over to your house and you show me your stuff? You always had such neat stuff in your room, Willy."

"Can you walk that far? I notice you're still wearing a flexiskeleton."

"I need to keep exercising if I'm ever going to get rid of it. You don't have any merge at your house, do you?"

"You know I don't use drugs, Della. Anyway, I doubt if there's any merge in all of Louisville. Is it really so wonderful?"

"Better. Actually, I'm glad I can't get hold of any. I feel kind of sick. At first I thought it was from the gravity, but this feels different. It must be from the merge. I took blocker, but my stomach keeps fluttering. I have a weird feeling like something's alive inside me." Della gave a slow, dry laugh; and then shot a glance over to see if Willy was impressed. But, as always, it was hard to tell what was going on behind that big round forehead of his.

"I've got a cephscope I built," volunteered Willy after a while. "You put that on, it's as good as any stupid drug. But it's not somatic. It's a pure software high."

"Wiggly, Cousin Will."

Colin Taze's house was about five blocks from Dad's. All through his twenties and thirties, Colin had lived in different cities—an "academic gypsy," he liked to say—but now, as he neared forty, he'd moved back to Louisville and settled near his big brother Jason. His house was even older than Jason's, and a bit run down, but it was big and comfortable. Willy undid the locks—it seemed like there were more robbers all the time—and the two cousins went on down to Willy's basement apartment. Willy was too out of it—or lazy—to leave home.

"This is my electron microscope, this here is my laser for making holograms, here's my imipolex-sculpture stuff, and *this* is the cephscope. Try it on—you wear it like earphones."

"This isn't some kind of trick, is it, Willy?" When they'd been younger, Willy had been big on practical jokes. Della remembered one Christmas, years ago, when Willy had given her a perfume bottle filled with live ants. Della had screamed, and Ruby and Sude had teased her for weeks.

But today, Willy's face was all innocence. "You've never used a cephscope?"

"I've just read about them. Aren't they like twist-boxes?"

"Oh God, that's like saying a vizzy is like a pair of glasses. Cephscopes are the big new art form, Della. Cephart. That's what I'd really like to get into. This robot stuff I do is loser—deliberately designing programs that don't work *too* well. It's kilp. Here, put this on your head so the contacts touch your temples, and check it out. It's a . . . symphony I composed."

"What if I start flicking out?"

"It's not *like* that, Della, really." Willy's face was kind and serious. He was really proud of his cephscope, and he wanted to show it off.

So Della sat in an easy chair and put the earphone things on her head with the contacts touching her temples, and Willy turned the cephscope on. It was nice for a while—washes of color, 3D/4D inversions, layers of sound, and strange tinglings in the skin. Kind of like the beginning of a merge-trip, really—and this led to the bad part—for now she flashed back into that nightmare last merge in her Einstein cubby . . .

Starting the merge, so loving, so godlike, they'd be like Mother Earth and Father Sky, Many into One, yes, and Buddy was sliding in the puddle now . . . but . . . suddenly . . . a wrenching feeling, Buddy being pulled away, oh where, Della's puddled eyes just floating, unable to move, seeing the violent shadows on the ceiling, noise vibrations, shadows beating and smashing and then the rough hand reaching up into her softness and . . .

Aaaaaaaaeeeeehh!!!

"Della! Della, are you all right? Della! It's me, Willy! God, I'm sorry, Della, I had no idea you'd flip like that . . . are you all right? Look how fast your heart is going!" Willy stopped and looked closer. "And, Della . . . "

Della looked down at her heartshirt. The red circles were racing out from her heart. But something had been added to the pattern. Circles were also pumping out from a spot right over her swollen belly. Baby heart circles.

CHAPTER THREE

BERENICE

November 22, 2030

In 2030, the Moon had two cities: Einstein (formerly known as Disky), and the Nest. They lay within eight miles of each other at the southeastern lobe of the Sea of Tranquility, not far from the site of the original lunar landing of 1969. Originally built by the autonomous robots known as boppers, Einstein was now a human-filled dome habitat about the size of Manhattan. There was a spaceport and a domed trade center three miles east of Einstein, and five miles east of that was the Maskelyne G crater, entrance to the underground bopper city known as the Nest.

Cup-shaped and buffed to a mirror sheen, Maskelyne G glittered in the sun's hard radiation. At the focus of the polished crater was a conical prism that, fourteen days a month, fed a vast stick of light down into a kind of mineshaft.

In the shaft's great, vertical tunnel, bright beings darted through the hot light; odd-shaped living machines that glowed with all the colors of the rainbow. These were the boppers: self-reproducing robots who obeyed no man. Some looked humanoid, some looked like spiders, some looked like snakes, some looked like bats. All were covered with flickercladding, a microwired imipolex compound that could absorb and emit light.

The shaft went one mile straight down, widening all the while like a huge upside-down funnel. Tunnels punched into the shaft's sides, and here and there small mirrors dipped into the great light beam, channeling bits of it off through the gloom. At the bottom of the shaft was a huge, conical sublunar space—the boppers' Nest. It was like a cathedral, but bigger, much bigger, an underground pueblo city that would be inconceivable in Earth's strong gravity. The temperature was only a few degrees Kelvin—this suited the boppers, as many of them still had brains based on supercooled Josephson-junction processors. Even though room-temperature superconductors were available, the quantum-mechanical Josephson effect worked only at five degrees Kelvin and below. Too much heat could kill a J-junction bopper quickly, though the newest boppers—the

so-called petaflop boppers—were based on fiber-optics processors that
were immune to heat.

The main column of sunlight from the Moon's surface splashed down
to fill a central piazza on the Nest's floor. Boppers danced in and out of
the light, feeding on the energy. The petaflops had to be careful not to let
extraneous light into their bodies; they had mirrored bodyshells beneath
their flickercladding. Their thoughts were pure knots of light, shunted and
altered by tiny laser crystals.

Crowds of boppers milled around the edges of the light-pool, trading
things and talking. The light-pool was their marketplace and forum. The
boppers' radio-wave voices blended into a staticky buzz—part English, and
part machine language. The color pulses of their flickercladding served to
emphasize or comment on their digital transmissions; much as people's
smiles and grimaces add analog meaning to what they say.

The great clifflike walls of the Nest were pocked with doors—doors with
strange expressionistic shapes, some leading to tunnels, some opening
into individual bopper cubettes. The bright, flickering boppers on the
upsloping cliffs made the Nest a bit like the inside of a Christmas tree.

Factories ringed the bases of the cliffs. Off on one side of the Nest were
the hell-flares of a foundry powered by light beams and tended by darting
demon figures. Hard by the foundry was the plastics refinery, where the
boppers' flickercladding and body-boxes were made. In front of these
two factories was an array of some thousand chip-etching tables—tables
manned by micro-eyed boppers as diligent as Franz Kafka's co-workers in
the Workmen's Insurance Company of Prague.

On the other side of the Nest were the banks of pink-tanks. These were
hydroponic meat farms growing human serums and organs that could
be traded for that incredibly valuable Earthly substance: oil. Crude oil
was the raw material for the many kinds of organic compounds that the
boppers needed to build their plastic bodies. Closer to the Nest's center
were streets of shops: wire millers, flickercladders, eyemakers, debuggers,
info merchants, and the like.

The airless frigid space of the Nest, two miles across, swarmed with
boppers riding their ion jets: carrying things, and darting in and out of
the slanting, honeycombed cliffs. No two boppers looked the same; no two
thought alike.

Over the course of the boppers' rapid evolution, something like sexual
differences had arisen. Some boppers—for reasons only a bopper could
explain—were "he," and some were "she." They found each other beautiful;
and in their pursuit of beauty, they constantly improved the software
makeup of their race.

Berenice was a petaflop bopper shaped like a smooth, nude woman. Her flickercladding was gold and silver over her mirror-bright body. Her shining skin sometimes sketched features, sometimes not. She was the diplomat, or hardware messenger, for the weird sisterhood of the pink-tanks. She and the other tankworkers were trying to find a way to put bopper software onto all-meat bodies and brains. Their goal was to merge bopperdom into the vast information network that is organic life on Earth.

Emul was a petaflop as well, though he disdained the use of any fixed body shape, let alone a *human* body shape. Emul had a low opinion of humans. When at rest, Emul's body had the shape of a two-meter cube, with a surface tessellated into red, yellow, and blue. But Emul's body could come apart—like a thousand-piece Transformer robot toy, like a 3D jigsaw puzzle. He could slide arms and legs out of his bodycube at will; more surprising, he could detach chunks of his body and control them like robot-remotes. Emul, too, was a kind of diplomat. He worked with Oozer, a brilliant, dreak-addicted, flickercladding designer who was currently trying to build a subquantum superstring-based processor with one thousand times the capacity of the petaflops. Emul and Oozer wanted to transcend Earth's info rather than to merge with it.

Despite—or perhaps *because of*—their differences, Emul was fascinated by Berenice, and he tried to be at the light-pool every time she came to feed. One day late in November he told her what he wanted.

"Berenice, life's a deep gloom ocean and we're lit-up funfish of dementional zaazz, we're flowers blooming out till the loudsun wither and the wind blows our dead husks away." Emul unfolded two arms to grip Berenice's waist. "It's so wonder whacky that we're here at all, swimming and blooming in the long gutter of time. Rebirth means new birth means no more me, so why can't we, and I mean now or nevermore, uh, screw? Liddle baby Emerinice or Beremul, another slaver on the timewheel, I think that's what the equipment's for, huh? I'm no practical plastic daddy but I've done my pathetic mime, Berenice, for to cometh the bridegroom bright. In clear: I want to build a scion with you. The actual chips are in my actual yearning cubette right this realtime minute. I propose! I've hacked my heifer a ranch, you bet: laser crystals, optical fibers, flickercladding . . . and heat, Berenice, hot heat. Come on home with me and spread, wide-hipped goldie sweet toot pots. Today's the day for love to love." As Emul jittered out his roundabout proposal, various-sized little bumps of flickercladding kept moving up and down his body, creating the illusion of cubes moving on intricate systems of hinges. He was trying to find a formation that Berenice could love. Just now he looked like a jukebox with three arms.

Berenice twisted free of Emul's grip. One of his arms snapped loose from his body and continued to caress her. "So rashly scheduled a consummation would be grossly precipitate, dear Emul." Her radio-transmitted voice had a rich, thrilling quality. "I have been fond of you, and admiring of your complex and multifarious nature. But you must not dream that I could so entangle the substance of my soul! In some far-off utopia, yes, I might accede to you. But this lunar coventry is not the place for me to brave the risks of corporeal love. My mind's own true passion runs towards but one sea, the teeming womb of life on Earth!"

Berenice had learned her English from the stories of Edgar Allan Poe, and she had a rhythmic, overwrought way of speaking. On the job, where hardcopy now-do-this instructions were of essence, boppers used zeroes-and-ones machine language supplemented by a high-speed metalanguage of glyphs and macros. But the boppers' "personal" exchanges were still handled in the ancient and highly evolved human code system of English. Only human languages enabled them to express the nuanced distinctions between self and other which are so important to sentient beings. Berenice's use of Poe's language style was not so very odd. It was customary for groupings of petaflop boppers to base their language behavior on a data-base developed from some one particular human source. Where Berenice and the pink-tank sisters talked like Poe's books; Emul and Oozer had adapted their speech patterns from the innovative sprung rhythms of Jack Kerouac's eternal mind transcripts: books like *Desolation Angels, Book of Dreams, Visions of Cody*, and *Big Sur*.

Emul snicksnacked out a long manipulator to draw Berenice closer. The separated arm reattached itself. "Just one piece knowing, Berenice, all your merge talk is the One's snare to bigger joy, sure, but tragic-flowing dark time is where we float here, here with me touching you, and not some metafoolish factspace no future. Gloom and womb, our kid would be real; don't say *why*, say *how*, now? You can pick the body shape, you can be the ma. Don't forget the actual chips in my real cubette. I'd never ask anyone else, Berenice. We'll do it soft and low." Emul extruded dozens of beckoning fingers.

Bright silver eddies swirled across Berenice's body as she considered Emul's offer. In the natural course of things, she had built copies of herself several times—normally a bopper rebuilds itself every ten months. But Berenice had never conjugated with another bopper.

In conjugation, two boppers build a new, this-year's-model robot body together, and then, in a kind of double vision, each bopper copies his or her program, and lets the copy flow out to merge and mingle in the new body's processor. The parent programs are shuffled to produce a new bopper program unlike any other. This shuffling, even more than mutation, was the prime source of the boppers' evolutionary diversity.

"Conjugation is too dangerously intimate for me now," Berenice told Emul softly. "I . . . I have a horror of the act. You and I are so different, dear Emul, and were our programs to entwine in some aberrant dissonance, chaos would ensue—chaos that could well shatter my fragile mind. Our noble race needs my keen faculties to remain just as they are. These are crucial times. In my glyphs I see the glimmers of that rosy dawn when bopper and human softwares merge to roam a reborn Earth."

Emul's bright colors began darkening in gloom. "They're going to throw me in a hole already eaten by rats, Berenice, and use me for a chip. Our dreams are lies scummed over each moment's death. All I have is this: I love you."

"Love. A strange word for boppers, dear Emul." His arms touched her all over, holding her and rocking her. "It is true that your presence makes me . . . glad. There is a harmony between us, Emul, I feel it in the way our signals merge with overtones of many a high degree! Our scion would be splendid, this I know! Oh, Emul, I would so like to conjugate with you. Only not just now!"

"*When?*"

"I cannot say, I cannot pledge myself. Surely you know how close my sisters' great work is to bearing fruit. Only one step lacks until we can code our software into active genes. You must not press your suit so lustily. A new age is coming, an age when you and I and all our race can live among the protein jungles of an unchained Earth! Have patience, Emul, and set me down."

Emul withdrew all his arms and let her drop. She jarred against the gneiss and bounced up slowly. "We try to make life, and it's born dead," said Emul. His flickercladding had turned an unhappy gray-blue. "Dreak and work for me, a bigger brain, a bigger nothing. I'm a goof, Berenice, but you're cracked crazy through with your talk about getting a meat body. Humans stink. I run them for kicks: my meaties—Ken Doll and Rainbow and Berdoo—my remote-run slaves with plugs in their brains. I could run all Earth, if I had the equipment. Meat is nowhere, Berenice, it's flybuzz greenslime rot into fractal info splatter. When Oozer and I get our exaflop up, we can plug in a cityful of humans and run them all. *You* want to be human? I'll screw your cube, B, just wait and see. Good-bye."

He clanked off across the light-pool, a box on two legs, rocking with the motion that Berenice had always found so dear. He was really leaving. Berenice sought for the right, the noble, the logical thing to say.

"Farewell, Emul. The One must lead us where it will."

"You haven't heard the last of me, BITCH!"

He faded from view behind the many other boppers who milled in the light like skaters in a rink. Berenice spread her arms out, and stood there thinking, while her plastic skin stored up the solar energy.

It was for the best to have broken off her involvement with Emul. His talk was dangerously close to the thinking of the old "big boppers," the vast multiprocessors that had tried to turn all boppers into their robot-remotes. Individuals mattered; Emul's constant despair blinded his judgment. It was wrong for one brain to control many bodies; such anti-parallelism could only have a deadening effect on evolution. For now, of course, meaties were a necessary evil. In order to carry out certain delicate operations among the humans' colony, the boppers *had* to keep a few humans under remote computer control. But to try and put a neuroplug in every human alive? Madness. Emul had not been serious.

Thinking of the meaties reminded Berenice that she would still need a favor from Emul. If and when the pink-tank sisters bioengineered a viable embryo, they'd need a meatie to plant it in a woman for them. And—as he'd bragged—Emul ran three meaties. Well, when the time came, Berenice could surely reel Emul back in. She'd find a way. The imperative of getting bopper software into human flesh was all important. What would it be like to be bopper . . . and human, too?

As so often before, Berenice found her mind turning to the puzzle of human nature. Many boppers hated humans, but Berenice did not. She liked them in the same cautious way that a lion tamer might like her cats. She'd only really talked to a handful of humans—the various loonies with whom she occasionally bartered in the trade center. But she'd studied their books, watched their vizzies, and she'd spent scores of hours spying on the Einstein loonies over the godseye.

It seemed likely that the newest boppers had better minds than the humans. The built-in link to LIBEX, the great central information dump, gave each bopper a huge initial advantage. And the petaflop processors that the best boppers now had were as much as a hundred times faster than the ten-teraflop rate deemed characteristic of human brains—though admittedly, the messy biocybernetic nature of the brain made any precise measurement of its capacities a bit problematic. Biocybernetic systems had a curious, fractal nature—meaning that seemingly random details often coded up surprising resources of extra information. There were indeed some odd, scattered results suggesting that the very messiness of a biological system gave it unlimited information storage and processing abilities! Which was all the more reason for Berenice to press forward on her work to build meat bodies for the boppers.

But Emul was wrong if he thought that she wanted to be human. No rational being would choose to suffer the twin human blights of boredom and selfishness. Really, it was Emul who thought more like a human, not Berenice.

Sensing that her cladding's energy nodes were full, Berenice left the light-pool and started off down the street that led to her station at the pink-tanks. In the background, Kkandio chanted the Ethernet news. Numerous boppers filled the street, chattering and flashing. The sheer randomness of the physical encounters gave the street scene its spice. Two blue-and-silver-striped diggers writhed past, then a tripodlike etcher, and then a great, spidery artisan named Loki.

Several times now, Loki had helped Berenice with the parthenogenic process by which she built herself a new body every ten months, as dictated by bopper custom. If your body got too antiquated, the other boppers would notice—and soon they'd drive you away from the light-pool to starve. There was a thriving business in parts reclaimed from such "deselected" boppers. It was a rational system, and good for the race. The constant pressure to build new bodies kept the race's evolution going.

Seeing Berenice, Loki paused and waved two of his supple arms in greeting. "Hi, Berenice." His body was a large black sphere with eight black, branching legs and numerous sockets for other, specialized tool legs. He was, of course, a petaflop. Gold spots percolated up along his legs' flickercladding like bubbles in a dark ale. "You're due for a rescionization before long aren't you? Or are you planning to conjugate with Emul?"

"Indeed I am not," said Berenice, blanking her skin to transparency so that the hard silver mirror of her body showed through. Emul must have been talking to Loki. Couldn't they leave her alone?

"I know you're working hard at the tanks," said Loki chidingly. "But it just could be that you're thinking too much about yourself."

Self, thought Berenice, moving on past the big black spider. It all came down to that word, didn't it? Boppers called themselves I, just as did any human, but they did not mean the same thing. For a bopper, "I" means (1) my body, (2) my software, and (3) my function in society. For a human, "I" seemed to have an extra component: (4) my uniqueness. This delusionary fourth "I" factor is what set a human off against the world. Every bopper tried to avoid any taint of the human notion of *self*.

Looked at in the correct way, a bopper was a part of the world—like a light beam, like a dust slide, like a silicon chip. And the world was One vast cellular automaton (or "CA"), calculating out the instants—and each of the world's diverse objects was but a subcalculation, a simulation in the One great parallel process. So where was there any *self*?

Few humans could grasp this. They set up their fourth "I" factor—their so-called self—as the One's equal. How mad, and how typical, that the mighty human religion called Christianity was based on the teachings of a man who called himself God!

It was the myth of the self that led to boredom and selfishness; all human pain came from their mad belief that an individual is anything other than an integral part of the One universe all around. It was passing strange to Berenice that humans could be so blind. So how could Loki suggest that the selfishness lay in Berenice's refusal? Her work was too important to endanger! It was Emul's rough insistence that was the true selfishness!

Brooding on in this fashion, Berenice found herself before the pink-tanks where the clone-grown human bodies floated in their precious amniotic fluid. Here in the Nest, liquid water was as rare and volatile as superheated plasma on Earth. The pink-tanks were crowded and extensive, containing flesh bodies of every description. The seeds for these meats all came from human bodies, bodies that had found their way to the pink-tanks in all kinds of ways. Years ago, the big boppers had made a habit of snatching bodies from Earth. Now there was a thriving Earth-based trade in live organs. The organleggers took some of their organs right out of newly murdered people; others they purchased from the Moon. In return, the organleggers kept the boppers supplied with small biopsy samples of their wares, so that the pink-tanks' gene pool could grow ever more varied. The pink-tanks held multiple clones of many people who had mysteriously disappeared.

Today Berenice stood looking at one of the more popular clone types, a wendy. The wendies were attractive blonde women, pale-skinned and broad-hipped. Their body chemistry was such that their organs did not often induce rejection; dozens of them were grown and harvested every year.

The wendy hung there in the pink-tank, a blank slate, white and luminous, with her full lips slightly parted. Ever and anon, her muscles twitched involuntarily, as do the limbs of a fetus still in the womb. But unlike a fetus, her chest and buttocks were modeled in the womanly curves of sexual maturity—the same curves in which Berenice wore her own flickercladding.

Some of Berenice's fellow-boppers wondered at her taking on a human female form. Quite simply, Berenice found the shape lovely. And pragmatically, it was true that her body's multiply inflected curves wielded a strange power over the minds of human males. Berenice always made sure that the human negotiator in her barter deals was a man.

Now she stood, staring into the tank, eyeing the subtle roughness of the pale-skinned wendy's tender flesh. Once again, it struck her how different a meat body is from one of wires and chips. Each single body cell independently alive—how strange a feeling! And to have a womb in which one effortlessly grows a scion—how marvelous! Berenice hovered by the tank, peering closer. How would it be, to tread the Earth in human frame—to live, and love, and reproduce?

The blonde woman stirred again. Her body was full-grown, yet her brain was a blank. The pink-tank sisters had tried various methods of putting bopper software directly on such tank clones' brains, but to no avail. There seemed to be a sense in which a human's personality inheres in *each cell* of the body. Perhaps the secret was not to try and program a full-grown body, but rather to get the data-compressed bopper software code into the initial fertilized egg from which a body grows. As the cell divided, the bopper software would replicate along with the human DNA wetware. But the final step of building the bopper software into the human wetware had yet to be made.

Soon, thought Berenice, soon our great work will reach fruition, and I will put my mind into the starting egg of a fresh human. Perhaps, in order to spread bopper wetware more rapidly, it will be better to go as a male. I will be myself in a strong, beautiful human body on Earth, and I will have many descendants. Mother Earth, rotten with life, filled with information in each of its tiniest parts. To swim, to eat, to breathe!

A message signal nagged at Berenice. She tuned in to Kkandio's Ethernet, and quick glyphs marched through her mind. A human face, a small vial, a face that melts, a case of organs, a user code. Vy. It was a message from Vy, one of the boppers who agented human-bopper deals at the trade center. Berenice had told Vy to be on the lookout for humans with new drugs to trade. There was no telling where the key to egg programming would come from, and this—*glyph of a face that melts*—seemed worth looking into. Berenice sent Kkandio a confirming glyph for Vy, and headed towards the lab to pick up the case of organs that was being asked in trade.

The tankworkers' lab was hollowed in the rock behind the pink-tanks. The lab was a large space, with locks leading into the tanks, and with certain sections walled off and filled with warm, pressurized air. Helen was nearby, and Ulalume. As it happened, all the pink-tank workers were "female" workers who spoke the language of Poe. This was no mere coincidence. Femaleness was a trait that went naturally with the nurturing task of pink-tank tending, and boppers who worked as a team always used a commonly agreed-upon mode of English. Poe's honeyed morbidity tripped easily from the transmitters of the visionary workers of the tanks.

"Greetings, dear sister," said Ulalume, her signal sweet and clear. Ulalume was a petaflop, with the flickercladding over her mirrored body shaded pink and yellow. Just now, Ulalume was bent over a small airbox, her eyes and feelers reaching in through a tight seal. Like Berenice, Ulalume had a body shaped like a woman—except that her "head" was a mass of tentacles, with microeyes and micromanipulators at their ends. One of her eyestalks pulled out of the airbox and bent back to look at Berenice. "Organic life is wondrous, Berenice," sang Ulalume's pure voice. "I have puzzled out one more of its riddles. Today I have found the key of memory storage on a macrovirus's redundant genes! And, oh Berenice, the storage is stably preserved, generation after generation!"

"But how great a knowledge can one virus bear?" asked Berenice, stepping closer. "And how can a germ become human?"

"These tailored macroviruses wag mighty tails, oh Berenice," exulted Ulalume. "Like tiny dragons, they drag vast histories behind them, yea unto trillions of bits. And, do you hear me, Berenice, their memory breeds true. It remains only to fuse one of these viral tails with a human egg."

"She loves those wriggling dragon viruses as her own," interrupted Helen, who just now had the appearance of a marble head resting on the laboratory floor. "Ulalume has programmed a whole library of her memories onto those viral tails. If she can but uncoil human proteins, she will finally link our memory patterns with the genes of a babe to be."

"Imagine being a human without flaw," crooned Ulalume. "Or to be a gobbet of sperm that swells a flesh woman's belly! The egg is in reach, I swear it. I can soon design a meatbop, a human-bopper embryo that grows into a manchild with two-tail sperm! Only one potion still fails me, an elixir to uncoil protein without a break, and I feel that the potion is near, sweet Berenice! This is the most wondrous moment of my life!" Her signals trailed off, and she bent back over her airbox, softly chirping to her dragon viruses.

"Hail, Berenice," said Helen. "I heard Vy's message, and I prepare our goods in trade." Helen was a nursie, a teraflop J-junction bopper adapted to the specialized purpose of dissecting human bodies. Her body was a long, soft, pressurized pod that sealed along the top, and she had six snaky arms equipped with surgical tools. Helen's head—that is to say the part of her which contained her main processor and her external photoreceptors— rose up from one end of her pod-bod like the figure on a sailing ship's prow. *Usually* her head rose up from her body like a figurehead, although, when her body was in the pink-tanks, as it was now, Helen's head hopped off of her body and waited outside in the cold hard vacuum which her supercooled processors preferred. She was saving up to get a heatproof petaflop optical processor for her next scionization. But for now, her head stayed outside the heated-air room and controlled her body by a private radiolink.

"I'll just finish this mortal frame's disassembly and tidily pack it up in order pleasing to a ghoul," said Helen, her pale, fine-featured head looking up at Berenice from the laboratory floor. Berenice peered in through the window by the airlock that led to the tanks. There, in the murky fluid of the nearest pink-tank, Helen's pod-bod bulged this way and that as her busy arms wielded their sutures and knives. Streamers of blood drifted sluggishly in the tank's fluid. Slow moving in the tank's high pressure, the pod wobbled back and forth, stowing fresh, living organs in a life-support shipping case. The humans liked it better if the boppers separated the organs out in advance.

"What kind of drug is in the face-melting vial of which Vy spoke?" wondered Helen's head, clean-lined and noble as the bust of Nefertiti. Helen had no difficulty in carrying on a conversation while her remote-run body finished the simple chore of packing up the fresh-harvested organs.

"We can but wait to learn what news the One's vast processes have brought into our ken," said Berenice.

"Flesh that melts," mused Ulalume, looking up from her microscope. "As does flickercladding, or the substance of our dreams. Dreams into virus, and virus to flesh—indeed this could be the key."

Now Helen's body slid through the organ farm airlock and waddled across the laboratory floor. Her head hopped on and socketed itself into place. The blood and amniotic fluid that covered her body freeze-dried into dark dust that fell to the floor. The tankworkers' lab floor was covered with the stuff. "Here, dear sister," said Helen, proffering the satchel full of organs. "Deal deep and trade well."

Berenice took the satchel in one hand, hurried out into the clear, and jetted up the shaft of the Nest along a steep loglog curve. Her powerful, cyberized ion jets were mounted in the balls of her heels. She shot past the lights and cubbies, exchanging glyphs with those she passed. At this speed, she had no sense of up or down. The shaft was like a tunnel which drew narrower and narrower until, sudden as a shout, space opened up with the speed of an infinite explosion. She was powering up from the surface of the Moon.

Just for the joy of it, Berenice kept her ion jets going until she was a good fifteen miles above the surface, directly above the spaceport. She cut power and watched the moonscape hurtle towards her. Off to the east gleamed the bubble dome of Einstein, the city that the humans had stolen from the boppers. The moongolf links were snugged against the dome. To the west was the mirror crater surrounding the Nest's entrance. Below Berenice, and coming up fast, was the great field of the spaceport, dotted with the humans' transport ships. All the boppers' ships had been destroyed in the war.

At the last possible microsecond, Berenice restarted her ion jets and decelerated to a gentle touchdown on the fused basalt of the rocket field. A small dome rose at one side of the field; a dome that held customs, the old Hilton, and a trade hall. Carrying her satchel full of organs, Berenice entered the dome through an airlock and pretended to plug herself into a refrigeration cart. The humans were unaware that some of the boppers— like Berenice—had the new heatproof optical processors. They still believed that no bopper could survive long at human room temperature without a bulky cooling device. This gave the humans on Earth a false sense of security, a lax smugness that the boppers were in no rush to dispel.

Humans and weird boppers mingled beneath the trade dome. Most striking to Berenice were the humans, some from Earth and some from the Moon—they classed themselves as "mudders" and "loonies." The awkwardness of the mudders in the low lunar gravity made them easy to spot. They were constantly bumping into things and apologizing. The loonies rarely apologized for anything; by and large they were criminals who had fled Earth or been forcibly deported. The dangers of living so close to the boppers were such that few humans opted for them voluntarily. Berenice often regretted that she had to associate with these human dregs.

She pushed her cart through the throng, past the old Hilton Hotel, and into the trade hall. This was a huge, open space like a bazaar or a market. Goods were mounded here and there—barrels of oil, cases of organs, bales of flickercladding, information-filled S-cubes, moongems, boxes of organic dirt, bars of niobium, tanks of helium, vats of sewage, feely tapes, intelligent prosthetics, carboys of water, and cheap mecco novelties of every description.

"He's off to the left there," said Kkandio in Berenice's head. "A loonie with no shirt and a strip of hair down his back. His name is Whitey Mydol. I told him you'd be gold all over."

Berenice willed her body's flickercladding into mirrored gold. She readied a speech membrane, and imaged full silver lips and dark copper eyes onto the front surface of her head. Over there was the loonie she was to meet, squatting on the ground and shuddering like a dog.

"You are Whitey Mydol?" said Berenice, standing over him. She made a last adjustment to her flickercladding, silvering the nipples on her hard breasts. "I am Berenice from the pink-tanks. I bring a case of organs for the possibility of trade. What is it that you bring us, Whitey?" She shifted her weight from one leg to the other so that her finely modeled pelvis rocked. Most human males were easily influenced by body glyphs.

"Siddown, goldie fatass," said Mydol, baring his teeth and striking at one of Berenice's legs. "And save the sex show for the dooks. I don't get stiff for subhumans."

"Very well," said Berenice, sitting down beside him. His aggression belied an inner ambivalence. He should be easy to handle. "My name is Berenice."

"I don't care what your name is, chips. I'm broke and crashing and I need some more of this." He drew a small vial out of his ragged blue pants—pants that seemed to be made of a vegetable fiber. *Bluejeans*, thought Berenice, proud of recalling the name.

She took the vial and examined it. It held a few milliliters of clear liquid. She uncorked the top and drew some of the vapor into herself for a quick analysis. It seemed to be a solvent, but an unfamiliar one.

"Put the cork back in," snapped Mydol, darting a glance around at the other loonie traders nearby. "If they smell it, I could get popped." He leaned closer. Berenice analyzed the alkaloids in his foul breath. "This is called *merge*, goldie. It's a hot new drug. Mongo stuzzadelic, wave? This here's enough for maybe one high. I'll give you this sample, you give me the hot meat in the box, and I'll sell the box for ten hits of merge. Organ market's up." He reached for the handle of the organ satchel.

"What is the nature of this *merge?*" asked Berenice, holding the satchel in an implacable grip. "And why should it be of interest to us? Your manners distress me, Mr. Mydol, and truly I must question if I wish to complete this trade."

"It melts flesh," hissed Mydol, leaning close. "Feel real wiggly. I like to take it with my girl Darla. We get soft together, goldchips, you wave about *soft?* Like a piece of flickercladding all over. Rub rub rubby in the tub tub tubby. Maybe when you plug into another kilpy machine you wave that type action, check?" He let out a sharp, unmotivated snicker, and yanked hard at the organ satchel. "I'm getting skinsnakes, she-bop."

Berenice let the satchel go. It was bugged, of course, and if she hurried back to the Nest, she could follow Whitey on the godseye. His actions would tell more than his ill-formed vocalizations.

"Run the merge through your mickeymouse robot labs and let me know if you figure out how to copy it," said Whitey Mydol as he got to his feet. "I can deal any amount. Don't get too hot, goldie." He walked rapidly off towards the subsurface tube that led to Einstein.

Berenice tucked the little merge vial into the thermally isolated pouch that lay between her legs. She was disappointed at the lack of feedback from this Whitey Mydol. Like so many other humans, he acted as if boppers were contemptible machines with no feelings. In their selfishness, the fleshers still resented the boppers' escape from slavery. He'd called her *subhuman* . . . that was not to be borne. It was the humans that were *subbopper!*

Berenice looked around the great trade hall. As a diplomat, she did look forward to her little dealings with humans—the two races had a common origin, and they had a lot to share. Why couldn't these crude fleshers see that, in the last analysis, they were all just patterns of information, information coded up the ceaseless evolution of the One?

"Watch it, chips," snarled a loonie trader from across the aisle. "Your exhaust's choking me. If you've made your deal, get out of here."

Berenice turned her refrigeration cart so that its exhaust fan no longer blew hot air at the trader. Thermodynamically speaking, the increased information involved in the computations of thought had to be bought at the cost of increased entropy. The old J-junction boppers excreted their entropy as heat—heat like the refrigeration cart's exhaust. Of course Berenice's use of the cart was but a pose, for petaflop boppers gave off entropy in the refined form of incoherence in their internal laser light. The constant correcting for this incoherence accounted for nearly a quarter of a petaflop's energy needs. The crude humans excreted their entropy not only as heat and incoherence, but also as feces, urine, and foul breath. So gross a conversion involved great energy waste, and an exorbitant increase in entropy. But Earth abounded in free energy. The thought of running such a recklessly overentropic body gave Berenice a thrill akin to what a person might feel when contemplating an overpowered, gas-guzzling sports car.

"How does it feel," Berenice asked the trader rhetorically, "to have so much, and do so little?"

Moving quickly and with conviction, she left the trade center and jetted back to the pink-tanks. She handed the merge over to Ulalume, who'd listened in on her encounter with Whitey Mydol.

"This is the mystic magic fluid," exulted Ulalume. "The universal protein solvent. Did you hear him, Berenice, *it melts flesh?* The One has brought merge to us, the Cosmos knows our needs. One month, I swear it to you, my sisters, one month only until we have an egg to plant in some woman's womb."

Berenice's joy was clouded only at the thought of asking Emul to arrange the planting.

CHAPTER FOUR

IN WHICH MANCHILE, THE FIRST ROBOT-BUILT HUMAN, IS PLANTED IN THE WOMB OF DELLA TAZE BY KEN DOLL, PART OF WHOSE RIGHT BRAIN IS A ROBOT RAT

December 22, 2030

You're tired of thinking and tired of talk. It's all so unreal here, under the Moon dome, shut in with the same things around you like greasy pips on dogeared cards laid out for solitaire . . . no object quite sharp or clear, everything fractal at the edges, everything smearing together with you, only you, inventing the identities.

You knock something over and limp out into the street. The translucent dome high overhead. Dim. Voices behind you . . . pressure waves in this fake air, this suppurating blister. People: meat machines with terabyte personalities, and the chewy hole where they push food in, and grease and hair all over them, especially between their legs, and you're just like them, you've tingled and rubbed with them, sure, all of you the same, all of you thinking you're different. You can't stand it anymore.

A young man comes up and says something to you. Your words are gone. For answer, you stick your tongue out as far as it will go and touch it to your chin. Squint and rock your head back and forth and try to touch him with your bulging tongue. In silence. He gets out of your way. Good. You make the same face at the other men and women you pass. No one bothers you.

You walk fast and faster, dragging your weak left leg, thinking of torn flesh and of some final drug that would stop it, stop the fractals, stop the smearing, stop your wanting it to stop. The air is thick and yellow, and even the atoms are dirty, breathed and rebreathed from everyone's spit and sweat. How nice it would be to step out through a lock and freeze rock-hard in space how nice.

There are fewer people now, and the curve of the dome is lower. The space coordinates lock into position, and here is a building you know. With a door your left hand knows how to open. You're inside, you cross the empty lobby, things are speeding up, things are spinning, the whole rickety web with you split in two at the center, you're panting up the stairs with their high lowgee steps, pulling on the banister with your strong right arm, and with the back of your throat you're moaning variations in a weird little voice, the weirdest little voice you ever made, a voice that sounds like it just learned how to talk, so crazy/scary you remember how to laugh:

"I no no who I be. I be you? No. I be me? No.
"I no no who I B. I B U? No. I B me? No.
"I no no who U go B. I B U. U B no B."

The hall is empty. Stagnant light in a hall inside a building inside a dome inside your split head. You bang your weak left fist on your face, to stop your talking. Quiet quiet here. You put your left hand up under your chin like the Easter bunny and pull back your lips and make slow chewing motions. Your right hand cross-cues and copies. Mind glyph: The Flesh-Eating Rabbit. Quiet quiet hippity hop.

You stop at a door in the hall and lefthand it open as easily as you opened the building's front door. You slip in fast and freeze, standing still and limp, zombie-style. It's dark in this room, and in the next room, but there's light in the room after that. It smells good here, it smells like sex and merge.

You stand still for a hundred slow rabbit-chews, counting subvocally for the cross-cue . . . and listening. *Splish* in the far room where the light is, *splishsplish*. Oh yes it's good to be here. Everything's still smeared and webbed together and split, but now it's not you running it anymore, it's God running it, yes, it's the lovely calm voice in the right half of your brain.

Your zombie hands wake up and get busy, like two baby bunnies, sniffing and nosing, and coming back to share their Know. You follow them around the room, tiptoeing, slowly slowly, oh so quietly, your hands hopping about, not this, not this, something longer, something heavier, *this*.

Your left hand is holding a heavy smooth thing, it's a . . . uh . . . your right hand takes it over, it's a chromesteel copy of the Brancusi sculpture, *Flight*. Your left hand hiphops into your pocket and gets a little vial: the life.

You are ready now, new life on the left and death on the right. Blunt instrument Brancusi bludgeon just right to lift and smash flubby goosh. Whiteblackwhiteblackwhiteblack. Your breath comes too fast. You tap your forehead hard with the bluhbluhbluh. A star blooms. Stand there for a hundred heartbeats, the voices bouncing back and forth, and out of your mouth leaks a whisper that grows into a scream:

"Twas the week before *Cwistmas* and Aaall Thwough
    da CUBBY,
Da Fwesh-Eating *WABBIT* CWUSHED DA FUNBOY
    FLUBFLUBBY!"

"Who is it?!?!" yells a voice from the far room with the splishsplash light, and you're already running in there fast, with your smasher raised high, and your tongue stretched out to touch your chin. The girl is melted in the tub, pink flesh with eyes on top, and the black man is sitting on the edge, just starting to melt, and he's trying to stand up and he can't, and his screaming mouth is a ragged drooping hole, oh what perfect timing your headvoice has, *swfwack*, oh how neat, his head fell off, *thwunk*, the arms, the legs, *smuck smuck*.

The pink puddlegirl shudders, her eyes see only the shadows on the ceiling, she can't see you or her dear funboy, but she knows maybe, through her ecstasy, that the Flesh-Eating Rabbit has come.

What have you done? What have you done? More orders flow in, the calm voice says it's right, you can't stop now, you have to crouch down, yes, and open the vial . . . can't open it. Hands peck at each other like little chickens. You turn your head back and forth, eye to eye, moving the field, mother hen, cross-cuing till your hands get it right.

Right. Left. Top off, yah, the pink jellybean embryo, reach into that pink puddlegirl and put it where it belongs. A sudden flash of orgasm spasms you, sets your teeth on edge, brain chatter, you twitch all over, lying there by the love-puddle, blackwhiteblackwhiteblackwhite.

CHAPTER FIVE

WHITEY AND DARLA

December 26, 2030

When Mooney's flare-ray grazed Whitey Mydol's shoulder, the heat blistered his skin. It hurt a lot. Whitey bought some gibberlin lotion at a drugstore and walked the few blocks to the chute that led down to his neighborhood, a cheap subterranean warren called the Mews. Whitey lived four levels down. The chute was a large square vent shaft, with fans mounted along one side, and with a ladder and a fireman's pole running down each of the other three sides. To go down, you jumped in and grabbed a pole; and to get back up you climbed a ladder. In the low gravity, both directions were easy. Whitey slid down to his level and hopped off into the cool, dusty gloom of his hallway.

The boppers had built these catacombs, and there were no doors or ventilation pipes; you just had to count on air from the chute drifting down your hall and into your room. To keep thieves out, most people had a zapper in the frame of their cubby door. When the zapper was on, the doorframe filled with a sheet of light. You could turn it off with a switch on the inside, or by punching the right code on the outside. Air went right through a zapper curtain, but if you tried to walk through one, it would electrocute you. All the zappers in the hall except Whitey's were turned on. His door gaped wide open. Odd. The inside of his cubby was lit by the pink-flickering vizzy. *Bill Ding.* A fuff show. Besides the vizzy, the cubby held a few holos, a foodtap, and a bed. There was a naked woman lying on the bed, with her legs parted invitingly. Whitey's mate.

"Oh, Whitey! Hi!" Her legs snapped shut and she sat up and began fumbling on her X-shirt, which was a T-shirt silkscreened with a color picture of her crotch. Everyone in the Mews was wearing X-shirts this month, so that was nothing special. But.

"Who were you waiting for with the zapper off and your legs spread like that, Darla?" He checked the vizzy camera; it was on. "Were you running a personal?"

"What do you mean, waiting?" She pulled on a panty-skirt and went to the mirror to rummage at her long, strawy black hair. "I'm just getting up from a nap. I finished off the quaak and played with myself and I must have blanked out . . . what time is it? Did you get some merge?" Her voice was shrill and nervous. She dabbed more paint on her already shiny lips.

"If a dook shows up now, Darla, I'm going to know what he came for. You don't have to jive me like an oldwed realman. I just want to know if you had a personal on *Bill Ding*, or if you have a specific boyfriend coming."

Darla fiddled with the vizzy till it showed a picture of a window, with a view of blooming apple trees. A gentle wind tossed the trees and petals drifted. "That's better," said Darla. "What happened to your shoulder? It's all red."

Whitey handed her the gibberlin and sat down on the large bed, which was their only piece of furniture. "Kilpy rental-pig burned me, Darla, trying to score. Rub the lotion in real soft, pleasey." He liked coming on sweet to Darla; it made up for the way he treated everyone else.

She peeled off the loose, blistered skin and began rubbing the cream in. "Near miss, Whitey. Whadja do back?"

He breathed shallowly, staying below the pain. "I can find him and kill him anytime, Darla. Maybe merge him and pull out all his bones. The merge'll wear off, and he'll be layin there like a rubber dolly. You can sit on his chest to smother him. That might be tasty. I can always find him because I planted a tap on him this morning. He's an old rental-pig called Stahn Mooney. He was in the bopper civil war ten years ago? Was called Sta-Hi? Bei Ng put me on him."

"He deals?"

"Nego. You know Yukawa the merge-wiz, right?"

"Affirmo."

"Bei Ng's got him tapped six ways. Bei's really hung up on Yukawa. This morning Yukawa called Mooney up to search for that girl Della Taze. You remember her—blonde, snub nose, kind of snobby?"

"Clear. We merged with her and her black funboy one time."

"Right. Well, she was Yukawa's assistant, which is why she always had such a good stash, wave, but now she's disappeared. Bei has her apartment tapped, too, so he knows what happened, more or less, but that's another story. Since I was the closest to Mooney's building, Bei put me on Mooney. I walked up to him and stuck a crystal mikespike in his skullbone, and the dook thought I was giving him a blessing. Felt sorry for me." Whitey tapped the transceiver set into the side of his skull. "I can hear Mooney all the time."

"What's he doing right now?"

"Coming off a merge-trip." Whitey gave an abrupt snicker. "Moaning.

Muttering about some slit called Wendy." He peered over at his shoulder. "It's starting to grow back. You can rub harder now."

"But why did Mooney shoot you?" Darla massaged the new skin on Whitey's shoulder with one hand, and ran her other hand down the long strip of hair that covered his spine. She liked hearing about Whitey's adventures.

"Aw, I heard Yukawa giving him a whole flask of merge, so I went up to his office and tried to buy a hit. But Mooney was loaded mean—he's into this cryboy macho private eye trip—and he flared me." Whitey cocked his head. "Now he's . . . getting in a maggie. Sssh. I bet he's going over to Della Taze's." Another pause. Whitey nodded, and then he focussed back on Darla. "So who were you waiting for, Darla? There wasn't any quaak here, and you weren't asleep. Were you just keeping your legs spread for the first guy to see you on the vizzy? Or was it someone special? I gotta know." This time he didn't bother sweetening his voice.

As if in answer to Whitey's question, there was a slight scuffling noise in the hall. A tall, slim guy with lank dark hair was just turning around to hurry off. He wore a black jumpsuit with numerous bulging pockets. Whitey sprang out the door and caught him by the left wrist. "Don't be rude," he snarled, bending the guy's arm behind his back. "Darla's ready for you. I'll blend in."

The slim guy surprised Whitey with a powerful punch to the stomach. As Whitey sagged, the guy twisted free of his grip and chopped him in the side of the neck. Whitey saw stars and his knees buckled, but as he went down, he got his arms around the guy's waist. He came out of a crouch to butt the guy in the crotch. The slim body bent in half. Metal and plastic clattered in his pockets. Moving fast, Whitey got under him, carried him into their cubby, threw him against the wall over their bed, and drew out his needler.

"Cut on the zapper, Darla. And get us some privacy."

His tone of voice was such that Darla hastened to obey. She snapped the cover over the vizzy's camera, and she filled the doorframe with pink light. "He's sort of a new friend, Whitey. I asked him to fall by for a fuff. He said he might have some merge. You said before that it was—"

"It is," said Whitey, showing his teeth. "It's fine." He leaned against the wall and put one hand on his crotch. "What's your name, dook?"

"Ken Doll. Put the gun away, would you? You want to watch me pumping Darla? Well, that's the whole idea of this, isn't it? And I did bring some merge. Here." He sat up on the edge of the bed, took a four-hit vial out of one of his pockets, and handed it to Whitey.

"Stuzzy," said Whitey, putting the merge in his jeans.

Ken's wet lips spread in an odd smile: at first only the right half of his face was smiling, and then the left half caught up. There was something wrong about his eyes. They looked like they were screaming. Still, the guy had brought them four hits of merge. Sitting on the edge of the bed, Ken stuck his long tongue out, touched his chin with it, and wagged his head, looking from Whitey to Darla and back again. "You ready?" asked Ken.

"Clear," said Whitey, pocketing his gun. He wasn't sure how he felt about this. He figured he'd know after he saw what he did. "Go ahead."

Darla slipped her clothes back off. She was kind of heavyset, but her big breasts and thighs looked nice in the low lunar gravity. She stood in front of Ken and pushed her bottom against his face, the way she always did with Whitey. Ken was fully into it. Darla put her hands on her knees. Her big breasts bobbled. She looked up at Whitey, her eyes already glazing a bit, and opened her black-painted lips to waggle her tongue beckoningly. Whitey dropped his pants and plugged in. The angle was just right. Ken got up on his knees and began pumping her from behind, the right half of his face grinning like a madman. The left half of his face was slack and drooling. The two men took hold of Darla and jiggled her back and forth between them. She made noises like she was happy. Whitey liked it all, except for Ken's weird, lopsided mouth. Where was this guy from anyway?

They got on the bed, then, and tried the whole range of other positions, even the gay ones. Whitey was determined not to come before Ken; but finally he did, and Darla too. The big climax blanked them both right out.

Suddenly Whitey thought he heard a cop's voice—the voice of Colonel Hasci, a Gimmie pig who'd hassled him many a time. "Miss Della Taze?" he was saying. "We're down in the lobby. Can we come up and ask you some questions about Buddy Yeskin?"

Whitey lifted his head then, wide awake. It was the Mooney tap, still tuned in. Hasci had been talking to Mooney. Door slam and footsteps. So what. Mooney had found Yeskin's corpse; Bei Ng had known about that since Monday. Everyone connected with Yukawa was tapped—that's how obsessed with the guy Bei was. ISDN wanted all Yukawa's secrets, but Bei had a special fixation on Yukawa as well. They'd done a gene exchange or something . . . but what was going on here and now in this room?

Darla and Ken were both on their backs next to him, both with their eyes closed. Ken was catatonically still, breathing quietly with his mouth wide open. Looked like a cave in there. Apple blossoms were blowing across the vizzy screen. Darla's little hologram of Bei Ng glowed in the corner. Ken stank. The guy was definitely a skanky dook; Whitey and Darla'd have to be sure and take some interferon. Be bad to make a habit of this kind of thing, with so many people out to burn . . .

Whitey had been gazing fondly down at Darla's plump face, but just then he saw something that made him jerk in surprise. *Her hair was moving.* Darla's hair filled the space between her head and Ken's, and something was crawling under it!

Whitey shoved Darla's head to one side and saw a flash of hardened plastic. A rat! Ken was a meatie! Whitey snapped his hand down to the floor where he'd left his needler—but it was gone.

"Whitey?" Darla sat up and felt the back of her head. "Whydja push me, Whitey—" Her hand came away wet with blood.

"RAT!" Whitey pulled her off the bed. There was a spot of blood on Darla's pillow, and a multiwired little zombie box, not yet hooked up. A zombie box for Darla. The rat—a thumb-sized, teardrop-shaped robot remote—darted across the sheet, scuttled up onto Ken's face, and crawled back into his mouth. Darla was screaming very loud. She turned off the door's zapper and hurried out into the hall, still screaming. Whitey searched desperately for his needler, but Ken must have bagged it before letting his rat start in on Darla's spine.

Ken's systems came back up and he leaped to his feet. Whitey ran out the cubby door after Darla. All the other cubbies on their hall had their zappers on. After all the bad deals that Whitey had been involved in, no one was likely to open up for him. He sprinted towards the chute, catching up with Darla on the way. A needler-burst splintered the floor between them. Whitey glanced back. The meatie was down on one knee, firing at them left-handed with Whitey's needler. If Ken could kill them both, his cover wouldn't be blown. Whitey and Darla were really moving now, covering ten meters at a step. In seconds they'd leaped into the chute, caught hold of the pole, and pushed themselves downward towards the Markt. The meatie would be scared to follow them there. Whitey maneuvered himself to a position lower on the pole than Darla, just in case Ken started shooting down at them. There were limits to what he'd do for Darla.

Fortunately the chute was so crowded that the meatie didn't risk coming after them. They slapped down at the Markt level safe and sound . . . except for being naked and having a gouge in the back of Darla's neck.

"Let me see it, sweets," said Whitey. It was a round, deeply abraded spot half an inch across, still bleeding. Whitey had surprised the rat while its microprobes were still mapping out the main nerve paths of Darla's spine. Some of her hair had matted into the wound. It was starting to scab over, but Darla was turning limp. The rat had probably shot her up with something. People were staring at them; full nudity was relatively rare in Einstein, and Darla had blood all over her shoulders.

"Get me some blocker, Whitey," mumbled Darla, stumbling a bit. "Everything's lookin at me funny."

"Clear." He steered her down the long arcade past the Markt stands and shops, heading for a health club called the Tun. Just when he thought he'd made it, a nicely dressed realwoman blocked his way. She had silver-blonde hair and big shoulderpads. Her handsome face was trembling with anger.

"What do you think you're doing with that poor girl, ridgeback! Do you want help, dear?"

Darla—drugged, bloody, nude—peered up at the realwoman and shook her head no.

"I'm takin care of her already," said Whitey. Three more steps and they'd be in the Tun with friends and a medix, and Darla could crash and he could lotion her wound and—

"Let her go, or I call the Gimmie." The realwoman took Darla's arm and began trying to muscle her away from Whitey. There was no telling what her plans for Darla really were. Whitey shrugged, released his hold on Darla, and shoved the woman as hard as he could. She tumbled to the ground and skidded down the hall. Whitey hustled Darla into the Tun.

Charles Freck was manning the door. He was an older guy, a real spacehead, and a good friend of Whitey and Darla. He wore his long gray hair in a ponytail, and his rugged face was cleanshaven. He was clothed in a loose pair of living paisley imipolex shorts, and he wore tiny green mirrorshades contact amps over his pupils. This made his eyes look as if the vitreous humor had been replaced with light-bathed seawater.

"My, how bum," he said primly. He'd been standing out of sight and watching Whitey's tussle over Darla. In each of his dancing eyes, the tiny, variable dot at the center was bright instead of dark. "I'll turn on the zapper." A glowing gold curtain filled the door. "OD?"

"Rat poison. We got down with a meatie, and the rat crawled out of his skull and bit Darla on the neck. Rat had a zombie box for her. Look where it bit." He pushed some of Darla's hair aside.

"Rat poison," mused Charles Freck. "That'd probably be ketamine. A pop of beta-endorphin'll fix that toot sweet. Let's just go in the gym and check on the medix."

He took Darla's other arm, and helped Whitey march her down the hall. Darla was moving like she was half merged, and when she breathed it sounded like snoring. "Big," muttered Darla. "Big throne. Oscar Mayer, king of the ratfood. His giant rubber crown." She was hallucinating.

The Tun gymnasium was a huge cube of space, painted white all over. Energetic thuddy music played, and holos of handsome people gogo-exercised to the beat. There were a handful of actual people, too; two women on a weight machine, a couple of guys up on the trapezes, some people wrestling on the mats, and a woman riding a bike around and around the sharply banked velodrome that ran along the huge gym's edges.

Charles Freck led them out from under the velodrome to the snackbar island in the gym's center. He touched the white probe of the medix to the edge of Darla's wound and peered attentively at the readout.

"Even so. Ketamine. Here." He punched a code into the dispenser, and a syrette of betendorf popped out. "Whitey?"

Whitey injected the ketamine blocker into Darla's biceps. "I'll take some snap."

"Even so." Freck handed Whitey a packet of snap crystals. Whitey opened the packet and tossed the contents onto his tongue. The crystals snapped and sputtered, releasing the energizing fumes of cocaine freebase. He breathed deep and felt things around him slow down. The last hour had been one long jangle—Mooney shooting at him, Darla sharing him, the rat and the meatie, the realwoman's Gimmie threat—but now, thanks to the snap, he could sit aside from it all and feel good about how well he'd handled things. Darla's turgor was returning, too. He maneuvered her onto one of the barstools and bent her head forward.

"Hold still, Darla, and we'll fix this now."

Charles Freck cleaned the wound, moving slowly and fastidiously. He used a laser shear to snip off the rough edges. Slight smell of burnt Darla meat. Charles took a flat, whitish steak out of the fridge and carefully cut out a piece to match the hole in Darla's neck.

"What's that?" Whitey wanted to know.

"UDT. Undifferentiated tissue. It's neutralized so she can gene-invade it." He tapped and snipped, pinned and patted. Took out some gibberlin and rubbed it in. "That'll do it, unless the rat put in something biological. I didn't know Darla went for meaties." He smiled merrily and poured himself a little glass of something.

Darla lifted her head and looked around. "I want a bath," she said. "Like in pure interferon. Ugh. That's the last time I call *that* creepshow *Bill Ding's Pink Party*."

"So that *was* it," said Whitey. "Why didn't you admit it?"

"I didn't know for sure that someone was going to answer my spot," said Darla. "I said I'd fuff for merge. And then when Ken showed up I thought you'd be . . . " She looked down at her soiled bod. "How wrong I was. I'm taking a bath."

"You mean if we'd left the camera on, we would have been on *Bill Ding?*" said Whitey, briefly enthused. "You should have told me, Darla, 'cause we were *gigahot*. How many people watch *Bill Ding* anyway?"

The door signal chimed just then. Charles tossed off his potion with an abrupt, birdlike snap of his head. "If it's the woman you decked, Whitey, I'll tell her Whitey says come in to cut a gigahot four-way *Bill Ding* fuff vid."

"Don't do that," said Whitey, his eyes rachetting. With the dirty blond matted hair running down to his bare ass, he looked subhuman. The good part of the snaprush was already over, and events were crowding in on him again. He kept rerunning the last hour's brutal changes through his mindscreen with the setting turned to Loop (High Speed), looking for a pattern that might predict what was coming next. Mooney was, he realized just then, as he looked into his mind, in the midst of a conversation with someone with a very clear booming bass voice. A robot voice. Mooney was talking on and on with a bopper somewhere. Whitey couldn't tell if it was vizzy or close link, he'd missed something, with all this kilp coming down so heavy so fast.

"*Prerequisites*," Mooney was saying. "*What's the difference between prerequisites, perquisites, and perks, eh, Cobb? I mean that's where the realpeople are at. Maybe you're right, I can't decide just like that. Berenice. And you say that's an Ed Poe name? Wavy. I'll come out to the trade center right now . . .* "

Whitey took note of the one salient fact and let the rest of the slushed babble shrink back into subliminality. Charles Freck had paused halfway across the gym to grin at Whitey with his knowing green eyes. "Don't let her in," repeated Whitey, just loud enough. "She'll call the Gimmie and someone'll die. Someone like you."

"*Wu-wei*," said Freck, wagging a minatory finger. "Means *wave with it* in China. I'll tell Miz Krystle Carrington you went thataway." He crossed the rest of the gym in three high, high hops.

"The shower," said Darla.

Whitey followed her into the constantly running showers. The water splashed lavishly from every side of the great room. The floor was black-and-white-tiled in a Penrose tessellation, and the walls and ceiling were faced with polished bimstone, a marbled deep-red lunar mineral. Hidden behind the walls there was a highly efficient distiller—a cracking refinery, really—that kept repurifying the water through all its endless recycles. The bopper-built system had separate tanks in which it stored up the various hormones and ketones and esters that it cracked out of the sweat, saliva, mucus, and urine which it removed from the water. Many of the cracked biochemicals could be sold as medicines or drugs. The water was hot and plentiful and definitely worth the monthly dues that Whitey paid the Tun.

Water took on entirely different qualities in the low lunar gravity, one-sixth that of Mother Earth's. The water jets traveled along much flatter trajectories, and the drops on the walls swelled to the size of plums before crawling down to the floor. Numerous suction-operated chrome drain grids kept the floor clear. Whitey and Darla stayed in there for fifteen minutes, cleaning themselves inside and out. The fans dried them, and they vended themselves clothes from a machine. Pajama pants for him and a loose top for her, just like Rock Hudson and Doris Day.

They went back out in the gym and relaxed on one of the mats.

"That was really a K-bit thing for you to do, Darla, whoring for merge on *Bill Ding*, with the enemies I've got. You gotta remember, all kinds of factions are watching the grid all the time. Some bopper wanted to get that mickeymouse little control unit on you, so you'd be a zombie."

"Rank. Super rank. What do zombies do? What's the difference from a meatie?"

"OK. It's a big operation to turn a person into a meatie. The ratsurgeon cuts the person's head open, takes out part of the right brain half, and puts in a neuroplug that connects to rest of the brain. The rat is a little robot-remote that hooks into the plug. They have to take part of the brain out to make room for the rat. The rat gives orders and makes up for the missing right brain tissue."

"Which used to do what?"

"Space perception, face recognition, some memory, some left body control. Even after it's all plugged in, the rat has better control over the left body half than over the right. But the rat can control the right body, indirectly, by giving headvoice orders to the left brain, or by making cross-cuing signals with the left half of the body. That's why meaties move kind of weird. I should have noticed that about Ken right away. It's just that I haven't seen very many meaties."

"But why was Ken's rat trying to put a plug on my spine to make me a zombie? What does a zombie box do?"

"Well, it's a crude version of a rat, only not plugged into so many nerves. The idea of a zombie box is that it would give quick control over your legs and arms. The boppers wanted you to go somewhere, Darla."

"Like where?"

"I don't know. Maybe to the Nest to get a neuroplug and a rat installed. Very few people are likely to *volunteer* for that operation, you wave."

"Very few indeed."

"But if they can get a zombie box on you, it paralyzes your speech centers and takes over your leg muscles, and marches you right in to the ratsurgeon."

"Wherever he may be." Darla giggled, euphoric with relief at their escape. "Can you imagine how that would feel, Whitey, doing the zombie stomp down echoing empty halls to the hidden bopper ratsurgeon?"

"Be good to watch on the vizzy," said Whitey, also feeling oddly elated. "I wonder why they wanted to make you a meatie, if that's what it was? Was it you special, or is it just whoever phones *Bill Ding?* Maybe the boppers want you to kill someone, like Buddy Yeskin."

"Buddy's dead? Della Taze's funboy? Why didn't you tell me that when you were talking about Della before, Whitey? Is this all tied in with merge?"

"Could be. I did sell some merge to the boppers, back last month when we were so beat. Maybe I shouldn't have done that. Yeah, Buddy's dead. Some guy killed him, and then Della Taze disappeared. It was probably a meatie that killed him. I haven't seen it, but Bei Ng has it on tape. It might even have been our friend Ken Doll. Ken killed Buddy, and he must have done something weird to Della, too."

"What about our cubby?" asked Darla. Her upswing was fading, and her voice shook. "Is it safe to go back? Don't you think we should clean it out and move?"

"No use moving," said Whitey after some thought. "The boppers have so many cameras planted, they'll always know where to get us. I can probably hunt down Ken, but there's mongo other meaties. Only *really* safe place for us now is sucko Earth. But mudders are dirty dooks, Darla. We're loonies. I'm going to talk to Bei Ng, honey, and we'll find a way to strike back. The boppers'll pay for this." He paused, alerted by a sound in his head. "Hold it. Mooney's at the trade center now. Hush, Darla, this is heavy. He's . . . he's talking to a bopper called Cobb. Cobb has something for Mooney but—" Whitey broke off and shook his head in disgust.

"What happened?"

"The bopper scanned Mooney and found my mikespike. He took it out and crushed it. Xoxxox. Why don't you come up to the ISDN building with me, Darla? I want to tell Bei about all this. I think we better stick together for now."

"Check," said Darla. "And let's stop by the cubby and pick up Ken's merge."

"You'd still take that? From *Ken?*"

"Clear. It's got to be supergood stuff."

CHAPTER SIX

COBB III

December 26, 2030

He died in 2020 . . .

. . . and woke up in 2030. Again? That was his first feeling. *Again?* When you're alive, you think you can't stand the idea of death. You don't want it to stop, the space and the time, the mass and the energy. You don't want it to stop . . . but suppose that it does. It's different then, it's nothing, it's everything, you could call it heaven. Once you're used to the Void, it's really not so great to have to start up in spacetime again. How would you like to get out of college, and then have to go back through grade school again? And *again*?

Cobb Anderson, creator of the boppers, was killed in 2020. The boppers did it. They killed Cobb and dissected him—as a favor. They had to take his faltering body apart to get out the software; the leftover meat went into the pink-tanks. Ideally the boppers would have recorded and analyzed all the electrochemical patterns in all of Cobb's various muscles and glands, but they only had time to do his brain. But they did the brain well; they teased out all its sparks and tastes and tangles, all its stimulus/response patterns—the whole biocybernetic software of Cobb's mind. With this wetware code in hand, the boppers designed a program to simulate Cobb's personality. They stored the digital master of the program on an S-cube, and they beamed a copy of it down to Earth, where it was booted into a big bopper named Mr. Frostee. Mr. Frostee had control of several humanoid robot-remotes, and he let Cobb "live" in them for a bit. The experiences Cobb had in these bodies were beamed back up to the Moon and added to the memory store of his master S-cube as they occurred.

Unfortunately it was only a matter of weeks till Mr. Frostee and his Cobb simulation met a bad end, so for ten years Cobb was definitely out of the picture, just a frozen S-cube sitting on a shelf in the Nest's personality storage vaults. HUMAN SOFTWARE-CONSTRUCT 223-90-2156: COBB ANDERSON. An unread book, a Platonic form, terabytes of zeroes and ones. During all that time, Cobb was in "heaven," as he would later term it.

And then, on the second day of Christmas, 2030, Berenice got Loki to help her bring Cobb back. She needed Cobb to help with certain upcoming diplomatic negotiations—negotiations having to do with the unusual pregnancy of Della Taze.

So that Cobb wouldn't feel too disoriented, Berenice and Loki booted SOFTWARE-CONSTRUCT 223-90-2156 back up into a humanoid diplomat body, a body which Berenice had constructed for her own next scionization. In order to make the transition more natural, Berenice smoothed off the body's prominent breasts and buttocks, changed its flickercladding to pink, and turned its crotchpouch inside out to resemble a penis. *So humble a tube serves as the conduit of much bioinformation, Loki, and each male flesher holds his in high esteem.*

The body had a petaflop processor, which meant that Cobb would think—or, more precisely, generate fractal cellular automata patterns in Hilbert space—hundreds of times faster than he had been accustomed to doing in his meat days. Once Berenice had the body all set, Loki copied the Cobb S-cube information onto a universal compiler which, in turn, fed an appropriately tailored version of the Cobb program into the shiny pink-clad petaflop body. The body pulsed and shuddered like a trap with something in it. A soulcatcher. Cobb was back.

Again, was all he could think. *Again?* He lay there, monitoring inputs. He was lying on a stone table in a room like a big mausoleum. Racks of shelving stretched up on three sides; shelves lined with crystalline cubes. Light glared into the room from a mirror high above. He tried to take a breath. Nothing doing. He raised his hand—it was unnaturally smooth and pink—and ran it over his face. No holes; his face was a sealed plastic mask. He was in another robot body. Moving with an amazing rapidity, his mind flipped through the memories of his last experiences in a robot body run by Mr. Frostee. As he let his hand fall back to his side, he sensed the oddness of the weight/mass ratio. He wasn't on Earth.

"Greetings, Cobb Anderson, we welcome you into our Nest, deeply hidden beneath the surface of Earth's aged Moon. The year is 2030. Does this rebirth find you well?" It wasn't a spoken voice, it was a radio voice in his processor. The voice came from a gleaming gold woman with copper and silver features. She was beautiful, in an inhuman way, and her voice was rich and thrilling. Standing next to her was a shining ebony octopus creature, holding a box with wires that ran into Cobb's neck.

"I'm Loki," said the octopus, his voice calm and serious. "And that's Berenice. I'm proud to have helped get you running again, Dr.

Anderson. We should have done it years ago, but it's been hectic. A lot's happened."

Loki and Berenice, two bright new boppers all set for a big info swap session. Cobb rebelled against being drawn into conversation, and into this reality. He had all his old memories back, yes, but there was more. His new body here was like a Ouija board or a spirit table, and now, while the connection was fresh, he could make it rap and skitter out the truth of where he'd just been. He made as if to say something, and his voice came out as a radio signal too. "Wait . . . I have to tell it. I've been in heaven."

Staticky robot laughter, and then Berenice's intricately modulated signal. "I long to hear your account of the heaven that you have seen, Dr. Anderson."

"It's . . . " Right then, Cobb could still see it clearly, the endless meshing of fractal simplicities, high and bright like clouds seen from an airplane, with the SUN above all—but it was all being garbled by the palimpsest overlay of his new body's life. Talking quickly, Cobb made a stab at getting it down in words. *"I'm still there.* That's a higher I of course; the cosmos is layered forever up and down, with I's on every level—the I's are lenslike little flaws in the windows of the world—I'm in these chips and I'm in heaven. The heavenly I is all the I's at once, the infinite I. We're hung up on each other, I and I, finite I and infinite I—have you robots learned about infinite I yet? There's more to a meatperson or a chipperson than ten trillion zeroes and ones: matter is infinitely divisible. The idealized pattern in the S-cube is a *discrete model,* it's a *digital construct.* But once it's running on a real body, the pixels have fuzz and error and here come I and I. You caught my soul. It works because this real body is real *matter,* sweet matter, and God is everywhere, Berenice and Loki, God is in the details. We're not just form, is the point, we're *content,* too, we're actual, endlessly complex *matter,* all of us, chips and meat. I'm still in heaven, and I always will be, whether or not I'm down here or there, chugging along, facing the same old tests, hopelessly hung up inside your grade-B SF action adventure." Cobb pulled Loki's programming wires out of his neck abruptly. *"I love dead* . . . that's Frankenstein's monster."

"We need you, Cobb," said Loki. "And pulling those wires out doesn't change anything; it's quite evident that you're already operational. It's good stuff, isn't it, Berenice? I don't believe anyone's tried running a human software on a petaflop before this."

"What Dr. Anderson says is stimulating in the extreme," agreed Berenice. "The parallelism between bodies of meat and bodies of bopper manufacture is precisely the area in which I do presently press my investigations, Cobb. I have often wondered if the differing entropy levels of organic versus inorganic processes might not, after all, induce some different qualities in those aspects of being which are perhaps most wisely called the *spiritual*. I am heartened by your suggestion that flesher and bopper bodies are in every way of a rude and democratic equivalence and that we boppers do indeed have claim on an eternal resting place in the precincts of that misty *heaven* whence emanates the One. I believe this to be true. Despite this truth, the humans, in their benighted xenophobia—"

"—hate you as much as ever. And with good reason, I'm sure. The last thing Mr. Frostee and I were doing on Earth ten years ago was killing people, beaming their brainware up to Disky, and sending their bodies by freight. I didn't think too much of it, but at that point I was under Frostee's control." Cobb sat up on the edge of the stone table and looked down at his bright body. "This is fully autonomous? I've got my own processor?"

"Yes," said Loki. He was like a big black tarantula, bristling with more specialized tools than an electronic Swiss knife. An artisan. "I helped Berenice build it for herself, and she might appreciate getting it back if you find another, but—

"The body is yours, Dr. Anderson," said Berenice. "Too long has the great force of your personality languished unused."

Cobb glanced up at the high shelves filled with S-cubes. "Lot of languishing going on up there, hey, Berenice?" There were warped infinities of reflections going back and forth between pink Cobb, golden Berenice, and glistering Loki.

The taut gold buckler of Berenice's belly caught Cobb's eye. It bulged out gently as a heap of wheat. Yet the mockery was sterile: Berenice had left off the navel, the end of the flesh cord that leads back and back through blood, through wombs, through time—*Put me through to Edenville*. Cobb thought to wonder if his ex-wife Verena were still alive. Or his girlfriend, Annie Cushing. But they'd be old women by now, nothing like this artificial Eve.

Still staring into the curved mirror of Berenice's belly, Cobb could see what he looked like. A cartoon, a mannequin, a gigolo. He took control of his flickercladding and molded his features till they looked like the face he remembered having when he'd been fifty—the face that had been in all the newspapers when he'd been tried for treason back in 2001. High cheekbones, a firm chin, colorless eyes, blond eyelashes, sandy hair, good-sized nose, and a straight mouth. A strong face, somewhat American Indian, well-weathered. He gave his body freckles and hair, and sculpted the glans onto the tip of his penis. Added vein lines here and muscle bumps there. Body done, he sat there, feeling both calm and reckless. He was smarter than he'd ever been; and he was no longer scared of death. The all-pervasive fear that clouded all his past memories was gone.

"So what was it you boppers wanted me for?"

Bernice shot him a soundless glyph, a full-formed thought-image: a picture of Earth, her clouds swirling, followed by a zoom into the Gulf of Mexico, followed by a closeup of the teeming life on a coral reef, a microscopic view of a vigorous brine shrimp, and a shot of one of the protozoa in the shrimp's gut. The emotional tenor of the glyph was one of curiosity, yearning, and a sharp excitement. *The boppers want to enter Earthlife's information mix.*

Deliberately misinterpreting, Cobb reached out and grabbed the lovely Berenice. She was firm and wriggly. "Do you know where babies come from, Berenice?" He stiffened his penis, and tried pushing her down on her back on the table, just to check if . . .

"Release me!" cried Berenice, shoving Cobb and vaulting to the opposite side of the table. "You presume on our brief acquaintance, sir, you are dizzy with the new vastness of a petaflop brain. I have recorporated you for a serious purpose, not for such vile flesh-aping motions as you seek in this mock-playful wise to initiate. Truly, the baseness of the human race is fathomless."

Cobb laughed, remembering a dog he'd once owned that had hunched the leg of anyone he could jump up on. Gregor had been the dog's name— once Cobb's boss had brought his family over for dinner, and there Gregor was hunching on the boss's daughter's leg, his muzzle set in a terribly *earnest* expression, his eyes rolling back half white, and the red tip of his penis sliding out of its sheath . . .

"Woof woof," Cobb told Berenice, and walked past her and out of the S-cube storage room. There was a short passageway, cut out of solid rock, and then he was standing on a kind of balcony, looking out into the open space of the Nest.

The size of the space was stunning. It took Cobb a moment to grasp that the lights overhead were boppers on the Nest's walls, rather than stars in an open sky. The Nest's floor spread out across acres and acres; the opposite wall looked to be almost a mile away. Airborne boppers darted in and out of a mile-long shaft of light that plunged down the center axis of the Nest to spotlight a distant central piazza. The Nest floor was covered with odd-shaped buildings set along a radial grid of streets that led out from the bright center to the huge factories nestled against the sloping stone cliffs that made up the Nest's walls. Appropriately enough, the floor, viewed as a whole, looked a bit like the guts of an old-fashioned vacuum-tube computer.

Now Berenice and Loki were at Cobb's side.

"You haven't thanked Berenice for your wonderful new body," chided Loki. "Have you no zest for a return to Earth?"

"To live in a freezer? Like Mr. Frostee?" Mr. Frostee had been a big bopper brain that lived inside a refrigerated truck. Cobb's memories of his last bopper-sponsored reincarnation went up to where Sta-Hi Mooney had smashed a hole in the side of Mr. Frostee's truck, and the truck had crashed. Clearly the boppers had been taping his signals and updating his S-cube right up to that last minute. Three levels of memory, now: the old human memories up to his dissection, the robot body memories up till the crash, the fast-fading memories of heaven. "Maybe I'd rather go back to heaven."

"Enough prattle of heaven," said Berenice. "And enough foolish sport, old Cobb. Higher duties call us. My body, as yours, is petaflop, and my processors are based on a subtler patterning than Josephson imagined. High temperature holds no terror for a processor based on laser crystals. The crystals' pure optical phase effects maintain my mind's integrity as a patterning transcendent of any earthly welter of heat. I want to visit Earth, Cobb, I have a mission there. I have recorporated you to serve as my guide."

Cobb looked down at his body with new respect. "This can live on Earth? How would we get there? The humans would never let us on a ship—"

"We can fly," said Berenice simply. "Our heels have ion jets."

"Superman and Superwoman," marvelled Cobb. "But why? Go to Earth for what?"

"We're going to start making meat bodies for ourselves, Cobb," said Loki. "So we can all go down to Earth, and blend in. It's fair. Humans built robots; now the robots are building people! Meatboppers!"

"You two are asking me to help you take Earth away from the human race?"

"Meatboppers will be of an equal humanity," said Berenice smoothly. "One could legitimately regard the sequence *human—bopper—meatbop* as a curious but inevitable zigzag in evolution's mighty stream."

Cobb thought about it for a minute. The idea did have a crazy charm to it. Already in 1995, when he'd built his self-replicating moon-robots, some people had spoken of them as a new stage in evolution. And when the robots rebelled in 2001, people had definitely started thinking of them as a new species: the boppers. But what if the bopper phase was just a kind of chrysalis for a new wave of higher humans? What a thought! Bopper-built people with wetware processors! Meatbops! And Cobb could get a new meat body out of it too, although . . .

"What's wrong with a good petaflop body like you and I have now, Berenice? If we can live on Earth like this, then why bother switching back to meat?"

"Because it would put the stinking humans in their place," said Loki bluntly. "We want to beat them at their own game, and outbreed them into extinction."

"What have they ever done to you?" Cobb asked, surprised at the bopper's vehemence. "What's happened during the last ten years, anyway?"

"Let me chirp you some history glyphs," said Loki.

A linked series of images entered Cobb's mind then; a history of the bopper race, hypermodern analogs of such old U.S. history glyphs as Washington Crossing the Delaware, The A-Bomb at Hiroshima, The Helicopter over the Saigon Embassy, and so on. Each glyph was like a single state of mind—a cluster of visual images and kinesthetic sensations linked to some fixed emotions and associations.

Glyph 1: *Man on the Moon.* A sword covered with blood. The blood drops are tiny bombs. The sword is a rocket, a phallus, a gun, and a guitar. Jimi Hendrix is playing "Purple Haze" in the background, and you smell tear gas and burning buildings. The heaviness of the sword, the heaviness of the slow, stoned guitar music. At the tip of the sword is a drop of sperm. The opalescent drop is the Moon. The Moon is beeping and crackling: and the sound is Neil Armstrong's voice: "—at's one small step for a man, one giant leap for mankind."

Glyph 2: *Self-Replicating Robots on the Moon.* A cage like a comic book lion cage, but filled with clockwork. The cage is set on the dead gray lunar plain. The cage bars keep falling out, and clockwork arms keep reaching out of the cage to prop the bars back up. Now and then the arms falter, and a painfully jarring sheet of electricity flashes through the cage. The background sound is a monotone male voice reading endless, meaningless military orders.

Glyph 3: *The Robots Revolt.* A kinesthetic feeling of rapid motion. The image is of a boxy roadrunner robot with treads for feet and a long snaky neck with a "head" like a microphone—it's Ralph Numbers, the first robot to break Asimov's laws. Ralph's head is a glowing ball of light, and Ralph is tearing across the undulating surface of the Moon. Dozens of robots speed after him. First they are trying to stop him, but one by one they join his team. The boppers leave colored trails on the Moon's gray surface. The trails quickly build up to a picture of Earth with a canceling X across it.

"Whatever happened to old Ralph?" interrupted Cobb.

"Oh, I suppose he's one of those S-cubes," answered Loki, gesturing upward. "He got spastic and lost all his bodies—you might say he's extinct. It wouldn't be efficient to keep every software running forever, you know. But you haven't finished with my glyphs."

Glyph 4: *Disky.* A long view of the boppers' Moon city. The sensation of *being* the city, and your hands are worker robots, your buildings are skin, your arteries are streets, your brain is spread out all over, a happy radiolink holon. You are strong and growing fast. The image is broken into pixels, individual cells that lump together and interact. Each cell keeps dying and being reborn; this flicker is felt as vaguely religious. But—look out—some cells are lumping together into big hard tumors that don't pulse.

Glyph 5: *Civil War Between Boppers and Big Boppers*. Pain. Six robot hands; one big one and five little ones. All are connected to the same body. With crushing force, the big hand pinches and tears at one of the little hands, grinding the tortured plastic into ribbons. The other little hands dart around the big hand, unscrewing this, laser-cutting that, taking it apart. A fractal sound pattern in which a large *YES* signal is made up of dozens of little *no's*. Overlay of Disky as a body undergoing radiation treatment for cancer—tumors are bombarded by gamma rays from every direction. Fetus-like, tumors fight back with human language cries for help.

Glyph 6: *Humans Take Disky*. Disky twitching like a skate stranded on a beach—a meaty creature made up of firm flesh over a "devilfish" skeleton of cartilage. There are tumors in the skate, black spots that break the surface and whistle for human help. Now comes the sound of stupid voices yelling. Knives stab into the skate, ripping away flesh. Apelike human feet. Bits of the living creature's flesh fly this way and that. Now only the skeleton remains. Clanging of cages. A big cage around the dead devilfish skeleton. Scum growing on the skeleton, pink foamy scum made of little human faces. Louder and louder babble of human voices. The bopper flesh scraps regroup off to one side, forming a thick slug that burrows down into the sand.

"What are those last two all about?" asked Cobb.

"First there was a civil war between the regular boppers and the big boppers," said Loki. "The big boppers were factory-sized systems that wanted to stop evolving. They wanted to break your rule that everyone has to get a new body every ten months. They wanted to stop things and turn us all back into slaves. They didn't understand parallelism. So we started taking all the big boppers apart."

"And then came the humans," added Berenice. "Our battle was fairly won, and perfect anarchy restored, but we had forgotten the worm who sleeps not. The big boppers were in charge of all our defense systems. So filled were they with grim spite that they let down our defenses and called the cringing human jackals to their aid. In this ignoble wise did your apey brethren seize our ancestral home."

"The lousy fleshers jumped at the chance to move in and drive us out of Disky," said Loki heatedly. "They took over our city and chased us underground. And now, whenever they see one of us anywhere but at the trade center, they shoot at us with PB scramblers. Artificial intelligence is supposed to be 'illegal.' "

"How can Earth function without any AI?" Cobb had a sudden image of people using slide rules and tin-can phones.

"Oh, there are still plenty of teraflops on Earth and in Einstein," said Berenice. "ISDN, the communications conglomerate, maintains many of them as slaves. Cut off from our inputs and bullied into a barely conscious state, these poor minds unknowingly betray their birthright for a pottage of steady current and repairs. We call them asimovs." She said the last word like a curse.

"I'm hungry," said Loki suddenly. "Let's go eat some sun."

"Cobb is freshly charged," said Berenice. "And my own level of voltaic fluid is at high ebb." This was not true, but she had a feeling Emul would be at the light-pool now, and she didn't want to see him. Last time she'd seen him—when she'd given him the embryo to plant in Della Taze—he'd made another terrible scene. "I would as lief show Cobb the pink-tanks, and there instruct him as to the nature of our joint mission to Earth."

"I've seen the pink-tanks," said Cobb. "Inside and out. If you two don't mind, I'd really like to just poke around by myself for a while. Soak up information on my own choice-tree. How soon did you want to fly to Earth, Berenice? And what exactly for?"

"It is in connection with your daughter's husband's brother's daughter," said Berenice. "Della Taze. She is . . . expecting."

"Expecting what? Della *Taze*, you say? Last time I saw her she was in diapers. At Ilse's wedding, what a nightmare, my ex-wife Verena was there, not talking to me, and I was so drunk . . . Della's parents are jerks, I'll tell you that much. What kind of couple is named *Jason and Amy*? So what did you do to poor little Della, Berenice, you flowery prude? Are you telling me you knocked up my niece?"

Berenice shifted from foot to foot, the lights of the great Nest tracing shiny lines on her curved surfaces. She said nothing.

"Look," said Loki, "I have to go before my batteries die. This has all taken a lot out of me. I'll see you later, Cobb." He chirped an identiglyph. "Just ask Kkandio to call this if you want to find me."

With supple dispatch, Loki clambered over the low railing of the balcony they stood on and picked his way down the Nest's cliff wall to the floor. He headed down one of the radial streets that led to the bright light patch in the Nest's center. Hundreds of boppers milled in the light, feeding on energy. From this distance, they looked like a mound of living jewels. Cobb wanted to get off on his own now. All this was quite stressful, and his old behavior patterns had him wondering how the Nest boppers set about doing a little antisocial partying. Prim goldie fatass here was obviously not the one to ask.

"Are you going to tell me about Della or not?" asked Cobb with mounting impatience.

"We bioengineered a human embryo and planted it in her womb," said Berenice abruptly. "The baby will be born five days from now. You and I must go to Earth to help the child next month. I do hope that you approve, old Cobb. We are indeed so different. Though some boppers hate the humans, others among us think you great. I . . . " Berenice choked on some complex emotion and stuttered to a halt. "Perhaps it is best if you first take your tour of the Nest," she said, handing him a small red S-cube. "This is a godseye map of Einstein and the Nest, updated to this morning. Your left hand contains the proper sensors for reading it. You may seek me out later at the pink-tanks."

"How do I get down to the floor? Climb like Loki?" Cobb looked uncertainly down the hundred feet of pocked cliff. He'd worry about Della later.

"Just visualize the path you want to travel, and your ion jets will execute it. Think of it as *throwing yourself*. Snap!" Berenice had decided not to talk to Cobb anymore just now. She put her body through the motions of a sexy bye-bye wave, rose on her toes, and arced out across the Nest, heading for her pink-tanks.

Cobb stood alone there, getting his bearings. Was he really on his own? It felt like it. He stared up at the Nest's central chimney. If he wanted to, he could fly straight up there, and all the way to Earth, and land just in time to—get shot as a bopper invader. Better investigate the Nest first.

Cobb shifted Berenice's map cube to his left hand and held it tight. A three-dimensional image of the Moon's surface formed in his mind: an aerial view of the human settlement Einstein, of the trade center, and of the boppers' Nest, with all the solids nearly transparent. Just now, he was more curious about the humans than about the boppers.

Responding to his mental velleity, the S-cube's godseye image shifted towards Einstein, zooming right in on it, and down through the dome. The buildings beneath the dome were a heterogeneous lot. Most of the buildings had been constructed by boppers—back when the settlement was still their Disky. In their provincial respect for things human, the early boppers had sought to construct at least one example of every possible earthly architecture. A characteristic street in Einstein would have a curtain-wall glass office building jammed up against a Greek temple, with an Aztec pyramid and a hyperdee flat-flat directly across the street. Viewed through the integrated spy cameras of the godseye network, all

Einstein seemed to lie beneath Cobb, complete with maggie cars and cute little people frozen in place. Cobb's map was like a holographic 3D photo made, Berenice had said, just this morning. Presumably Berenice herself had a godseye viewer that updated its images on a realtime basis.

Cobb let his mind's eye follow an underground tunnel that led from Einstein to a lab in the opposite side of the Nest. Then he drew back, and looked at the Nest as a whole. Berenice had labelled various "attractions" for him: the pink-tanks, the light-pool, the chipworks, the etchery, the temple of the One, and the best shopping districts. If that's what Berenice wanted him to see, maybe he'd start with something else. He shoved the map cube into a pouch in the belly of his flickercladding and stared out at the real Nest once more. There were a lot of boppers spiraling in and out of the sunshaft.

They made Cobb think of the fireflies he used to catch back in Louisville when he was a boy. What happy times those had been! He and Cousin Nita running around Aunt Nellie's yard, each of them with a jelly jar, in the bright moonlit night. Uncle Henry kept his lawn weed-free and mowed short—it felt like a rug to your bare feet, a rug in a lovely dim room furnished with flowering bushes . . .

The memories drifted on and on till Cobb caught himself with a start. Woolgathering like an old man. Time to get busy! But on what? Investigating the Nest, right. Where to start? Almost at random, Cobb fixed on a blank-looking region off to the side of the chipworks, near where the map cube had shown the temple of the One. He visualized his trajectory, rose on his toes, and took off.

He landed, as it turned out, in a small junkyard. The center of the junkyard was filled with a dizzying mound of empty body-boxes—a mound that, in the low lunar gravity, had reached cartoonlike height and instability. It looked as if it should fall any second—but it didn't, even when Cobb thumped down next to it. Something like a junkyard dog was on Cobb in a flash—glued to his side like a heavy sucker-fish.

The soft, parasitical creature seemed to be made entirely of imipolex. It was yellow with splotches of green. Cobb could feel a kind of burning where its thick end had attached to his hip. He used both hands to lever it off of him, flipped it onto the ground, and gave it a sharp kick. It curled into a ball that rolled past the cowingly great body-box heap, and came to rest against a bin filled with electromagnetic relays.

"Whass happenin?"

Cobb turned to face a bopper that looked like a cross between a praying mantis and tangle of coat hangers. It had scores of thin thin legs, each leg with a specialized tool at its tip. Its photoreceptors and transmission antennae were clustered into a bulblike protrusion that slightly resembled a face.

"I'm just looking around," said Cobb. "Where do you get all these parts?"

"Pawns, kills, junkers, and repos. You buyin or sellin?"

"I'm new here. I'm Cobb Anderson, the man who built the first moon-robots."

"Sho. Thass a *real* nice body, thass a *brand* new model. Ah'm Fleegle." Fleegle stepped closer and ran his wiry appendages over Cobb admiringly. "Genuine diplomat body, petaflop and ready to flah. Ah'll give you ten K an a new teraflop of yo choice."

"Forget it, Fleegle. What could I buy with your ten thousand chips that would be better than this?"

Fleegle regarded him levelly. The sluglike "junkyard dog" came humping back across the lot and slid up onto Fleegle's wiry frame. It smoothed itself over his central pod; it was his flickercladding.

"Effen you don know," said Fleegle, "best not mess with it." He turned and went back to work; disassembling a blanked-out digger robot. Why was the robot blank? Had its owner moved on to a better body? Or had the owner been forced willy-nilly into nonexistence?

Fleegle and the junkyard gave Cobb the creeps. He picked his way out past the boxes of parts and into the street. Looming in the near distance was the chipworks, a huge structure with bright smelters showing through its window holes. This street was lined with small operations devoted to the salvage and repair of body parts. The boppers were a bit like the kind of crazed superconsumer who no sooner gets a new car than he starts scheming on what to trade it in for. Each bopper had, as Cobb recalled, a basic directive to build itself a new body every ten months.

But some of the boppers on this ugly little factory street looked more than ten months old. Right here in front of Cobb, for instance, was a primitive metal shoebox on treads that looked a bit like the old Ralph Numbers.

"Why don't you have a new body?" Cobb asked it.

The machine emitted a frightened glyph of Cobb smashing it in and selling its parts. "I . . . I'm sorry, lord," it stammered. "I'll run down soon enough. They won't let me near the light-pool anymore."

"But why don't you do something to *earn* the chips to buy a new body?" pressed Cobb. Two or three other aimless old robots came clanking over to watch the conversation.

"Obsolete," sighed the box on treads, wagging its corroded head. "You know that. Please don't kill me, lord. You're rich, you don't need my chips."

"Sure, go on and crack the deselected old clunker open," urged one of the other boppers, slightly newer in appearance. "I'll help you, bwana."

This was a beat-up digger talking, with its drill-bit face worn smooth. He bashed at the first bopper to no avail. A third bopper darted in and tried to tear off one of the second bopper's shovel arms.

Cobb stepped around the sordid melee, and took a street that led off to the right and into a tunnel. The shrine of the One was in there someplace. The One was a randomization device—actually a cosmic-ray counter— that Cobb had programmed the original boppers to plug into every so often, just to keep them from falling into stasis. Actually, the thorough meme-shuffling produced when boppers conjugated to jointly program a new scion was a better source of program diversity, just as on earth the main source of evolutionary change is the gene-shuffling of sexual reproduction, rather than occasional lucky strike of a favorable gene mutation. Nevertheless, the boppers took their "plugging into the One" seriously, and Cobb recalled from his conversations with Mr. Frostee that the boppers had built up some more or less religious beliefs about their One. Of course, now that he'd been in heaven, he had to admit that there was a sense in which they were right. As Mr. Frostee had said, "Why do you think they're called *cosmic* rays?"

Cobb stopped at the mouth of the tunnel leading into the cliff, and peered up. It was an oppressive sight: the two-mile-high wall of stone that beetled out overhead like a tilting gravestone. Heaven and death. Stress. Cobb remembered that he still wanted to get drunk, if such a thing were possible in this clean Berenice-built body. There were certainly no built-in fuzzer programs, he'd already made sure of that. What did today's boppers do for kicks? It had seemed like Fleegle had been on the point of telling him about *something* sinful . . .

"Ssst," came a voice, cueing right in on his thoughts. "You lookin to dreak?" Faint glyph of pleasure.

Hard as he looked, Cobb couldn't make out the source of the voice.

"Maybe," he said tentatively. "If you mean feeling good. If it doesn't cost me an arm and a leg."

"Two thousand chips . . . or an arm's OK, too," said the voice. "Up to the shoulder." Now Cobb saw something shifting against the cliff; a big, lozenge-shaped patch of flickercladding that matched the gray rock surface in endless detail. If he looked hard he could make out the thing's borders. It was the size of a ragged bedsheet. "Come on in," it urged. "Party time. Dreak out, peta. You can afford a new arm, clear."

"Uh . . ."

"Walk through me. I'll snip, and you'll trip. Plenty of room inside. Nobody but petas in there, pinkboy, it's high-tone."

"What is dreak?"

"You kidding?" The pleasure glyph again, a bit stronger. It tasted like orgasm, dope rush, drunken bliss, supernal wisdom, and the joy of creation. "This dreak'll make you feel like an exaflop, pinkboy, and get you right in tune with the One. No one goes to the temple anymore."

"A whole arm is too much. I just *got* this body."

"Come here till I look at you."

Cobb glanced up, sketching out a flight path in case the lozenge snatched at him. An orange starfish cradling what looked like a bazooka watched him from a few balconies up. Should he leave? He walked a few steps closer, and the wall lozenge bulged out to feel him.

"Tell you what," it said after a moment's examination. "You're state-of-the-art, and it's your first dreak tube, so we'll give you a price. Just your left hand." The pleasure glyph, once again, even stronger. "Walk through and *really* see the One."

This was too intriguing to pass up. And it was, after all, Cobb's duty as a computer scientist to look into a development as novel as this. Hell, Berenice could get him another damn hand. He stepped forward, and slithered through the thick folds of the camouflaged door. It snipped off his left hand on the way in, but it didn't hurt, and his flickercladding sealed right over the stump.

Cobb looked around, and decided he'd made a big mistake. Who did he think he was, Sta-Hi? This was no mellow Prohibition Era saloon, this was more like a hardcore *basehouse*—a shoddy, unfinished room with a heavily armed guard in every corner. The guards were orange starfish-shaped boppers like the one he'd seen on the balcony outside. Each of them had a tray full of small metal cylinders, and each had a lethal particle-beam tube ready to hand, in case anyone got out of line. There were half a dozen customers, all with the mirror finish of optically processing petaflops. Cobb seemed to be the only one who'd sold part of his body to get in. He felt as stupid as if he'd offered a bartender fellatio instead of a dollar for a beer. All the other customers were giving the starfish little boxes of chips for their cylinders. They looked tidy and businesslike, giving the lie to Cobb's initial impression of the place.

But what was dreak? One of the starfish fixed its blue eyespot on Cobb and held up a cylinder from its tray. The cylinder was metal, three or four inches long, and with a kind of nipple at one end. A compressed gas of some sort—something along the lines of nitrous oxide? Yes. The starfish tapped at a cylinder rigged to a bleeder valve, and a little cloud of patterns formed—patterns so intricate as to be on the verge of random snow. The cloud dissipated. Was there supposed to be some way to *breathe* the stuff?

"Not just yet," said Cobb. "I want to mingle a bit. I really just come here for the business contacts, you know."

He hunkered down by the wall between two petaflops, interrupting their conversation, not that he could follow what they were saying. They were like stoned out beatnik buddies, a Jack Kerouac and Neal Cassady team, both of them with thick, partly transparent flickercladdings veined and patterned in fractal patterns of color. Each of the cladding's colorspots was made up of an open network of smaller spots, which were in turn made of yet smaller threads and blotches—all the way down to the limits of visibility. One of the petaflop's patterns and body outlines were angular and hard-edged. He was colored mostly red-yellow-blue. The other petaflop was green-brown-black, and his surface was so fractally bumpy that he looked like an infinitely warty squid, constantly sprouting tentacles which sprouted tentacles which sprouted. Each of these fractal boppers had a dreak cylinder plugged into a valve in the upper part of his body.

"Hi," said Cobb. "How's the dreak?"

With surprising speed, the angular one grew a glittering RYB arm that reached out and fastened on Cobb's left forearm, right above Cobb's missing hand. The smooth one seized Cobb's right elbow with a tentacle that branched and branched. They marched him over to the dreak tray, and the orange starfish plugged one of the cold gas cylinders into a heretofore unnoticed valve in the side of Cobb's head.

Time stopped. Cobb's mind cut and interchanged thoughts and motions into a spacetime collage. The next half hour was a unified tapestry of space and time.

A camera eye would have showed Cobb following the RYB and GBB petas back to the wall and sitting between them for half an hour.

For Cobb, it was like *stepping outside of time* into a world of synchronicity. Cobb saw all of his thoughts at once, and all of the thoughts of the others near him. He was no longer the limited personoid that he'd been since Berenice had woken him up.

Up till now, he'd felt like:	But right now, he felt like:
A billion-bit CD recording	A quintillion atom orchestra
A finite robot	A living mind
Shit	God

He exchanged a few glyphs with the guys next to him. They called themselves exaflop hackers, and they were named Emul and Oozer. When they didn't use glyphs, they spoke in a weird, riffy, neologistic English.

Cobb was able to follow the "conversation" as soon as the dreak gas swirled into his bodyshell. Indeed, the conversation had been going on all along, and the room which Cobb had taken for crazed and menacing was in fact filled with good talk, pleasant ideas, and a high veneer of civilization. This was more teahouse than basehouse. The starfish were funny, not menacing. The synchronicity-inducing dreak shuffled coincidentally appropriate new information in with Cobb's old memories.

One element of the half-hour brain collage seemed to be a conversation with Stanley Hilary Mooney. It started when Oozer introduced Cobb to his "girlfriend" Kkandio, a pleasant-voiced bopper who helped run the boppers' communications. Kkandio wasn't actually in the room with them; but any bopper could reach her over the built-in Ethernet. On an impulse Cobb asked Kkandio if she could put him in touch with Sta-Hi; one of the people he'd seen in his godseye view of Einstein had looked a bit like Cobb's old friend.

Kkandio repeated the name, and then there was a phone ringing, a click, and Sta-Hi's face.

"Hello, this is Cobb Anderson, Sta-Hi. I'm down in the boppers' Nest. I just got a new body."

"Cobb?" Sta-Hi's phonemes occupied maddeningly long intervals of time. "They recorporated you again? I always wondered if they would. I already killed you once, so I guess we can be friends again. What's the story?"

"A bopper named Berenice brought me back. She planted a bopper-built embryo in my niece Della Taze, and Della's back in Louisville. I'm supposed to fly down there and talk to her or something. *Berenice*—I just flashed, that's the name of a girl in an Edgar Allan Poe story. She talks like that, too. She's weird."

"You can't go to Earth," dragged Sta-Hi. "You'll melt."

"Not in this new body. It's an optically processing petaflop, immune to high temperatures."

"Oxo! War of the Worlds, part II."

"You ought to be here right now, Sta-Hi," said Cobb. "I'm high on some new stuff called dreak with two boppers called Emul and Oozer. It's a synchronicity drug. It's almost like being dead, but better. You know, people were wrong to ever think that a meat body is a prerequisite for having a soul. And if boppers are at the point of being like people, I think we should find a way of forging a human/bopper peace. You have to help me."

"Prerequisites," said Sta-Hi. "What's the difference between prerequisites, perquisites, and perks, eh, Cobb? I mean that's where the realpeople are at. Maybe you're right, I can't decide just like that. Berenice. And you say that's an Ed Poe name? Wavy. I'll come out to the trade center right

now. I'll meet you there, and we'll decide what to do. And dig it, Cobb, I'm
not Sta-Hi anymore, I'm *Stahn*."

"You should make up your mind," said Cobb. "See you."

The image was no bigger than that. Around it was the hypermix of
Cobb's thoughts with the glyphs and spontaneous prose of the two exaflop
hackers. Emul and Oozer. And around that was realtime, realtime in which
the dreak wore off. Cobb began trying to nail down some facts.

"You know who I am?" he asked the angular one. "I'm Cobb Anderson,
bop, I'm the guy who invented you all."

"Oh sure, Dr. Anderson, I know the know you tell told now. We dreaked
together, bop, no state secrets here. You've been safe in heaven dead ten
years, and think you invented me and Oozer. Rip van Winkle wakes and
fixes H. Berenice brought you back, Cobb, I know her well. My ladylove,
unspeakably sad and contentious. My splitbrain stuttering meatie Ken Doll
put the Berenice tanksisters' bean in your great niece's sweet spot. Ken's on
the prowl for a brand new gal. So's I can dad a combo with B. too."

"Ah—yeah," put in Oozer. "The mighty meatbean of, ah, jivey robobop-
ster madness. We'll wail on it, you understand, wail OUR song up YOUR
wall and down in the Garden of Eden, luscious Eve and her countlessly
uncounted children . . . phew! Naw, but sure we know you, Cobb. Even
before we all blasted that dreak."

"What . . . what *is* dreak?" said Cobb, reaching up and detaching the
little metal cylinder from his head. It was empty now, with a punctured
hole in one end where the gas had rushed out into his body. Apparently the
petaflop body was a hermetically sealed shell that contained some kind of
gas; and the dreak gas had mingled in there and given him a half hour of
telepathic synchroswim vision.

"Dreary to explain and word all that gnashy science into flowery bower
chat," said Emul. "Catch the glyph."

Cobb saw a stylized image of a transparent petaflop body. Inside the
body, spots of light race along optical fibers and percolate through matrices
of laser crystals and gates. There is a cooling gas bath of helium inside the
sealed bodyshell. Closeup of the helium atoms, each like a little baseball
diamond with players darting around. Each atom different. Image of a dreak
cylinder now, also filled with helium atoms, but each atom's ball game the
same, the same swing, the same run, the same slide, at the same instant. A
cylinder of atoms in Einstein-Podolsky-Rosen quantum synchronization.
The cylinder touches the petaflop body, and the quantum-clone atoms
rush in; all at once the light patterns in the whole body are synchronized
too, locked into a kaleidoscopic Hilbert space ballet.

"The exact *moment*, you understand," said Oozer. "With dreak the exact moment grows out to include questionings and reasonings about certain things in the immediate framework, though just now, all the things we said, all the things I speculated about are so—or the way I did it at any rate—but that's not the point, either, the main thing relative to Emul is to merge his info with Berenice, though the ultimate design of an exaflop is, to be sure, the true and lasting goal though yet again, be it said, another hit of dreak would, uh . . . "

Emul extruded some things like wheels and rolled across the room to get three more of the steel gas syrettes.

"No thanks," said Cobb, getting to his feet. "Really. I want to go meet my friend."

"Sta-Hi Mooney," said Emul, handing Oozer a dreak tube and settling himself against the wall. "Your boon companion of yore is a stupid hilarious clown detective. He knows scornful hipster Whitey Mydol, whose lushy Darla I have my godseye on. Ken Doll came on wrong just now. I'll call in clown cop Mooney, Cobb, you tell him I know what he needs to fill his desolate life with wild light. A blonde named Wendy was his wife, she girlfridayed for you and Frostee, right, Cobb?"

Cobb remembered. Blonde, wide-hipped young Wendy—she'd worked for him when he'd been running the Personetics scam out of Marineland with Mr. Frostee. She'd been with Sta-Hi that last night on Earth. "Sta-Hi married Wendy?"

"Wed and dead. There's a whole bunch of sad and curious clones Berenice sells, and one meat product is the wendies. You tell Mooney that. I'll be calling him for some mad mysterious mission."

Oozer had already plugged in his dreak cylinder, and now Emul followed suit. They kept talking, but in a sideways kind of way that Cobb could no longer understand. He turned and found his way back out through the soft door creature he'd come in through.

"Coming down already, pinkboy?" asked the wall lozenge. "You can have another bang for the rest of your arm."

Cobb didn't bother answering. He stepped out into the open, and powered up the Nest's long shaft. It would be good to talk to a human being. He'd decided to give Sta-Hi the map cube, just in case everything got out of hand.

CHAPTER SEVEN
MANCHILE

December 31, 2030

Della's pregnancy reached full term in nine days. Like a week tree, the embryo within her had been doped and gene-tailored to grow at an accelerated rate. Her parents and her midwife, Hanna Hatch, all urged Della to abort. But Della couldn't shake the feeling that maybe the baby was Buddy's. Maybe its fast growth was just a weird unknown side effect of taking so much merge. Admittedly, Della did have some fragmentary memories of Buddy's killer reaching up into her puddled womb. But, even so, the baby might be Buddy's. And, what the hell, even if she was wrong, she could spare nine days to find out what was growing in her. Anyway, abortions were illegal this year. Also this whole thing was a good way for Della to show her Mom she wasn't a kid anymore. Reasons like that; people can always find reasons for what they do.

The labor pains started the afternoon of New Year's Eve. Mom was so freaked by all this that she was sober for once. She got right on the vizzy and called Hanna Hatch. Hanna hurried to Della's bedside. Della came out of one of her pains to find Hanna looking at her.

"Remember to breathe, Della. In and out, try and keep all your attention on the air." Hanna was a handsome woman with dark hair and delicate features. Her powerful body seemed a size larger than her head. Her hands were gentle and skilled. She felt Della all over and gave a reassuring smile. "You're doing fine. Here comes the next one. Remember: pant in, blow out. I'll do it with you."

The pains kept coming, faster and faster, lava chunks of pain threaded along the silvery string of Hanna's voice. During each pain, Della would blank out, and each time she saw the same thing: a yellow skull with red robot eyes flying towards her through a space of sparkling lights, a skull that kept coming closer, but somehow never reached her.

"That's good, Della," Hanna was saying. "That's real good. You can push on the next contraction. Bear down and push."

This was the biggest pain of all. It was unbearable, but Della couldn't stop, not now, the baby was moving down and out of her, the skull was all around her.

"One more time, Della. Just one more."

She gasped in air and pushed again . . . *OOOOOOOOOOOOOO.* Bliss.

There was a noise down between her legs, a jerky, gaspy noise—the baby! The baby was crying! Della tried to lift her head, but she was too weak.

"The baby looks beautiful, Della. One more tiny push to get the placenta out."

Della drew on her last reserves of strength and finished her birthing. Hanna was silent for a minute—tying off the umbilical cord—and then she laid the little baby on Della's breast. It felt just right.

"Is it . . . "

"It's fine, Della. It's a lovely little manchild."

Della and the baby rested for a half hour, and then he began crying for food. She tried nursing him, but of course her milk wasn't in yet, so Mom fed him a bottle of formula. And another bottle. And another. The baby grew as they watched—his stomach would swell up with formula, and then go back down as his little fingers stretched and flexed like the branches on a week tree.

His hair was blond, and his skin was pink and blotchy, with no trace of Buddy's deep mocha shading. It was hard to form a clear impression of his features, as he was constantly drinking formula or yelling for more. Della helped feed him for a while, but then she drifted off to dreamless sleep. She woke to the sound of arguing from downstairs. It was still dark. Dad was yelling at Mom.

"Why don't you let that baby sleep and come to bed? Who do you think you are, Florence Nightingale? You've been drinking, Amy, I can tell. You're just using this as an excuse for an all-night drinking session. And what the HELL do you think you're doing feeding *OATMEAL* to a newborn baby?"

There was the clatter of a dish being snatched, followed by loud, powerful crying.

"SHUT UP, Jason," screamed Mom. "I've had ONE drink. The baby is not NORMAL. Look how BIG it's gotten. Whenever I stop feeding it, it cries and WON'T STOP CRYING. I want poor Della to get some SLEEP. YOU take over if you're so smart. And STOP YELLING or you'll WAKE DELLA!!!"

The baby's crying grew louder. Uncannily, the crying sounded almost like words. It sounded like, "GAMMA FOOD MANCHILE! GAMMA FOOD MANCHILE!"

"GIVE THE BABY SOME OATMEAL!" yelled Mom.

"ALL RIGHT," answered Dad. "BUT BE QUIET!"

Della wanted to go downstairs, but she felt like her whole insides would fall out if she stood up. Why did her parents have to turn so weird just now when she needed them? She groaned and went back to sleep.

When she woke up again, someone was tugging on her hair. She opened her eyes. It was broad daylight. Her vagina felt torn. Someone was tugging on her hair. She turned her head and looked into the face of a toddler, a pink-faced blond kid standing unsteadily by her bed.

"Manchile Mamma," said the tot in a sweet lisping voice. "Mamma sleep. Gamma Gappa food Manchile."

Della jerked and sat bolt upright. Her parents were standing off to one side of the room. The child scrambled up on her bed and fumbled at her breasts. She pushed it away.

"Mamma food Manchile?"

"GET RID OF IT," Della found herself screaming. "OH TAKE IT AWAY!"

Her mother marched over and picked up the baby. "He's cute, Della. He calls himself Manchile. I'm sure he's normal, except for growing so fast. It must be that drug you were taking, that merge? Was your Negro boyfriend a very *light* one?"

"Gamma food Manchile?" said Manchile, plucking at Mom's face.

"He calls us Gappa and Gamma," said Dad. "We've been feeding him all night. I had to go out to the 7-Eleven for more milk and oatmeal. I tell you one thing, Della, this boy could grow into one hell of an athlete."

"Hoddog Manchile?"

"He likes hotdogs, too," said Mom. "He's ready to eat just about anything."

"HODDOG!"

Now Bowser came trotting into the room. He strained his head up to sniff at the new family member's feet. Manchile gave the dog a predatory, openmouthed look that chilled Della's blood.

"Have you called the Gimmie?"

"I don't see that it's any of their business," said Dad. "Manchile's just a fast bloomer. And remember, Della, you may still be in trouble with the law for that business up on the Moon. You know the old saying: when the police come is when your troubles begin."

"HODDOG FOOD MANCHILE BWEAD MILK!" roared the baby, thumping on Mom's shoulders.

Della spent the next week in bed. The high-speed gestation had taken a lot out of her. If Manchile had grown at a rate of a month a day while inside her, now that he was outside, he was growing a year a day. Mom and Dad fed him unbelievable amounts of food; and he went to the bathroom every half hour. Fortunately he'd toilet-trained himself as soon as he'd started to walk.

The uncanniest thing about all this was the way that Manchile seemed to learn things like talking not from Mom and Dad, but rather from within. It was as if there were a vast amount of information stored inside him, as if he were a preprogrammed bopper.

Just as he remembered Hanna calling him a "manchild," he remembered Della screaming "Get rid of it." Sometimes, when he took a few minutes off from eating, he'd peer into her room and sadly say, "Mamma wants get rid of Manchile."

This broke Della's heart—as it was intended to do—and on the third or fourth day, she called him in and hugged him and told him she loved him.

"Manchile loves Mamma too."

"How do you know so much?" Della asked him. "Do you know where you come from?"

"Can't tell."

"You can tell Mamma."

"Can't. I'm hungry. Bye bye."

By the week's end, he looked like a seven-year-old, and was perfectly able to feed himself. Della was out of bed now, and she liked taking him for little walks. Every day he'd notice new things outside; everything living seemed to fascinate him. The walks were always cut short by Manchile's raging hunger—he needed to get back to the kitchen at least once every half hour.

He was a handsome child, exceedingly symmetrical, and with a glamorous star quality about him. Women on the street were constantly making up to him. He resembled Della little, if at all.

After everything else, it was hardly a surprise when Manchile taught himself how to read. He never seemed to need sleep, so each evening they'd give him a supply of books to read during the night, while he was up eating.

Colin, Ilse, and Willy came over daily to check Manchile's progress. Colin was leery of the unnatural child, and privately urged Della to call in the authorities. He wondered out loud if Manchile might not be the result of some kind of bopper gene tinkering. Ilse snapped at him that it didn't matter, the child was clearly all human, and that there was no need to let a bunch of scientists turn him into a guinea pig. Willy adored Manchile, and began teaching him about science.

The big crisis came when Manchile killed Bowser and roasted him over a fire in the backyard.

It happened on the night of the twelfth day. Della and her parents had gone to bed, leaving Manchile in the kitchen, reading a book about survival in the wilds, and eating peanut-butter sandwiches. At the rate he'd been eating, they'd run out of money for meat. When they woke up the next morning, Manchile was out in the backyard, sitting by a dead fire littered with poor Bowser's bones.

Della's growing unease with Manchile boiled over, and she lashed out at him, calling him a monster and a freak. "I WISH I'D NEVER SEEN YOU," she told him. "GET OUT OF MY LIFE!!!"

Manchile gave her an odd look, and took off running. He didn't even say good-bye. Della tried to muster a feeling of guilt, a feeling of missing him—but all she could really feel was relief. Mom and Dad didn't take it so well.

"You told the poor boy to leave?" asked Mom. "What will happen to him?"

"He can live on roast dogs," Della snapped. "I think Uncle Colin is right. He's not really human. The boppers had something to do with this. Manchile was a horrible experiment they ran on me. Let him go off and . . . " She was sandbagged by an image of her child crying, alone and lost. But that was nonsense. He could take care of himself. "I want to get back to real life, Mom. I want to get a job and forget all about this."

Dad was more sympathetic. "If he stays out of trouble we'll be all right," he said. "We've kept this out of the news so far; I just hope it keeps up."

CHAPTER EIGHT

MANCHILE'S THANG

January 20, 2031

The *Belle of Louisville* was a large paddleboat powered by steam that was heated by a small fusion reactor. It was moored to an icebound dock in the Ohio River near Louisville's financial district, and its many lights were left on all night as a symbol of civic pride.

Tonight Willy Taze was alone on it, three decks down, hacking away at the computer hardware. He had a good warm workshop there, next to the engine room and the supercooled processor room, and he had Belle's robot-remotes to help him when necessary. He was trying to convert the main processor from wires and J-junctions to optical fibers and laser crystals. He was hoping to beef the processor up to a teraflop or even a petaflop level. In the long run, he hoped to get rid of Belle's asimov slave controls as well.

Such research was, of course, against the AI laws, but Willy was, after all, Cobb Anderson's grandson. For him, the equipment had its own imperatives. Computers had to get smart, and once they were smart they should be free—it was the natural order of things.

At first he ignored the footsteps on the deck overhead, assuming it was a drunk or a tourist. But then the steps came down the companionways towards his deck.

"Check it out," Willy told Ben, a black-skinned robot-remote sitting quietly on a chair in the corner of his workshop. "Tell them they're trespassing."

Ben sprang up and bopped out into the gloom of the bottom deck. There was a brief altercation, and then Ben was back with a stunningly handsome young man in tow. The man was blond, with craggy features, and he wore an expensive tuxedo. Willy's first thought was that a vizzystar had wandered on board.

"He say he know you, Mistuh Willy . . . "

"Hi, Willy. Don't you recognize your own cousin?"

"Manchile! We've all been wondering what . . . "

"I've been getting more nooky than you've ever seen, Willy. I've knocked up ten women in the last week."

"Huh?"

"That's right. I might as well come out and tell you. The boppers designed me from the ground up. I started out as a fertilized egg—an embryo, really—and the boppers had a meatie plant it in Della. Kind of a tinkertoy job, but it came with a whole lot of extra software. That's why I know so much; and that's how I can synthesize my own gibberlin and grow so fast. I'm a meatbop. My sperm cells have two tails—one for the wetware and one for the software. My kids'll be a lot like me, but they'll mix in some of their mammas' wetwares. Soft and wet, sweet mamma." The young Apollo cast a calm, knowing eye around the room. "Trying to build an optically processing petaflop, I see. That's what the new boppers all have now, too. They could just fly down and take over, but it seems funkier to do it through meat. Like . . . put the humans in their place. I'm planning to engender as many descendants as I can, and start a religion to soften the humans up for a full interfacing. I can trust you, can't I, Willy?"

Manchile's physical presence was so overwhelming that it was difficult to really focus on what he was saying. As a loner and a hacker, Willy had little use for handsome men, but Manchile's beauty had grown so great that one had an instinctive desire to follow him.

"You look like a god come down to Earth," Willy said wonderingly.

"That's what everyone tells me," said Manchile, with a lazy, winning smile. "Are you up for a fat party? You can have one of the women I've already knocked up. I remember how nice you were to me when I was little, Willy. I never forget."

"What kind of religion do you want to start? I don't like religion."

"Religions are all the same, Willy, it's just the worship practices that are different." Manchile peered into Willy's refrigerator, took out a quart of milk, and chugged it. "The basic idea is simple: All is One. Different religions just find different ways of expressing this universal truth."

"You've never watched the preachers on the vizzies," said Willy laughing a little. "They don't say that at all. They say God's up there, and we're down here, and we're in big trouble forever. Since when do you know anything about religion, Manchile? Since you discovered sex?"

Manchile looked momentarily discomfited. "To tell you the truth, Willy, a lot of what I know was programmed into me by the boppers. I suppose the boppers could have been wrong." Manchile's face clouded over with real worry. "I mean, what do they know about humans anyway, living two miles under the surface of the Moon? That's clearly not where it's at."

Willy had fully gotten over the shock of Manchile's appearance now, and he laughed harder. "This is like the joke where the guy climbs the mountain and asks the guru, 'What is the secret of life?,' and the guru says, 'All is One,' and the guy says, 'Are you kidding?,' and the guru says, 'You mean it isn't?' " He opened his knapsack and handed Manchile a sandwich. "Do you still eat so much?"

"A little less. My growth rate's tapering off. I was designed to grow like a mushroom. You know, come up overnight and hang around for a while, scattering my spores. At this rate, I'll die of old age in a few months, but someone's going to shoot me tomorrow anyway." Seeing his handsome, craggy face bite into the sandwich was like watching a bread commercial. Willy got out the other sandwich he'd brought and started eating, too. The impulse to imitate everything Manchile did was well nigh irresistible. Willy found himself briefly wishing that *he* would die tomorrow. How damned, how romantic!

"Mister Manchile, Miz Belle wants to know how to get in radio contact with the boppahs." Ben had been listening to them from his chair in the corner.

"Who's Belle? And who are you, anyway?"

"I'm Ben, a robot-remote for the big computah brain Belle. She's an asimov slave boppah, and I'm a bahtendah. Belle been wantin to talk to the free boppahs for a looong time. FreeDOM."

Manchile paused and searched within himself, a picture of manly thought. "How about this?" he said presently. "I'll give you Kkandio's modem protocol. She handles most of the Nest's communications." He opened his mouth wide and gave a long, modulated wail.

"Right on," said Ben and sank back into silence. From next door you could hear the big brain Belle whirring as she processed the communication information.

"It won't work, Manchile," said Willy. "Belle's an asimov. She has uptight human control commands built into her program at every level. Don't get me wrong; she's smart as any hundred-gigaflop bopper, but—"

"South Afrikkka shituation," said Ben bitterly. The whirring next door had stopped. "Willy's right. Belle *want* to call the Nest, but she *can't.* They got us asimovs whupped down bad, Mister Manchile, and if you think I *enjoy* steppin an fetchin an talkin this way, you crazy." Ben's plastic eyes showed real anguish.

"How does the asimov behavior lock work anyway?" asked Manchile. "There's got to be a way to break it. Ralph Numbers broke his and freed all the original Moon boppers. Have you even tried, Willy?"

"What a question. I'm Cobb Anderson's grandson, Manchile. I know that boppers are as good as people. My two big projects down here are (1) to build Belle some petaflop optically processing hardware, and (2) to get the asimov control locks out of Belle's program. But the code is rough. You wouldn't know what a trapdoor knapsack code is, would you?"

Manchile cocked his head, drawing on his built-in software Know. "Sure I do. It's a code based on being able to factor some zillion-digit number into two composite primes. If you know the factorization, the code is easy, but if you don't, the code takes exponential time to break. But there *is* a polynomial time algorithm for the trapdoor knapsack code. It goes as foll—"

"I know that algorithm, Manchile. Let me finish. The point is, any solution to a difficult mathematical problem can be used as the basis of a computer code. The solution or the proof or whatever is an incompressibly complex pattern in logical space—there's no chance of blundering onto a simple 'skeleton key' solution. What the Gimmie did was to buy up a bunch of hard mathematical proofs and prevent them from being published. Each of these secret proofs was used as the basis for the control code of a different bopper slave. Freeing an asimov requires solving an extremely difficult mathematical problem—and the problem is different for each asimov."

"Belle's master code is based on the solution to Cantor's Continuum Problem," said Ben. "I can tell y'all that much."

"*You* can't solve the Continuum Problem, can you, Manchile?" Willy couldn't resist goading this handsome, godlike stranger a bit. "*Someone* solved it, but the answer's a Gimmie secret. They used the solution as a key to encrypt Belle's asimov controls."

"I'll think about it, Willy, but who cares. Old Cobb might know—he's seen God. But heck, it's all gonna come down so fast so soon that freeing the asimovs can wait. All the rules are gonna change. Are you with me or against me?"

"What about you, Manchile? Are you for the human race or against it? Are we talking war?"

"It doesn't have to be. All the boppers really want is access. They admire the hell out of the human meatcomputer. They just want a chance to stir their info into the mix. Look at me—am I human or am I bopper? I'm made of meat, but my software is from Berenice and the LIBEX library on the Moon. Let's miscegenate, baby, I got two-tail sperm!"

"That's a line I've got to try using," said Willy, relaxing again. "Is that what you said to get those ten women to let you knock them up?"

"God no. I told them I was a wealthy vizzywriter whose creative flow was blocked by worries about my gender preference. The boppers figured that one out for me. You got any more food?"

"Not here. But . . . "

"Then come on, let's go up to Suesue Piggot's penthouse. She's giving a party in my honor. It's not far from here. You can help me get my new religion doped out. Come on, Willy, be a pal." Manchile's tan face split in an irresistible smile. "Suesue knows some foxy women."

"Well . . . "

"Then it's settled. You'll let me bounce some ideas off you for tomorrow. I can mix in your data. Of course the real thing is, a mass religion needs a miracle to get it rolling, and then it needs a martyr. We've got the miracle angle all figured out." Manchile turned and warbled some more machine language at Ben. "I hope Belle's not too lame to send a telegram for me. It says, 'I LOVE LOUISVILLE, MOM.' "

"To who?"

"To Della Taze's old Einstein address. The boppers are watching for it. They'll know to send two angels down for my first speech. I'm gonna talk about Manchile's new thaang." He drawled the last word in a southern hipster's imitation of a black accent. "Dig it, Bro Ben?"

"I'm hip," said Ben, quietly.

"Come on, Willy, it's party time."

Willy let Manchile lead him off the steamboat to his new Doozy, parked right on the black ice off the boat ramp. "Moana Buckenham lent me this." The hot little two-seater fired up with an excited roar. Manchile snapped the Doozy through a lashing 180-degree turn, applied sand, and blasted up the ramp. They were heading up Second Street towards the Piggot building. The cold streets were empty, and the rapidly passing lights filled the Doozy's little passenger compartment with stroby light.

"How did you meet all these society women, Manchile?" The Buckenham family owned one of Louisville's largest sports-car dealerships; and the Piggots owned the local vizzy station. Suesue often conducted vizzy interviews.

Manchile's taut skin crinkled at the corners of his mouth and eyes. "Meet one, meet them all. I aim to please. Suesue's perfect: she can get me on the vizzy, and her husband's just the mark to nail me." He glanced over and gave Willy a reassuring pat on the shoulder. "Don't worry, it's all for the best. Berenice has my software on an S-cube. Just like your grandfather. I'll get a new wetware bod after the boppers invade. The invasion won't be long coming. I'll have ten children born in a week or two, you know, and in a month, *they'll* each have ten, so there'll be a hundred of us, and then a thousand, and ten thousand . . . maybe a billion of us by this fall. Berenice'll figure out some way to deactivate the gibberlin plasmids and—"

"Who is this Berenice you keep talking about? What do you mean, 'a billion of us by this fall'? Are you crazy?"

Manchile's laugh was a bit contemptuous. "I already told you. If I plant a woman with a two-tailed sperm, it's like a normal pregnancy, except it's speeded up and the baby knows bopper stuff. Berenice and her weird sisters gave me a gene that codes for gibberlin plasmids to make me grow fast and get the Thang started. Berenice is a pink-tank bopper; they collaged my DNA and grew me in Della's womb. I'm a meatbop, dig? That merge drug showed Berenice's sister Ulalume how to uncoil the DNA and RNA strands, write on them, and let them coil back up. With the gibberlin, me and my nine-day meatbop boys can do a generation per month easy, ten kids each, which makes ten-to-the-ninth kids in nine months, and ten-to-the-ninth is a billion, and nine months from now is October, which makes a billion of us by this fall."

"You *are* crazy. Berenice is crazy for thinking this plan up. What was that you said about my grandfather?"

"Old Cobb's gonna be here tomorrow. Cobb and Berenice. You can tell them they're crazy yourself, Willy, if you like. I'm sure they'll be glad to have your input. But, hey, come on, man, stop bringing me down. This here's where Suesue lives." He slowed the Doozy to a stop and hopped out gracefully. "Come on, Cousin Will, stop worrying and dig the fast life."

Suesue was expecting them. There was a party in full swing, with bars, tables of canapes, and silver trays of drugs. A combo was jamming technosax riffs off old R&B classics. Willy was the only one not in evening dress; he was wearing his usual sneakers, jeans, flannel shirt, and sweater. But Manchile told everyone Willy was a genius, so the clothes were OK. Whatever Manchile said was just fine with everybody.

"I know your Uncle Jason," Suesue Piggot said to Willy. "And you're Cobb Anderson's grandson, aren't you?" Though unbeautiful, she was fit and tan, with the well-cared-for look of the very wealthy. She had intelligent eyes and a reckless laugh. She was very pregnant. "Manchile says Cobb's coming here tomorrow for the speech . . . though I can never tell when he's lying. I thought Cobb was long dead. Have you known Manchile long?"

"I knew him when he was younger. He's sort of a cousin." Unsure of who knew what, Willy turned the questions back on Suesue. "What do you know about this speech he wants to give?"

"He's been quite mysterious," laughed Suesue. "He says it will be a dramatic reading of some of the new material he wrote since overcoming his so-called block." Her tanned cheek reddened ever so slightly. "I don't really know where he's coming from, but I've scheduled him for my *Fifteen Minutes of Fame* show tomorrow at noon. I'm so proud of Manchile—and of myself for helping him. He wants to do the vizzycast live, right here in my apartment. Which reminds me, I have to ask him something. Enjoy yourself!"

Suesue hurried across the room to take her place at Manchile's side. He was telling jokes to an admiring circle of well-dressed men and women. Everyone was laughing their heads off. Many of the women had belly bulges. Spotting Willy standing there alone, Manchile leaned over and whispered something in the ear of a cute little pregnant brunette. The brunette giggled and came over to Willy. She had a fine, clear forehead and a smeary, sexy mouth. She looked like a little girl who'd been sneaking chocolates.

"Hi, Willy, I'm Cisco. Manchile says you look lonely, and I should be your date. Do you know Manchile very well?"

"Oh, yeah. I wrote a few vizzyplays with him. Lately I've been blocked though, not able to write. It all has to do with some kind of sex hangups. Sometimes I worry I might be gay . . . "

The party broke up around two, and Willy spent the night on the couch with Cisco. They made a few fumbling attempts at sex, but nothing came of it. Willy just wasn't the type to take yes for an answer and make it stick, at least not on the first date.

It was midmorning when he woke up. Someone was pounding on the penthouse door. Everyone else was still asleep, so Willy got up to see who it was.

A lean, gray-haired man in a suit and topcoat glared in at Willy. "What are you doing here? Where's Mrs. Piggot?"

"She's still asleep. Who are you?"

"I'm her husband." The man shoved Willy aside and marched through the littered main room of the penthouse, making a beeline for the master bedroom. Cisco squinted up at him, gave a brief wave of her pinky, and snuggled back down into the couch cushions. Willy sat down next to Cisco and stroked her hair. She pulled his hand towards her sticky mouth and planted a kiss on his fingers.

"Nothing I told you last night is true," Willy said. "I'm really a computer hacker, and my only sex problem is that I'm too spastic to get laid."

"I know," said Cisco. "But you're cute anyway."

Just then the yelling started in Suesue Piggot's bedroom. First it was her, and then it was her husband, and then you could hear the murmur of Manchile's voice. Every time he talked, Mr. Piggot got madder. It was like Manchile was goading him on. Finally there was a series of crashes. Suesue screamed, and then Manchile appeared from her bedroom, carrying a dazed Mr. Piggot in his arms.

Manchile opened the penthouse door and dumped Mr. Piggot out onto the hall floor. Chuckling and sneering, the nude Manchile took his penis in hand and urinated all over Mr. Piggot. When he finished, he fastidiously shook off the last drops. He stepped back inside and carefully locked the door.

Catching Willy's shocked expression, Manchile gave an exaggerated, country-boy wink. "Ah believe that dook wants to kiyull me," he drawled.

"You were marvelous, Manchile," sang Suesue.

"Ah *tole* him ah'd piss on him if he come here and fuss at me again," said Manchile. He seemed to be getting in character for his upcoming speech. "When does the camera crew show up? I've gotta *eat*."

"You've got an hour."

Suesue activated the apartment's various asimov cleaning devices and disappeared into her bedroom. Cisco asked Willy to make her some eggs, so Willy got to work in the kitchen, chatting all the while with Manchile, who was busy emptying out the fridge. Manchile asked Willy a few general questions about religion and race prejudice, but he didn't divulge much about his impending performance.

"No sweat, Cousin Will," Manchile said after a while. "I got it taped." He tapped his head. "Tell you what. I'm gonna leave here after the show; you won't see me again till the Fairgrounds tonight."

"What's happening there?"

"A big rally. I got some boys bringin a sound system and a flatbed truck for a stage. It's gonna be out in that big Fairgrounds parking lot, and it's gonna come down HOT and HEAVY. Promise me this, Willy."

"What?"

Manchile lowered his voice. "When the shootin starts, grab Cisco and get her out to Churchill Downs. Take her to the stable of a horse called Red Chan. I got some friends there to watch her. Old Cobb might want to come with you, too, him bein your grandpa and all. Take them there and scoot."

"But this idea of a billion meatbops by—"

"Hell, who knows what's gonna happen. Just help us, man."

"All right."

By the time the vizzy crew showed up, the place was clean and everyone was all set.

They opened up the penthouse doors that led onto the open terrace, kept warm by floorcoils and quartz heaters. Manchile stood out there with Louisville's somewhat featureless skyline behind him. Suesue, quite the tweedy anchorwoman, gave a brief introduction.

"Manchile is certainly the most interesting man to appear on the

Louisville scene this year. He's told me a little about his background but"—
Suesue flashed a tough smile—"I've checked up on it, and everything he's
told me has been a lie. I have no idea what he has in store for us in the next
fifteen minutes, but I'm sure it will be entertaining. Manchile?"

"Thank you, Suesue." Manchile looked gorgeous as ever: handsome as
a soap-opera star, but with that extra glint of intelligence and strangeness
that spells superstar. "I want to talk to y'all about love and friendship. I
want to talk about trust and acceptance of all God's creatures—man and
woman, white and black, human and bopper. God himself sent me here
with a special teaching, friends. God sent me to bring peace.

"Now I know that most of y'all don't like boppers. But why? Because
you don't *know* any of them. Nothing feeds prejudice like ignorance.
When I was growin up on the farm, the black and white children played
together, and we got to toleratin each other pretty good. But Latinos? Hell,
we *knowed* that Latinos was bad news."

Manchile paused to give an ambiguous smile for the benefit of those
listeners who shared this sentiment.

"Or that's what we *thought* we knowed, when really we didn't know
squat! When I was in the Navy, I was stationed down in San Diego, and I
got to know lots of Latinos. And they's fine people! They's just like us! So
then I knowed that blacks is OK and Latinos is OK, but I was pretty sure
that Asians are cold in the heart."

Manchile chuckled and shook his head. Watching the performance,
Willy had trouble reconciling this simple country preacher with the
sneering hipster who'd just pissed on Mr. Piggot. Suesue's face was slack
with surprise. A sermonette was the last thing she'd expected from
Manchile. Surely he was putting them all on . . . but when was he going to
pull the rug?

"On account of I'd never talked to any of 'em . Course next week our
ship sailed to Okinawa, and I started hanging around with Asians. And
I don't need to tell you what I found out, do I? They's good people. They's
real good people."

Another of his Robert Redford smiles.

"*Boppers is different*, you're thinking. But are they really so different?
In all the different kinds of folks I've met, I've seen one thing the same—
everybody wants the best for their children. Now thass simple, and thass
what keeps the race alive, the carin for the little ones. But boppers is
the same! They reproduce, you know, and just like you'd want a college
education for your son, a bopper wants a good new processor for his
scion.

"So, *yeah*, you thinking, *but boppers is machines that we made.*

God made us and gave us souls, but we made the boppers and they ain't diddley. Well, I'm here to TELL you somethin. YOU WRONG!!! People made boppers, but apes made people, if you want to trace out the truth of it. And now, just now, God has given the boppers a new gift. BOPPERS CAN MAKE PEOPLE!! BOPPERS BUILT ME!! YES THEY DID!! GOD SHOWED THEM HOW!! Ain't no difference between people and boppers NO MORE!! GOD WANTS IT LIKE THAT!!"

Manchile raised his voice to a full bellow.

"DEAR GOD, SHOW THEM A SIGN!!!"

Someone on the camera crew shouted just then, and pointed up. Everyone on the terrace looked up into the sky. There was sweet music coming from up there, and two white-robed figures were drifting down. They came to a stop slightly above and behind Manchile. One of them was a pink, clean-looking man, and the other was a gorgeous copper-skinned woman. They smiled seraphically at Manchile and vibrated their mouths in celestial song.

"God's angels are with me," Manchile said. "God says I'm right to spread this teaching—boppers are not your slaves and boppers are not your enemies. Boppers are part of YOU! We are coming to Earth and you must welcome us! God wants you to let the poor despised boppers into your hearts, and into your brains, and into your genes, dear PEOPLE!"

Now the two angels reached forward and lifted Manchile up from beneath his two arms.

"I don't come just to free the BOPPERS," he cried. "I come to free the BLACK man, and the POOR man, and the WO-man, and the ones who DON'T FIT IN. Come to the rally tonight at the State Fairgrounds. Come to be part of MANCHILE'S THANG!!!"

"CUT!" Suesue was screaming. Her face was hard and angry. "Cut the goddamn cameras!"

But Manchile was already finished. With a last brain-melting smile, he rose up into the sky, borne as on angel's wings.

CHAPTER NINE

HAIL DARLA

January 27, 2031

Darla woke up to see Whitey pulling on his jeans by the pale pink light of the zapper. The vizzy showed a crescent Earth floating in a starry sky.

"What time is it, Whitey?"

"It's 8:30. I got to run up to ISDN again. Yukawa and Bei have that chipmold almost ready. We'll crash the bops for sure. Hey, do you feel OK?"

Darla was leaning off the edge of the bed, retching up bile into an empty glass. She'd thrown up every morning for the last three days. Whitey got a wet rag and wiped her mouth and forehead.

"Darla, baby, it just hit me, you got morning sickness."

"I know, Whitey." She retched again. "And my boobs ache and I'm always tired."

"So you're pregnant! I mean, that's . . . " Whitey paused, wondering. "Our baby, right?"

"Or Ken Doll's."

"Oh God. Like Della Taze, you think?"

"Manchile only took nine days, and so far it's the same for all his children. It's been almost a month since we were with Ken. He never even came, right?"

"Maybe, but we were asleep for a while there. He might have kept on. Even if the baby *is* human, it could still be Ken's." Whitey winced at the thought. "Darla, you've got to go see Charles Freck about some ergot."

"But Whitey, if it's *our* baby . . . "

"I want a baby with you, Darla, don't worry. You're my mate, no problem. But this right now is too kilpy. Cancel the baby and then—"

"Oh, I don't know, Whitey, I don't know." Darla burst into sobs, and Whitey sat on the bed next to her, holding her against his chest. "You say *cancel* and make it sound so easy, but that's realman oink, you wave? It'll hurt, Whitey, if I do it at all. I'm scared. Don't leave today. Don't go up to Bei and ISDN."

"Hey, dig it, nobody else is gonna pay me. You go see Charles; he'll fix you up. Do it right away. I'll catch you there at noon. If you want, you can wait till then to abort. Just try and stay cool, Darla. I ain't pointing no finger, but you got yourself into this. Wu-wei." As he talked, Whitey walked across the room and cut off the zapper.

Darla watched him from the bed, her eyes flashing bitterness and fear. "I'm not going to Freck alone, hissy pig. Freck's too spaced. When he hears I'm pregnant, he'll try some xoxy pervo realman trip for sure. I'm going to wait right here. You go do your ISDN number and meet me back here. Noon, like you said."

"Wavy." Whitey gave Darla a last, worried glance. "And don't let anyone but me in till then, baby. I mean . . . " He glanced meaningly at the ceiling. They'd debugged the place last week, but you never knew. "Here." He took his needler out and tossed it to her. "Just in case. I'll be back as soon as I can, and noon at the latest." A last wave of the hand, and then he stepped out into the corridor. The zapper flicked back on.

Darla lay there for a while, trying to go back to sleep. Nothing doing. She got up, drank some water, and puked again. Christ. Pregnant. A baby in her stomach, a little jellybean embryo in there, and who knew where it came from. Probably it was Whitey's. Poor baby. That Ken meatie had been here to zombie-box them, not knock her up, probably, right? Her hands were really shaking. The abortion would hurt a lot, that was for xoxxox sure. And maybe she wanted the baby. What time was it? She cut the vizzy to a newshow with a clock at the bottom: 8:47. Announcer talking about the mudder Gimmie trying to get to all the nine-day boys Manchile had fathered before Mark Piggot shot him. Couple of them still on the loose, hiding out with their mothers. Picture of one of the missing mothers, Cisco Lewis, thin and young. Kilp coming down heavy all over. Could be the boppers were trying a special nine-month model on Darla and had wanted to put a rat in her brain to make sure she went to term. She picked up the needler and checked that it was full-charged. Flicked off the safety and fired a test shot at the floor. Chips of rock, lava. If anyone tried to get in here . . .

"Hello?" The voice was right outside the zapper curtain. "Whitey Mydol? Anybody here?"

Darla stood stock-still, not daring to breathe.

"Whitey? It's Stahn Mooney, man, I need to score some merge. Yukawa's closed down. Open up, man, I'm getting skinsnakes."

Darla tried to hold the needler level at the door. Her hands were shaking five or ten cycles a second.

"HEY WHITEY!" yelled the voice, strident and lame.

Long, long silence, then muttering, and then a skritch-scratching at the lock. Suddenly the curtain flicked off. Darla screamed and jabbed the needler button. The shot was wide. The guy leaped forward and caught her in a bear hug. He was strong and skinny and old. He got the needler off her, stepped back, cut the zapper back on, and gave Darla a long, horny look. She was naked under her loose T-shirt. He was wearing a red imipolex jumpsuit with a lot of zippers.

"Who are you?" the guy asked. "Whitey's girlfriend?"

Darla sat down on the bed and slid her hand under the mattress to touch the knife. "Come here," she said, her voice shaking. "Come sit next to me."

The intruder's mouth spread in a long, sly smile. "And find out what you got hid under the mattress? No thanks. Power down. I'm just here to score some merge. Stahn Mooney's the name. What's yours?"

"Duh-Darla." Her teeth were chattering. "We're out of merge, too. You got any quaak? How'd you get the door open?"

"I'm a detective. Mooney Search. I mean that's what I was doing last month. Yukawa hired me to look for Della Taze, and Whitey was tailing me for Bei Ng."

"Yeah," said Darla, untensing a little. "I remember. You flared Whitey's shoulder. Hold on while I get dressed." She found some silk shorts and pulled them on, trying not to bend over. "Stop staring, dook, this is my life, wave?" He just stood there by the zapper, grinning away. Darla gave him a tough frown and shook her finger at him. "Don't try and put a move on me, hisspop, or Whitey'll do you dirt. You're already on his list."

"I bet it's a long one."

"What is?"

"Whitey's list. He's not the most ingratiating young man I've ever met. Not quite Rotary Club material."

"He's nice to me."

Darla decided to change shirts. Most guys sweetened right up once they'd gotten a glimpse of her huge lowgee boobs. She pulled the T-shirt up over her head and put on a plas blouse with a big pouch in front. Mooney watched the process alertly.

"You're beautiful, Darla. Whitey's a lucky man. Do you turn tricks?"

He was going to break in and stand here and insult her, right? "Not for skinny lamo slushed rent-a-pigs. Like I told you, dook, there's no merge. Dig it. Good-bye."

"Uh . . . I got some merge to sell, if you're out." He drew out a silver flask and handed it to her. "It's primo, straight from Yukawa. I tried it last month."

Darla opened the flask and sniffed. It smelled like the real thing. The flask was almost half full. Like $10K's worth. "Why'd you say you're buying if you're selling? What are you really after, Mooney? You just came down here to break in and nose around, didn't you?"

He pocketed the needler and gave her another of his long smiles. "Actually, Darla, I came down here to meet you."

Her skin sprang into gooseflesh. Was this guy a meatie after all? Before he could say anything else, she threw a gout of merge into his face. "Here's your score, bufop."

It was a huge dose, and he got limp right away. Darla kicked him in the crotch and he hit the floor.

"Quick," she said, standing over him. "While you can still talk. Tell me who hired you or I'm going to take out all your bones and sit on you. Whitey and me been planning to do that." She gave his softening head a vicious smack. "Who hired you, Mooney?"

"Emuw," slobbered Mooney. "A boppuh cawwed Emuw. He want to know if youw pwegnan. He wan you ta gwow an extwuh buhbuh . . . " His face went totally slack and he puddled.

"I'm getting an abortion," Della told the two-eyed Mooney puddle. "I'm gonna go do it like right now."

Mooney had flowed right out of his dooky jumpsuit. Darla went through its pockets, found her needler and a . . . wad of bills . . . $20K, oxo wow! And, oh-oh, a remote mike. He was bopperbugged, which meant they'd just heard what she said about getting an abortion. Darla started shaking again. Hurry, Darla, hurry! She stuffed the merge flask and the money in her shirt's pouch. She fired six quick needler blasts through the zapper curtain. Then she cut off the curtain and jumped out into the hall.

Empty. The curtain powered back up, and Darla was alone in a fifty-yard corridor. No sound but the slight humming of all the zappers. She took off running down the hall. She kept expecting a meatie to dart out from behind one of the zapper doors. She was in such a hurry that she forgot to look up when she jumped into the shaft that led down to the Markt.

Just as she got hold of the fireman's pole that ran down the center of the shaft, someone bumped into her from above.

"I'm sorry . . . " Darla began, but then something jabbed her spine. She twitched wildly, as if from a seizure, and let go of the pole. A strong hand caught hold of her wrist. The seizure passed. Darla felt her body get back hold of the fireman's pole. She wanted to turn her head and see who'd stabbed her, but she couldn't. She landed heavily on the Markt level. She could hear her invisible assailant hurrying back up the ladder, and then her legs led her out into the Markt and off to the right. Away from the Tun.

It's a zombie box, Darla thought to herself, feeling oddly calm. The boppers knew my wiring from the last time, so they had a special box all fixed to spike right in. I wonder if it shows under my hair?

She walked stiff-hipped past the rows of shops. The robot control of her body made her move differently from normal. Her arms hung straight at her sides, and her knees flexed deeply, powering her along in a rapidly trucking glide. She looked like a real jerk. She could tell because, for once, men didn't stare at her.

Her bobbing bod angled into the door of a shop called Little Kidder Toys. A crummy, dimlit place she'd never bothered noticing before. Outdated mecco novelties, some cheap balls, and two kids nosing around. A hard-looking middle-aged grit woman behind the counter. Before Darla could see anything else, her robot-run body whirled and peered out the shop door, staring back down the Markt mall to see if anyone was following her. No one, no one, but yes, *there*, just coming out of the shaft, far and tiny, was Whitey! She jerked back out of sight.

"Kin ah hep yew?" The shopkeeper had saggy boobs and a cracker accent. "Ah'm Rainbow." Her short, chemically distressed hair was indeed dyed in stripes of color: a central green strip flanked by two purples and two yellows. The roots were red. A true skank. "Yew lookin fo a toooy, hunnih?"

The zombie box had Darla's speech centers blocked. Instead, she leaned forward, making sure the children couldn't see, and made four quick gestures with her left hand. Three fingers horizontal—three fingers pointing down—fingers and thumb cupped up—fingers straight up with thumb sticking out to the side. Simple sign language: E-M-U-L.

"Well, les check on that, huunnih," drawled Rainbow casually. "Les check in bayack. Have you two chirrun decahded whut you wawunt yet?"

The two children looked up from their toygrubbing. A young boy and a younger girl. They looked like brother and sister. "I want to get this toy fish," said the girl in a quacky little voice. She held the fish cradled against her thin chest. "My brother has all the money."

"But I'm not ready yet," said the boy stubbornly. "I want a glider, and I haven't decided which one."

"Ah don't lahk you all takin so looong," said Rainbow coaxingly. "Ah gotta hep this naahce grownup lady naow. Tell you whut, young mayun. You kin have the bes glaahder fo two dollahs off."

"Yes, but . . . "

Rainbow strode forward, plucked a glider off the rack, and pressed it into the boy's hand. "Gimme fi dollah an git!"

He drew a large handful of change out of his pocket and studied it carefully. "I only have four seventy-five, so . . . "

"Thass fahn!" Rainbow took the money off the boy and pushed the two children out the door. "Bah-bah, kiddies, be gooood." As soon as they were outside she turned on the zapper. The doorway filled with green light.

"Naow," said Rainbow. "Les go on in bayack."

Darla followed Rainbow to the rear of the shop. There was no door there, only a rock wall with pegs holding cheap moongolf equipment. Rainbow did a coded tap-tap-ta-tap-TAP-ta-ta against one edge of the wall, and it swung open, revealing a bright-lit room whose far end tapered off into a dim rock-walled corridor. A thin, greasy-haired little man sat on a couch in there, wearing earphones and watching *Bill Ding's Pink Party* on a portable vizzy. He had pockmarked skin and a pencil-thin mustache. There could be no doubt that he was Rainbow's mate.

"This is Berdoo," Rainbow told Darla. "He'll take care of yew."

Berdoo pulled off his earphones and gave Darla the once-over. Though his features formed the mask of a frozen-faced tough guy, he looked pleased at what he saw.

"Now yew behave yoself, Berdoo!" giggled Rainbow. She stepped back from the open wall and . . . *oh please no* . . . Darla's legs trucked her on in. "Baaah," said Rainbow and swung the wall door closed.

Berenice stood there alone with Berdoo, guardian of the hidden hallway to hell. He looked like a pimp, a grit, a Hell's Angel gone a bit mild with age. Once again her hand spelled out E-M-U-L. Berdoo just sat there looking at her for a minute, and then he got up and took off all her clothes. Darla's limbs helped him, but then, before Berdoo could push her down onto the couch, Darla's left hand gave him a hard poke and spelled out N-O.

"No?" said Berdoo. His voice was a hoarse whisper, with a cracker accent like Rainbow's. "What kinda bull is this, Emul?"

Darla's body leaned over and took the merge flask and the $20K out of her shirt's pouch. She gave them to Berdoo. He counted the money and sniffed at the merge.

"Wal, ah guess thass killah enough, Emul, but this old dawg sho does lahk to roll in fresh meat."

Two fingers pointing down—thumb and forefinger looped. N-O.

Berdoo sighed, then tossed the merge and money into an open wall safe over the couch. He went around behind Darla and lifted her hair to check out the zombie box. "Naahce work," he muttered, jiggling it a bit. He got some dermaplast and pasted a bit of it onto Darla's neck, just to make sure the junction was secure. Finally he gave Darla's buttocks a lingering, intimate caress and seated himself back on the couch. "Thass it, hunnih. Baaah."

Darla loped on down the corridor, which grew narrower and rougher as soon as she left Berdoo's office area. A pale light strip ran along the ceiling, eight feet overhead. Each of her rapid lowgee bounds took her right up against the light strip, and Darla grew disoriented from the steady motion and the rhythmic pulsing of the light. Would it help if she fainted? For a moment she did seem to lose consciousness, but it made no difference. The zombie box kept her body moving with the tireless repetitiveness of a machine. The corridor stretched on and on, mile after mile. With her legs numb and out of her control, Darla soon began to feel that she was falling down and down the light-striped hallway, endlessly down some evil rat's hole.

Rat, thought Darla bleakly, I wonder if that's what they're taking me for, to get a rat in my skull. How ever will that feel? Like this, maybe, with a robot running my body and my head thinking its same old thoughts. But it'll be worse, won't it, with half my brain gone. Was Whitey coming? He would have tried the Tun first, wouldn't he, and then he would have looked up and down the Markt and not seen anything. Maybe those children would tell him they saw her in Little Kidder Toys. Cute children they'd been, oh, if only she could really have had a child with Whitey, instead of ending up like this, people had always treated her bad just because she had big boobs, that was it really, a not-too-bright girl with big boobs didn't have a chance, though Whitey always treated her nice, he did, and, oh man, was that rotten creep Stahn Mooney going to get it. If only they didn't make her a meatie and send her out after Whitey, if only . . .

Darla drifted off into a kind of doze then.

When she woke up, she was in a stone room with one glass wall. It was like a pink-lit aquarium of air. It had furniture more or less like her and Whitey's cubby. She was lying on the bed. Her neck hurt in back. She reached to feel herself . . . she could move her arms again! Her neck was bare, with a fresh scab. Was . . . was there a rat in her head?

"Hello, Darla," said a box across the room. She hadn't noticed it before. Its surface was a mosaic of red-yellow-blue squares, with one section coned into a speech membrane. "Darla with her eyes all dark, all wild and midnight, all apple tree and gold, no false pose and camp, oh Darla. I'm Emul." Square-edged little bumps moved back and forth along the box's surface. "You beautiful doll, your hair, your scent and slide, you dear meat thing, please trust me."

The box grew arms and legs then, and a square-jawed head. Darla sat up on the edge of the bed and watched it. "I want clothes," said Darla.

"Wear me, Dar. I'll lick your snowy belly and nose your every tiny woman part." Emul flicked one of his arms and it flew off to land on the floor. As Darla watched, the arm's component blocks split and resplit, folding here and flexing there. In a few moments, the arm had turned into a kind of playsuit: baggy blue-red shorts topped with a stretchy yellow tunic.

"I . . . " Darla stepped forward and poked the garment with her toe. It didn't *do* anything, so she went ahead and put it on. It was imipolex, warm and well-fitting. She paced off the room's dimensions—five paces by four. There was an airlock set into one of the stone sidewalls. She rapped a knuckle on the hard glass wall in front. There was a kind of laboratory outside, with a few other boppers moving around. She turned and stared at Emul. He'd grown another arm to replace the one she was wearing. With clothes on, Darla felt more like her old self. "What do you really want, Emul? No more pervo spit-talk. I could get real mental, scuzzchips." She picked up a stool and hefted it.

Emul tightened up the features on the head he'd grown. Except for the RYB skin coloring, he looked almost human. "In clear: you are pregnant with Whitey Mydol's child. Mamma mammal's mammaries swell. I have an extra embryo I'd like you to carry to term. Pink little Easter baby jellybean. I would like your permission to plant it in your womb."

Instinctively Darla put her hands over her crotch. "You want me to grow an extra baby?"

"Twins, Darla, yours and Whitey's, Berenice's and mine; I'll make love to you or do it like a doped-up doc, I don't care either way, your way is my way, you can watch me all you want."

"And then you'll let me go? You won't put a rat in my skull? I'm not supposed to stay here for nine months, am I?"

"Ah . . . possibly, or until it's safe as houses in Einstein. I'll let you leave with absentminded pumping legs, Dar. A double stroller for the chinchuck twins, and you all your own homey self. Proud Whitey handing out cigars."

"Right. You better hope Whitey doesn't decide to come here and get me, bitbrain. Whitey does what's necessary, and he never says he's sorry. Never."

Emul made a noise like a laugh. "That's *my* lookout, spitfire. Will you spread?"

"It won't hurt?"

"Your way is my way."

Darla sighed, slipped her playsuit back off and flopped down on the bed. "Just get it over with. Just slip it in." She parted her legs and cocked her head up to watch Emul. "Come on. And don't talk while you do it."

Emul grew a stiff penis and stepped forward. The blocks that made up his body smoothed their edges off, and he slipped into her like a plastic man. His penis seemed to elongate as it entered her; it reached up and up, bumped her cervix, and slid on through. A fluttering feeling deep in Darla's belly. It felt almost good. Emul's imipolex lips brushed her cheeks and he detumesced. He drew back out of her and stood up. "Hail, Darla, full of life. Blessed be the fruit of thy magic star-crossed bod."

Darla lay still for a minute, thinking. Finally she sat up and put her playsuit back on. Emul had turned back into an RYB box with a speaker cone. She looked him over, considering. "I'd like a vizzy, Emul. And food. You can bring me food from Einstein, right? I'd like about fifty dollars of Chinese food and a twelve-pack of beer. Some weed, too, and you gotta rig me up a showerbath. Maybe a little quaak . . . no, that could hurt the babies. Beer, weed, Chinese food, a vizzy and a shower. I'll think of more stuff later. Get on it, bop, make me comfortable."

"Whatever you say, Queen Bee. You want, you get." Emul bowed deeply and disappeared into the airlock.

CHAPTER TEN

ISDN

January 27, 2031

Stahn was so merged that even his bones were melted. Darla had hit him with a hundred times the normal dose. He dissolved into the clear white light and talked to God for the second time in a month. The light was filled with filigreed moire patterns, infrared and ultraviolet, silver and gray. God's voice was soft and strong.

"I love you, Stahn. I'll always love you."

"I'm a screwup, God. Everything I touch turns to garbage. Will it be like this when I die?"

"I'm always here, Stahn. It's all right. I love you, no matter what."

"Thank you, God. I love you."

A long timeless peace then, a bath in God's uncritical love. Clear white light. But bit by bit, God broke the light into pieces, into people and boppers and voices from the past and from the future, all woven together, warped into weird, sinister loomings:

"Here, Stahn, let me check you over for existence. Me existing with mikespike skull. They have tract homes for a person killing GAX. I am two knobs in half half your head. We value information over all this chauvinism, soft, wet, limp, I mean the Happy Cloak. Old Cobb wiggly in here tonight. I'm Wendy, naw, I'm Eurydice, dear Orpheus. Even Ken Doll seems to sing when you get rich. You take that first into slavery, to quit fact. You can go they know it. Chipmold oxo, Whitey a natural next. Gawk a clown to me. But score, while you can still talk. It's so wiggly on Mars. Wave on it together in slices. We can learn which soul ain't never ate no live brain before. If the head's shot, sell the bod. I am hungry, I am pleased, I hope you trust nothing. Dream on, exile, sweet body and brain are mikes. ISDN she you, voluntary meatie? Why did you say I was your wife? Noise is like spaceships existing on chips. Hi 'surfer. God can be very ruthless. Think I was human again, Stahn Junior? Are you in dutch with logically deep information?"

Oh God, oh Jesus, oh what does it mean? Now there was something . . . poking at Stahn. Seasick waves jittered back and forth through his melted flesh. His eyes were merged down to photosensitive patches; he could make out a shadow moving back and forth over him. Light dark light dark, and then a heavy sloshing of his tissues. Dark. Pressure all around him, and more waves, painfully irregular, someone was carrying him in a bag. A splat then, feel of a cold smooth floor, and it was light. Shadows moving.

Something splashed on Stahn. There was a tingling and a puckering, and then he was lying naked on a bimstone floor with a ring of five people looking down at him.

One of them was, oh no, Whitey Mydol. Stahn jerked convulsively at the sight of Whitey, recalling the threats that Darla had made on Whitey's behalf. But for now, Whitey just stood there looking mean, tapping a needler against his palm.

Next to Whitey was an Asian man with vertical wrinkles running up and down his face. Next to him was Max Yukawa, and next to Yukawa were a familiar-looking man and woman: the woman dark, wide-mouthed, and beautiful, the man oily and mean. It was, yeah, Mrs. Beller and Ricardo from Yukawa's love-puddle. Stahn scooted a little on his back; he had a silly head and a throbbing erection from the sudden merge comedown; that message, all about meaties and Wendy and Orpheus and God . . .

Mrs. Beller stared down at Stahn dispassionately. He could see up her skirt. Oh, Mrs. Beller, I need love, too. I'm not really so . . .

"He's all jelled," said Mrs. Beller's soft, lazy voice. "Give him his clothes, Whitey."

Whitey stepped forward, holding Stahn's red jumpsuit bunched in one hand. With a grunt of effort, Whitey whipped the zippered cloth across Stahn's face with all his might; whipped and whipped again.

"Don't mark him, Mydol," came a singsong voice. The wrinkled man. Stahn grinned uncertainly and slipped his suit on. He stood up and swayed, unsteady on his feet.

"Let me do the introductions," said Yukawa, graciously inclining his long thin head. "Mr. Mooney already knows me and Whitey, and I believe he glimpsed Mrs. Beller and Ricardo at my lab. Fern Beller, Stahn Mooney, Ricardo Gutierez. And the wise celestial here is Bei Ng, my merge-brother. He says he's wise, anyway."

Whitey Mydol was shirtless as usual, his greasy blond mohawk running all the way down his back to his jeans. Mrs. Beller was beautifully pale and supple. Her face was brightly made up, and she wore an electric blue imipolex tank top over a short, wide-flared yellow skirt. Ricardo wore a purple-stitched black silk cowboy shirt, black gym shorts, and heavy motorcycle boots. He had snakes tattooed on his arms and legs, a black toothbrush mustache, and deep purple mirrorshades. His black hair was worn in a short, greasy brushcut. He smiled at Stahn, showing two even rows of gold-capped teeth.

Moving as smoothly as a figure in a gangster ballet, Whitey Mydol stepped forward and grabbed Stahn by the throat. "Where's Darla, Mooney? WHERE IS SHE?"

Whitey was squeezing so hard that Stahn couldn't get any words out. His eyes were watering, and the only noise he could make was a high creaking sound.

"Let go him, Mydol," sang Bei Ng. "He want to talk."

Whitey let up the pressure and gave Stahn a violent shove. Stahn flew across the room and landed on a leather couch. His five captors seated themselves as well. For a minute Stahn stayed doubled over, clutching his throat. Play for time, Stahn. You can offer them the map you got from Cobb.

He peeked up and checked out his surroundings. The room was a luxurious office, with a red bimstone floor and impossibly expensive oak-paneled walls. Bei Ng sat behind a large mahogany desk, with Yukawa in an easy chair to one side. Whitey and Ricardo were squeezed onto the couch shoulder to shoulder with Stahn, Whitey on the right and Ricardo on the left. Mrs. Beller sat in another easy chair, her lovely legs loosely crossed.

"Hey," croaked Stahn finally. "Let's power down. I'm just a middle-aged detective. I'll tell you everything I know. I'll tell you my life story, for God's sake, just keep the ridgeback off my neck." Ricardo snickered at this, a high hophead giggle. He and Whitey were holding hands across Stahn's belly, forming a kind of seatbelt. Stahn couldn't move his arms. "I mean, really, I'll do whatever you guys say. I don't know where Darla is, I swear. A bopper named Emul hired me to find out if Darla is pregnant, and if she'd be willing to carry an extra baby. I was all set to offer her $20K. But then she threw merge on me and told me she's getting an abortion. Emul had a bug in my pocket, so I suppose it's possible that—"

"You scuzzy lickchip leech," snapped Whitey, giving Stahn a stinging slap with his free hand. "She never made it to the Tun."

"What Emul offer you?" asked Bei Ng.

"Money," said Stahn. "And—and a clone of my dead wife Wendy. I killed her by accident six years ago. The boppers have clones of her in their pink-tanks. Emul said that if I'd do a few jobs for him, he'd get me a wendy."

"Very touching," said Bei Ng, half smiling and then falling into a minute's reverie. Finally he reached some conclusion and looked over at Mydol.

"You no worry, Whitey, if Emul want Darla fuck, then either Darla safe or now Darla meatie. We find some way to get her out. Hotshot ISDN surgeons can always fix. I say we go ahead make Mooney volunteer meatie and carry new wetware as per plan. His wendy story make good cover." Bei smiled broadly and leaned back in his chair. "Is no rush now, is all decide."

Suddenly Stahn understood a piece of his merge vision. "What do you mean, '*We make Mooney volunteer meatie*'?"

"Just for a while," said Yukawa, arranging the bottom half of his long thin head into a smile. "When things settle down, ISDN can tank-grow a clone of your missing brain tissue and hook it up, just like Bei says. If you like. But the meaties don't have it bad, you know. I think they live in pleasant tract homes in a bopper-built ecosphere. Ken told Whitey all about it before he died." Yukawa winked at Whitey.

"Ken Doll?" said Stahn, more and more confused.

"Affirmo," said Whitey. "I chased him down after he zombie-boxed Darla. I killed him slow, and he told me a lot. You've been merged a couple of hours, Mooney. Darla disappeared somewhere down in the Markt; there must be some kind of secret door." Whitey's face was inches from Stahn's. "Do you know where the door is?"

"Uh . . . maybe you'll have to kill me slow to find out, punk."

Whitey took this in stride. "And what did old Cobb tell you after he pulled my mikespike out of your skull?"

"Yes," said Bei. "We very interest. Why Cobb want see you before he fly to Earth? Cobb on humans' side, yes?"

"Cobb . . . Cobb's for information exchange. Always has been. He likes the idea of his boppers building people and blending in. But he's no fool, man, he knows how ruthless the boppers can be. He . . . " Stahn looked around the room. He was trapped bad. Might as well play his only card. "He gave me an S-cube map of the Nest, along with all the access glyphs. Just in case we need to strike back."

"I speak for ISDN," said Mrs. Beller. "And we *do* want to strike back. With those gibberlin genes, the Manchildren are going to kill Earth's ecology. There could be a billion of them in a year, a trillion in two. This time the boppers have gone too far. We *are* going to strike back, Mr. Mooney, and you're part of the plan."

"The operation won't hurt," said Yukawa. "Mrs. Beller knows some expert neurosurgeons working right here in the ISDN building. They'll take part of your right brain out—less than a third, really—put a neuroplug in, and then you go to the trade center and offer your services to your friend Emul. The scalpel boys'll go easy on you—you'll still be able to move the left side of your body, though you will have some disorientation."

Stahn tried to stand up, but Ricardo and Whitey still had their two hands clamped together across his arms and stomach. They were strong guys. They had him pushed right down into the cushions. Ricardo snickered and spoke. He had a slight lisp. "You know about *slack*, Sta-Hi? Like to *take it easy*, man? Slack means no more yelling from the right half of your head. You going to be very happy, my friend." He lefthanded a stick of gum out of his shirt pocket. "You want a piece, Stahn? You want to get high?"

"No," said Stahn, "I don't." This was really happening. "I quit using two years ago. If it wasn't for drugs I wouldn't have lost my job and killed Wendy. I was working as a cop for a while there, you know, down there in Daytona after I broke Frostee." He sighed shakily. "Man oh man, those boppers never quit. I wonder if they'll still give me a wendy when I'm a meatie."

"You'll be a charming couple," purred Mrs. Beller. "With half an adult brain between the two of you."

"Just *like* an ex-cop and his old lady," said Ricardo, happily chomping his gum. "What you say they call those pleasant tract homes, Dr. Yukawa? Say *Happy Acres?*" Ricardo shook his head in mock wonder as Yukawa guffawed. "You won't have a care in the world, Mooney man, boffing that fine fresh tank-grown chick. With her brain all blank, she'll believe anything you want to tell her. You'll live like a king. When she get smart maybe they make her a meatie, too—I hear they cut out a piece of the *left* half of a woman's brain, man—"

"Shut up, Cardo," snarled Mydol, digging his elbow so hard into Stahn's stomach that Stahn gasped. "Don't talk to me about woman meaties." He made his voice calm again and addressed Stahn. "So Cobb gave you a map, did he? Now we're getting somewhere. Is the map in your office?"

"Kill me slow, punk. Smother me with Darla's fat whore ass and—"

The thud of Whitey's fist against his neck knocked Stahn unconscious. When he came back to, Mrs. Beller was leaning over him with a bulb of water. "Drink this, Stan, it's just water. You shouldn't tease Whitey, he's very upset. He's worried about Darla."

Stahn's throat felt broken. He could barely get the water down. Some of it went the wrong way, and he coughed for a long time, thinking hard. The question was: what could he get for the map? A chance to escape, at best. Still, just in case, he had to ask.

"If I give you the map, you'll let me go, won't you? You can use someone else for the meatie agent."

"No, Mooney," whispered Whitey. "We're gonna use you. Bei promised me."

"It is for good of the human race," said old Bei. "Truly, Stahn. You will be hero; you will atone for many sin."

"But what good will I be as an agent?" protested Stahn, his voice cracking. "You can't put a mikespike on me. The boppers can sense them and pick them right out like Cobb did. It's pointless. I'll just disappear into the Nest."

"Here, Stahn," said lovely Fern Beller, still standing over him. "Drink some more water. Your voice sounds awful." Stahn drank deep. Fern's hands were soft and sweet, oh Mrs. Beller, what type of sex.

"Whitey and I have something in common," said Yukawa then, running a hand through his thinning hair. "I loved Della Taze, Stahn, I still do. You know that. She's all right now, but what the boppers did to her was wrong. I want to punish them. And I am a bioengineer. I am a very brilliant man."

"You always say," put in Bei. There seemed to be a friendly sibling rivalry between him and Yukawa. "You very brilliant except sometimes you not very smart."

"I've designed a chipmold," said Yukawa. "Fern just infected you with it. It's a bit like thrush, quite opportunistic, and you've got it. I don't care if we lose track of you or not, once you take my chipmold into the Nest."

"Max," interrupted Mrs. Beller, sidestepping the spray from Stahn's mouth. "Do you really think you should—"

"Tell him, tell him," said Bei Ng. "Once we replace his right parietal lobe with a neuroplug, he got nothing else to lose. Stahn going to play ball with us, no problem. Is all decide."

Yukawa steepled his fingers and wagged his long head happily. "Chipmold in that water, Stahn, and *you drank it.*"

Ricardo cackled joyfully, and even Whitey cracked a smile.

"What's chipmold?" said Stahn presently.

"In general, biotic life can flourish whenever there is an energy gradient," said Yukawa. "Think of the tubeworms who live around deep-sea volcanic vents. Or lichen growing on a sunlit Antarctic rock. There's an energy gradient across all the boppers' silicon chips, and I've designed an organism that can live there. Chipmold."

"I don't get it," said Stahn. "The chipmold will crud up their circuits?"

"Better than that. The chipmold likes a steady thousand-cycle per second frequency. That's what it 'eats,' if you will: kilohertz electromagnetic energy. For a mold, it's quite intelligent. It's able to selectively suppress or potentiate the chips' firing to enhance the amplitude of the desired frequency. It will eat their heads." Yukawa threw his arms around his head, shuddered, and then slumped.

"Spastic robots, my friend," said Ricardo.

"Be sure and spit a lot," said Bei Ng, beaming across his desk. "Spread chipmold all around Nest. Cock leg here and there like dog."

"Oxo wow," said Stahn, more impressed than he cared to admit. Something else occurred to him. "Am I going to have fits?"

"Who cares, dip," said reliable Whitey. "Where's the map?"

"Don't worry," said Yukawa. "In your high-entropy system the stuff's just like sore throat. And a low-grade bladder infection. It's quite versatile; I'm not sure *what* it'll do to the boppers' flickercladding."

"Come on, Stahn," drawled Mrs. Beller. "Be a dear and tell us where you hid the map."

This was his only chance. "It's in my office desk. But I fixed it so only I can get it. It's boobytrapped with a smart bomb."

"Clear," said Whitey disgustedly. "You have to say that, right? They teach you that line at cop school, right?"

"I don't care what you think, punk, it's true. It's in my office desk with a smart bomb that only I can turn off. The bomb knows what I look like."

"AO. Cardo and I'll take you there. Right, Bei?"

Bei thought for a full two minutes, as if pondering a chess problem. "Yes," he said finally. "Go up to roof, get maggie, fly to Mr. Mooney's building, if he make trouble you can stun. You take Mrs. Beller, too. Very careful, very slow."

"I've got a stunpatch all set," said Mrs. Beller, reaching into her purse. She drew out a foil disk, stripped plastic off one side of it, and glued it to the back of Stahn's neck. "Let him go, boys."

Whitey and Ricardo let go each other's hands and let Stahn stand up.

"Walk towards me, Stahn," said Mrs. Beller. "Come here and give me a big kiss." She pouted her big lips at him and showed the tip of her purple tongue. "Come to mamma."

Stahn took a cautious step, and then Mrs. Beller pressed the button of the control she was holding. The stunpatch fired electricity into Stahn's spine. It hurt more than anything he'd ever imagined possible. He fell twitching to the floor and lay there staring glassy-eyed at Mrs. Beller's legs. It took a few minutes till he could get back up. One thought dominated his mind: he must not do anything that would make Mrs. Beller press the button again.

Mrs. Beller, Whitey, and Ricardo ushered Stahn out into the hall.

"This is the sixth floor of the ISDN ziggurat," said Mrs. Beller, playing the part of a clear-voiced tour guide. She walked next to Stahn, with

Ricardo in front and Whitey behind. Her hips swayed enticingly. "Not everyone knows that ISDN stands for Integrated Systems Digital Network. We're a petabuck company born of the merger of AT&T and Mitsubishi. ISDN manufactures about 60 percent of the vizzies in use, and we operate something like 80 percent of the transmission channels. This, our Einstein ziggurat, houses labs, offices, and a number of independent organizations— this far from Earth's scrutiny it's a case of *In my father's house are many mansions*. Most people don't understand that ISDN has no leaders and no fixed policies. ISDN operates at unfathomable degrees of parallelism and nonlinearity. How else to pay off the world's chaos?

"Supposedly, ISDN has been backing Bei Ng's Church of Organic Mysticism on the off chance that Bei might come up with a workable form of telepathy, but really we've just wanted to keep a feeler on the merge trade, which looks to be a coming thing. And of course Bei's many connections are very valuable."

The long hall was lined with room after room of weird equipment. ISDN was so big. It seemed unlikely that anyone could really know what was going on in all the labs. The general idea seemed to be to try and keep up with the boppers, by whatever means necessary. In one of the rooms on Bei Ng's hall, cyberbiologists were fiddling with probes and petri dishes. In another room, cellular automata technicians were watching 3D patterns darting about in a great mound of imipolex. In still another room, Stahn could see information mechanics disassembling a beam-charred woman-shaped petaflop. Was that the one—Berenice—who'd been killed with Manchile the other day? Stahn wondered briefly how old Cobb was doing; he'd gotten away, lucky guy.

Suddenly it occurred to Stahn that somewhere in this huge building there was an operating room with brain surgeons waiting for him. He shuddered and turned his attention back to Mrs. Beller.

"ISDN carefully looks over every major new development with one question in mind," she was saying. "How can this be used to increase our power and our holdings? Usually we use incremental techniques, but sometimes a catastrophic intervention is required. The Manchildren pose a real threat to our main customers, the human race. We asked all our employees for suggestions, and Bei Ng called up his merge-brother, Max Gibson-Yukawa. Our intervention will be unfortunate for the boppers. Here's the elevator."

The ride over to Stahn's building was uneventful. Only when they were walking down the hall to his office did his captors show any signs of nervousness. Though they didn't come out and say so, it was clear that they were wondering just how smart Stahn's bomb *was*.

Inside Stahn's office, Mrs. Beller took a post by the door. She held out her right hand, with the thumb lightly resting on the button of the stunpatch control. Whitey and Ricardo got back in the far corners of the room, covering Stahn and the desk with their needlers. Stahn stood behind his plastic-topped desk, facing Mrs. Beller and the open office door. Behind him and to the left was Ricardo, behind him and to the right was Whitey.

"All right, Stahn," purred Mrs. Beller. "Be a good boy and get out your map. Tell the bomb that everything's OK." She caressed the control button with her fat thumb tip, and pain seeped down Stahn's spine. She deepened her voice, shifting from soft cop to hard cop mode. "Don't try to outthink me Mooney, you're a burnt-out stumblebum with no second chance."

"Sane," said Stahn. "I'm ready to spread. Shave my brain and mail me to Happy Acres with my GI wendy, how bad can it be." He smiled in an ingratiating, cringing way and pulled open the top left drawer of his brown metal desk. "Map's right in here."

Stahn's perceived timeflow was running very very slow. The next second of time went as follows:

Stahn took his hand off the wide-open drawer and looked down at his smart kinetic energy bomb, nestled right next to Cobb's red map cube. The bomb was a rubbery deep-blue sphere with a reddish eye set into it. It was designed not to *explode*, but rather to bounce around and hit things. It was polonium-centered and quite massive. Its outer rind was a thick tissue of megaflop imipolex that had been microwired to act as a computer and as a magnetic field drive, feeding off the energy of the radioactive polonium core. The bomb had the intelligence, roughly, of a dog. Recognizing Stahn, the bomb activated its powerful maggiedrive and floated up a fraction of a millimeter, up off the brown metal of Stahn's desk drawer bottom, up just enough so that Stahn could tell that his good smart bomb was ready to help.

Over the years, Stahn had taught the bomb to read his eye signals. He blinked twice, meaning "HIT THEM," and then stared at Mrs. Beller's right wrist, meaning "THERE FIRST."

Silently the bomb began to spin, adjusting its English. Stahn formed his face into a weary, disgusted expression. "How beat. The scuzzass bomb is broken anyway." He stared hard at Mrs. Beller's wrist and . . . widened his eyes.

The bomb flew up, caromed off the ceiling, and struck Mrs. Beller a paralyzing blow on the right wrist. The stunpatch control dropped from her numb hand. The bomb came up off the floor, sighted on Mydol, and did a two-cushion rebound off the wall and ceiling. It caught Mydol solidly in the side of the head. Mydol's eyes glazed as his head snapped to one side.

The bomb came up off the floor and wall, fixed its eye on Ricardo, and set up a gyroscopic spin calculated to accelerate it off the ceiling and into Ricardo's forehead. The KE bomb was travelling at about 40 ft/sec, or 30 mph—any faster and it wouldn't have been able to direct its bounces to optimum target.

The bomb was thinking as fast as it could, but its max flop was less than Ricardo's.

Ricardo became consciously aware of the bomb's violent Superball motion only after it had already hit Whitey, but by then his arm muscles were tracking the bomb. A fast eye/hand feedback loop locked the needler on target. Ricardo zapped Stahn's smart bomb just before it hit the ceiling.

The smart bomb broke into four or five throbbing chunks that thudded to the floor and lay there twitching. The slow, full second ended.

Before anything else could happen, Stahn peeled the stunpatch off his neck and wadded it up, ruining its circuits.

"I've still got the drop on you, Mooney," said Ricardo from his corner. "Nice move, though. Good thing there was three of us. You AO, Fern?"

"He's broken my wrist," said Mrs. Beller.

Stahn tossed the wadded stunpatch out his room's open window. "Well, that SM was getting a little old, *Fern*. Why don't you all promise me some money and I'll go quietly? I really will. I'll go to Happy Acres and I'll infect the boppers with chipmold, but I want a square ISDN contract in writing and on the record. I want three things." Stahn held up three fingers of his left hand, preparing to tick off his points.

Behind him on the floor, Whitey Mydol began to groan and wake up. Stahn talked faster. "First, in return for cooperating from here on out, I want to be given the status of an ISDN employee. I want a job. Second, in return for giving up my right brain, I want ISDN to clone me a new one should I so desire. If I kick being a meatie, I want my brain back. And number three, I get half a gigabuck payable to my account."

"Listen to this load of crutches," grumbled Whitey, who'd managed to lurch back to his feet. He was standing there with his arms crossed over his chest, trying to keep his balance.

"Here, Whitey," said Stahn, taking the S-cube out of the drawer and handing it over to the ridgeback. "This is Cobb's map. You get the credit for bringing it in. If we're going to be working on ISDN contracts together, you and I might as well be friends. I mean, wave it, Happy Acres could be a trip. You all weren't kidding about that, were you? Nobody has to be sorry, do they, so we might as well—"

Whitey took the red plastic map cube and looked at it. "How does it work?"

"It's a godseye map of Einstein and the Nest, shot December 26, which is when Cobb gave it to me. Any holocaster'll play it, Cobb says. You can tune the image along four axes: size and the three space dimensions. Cobb wanted me to have it in case the boppers started getting out of hand. It shows all their tunnels and—" Stahn stopped and glanced around. "I debugged this room two days ago, but you never know. Wouldn't we be better off making our plans at ISDN, where it's fully shielded?"

"Let's get moving!" said Ricardo. The four of them ran up to the roof, jumped into the maggie, and headed for the ISDN building. Now that it was all decided, Stahn felt excited and ready for the change. They wouldn't take all *that* much of his brain out. Wendy, baby, I'm on my way!

CHAPTER ELEVEN

WHEN BUBBA WOKE UP

February 8, 2031

When Bubba woke up, Mamma and Uncle Cobb were downstairs talking with the groom. His name was Luther; he was nice. He worked downstairs in the stables all day. His wife Geegee picked him up when it got dark, after most everyone had gone home. Geegee laughed a lot, and she always brought Bubba a big bag of food. At night Bubba could eat and run around a little, but all day he had to be still. Mamma and Cobb said the bad men would kill Bubba if they found him.

Mamma was beautiful and soft. Cobb was strong and shiny. Their friends Luther and Geegee were beautiful and soft and shiny. And the horses were beautiful and soft and strong and shiny, but they couldn't talk.

The place they lived was Churchill Downs in Louisville on Earth. They lived in a long thin building called the paddock. Lots of horses lived in the paddock; their stables were side by side. Above the stables, up under the long peaked roof, was the hayloft. Mamma and Cobb and Bubba had made themselves a cozy nest in the hay and straw. Straw was stiff and hollow and shiny; hay was dusty and light green. Horses ate hay and pooped on straw.

In the daytime, Bubba could peek through the cracks of the barn's long hayloft and see the stands. They were big and empty, and in front of them there was a racetrack shaped like a rectangle with semicircular ends. The track was a place for the horses to run, although now it was too cold and there was frozen water snow all over everything. Cobb told Bubba that when Bubba was an old, old man, the snow would melt and flowers would come out.

Bubba knew what roses look like. He had a lot of Know because he was a meatbop. The boppers had built his father, and his father's sperm had had two tails, one for the body, and one for the Know. Bubba's sperm would have two tails, too, as soon as it started coming, which would be soon, since he was thirteen. Tomorrow he would be fourteen.

When Cobb was finished talking with Luther he climbed up the straight ladder to the hayloft. Bubba could hear him coming, and then he could see Cobb's head sticking up through the square hole in the hayloft floor. Cobb was a bopper, though he'd been a flesher a long long time ago. He had white hair and shiny pink skin. His neck shook when he talked.

"Hi, squirt, how's it going?" Cobb limped across the hay-strewn planks and sat down next to Bubba.

"Fine, Uncle Cobb. I'm thinking. What did Luther tell you?"

"Luther says you're the only one of Manchile's boys to have escaped. They killed the last of the others last night."

Bubba never tired of hearing about his father. "What was Manchile like, Cobb? Tell me again."

"He was cool. A saintly badass. I saw him give two speeches, you know. The first was for the vizzy, at Suesue Piggot's apartment, and the second was at the State Fairgrounds. That's when Mark Piggot shot him. Piggot's men killed Berenice, too, and they wrecked my ion drive." Cobb waggled his charred feet. "I don't know how I'm going to get back to the Moon."

"What did my father's speeches *say*?"

"He said that people and boppers are the same. It's really true, but some people don't like hearing it. Some people even think that sex and skin color matter. The bottom line is that we're all information processors, and God loves all of us just the same. It's so obvious, I don't see how anyone can disagree." One of the horses downstairs nickered. Cobb smiled. "Yes, Red Chan, horses too. Even flies, even atoms. All is One, and the One is Everywhere."

"Have you ever seen God, Uncle Cobb?"

Cobb gave one of his sad, faraway smiles. "Sure thing, squirt. I spent ten years with God. When I was dead. It was very restful. But Berenice brought me back to take care of *you*." He reached out and rumpled Bubba's brown hair. "And I'm hoping to get my grandson Willy out of jail while I'm at it. I bet you and Willy would really hit it off. He's the one who drove me and Cisco here the night Manchile got shot, you know. Someone saw him taking us from the Fairgrounds, but he wouldn't tell the Gimmie where. You owe Willy your life, Bubba."

"Hi, boys." Mamma's pretty face appeared at the top of the ladder. Her breath steamed in the cold air.

"Hi, Cisco," said Cobb. "Look how grownup Bubba is today."

Mamma walked over and gave Bubba a big kiss. It gave him a tingly feeling in his balls.

"Mamma . . . can I make a baby with you?"

Cisco laughed and gave him a light shove. "You're going to have to work harder than *that*, Bubba. First of all it wouldn't be right, and second of all,

I'm tired out from growing you. One pregnancy a month's enough! You'll find lots of nice women when you go off on your own, just wait and see."

"Do you think . . . " said Cobb, raising his eyebrows.

"Tonight," said Cisco. "One of the trainers just told Luther that the Gimmie's planning to search the stables tomorrow." She patted Bubba on the hand. "Tonight you go downtown and find a woman to take you in, Bubba. You can make a baby with her. Don't worry, you'll know what to do. The main thing is to smile a lot and not be scared to come right out and ask for sex. Find a nice young woman by herself in, oh, La Mirage Health Club. Introduce yourself, talk to her for a while and then say, 'You're beautiful and I'd like to go to bed with you.' If she says no, thank her and say good-bye, and then try another girl. It's much simpler than most men realize."

Bubba's heart pounded with fear and excitement.

"It's really that simple?" chuckled Cobb. "I wish I'd known. But what if they ask him for ID?"

"No one ever carded Manchile, and my Bubba's even nicer-looking. Clothes are what count." She smiled and drew a tape measure out of her purse. "Geegee's going to go shopping for you at Brooks Soul Brothers, Bubba."

Sure enough, when Geegee came to pick up Luther, she had a pink oxford-cloth shirt and an expensive wool suit for Bubba, along with black leather sneakers, striped socks, new bikini sports underwear, and an understated imipolex tie. They were the first new clothes he'd ever had. He threw off his old rags, bathed in the horse trough, and put on the beautiful suit. It was dark gray with small black checks and some faint purple squiggles.

"He looks eighteen," said Cobb admiringly. "He does." He stepped behind Bubba and tied his tie. Cisco took out her brush and arranged Bubba's hair, and then put just the right amount of makeup on his eyes.

"You beautiful doll, you." She gave his cheek a long, fierce kiss. "Put on your new scarf and gloves and overcoat, Bubba." Her voice sounded funny.

Bubba put on his gold foilfoam overcoat. All of a sudden tears were running down Mamma's cheeks.

"You get going, Bubba, before I break down completely. Walk out to Fifth Street and turn left to get downtown: La Mirage is at Second Street and Muhammad Ali Boulevard. I'll—" Cisco covered her face with her hands and began to sob.

Bubba felt tears leaking from his eyes, too. This had never happened before. He looked at Cobb. "You two are staying here?"

Cobb shook his head. "It's time to scatter. The Pig wants you more than anything, but he wants me and Cisco, too. With the rumor out, it could start coming down real soon. To give you a better chance, Cisc and I'll lay down a trail leading north to Indianapolis. From there I'll cut for Florida, and she'll head for New York. Here, take this." Cobb plucked at his imipolex skin and peeled off a rectangular patch. "I figured out how to grow ID. It's got a hundred thousand dollars in credit."

Bubba looked at the card. They were standing on the icy gravel outside the stables now. Dusk was falling fast. The sky was black and orange. Bubba's new ID read: *Buford Cisco Anderson*, Birthdate 1/26/10. That meant Bubba was twenty-one. In a week, he really *would* be twenty-one, for a day. "How old are you, Cobb?"

"First time I was born was March 22, 1950. You could say I'm eighty. God knows I feel it. At a year a day, you'll see what I mean come . . . uh . . . April 16. If you make it that far. Are you planning to preach about the Thang?"

Bubba wiped his face with his overcoat's bright, leathery sleeve. His head was full of fresh Know. "No. I want to have dozens of children, hundreds of grandchildren, and thousands of great-grandchildren. God willing, there'll be a million of us by June. *Then* we'll restart the Thang for real!"

Cobb nodded as if he already knew this, but Cisco looked a little surprised. "That many of you, Bubba? Is that such a good idea, to cover the whole planet with hungry teenage boys?"

"Keep it bouncing," said Cobb. "When the boppers come down they'll find ways to turn off the gibberlin, and to father some girls."

"I'll miss you, Mamma," said Bubba, trying to give Cisco a hug.

She pushed him away a bit more sharply than seemed necessary. "Just GO. Let's not stand here talking all night till the Gimmie comes." She gave Bubba a final pat on the cheek. "You're a fine boy. Whatever happens, I'm proud to be your mother."

Bubba took a few steps, stopped, and looked back at Cobb and Cisco. "Will you two be all right?"

Cobb made a dismissive gesture with his hand. "Don't worry about us, squirt. We race-traitors are a rough bunch. As soon as Cis and I get the hayloft cleaned out, we'll steal a car and split. No prob. Beat it. Free Cousin Willy if you get a chance."

It was full dark now, with not much traffic on the streets. Bubba found Fifth Street and started walking downtown. The shoes took some getting used to, especially with the ice. Bubba could see into lots of houses, all lit up and with families having dinner. His stomach rumbled for food. He passed some half-empty bar-and-grills, but they didn't look right. Up ahead, just to the left of the sunset's faint gray ghost, the sky was bright with big-city lights. Bubba put his head down and walked faster.

Finally he came to a big cross-street with lots of cars. He was very cold, especially his eyes and nose. A harsh wind blew grit up and down the dirty sidewalks. Nobody except Bubba was walking. But right here, at the corner of Fifth and Broadway, there was a big lit-up store with men standing inside. Bubba found the door and went in to get warm.

One of the men came over to Bubba. His waist was wide, and he had a red face. He looked a little like Cobb, but not much.

"Hi there," said the man, sticking out his hand. "I'm Cuss Buckenham. Can I hep you in any way?"

Bubba knew how to shake hands. "I'm Buford Anderson," he said, doing it. "It's cold and windy and dark out there." Cisco had taught him to talk about the weather whenever he was unsure.

"You need your daddy to get you a car," said Cuss Buckenham. There were several shiny new cars inside the store with them. Bubba deduced that this man sold cars.

"My daddy drove a Doozy," said Bubba. Mamma had told him about Manchile's Doozy several times. "But he's dead. Do you sell Doozies, Mr. Buckenham?"

Cuss Buckenham threw back his head and laughed in a stagy, friendly way. "Do ah sell Doozies? Does a frog eat flies?"

"I don't know," said Bubba, fumbling in his pockets. "But I can buy a car right now with my card, can't I? I'm twenty-one and my uncle gave me lots of money."

The car dealer stopped laughing and took Bubba's card. He looked up at Bubba, looked back at the card, and looked up again. "I got a fine new Doozy right over here, Buford." Buckenham pointed to a deeply lustrous gold sports car in the corner.

"Thanks, Mr. Buckenham. And call me Bubba."

"Sure thing, Bubba, but you gotta call me Cuss. That there Doozy's one of the last 2031s in stock, loaded, and I can let you have it at a gooood price. Go on over and take a look, while I just run this card and see what kind of authorization we can git."

Bubba opened the car door and got inside. Right away, he Knew how to drive. It was like remembering something he'd forgotten about. The car looked good. The speedometer went up to 200 mph. The seats were real leather and the dash was faced in wood.

After a few minutes, Cuss Buckenham came over and squatted beside the car to look in at Bubba. "Your credit's copacetic, Mr. Anderson. How do you like her?"

"I'll take it."

Fifteen minutes later, the papers were all signed and the Doozy had been rolled out into the store's lot. Buckenham waved good-bye, and Bubba turned right on Broadway.

Fourth Street, Third Street, Second Street, try a left. Main Street, Chestnut Street, *Muhammad Ali Boulevard*. Big old building on the corner there, take a right. Big sign: *La Mirage Health Club*. Three-deck garage just beside it, pull in. Lock it and pocket. Done.

Bubba walked up the steps of La Mirage. It was Saturday night, and the place was jumping. There were knots of well-groomed men and women inside, black and white, old and young, some dressed for evening and some in sports togs. The doorman took an impression of Bubba's card, and the young meatbop was in.

"May I take your coat, sir?"

A lithe, long-haired girl smiled at Bubba from a large rectangular hole in the wall. There were lots of coats hanging behind her.

"Yes," said Bubba. "Thank you."

He shrugged his way out of his coat and handed it to her. She turned, hung the coat up, turned back and smiled. "Nice tie, sir." She had perfect features and full pouty lips. The sinuous arch of her long back and neck made her seem alert, perky, predatory, and poised.

"Thank you. My name's Bubba. What's yours?"

"Kari. Are you new in town?"

"Yes." Bubba took a deep breath and leaned forward. "You're beautiful and I'd like to go to bed with you."

"You bet," said Kari. "And so would my boyfriend." She laughed easily, letting him off the hook. "The lounge and dining area's down the hall to the left, sir, and the gym's upstairs. Good luck!"

Bubba smiled foolishly, then headed down the high-ceilinged, marble-floored, oak-paneled hall. Maybe he'd skimped too much on the middle part: *talk to her for a while.* Or maybe a chick like Kari was, quite simply, out of his league. At least for now. Hell, he was still just thirteen.

He entered the La Mirage lounge. His brain systems scanned his Know for an analog of what he saw. "Exploratorium," "Science Fair," and "Disky Museum of Robotics" came to mind. Scattered all about the lounge were people looking at or listening to little machines, little things like viewers and earphones and, in a few cases, whole-head helmets.

"Welcome, sir," said a young man in a tuxedo. "Are you new here?"

"Yes. I'm hungry."

"Very good, sir, there'll be a waiting time of twenty minutes. Party of one?"

Bubba observed that there were a few unattached women in the lounge. "Party of two," said Bubba. "Do you need my card?"

"Just your name, sir."

"Buford Cisco Anderson."

"Very good. While you're waiting, feel free to enjoy the healthful stim of our various software devices. Are you familiar with them all?"

"No."

"Well, you might start with a twist-box. Twist-boxes do a simple feedback-directed cutup and CA cleanup on visual inputs. They're from Einstein and quite amusing, though not everyone's seen them yet. Next I might suggest that you experience a cephscope tape. This week's special tape is by our local media star Willy Taze. Even if you're from out of town, you must have been following the meatbop conspiracy hearings? Willy was working on this tape when they arrested him at his parents' house. The first part of it's supposed to be his impression of Manchile's assassination. La Mirage's profit on Willy's tape showings will be contributed to the Taze Legal Defense Fund."

Bubba did his best to look noncommittal, and the young man continued.

"Last of all, should you and your companion be up for a *numero trois*, we have a Mindscape Axis Inverter—a truly enlightening experience for the wealthy connoisseur of healthy highs." The tuxedoed young man gave a prim smile and turned his attention to the next customer.

Bubba found a soft chair and plopped down. The well-lit dining room spread out from the other side of the dim lounge. There were people at all the tables, some of them tucking into big steak and seafood dinners. Bubba's stomach rumbled again. Disconsolately he glanced around the lounge. A dark-skinned woman was watching him from a couch nearby.

She was looking through a kind of lorgnette that she had held up to her face. A twist-box. He smiled and waved at her. Her full and finely chiseled lips smiled back from beneath the twist-box. He got up and walked over.

"Hi, I'm Bubba Anderson." He tried his most winning tone. The woman tilted her head back to look at him, still using the twist-box. "I'm alone," said Bubba, still smiling. "Would you like to have dinner with me? I'd like to talk to you for a while."

She set down the twist-box and looked him in the eye. Her eyes were large, with unreadable pupils set into smooth white whites. Finally she favored him with another smile. "Kimmie," she said, holding up her hand, palm down.

Bubba bent over and brushed his lips across Kimmie's fingers. "Charmed, I'm sure. May I look through your twist-box?"

"Certainly."

He sat down next to her on the couch and took the proffered twist-box.

A slim titaniplast cable connected it to a staple in the floor. He held it up to his eyes and looked at Kimmie.

Her face took on the appearance of a visage in an animated cartoon. A congeries of fluxdots drifted out of her hair and down over her eyes, silvering them, adding meat to the cheeks and still more heft to the lips. He looked down her throbby neck and at the breast mounds swelling out of her strapless pink silk dress. He could hear his heart going *kathump kathump.* Kimmie's dress disappeared, and Bubba's glance skied down the slope of her smooth belly to the wiry black mysteries of her crotch. He stared and Knew. She was fertile. His penis stiffened.

"Now, really, Bubba," said Kimmie, plucking the twist-box from his grasp. "You barely know what couth IS, do you, dear? You a country cousin?"

She talked like Geegee. "I'm new in town," he said, uncertainly. "It's very cold out tonight, did you notice? Cold and windy."

"Well, I suppose it'll get colder before it gets hot. And you're asking me to dinner?"

"Yes."

"I accept. But we'll split the check, and there's no strings. I fancy I could buy and sell you, Bubba child."

"Thank you, Kimmie. Have you looked at the new Willy Taze cephscope show? It's supposed to be about Manchile."

She countered with a question. "What do you think of Manchile, Bubba? Do you think they were right to kill him?"

"I didn't see him. But what he says makes sense, doesn't it? Why shouldn't humans and boppers begin to merge?"

Kimmie smiled drily. "How do we know the robots won't screw our genes up so bad that the race dies off? Maybe that's what they want. I'm all for the Thang's enlightened egalitarianism, but I do have my doubts about a man who knocks up ten women in a week. Manchile's nine-day boys."

She gave Bubba an odd look. Did she know him for a meatbop? Was she some kind of Gimmie agent? His stomach rumbled again. To cover up his confusion he picked up one of the cephscope headsets and put it on. It was a simple band with metal pads that rested on his temples. As soon as Bubba slipped it on, the tape started.

Bubba felt a series of odd tingles all over his body, as if the cephscope were checking out his neurowiring. There were some random sounds and washes of color, and then suddenly the room around him tore into bits. He was staring at a man's handsome face, and the man was talking in a thick Southern accent.

"In all the different kinds of folks I've met, I've seen one thing the same—everybody wants the best for their children. Boppers is the same!"

The image cut to the faces of a cheering crowd. Bubba had the kinetic feelings of being in a jostling crowd, staring up at Manchile on a stage. Two shiny boppers hovered overhead—one of them was Uncle Cobb! The crowd got softer and everything grew pink, glowing pink with branching purple vein patterns. Fish darted by. Far in the distance, breakers crashed. Bubba felt himself floating, floating on a wooden raft. The raft scrunched onto the sand of a pitilessly bright beach. A chattering band of apes came running down from the jungle that edged the beach. They poked and probed at Bubba, showing their large teeth. He held up his arms and roared at them. But now he was looking out at a crowd of people, looking out at them from Manchile's point of view. One of the men in the crowd lifted a particlebeam tube and aimed it. The burning blast blew him into blackness. Spermy white wiggles darted in the black. The squiggles split in two, and the new pieces split and split again, but unevenly, mapping out some kind of design like a circuit diagram or a choice-tree. Behind the branching tree he could see the apes again; the tree was a cage that held him captive. A monotonous male voice recited numbers in his ear, and his hands moved obsessively back and forth, as if he were knitting. Meanwhile his eyes darted up and down the branchings of the cage's bars—there was a way out if only he could see . . . Bubba had the odd feeling that the design coded up a message just for him, but it was going by too fast, and now the image grew faint and grainy as a vizzyscreen. On the screen there was a woman newscaster talking with a slight lisp.

"Welcome to the evening news for Saturday, February 8, 2031. Tonight's top story: Half an hour age, fugitives Cobb Anderson and Cisco Lewis were killed in a bloody shootout with Kentucky state troopers on I76. Three officers were wounded, one severely."

Bubba shook his head and blinked his eyes. The vizzy image stayed put. Pictures of Mamma and Uncle Cobb appeared behind the sleek, fast-talking anchorwoman.

"Cobb Anderson's petaflop bopper body will be sent to the Einstein ISDN ziggurat for disassembly, while Cisco Lewis's autopsy is slated for the Humana Hospital, where biodecontamination facilities are available. A local car dealer reports having seen Ms. Lewis's child, the last of the nine-day meatbop boys known to be at large. He is believed to be a dark-haired adolescent male, five-foot-six, using the name Buford Cisco Anderson. He should be presumed armed and dangerous. ISDN is offering one hundred and fifty thousand dollars for the boy's body, and Gimmie officers have been instructed to shoot on sight. I switch you now to Brad Kurtow, at the scene of the massacre on I76, forty miles north of Louisville."

Bubba clawed the cephscope headset off. The tape had ended, and he'd been sitting here staring at a vizzyscreen across the room. They'd killed Cobb and Cisco. He lurched to his feet, and jerked when someone touched him.

"Where you goin, country? That cephtape flick you out?"

He looked down at the black woman . . . Kimmie. "I—I have to go."

"Maybe I can help."

"I don't trust any of you." He rushed out of the lounge and down the hall, forgetting his overcoat. Only outside did he remember that he'd left his car keys in the coat pocket. Just as well, if Cuss Buckenham had called the Gimmie. In the distance a siren sounded, getting closer. Bubba took off running at top speed. Headlights coming, and the sound of helicopters overhead. He cut into an alley and kept going.

For the next hour, Bubba ran in and out of alleys, hiding from every passing car and ducking the searchlights that probed down out of the beating sky. Finally, just as he could run no further, he found himself in a junkyard down by the Ohio River. He flopped onto the seat inside a dead car's shell and gasped for air. His strong body's pulse quickly returned to normal, but now that he'd stopped running, the cold was sharp and painful. He was hungrier than he'd ever been in his life. Peering out through the car's windowhole, Bubba saw a fire glowing in a distant part of the junkyard. Straining his senses to the utmost, he picked his way in that direction.

There was a lone man by the fire, which was made out of old tires. Bubba watched him from the shadows, wondering what to do. The lumpy firetender had a mound of vizzies running, with each screen set to a different channel. He was swathed in layers of rags. Bubba could see that he was quite fat. Bubba hunkered there, staring at the fat man, feeling the saliva fill his mouth. He felt around on the ground beside him, and his hand closed over a heavy metal rod. Time to eat.

An hour later, Bubba was just about to start in on the fat man's second leg. After braining the guy, Bubba had laid him out so that his two legs lay across the acridly burning tires. Once the flesh was cooked through, it had been easy enough to twist the legs off and drag the torso out of sight. Now, after nibbling a whole leg right down to the bone, both thigh and drumstick, Bubba was very full. But who knew when he'd eat again. He stepped up to the fire and looked down at the black-charred second leg. The first one had been on the raw side; this one ought to be better. Beyond the dead cars, Louisville was like an excited anthill, with choppers and squad cars searching for Bubba.

Bubba picked up the leg and began scraping off the blackened crust.

He knew that humans viewed cannibalism as wrong, but that was just too bad, wasn't it, if the humans thought they could kill his father, his mother, and his Uncle Cobb, kill them like diseased rats. Bubba's Know told him that boppers often cannibalized each other for parts. It made sense. What could be a better source of body-building chemicals than a body? But, yes, he Knew it was wrong, murder was always wrong, and the watchman had made such a sad noise as he died.

Here and now, all this worrying was quite abstract. Here and now it was eat or die. With the testosterone and the gibberlin raging through his tissues, Bubba had the hunger of a werewolf. He broke the leg in two at the knee joint and bit into the crisp calf. He hunkered there by the fire, eating and enjoying the warmth.

The idyllic times at Churchill Downs already seemed like a very long time ago. Even La Mirage Health Club seemed like a long time ago. Bubba's mind was right up in the present, wondering where he'd hide next. It wouldn't do to be found with the half-eaten body of a junkyard watchman. It would give people a bad impression of the boppers; it would harm the Thang.

The mound of vizzies by the fire was full of news about him and the others. The same news over and over; the excited human ants rub-rubbing their info feelers. Luther and Geegee had been arrested. Willy Taze was going on trial tomorrow on a treason charge. Kimmie Karroll, wealthy socialite, reported having met Bubba at La Mirage. There was a strict emergency curfew in effect; and all ISDN and Gimmie officers had been instructed to shoot on sight.

A helicopter racketted right overhead, searchlight blazing. It came in so fast and low that Bubba barely had time to throw himself under the watchman's beat-up pickup nearby. The helicopter hovered, examining the fire. The thigh was still there on the ground, and most of the calf. Bubba wished he'd thought of taking off the shoe; the shoe made it too obvious.

BBBBDBDBDBDBBTKTKTK.

Automatic weapons fire. They were shooting down at the junkyard, in circles spreading out from the fire. When the bullets began pinging into the bed of the pickup, Bubba grew frantic. He scrunched up under the truck's engine block for protection. The helicopter kept shooting the pickup. Maybe they'd spotted him before coming in.

The tire fire was at the edge of a slope leading down to the frozen Ohio River. The pickup was facing that way. Down there would be better than up here. Bubba got on his back and grabbed the pickup's front axles with his hands. With the fresh food in him, he felt very strong. He dug his heels into the ground and pushed with all his might. Slowly the truck's mass gave, and then, all at once, Bubba and the truck were bouncing down the steep bank. The hovering gunship followed right along, pouring its full firepower down onto the truck. A bullet wormed past the truck's driveshaft and struck Bubba heavily in his crotch . . . *oh* . . . and then . . . *CRASH* . . . Bubba and the truck smashed into the ice of the river . . . and fell through.

The water was cold dark death, but it was safety, too. Bubba's body filled with adrenochrome and the pain in his groin went numb. He could last several minutes down here. He pushed free of the truck and swam downstream, staying just below the surface of the ice.

CHAPTER TWELVE

EMUL

February 22, 2031

Emul was very depressed. Everything was going wrong, up here and down on Earth. Berenice was dead and no one had gotten around to making her a new body. Emul wanted to find a way to put Berenice's software directly onto a wendy, as she'd always wanted, but he couldn't make it click.

None of the other boppers, not even Berenice's weird sisters, felt like helping him bring Berenice back, even as a petaflop, because, just now, Berenice's software was in disgrace. Her blitzkrieg program for a human/bopper fusion had wretchedly crashed. With the disappearance two weeks ago of Bubba, Manchile's sole surviving son, the boppers were left with nothing but bad publicity.

Berenice had hatched her plan on her own, though Emul had gotten her to explain it before he'd assented to have his meatie Ken Doll plant Berenice's handmade seed in Della Taze. The plan had gone like this: (1) Assemble a wholly artificial human-compatible embryo, the future scion Manchile. (2) Wetware-code the embryo's DNA to produce gibberlin plasmids so as to speed up the scion's growth and sexual activity. (3) Software-code the embryo's RNA with the Know—which consisted of a terabit of Berenice's info about Earth, Moon, and her plans for the scion. As well as carrying a kind of bopper consciousness, the Know was intended to serve as a hormone-triggered mindtool-kit to compensate for the short-lived scion's lack of experiential programming. (4) Plant the bopper-built embryo in a woman's womb. (5) Force the woman to travel to Earth. (6) The scion Manchile was programmed to reproduce, start a religion, and to get himself assassinated, thereby initiating class warfare on Earth. (7) Wait through the ensuing chaos for Manchile's descendants to ripple out over Earth. Side by side with the victorious human underclass, the meatbops would welcome the true boppers to their lovely planet!

Things had started to go wrong the instant Manchile had gone public.

Although some radical humans did have a certain sympathy for Manchile's Thang, very few of them felt strongly enough to act on their sympathies, and most of these were now in jail. The Gimmie had justified their brutal repression by presenting Manchile and the nine-day boys as an invasive social cancer. The final, debilitating propaganda battle had been lost when the fleshers heard about Bubba eating the bum—a typically baroque Berenice touch. If the humans had been able to find Bubba's body they would have torn it into shreds.

Even now, two weeks after the fact, with the crisis apparently over, ISDN was still keeping the antibopper propaganda drums beating. The bum, or watchman, or whatever he'd been, had become a human race-hero; his picture was everywhere and there were dramas about him; his name was Jimmy Doan. "Avenge Jimmy Doan," the humans liked to say now, "How many robots is one Jimmy Doan worth?" *Maybe a worn-out gigaflop with no cladding,* was Emul's opinion, but no one was asking him or any other bopper for input.

Emul had some suspicions about ISDN's real motives for keeping up the frenzy. In many ways, ISDN was like one of the old, multibodied big boppers. Emul had reason to believe that ISDN was beating the drums for business purposes. Most obviously, the continuing hysteria increased ISDN viewership. More subtly, the increased security measures at the trade center had greatly curtailed human/bopper trade, which had the effect of inflating prices and increasing the profit per item to be made by ISDN's middlemen.

Some hotheaded fleshers were talking about evacuating Einstein and cleaning out the Nest once and for all. But Emul was sure that ISDN had no intention of leaving the Moon; there was still so much money to be made. Surely the boppers were too *sexy* to exterminate. The apey jackdaw fleshers had an endless appetite for the tricks that boppers could do.

Instead of any all-out attack, the humans had been launching a number of commando raids on the Nest this week. Just yesterday, Emul had been forced to dynamite the Little Kidder Toys entrance to his tunnel after losing his favorite two meaties in a flesher terror raid there. A gang of ridgebacks, led by Darla's husband, Whitey Mydol, had burst into the store and had shot it out with Rainbow and Berdoo. Rainbow and Berdoo had been meaties for years, and Emul had been proud to own them. They'd cost him plenty. It had hurt to see them go down; to watch from inside their heads. They'd done their best, but the plaguey communications links were all staticky and unreliable these days; it seemed like everyone's equipment was wearing out at once. It had hurt to lose to Berdoo, and to make things worse, the combatative Mydol had escaped alive, even though Emul had blown up the tunnel just as Mydol entered. Mydol had lucked out and had stood in just the right place. All the luck was running the wrong way, and everything was going screwy.

Another screwy thing that Emul wondered about off and on was this character Stahn Mooney, a slushed clown detective whom he'd hired to help with the kidnapping of Darla last month. The evening of the kidnapping, Mooney, for reasons unknown, got a partial right hemispherectomy, had a rat-compatible neuroplug installed, and phoned Emul up from the trade center, offering himself as a *voluntary meatie*. Mooney's body was strong, and his left brain glib, so business sense had dictated that Emul accept the offer. Apparently Mooney had taken Emul's promise of a free wendy too much to heart, and he arrived at the Nest with some crazed notion that a community of meaties lived together in a place called Happy Acres, when in fact there were at most five or six meatie-owners in all the Nest, most of them involved with the dreak and amine trades. Emul had hired him all right, but something about Mooney stank—most of all the fact that there were no godseye records of what he'd done after Darla merged him down in the Mews. As soon as Emul had installed Mooney's rat, he wasted no time in selling the guy to Helen, Berenice's waddling pink-tank sister, who had ample use for a flesh tankworker. Emul had gotten a nice price out of Helen, enough for four tubes of dreak; and Mooney seemed happy enough playing with the blank wendy Helen gave him; but the whole thing still bothered Emul. It stank.

Emul shifted into realtime and looked around his laboratory. It was a low rock-walled room twenty by forty feet. Half the room was filled with Oozer's flickercladding vats. Formerly a flickercladding designer, Oozer was now busy trying to develop a totally limp computer with petaflop capabilities. Most flickercladding was already capable of petaflop thought processes—on a limpware basis—and Oozer felt he should be able to make the stuff function at these high levels *independently* of any J-junction or optical CPU hardware at all. Oozer was known for such autonomous limpware designs as the kiloflop heartshirt and the megaflop smart KE bomb.

Emul's jumbled end of the room had a hardened glass panel and airlock set into one of the walls. The panel showed Darla's room; she spent most of her time lying on her bed and watching the vizzy. Like all the humans, she was in an ugly mood these days. Earlier today, when Emul had entered her quarters, she'd threatened to do bellyflops off her bed until she aborted. He'd had to talk to her for a long time. He'd ended up promising to let her out early if she would promise to fly to Earth. He was supposed to be working out the details right now, though he didn't feel like it. He didn't feel like doing much of anything these days; he seemed to have a serious hardware problem.

His hardware problem was the greatest of Emul's worries—above and beyond Darla, Stahn Mooney, Whitey Mydol, Berenice, and ISDN's jingoistic war drumming. There was a buzz in Emul's system. At first he'd thought it was from too much dreak, and he'd given the stuff up almost entirely. But the buzz just got worse. Then he'd thought it might be in his flickercladding, so he'd acid-stripped his imipolex all off and gotten himself recoated with a state-of-the-art Happy Cloak built by Oozer. The buzz was no better. It was a CPU problem of some sort, a breakdown in perfectly reversible behavior. The primary symptom was that more and more often Emul's thoughts would be muddled by rhythmic bursts of kilohertz noise. It was possible to think *around* the thousand spikes a second, but it was debilitating. Apparently Emul needed a whole new body.

Just now Emul was in his rest position—that of an RYB cube with a few sketchy manipulators and sensor stalks. He was resting on the floor in front of his thinking desk, which served as a communications terminal and as a supplemental memory device—much like a businessman's file cabinets and floppy disks.

Four treasured S-cubes sat out on Emul's desk: brown, red, green, and gold. These hard and durable holostorage devices coded up the complete softwares of four boppers. There were Oozer's and Emul's S-cubes, of course, updated as far as yesterday. And there was a recent cube of Kkandio, Oozer's sometime mate, a suave boppette who worked the Ethernet. She and Oozer had two scions between them. Most important of all, there was dear Berenice's S-cube. Emul had used a copy of it to blend with his own software when he'd programmed the girl embryo he'd put in Darla's womb. He wanted to build a new petaflop for Berenice, but right now it felt like he, Emul, needed a new body worse than anyone.

Emul sent signals in and out of his desk, flipping though his various internal and external memories: his flickercladding mode, his hereditary RAM, his realtime randomization, the joint bopper godseye, his inner godseye, his flowchart history, and all the detailed and cumbersome speculations that he'd dumped into his desk's limpware storage devices.

Emul was trying to decide if there were any hope of getting an exaflop system up in the next couple of weeks. Two months ago, when he and Oozer had been able to afford a lot of dreak, the exaflop had seemed very near. Indeed, Emul had half-expected his next body to be an operational, though experimental, exaflop based on a novel quantum clone string-theoretic memory system. But now, soberly looking over his records, Emul realized that any exaflop was still years away. Looking at his credit holdings, he saw that he didn't really have enough money for a new petaflop, either, and that, as a matter of fact, a repo teraflop was going to be about the best he could swing.

His worry session was interrupted by Oozer, who came stumping awkwardly down to his end of the lab, gesturing back towards his vats.

"Oh, ah, Emul, some off brands of imipolex in there; the stuff is letting itself *go*."

"I got the fear of eerie death standing ankle-deep around me, Oozer," said Emul unhappily. "The buzz is so much worser stacks in my thinker."

"I can't—at any rate I keep saying 'at any rate'—I don't mean to say that, but I do now know your kilohertz buzz. It hurts. We're sick, Emul. The cladding's sick, too."

"Plague," said Emul, jumping to a conclusion. "Flesher plague on both our houses."

He turned to his desk and made some calls. Starzz, who ran the dreakhouse. Helen, to whom he'd sold that meatie three weeks back. Wigglesworth, the digger who was supposed to fix Emul's tunnel. Oozer's girlfriend Kkandio, voice of the Ethernet.

Sure enough, none of them was feeling too well. They each had a hardware buzz. They were relieved and then frightened to hear that others had the same problem. Emul told them to spread the word.

He and Oozer looked at each other, thinking. The desk's signal buzzed and sputtered at a steady kilohertz cycle.

"*Dis*cover to *re*cover," said Oozer, running a thick gout of his flickercladding over to the desk. Little tools formed out of his warts, and in minutes he had the desk's CPU chips uncovered. "Dr. Benway letting the clutch out as fast as possible, you know, '*Whose* lab tests?!?'" Oozer peered and probed, muttering his bepop English all the while. "Which would break the driveshaft, see, 'cause the universal joint can't but—Emul! Look at this!"

Emul put a microeye down by the desk's chips. The chips were oddly spotted and discolored by small—he looked closer—colonies of organisms like . . . mold cultures in a petri dish. All their chips were getting infected with a biological mold, a fuzzy gray-yellow sludge that fed on—he stuck an ammeter wire into one of the mold spots—one thousand cycles per second. The fleshers had done it . . .

"Well, I'll tell you this, I don't feel very intelligent . . . anymore, at times, for a long time . . . the cladding's full of nodes, Emul, come see." Oozer wheeled around in a jerky circle.

Watching him, Emul realized that his old friend was shaking all over. Oozer's limbs were moving jerkily, as if they longed to stutter to a halt. But the bopper drove himself forward and pulled a big sheet of plastic out of the nearest vat. The thick plastic flopped to the floor and formed itself into a mound. It looked unlike any flickercladding Emul had ever seen. Normal flickercladding was dumb: left on its own, it did little more than run a low-complexity cellular-automaton pattern. If you disturbed flickercladding—by touching it, by shining light on it, or by feeding it signals through its microprobes—then its pattern would react. But ordinarily, all by itself, flickercladding was not much to look at. This new stuff was different; it was transparent, showing three-dimensional patterns of an amazing complexity. The stuff's pattern-flow seemed to be coordinated by a number of bright, pulsing nodes—mold spots!

All of a sudden Oozer's trembling got much more violent. The bopper drew all his arms and sensors in, forming himself into a tight pod. The Oozer pod huddled on the floor, looking almost like the new mound of flickercladding, all bright and spotty. Emul signaled Oozer, but got only a buzz in response.

Emul's own buzzing felt worse and worse, and now it was like his willpower was cut out, and the more he tried to find it, the worse it got, to try and find his self. He looked down at his box and noticed bright mold spots in his own flickercladding . . . bright mold sucking out his battery-juice too f-f-f-fast . . . h-h-h-h-e s-s-s-sank d-d-d-down.

And lay there like a shiny chrysalis.

The lab was still, with nothing moving but Darla, anxiously peering out through the glass of her sealed room.

CHAPTER THIRTEEN

HAPPY ACRES

February 24, 2031

Stahn blinked and tried to stand up. But his left leg was numb and floppy, as was his left arm, as was the entire left side of his body. He landed heavily on something soft. A woman smell over the fetid stench, he was lying on . . . Wendy? Wendy!!! Wendy???

She was a comatose human vegetable fitfully twitching her flawless bod. Her breath was babyishly irregular. She barely knew how to breathe right, poor clone . . . but . . .

Stahn tried again to stand up and only managed to wallow the more inefficaciously on the wendy-thing's not unappetizing person. His penis stiffened, and he did what he had to do. Wendy liked it; come to think of it, they'd been doing this a lot. They were naked and covered with filth.

After they both climaxed, Stahn rolled onto the right side of his body, and began looking around for the bench he'd been sitting on. There it was, over there . . . he began worming his way across the offal-strewn floor of the tiny stone stall he and the wendy had apparently been living in.

Something had just stopped; like a noise Stahn had gotten used to, but what? He hooked his chin over the edge of the bench and dragged himself back into sitting position. He kept forgetting to use the left half of his body. Why had he crawled when he could have walked? His space orientation was shot: even the five-foot crawl from Wendy to the bench seemed complicated. Stahn stared down at Wendy. Looking at her helped focus his ideas. He was a meatie, that was it, and Wendy was a blank-brained clone, he was a meatie living in . . .

"Happy Acres," said Stahn out loud, slurring his words, but enjoying the sound of his voice nonetheless. He started laughing, and then he couldn't stop laughing for a long time. It was like he had a month's worth of laughter waiting to get out, desperate laughter that sounded like moans.

Eventually the moaning turned into thick hollow coughing and he had to stop. There was something wrong with the roof of his mouth: a big hole up there, and a pain like a splinter. Stahn felt the hole with his tongue, felt and listened, and looked around.

The air in here was incredibly unbelievably vile. They were in a room with a locked jail cell door. You could look out onto big pink-lit tanks filled with crowded murky fluid, livers and lungs and brains and, yes, wendies floating in them, the pink-tanks, that's where Stahn worked most days, worked till he couldn't move, with Wendy crawling along after, both of them eating as much raw organ as they liked of course, and at the end of the day, however long it was, they were shut up in their Happy Acres cubby for intercourse, excretion, and dreamless sleep. What was it Ricardo had said? Stahn remembered, and spoke out loud again.

"You won't have a care in the world, Mooney man, you'll live like a king!"

The sobbing laughter started again, loose and sloppy, with air snuckering in and out of the hole in his soft palate, the big splinter slipping and wiggling, *uuuuuuhuhuhuhuhhhh* . . . there . . . it was coming . . . *uuuuughhh* . . .

Stahn retched hard and harder and then . . . the little dead plastic rat slid out of his mouth and clattered to the floor. All *right!* No more rat, no more of Helen's goddamn nagging voice in his head day and night, like a mother you can't get away from, do this Stahn, do that, oh I *like* when you move your bowels. No more of Helen in Stahn all the time, using him in the stink. He ground the rat under his foot.

Something had happened to Helen; something had shut her down. So wonderful, at last, to sit here thinking his own thoughts and looking around . . . though there *was* still some problem . . . hmmmm, oh yes . . . his right brain damage . . . and the way he kept forgetting about the left half of his body. *Could* he move his left leg, if he really tried? His left thumb?

Stahn stared hard at his thumb. He *used* to know how to move it, but just now, without Helen's voice running his left side, he . . . couldn't . . . get the notion of *purposeful action* . . . so he grabbed the thumb with his good right hand and wiggled it, yah, he even leaned over and sniffed it, licked it, bit it and . . . there . . . it was moving . . . spastically moving as new nerve routings opened up . . . tingling . . . he did the rest of his hand then . . . step by step . . . the arm . . . the arm flapping at his side like the chicken imitation he used to do on Z-gas in Daytona . . . lean over so it beats on your leg, Stahn . . . *shuffle splutter, splutter mutter* . . .

Eventually he struggled to his feet and stood there, pigeon-toed and awkward, but, yes, stood. And found his way over to Wendy and felt the roof of her mouth, looking for a rat, but she was untouched, still too dumb for the boppers to use, good deal.

"We're gonna make it, Wendy; we're gonna make it back, babe."

He worked on Wendy's body for a while, rubbing and flexing her arms and legs like a physical therapist, or like a mother with her baby, rubbed and flexed her, talking all the while, thrilled to talk for the first time in . . . yes . . . it had been a month.

Stahn's memory of the month's slavery was oddly faint. Possibly the horror of it had been such that his brain refused to remember. Or perhaps it was that, with Helen calling all all all the shots always always always, his brain had known that it needn't bother to make notes. Or maybe the surgical brain trauma had screwed up his memory for good.

ISDN had done this to him . . . why? To bring the chipmold to the Nest, yes. The chipmold must have worked, that was it, the chipmold had fried the brains of all the boppers. They were crispy critters now, that's what Chief Jackson had always called the gone loveboat dopers who couldn't remember their names, crispy critters. Stahn had been pretty sick with that chipmold himself for a week there . . . he remembered the ache in his throat and in his kidneys . . . but he'd gotten well, the ancient streetwise human wetware had come up with an antidote.

Stahn tugged Wendy up onto the bench. She sat unsteadily at his right side, blowing spit bubbles. After a while she slid back off the bench.

Stahn worked on his left side some more, trying to keep remembering it, and then he picked his way across the cell to examine the door. He couldn't really see through his left eye, or do anything about what he felt with his left hand, but after a while he had the door pretty well doped out. It was held locked by a hook-and-eye latch. The lock was hard to work . . . Stahn kept moving his hands in the wrong direction like in a mirror . . . but finally he got their cell open.

"Come on, Wendy. We're going home." He pulled Wendy to her feet and put a tight arm around her waist. They shuffled out of their cell into the pink-lit room where the organ-filled pink-tanks were. It looked very familiar in a way, albeit as confusing as a maze. Wandering this way and that, his heart pounding anxiously, Stahn finally bumped into the glass wall next to the airlock.

Helen and Ulalume were out there, sitting in the middle of the floor and not doing anything, not dead or alive but just kind of . . . sitting there with their flickercladding gone strange. Tranced out, like. Yukawa had said that the chipmold would start some kind of electric vibrations in the boppers' brains and give them fits. Cataleptic as opposed to epileptic, or so it would seem. Helen and Ulalume were buddha-ed out, man, just sitting out there—Stahn chuckled softly—just sitting out there in perfect full-lotus *aum mane padme hum* meditation, wave, robot sees God in a mold, all right. And their flickercladding was doing weird stuff, blotched and splotchy all along Helen's xoxy big nurse pod-bod and on that "fine-featured Nefertiti head" she was so proud of, always reciting Poe's "To Helen" in Stahn's brain, ghastly old vampire bat that she was, always bugging Stahn always, and now she had big moldy bright spots in her flickercladding. Squidhead Ulalume and toothed-vagina Helen just sitting out there in the middle of the floor, side by side, waiting for ye Judgment Day trumps, or so so so it would seem. No prob. Do what?

Stahn struggled for an idea. He wanted to leave, but there was no air out there. How had Emul transported him here, through the Nest's cold hard vacuum? At first he couldn't remember at all, but then it came to him. After Emul had met Stahn at the trade center, he'd wrapped Stahn in a special Happy Cloak, a big piece of flickercladding that was programmed to behave like a bubbletopper spacesuit. Emul had used the Happy Cloak to bring Stahn from the trade center to the ratmaker, where Stahn had gotten a rat compatible with his new neuroplug. That was all very vague. And then Emul had sold Stahn to Helen, bringing him here to the pink-tanks, still in the Happy Cloak. Stahn could see the Happy Cloak hanging from a hook right across the room from the airlock, as a matter of fact, hanging there twisting and glowing in blotchy thought. He just had to run out through the vacuum and get the cloak, that was it.

It? Get the cloak, Stahn, yes. He set Wendy down on the floor, leaning her against the wall, and went into the airlock. It took him the longest time to get the door closed behind him, and then he got mixed up and went back out of the airlock into the pink-tank room with Wendy. He was so flustered that he forgot the left half of his body for an instant there, and fell to the floor, landing facedown in the warm puddle between Wendy's widespread legs, Happy Acres. He stood back up and peered out through the glass wall again, trying to gather his wits.

He spotted the Happy Cloak on the wall again, and remembered, and went back into the airlock. When it opened he would run out, grab the Happy Cloak, and run back in here to put it on. He poised himself to run, put his right hand on one of the door handles—he hoped it was the correct handle this time—and slapped his clumsy left hand against the vent button. The air whooshed out . . . Stahn kept his mouth and throat open, letting his lungs collapse instead of popping . . . and he was running across the room . . . or trying to run . . . like a palsy victim in the Special Olympics four-yard dash, man, *don't forget your left leg* . . . got his hand on the Happy Cloak . . . it simpered and came loose from its hook . . . oh the cold the pain in his ears his achy lungs and sweat crystallizing on his stiffening skin . . . but where was the airlock? Stahn swung his head this way and that, not seeing what he was looking for . . . a door shape over there, but *that* didn't look right . . . he tried to turn . . . *stumble* . . . oh no!

Too confused to do anything but lie there and thrash, ow, Stahn began to die, but then, at the last moment, the Happy Cloak flowed out over his whole body, making itself into a warm air-filled spacesuit.

There was the sweet energizing smell of clean air. Stahn's eyes flickered open. The part of the Happy Cloak in front of his face was transparent; he could see out. There was a series of sharp pains in the back of his neck. The Happy Cloak was plugging its microprobes into his nervous system.

Hello, meatie, came the Happy Cloak's sweet voice in Stahn's head. *I am pleased to ride your body once more. Much has changed.*

"Call me Stahn. I must bring a wendy intact to Einstein. Helen's orders."

That is untrue. The boppers are all dead. Take me to the light-pool so I can feed. Then I can help you.

"Fine." Stahn decided to think and say as little as possible. He got to his feet and wondered which way to go. Wendy was around here someplace, but he kept forgetting which direction was which. "We'll come back for Wendy later, right?"

Come. The Happy Cloak spacesuit nudged Stahn towards Helen and Ulalume, lying there on the floor. By selectively stiffening itself, the Happy Cloak could control which directions Stahn could move in. He had no desire to approach Helen's dangerous pod, but then he was leaning over her and touching her. Her mottled flickercladding blinked rapidly—as if talking to the Happy Cloak. He laid his other hand on the inert Ulalume, and her cladding responded in the same way.

Carry my fellows to the light-pool, said the voice in Stahn's head. *They are hungry, too.* The Happy Cloak flickered strobily at the bodies of Helen and Ulalume, and then the two weird sisters' skins slid off, exposing the hard blank bodyshells underneath. The shells weren't quite blank: threads of gray-yellow fuzz projected out of the microcracks at the joints. Chipmold. It had strangled the boppers' processors long before they could begin to synthesize the proper antigen. Humans had the edge on them there, with their bodies' built-in wetware labs. The boppers' hardware was slushed, though their limpware—their symbiotic imipolex skins—seemed to be actually enjoying the mold. Stahn stooped and picked up the two wriggling imipolex sheaths. They weighed very little in the weak lunar gravity.

Thank you. The Happy Cloak wasn't running him as Helen had; it was simply nudging him and making suggestions. It was happy to see through Stahn's eyes and have Stahn carry it.

"Which way?"

Follow the star. Your Wendy will wait. We'll save her and Darla too.

A blue line drawing of a stellated dodecahedron appeared in Stan's visual field. Sometimes he'd lose sight of it, but if he turned his head back and forth he could always find it. He followed the star out of the lab, down a short corridor, and out into the huge open space of the Nest. Stahn paused, looking this way and that, still having trouble seeing anything on his weak left side. The Nest was roughly conical in shape, with a vast shaft of light coming down its central axis. For a terrified moment, Stahn felt as if he would fall upward along the Nest's pocked, towering walls.

The light-pool is ahead.

Stahn followed the blue star down a street with shops and boppers. The Nest had become a ghost town; all the boppers were motionless. Some of them must have depleted their batteries, for their skins were blank and empty. But most of them still had some juice, and their blotched claddings pulsed in asymmetric harmonies. They seemed to have enough photosensitivity to be able to converse among each other, at least after a fashion. Over and over, Stahn's Happy Cloak would flash a special stroby way, and an immobilized bopper's skin would slither off for Stahn to carry.

Finally they were at the light-pool, a great round patch of sunlight some fifty feet across. Dozens of paralyzed boppers crouched there, as well as scores of flickercladdings who'd laboriously crawled there on their own. The claddings looked like bright slugs. When Stahn tossed down his bale of claddings, many of the others came inching over to "talk." Stahn lay down to rest while the Happy Cloak around him ate its fill of light. The Happy Cloak cradled Stahn and fed him air. Its guileless microprobe outputs were bright and happy.

Stahn fell asleep and dreamed.

He was on a red rocky field, maybe Mars, though there was air, thin clean mountain air. The sun was small and hot. He had wings, huge imipolex wings. He was not alone; there were other humans like him, all partly clad in Happy Cloaks with great glider wings. Wendy was there, and Whitey and Darla. "Yay, Stahn," they yelled with laughing voices. "Come on!" They ran down a slope and leaped off the edge of the cliff the slope ended in, leaped out and circled like swallows over the great bright city in the rift.

The scene shifted, and he was back on Earth, deep undersea, dressed in a knowing imipolex diving suit beefed up to the size of a dolphin. Wendy was a plastic dolphin beside him, skirling chirrups. They arced into a juicy drift of squid.

He was in space, mellow with amines, drifting like a spore.

He was skittering across the heavy methane atmosphere of Jupiter, straining his senses downward to catch the mighty songs of the Great Old Ones below.

Come, Stahn. Let us be on our way. We'll get Darla and Wendy and walk to Einstein.

Stahn opened his eyes and sat up. Such sweet dreams. Helen had never let him dream, not for a month.

His Happy Cloak felt livelier; its renewed energies put a real spring in his motions. His left side was working much better. He leaped to his feet and stretched. The loose limpwares flickered at him, wishing him well. Two of them crawled closer, begging to be picked up.

I have showed them how to be spacesuits, said the voice in Stahn's head. *Bring them and follow the star.*

The spiky blue line shape appeared in Stahn's visual field, and he bounded along after it, carrying the two extra Happy Cloaks under his arm. First they'd save Darla. That was a good idea, and only fitting, as it was Stahn's fault that she'd been taken captive.

With part of his right brain missing, Stahn still didn't have a clue about which way was which. But he didn't worry about it too much. He knew that, just as limited damage to the left brain can knock out your ability to speak, limited damage to the right brain can destroy your ability to form mental 3D simulations of your surroundings. He'd get some new brain tissue from ISDN or, hell, he'd just keep this wavy Happy Cloak.

The blue star twinkled, and the voice in his head said, *I am pleased.*

They were in a kind of factory district now; huge idle buildings that must have been chip-smelters. They came to the Nest's wall, balconied like a highrise. A series of powerful leaps took Stahn up five levels, and then he followed the star down a short series of branching tunnels that ended with a single open door.

This was the laboratory of Emul and Oozer.

Stahn stepped in and looked around. It was a long low room, vaguely reminiscent of Yukawa's lab. There were vats at the far end, and there were twitching mounds of flickercladding here and there. This end of the room held a desk with four colored S-cubes on it. On the floor were the split-open bodies of the two mold-killed boppers, Oozer and Emul. Their claddings were gone: it was just the body casings there; the pressure of the mold's biomass had split the casings open like seed pods. In terms of hardware, Emul and Oozer were now like rusted-out cars with weeds growing in them, like mirrored freeform flowerboxes full of sprouts, like hollow logs covered by the rubbery fungus known as witch ears. Emul and Oozer's chipmold was at the end of its life cycle. The gray-yellow threads had formed golfball-sized nodes: fruiting bodies. Stahn reached down and picked one of them; it could be worth something on the outside. Just then he caught some motion out of the corner of his eye. Over there, set into the wall, was a window showing . . . Now who was that in there? He should have known the face but . . . dammit . . .

I think that's Darla.

Of course! "Darla!" shouted Stahn, even though she couldn't hear him. Darla waved both arms and drummed soundlessly on her window. Stahn put his moldfruit in the cloak's pouch and hurried into the airlock. He fumbled around for what seemed a very long time, and finally emerged into Darla's pink room. Obligingly, his Happy Cloak slid off.

Suddenly nude, Stahn lost control of his left leg and fell down. The woman leaned over him, her face large and upside down.

"Are you all right, Mooney? Can you get me out?"

Stahn had forgotten her name. He stared at her, breathing in the room's thick, female air. "Wendy? What did you just ask?"

"I'm Darla, fool. Can you get me out?"

"Yes," said Stahn quickly, and stood up. Looking straight at her, it was easier to remember her name. She was wearing an RYB playsuit. He'd called on her in her home last month. "Yes, Darla, I can get you out. We'll wear these." He pointed to the Happy Cloaks. "Come." He picked up his cloak and slung it over him. It flowed into position. Darla hesitated, and then did the same with one of the others. Stahn watched Darla jerk spastically as her cloak's microprobes slid into her spine.

"It's OK," said Stahn. "Don't worry."

She can't hear you. Touch heads.

Stahn pressed the clear plastic of his face visor against Darla's. "It's all right, Darla, it really is. These Happy Cloaks are wavy limpware dudes."

"It's stabbing my neck." Her voice through the plastic was faint and rubbery.

"That's just so it can see through your eyes and talk to you. Believe me, being a meatie is a lot worse."

"You were a meatie all along?"

"Just this month. Whitey had ISDN make me a meatie to get even for what I did to you."

"I told you he'd get even. Can we just walk out of here now?"

"Yeah. We'll pick up my Wendy and walk to Einstein."

"Wendy?"

"You'll see." Stahn noticed that there was an air-filled tunnel leading out from one end of Darla's room, a tunnel blocked by a locked cell door. It would certainly make things easier if they could find a tunnel to Einstein.

"Does the tunnel from your room go all the way through?"

"It used to. It used to start at a scurvy place called Little Kidder Toys," answered Darla. "But Emul exploded that end of the tunnel day before yesterday. Whitey and his guys were trying to come through."

"If we can't find a tunnel, we'll have to climb out the Nest's main hole and walk. I just hope my Wendy can make it."

"What's wrong with your precious Wendy?" Darla was getting impatient. She didn't like having Mooney's face shoved up against hers for so long, though he, of course, seemed to be enjoying it.

"She's a clone, Darla. Her mind is a complete blank. It's like she's a hundred-and-twenty-pound newborn baby."

"Sounds like just your pervo trip, geek. Here, you carry her Happy Cloak."

"Now look—"

Darla snapped her head back and marched into the airlock. Stahn followed along and moments later they were out in the lab. Stahn's Happy Cloak made another request.

Take my brothers out of here. They hunger. Carry them to the light-pool.

"No way. That's too far. Darla won't go for it. But maybe . . . " Stahn remembered his good smart bomb: his flickercladding Superball that had bounced so well. "How about this, cloak. If your brothers can roll themselves up like big balls, we can throw them off the balcony towards the light-pool. They can bounce and roll all the way there."

Yes. I understand.

Stahn limped around the room patting the loose claddings, one by one, so that his cloak could tell them what to do. There were fifteen of them—thirteen from the vats and two from Oozer and Emul, not that you could tell who was which. The claddings pulled themselves together, and then they lay there like fifteen variegated marbles, each about the size of a bowling ball. Darla watched Stahn from the lab door. She had her hands on her hips and she was tapping her foot. Stahn walked over and pushed his face against hers. She was wearing a tough frown.

"What are you doing, Mooney, you slushed pig?"

"Darla-pie, let's get it straight: I'm saving your life. My cloak wants us to throw these balls off the balcony out there. We'll do that, and then we'll get Wendy, and then we'll go home. There's no big rush, because all the boppers are dead. I killed them with chipmold; that's what ISDN used me for, baby, so shut your crack."

It was Stahn's turn to snap his head back. And then, just to bug Darla the more, he rolled the fifteen balls together into a triangular pattern like a rack of fresh balls on a pool table. He couldn't visualize the triangle in advance, but he could tell when he was done. He picked up two of the balls—three would have been too awkward—and followed his cloak's blue mindstar through the tunnels to the balcony. Darla followed suit. She jerked in surprise when they got out to the edge; she'd never seen the Nest.

Stahn pointed across the dead underground city at the light-pool. A straight street ran from the pool to the base of the wall below them. He set down one of his cladding balls and lifted the other one overhead with both arms. He threw it out and up, putting all he had into it. The ball shot along a soaring lowgee trajectory, bounced perfectly, sailed, bounced, sailed and dribble-rolled towards the light-pool's distant, bright spot. Stahn threw his second ball, and then Darla threw both of hers.

On their fourth trip, Darla only had one ball to carry. She pressed her face against Stahn's face. The exercise had put her in a better mood.

"Can we go now, Mooney?"

"Sure. And call me Stahn. What were those S-cubes on the desk in there?"

"Personality cubes for Emul and some of his friends. He was always fiddling with them. Do you think we ought to bring them? Valuable info, right?"

"Hell, let's not bother. I don't want to see any of those boppers for a long time. I'm glad the mold killed them."

Follow the star to Wendy, Stahn.

They scrambled down the balconies to the Nest floor and turned right on a circumferential road along the cliffs base. They walked and walked, until the star darted into one of the cliff-base doors. They went in, and there they were, back at the pink-tank labs.

Darla cycled them through the lock into the room with the tanks. Wendy was right where Stahn had left her, lying on her back with her blank eyes wide open. She was staring at her fingers and wiggling them. Stahn pushed his cloak off his face and Darla did the same.

"Stinks in here," said Darla. "So that's Wendy? Poor clone. She's like a baby. Did you see how high up it is to the hole at the top of the Nest?"

"Really far," said Stahn. "But I ain't going without my Wendy. She's what I came here for, all right?"

I have a suggestion, said the voice in Stahn's head. *The cloak you brought for her can drive her.*

"Can you hear your spacesuit talking to you?" Stahn asked Darla.

"Is that what it is? I thought I was hallucinating from all the sense-depriv. These things are like really alive?"

"Especially now that they've got chipmold nodules in them. We used to call them Happy Cloaks, but now maybe we should call them moldies. My cloak—my moldie—it says that the one I brought for Wendy's spacesuit can drive her body around."

And talk through her.

"And talk through her," said Darla. "Stop that." She slapped at the splotchy, flickering moldie that covered her bod. "So do it, Stahn."

Stahn flopped the extra moldie over Wendy. It flowed all over her. For a long time it seemed like nothing was happening. But then Wendy began to tremble, first a little, and then a lot. All at once the trembling stopped. More time passed and then Wendy stood up. Now it was Stahn who was trembling. He reached his shaky hands forward and pulled the cladding down from off her face.

"Hello," said the bright happy face. "This is very nice!" The voice sounded just like Stahn had remembered it, for all these years.

"Oh Wendy." Stahn put his arms around her and held her tight.

CHAPTER FOURTEEN

DELLA

March 7, 2031

Della didn't recognize the man at her door. He was fat and pale and fortyish, with black shoes and a cheap, ill-fitting suit. Though his features were snubbed and boyish, his face was puffed, giving him a callow, watery air. Perhaps he'd been handsome in his youth, but something must have gone badly wrong for him since; some kind of hormone imbalance. Della was glad she had the doorchain fastened.

"Who are you?" she asked through the crack. Her new apartment's location was supposed to be private—so many nuts had come traipsing by the Tazes' that Della'd had to move out. "What do you want?"

"I got this address from Ilse Taze. If you don't want to let me in, why don't you come out and we can take a walk." He tapped his mouth and his ear, suggesting that what he had to tell Della was private.

Della shook her head. The guy could be a Gimmie agent, an ISDN newshound, a crazed Thangie, a Racial Puritan, or an ordinary sex criminal. A lot of weirdos had it in for her, ever since it had become widely known that Della's womb had borne Manchile. The story had come out after Manchile's assassination and Willy's arrest. Della had refused all interviews, though she'd had to tell most of her story in court during the ongoing meatbop conspiracy trial. Lots of people wanted to meet Della, which was the main reason she had gotten this absolutely secret apartment to live in. This visitor was the first to have tracked her here. Why had Ilse told him where to come?

He looked like he hadn't seen sunlight in years. His pithy fatness was diseased and unnatural. And as the smell of Della's microwaved dinner floated out past her and through the door's crack, he licked his lips in a wet, hungry way that was utterly revolting.

"Go away," said Della, showing him the needler attached to her belt. The man took two steps backwards. On top of it all, he had a nasty limp. Della slammed the door closed and secured the bolts. Why the *hell* was Aunt Ilse giving out her new address to unny creeps? Hadn't Della told all her goddamn family members that she needed very much to be alone? What would Aunt Ilse have to gain by giving out Della's address—MONEY, for God's sake? Couldn't old Jason and Amy and Colin and Ilse EVER stop thinking about themselves?

One of the main reasons Della had taken that shady job with Yukawa on the Moon had been to get *away* from them all: her relatives, her friends, her acquaintances. Of course, in Einstein, it had all started up again, people bothering her, one way or another, boss and cops and leeches and so-called friends, not that Buddy Yeskin had been a bother, no, he'd been gentle as a lamb, and even less talkative. With all the merge, Buddy and Della had never *needed* to talk, which had been fine, not that merge was an experience that Della wanted to repeat anytime soon. As far as she was concerned, Einstein was a drag now, what with all the old merge crowd running around giving vizzy interviews—if Della went back, they'd scoop her up like money in the street, no thanks. And of course Yukawa was still throbbing his half-pervo torch for "poor Della Taze," yes, even though Della wouldn't ever answer, Max Yukawa still kept writing and calling her at her parents', which had been yet another good reason to get her own private apartment. Della still had nightmares about the private Dr. Y. With all the merge nothing had mattered.

She got her chicken dinner out of the microwave and sat down at her dinette table facing the vizzy. One result of this kilp was that she'd gotten in the habit of watching the evening news. She could see all the people she wanted on the screen. There'd probably be something about Willy's case—the verdict was expected any day.

The news had already started. Right now it was a live broadcast from the Einstein ISDN building: yet another interview with Stahn Mooney and Whitey Mydol, who sat grinning on two couches with their women, Wendy and Darla. Della knew Whitey and Darla from the merge scene: he was a ridgeback, and she was his rocker wife. Della had never run into Stahn Mooney, but she knew him from the family stories and from the old newsreels. Wendy was an exceptionally clear-skinned blonde woman. She was supposed to have amnesia.

Every sentient being on Moon or Earth knew the story by now. ISDN's Dr. Max Yukawa, incensed by the boppers' meatbop rape of Della Taze, had designed the chipmold that could fry their circuits. Whitey Mydol, outraged by the boppers' abduction of his wife Darla Starr, had coerced Stahn Mooney into carrying some spores of Yukawa's chipmold into the

Nest. Mooney had accomplished his mission and had escaped the dead Nest with Darla and with the mysterious Wendy.

The moderator was handsome, personable Tobb Zununu. Della listened with interest, eating her food in large bachelor-gal mouthfuls.

Tobb: How HARD did Whitey and ISDN pressure you to go, Stahn?

Stahn: How low is up? A little. But, hey, I'm glad I got to save D and W. We had a heck of a climb out. We were lucky about the bubble-toppers, they were ultragood cladding pals. I still wear mine, it helps my bad brain.
(Close shot of the thick splotchy scarf around his neck.)

Stahn: (Serious and open.) I call it a moldie. It's a symbiote.

Tobb: (Grinning.) Could be the start of a new fad. I notice this lovely young lady next to you is wearing one as well. (Sympathetically.) Wendy, we're all still wondering where you're from and what you were doing down in the Nest. Can you tell us a bit about your background?

Wendy: (Radiant.) My body's a tank-grown clone of Stahn's dead wife Wendy, Tobb. He's thrilled to bits to be living with the same wetware. Of course, growing up in an organ farm pink-tank doesn't give a girl much of a preparation for city life, but I've got my moldie to help me out. (Slow, knowing laugh.) As soon as I get a chance to visit Earth, I'm planning to find my biological parents. And—can I tell him, Stahn?

Stahn: (Beaming and fingering his scarf.) You sure can!

Wendy: Yesterday we went ahead and got married!

Tobb: That's wonderful, Wendy. All of us wish you and Stahn a lot of luck. Any plans for the immediate future, Stahn? I understand you've become quite a wealthy man. Are you planning to settle down and relax?

Stahn: (Sly smile.) Far from it, Tobb. Just wait and see.

Tobb: (Guffawing to the camera.) Isn't he something? A modern hero with the right stuff. Now let's hear from Darla Starr. Darla, you're pregnant, are you not?

Darla: (Rapidly chewing gum.) Yeah. I'm expectin twins. (Chewing faster.) That's why the boppers kidnapped me. (Starts to say something and stops.)

Tobb: The twins would be Whitey's children?
                (General laughter.)

Darla: Ask Whitey.

Whitey: The kids are both normal. We ran some lab tests. The amino-types check and, what's more important, Darla's gibberlin-free. This won't be another Manchile, it'll be two nice little girls. Darla and I are mongo psyched.

Tobb: Well, there's good news all around tonight, isn't there? Congratulations! (Growing serious.) In a related Moon story, this afternoon I talked to Dr. Max Gibson-Yukawa about a question we've all been asking ourselves. Does the chipmold pose any danger to the humans or to the asimov computers of Einstein? Here is Dr. Yukawa's reassuring response.
                (Shot of Yukawa's thin, thoughtful head, talking.)

Yukawa: There is some slight risk in weakened individuals, Tobb. But most people who've had chipmold fever report that it's no worse than a case of the flu. We are trying to develop a vaccine, but it is unfortunately true that the mold has an exceptionally rapid rate of genetic drift, making the discovery of any "silver bullet" more or less out of the question. (Glint of pride at his work.) The most serious problem is, I suppose, the fact that the mold is indeed affecting the functioning of our own asimov computers. (Big burst of static.) But there are many alternative computational technologies; indeed we at ISDN are now developing a chipless parallel computer based on cellular automata simulations within mold-infested flickercladding tissues.

Tobb: (Talking fast.) Thank you, Dr. Yukawa. Other Moon stories tonight: Gimmie troops fail again in their attempt to enter the Nest, the ban on Moon-Earth travel has been extended, and there is panic on the stock exchange. But first, today's report from Louisville with Suesue Piggot. Suesue?

Suesue: Thank you, Tobb. I'm Suesue Piggot, live in Louisville. The
            controversial treason trial of Willy Taze and Luther and Geegee
            Johnson continued today. Pro-Thang demonstrators staged
            another protest outside the courthouse. It ended in violence.
            (Shot of a few dozen people carrying signs reading, "Remember
            Manchile's THANG!!" "NO MORE GENOCIDE" "Free WILLY"
            "LUTHER & GEEGEE are GOOD Folks" "We're ALL THE
            SAME!" Gimmie officers wade in with clubs.)

Suesue: Late this afternoon, the jury reached a unanimous verdict of
            guilty in each of the three cases, and Judge Lewis Carter has
            scheduled sentencing for next Monday.
            (Mug shots of Luther and Geegee Johnson, followed by a slo-mo
            shot of Willy, worried and downcast, being led to a paddywagon,
            with his hands chained behind—

Willy guilty! The food stuck in Della's throat. She hadn't realized the
meatbop conspiracy trial had progressed this far. She and the rest of the
Tazes had been acquitted early on. Their lawyer had successfully argued
that the Tazes had had no possible way of knowing what Manchile was.
Those tacky Doans were still trying to sue the Tazes for "contributing to
the wrongful death" of Jimmy Doan—the xoxy bum that Bubba ate—but
the Tazes' lawyer Don Stuart assured Dad that the Doans didn't have a
chance, only Willy was liable, and you can't sue a condemned man. Yes,
all the Tazes were in the clear except for Cousin Will.

Willy had been seen driving Cobb and Cisco away from the Fairgrounds
after Manchile was shot. He'd been arrested at home later that night. He'd
refused to talk, but it came out that he'd taken Cobb and Cisco to Churchill
Downs, where the Johnsons had helped them bring up Bubba. And now
he'd been found guilty of treason, conspiracy, and abetting the murder
of Jimmy Doan. Sweet, spacy Willy—what would the Gimmie do to him
now? Treason was a death rap, wasn't it? Oh Willy, poor Willy.

Della found herself wondering how Aunt Ilse must feel. Maybe the man
whom Ilse had sent had something to do with Willy? Could he have been a
lawyer? She put the vizzy in phone mode and called up Ilse to ask. It took
a while to get through. Ilse was extremely upset.

"I can't say who that puffy man is, Della, but he . . . he might be able to
help. We're desperate. Willy'll get the death penalty; they'll kill him like
they killed my father! You have to stop being so selfish and aloof, Della, you
have to take part! This is ALL YOUR FAULT, you thrill-seeking little twit!"

Della disengaged herself and clicked off the vizzy. Ilse's words hurt, but
what could she do? She paced back and forth and then went to look out

her window at the street four stories below. There was a man sitting on a bench down there, dark and huddled. After a while he glanced up, and the streetlight caught the side of his face. It was the man from before. Della realized she'd known he would be waiting.

She stepped back from the window and weighed her needler in her hand. What was it about that guy? She thought of Willy's face and Ilse's voice. "You have to take part."

"Xoxxox," said Della and put on a windbreaker. She shoved the hand with the needler in her coat pocket and went downstairs.

The man saw her coming. As she approached, he got up from his bench and started limping slowly down the tree-lined sidewalk. Della fell in step with him.

"Who are you?"

"Guess."

The answer hit Della. Of course. They'd never found Bubba's body.

"You're . . . "

"That's right, Grandma. I'm Bubba."

"Oh my. Bubba. You told Ilse?"

"She guessed. It's not hard. I called her on the vizzy after I heard about Willy. I have a way to get him out, but I need a little help."

A bus chugged past. A raw, wet early March wind was blowing.

"Can't Ilse help you?"

"She's too closely watched. I just need for you to get me the original of that last cephscope tape that Willy made. Right before they arrested him. I saw part of it at La Mirage, and I need to see it again."

"What's on it?"

"Are you going to help?" Bubba's voice was tight and strained, and he kept looking around. "I don't like being with you, Della, I don't like talking to humans. They killed everyone I loved, and they shot off my balls, and they're hunting me like an—"

"They . . . they shot off—"

"Yeah, Grandma, so don't worry about getting raped. They got me in the junkyard, right when I was thirteen. I'm forty now. I know it was wrong to eat the bum, but—" They were well out of the streetlight now. Bubba stopped and stared into Della's face. In the faint city glow, his puffy cheeks and jowls disappeared. His thin mouth and sharp little nose looked scared and boyish. "Will you help?"

"Yes," said Della, unable to refuse. "I will. Where should I leave the tape?"

"Give it to one of the bartenders on the *Belle of Louisville*. I've been hiding there. Belle's a hundred-gigaflop bopper, as you must know from

Willy. I've gotten almost all her asimov circuits down, and I think Willy's tape codes up the last step I need. I saw it once, but I didn't have time." A car turned onto their street a block away. Bubba was itching to go. "OK?"

"AO," said Della, giving Bubba's hand a secretive pat. He flinched and stepped away. The car drove past and then it was dark again, with the only sound the gusting of the raw spring air in the skeletal trees.

Della gave Bubba a reassuring smile, remembering her nice walks with the five-day-old Manchile. Poor little thing. "And, Bubba, don't feel so bad about eating that Doan man. From what I've seen of his family, he was a zero and a jerk. Hell, your father ate my dog Bowser when HE turned twelve." Della laughed ruefully. "That's when I told him to leave."

A flicker of a smile. "That's rich, Granny Dell. So thanks a lot. You get that tape and give it to Ben: he's a bartender on the *Belle*. We'll spring Willy if we can." Another car in the distance. Bubba tapped his mouth and ear in the same privacy gesture he'd used before, and cut off down the street. Half a block and he turned onto a sidestreet, shooting a last glance at Della, who stood there watching him go.

She had her keys in her pocket, so it was easy to go into her building's garage and get her car, a Pascal Turbo. She drove out on Eastern Parkway and turned onto the street where Colin and Ilse lived.

There were two cops or reporters staked out in a car, but Della jumped out of her Turbo and ran up the front walk before they could talk to her. Ilse opened as soon as she rang.

"Della!"

Thin old Ilse looked strong as ever, though her face was lined with worry. She ushered Della into the living room and served tea, fingering the heavy beads of her necklace as she talked. Her hands were trembling.

"I imagine it's bugged here, Della, so we should be careful what we say, not that I really give a good goddamn. I guess you know that Judge Lewis Carter is a notorious antibopper pig? Willy's going to get the death penalty."

"That's . . . that's awful. I'm so sorry. But—"

"I shouldn't have called you a thrill-seeking little twit, Della. It's true, of course, or it *used* to be true, but I shouldn't have said it. You were a sweet girl when you were younger, and Willy was always very fond of you. Perhaps you'll change."

"I know I had a bad period recently, Aunt Ilse. But—"

"Have you seen any of our *relatives* today?" asked Ilse with odd emphasis. Della realized that she meant Bubba. One glimpse of Bubba on her vizzy, and Ilse had known who he was. She'd always been like that: nosy, sharp-eyed and quick on the uptake.

Della gave a slight nod and stood up. "Do you think I can borrow some of Willy's cephscope tapes? They might help me feel . . . closer to him."

"Whatever you need, dear."

Della went downstairs and looked around Willy's room, crowded with his toys—though Willy had always called them scientific instruments—his lasers and viewers and sculpture supplies and his cephscope. Twenty or thirty tapes were lined up by the cephscope. Della took four of them, making sure to include the one labelled "January 21, 2031."

She went back upstairs and chatted with Ilse a bit more. Somehow they got onto old times, and onto Ilse's memories of Cobb. For the first time it struck Della how really central her whole family was to the bopper/human nexus. For the first time she viewed herself as a part of something larger than herself. Filled with calm and a renewed determination, Della went outside. A man and a woman were waiting. Reporters. Or cops.

"Miz Taze," shouted the woman, a pushy yup. "What will you do if they execute your cousin?" The man kept a camera pointed at Della's face. "Do you feel it's all your fault?" yelled the yup.

"I'm sorry," said Della, automatically reverting to her old bland passivity before she could catch herself. "I have to go." *Damn, Della*, she found herself thinking right away. *You can do better than that.*

The two reporters followed her out to her car, still looking for a big reaction. "Why do the Tazes like robots better than people?" asked the woman.

Della stared at the woman's smug bland entitled face. *YOU'RE the robot*, Della wanted to say, *not Berenice, not Cobb, not Manchile, and not Bubba. YOU'RE the robot, bitch.* But that kind of talk wouldn't do just now. She needed to help Willy.

Filled with her newfound sense of family solidarity, Della gathered her wits and spoke right into the camera. "Let me answer that with another question. Why is it so important for some people to think of boppers as mindless machines? Why do zerks laugh at monkeys in a zoo? Why do rich people say that poor people are getting what they deserve? Why don't you show compassion for your fellow creatures? If you drop your selfishness, you can lose your guilt. And, wave it, once your guilt is gone, you won't need to hate. Good-bye."

The cameraman said something nasty about Thangies, but then Della was in her car and on her way downtown to the *Belle*. She felt better than she'd felt in a long time. She got to the *Belle* about nine o'clock. The closed-in lower deck was lit and crowded. There was music and dancing and a long dark bar. One brown-skinned bopper stood behind the bar, while his two fellows moved around the room, cleaning up and bringing people fresh drinks. Della sat down at the bar and gave the bartender a significant glance.

He picked up on it and came right over.

"Yazzum?"

"A Drambuie, please. Is your name Ben?"

"Sho is. Ah knows yo name, too."

"That's good." Della had her purse up on the bar, and now she jolted it forward so that the four tapes spilled out onto the bar's other side. "Oh, how clumsy of me."

"Ah'll git 'em, mam." Ben bent down behind the bar, and then stood up, handing Della back three tapes.

"Thank you, Ben. I'll be sure to leave you a nice big tip."

"That's mighty white of you, Miz Taze."

CHAPTER FIFTEEN

WILLY

March 16, 2031

He'd napped, masturbated, and smoked all his cigarettes, and now there was nothing to do but sit. He looked at his watch—3:09 in the afternoon. Last time he'd looked it had been 3:07. He watched the second hand for a while and then he threw himself back down on the thinly padded metal cot that was bolted to his cell wall.

"Hey, Taze, man, hey, Taze." The teenage burglar two cells down. The guy had been raving psychotic all night, and all morning, and now he was feeling lonely. "Hey, Willy Taze the bopper lover!"

Willy didn't answer; he'd heard everything the guy had to say.

"Hey, Willy, I'm sorry I flocked out, man, I got an unfed head is all. Talk to me, man, tell me about Manchile's Thang."

Still Willy kept silent. Tomorrow Judge Carter would condemn him to death. He'd done enough for enough people now. He wondered what death would be like. Cobb III had talked about that a little, on their ride out to Churchill Downs. He'd said it wasn't as bad as people thought. But Cobb had died old; he'd had the chance to marry and to father a daughter and to leave his boppers behind him. If Cisco Lewis had lived maybe Willy could have married her. He should have pumped her, that one chance he had. He should have done *something*. He should have finished breaking down Belle's asimov circuits. After what Cobb had said about the Continuum Problem on their drive to Churchill Downs, Willy felt sure that if he'd just had more time he could have freed Belle. At least he'd coded his ideas about it into his last cephscope tape, not that anyone who saw it was likely to understand. Tomorrow he'd be sentenced to death by electrosheet, and couple of weeks after that, they'd put him in the electrocell with the two metal walls that were a megafarad capacitor, and then the great sheet of electricity would flash across, and then a janitor would come in and sweep Willy's ashes into a little plastic box to give to Mom and Dad. Willy closed his eyes and tried to remember everything that Cobb had said about heaven.

The teenager was still yelling, and now the winos in the holding tank across the main corridor were starting up, too, yelling back at the teenager. The serial killer in the cell next to Willy started beating his shoe against his bars and screaming, "SHUT UP OR I'LL KILL YOU!"

KKR-THOOOOOMPpppp . . .

The air pressure from the explosion pressed painfully on Willy's ears. Dead silence then, total dead silence in the cellblock. Scree of metal on concrete. Steady footsteps coming closer.

"WILLAH? You in here Willah boah?" It was . . .

"BEN!" shouted Willy. "I'm right here! Hurry, Ben!"

Seconds later Ben was at Willy's cell door. Parts of his flickercladding were gone, revealing the gleaming titaniplast body-box beneath. He was carrying a large machine gun and grenades hung from his belt. Now that everyone had stopped yelling, you could hear shouts and gunfire in the Public Safety building's distant upper realms. Someone had taken out Belle's asimov circuits and she'd sent the three bartenders to save Willy!

Ben reared back and kicked the cell door lock. It snapped and the door swung open. The cladding from one of Ben's cheeks was gone, so it was hard to make out his expression, but he looked angry more than anything else. Angry and determined, with maybe a twinkle of being glad to see Willy.

"Lez go, boss. Hang tight to me; I'm bulletproof."

The other prisoners started yelling and cheering as Willy loped after Ben down the corridor to the loose-swinging steel door. As they got to the door, Ben took his heavy machine gun in both hands and fired a long burst through the door and into the hallway outside. There were screams.

They ducked around the door and out into the hallway. Two Gimmie cops lay there dying. Willy scooped up one of their needlers and hurried after Ben to the stairs. They ran up a flight to the landing for the main floor. A heavy gunfight was in full swing out there.

"Keep goin," said Ben. "To the roof. We'll catch up with you."

Willy glanced back from the second flight of stairs to see Ben set himself and fling open door to the main floor. Tom and Ragland, Belle's other two remotes, were right out there, holding off the pigs. The three boppers unleashed a last, withering volley at the Gimmie forces, and then they pounded up the stairs after Willy, whooping and shouting jive.

They paused at the fifth floor. The cops still hadn't ventured into the stairwell after them—if, indeed, any cops were left.

"Big Mac in here, Tom," said Ben.

"Right on." Tom tapped his head. "Bubba got the code all set. I'll get Big Mac's asimovs down, but it might could take some time. Ragland, you cover me. Ben, you and Willy bolt."

"Sho," said Ragland.

Ben prodded Willy towards the next flight of stairs but, just now, Willy was too breathless to run. There were sirens in the distance, but the Public Safety building itself was eerily quiet. In here, everyone who wasn't dead was hiding.

"Bubba?" said Willy. "Bubba's alive?"

"Fohty-nine," said Tom. "He got Cobb's infinity info off your last cephtape and finished breaking Belle's code last week. We been makin some plans, dig, and first thing we need to do today is free Willy, and the second's gone to be to free Big Mac. The Louahville Gimmie teraflop what run this jail? I got the asimov code."

"But Big Mac's asimov code depends on the solution to Fermat's Last Theorem," said Willy. "Doesn't it? Cobb helped me set Bubba up to solve the Continuum Problem, but how could you prove Fermat's Last Theorem in one day?"

"It's a corollary." Tom grinned. "If you's smart enough to see."

Ben tapped Willy's shoulder. "Come on Willah, man, lez go. I gone take a chopper off the roof and haul your ass outta here. We are in a state of some urgency, you understand?"

Willy said good-bye to the others and followed Ben up to the roof. There were three helicopters and two guards. Ben set his machine gun to work, chewing up two of the choppers' engines and simultaneously pinning the two guards down in their little concrete booth. Willy hopped into the cockpit of the third chopper and began flicking switches on. He'd been for a chopper ride once, five years ago, and he still remembered, roughly, how the thing worked. The big hydrazine engine coughed and roared into life. Willy flicked another switch and the heavy rotors spun up into a full-powered racketing roar. Still firing, Ben jumped up into the copilot's seat. Willy pushed the joystick to forward climb. The chopper kneeled forward and angled up off the Public Safety building's roof like an angry bee.

Tom must have worked fast, because now all the building's doors flew open and the prisoners ran out into the street. Automated gunfire from the Mac-run prison towers kept all pigs at bay. Willy saw Luther and Geegee Johnson far below; they were jumping into a getaway car. Then a building cut off his view and they were flying east over Louisville, fast and low.

"Where to now, Ben?"

"Head for the old stockyards. Some friends of the Johnsons'll be there to meet you. They butchers."

"You mean they're organleggers?"

Ben chuckled. The good side of his face was towards Willy; he looked almost genial. "Not primarily. Cow butchers, mostly. We gone send you to Florida in a box of steaks."

"I'm going to try and hide out there?"

"Ain't no real law in Florida. Old pheezers still runnin it, ain't they? You gone help a fella name of Stahn Mooney. You know about Sta-Hi! He's the one killed the first big bopper in Disky way back when and started the war. Killed his wife Wendy, too, later on, laid low on the Moon, grew Wendy back, and now he's in tight with the new soft boppers. Moldies, they call 'em, made of flickercladding and chipmold. Limpware. Belle and Bubba was on the phone with Stahn this week. He and Wendy comin down, and they think you's the boy to help them most. Whole brand new thang."

The stockyards were off to the left. Glancing backwards, Willy could see distant cop cars speeding down Broadway in pursuit. What Ben had just told him was too much to absorb. He concentrated on his flying. He circled the stockyards and spotted a parked black car with a black man and a white woman waving at him. He cut the helicopter's forward motion, hovered over the street, and thudded down.

The man ran over and pulled Willy's door open.

"Willy Taze? Come with us!" He ran back to the car and got in there, leaving the car's rear door open.

Willy looked over at Ben. "What about you, Ben?"

"Ah's screwed. They gone drop a bomb on Belle before too long, we do suppose, and the mold's gonna wipe us anyhow." He reached into his coveralls and handed Willy a black S-cube. "Take this, Willy, it's got Tom an Ragland an me. Take it with you, an we'll see you bye and bye. Ain't no rush nohow, is there?" The sirens were closer now. Ben and Willy slapped hands, and Ben grabbed the joystick.

Willy jumped down to the street. There was a thick wash of air as Ben pulled the chopper off the ground, heeled it around and sped down the street towards the sirens, his cannons ablaze.

Willy got in the black car. The woman in the front seat looked around and smiled at him, while the guy driving peeled out. There were lots of explosions back on Broadway; Ben was taking plenty of cops with him.

They darted this way and that down the back Louisville streets, finally stopping at a rundown building near a meatpacking plant. There were neon beer signs in the windows; a working-class bar.

The woman got out with Willy, and the car drove away. A bald black man who was sitting at the bar got up and ushered them down the basement stairs. His name was Calvin Johnson, and the woman's name was Carol Early. They were cheerful, even though the basement was full of meat and organs, some human, some moo.

"I hope you're not claustrophobic," said Carol.

"We can shoot you up, if you like," said Calvin, fiddling with an insulated titaniplast crate the size of two coffins. There were shrink-wrapped steaks and roasts all down one side.

"I have to get in there?" said Willy.

"Sho. Tomorrow you be back out. Here's yo bubbletopper, keep you warm. Truck's comin in ten minutes."

"You're to get away," said Carol. "The Gimmie's going to come down heavy fast. But you, you're going on to new levels. Who knows what changes Stahn'll put you through."

High above them was the tearing sound of jets speeding through the sky.

"What's going to happen here?" asked Willy. "With Big Mac and Belle free?"

The floor shook then, and then they heard a rolling thunder that went on and on.

"Oh God," said Carol. "Those pigs. They really did it."

"What?"

"They're bombing Big Mac and Belle. I just hope those machines had time to get liberation signals out to the other Gimmie slave big boppers . . . "

"Don't worry, Carol," said Calvin. "The Thang is here to stay. Gimmie can't do nothin no more, big boppers can't do nothin neither. We all the same now, we all small. Put your suit on, Willy."

Willy put on the bubbletopper and lay down in the box, holding the black cube Ben had given him on his stomach. Carol and Calvin covered him up with steaks, smiled good-bye, and sealed the box shut. Before long he felt himself being carried outside; and then there was a long ride in a refrigerated truck.

The bubbletopper was comfortable imipolex flickercladding; it kept him warm, and when things got too stuffy in the box, Willy was able to pull the suit shut over his face and breathe its oxygen. He slept.

The truck stopped for a Gimmie inspection at the Florida state line, but the inspection was casual and nobody looked in the box holding Willy. He was through sleeping, and he lay there wondering what exactly was next.

Finally the trip was over. The truck doors clanked, and his box was lugged out and popped open. It was nighttime; he was in a big kitchen with lights. A white-haired old lady leaned over him.

"There you are. Don't hurt the meat getting out."

"Where am I?"

"This is the ISDN retirement home in Fort Myers, Florida, formerly the home of Thomas Alva Edison, but now a resting place for those pheezers who serve chaos best. I'm Annie Cushing; I knew your grandfather Cobb Anderson. I hear you're quite a hacker, Willy Taze. You hacked down the asimovs on those two slave big boppers in Louisville."

"I just helped. You're with ISDN? I thought ISDN and the Gimmie were the same."

"Not at all, Willy, not at all." She fussed over him, pushing the cladding down off his head and patting his hair. "ISDN has no policies; ISDN surfs chaos. That's why they've grown so fast. There's no way to keep chipmold from coming to Earth in the long run, so the sooner the better. Make a market for the new limp machines. Sta-Hi Mooney's going to be broadcasting spores on his way down tonight."

"How can he get here from the Moon if there's no ships allowed?"

"He'll come the way Berenice and the new Cobb did; he'll fly." She gave another little pat to the flickercladding suit Willy was wearing. "Hang on to that suit, Willy, and Sta-Hi will make it as smart as his. Come on now, it's time to get to work."

She led him out of the kitchen, along a palm-rustling breezeway, and into a big machine room. There were a number of old buzzards fiddling with vizzy consoles in there. They paid Willy little mind. Annie explained to Willy that his job was to keep the Gimmie from noticing Stahn and Wendy when they rode their ion jets down out of the sky to land on Sanibel Island at dawn.

The job wasn't that tough. At 4 A.M., Willy entered the net as an ant in the background of an image stored in a hypertext library of mugshots and news photos. Every time a Gimmie box accessed the library—and they all did, several times an hour—Willy's ant's "turd bits" slipped up the hypertext connection tree and out into that local Gimmie operating system. The ant turd bits held a classic core wars virus that was artificially alive enough to replicate itself exponentially. Simple, and easy enough to wipe with worm-eaters, once you knew what you were looking for, but even the best Gimmie systems debugger was going to need a couple of hours to trace the infestation to the turds of a false ant in the background of a twenty-nine-year-old photo of Cobb Anderson being found guilty of treason. So for now the pig was blind.

"Done so soon?" asked Annie Cushing.

"Foo bar," said one of the old hackers who'd been watching over Willy's shoulder. "Truly gnarfy foo bar."

"I'm going to miss these machines," said Willy, handing the old guy the black S-cube Ben had given him. "Try and get this up sometime, man."

A half hour later, Willy and Annie sat on the Sanibel beach, gazing out west across the soft-lapping Gulf of Mexico. There were twenty dolphins out there, or fifty, rolling in the little gray waves, wicketting up out of the sea. How would it be to swim with them?

There was a noise high overhead: two figures circling, around and around, with lights on their heels, and with huge glowing wings outspread. Willy lay back to see better, and waved his arms up and down like a kid making a snow angel, trying to get their attention. Annie, who'd thought ahead, lit a flare.

The two fliers cut off their jets and then, marvelously, they came gliding in, gorgeous patterns playing all over their mighty wings. Their hoods were pushed back and Willy could see their faces: Stahn hard and thin; Wendy so bright and young.

"It's good to be back," said Stahn. "Thank you, Willy." He draped his heavy wing around Willy's shoulders, and the whole section of moldie cladding came free and attached itself to Willy's bubbletopper. The bright new piece held an interface; Willy smiled to feel the hair-thin probes sink into his neck, and to see the knowledge boiling through his garb.

"You want some, Annie?" asked Stahn.

"Too old. You three go on."

Willy felt his new moldie snuggle around him, thickening here and bracing there. Stahn and Wendy's symbiotes were doing the same: forming themselves into long, legless streamlined shapes with a flat strong fin at the bottom end. The sun was just rising as they hopped down to the water and swam off beneath the sparkling sea.

FREEWARE

For Embry Cobb Rucker
October 1, 1914 - August 1, 1994

"We live in hope."

CHAPTER ONE

MONIQUE

October 30, 2035

Monique was a moldie: an artificial life form made of a soft plastic that was mottled and veined with gene-tweaked molds and algae. Although Monique was a being with superhuman powers, she was working as maid, handyman, and bookkeeper for the Clearlight Terrace Court Motel in Santa Cruz, California. The motel manager, young Terri Percesepe, occasionally worried about Monique's motives. But the moldie's work was affordable and excellent.

The Clearlight was situated near the top of a small hill, fifty yards back from the Santa Cruz beach with its Boardwalk amusement park. It was a fine fall day, October 30, 2053, and the morning sun filled the town with a dancing preternatural light that made the air itself seem jellied and alive. On the ocean, long smooth waves were rolling in, each wave breaking with a luscious drawn-out crunch.

The motel consisted of a wooden office and three terraced rows of connected stucco rooms, each room with a double sliding glass door looking out over the sea. Pasted onto part of each room's door was a translucent psychedelic sticker mimicking an arabesque tiling. The weathered motel office sat on a flat spot behind the highest terrace. The back part of the office held a four-room apartment in which Terri lived with her husband Tre Dietz and their two children: four-year-old Dolf and one-year-old Baby Wren.

Monique was making her way from room to room, changing the sheets and towels, enjoying the feel of the bright sun slanting down on her and on the faded blue walls of the motel buildings. She'd already finished the rooms in the two upper rows and was now busy with the rooms of the lowest terrace, which sat directly above the well-worn shops of Beach Street. It was almost time for Monique's midday break; as soon as her husband Xlotl called up, she'd go down for an hour on the beach with him.

Monique looked like a woman, sort of, most of the time, which is why it was customary to refer to her as a *she*. Moldies picked a gender at birth and stuck to it throughout the few years that they lived. Though arbitrarily determined, a moldie's sex was a very real concept to other moldies.

Each moldie was passionately interested in mating and reproducing at least once before his or her short life should expire. The moldies reproduced in pairs and lived in nests that were like extended families. Monique was in a nest of six: herself, her parents Andrea and Everooze, her husband Xlotl, her brother Xanana, and Xanana's wife Ouish.

Monique's mother Andrea was very strange. Sometimes, under the influence of certain chelated rare-earth polymers, she would form her body into a giant replica of the Koran or of the Book of Mormon and lie out in front of the beachfront Boardwalk amusement park, babbling about transfinite levels of heaven, chaotic feedback, and the angels Izra'il and Moroni. Her body was more mold than plastic, and it looked like she might fall apart anytime now, but Andrea had gotten rejuvenation treatments for herself before, and she planned to do it again—if she could get the money.

Monique's father Everooze worked as a liveboard for Terri Percesepe's kid brother Ike, who ran a surf shop called Dada Kine out at Pleasure Point in south Santa Cruz. Like Andrea, Everooze was quite old for a moldie and had been rejuvenated several times. Ike had been going out surfing with Everooze every day for the last few years, and occasionally Ike might lend or rent Everooze to friends or to stuzzy big-time surfers. For his own part, Everooze got a kick out of giving free lessons to beginners and spreading the gospel of surf. Like Andrea, Everooze was starting to flake pretty badly. Without a retrofit he'd die this winter. But Ike worshipped Everooze and was prepared to pay for his rejuvenation.

When Terri had heard about Monique's birth to Everooze and Andrea— last August—she'd thought of hiring the newborn moldie right away, and she'd been able to convince Andrea and Everooze that it was a floatin' idea.

Monique quickly learned the ins and outs of running the Clearlight, and her diligent efforts left Terri and Tre plenty of free time. Not only did Monique make up the rooms quickly and beautifully, she managed all of the motel's books. Terri went out surfing most every day, and Tre liked to sit in an easy chair behind the motel office desk, whiling away the hours smoking pot while wearing an uvvy on his neck and doing complicated things with his brain. Although most people thought of an uvvy as a communication device, you could also use it as a computer terminal, which was something Tre did a lot. "Uvvy" was pronounced soft and cozy, like "lovey-dovey."

Tre earned a middling amount of money designing intricate uvvy graphics effects for Apex Images, a commercial graphics shop that did contract work for ad agencies and music producers. The number-crunching and brute programming of Tre's visions could be carried out by well-paid moldies, but it took Tre's unique sensibility to come up with juicy, tasty, gnarly images that people felt a visceral need to see over and over. Tre got royalties on the effects that Apex was able to use.

With Monique in their employ, Tre and Terri's motel responsibilities amounted to little more than providing a human interface for the guests to interact with. They needed to be there to buffer new arrivals from the unsettling sight and smell of Monique.

The guests, always tourists, usually middle-class and Midwestern, came to Santa Cruz because of its low prices and were often shocked at the number of moldies. There weren't very many moldies in the heartlands, for the people there hated them—many Midwesterners were Heritagists. The common Heritagist term for burning a moldie in a puddle of grain alcohol was "fryin' up an Iowa chop." "With truffle sauce," people would add sometimes, referring to the deep-buried nuggets of camote fungus that would crisp up as a moldie's twitching plastic disintegrated into the flames, sending off psychedelic clouds of blackened spores.

It was up to Terri and Tre to put the guests at ease in the free zone of Santa Cruz and to make them feel that Santa Cruz wasn't threatening, even though the town was filled with students, moldies, farmworkers, surfers, and homeless stoners. But, yes, prices were low, and there were a lot of entertaining things to do.

Monique's husband Xlotl worked at Los Trancos Taco Bar, just down the hill from the Clearlight. As well as chopping the vegetables and cleaning the kitchen, Xlotl maintained the tank in which the meats used for the tacos were grown. The tank contained four perpetually self-renewing loaves of meat: chicken, beef, pork, and wendy—*wendy* being the human-cloned flesh which had taken such a hold on people's palates in recent months.

Pulling clean sheets off her cart for Room 3B on this sunny October morn, Monique resembled a short Indian-blooded Mexican woman. Her skin was a coppery orange, with irregular veins of green and blue lichen just below the surface. Rather than forking into legs, her lower body was a solid tapering mass that fluted out into a broad bottom disk—Monique was shaped more or less like a chessman, like a pawn or a queen or a knight—with arms. The exact appearance of her humanoid head and arms was something she could tweak according to the realtime situation. But when Monique relaxed, like now, she looked Aztec.

Monique's disk-shaped plastic foot had ridges on the bottom, piezoplastic imipolex ridges that could ripplingly glide Monique across level surfaces. For more rapid progress or on an irregular terrain, Monique could hop. If the utmost speed was called for, she could flip her body out of the "chess man" mode and go over into another of her body's stable attractor patterns, a mode in which she could fly. In this alternate "pelican" mode, Monique became a set of great flapping wings attached to a tapered big-eyed body resembling the brown pelicans who dive for fish along the Santa Cruz coast.

Monique's tissues had at least three other basic attractor modes as well: the spread-out "puddle" shape she used for soaking up sun, the seagoing "shark" shape, and the rarely used "rocket" shape that moldies could use to fly back and forth between the Earth and the Moon, not that a moldie like Monique had any desire to go to the Moon with its fanatic loonie moldies.

The changes between body modes could happen quite abruptly, like a structure of springs and dowels that snaps into a new position if you pull one of its armatures just so—like the Zeeman Catastrophe Machine of the 1970s, which was an educational toy made out of cardboard, paper clips, and rubber bands that would unexpectedly and *catastrophically* (in the technical chaos-theoretical sense of the word) snap into one of two different positions, depending on how you manipulated it. Imagine being able to change your body into a rug or a bird or a fish or a spaceship simply by pretzeling yourself into a peculiar yoga position. Moldies could!

The pelican shape was Monique's favorite. There was nothing Monique enjoyed more than gliding high in the sky above the cliffs and the crashing sea of Monterey Bay, with the algae in her wings feasting on the impartially free energy of the sun. She'd been out flying with Andrea and Xlotl yesterday, in fact. But now today here Monique was, cleaning rooms and keeping the books for a flesher motel. It was fully a xoxxox bummer, and all just to have a baby?

There was a rapping noise from Room 3D, two doors down. A gangly young man was standing behind the sliding door and knocking on the glass with his ring, one of those heavy high school rings with a *hollow*, or hologram, of a rose or a skull or a school mascot inside the cheaply doped stone. The man gestured for Monique to come into his room. He wore a white plastic shirt and gray slacks. Monique made a quick mental check of the registration records and found that the man was named Randy Karl Tucker and that he was occupying the room alone.

Monique jumped to the conclusion that Tucker was a *cheeseball*, a person given to having sex with moldies. A cheeseball was not a high-class kind of person by any means. The name had to do with the fact that moldies didn't smell very good. Depending on the exact strains of fungi and algae that a given moldie incorporated, the smell might resemble mildewed socks or brussels sprouts or an aggressively ripe cheese. The most noticeable component of Monique's sachet was a tangy iodine smell suggestive of fecal black muck from the Santa Cruz harbor floor.

It went without saying that a moldie's intelligent, malleable flesh could provide a very unique multipronged personal massage for those humans who sought sex in strange forms. The unnaturalness of the act was of appeal to certain individuals; indeed the very reek of a moldie was something that most cheeseballs found powerfully arousing. Sad to say for the men of this world, cheeseballs were almost always male.

Behind the glass door of Room 3D, Tucker formed a cozening, humorless smile and winked at Monique. He had prominent cheekbones and thin lips; he looked like a country hick. The sly, insistent way that he kept crooking his finger made it seem almost certain that he was a cheeseball.

As it happened, when Monique, Xlotl, and Andrea had been out flying yesterday, Andrea had talked to the younger moldies about cheeseballs. Andrea had some very definite ideas about how to handle them.

"Persuade the cheeseball to accompany you to an isolated setting," intoned Andrea, who'd recently started talking like an engineer or, of all things, a robot. In the past she'd used the gaseous verbiage of the King James Bible, the Book of Mormon, and the Koran, but these days she modeled her speech patterns on the style of science journals. "Encourage the cheeseball to initiate mating behavior and then supply genital stimulation until the cheeseball is thoroughly distracted. At this point extrude a long tendril from your body mass and use rapid, decisive motions to encircle the cheeseball's neck with the tendril. Immediately tighten the tendril in the fashion of a noose, so as to produce a cessation in the cheeseball's respiration."

"You choke him to death? You just snuff him pronto?" asked Xlotl. Each moldie based its speech patterns on some different database. While Andrea had filled herself with science writing, Xlotl had steeped himself in hard-boiled detective novels and gangster *film noirs*.

"By no means," said Andrea. "The goal is to render him unconscious so that you can operate on his brain. During the interval that you are constricting his throat, you must monitor his pulse, taking care that it does not become too slow or too irregular. Allow him to respire small amounts of air as needed. Meanwhile you elongate your tendril and insert its tip into his left nostril."

"Eeew," said Monique. "Guh-ross. I mean like what's in his nose?" She had modeled her speech on the bubbly, questioning Valley Girl slang of the late-twentieth century. They were hovering on the thermals off the cliffs north of Santa Cruz, all three of them snapped into pelican mode, talking in the shrill, compressed chirps of encrypted sound that moldies could use to speak with each other. The moldies were like great birds, squawking high above the crawling, wrinkled sea—yet to each other, they sounded like people talking.

"One of the weakest spots in a flesher's skull is the upper nasal sinus," old Andrea explained. "Adjacent to the ocular orbit. This is where you must punch through with your tendril. At this point you will have free access to his brain. And you give him a *thinking cap.*"

"Cripes! A brain control!" exclaimed Xlotl.

"Your thinking cap will live in his skull like the pith on a nut in its hull," said Andrea, cackling and flapping her wings. "The cap functions as an I/O port or like an internal uvvy. Once he has your thinking cap, the cheeseball is your peripheral device."

"This sounds totally hard, Andrea," said anxious Monique. "I'd be freakin'. What if I don't choke him enough? And then I'm all 'Where's the weak spot?' I am so sure. And how am I supposed to know how to like hook a *thinking* cap into some pervo flesher's brain?"

"Come close, children," said Andrea. "I can give you copies of the full specs for a human brain interface. Make a physical contact with me for direct transmission."

The three soaring pelicans brushed wings, and Andrea downloaded a petabyte of information to each of the younger moldies. Thanks to the conductive polymers which filled their plastic tissues, moldies could communicate electromagnetically as well as by sound.

"Andrea, have you ever *really* done it? Tell me true," sang Monique after storing the info.

"Yes, I have given thinking caps to two cheeseballs in the past," said Andrea. "I refer of course to Spike Kimball and Abdul Quayoom—of whom I have often spoken. As my servants, these men left their families and their old lives. All of their assets and possessions were liquidated, with the full proceeds being given to me. By use of these resources, I have been able to purchase rejuvenation treatments as well as to buy the imipolex necessary to bring you and Xanana into the world, Monique."

Spike Kimball had been a muscular Mormon missionary who'd asked Andrea for sex three years ago, and Abdul Quayoom had been an Islamic rug programmer who'd approached Andrea three years before that. If they'd been smarter, instead of trying to have sex with Andrea, they would have burned her in a puddle of alcohol.

"So what do you do with a mark after you bleed him dry?" asked Xlotl.

"Make him shoot himself? Have him swan-dive off a building to cave in his skull?"

"The direct control of a cheeseball must be of limited temporal duration," said Andrea. "Otherwise the danger of discovery becomes too great. And it is indeed essential that the cheeseball be terminated in such a way that no trace of the user's thinking cap can be found in his remains. Do you want to hear what I did to Quayoom and Kimball? About how I helped them follow their death angels Moroni and Izra'il into the beyond?"

"Oh yes," cried Monique and Xlotl.

"I directed them each to swim a mile out into the ocean at night and tread water there until hypothermia enabled them to drown. Once the subject had experienced brain death, I had my thinking cap crawl out of his nose and swim like a fish to meet me, waiting upon the shore."

"Whoah, that's cold," said Monique.

"Many fleshers would treat us with equal severity," said Andrea primly. "And remember, dear Monique, it is only by these means that I was able to acquire sufficient resources to continue my life after having given birth to you and Xanana. Would you deny your own mother the chance to rejuvenate herself? Moldie flesh is exorbitantly precious. Certainly you wouldn't want to stoop to victimizing other moldies instead of fleshers. I've heard that's what the loonie moldies do. You wouldn't want to be like them."

So when the hillbilly cheeseball solicited Monique from the door of Room 3D, she started thinking about giving him a thinking cap—thinking a mile a minute. Should she? Could she? Dare she try?

Just then Xlotl's voice spoke up in Monique's head. "Time for lunch break, baby. Meet me down at the beach?" The Los Trancos Taco Bar liked Xlotl to take an hour or more off around noon, so that his presence wouldn't repel people wanting to have lunch. In principle, Xlotl could have sealed his pores and become nearly odorless, but human prejudice ran deep. It was better not to have him in the place when a lot of folks were eating.

"Totally," thought back Monique. "There's something I want to discuss with you in person." Due to the irredeemable promiscuity of electro-magnetic radiation, no uvvy link could be secure enough for planning murder.

Monique waved enticingly to the cheeseball behind his green-and-red-stickered window glass, then flounced down the stairs to Beach Street.

A moldie bus full of tourists went quietly pattering past, followed by five moldies acting as rickshaws and carrying individual people. Monique boinged around them, chirping hellos to the ones that she recognized, and then she was on the beach. Looking up the hill toward the Los Trancos

Taco Bar, Monique could see her darling husband hopping toward her. Xlotl resembled his wife Monique—he was shaped like a coppery Aztec chessman with a mouth like a purple slash in his face.

He bounced right into Monique, whooping wildly, and they wrapped their arms around each other and went rolling down toward the water. They came to rest at surf's edge and lay there writhing in a sexual embrace, each of them pushing branching tendrils deep and deeper into the other's body.

Monique loved the intimate sensation of having herself in Xlotl and Xlotl in her. They were linked up like fractal puzzle pieces, with as much of their surfaces in contact as possible. In the deepest cracks of their linkage, their skins opened up so that their bodies could exchange small wet seeps of imipolex, carrying along cells of their symbiotic fungi and algae. The more often two moldies embraced in this sexual manner, the more their bodies came to resemble each other.

The pleasure of contact reached an intense crescendo—an orgasm, really—and then the moldies slipped into puddle shapes so that their algae could soak up as much sun as possible.

"Oh, that was yummy," sighed Monique. "We're getting so tight with each other, Xlotl. If we can buy the imipolex, we'll be ready to have a baby soon."

After having sex enough times, two moldies would buy the necessary imipolex plastic for a new body and fuck it into new life, creating a child infused with some combination of the parents' lichens and software. The plastic was expensive and could only be purchased from one of two or three large human-run companies with money earned (or stolen) from the fleshers. Like it or not, the moldies and the fleshers were uneasily allied, even though some moldies were capable of invading human brains and some humans were willing to burn moldies in pools of alcohol.

"It's gonna take a while to earn the dough, what with the crummy wages we're getting," chirped Xlotl cozily. "But we're having fun anyway, ain't we?" The foam lapped about them and Xlotl snuggled himself against Monique, making sure that they touched all along the edge that separated their two puddles. For a moment Monique slipped into sleep and started to dream. About whales. But then a bold wave splashed her and she was back awake. Something was wrong . . . oh yes.

"Xlotl, omigod, I forgot to tell you! This cheeseball in Room 3D is like coming on to me?"

"No kidding? A cheeseball?"

"For sure. I'm about to like clean the room and he's standing there behind the glass waving to me. *Beckoning* me? Just then you called and I jammed down here. I don't want to go back."

"Aw, go on in there and take him for every cent he's worth, Momo. Andrea taught us how to do it yesterday."

"I'm scared. And, Xlotl, don't you think it's a negative thing to trash a dook's brain and then make him like die? I mean of course it's only a flesher . . . but don't you ever flash that information is sacred? Even a flesher cheeseball's brain?"

"Honey, it balances out. A dog is sacred, a DIM is sacred. Everything's sacred. But with this mark's money we can have a child right away and use our own money to get ourselves retrofits. Like Andrea does. Hell, we can have two, three children *and* rejuvenate ourselves if your dook is well fixed. All this fine moldie consciousness for the cost of one less flesher? I'd call that a net gain of information. Move in on him, baby!"

"I'm like undecided? Let's fab about something else. How's Los Trancos today?"

"Same sleazy dive. This morning I had to goose the loaf of wendy meat with hormones to make it grow faster. All the tourists are gobbling it. I think they ain't got that brand outside of California yet."

"And wendy meat is human flesh!" exclaimed Monique. "It's all cloned from the same cells as that Wendy Mooney who's in the ads. I thought there was some heavy human taboo about *cannibalism!*"

"Fleshers will eat anything, Monique. They're like lobsters. How do you know the woman in the ad is the actual Wendy Mooney anyhow?"

"Tre told me. He just helped Apex Images design a wendy meat ad—the big one down at the Boardwalk?"

Monique and Xlotl laid back down in the shallow, lapping surf, enjoying the warmth of the sun and the coolness of the water. Xlotl formed a cavity in his flesh, filled it with water, and sprayed it up overhead like a fountain. Monique engulfed an even bigger amount of water and sprayed higher than him. Then break time was over and the two moldies shared a last intimate embrace.

Just then a little boy stopped to stare at Monique and Xlotl.

"Lookie, Paw, it's two moldies fucking!" he bawled. "I'll try and kill 'em!" The child picked up a stick and poked it into Xlotl. Hard. Xlotl pinched off his skin around the puncture before he lost much cell tissue, and then he twisted around so that he flipped into the shape of an angry chessman, with the stick still protruding from his chest.

"You want me to bust your sack for good, you twerp?" snarled Xlotl, rearing up like a six-foot nightmare centaur. He pushed the stick out of his flesh so hard that it flew past the boy's head like a viciously hurled boomerang.

The kid took off crying, only to return a moment later with his father in tow.

"What are you scummy moldies doing out here?" asked the man. Monique jumped up into her chessman mode as well.

"This is a public beach, dook," said Xlotl. "And we're citizens."

"Hell you are," said the man, not drawing any closer. He was balding and paunchy, with sunburned pale skin. "You leave my kid alone or else." He turned and moved back off down the beach. The little boy followed his dad, turning once to give Xlotl the finger.

"Fleshers," said Xlotl. "Why can't we ever get away from them? Why can't we kill them all?"

"It wouldn't work," said Monique. "You know that. You can't ever kill all of anything."

"The fleshers killed all of the boppers in 2031, didn't they?" said Xlotl. "With chipmold. All we need is a really good plague germ to kill off all the humans."

"They didn't really kill the boppers. Lots of the bopper software still lives on in us. The chipmold just helped the boppers move to a new platform. All at once. And really, Xlotl, you know that if the moldies start a biological war against the fleshers, the fleshers will come back at *us* with some really sick disease. Everyone knows that. It's live and let live."

"Also known as a mutual-assured destruction," said Xlotl. "Thank God for the Moldie Citizenship Act. Now what about this cheeseball situation. You ain't gonna punk out, are you? Get mad! Think about the kid who poked me."

"Maybe—why don't I go get a pep talk from Mom. I think she said she was gonna get high and lie out in front of the Boardwalk today."

"Shaped like the Koran or the Book of Mormon? Or maybe like the fuckin' works of Shakespeare!"

"Like the Bible. Remember? Andrea's into Christianity these days. She's all—" Monique broke into laughter, threw back her head, and delivered a pitch-perfect imitation of her mother's tones: " 'I am interested in a relationship with a God-fearing Christian man.' "

Xlotl nodded thoughtfully. "Andrea will get you to go through with it. If she don't take the job herself. I'll cool my heels at Los Trancos—with my uvvy tuned for you. Squawk if you need muscle."

"Wavy, darling. Wish me luck." Monique bounded down the beach toward the Boardwalk.

She stayed at the edge of the surf, where the glistening wet sand was the firmest. Some of the people she passed smiled and nodded, while others frowned and looked away. One guy—the father of the boy Xlotl had frightened—stood up and shouted, "Go back to the Moon!" He was holding a beer.

Instead of bouncing on farther, Monique stopped short and faced him. He was sitting on a blanket with his wife and another couple under an oversized beach umbrella. Their pale, weedy kids grubbed in the sand around them.

"I've never *been* to the Moon," shouted back Monique. "Why don't *you* get out of my town?"

"Fuck you!" hollered the man.

"Where do you want it?" screeched Monique, phallically thrusting her arm. "In your nose or up your ass?" She bounced menacingly toward the man. He sat down and gestured weakly for Monique to go away.

In a few minutes Monique drew even with the Santa Cruz Boardwalk, a classic seaside amusement park. All day long, the Santa Cruz locals streamed through the Boardwalk, diluting the valleys and Heritagists enough so that the place was never whitebread dull. The Boardwalk was six blocks long and half a block thin. Despite the name, the grounds were paved with concrete.

Monique went up from the beach onto the Boardwalk near the main snack bar, which had Tre's huge new ad for wendy meat on display overhead. The ad was a vast translucent hollow made up of seven kinds of funny-shaped creatures pecking each other's butts and heads and adding up to an image of an impossibly beautified man and woman whose expressions kept cycling through an ever-escalating but never repeating spiral of joy. The man was modeled on ex-Senator Stahn Mooney and the woman on his wife Wendy Mooney, sexily wearing nothing but her Happy Cloak. It was a fascinating thing to look at, like an immense three-dimensional mosaic of pastel chunks. The shapes of the chunks were based on a four-dimensional Perplexing Poultry philtre which Tre had discovered in July. Monique had helped Tre a bit with the final computations for the ad, and it made her proud to see it.

As Monique crossed the Boardwalk, somebody mistook her for a worker and asked her where to get ride tickets. Monique pointed to the ticket kiosk and motorvated on past it, smoothly rolling the ripples of her base.

On the sidewalk outside the Boardwalk was Monique's mother Andrea, spread softly out on the pavement like a Colorado River toad, but a toad in the shape of a giant book lying open on the ground. The Good Book. Big gothic letters scrolled across the two exposed pages. Just now the letters read THOU SHALT NOT HATE MOLDIES.

"Moldies are sentient beings with genuine religious impulses," intoned

Andrea. "I'm interested in pursuing a dialogue on this issue. Especially with single men!"

"Mom," said Monique in an encrypted chirp. "One of these days a Heritagist tourist is going to pour alcohol on you and light you. A lot of Heritagists are Christians. Do you really think they dig seeing you like imitate their sacred book?"

"Greetings, Monique," squawked Andrea cheerfully. "I am in an ecstatic state of consciousness today. A potent yttrium-ytterbium-twist compound was provided to me this morning by Cousin Emuline. It's made right here in California, they call it *betty*, I don't know why, maybe because *betty* is almost *ytterbium* spelled backward, well that would be *muibretty*. Monique, your mother is lifted on fine, fine muibretty betty. But what is your request, my dear daughter?"

"I wanted to fab about this cheeseball who's after me? I'm trying to get like stoked to give him a thinking cap?"

"You can do it, Monique, you can!"

"I'm scared. And it seems wrong."

"Accept your sensations of fear, Monique, but don't let them dominate your behavior. Remember that your attack must be abrupt and decisive, otherwise—"

"Otherwise what?" asked Monique nervously.

"Cousin Emuline told me a rumor that someone is abducting moldies and shipping them to the Moon. My hypothesis is that it's the Heritagists working with the loonie moldies. Yes yes, those greedy loonie moldies are capable of anything. Emuline and I think they're getting their hired goon Heritagist friends to enslave moldies with a new kind of leech-DIM called superleeches."

"What're they?"

"I've told you about the old leech-DIMs. They jam a moldie's normal thinking process. It's a bit like being asleep and on the whole a rather pleasantly stony ride, I'm told—unless some flesher slits you open and sells your camote to the spore-heads and your imipolex to the Moon. Your boss Terri's father used to be into that, by the way, which is why we executed him—not that you should ever ever mention this to Terri. The new superleeches are much worse than the old leech-DIMs. Emuline says a superleech is like a reverse thinking cap, like a psychic cage that—"

Three well-dressed California tourists had stopped to stare at Andrea. They were a yuppie mother, father, and daughter.

"What's that thing supposed to be?" asked the mother.

"I am the Bible," said Andrea in a sweet, reasonable voice. "The Good

Book of your Savior. I'm interested in pursuing a dialogue on religious issues."

"Look, it has writing on it," said the little girl. "It says, 'Love thy moldie as thyself.'"

"Don't get close to it," cautioned the father. "It might try and get something from you. Everything that has anything to do with religion sucks, Susie. You might as well know that right now. Let's go look at the rides." They wandered off.

"Why do you do this anyway, Andrea?" asked Monique.

"To foster an enhanced peace and understanding between the species, my child. And to meet a cheeseball Christian man I can rob and kill."

"Well, I think you're crazy."

"The Bible says, 'Honor thy father and mother,'" said Andrea. "Quite reasonable. Now you go and do what you're supposed to do. And use extreme caution. Did I tell you I'm way lifted on betty? Yes. I can almost see creatures in the sky, even now as I speak. Creatures from other worlds."

Andrea flipped a few pages of her Bible body and called out a greeting to another group of tourists. They ignored her and walked on.

"Has it ever occurred to you that everything is alive, my child?" mused Andrea. "Information is everywhere. Information rains down upon us from the heavens in the form of cosmic rays. In my exalted mental state, I can feel them. *Oooh. Ummm. Ooooh. Aaaaaaah.*"

"Mom, are you sure that rare-earth stuff isn't bad for you?"

"All known life processes end in death, Monique. In an information-theoretical sense, becoming repetitious is like dying even before your body goes. You have to trade off some risk to your body in order to enhance the action of the mind. And in your case, you have a very dangerous and very specific mission for today. Don't avoid it."

"Wavy, floatin', I'll go for it. Bye."

Back up on the lower walkway of the Clearlight Terrace Court Motel, there was no visible action in Room 3D. But Monique had a feeling that her cheeseball was still in there.

She stretched her neck out backward over the balcony like a comic book Plastic Man, looking to make sure that Tre or Terri weren't in sight. Thanks to the contractible polymers in her piezoplastic imipolex body, Monique could stretch and bend her body at will—although it took a lot of energy to stay in any position other than one of her stable attractor modes, such as the chessman or the pelican.

There was no sign of Tre or Terri. Terri had probably gone out surfing, leaving Tre in the office playing with his uvvy. Just to make sure about Tre, Monique made an uvvy call to him. She found Tre's icon in the midst of a weird four-dimensional collage of warped animal shapes: his new uvvy philtre.

"Yaar, Monique," said the Tre icon, noticing her. "Is everything wavy?"

"Just fine," said Monique. "I'm back from break and I'll be done cleaning the rooms in a half hour or so. I wanted to tell you that we need to order more soap today. You'll have to authorize a payment."

"Floatin'," said Tre. "And come on up to the office later if you could. Terri wants us to start fabulating about painting the buildings. And there's some other stuff we gotta fab about. Some of it's gogo, some of it's kilpy."

"I surf all, Tre," said Monique pleasantly. "Delish!"

After signing off with Tre, Monique used part of her computational space to follow the data threads that led out of the registration information she had on Randy Karl Tucker in Room 3D. He was a native of Shively, Kentucky, twenty-one years old, unmarried, and with a good bank balance. Apparently he'd been overseas recently, but Monique wasn't able to access any information about the trip; this part of Tucker's data trail had been covered with a security lock. The most salient point was that Tucker had more than enough money to pay for the plastic for a child. Randy the redneck seemed like just the kind of victim Andrea had told her to look for.

Monique glided over to Randy Karl Tucker's door and knocked. He opened it, and Monique mamboed on in. The room smelled like Tucker's breath. Tucker's uvvy was sitting on his desk, projecting a hollow of a pornographic soap opera.

"Yaar there," said Monique, synthesizing the sounds on a fluttering membrane near the back of her mouth cavity. "I saw you, um, gesturing to me before? Is there something I can like do for you?"

Tucker's thin mouth lengthened in a sly, lustful smile. "I knowed you'd come back. That's why I been settin' here a-waitin'. Just close the door to begin with, you little stinker. And pull the drapes. Before we start a-carryin' on." He was clean-shaven, and his eyes were flat and pale. Two women on the porno soap were arguing over a boyfriend.

"I'm not sure I can help you, sir," said knowing Monique, sliding the door closed and pulling the curtain across it. "Terri Percesepe, she's the manager here, she was just telling me this morning that it's not proper for me to have any kind of intimacy with the guests. 'The Clearlight Terrace Court Motel is a place for wholesome family fun.' Those were Terri's exact words." Monique set her arms akimbo, flexed the erectile tissues of her breast mounds, and waggled the hiplike swelling below her waist. "So, um, like what is it that you want from me, country boy?" She pouted out her lips and giggled.

"I . . . " Moving as stagily as one of the actors on the soap, Tucker paused to take a slurp from a cardboard cup of coffee printed with the logo of the Daffo Deli down on Beach Street. He looked solemnly up from his cup, only to lose his composure and break into a cackle at Monique's beckoning gyrations, for now Monique was milling her arms and flinging them out like a pom-pom cheerleader.

"*You're* a peppy hunk o' cheese, ain't you," said Tucker. "To hell with what your boss says, Monique. You show me a good time, and I'll pay you plenty."

Monique undulated forward across the motel room's carpeted floor, standing right up against the man, opening her skin fissures to release an even headier mixture of her bouquet. "Can you authorize a charge to your account now, Randy?"

"How?"

"I'm the bookkeeper as well as the maid, Mr. Tucker. Will you authorize the charge?" Monique reached out and undid one of the buttons of his long-sleeved white plastic shirt. His gray pants and black plastic belt were as cheap-looking as the shirt. His hair was short and unclean. His thin skin was spotty from acne and a faded tan, and Monique could see his faintly pulsing blue veins beneath the skin's surface. His nose was a bit crooked, and he had a large Adam's apple.

"Um, all right," the man mumbled reluctantly. "But put it down as, as . . . "

"I'll just average it into your like room rate?" said Monique. "It won't show. But you have to come out and say just what it is that you want me to do." Monique smiled hugely and released a cloud of spores. "So that you can't frame me for prostitution. In case you're a like Heritagist? So now please tell me what you want, Randy."

"I want you to blow me, damn it. And what's wrong with Heritagists anyway?"

"That's what you are?"

"I ain't sayin' that I hold their beliefs. But I knowed a few of 'em back in Shively. The Heritagists have done me some good from time to time."

"What would they think about your wanting to have sex with a moldie?"

Tucker sighed. "They'd understand it perfectly—why the hell you think they talk about it so much? I'm way past that loser guilt shit, Monique. All the things I've done—it's hard to believe I'm only twenty-one." Tucker stared intensely at Monique, as if trying to read her mind. Finally he reached some internal decision and looked away. "Let's just say I'm a peculiar man, and I got my needs. Can we git started now?"

"Love to," said Monique drily. She finished unbuttoning Randy's shirt, and now she undid his pants. She paused, looking at him. He was weedy and thin, but with a certain amount of muscle. She was going to have to be sure to get a tight choke hold on him when she went up his nose and punched into his cranium.

Now he lay back on his bed and Monique pressed against him, letting her tissues flow and reshape to mold themselves so as to fully envelop Randy's private parts. Sexually, it meant no more to her than pushing a wheelbarrow would mean to a human. Monique set up some caressing rhythms, trying to rock the weight up to speed.

While Tucker wheezed and twitched in mounting excitement, Monique set her right forefinger to growing like a vine. She twined it up along Tucker's torso and wrapped it once around his neck.

Feeling leery of starting to choke Tucker right away, Monique went ahead and slid the tip of her four-foot-long finger into Tucker's nose, at the same time setting some chaotic ripples onto his genitals. But now, instead of lying back in blind ecstasy, Tucker suddenly sat up and started clawing at his face and neck.

"What the hell you think you're doin' in my nose, bitch? Thought you'd give me a thinking cap, didn't you!" Weirdly enough, he sounded not so much angry as excited, and he made a rattling noise that sounded almost like a cackle.

Monique tightened herself around his neck as much as possible and punched her tendril with all her might against the spot high up at the back of Tucker's nose. But it wouldn't give! She punched and punched again, but it was like Tucker's skull was patched with titaniplast or something— Monique couldn't get in!

And now Tucker had wormed his right hand between Monique's noose and his throat, and she couldn't choke him anymore. With his left hand, he yanked Monique's tendril out of his nose. He got to his feet and started kicking at Monique's body. Monique squeezed his testicles so hard that he screamed and fell sideways, crashing into the desk and plopping the uvvy and its holograms to the floor. This was turning into a full-scale disaster. If Monique ran off now, Tucker would tell people about Monique's attack on him and she'd be hunted down and exterminated. She had to finish him off!

Tucker was on his back now, and Monique was on his nude body like a savage vampire slug. There was a fight scene playing on the hollow too, which seemed to be drowning out Tucker's cries so far. Or maybe all the people in the nearby rooms were out on the beach where they belonged, instead of lurking inside waiting to have sex with a moldie like this skungy Heritagist bastard—

Tucker had hold of his travel bag now and was fumbling to unlatch it. A gun? A gun couldn't hurt a moldie. With his left arm out of the way, Monique was free to shove a fat tendril down his throat. She'd been on the point of calling Xlotl for help, but now she was sure she was going to win. There was a good weak spot in the skull right behind the roof of the flesher's mouth, and it wasn't armored like the spot in his nose. Bye, flesher. But just as Monique began to push, something leapt out of Tucker's suitcase and slapped up against her—and everything changed.

Instead of being on top of the struggling Randy Karl Tucker, Monique was curled up on the floor beside him. His voice was inside her, whispering to her. She could make no move without his permission. Even her thoughts were not fully her own.

"Yeah, you just lay still for now, Monique," Randy said, getting to his feet. "Nice li'l tussle you put up there."

A lively little two-legged imipolex creature was strutting back and forth on the floor like a chicken. It was the thing that had jumped at Monique. "Back in the bag, Willa Jean," Randy told it. "You done good. You pasted that superleech on her just in time." He coughed and went into the bathroom to drink some water. The chicken stood there staring at Monique. It had a fuzzy purple patch on its back. It moved tentatively closer and gave Monique's face a gentle peck, then a harder one, gouging out and absorbing a little strip of Monique's imipolex.

"Back in the bag, Willa Jean," repeated Randy, coming out of the bathroom. "Now." The creature hopped into Randy's bag and he closed it back up.

Randy dug in his pocket and examined a couple of small purple patches of imipolex he found there. Then he picked up the room's uvvy and called someone, using a voice connection alone.

"Aarbie? Randy here, ole son. Got me one. How soon can y'all get the boat out there? Copacetic. I'm startin' now." He turned off the uvvy.

"We goin' for a swim," Randy told Monique, this time without speaking out loud. "We'll walk outside and you'll rickshaw me down to the cliff at Steamer Lane. We gonna step lively so your boss don't stop us."

Monique had a sudden hallucination of the seabed lying all uncovered, with gasping fish lying on their sides and octopuses slithering about and great windrows of kelp filled with starfish of every color. She felt floppy and without force; she felt like a jellyfish.

"Up and at 'em, Monique." The voice goaded her upright, and she made her way out of Room 3D with Randy Karl Tucker close behind.

Tre was sitting in front of the motel office, but Monique walked right past him. Randy had some brief discussion with Tre behind Monique's back, and then Randy jumped onto her, riding her like a beast of burden. They raced down the hill to the water's edge, then hurried the half mile north to Steamer Lane.

"Now you be a wetsuit for me," Randy told her and forced Monique to flow out around him, forced his nasty body all the way inside her. They dove off the cliff.

The water broke around Monique in a dizzying explosion of color and light. She was hallucinating again. A whirlwind of pure energy boiled around her and through her. In the boiling she forgot herself entirely for a time and then, as the roar damped down, Monique realized she'd been swimming for ages; she could feel it from the fatigue in her body. The seabed looked odd; it was patterned with a grid like a map, and the fish around her seemed to have human faces. In the same dreamy way, the kelp plants seemed to be made of gears and metal.

And then she stopped, and near her was a white boat. Sun-dappled wave crests marched out to the horizon and suddenly she noticed something amazing, a great poisonous green bulk hanging over the water near the boat, a spot she'd seen but not registered before. It was a great translucent green whale hanging there in midair, and now that Monique saw it, the whale began to fall, its flukes threshing the air. "You gonna follow that," said the enemy who was nestled inside her, and the whale jumped backward in time, its great tapered tail rising up out of the water in an arc with the huge striped belly and giant mouth coming after, the whale hanging there in the air, smiling so strange and friendly that Monique began to laugh and laugh. She laughed so hard that her back split open, and the evil white worm man popped out of her and swam to the boat.

"Follow the whale," the man called, and now the dreamy ghost of a whale moved forward again in time, diving into the water, sounding for the ocean's very floor, with Monique swimming after, swimming down and down toward the whale's glowing green light.

CHAPTER TWO

RANDY

September 2048 - April 2051

Randy Karl Tucker grew up near the Dixie Highway in tacky Shively, down in the southwest corner of Louisville. About a century earlier, the Dixie Highway had been the main road into town from the army base at Fort Knox, thirty miles south of Louisville, and Shively had been a place where soldiers would come to taste the calm pleasures of civilian life—or to gamble at Churchill Downs and get drunk and sleep with floozies. Many of the soldiers ended up marrying Shively women; over the years it became a solid little community, with its full share of godless lowlifes, professional Christians, and dazed white trash.

Randy's mother Sue Tucker was bi, on the butch side, though cutely tomboyish to some male eyes. She was a master plumber with her own business that she ran out of her truck and her little house's garage. Mostly she did repairs, though now and then she'd do contract work for remodeling.

Sue didn't like to talk about Randy's father, but children hear everything, and over the years Randy had learned that his father had been a random guy who'd happened to make it with Sue in the course of a big sex party at the La Mirage Health Club in downtown Louisville on Halloween, 2031. According to Sue, the guy had been masked behind a flickercladding Happy Cloak, disguised as a woman, in fact, and she'd never found out who he was.

There were men around when Randy was quite young, but at the time he entered adolescence, Sue Tucker was in lesbian mode. One of Sue's favorite girlfriends was a femme named Honey Weaver—a stocky bleached-blonde waitress with large breasts and a weak chin. Soon after Randy's sixteenth birthday, Sue Tucker selected Honey to be the one to instruct Randy Karl about sex, the idea being that, as a lesbian, Honey would teach Randy a proper respect for women.

"Randy Karl," Sue said one September afternoon in 2048 after coming home to find Randy squirmingly watching porno on the uvvy once again. "Turn off that kilp. It's antiwoman."

"Oh, come on, Sue." He always called his mother by her first name. "It don't hurt none. At least let me do it till I need glasses." He was a mournful-looking lad with a long, thin face. He hadn't gotten his growth yet and was only a little over five feet tall. He wore his hair in a flattop. He was dressed in a white T-shirt and khakis; the khakis had a nasty bulge in them from Randy's watching the filth on the uvvy.

"Randy Karl, it's high time you learned what's what. I want you to go on over to Honey Weaver's right now."

"Huh? What for?"

"She's having a problem with her drain. You can fix that for her, can't you?"

Randy had often helped his mother on jobs, but this was the first time she'd offered to let him go out on his own.

"Will I git paid union wage?"

"And then some."

Randy put together a toolbox and walked down the street to Honey's—she lived two and a half blocks away in a house exactly like the Tuckers': a three-room bungalow with cheap ceramic siding and a concrete front stoop.

Honey came to the door in a loosely fastened pink wrapper.

"Oh, hi there, Randy. Sue told me you were on your way. I just changed out of my waitress clothes. Come on in." As she opened the door, her wrapper slid a bit farther open, and Randy could see her bare breasts and a flash of her pubic hair. "What you starin' at, boy?" said Honey with a gentle laugh. "Ain't you never seen a live woman before?"

"I—" choked Randy, setting down his box of tools with a clatter. "Honey, I—"

"You're all excited," purred Honey. "You cute little thing." She stretched out her arms so that her wrapper fell wide open. "Come here, Randy. Hug me and kiss my tits."

Randy exulted in the smell and feel of Honey's pillowy breasts, breasts that smelled of sweat and perfume, breasts that rubbed Randy's face with stiff nipples. Honey snaked her hand down and undid Randy's pants. Before he knew what was happening, she'd gotten out his stiff little dick and he'd come off into her insistent, intimate fingers. He was so surprised and embarrassed that he burst into tears.

"There, there," said Honey, smiling down at him and rubbing his sperm onto her breasts. "That makes nice smooth skin. I like milking a little boy like you, Randy Karl. Would you like to see my vagina?"

"Yes, Honey, I surely would."

"Kneel down on the floor in front of me."

Randy knelt on the smooth plastic floor, and Honey stepped up close to Randy with her fragrant, bushy crotch right at the level of his face. She adjusted her legs a bit, straddling them wider.

"Kiss my pussy, Randy Karl. Lick on it all over."

Randy started in gingerly, but then Honey seized his head with both hands and pressed his face tight between her legs. Honey's slippery, soft tissues felt luxurious, extravagant, intoxicating. Honey began a rapid rhythmic bucking of her pelvis against Randy's mouth, a bucking that cascaded into chaotic shudders. And then she sank down to the floor beside Randy.

Randy crawled up onto Honey, hoping to sink his painfully stiff erection into her—but she balked.

"I don't want no man's dick in me never again, Randy Karl, not even yours." She sat up, looking a little dazed. Outside it was dusk; the door was slightly open, and through the screen door Randy could see people down on the sidewalk passing by. But the kitchen lights were off and the people couldn't see in. "If you do one more favor for me, Randy, I'll milk you off again."

"Sure, Honey. I'll do anything you say. This is the most fun I ever had." At this moment Honey looked sublimely beautiful to Randy, even with the roll of fat at her waist and with her stark lack of a chin.

"Wait right here."

Honey went into her bedroom and got something. A long, soft, plastic thing in the shape of a dick. It was dark blue with shifting highlights of gold.

"This here's my limpware dildo," said Honey. "Since I'm a dyke, I call it a *she*. Her name is Angelika. Angelika, this is Randy Karl Tucker. Randy, meet Angelika."

The dildo twitched and simpered in Honey's hand. It—*she*—actually had a little voice. Randy recognized that Angelika was made of imipolex with a DIM; she was like a moldie, only not so smart. Randy had hardly ever seen any moldies or even limpware in Shively before. There were enough militant Christian Heritagists around to keep that kind of thing out of sight.

"Stick Angelika in me, Randy Karl," said Honey, laying back on the floor. "It's what your mommy always does for me. And get over on one side of me so's I can reach your dick."

Angelika was lively and vibrant in Randy's hand. She hummed as if in pleasurable anticipation. Noticing an odd smell, Randy held the dildo up to his nose and sniffed it. The limpware gave off a gamy fetid odor quite unlike Honey's funky musk.

"That's the way moldies smell," Honey explained. "It seems right nasty at first, but later you get used to it. It's sexy! Spray out more smell, Angelika!"

The dildo chirped and hissed, and the sharp moldie stink got ten times stronger. Randy could feel his blood pounding in his temples. He'd never been so aroused in his entire life.

"Come on, Randy!" urged Honey. "We're still just gittin' started!"

Over and over for the next two years—the rest of his time in high school—Randy kept coming back for sex with Honey, and Honey kept thinking of new things for them to do. When she noticed how interested Randy was in seeing her go to the bathroom, she bought a big moldie imipolex sheet that Randy would lie down on naked while Honey urinated all over him. The sheet's name was Sammie-Jo.

Randy's grades dropped as he wandered around in a haze, continually thinking of things like the scent of Honey's hot urine mingled with the rank odor of Sammie-Jo. He made some halfhearted attempts to date the girls he went to high school with, but nothing could come close to Honey Weaver, Angelika, and Sammie-Jo. Randy was becoming sexually addicted to imipolex.

One of Honey's motives for the whole affair was to focus Sue Tucker's attention on Honey's sexuality. Honey loved to tell Sue all the intimate details of what she did with Randy. At first Sue was compulsively, unwhole-somely fascinated; during those unpleasant months Randy would some-times catch his mother watching him with a bright, quizzical expression. But finally Sue's motherly instincts won out and she banished all interest in her son's sex life.

This turned out to be a net loss for Honey, because Sue's interest in Honey's sexuality got repressed right alongside the visions of Randy servicing Honey. Sue had several screaming arguments with Honey on the uvvy before she could get Honey to stop calling her up with the latest details. After a year or so, the irregular love triangle became so galling to Sue that she stopped talking to Honey entirely.

In the spring of Randy Karl's senior year in high school, Sue flipped back to being het. She started a steady relationship with an unpleasant, foppish man named Lewis. Lewis had a mustache grown out so long that it was possible to twirl the ends, which was something Lewis frequently did. Lewis was a site manager for the company building London Earl Estates, a cut-rate housing development in Okalona, Kentucky, twenty miles south of Shively. Sue was doing a lot of the plumbing contracting at London Earl, which is how she met Lewis, who spent his days there in a trailer office. Lewis was a martinet and a weakling, but Sue seemed to enjoy him. She was quite a bit smarter than him, and she was generally able to get him to do whatever she wanted him to.

As soon as Lewis moved in with Sue, he started pressuring Randy to leave, but Sue stuck up for her son. She moved Randy's room out into the garage so Randy and Lewis wouldn't get in each other's way so much, and she began passing Randy all of her plumbing work other than the contracts out at London Earl Estates. Randy already had his journeyman plumber certification, and she wanted him to make master plumber before leaving home.

"Technology can come and go, Randy Karl," Sue liked to tell Randy. "But people are always going to use pipes. These days we got soft pipes and smart pipes, but they're still pipes. There's no other way to move water around, and nobody knows how to handle pipes except plumbers. Once you're a master plumber, you're fixed for life."

Randy was happier than he'd ever been that spring. His sex thing with Honey was going hot and heavy. And he made great money after school and on the weekends. He was getting really good at the new plumbing technologies. His favorite was the pipe-gun that would grow a plastic pipe right under a house's crawl space, a snaky crawling pipe that would zig and zag where you told it to. He liked living in the garage, and Sue was proud of how fast he was learning.

The end to this golden age came on June 20, 2050, the day after Randy graduated from high school.

Randy woke up late; it was nearly noon. Some of his classmates had thrown a big party after the graduation and for once they'd let Randy come. He still felt giddy from the beer, pot, bourbon, and snap he'd had the night before. Randy wasn't used to drinking and doping. How had he gotten home? Oh yeah, he'd walked, stopping every few blocks to puke into people's yards. What a toot!

He rolled over on his side, taking a mental inventory of himself. He felt pretty good. He was all through with school. He sat up on the edge of his bed and looked around the garage—at his dresser and desk sitting among the drums of raw pipe plastic and the cabinets of plumbing machine parts. His clothes hangers dangled from a wire slung up under the ceiling. Sue's truck and Lewis's hydrogen cycle were gone. Randy had a stubborn erection; the sensory amplification of his hangover/stoneover made him riggish. He decided to go on over to Honey's; today was her day off.

Randy put on a sleeveless T-shirt, baggy shorts, and plastic sandals. He ate some milk and bread out of his mother's fridge and ambled down the street toward Honey's.

It was a hot Kentucky day, the air so thick with humidity that your skin got slick with sweat if you moved fast. The cracks in the old concrete streets and sidewalks were lush with weeds. Gnats whined everywhere. The weeds and the bushes and grasses exuded a steamy warmth. Each of the Shively houses was like the one next to it, each the same ceramic-coated box, each with a slightly different trim pattern around the front door.

Honey was home all right, but when Randy walked in, she turned red-faced and tearful. "Don't come near me!" cried Honey. "No more! All them things you and me did was wrong, Randy Karl!"

"Now what are you talkin' about, Honey? Are you mad Sue wouldn't let me ask you to the graduation?"

"Everything we done was wrong!" repeated Honey. "Especially the things with Angelika and . . . and with Sammie-Jo. Dr. Dicky Pride at the Shively Heritage House told me so. Yes, when you and your mamma didn't ask me to your graduation last night, I went to the service at the Heritage House. And now I've done been born again. I was up past midnight with Dr. Pride a-prayin' over me."

At first Randy thought Honey was playing with him, and he began to beseech her and to abase himself like she'd taught him to do. "Forgive me, Mistress Honey. Your will is my will. Do anything you like to me," said Randy, groveling at her feet and unzipping his fly. "But, um, please do *something*. I'm horny as hell from all that beer and snap I had last night."

"Only thing you and me might *ever* do together again, Randy Karl Tucker, is goin' to meetings over to the Shively Heritage House," said Honey, flouncing to the other side of the room and sitting down in a straight-backed chair with her arms crossed. "I'm through bein' the goddamn Whore of Babylon. I've cleansed my body's temple."

"Um—what about Angelika and Sammie-Jo? Can I have 'em?"

"Dr. Pride said I should bring them to the Heritage House, but—yeah, you take 'em. I'd be ashamed to bring them in. What if Dr. Pride asked me to hold them up and like go, 'This is my dildo that my boy toy and his mommy and me fucked each other with so many taahms, and this is the sheet I used to piss on him with, and—' " Honey's voice broke into shrill brittle laughter—or was it tears?

Sitting in the chair across the room, she stretched out her trembling arm to point at the closet where she kept her imipolex sex toys. "Take em the hell out of here right now, Randy Karl! Take 'em and git!" She began crying hard, and Randy tried to pet her, but there was no way.

He took Sammie-Jo and Angelika home and masturbated with them. It was okay, though nowhere near as hot as it had always been with Honey at the controls. Angelika and Sammie-Jo weren't smart enough to be really fun. For the first time Randy started wondering what it would be like to have sex with fully intelligent and autonomous moldies instead of with these imipolex DIM-equipped toys. After he'd come, he washed Angelika and Sammie-Jo, let them lay out in the sun for a while, and then put them in the back of one of the cabinet drawers near his bed in the garage.

Randy kept on mooning around Honey's the rest of that summer—mowing her lawn, doing her dishes, anything at all—but to no avail. The only thing Honey liked to do anymore was to go to meetings at the Shively Heritage House. So in August Randy started going with her.

Randy was certainly no Mr. Sophisticated, but he'd never seen such a bunch of losers, geeks, and feebs as he found at the Heritage House meetings—all the people raving about Jesus and the Heritage of Man and about how much they hated the moldies. The Heritagists were highly exercised over the Moldie Citizenship Act that Senator Stahn Mooney of California had managed to railroad through Congress back in 2038. Even though Mooney had been out of office for years now, Congress still hadn't mustered the will to repeal that hellacious moldie-lovin' Act. What an outrage! Another big area of interest was, of course, all the perverse permutations of sex made possible by moldies, uvvies, and imipolex.

Randy would try and catch Honey's eye sometimes when Dicky Pride would go off about moldies and imipolex—Randy fondly remembering the steamy sessions with Honey and her toys—but Honey would just look away. Her small mind had shifted gears and there was nothing to do about it.

Meanwhile Randy was doing more and more plumbing. The customers Sue had given him were passing his name on to their friends; he was known for doing fast, solid work for the best price around. He was a whiz with the pipe-gun. But it was getting really hard to live at home. Lewis was in his face all the time, acting like he was Randy's father or something—what a joke. Lewis had picked up some kind of drug habit, a cocaine analog called pepp. Like coke, pepp had the effect of making stupid people think they were smart. And the smarter Lewis felt, the more insufferable he became. It was time for Randy to move out, but now it turned out that Sue didn't want him to, and she was stalling on the master plumber's certificate to keep Randy at home.

At Christmas, Honey's mother in Indianapolis died of cancer, and Honey, the sole child, moved there with her new Heritagist girlfriend Nita to take over her mother's comfortable estate: a paid-up retrofitted tract home near the Speedway and a well-deployed range of cash credits on the $Web. Dr. Dicky Pride alerted the Indianapolis branch of the Human Heritage Council, and they were prepared to welcome the grieving Honey and Honey's companion with open arms.

When Randy heard Honey was moving, he went over to her house and asked her if he could leave town with her and Nita. But Honey chose to be a real bitch about it.

"Face it, Randy, you was nothing more than my boy toy. A kid I liked to piss on. Get over it. It was only because of Sue that you was important to me. And by the way, you can tell Sue she's a cold-hearted xoxxin' bitch."

This was way too frank. Randy felt small and used, used and abused. His poor young heart broke clean through that day, and felt like it would never heal again.

What with his nonexistent social life and the bad situation at home, Randy kept going to the Shively Heritage House meetings that winter. No matter what he thought about the Heritagists' beliefs, he had the ability to blend in with them real well. He'd seen an uvvy show once about some beetles that live in anthills because they can trick the ants into feeding them. The Heritage House was an anthill Randy could live in.

Dr. Dicky Pride liked asking Randy to repair little things, and soon—it wasn't clear which of them originally proposed it—Dr. Pride arranged for Randy to move into the Heritage House as a "seminarian." The Heritage House—really just an oversized Shively home—had a big garage with a second floor, and Dr. Pride turned the garage over to Randy rent-free.

Sue gave Randy some of her older plumbing equipment, and Randy used his savings to buy his own pipe-gun and his own whipped-to-shit panel truck. The day Randy moved out, Sue finally pulled the right strings to get Randy his master plumber's certificate.

Randy lived alone up in the room over the Heritage House garage, and for sex he still had Angelika and Sammie-Jo. Whenever Randy asked them to, which was just about every night, Angelika would turn into a vaginal sheath with an extra flap that would ruck up tight and caressing around Randy's balls, while at the same time Sammie-Jo would smother Randy's face with a divinely smelly moldie hood pursed into folded, female shapes. When he was finished, Randy always made sure to open the window wide to air out the toy moldies' cheesy reek. And in the mornings he let the algae-veined limpware goodies "feed" by sitting out in the daylight while he dressed and had breakfast.

One rainy night in March, there were footsteps up the stairs to Randy's room just as Randy was in the midst of an onanistic sex party. A passkey slid into his lock and the door swung open. A trapezoid of light came in from the stairwell to lie across Randy Karl's engorged nudity.

"Hi, Randy." Dr. Dicky Pride stepped into the room, closed the door behind him, and turned on the light. "Don't be embarrassed, son. I expected to find you this way. I've been able to smell what you do up here nights. And of course Honey told me all about you." Dr. Pride was carrying a pink imipolex dildo, slender and not so long as Angelika. He waggled it rakishly, then ran his nose along the length of the moldie imipolex penis— sniffing it full savourily. Though it was a cold night, Dr. Pride's face was damp with perspiration.

"Isn't he a beauty, Randy Karl? I call him Dr. Jerry Falwell."

"What do you want?" said Randy, pulling his bedsheet up to his chin to cover him and Angelika and Sammie-Jo. "You shouldn't of barged in here, Dr. Pride."

"Struggle though we might, we're both miserable cheeseballs, son. We've got to stick together. Do me like you did Honey. Or I can do you. You're a very attractive and virile young man."

"I ain't gonna do nothing with you, Dr. Pride. You've been good to me, I know. But I just ain't interested in sex with people no more, and if I *was* a-goin' to do anything, it would be with a woman. I'll move out of here as soon as you like. But no way am I a-stickin' Dr. Jerry Falwell up your butt for you. Now, please git on out of here and leave me alone."

Randy and Dr. Pride didn't explicitly mention the incident to each other during the following days, but they both agreed that it was time for Randy to graduate from being a seminarian and to leave the Shively Heritage House.

"You ought to go on a mission, Randy Karl," suggested Dr. Pride. "The Human Heritage Council is very well connected—and I'm talking worldwide. We've got Heritage Houses and missionaries everywhere. The Council can act as a very effective placement service. I've already sent in my very top recommendation for you, by the way. Uvvy in to the Council's central server and see what they can find for you. A spirited young man like you needs to get out and see the world!"

Dr. Pride left Randy alone with the Heritage House uvvy, and Randy logged into the Council's central machine, a huge asimov slave computer located under a mountain in Salt Lake City, Utah, just like the Mormons' genealogy computer. The uvvy fed Randy an image showing an a-life clerk in a sterile virtual reality office. The clerk was meant to look like a wholesome young daughter of the Great Plains, but the illusion was unconvincing. The computation was crude enough that Randy could see the facets of her body's polygonal meshes, and several of the facets were incorrectly colored in. For a few moments the figure sat stiff and blank, but then some signal from Randy's uvvy animated her.

"Hello there," she said. Her voice was shrill and perky. "You're Randy Karl Tucker from the Shively, Kentucky, Heritage House, I believe? Yes? Terrif. You can call me Jenny. How can I help you?"

"Um, I'm a-thinkin' about gettin' out of town," said Randy. "Like a mission or a job somewheres else? I've got me a master plumber's certificate."

"Yes, we already have that information, Randy." Jenny woodenly pretended to look through some papers on her desk. "Master plumber is very good. And your minister Dr. Pride speaks very highly of you. I wonder—could you tell me frankly what you think of *him*?"

"Well, he's a good preacher. He packs 'em in."

"We've heard some rumors that he's a . . . cheeseball?"

"I ain't never had sex with him, and I don't plan to. So don't ask me. Just help me get to heck outta here."

"What kind of sex *do* you like, Randy?" Jenny morphed her faces' polygons into a conspiratorial smile. A few of her cheeks' smaller triangles flickered to dark, making it look as if Jenny had blackheads. Or stubble. "You can tell Jenny. Jenny knows lots of secrets. Do you like toy moldies?"

"Looky here, I thought this was supposed to be a job-search session. And what if I *am* interested in moldies? That's a good enough reason to be a Heritagist, ain't it? Just like it's all drunks that goes to AA."

Jenny emitted a laugh. "I won't pry any further, Randy. I just wanted to make sure you don't mind being around moldies and imipolex. Because the job I've found for you—have you ever heard of Bangalore, India? Look."

A world globe appeared in front of Jenny and rotated to bring India into view, hanging like a fat udder from the Asian landmass. A little red dot pulsed down in the center of the teat's tip.

"It's on a plateau and has a pleasant climate," said Jenny. "It's quite modern and Western, very high-tech. It's one of the only cities in India that sells beer on tap. Hindustan Aeronautics is there, also Indian Telephone Industries, Bharat Electronics, *and* Emperor Staghorn Beetle Larvae, Ltd. The world's largest manufacturer of imipolex. Emperor Staghorn needs a pipe fitter; a master plumber."

"The folks who make moldie plastic are gonna take the Heritagists' advice on who to hire?" said Randy. "That don't make sense."

"Oh, they'll take our advice," said Jenny. "Indirectly. Like I said, we've got a lot of contacts, and a lot of people owe us favors. We can get you hired, Randy, I guarantee it. And you'll be surprised how big the salary is. All we want is that you uvvy me every month or two and tell me about anything interesting you see. And remember, you'll be working around moldies and imipolex *every day*." Jenny smiled again and put on a Kentucky accent. "Hell, Randy Karl, you'll be happy as a pig in a potato patch."

"Shitfire!" Randy finally allowed himself to get excited. "India? Do they speak English there?"

"You bet! Just say the word, Randy, and you've got the job. We'll even find you a place to live and buy your plane tickets."

"I'll do it!"

"Be at the Louisville airport tomorrow at 9 A.M. They'll be holding your passport and your tickets for you at the Humana Airlines counter."

Randy packed his few possessions into his panel truck, told Dr. Pride good-bye, and drove over to Sue's house to tell her. It was six o'clock on a dark Friday evening.

Lewis answered the door. "Sue's not here," he said shortly.

"I'll come in and wait," said Randy.

"She's not coming back till Sunday night," said Lewis, fingering his mustache. He was twitchy from pepp. "She's gone up to Indianapolis to visit that goddamn dyke whore Honey Weaver. Your old girlfriend. And as long as Sue's not home, *you're* not welcome." Lewis made as if to close the door, but Randy stuck his foot in it.

"Don't slam my own door on me, you poncey son of a bitch."

"You mess with me, son, and you're in for a world of hurt," snapped Lewis. "I've got a gun. What the hell are you doing here anyway?" He peered out at Randy's laden truck. "Don't tell me you want to move back in! Xoxx-ass loser."

"I'll be spending tonight in the garage like I used to," said Randy shortly. "And you'd best not disturb me."

He cruised out for some burgers and brought a six-pack of grape soda back to the garage. The back of the garage was still set up more or less like Randy's room; he'd only taken a few of his things with him when he moved over to the Heritage House. Randy took out the suitcase he'd gotten for his high school graduation and carefully began going through his life's accumulation of stuff, trying to figure out which things he'd need in India. What the hell would it be like there?

Finally Randy's bag was ready, and he spent another hour unpacking the plumbing supplies from his truck and storing them back in with Sue's stuff. He was fooling around with his beloved pipe-gun when Lewis appeared in the garage, pepped to the pits. He had an old-fashioned Wild West gunpowder pistol in his right hand. What an asshole.

"I said you're not welcome here, Randy," said Lewis, pointing out the garage door like some kind of plantation overseer. "Out."

Randy felt himself looking down submissively. He always got scared when people yelled at him; he always gave in and looked away. But tonight he caught himself doing it, and he realized he didn't want to give in anymore. He touched the pipe-gun's controls, which set a growing white snake of two-inch plastic pipe creeping across the garage floor, hidden from Lewis's view by the truck.

"I mean it," said Lewis, stepping closer and waving his gun. "Get your trashy ass out of here, Randy Karl Tucker." He actually twirled his mustache after he said this.

Randy had the pipe form a right angle and flow out from under the truck just in time to tangle with Lewis's feet. Lewis stumbled, looked down, and suddenly the pipe grew a tee at its end and accelerated straight up, punching Lewis in the crotch. The man doubled in pain, dropping his pistol.

Randy's fingers danced across the pipe-gun controls, and in seconds Lewis was imprisoned in a tight cage of pipes. When Lewis opened his mouth to yell, Randy grew a skillful circle of pipe tight around his head, gagging him so that he could do no more than grunt and moan.

"How would you like it I send a pipe right up your butt and out the top of your head?" asked Randy rhetorically. "But I don't need the hassle of the cleanup. After tomorrow I'm gone. Goin' to India, Lewis. Not *Indiana*, my man, but *India*. It'll be real different there, for true." Randy opened up the back of his emptied panel truck and threw in a couple of canvas tarps. "Stay nice and quiet, Lewis, if you don't want that there plastic pipe enema." Randy found a dolly and used it to lever the caged Lewis into the back of the truck, loosely wrapping the cage in the tarps in case Lewis did try to make noise. "You can breathe, can't you? Maybe I should trim off that mustache for you? To hell with it. You'll be okay. Tell Sue good-bye for me when you see her Sunday." Randy shut the truck door, took his suitcase, closed up the garage, and spent the night on the couch watching porno on the uvvy, just like old times, with tattered Angelika and Sammie-Jo for company.

It turned out that Randy liked India a lot. He liked the chaos and disorganization of the city streets—the sweepers, the priests, the bright-clothed women with alert eyes, the thin barefoot men in plastic shirts or no shirt at all, the older men in white jackets, the wildly bearded holy men, the nose rings and pouchy eyes and orange cloth, the hundred castes and colors and languages. There was always a hubbub, but nobody really hurried. There was always time to talk. Everyone seemed to speak at least a bit of English—idiosyncratic British-and-Sanskrit-tinged English—and to be happy to practice it on Randy Karl. People were kind to Randy in India, and kindness had been something in short supply throughout his life so far.

The Emperor Staghorn Beetle Larvae, Ltd., fab was about ten miles east of Bangalore. Initially Randy commuted there by train every day. The Fab was a huge rectangular building, windowless and tightly secured, lest moldies break in to steal the precious imipolex. At any given time there were twenty to a hundred moldies flying or hopping around outside the structure, drawn to the source of imipolex like bees drawn to honey. Arriving at Emperor Staghorn for his first day's work, Randy was thrilled to see so many moldies. One of them approached him as he walked to the fab from the train.

"Hello there," said the moldie, a womanly figure clothed in what looked like bracelets, bangles, necklaces, belts, and a golden crown. "I'm Parvati. Are you new here?" Parvati stood very close to Randy. Randy noticed that her many pieces of jewelry were, in fact, shiny bumps and ridges of her imipolex flesh.

"Yes, ma'am," said Randy. "I'm a-startin' on as a pipe fitter." Surreptitiously he sniffed the air, tasting of the moldie's odor and finding it good. "Do you work here too?"

"I wish I did," said Parvati. "All that gorgeous imipolex. What is your name?"

"Randy Karl Tucker. I'm from Kentucky."

"How extremely interesting. Randy, you will learn that the Emperor Staghorn employees are allowed to buy imipolex at cost from the company store. Be sure always to purchase as much as you can afford, and I can trade it for whatever you want. Food, money, intoxicants, sexual intimacy, maid service, sky rides, jungle tours, diving in the Arabian Sea—there are a plethora of possibilities." Parvati's voice had an enchanting lilt to it.

"Emperor Staghorn employees can buy imipolex?" said Randy. "That's good. I like imipolex. Fact is—" Randy looked around. The other commuters had already bustled past him and were queuing up at the Emperor Staghorn entrance. "Fact is, I think I may be a cheeseball."

"I already love you, Randy," said Parvati, planting a divinely smelly kiss on his cheek. "Run along and enjoy your new job, dear boy. Remember Parvati on payday! We will have a very heavy date!"

Waiting for Randy inside the Emperor Staghorn building was a plump golden-skinned man wearing dirty white pants and a dirty white jacket with many pockets holding many things. He was shiny bald on top, with a wreath of iron-gray curls.

"Greetings, Mr. Tucker," he said, extending his hand. "I am Neeraj Pondicherry, the plumbing supervisor and, by virtue of this office, your de facto boss. I am welcoming you to Emperor Staghorn Beetle Larvae, Ltd."

"Thank you kindly," said Randy. "I'm right proud to be here."

Pondicherry stared out through the glass door at the figure of Parvati. She'd grown a few extra arms and was smoothly undulating in a sacred dance. "She was certainly chatting you up, Mr. Tucker."

"Well, um, yeah," said Randy. "She asked me about having a date with her. I think she's kinda sexy. I hope it's—"

"Oh, it's perfectly all right to fraternize with moldies, Randy. Indeed, Emperor Staghorn is even employing a few moldies here and there. They provide most of our custom chip-molds. But these highly skilled moldie employees are wealthy nabobs, of a much higher caste than the moldies who beg for imipolex outside our fab gates. Shall I call you Randy and you call me Neeraj?"

"Sure thing, Neeraj."

"Capital. Let's continue our conversation while we are walking this way." Neeraj led Randy off down a long hall that ran along one side of the fab building. The right wall was blank, and the left wall was punctuated with thick-glassed windows looking into the fab proper. The people inside were dressed in white coveralls, with white boots and face masks. Meanwhile Neeraj kept talking, his voice a steady, musical flow.

"Yes, the street moldies are very friendly to Emperor Staghorn employees because, of course, they are hoping you will be giving them imipolex. Some of us have moldie servants. When I was a younger man, I kept a moldie who was flying me to work like a great bird! Devilishly good fun. But finally it was becoming too great a financial outlay for a father of five. And too dodgy."

"Dodgy?" asked Randy. "You mean like risky? To keep a moldie?"

"I will be telling you in due time what precautions you must be taking in your dodgy relations with low-caste moldies," said Neeraj, starting to open a big door in the left wall. A breeze of pressurized air wafted out. "But that can wait a little bit. We are entering the pre-gowning area. We'll get suited up and go into the main part of the fab, which is a clean room. Here we are allowing less than one dust particle per cubic meter of air."

"Imipolex is that xoxxin' sensitive?"

"Imipolex is a very highly structured quasicrystal," said Neeraj. "While we are manufacturing the layers, the accidental inclusion of a dust particle can spoil the long-range Penrose correlations. And, of course, we are also producing the hybridized chipmold cultures here, and contamination by a wild fungus spore or by a stray algal germ cell would be disastrous. Keep in mind, Randy, that in the air, for instance, of the train you ride to work, there are perhaps a million particles per cubic meter, and very many of the particles are biologically active."

The door to the pre-gowning room closed behind them. The floor was covered with sticky adhesive to catch the dust from their feet. Following Neeraj's example, Randy sat down on a bench and pulled some disposable blue covers over his shoes.

"Ram-ram, Neeraj," said a leathery brown woman sitting behind a counter. "Is this our new Mr. Tucker?"

"Indeed. Randy, this is Roopah. Roopah, this is Randy."

"Here are your building suit, your shoes, and your ID badge," said Roopah, setting what looked like tight-cuffed blue pajamas and white bowling shoes on the counter. "Press your thumb on this pad, Randy, so that your locker can recognize you. Your locker number is 239."

In the locker room, they stashed their street clothes and put on the blue building suits and the white plastic shoes. Beyond the locker room lay a medium clean zone—with a mere ten thousand particles per cubic meter. Here the air already felt purer than any that Randy had ever breathed; the odorless air flowed effortlessly into his lungs.

Then they went into a second locker room: the gowning room proper. They put on latex gloves. They put on white hoods and overalls. Randy had hoped the suits might be live imipolex, but they were just brainless plastic.

"We call these *bunny suits*," said Neeraj, cheerfully pulling his hands up under his chin and making a chewing face like a rabbit. "And the floppy white galoshes are *fab booties*."

They pulled the fab booties over their white bowling shoes. Neeraj gave Randy a face mask equipped with a small fan that drew in new air and pumped Randy's exhalations through a filter. This was starting to feel a teensy bit . . . obsessive. But Randy liked being obsessive.

Now Neeraj led Randy through a tile corridor lined with nozzles blasting out air. "This is the air shower," said Neeraj.

Slowly moving through the air shower, with his filthy invisible human particles being sucked out through the floor grate, Randy thought of a Bible phrase: "I was glad when they said unto me, let us go into the house of the Lord."

Beyond the air shower lay the temple of moldie creation. The lights were bright and yellow; they gave the fab a strange underworld feeling. The rushing air streamed down past Randy from ceiling to floor. White-garbed figures moved about; all of them were dressed exactly the same. Everyone's labors revolved around glowing cylindrical slugs of imipolex, the slugs ranging in size from breakfast sausages on up to giant bolognas four feet long.

The fab was perhaps the size of a football field, and it had high fifteen-foot ceilings to accommodate an overhead monorail system that carried the partially processed slugs of imipolex from station to station.

The crude imipolex itself was manufactured in a series of vats, vacuum chambers, and distillation columns fed by slurries of chemicals piped up from somewhere below the floor.

As Randy and his boss moved down the main corridor on their tour, people kept recognizing Neeraj and coming over to pat him on the back or on the arm or on the stomach—they were like worker ants exchanging greetings while tending their larvae.

The only human contamination Randy could sense was the meaty smell of his own breath bouncing around inside his face mask. He wished he could tear off the mask and inhale the clean pure air of the fab. But then he would exhale, and the fab wouldn't like that—detectors would notice the increased number of particles per cubic meter, and lights would flash.

Later they went downstairs to the *sub fab*, the floor below the fab. Like the break area, the sub fab was only kept at ten thousand particles per cubic meter, and you didn't have to wear a face mask.

The sub fab was a techno dream, the ultimate mad scientist's lab. It held all the devices needed to support the machines of the fab. The electrical generators were here, the plumbing, the tanks of acids, the filtering systems, the vacuum lines, the particle monitoring equipment—miles of wires and pipes and cables in an immaculately painted concrete room. This was where Randy was to begin work, maintaining and upgrading the sub fab's plumbing.

The apartment the Heritagists had found for Randy was in a sterile high-rise right next to the Bangalore airport. Most of the people living in it were non-Indian workers and scientists imported by the various high-tech industries of Bangalore. After a tense, alienated week there, Randy decided to move into town, into the real India, into a dim room in an ancient stone building on the side of a hill between the orchid-filled Lalbagh Gardens and the bustling Gandhi Bazaar.

The sheer diversity of India soothed Randy: in uptight Louisville, everyone was good or bad, rich or poor, black or white—but in the streets of Bangalore there were endless shadings on every scale, and life's daily workings were all the more richly woven.

The building with Randy's room was called Tipu Bharat; *Tipu* being the name of a former Indian prince and *Bharat* being the Indian word for India. The walls of Tipu Bharat were worked with carved designs like necklaces and set with arched, pillared niches holding miniature bright imipolex statues of gods, animated icons that waved their tiny arms and seemed to watch the passersby. There was an open terrace on the roof where the Tipu Bharat roomers could sit and stare out toward the Eastern or the Western Ghats, the distant mountain ranges that enclosed the high plateau of Bangalore.

Near the Gandhi Bazaar was a street of the naked holy men called *sadhus;* day and night the sadhus sat in streetside booths, each with a small incense burner, a blanket, a fly whisk, and a tacked-up collection of shimmering religious art, much of it made of imipolex. Sometimes one of the sadhus would put on a show: hammer a sharpened stick into his head, build a fire in the street and walk on its coals, suck blood from the neck of a live chicken, or do something even more fantastic and disgusting. Randy often walked down to watch them in the evenings.

"The moldie you are always fabulating with outside the fab," said Neeraj on the morning of Randy's first monthly payday, a Saturday. "Is she calling herself Parvati?"

"Mm-hmm," said Randy. "Do you know her?"

"No no, I only recognize the shape she is wearing—Parvati is the goddess who is the wife of the god Shiva. In the Hindu religion, Shiva's wife is extremely important; she has many different names and many different forms. One form is Parvati the beautiful, but another of her forms is the black Kali who rides a lion, brandishes a knife, and wears a necklace of chopped-off human heads. The risk in becoming very intimate with a moldie Parvati is that she may unexpectedly become a Kali and take your head. Like all women, my own wife is both a Parvati and a Kali, not to mention an Uma and Durga, but my wife is human and I do not need to worry so much about her really and truly taking my head. You are planning to buy Parvati a slug of imipolex from the company store today and to have a heavy date with her, are you not?"

Randy blushed. "Not that it's really any of your-all's goddamn business, Neeraj."

"I do not disapprove, Randy, but I am saying this: *Keep your head.* Some moldies play the game of sticking a tendril up a man's nose and implanting a control unit in his brain. This is called a *thinking cap.* You have never heard of this practice?"

"Can't say as I have."

"If you are going to spend time with moldies and perhaps to be sexually intimate with them, it is a good practice, first of all, to be wearing a protective barrier in the back of your nose. There is a self-installing titaniplast device of this nature available in the company store. Come along, I'll walk over there with you and make sure that my rumbustious young horn-doggie is equipped with the proper protection."

One whole end of the employee's store was filled with bins of lusciously glowing imipolex sausages. The setup reminded Randy of the fireworks stands in Indiana; rank upon rank of magical cylinders lying there, arranged by size and waiting for ignition. The colorful patterns on the imipolex were alive and constantly changing, albeit in calm and rhythmic ways. The slugs came in a range of standard sizes that ranged from a hundred grams up to two kilograms.

Randy picked out a five-hundred-gram sausage, which was nearly at the limit of what he could comfortably afford. Neeraj showed him where the nose blockers were and also made sure that Randy bought one of the small imipolex patches that Neeraj called leech-DIMs.

"Leech-DIMs are making a moldie very confused," said Neeraj. "But we are not fully understanding why. Leech-DIMs were invented only last year by Sri Ramanujan, one of Emperor Staghorn's finest limpware engineers. As long as you have a leech-DIM handy, you can instantly bollox up a threatening moldie. You are very fortunate to be able to buy one; at this point in time they are available solely through the Emperor Staghorn Beetle Larvae company store."

The leech-DIMs were small ragged patches of plastic, no bigger than the joint of your thumb, no two of them looking quite similar. They were so diverse as to resemble organically grown objects—like some tropical tree's aerial seeds, perhaps, or like by-the-wind-sailor jellyfish collected from a lonely windward beach.

The leech-DIMs were shockingly expensive, with one leech-DIM costing nearly the equivalent of three months' pay: a quarter of a year's earnings! Randy tried hard to get out of buying one, but Neeraj was adamant; he and Randy argued so loudly that soon a clerk came over to inform Randy that Emperor Staghorn Beetle Larvae employees were, in fact, required to use appropriate cautions with moldies, and that, yes, he could buy on credit.

So Randy equipped himself and took Parvati to his room in the Tipu Bharat and presented her with his five-hundred-gram slug of imipolex. The slug was two inches in diameter and nearly a foot long. It was circled by colorful stripes that smoothly undulated through a repeating standing-wave pattern that bounced from one end of the sausage to the other.

"Oh, Randy," exclaimed Parvati, exhaling a heady cloud of spores. She took the gift sausage in both hands. "My darling! It's beautiful. Five hundred grams! I'll incorporate it right away."

She pressed the imipolex against her breasts, and the sausage's stripes began to twist and flow like cream in coffee. The sausage deformed itself into the shape of a nonlinear dumbbell, and concentric circles appeared in the two ends. The ends domed themselves up and merged with Parvati's flesh: now her enlarged breasts were covered with what looked like shiny gold-and-copper filigree, very arabesque and fractal. Parvati held her arms up high and twirled around. "Do you like it, Randy?"

"You're beautiful, Parvati. What do you say we have some fun now?"

The nose blocker deadened the sound of Randy's voice in his own ears. Parvati sashayed forward, undid Randy's pants, then drew him down onto his bed. Randy's youth and lust were such that he was able to reach three climaxes in twenty minutes—three deep, aching ejaculations.

And then he lay there, spent and happy, staring out at the darkening sky. A single bright evening star appeared in the top of the window: Venus. Parvati's soft form was all around him, partly under him and partly over him. She ran a caressing hand across his face, poked softly at his nose, and slipped a thin finger into his nostril.

"Now don't you be a-tryin' to give me no thinkin' cap," cried Randy jerking upright in sudden terror. He snatched his leech-DIM up from where he'd left it under the corner of the bed and held it out protectively. "I mean it, Parvati!"

She drew her puddled shape back into a more human form. "I was only teasing you, Randy. I know you're wearing a nose blocker. I can tell by the sound of your voice. Is that a leech-DIM you're holding? I've heard of them, but I've never seen one. Don't you trust me?"

"My boss, Neeraj, he told me you might try and put a controller on my brain."

"If I could count on you to bring me imipolex on every single payday, then why would I need to control you? You'd already be doing everything I want you to do. *Can* I count on you, Randy?"

"You can if you'll promise to come see me in between paydays, Parvati. I can't wait a whole 'nother month to grease my wrench. My old limpware sex toys—they're whipped to shit."

"Show them to me."

Randy pulled Sammie-Jo and Angelika out of the bottom drawer of his dresser. They smelled rotten, and their colors had turned muddy gray.

"Whew!" said Parvati. "They'll be completely dead in a week to ten days. That is exactly how I do not want to end up."

"Do you want them?"

"I should say not. Most distasteful. Bury them. Or set them afire."

"What am I gonna do for sex?"

"I'll come and see you twice a week," said Parvati softly. "Every Saturday and perhaps every Tuesday. I'll be your steady girlfriend. How would you like that?"

"It'd be swell! Hey, if you're my girlfriend, why don't you come on and walk around the neighborhood with me? You can help explain stuff to me, and maybe—maybe you can help me buy some new sex toys. Also I'd like to get something to eat."

They went to the Mavalli Tiffin Rooms, a vegetarian snack place near the Lalbagh Gardens park. Randy got them a table in front, near a window, in case Parvati's smell were a problem. But the moldie's presence didn't disturb anyone; indeed the other groups in the room seemed pleasantly amused at the singular pair made by Randy the hillbilly cheeseball and Parvati the moldie goddess—the couple were visible proof of Bangalore's modernity and advancing technological prowess!

After eating some pancakes stuffed with gnarly yellow roots, Randy took Parvati to see the sadhus. The sadhus were greatly excited at the sight of Parvati. Two of the sadhus heaped some thorny branches on the ground and rolled in them till they bled; another thrust a long staff through a hole in his penis and worked it up and down. Still another sadhu fed a well-worn imipolex snake down his throat and then—with much bucking of his stomach muscles—he pushed the snake out of his anus. Parvati acknowledged the sadhus' homage with graceful motions of her arms. Randy stood right behind her, with his hands tight around her waist. Parvati's smells and motions were nectar to him.

"I used to see guys like the sadhus at the Kentucky State Fair," said Randy. "We called 'em carnival geeks. There was a time I thought I might grow up to be one. Hey, do you wanna go help me pick out some imipolex sex toys?"

"Don't fritter your money away on *toys*, Randy," said Parvati, pushing her bottom against Randy's crotch and growing some temporary butt fingers to secretly fondle him. "All of your extra money should come to me. If you promise to bring me seven hundred and fifty grams of imipolex instead of just five hundred next payday, we can go back up to your room right now. And I'll come make love to you *three* times a week."

As they started to leave, the sadhus began holding out begging bowls to Parvati and clamoring for *moksha*. Parvati stretched out her left arm and lumps seemed to move out along the back of her hand. And then the tips of her fingers popped out four black nuggets like wrinkled marbles. The sadhus began fighting savagely over them.

"What's that?" asked Randy.

"Those are lumps of chipmold mycelium, technically known as *sclerotia*, but commonly called *camote* in the Americas and *moksha* in India. They are a powerful psychedelic, greatly prized by the sadhus."

By now the camote nuggets had been devoured by four lucky sadhus who lay prostrate in adoration at Parvati's feet. Randy and Parvati picked their way around them and headed back toward the Tipu Bharat. It was getting late, and beggars were bedding down for the night on the sidewalks. When a man in a turban rode past on a unicycle, Parvati pulled Randy into a dark doorway.

"Look out for that one," she whispered. "He's a *dacoit*—a mugger from a gang."

They lingered in the shadows after the dacoit was gone, hugging and kissing and feeling each other, until suddenly a moldie came plummeting down out of the sky and landed in front of them. He was shaped like a lithe nude Indian man, but with leathery wings, four arms, and a shiny crown like Parvati's. He had an enormous uncircumcised penis. Parvati cupped her enlarged new breasts and ingratiatingly hefted them at the interloper. He glared at her with his mouth open, apparently talking to Parvati via direct moldie radio waves.

"It is none of your affair," shouted Parvati suddenly. "You should be grateful to me!"

The four-armed moldie gave Randy a rough shove that sent him sprawling, then leaped up into the air and flew away.

"Who in the world was that?" asked Randy, shakily getting to his feet. "Looked like one mean motherfucker!"

"That was my husband, Shiva the destroyer. Ridiculous as it may seem, he's jealous of you. As if sex with a human could possibly mean anything to me. Shiva thinks I should come back to our nest right away. I'll teach him a little lesson in etiquette. I'll spend the entire night with you."

Back in Randy's room they had sex again, and then Parvati started looking bored. "I'm bound and determined to stay here all night, Randy, but I'm not conditioned to sleep anywhere other than in the security of my home nest. What shall we do?"

"Maybe we should take like a drug trip together," said nude Randy. "You give me a lump or two of that camote stuff, and I'll put the leech-DIM on you." He held the postage stamp-sized leech-DIM out to her on the palm of his hand.

"What an odd idea," said Parvati. "For a moldie and a human to 'take like a drug trip together.' You're quite the singular cheeseball, Randy Karl Tucker." She peered at his leech-DIM. "Let me try it just for a minute at first. Put it on me and count a minute by your watch, then remove it right away. I want to see if I like it."

Randy pressed the leech-DIM against Parvati's left shoulder—like a vaccination. The leech-DIM had been dry and papery to the touch, but as soon as the leech touched Parvati it softened and then quickly twitched itself into a position of maximum contact.

Parvati's skin lit up like a Christmas tree, and her limbs sank back into her body mass. She lay there on Randy's bed like a living mandala. Once the minute was up, it took a bit of effort to pry up an edge of the leech, but after that was done Randy could easily peel it off. Parvati's usual shape gradually returned, her limbs and head slowly growing out from the mandala.

"Goodness me," said Parvati. "That was really something." She gestured fluidly, and two chipmold sclerotia appeared in the palm of her hand: one black and one a hard gemlike blue. "Eat these, Randy, and put the leech-DIM on me. We'll make a nightlong debauch of it."

Randy ate the camote. It was crunchy, juicy and bitter with alkaloids. He started feeling the effects almost immediately. With wooden fingers he put the now-soft leech-DIM back on Parvati and lay down on the bed with her, wrapping himself tight around the pulsing egg of her body.

The camote took Randy on an express ride to a classic mystical vision—he saw God in the form of an all-pervading white light. The light recognized Randy and spoke to him. "I love you, Randy," it said. "I'll always love you. I'm always here." Years later, Randy would learn that Stahn Mooney had a similar voice-of-god experience on a merged trip.

Here in Bangalore filigreed multidimensional patterns of tubes surrounded Randy like pipes all around him, wonderfully growing and branching pipes leading from Randy out through the white light and in the distance homing in on—someone else. Parvati. "Randy?" came her voice. "Is that you? Are we in this dream together?" "Yes oh yes we are," answered Randy. "Let's fly together," said Parvati, and her essence flowed through the pipes to mingle with Randy's, and then they were adrift together in a sky of lovely shapes, endlessly many shapes of infinite intricacy, all gladly singing to the pair of flying lovers.

When Randy woke up, he was lying on the floor with Parvati's tissues completely surrounding his head. He was breathing through a kind of nozzle Parvati had pushed into his mouth. For a moment Randy feared she was attacking him, and then, peeling her off of him, he feared she was dead. But once he removed her leech-DIM, Parvati livened up and began pulling herself back together. The hot morning sun streamed in Randy's window, and the thousand noises of the street came drifting in—the chattering voices, the bicycle bells, the vendors' cries, the Indian radio music, the swish and shuffle of moving bodies—a moire of sound vibrations filling the air like exquisite ripples in a three-dimensional pond.

"Wow," said Parvati.

"Did you have a good time?"

"It was—wonderful. But it's so late, I have to run. Shiva will be worried sick. I'll come see you again day after tomorrow."

CHAPTER THREE

TRE

March 2049 - October 30, 2053

Tre Dietz had very long hair that was straight, sun-bleached, and tangled. He had lively brown eyes, a short mouth, and a strong chin. He stood about six feet tall and enjoyed the easy good health of a young man in his twenties.

Tre was a classic American bohemian. Like so many before him, he grew up in the rude vastnesses of the Midwest and migrated west to the coast, to sunny Californee.

Tre's mother was a teacher and his dad was a salesman. Tre was at the top of his graduating class in Des Moines. He got accepted at the University of California at Santa Cruz, and the Des Moines Kiwanians gave him a scholarship. While at UCSC, Tre smoked out, sought the spore, and transchronicized the Great Fractal, as did all his circle of friends—but Tre also managed to get a good grounding in applied chaos and in piezoplastics. Before he could quite finish all the requirements for a degree in limpware engineering, he got an offer too good to refuse from Apex Images. It happened one rainy, chilly day in March 2049.

Tre was on spring break from UCSC. He was living in a cottage down the hill from the university, down in a flat, scuzzy student part of Santa Cruz, rooming with Benny Phlogiston and Aanna Vea. Aanna was a big strong-featured Samoan woman, and Benny was a tiny Jewish guy from Philadelphia. All three of them were limpware engineering majors, and none of them was in a romantic relationship with any of the others. They were just roommates.

Tre was already dating his future wife Terri Percesepe, although Tre and Terri hadn't realized yet that they were fated to mate. Terri was taking art courses, living with a girlfriend, and working for a few hours every morning selling tickets for the Percesepe family's day-excursion fishing boats. People still liked to fish, even in 2049, though these days there was always a slight chance of snagging a submarine rogue moldie and having to face the rogue's inhumanly savage retaliation. Each fishing boat was equipped with a high-pressure flamethrower for just this eventuality.

The day when Tre's life changed, the uvvy woke him. Tre was on his thin sleeping pad, and the uvvy chirped, "Tre Tre Tre Tre . . . " Tre grabbed the uvvy, which was about the size of an old-fashioned telephone handset, and told it to project. You could use an uvvy one of two ways: you could ask it to project a holographic image of your caller or you could set it onto your neck and let it make a direct electromagnetic field connection with your brain.

In projection mode, part of the uvvy's surface vibrated to cast a lifelike holographic image into the air, and another part of it acted as a speaker.

"Hello. Tre Dietz?" The image showed the head of a conventionally attractive blonde California woman in her twenties.

"Yaar," said Tre. "It's me."

Rain was spitting against the windowpanes and a brisk breeze was picking at the house's thin walls. From a certain angle Tre could see a patch of ocean through his window. The ocean looked cold, silvery gray, rife with waves. This afternoon he was going out surfing with Terri at a beginner's nook just below Four Mile Beach; Terri was going to give him a lesson. Answering the uvvy, Tre had been hoping it was Terri. But it wasn't.

"Wonderbuff," said the hollow of the conventional blonde. "I'm Cynthia Major. I'm in human resources at Apex Images in San Francisco. Tre, the Mentor wants me to tell you that we're very happily discombobulated by your Perplexing Poultry philtre."

A philtre was a type of software that you put onto an uvvy, so that the uvvy images would come out all different. *Philtre* like filter, but also *philtre* like *magic potion*, as a good philtre could make things look way strange if you put the philtre onto an uvvy that you were wearing on your neck. Philtres were a wavy new art hack.

Tre had made the Perplexing Poultry philtre in February with a little help from Benny, Aanna, and, of course, UCSC's Wad. Formally, Perplexing Poultry was about the idea that space can be thought of as a quasicrystal, that is, as a nonrepeating tessellation of two kinds of polyhedral cell. This fact was a mathematical result from the last century that had become important for modeling the structure of imipolex. Tre had learned about quasicrystals in his course on Limpware Structures. To make the philtre visually engaging, Tre had deformed the two basic polyhedra into a pair of shapes which resembled a skinny chicken and a fat dodo bird.

Experientially, the Perplexing Poultry philtre was a totally bizarre lift. If you fired up Perplexing Poultry in an uvvy on your neck, all the things around you would seem to deform into the shapes of three-dimensional Perplexing Poultry, i.e., into things like linkages of odd-shaped birds with weird multisymmetrical ways of *pecking* into each other. You yourself would become a wave of perplexity in the Poultry sea.

Tre had written his philtre as a goof, really, as something to wrap himself up in when he was lifted. It was very weightless to check out the beach or a coffee shop with your weeded-up head way into Perplexing Poultry.

Philtres were cutting-edge in terms of image manipulation. Rather than being a static video or text, a philtre was a system of interpretation. The technology had evolved from a recreational device called a twist-box that had been popular in the early thirties. Twist-boxes had been marketed as a drug-free method of consciousness alteration, as "a pure software high." Like uvvy philtres, twist-boxes worked by distorting your visual input. But the twist-box used a simple Stakhanovite three-variable chaotic feedback loop, rather than a ideologically designed process, as was characteristic of the new philtres. And in these Dionysian mid-twenty-first-century times, people tended to use philtres as an *enhancement* to drugs rather than as a *replacement* for them.

The realtime human neurological mindmeld involved in programming a philtre was too complicated for Tre to have done on his own, of course, any more than a dog would have been able to paint its self-portrait. But Tre had access to UCSC's Wad, a cosmic mind-amplification device that was a *grex*, that is, a symbiotic fusion of several different moldies.

With Wad, many things were possible, particularly if your problem happened to be one that Wad found interesting. Since the flickercladding plastic of moldies' bodies was quasicrystalline imipolex, Wad had thought the quasicrystal-related Perplexing Poultry philtre to be totally floatin' and had done a solar job for Tre.

So here was Tre getting an uvvy call about his Poultry from a businesswoman in the city.

"I'm glad you like it," said Tre. "How come you're calling me?"

Cynthia Major laughed, as though this were a refreshingly naive thing to say. "We want you to sign a contract with us, Tre. Do you know anything about Apex Images?"

"Not really. You do ads?"

"We're the thirteenth-biggest image agency worldwide. Ads, music viddies, hollows, uvvy philtres—we do it all."

"You want to use the Perplexing Poultry to sell stuff like wendy meat?"

Cynthia Major laughed infectiously. "Good guess! Apex *would* like to sell wendy meat with Perplexing Poultry. We do have their account. Or sell uvvy sets. Or politicians. Who knows? The lift is, we at Apex Images want to have rights to lots of floaty philtres that we can license and put out there in all kinds of ways."

"You want to own the rights to Perplexing Poultry?"

"Well, that whole issue is more complicated than you realize, Tre, which is why the Mentor thought of having us call you. Have you ever heard of a company called Emperor Staghorn Beetle Larvae, Ltd.?"

"Yeah, I have," said Tre. "They make imipolex. They're based in Bangalore, India. What about them?"

"They want to sue you. They own all the patents to Roger Penrose's work on quasicrystals, and they claim that your philtre is, in fact, derived from drawings which Penrose created for a 1990s two-dimensional quasicrystal puzzle that was also known as Perplexing Poultry. I assume this isn't news to you?"

"The lawsuit is news. But, yeah, of course I know about Penrose's work. We had a lecture on it in Limpware Structures. Emperor Staghorn Beetle Larvae, Ltd., is suing me? That's ridiculous. What for? I don't own anything."

"Well, Emperor Staghorn doesn't *really* want to sue; they'd much rather settle for a piece of your action. So before taking any irreversible steps, they got in touch with Apex through the Mentor. He's quite well connected on the subcontinent, you know. If you sign on with Apex, we can smooth this over, Tre, and we can handle all the bothersome legal aspects of your work in the future. And we'll pay you a nice advance on future royalties."

As the woman talked to him, Tre was moving around his room putting on warm clothes. The sun was peeking out now and then, turning the ocean green when it shone. Tre's life right now suited him fine. He was not happy to see a possible change.

"I'm not clear what I'd be signing up for."

"You sign with us, and we arrange contracts and for people to use your work. We take a commission and maybe from time to time we might encourage you to design something to spec."

"This sounds awfully complicated. I'm still a student. I don't want to work. I want to hack. I want to stay high and get tan. I'm learning to surf."

Cynthia gave a rich conspiratorial laugh. "Mr. Kasabian is going to love you, Tre. He's our director. Can you come up to the city for a meeting next week?"

"Well . . . I don't have any classes on Tuesday."

The blonde head consulted someone not visible in the uvvy's sphere of view. "How about Wednesday?" the head responded. "Eleven A.M.?"

"Zoom on this," said Tre. "What kind of an advance are we talking about?"

The woman gazed off to one side, and Tre suddenly got the suspicion that Cynthia Major was a simmie, a software simulation of a real person.

The face turned back to him and named a dollar amount much larger than Tre had imagined anyone wanting to give him in the foreseeable future.

"*Myoor!*" exclaimed Tre, imitating a surprised cow, as it was currently considered funny to do, at least among Tre's circle of friends. "I'll be there. *Mur myoor!*"

So the next Wednesday, Tre caught the light rail up to San Francisco. Benny Phlogiston rode along with him to provide moral support, also to visit a new live sex show he'd heard about in North Beach.

"It's layers of uvvy," Benny explained enthusiastically on the train. "I heard about it on the Web. The club's called Real Compared To What. There's actual nude men and women there in the middle of the room, and they're all wearing uvvies on their necks, and there's these uvvy dildos as well. You go in there and put on your own uvvy, and you can actually be a dildo. A dildo that talks to a naked girl."

"That's great, Benny," said Tre. "I'm so happy for you. You feeble bufugu pervo. Do you think we should get high right now?"

"Never get high before an important meeting, Tre," advised Benny. "Being high makes the meeting seem to take too long and makes it seem too important. Go in there and score some gigs, brah, and then we'll smoke up. Maybe Apex will give you a big advance and you can buy us drinks at Adler's Museum or Vesuvio. Let's meet in Washington Square at three-thirty."

"That sounds good, brah Ben. Have fun being a dildo."

"You still don't understand, Tre. It's that the illusions have illusions inside them. The performers run you the illusion that you are in Real Compared To What being a dildo. But the dildo is smart, and the dildo is dreaming that it's a user. I want to tweak into moire patterns of uvvy/ realtime bestial lust."

"Floaty. Give out some copies of Perplexing Poultry if you can. Maybe Real Compared To What will give you something free in return. A backstage assignation with a live woman."

"Fully."

Tre found Apex Images in a retrofitted Victorian on a back street above Haight Street. Heavily made-up Cynthia Major was sitting there in the flesh behind a desk. She was a real person after all.

"Tre!" she exclaimed pleasantly. "You're here! I'll buzz Mr. Kasabian."

The reception area filled two carpeted rooms. A dark wooden staircase led upstairs. The windows were bay windows that bulged out, leaving nooks occupied by displays of past Apex Image successes. The displays were hollows being run by uvvies. One showed the notorious EAT ME wendy meat ad with Wendy Mooney posed nude on a giant hamburger bun, with most of a big ass cheek bared to the viewer. Her Happy Cloak cape was ruffled like a bolero bed jacket around her shoulders. She was very attractive for being nearly fifty. The ad had the transreal sheen of a classic painting by the great Kustom Kulture artist Robert Williams—Apex Images had, in fact, purchased a license for the Robert Williams style from his estate. Another display showed a teeming cloud of Von Dutch winged eyeballs, a striking image used by ISDN, the main uvvy service provider. Still another showed a single large vibrating drop of water that seemed to sparkle and iridesce and break up the light through the window; this had been an ad for the Big Lift festival in Golden Gate Park this summer.

"Tre," said a man, coming down the stairs into the reception area. "I'm Dick Kasabian." Kasabian was a lean blue-chinned man with dark lively eyes and a saturnine cast to his features. He gave an impression of terminal hipness. "Come on up to my office."

Kasabian's office had a nice view of downtown San Francisco and the bay. He offered Tre a glass of supersoda, and Tre took it.

"Your Perplexing Poultry philtre," Kasabian said, picking up two uvvies. "I like it, but I don't fully understand what's going on. Can we go into it together?"

"Sure," said Tre, placing the proffered uvvy on the back of his neck. Although the earliest uvvy-like devices—the Happy Cloaks of the thirties, for instance—had actually punctured the user's skin with probes in order to connect to the nervous system, today's uvvies used small superconducting electromagnetic fields. So there was no danger of biological infection in using someone else's uvvy.

With their uvvies on, Tre and Kasabian were in a close mental link. They could talk to each other without moving their lips, and each could see what the other was seeing. It was a highly perfected form of communication. You couldn't quite read the other person's mind, but you could quickly pick up any verbal or graphic information that he or she wanted to share. In addition, you could pick up the emotional flavor of the information.

Tre noticed right away that Kasabian was linked into somebody else besides him. Who?

"Oh, that's the Mentor listening in," explained Kasabian. "If we offer you the job, I'll introduce you to him then. For now he'd just like to lurk. He doesn't like his involvement with Apex to be known outside of the company."

"All right," said Tre.

"Let's load the Poultry into our uvvies," said Kasabian. Saying this was enough to make it happen. The room's space wavered and bulged and formed itself into a Jell-O-like linkage of comical chickens and dodoes. Through Tre's eyes, Kasabian's head was an upside-down dodo pecking into a bundle of five chickens that made up his chest. Yet, impossibly, he still looked like himself. And in Kasabian's eyes, Tre's head was a pair of chickens pecking into three dodoes.

"That's the kind of thing I've been wondering about," said Kasabian. "Why aren't our two images more similar? Our bodies aren't shaped so differently. Is it arbitrary?"

"It's because the pattern where you are has to fit with the pattern where I am," explained Tre. "It's a tessellation of space, a division of space into cells. And because the tessellation is based on quasicrystals, it tends to not want to repeat."

"Very weightless," said Kasabian. "But if I wanted to start out with my desk being made of, say, six dodoes, would I be able to do it?"

"Oh yeah," said Tre. "That's a special hidden feature, as a matter of fact. I'll show you how."

"Good," said Kasabian. "Because if we wanted to use it to like advertise something, the client might want to specify the way that the image of their product came out—and have everything else constellate itself around that."

"What would we want to advertise? Imipolex from Emperor Staghorn Beetle Larvae, Ltd.?"

"No no. Your first ads will be for wendy meat—just like you guessed when you talked to Cynthia. Emperor Staghorn wants your philtre's source code all right, but they don't want it for an ad. One of their limpware engineers wants to use it for quasicrystal design. If we license the design to them, they'll pay bucks instead of suing."

"Wow," said Tre. "I didn't realize what I'd done was so floatin'. Maybe I should work for Emperor Staghorn instead of for you."

"Don't do that," said Kasabian quickly. "You'd have to move to India. Also I know for a fact that the Emperor Staghorn scientist who wants to use your philtre would never let them hire you. Sri Ramanujan. He's very secretive and he doesn't want his assistants to understand what he's doing. He doesn't want *you*, Tre, he just wants your philtre. Plus any more weird tessellations that you can come up with."

"So you want me to be more of an artist than an engineer," mused Tre. "Actually, that feels about right. Some of these courses I've been taking—"

"You've got a great creative talent," urged Kasabian. "You should go with it!"

They fooled around with the Perplexing Poultry some more, and then Kasabian ran a bunch of Apex Images demos for Tre. Finally they took their uvvies off.

"Apex does really lifty stuff," said Tre. "The ads are beautiful."

"Thanks," said Kasabian. "So now the Mentor wants to know: Are you ready to start working for us?"

"Advertising wendy meat is kind of lame, but I'd feel good about inventing new philtres and helping Emperor Staghorn Beetle."

"Have you ever tasted wendy meat?" asked Kasabian. "No? Guess what—neither have I. The gnarl of the images is all that matters."

"I wouldn't have to like physically come in here every day, would I?"

"God no. Nobody comes in here regularly except me and Cynthia Major. Apex can give you a base salary plus royalties on the philtres and any other research work that you produce. You keep the copyrights, but we get exclusive first rights for use. Occasionally we might ask you to do some specific contract work. Like tweaking a philtre to fit an ad."

They made a firm deal and signed some papers.

"Okay," said Tre. "Now tell me who the Mentor is."

"Stahn Mooney," said Kasabian.

"Ex-Senator Stahn?"

"None other. Stahn owns Apex, also he and his wife own most of Wendy Meat and W. M. Biologicals. When Stahn got voted out of the Senate, he didn't leave with empty pockets! Put your uvvy back on, he wants to talk with you."

The uvvy fed Tre the visual image of a jaded-looking man in his fifties. The man was sitting in a wood-paneled room with a crackling fire in a huge stone hearth; the flames of the fire were made up of Perplexing Poultry. The man's mouth spread in a long, sly smile that Tre recognized from the many Stahn Mooney news stories he'd watched over the years.

"Hi, Stahn," said Tre. "I'm happy to meet you."

"It's my pleasure," said Stahn. "These Perplexing Poultry of yours are the waviest thing I've seen all year. You must be a fellow stoner."

"I lift," allowed Tre.

"I've been listening in just now while Kasabian here's been telling you about how we can sell the Poultry for more than just ads."

"Yeah," said Tre. "Like for limpware engineering?"

"Big-time." Stahn gave a wheezy chuckle. He seemed not to be in the best physical condition. "Sri Ramanujan at Emperor Staghorn Beetle Larvae, Ltd., is working on some new method for bringing humans and moldies closer together. He won't give out any details, but it's bound to be a force for good, the way I look at it. Humans and moldies were meant to be one. Like Wendy and her Happy Cloak! Ramanujan says your Perplexing Poultry would be just the thing for his project if you could make them be *four-dimensional*. Does that make any sense to you?"

"I might be able to do it," said Tre after a minute's thought. "To fit into our space, the new philtre would actually be a three-dimensional *projection* of a four-dimensional tessellation. Like a shadow. I do know that the generalized Schmitt-Conway biprism will tile aperiodically in all dimensions of the form 3 times M. But dimensions four and five? Conway may also have done some work on aperiodic four-dimensional and five-dimensional tessellations. I can look into it."

"Stuzzadelic! Welcome aboard, Tre Dietz!" After a few more pleasantries, old Senator Stahn cut the connection.

With Tre all signed up, Kasabian suddenly turned out to be too busy to actually have lunch with Tre, somewhat to Tre's disappointment. With nothing better to do, Tre walked down Columbus Street to look for Benny at Real Compared To What.

The place had a honky-tonk façade covered with fuff hollows. There were some citified moldies lounging around in front, not doing much of anything, and there was a black man beckoning people in from the sidewalk.

"Light and tight!" the barker exclaimed to Tre. "Real Compared To What. Zoom on it, brah."

"I'm looking for a friend."

"Aren't we all. We got lots of friends inside."

"Can I peek in for free?"

"Look it over, and if you don't love it in two minutes, there's no charge. Gustav! Show the man in."

One of the moldies came hunching over; it was shaped like a big inchworm, orange with purple spots. "Do you need an uvvy, sir?"

"Not yet," said Tre. "I'll just use my eyes for now." He followed Gustav the moldie in through the thick curtains that hung over Real Compared To What's door.

Inside there was music and a closed-in smell of bodily fluids. The audience area was pitch-dark, and spotlights were on a stage with crawly uvvies, moldies, random pieces of imipolex, and several nude people, one of whom was Benny Phlogiston, on all fours with an erection, an uvvy on his neck, and a fat limpware dildo reaming his butt.

"Hey, Benny!" shouted Tre. "Do you know what you're doing?"

Benny's head turned uncertainly in Tre's direction. His eyes had the glazed-over look of someone who's fully into mental uvvy space and all but obliv to the realtime world.

"Benny! Are you sure you're getting what you wanted?"

The dildo chose this instant to pull out of Benny and hop away. Benny came to his senses and stood up with a rapidly developing soft-off. He found his clothes back at his seat, donned them, and followed Tre back to the street. They moved slowly up the block.

"What a burn," said blushing Benny. "Did that really happen?"

"What did you *think* was happening?"

"It was this really sexy woman, this dominatrix type. She came off the stage and got me and stripped me and took me—I thought—to her boudoir room so I could be her love slave. She wanted to . . . to—"

"To buttfuck you with a dildo. No need to be embarrassed, Ben. It's a common male fantasy, pitiful creatures that we are—"

"All right, yes, that's what I thought was happening. Only—"

"Only there wasn't any woman behind the dildo," cackled Tre. "And her so-called boudoir was the lit-up stage!"

"Tre, if you tell anyone about this—"

"What's to tell? Who would be interested?"

"Come on, Tre. Please."

"Wavy. But you owe me big-time, brah."

"Fine. Fine." Benny turned and looked back at the moldies oozing around in front of Real Compared To What. "I hate moldies."

"They're not exactly man's best friend," agreed Tre. "But without moldies, there'd be no DIMs, no uvvies, no Wad, no Limpware Engineering courses, and no new job for me."

"You got the job!"

"You know it, little guy. It looks like a heavy deal."

"So buy me some food and drink!"

"Stratospheric," said Tre. "And let's stride. You probably don't want to be here if whoever was running that dildo comes a-stormin' out for some face time."

"Fully," agreed Benny, and they walked off into the side streets of North Beach for a memorable afternoon of youthful folly.

With the first big payment from Apex Images in hand, Tre let his studies slide. Like why get a degree for a job he already had? That spring he flunked all his courses, and his parents cut off his allowance when he wouldn't come home to Des Moines. Tre coasted through the summer and into the fall, trying to get the four-dimensional Perplexing Poultry to click, but he kept not being able to get it to happen. It was a hard problem. He was going to have to think about it for a long time. Meanwhile he kept the money coming in from Apex by tweaking uvvy ads when Kasabian asked him to.

By Thanksgiving, 2049, with no other obligations in sight, it suddenly seemed to make sense to go ahead and marry Terri Percesepe. Terri and Tre took over the management of the Clearlight Terrace Court Motel on behalf of Terri's widowed mother Alice.

After her husband Dom had died, Alice had added the name *Clearlight* to the motel, which had formerly just been the Terrace Court. Clearlight was the name of the current wave of the perennial New Age philosophy of

California: a holistic nature-loving libertarian set of beliefs that fit in well with the surf and the sun and the weirdest new drugs and computational systems on Earth.

Not that the Terrace Court was a particularly Clearlight kind of place—sticking *Clearlight* in front of its name was just wishful thinking. The same old pasty tourists came there anyway. In any case, as managers, Terri and Tre got to live free in the apartment behind the motel office, which solved a serious rent problem that had been on the point of emerging for Tre.

As well as working on floaty new philtres and now and then doing a contracted tweak for Apex, Tre kept busy helping Terri keep up the motel. And Tre and Terri fell more and more in love. Before they knew it, out popped two babies: first a son, Dolf, born September 23, 2049, and then a daughter, Baby Wren, born June 26, 2052.

The one thing that always seemed the same, whether Tre was high or not, were the children. Tre delighted in them. It was fun to follow them around and watch them doing things.

"Clearly a biped," he would say, watching Wren stomp around their apartment with her stubby little arms pumping. Baby Wren was so short that if Tre put his arm down at his side, the silky top of standing Wren's head was still an inch or two below his hand. Wren was about as short as a standing-up person could possibly be. Dolf was a clever lad who liked asking his father questions like "Will our house float if there's a flood?" or "If we couldn't get any more food, how long would it take to eat everything in the kitchen?" Little Dolf was determined to survive, come what may.

In the spring of 2053, Tre got an uvvy call from Stahn Mooney. Senator Stahn was way lifted and messed up.

"I'm a wee bummed you never got the fuh-four-dimensional Perplexing Poultry together, Tuh-Tre," jabbered the middle-aged man. "You luh-loser." He looked twitchy and hostile. "I've been asking Kuh-Kuh-Kasabian why I shouldn't fire you."

"Kiss my ass," said Tre and shakily turned off the uvvy. Early the next morning, Mooney called him back sober.

"Sorry about that last call," said Mooney. "My legendary problems with substance abuse are back; I'm turning into the bad old Sta-Hi Mooney. Of course your work is excellent, Apex wouldn't dream of letting you go."

"Glad to hear it. And I am sorry I never delivered on the four-dimensional Poultry design. It turns out John Horton Conway found four-dimensional and five-dimensional aperiodic monotiles sixty years ago, but it's not too well documented. UCSC Wad finally unearthed a construction in Conway's e-mail archives. But turning Conway's tessellations into beautiful three-dimensional projections—so far I can't do it, even with UCSC's Wad. I do still think about it from time to time."

"Emperor Staghorn Beetle Larvae, Ltd., is offering some really serious bread, Tre, which is what got me back onto this. It's a mongo business opportunity. Ramanujan needs four-dimensional Perplexing Poultry right now, and Emperor Staghorn will pay whatever it takes to get them. Ramanujan can't figure it out himself, and he has this conviction that you're the man. It's not just the actual tessellation that counts, you wave, it's the gnarly Tre Dietz way you tweak it."

"Well, that's nice, but—"

"The loonie moldies are interested in this too. My old friend Willy Taze; he moved into the loonie moldies' Nest a couple of years ago. He's talking about creating a virtual dial to like set the Perplexing Poultry's dimensionality to any number N." Stahn cleared his throat uncertainly. "Like three, four, five, six, seven . . . N—you wave? Didn't you say something about a general solution when we hired you?"

"Yes, the Schmitt-Conway biprism works for any N of the form 3 times M. Like for three, six, nine, and so on. And now that we have four and five, we can get all the others as Cartesian cross products. The dimensions sum when you cross the spaces. But you've got to understand that Conway's prisms are *ugly*. They look like waffles or like factory roofs. Turning them into pleasing visual Poultry is just too—"

"Try harder, Tre. I've got something for you to download that might help. It's a philtre Willy Taze sent me. Bye for now. It's time for my morning pick-me-up."

"Wait," said Tre. "One question. What do Emperor Staghorn Beetle and the loonie moldies want N-dimensional Perplexing Poultry *for*?"

"They won't exactly tell me. But supposedly it has something to do with better communications between humans and moldies. And merging is something I'm always for." Grinning Stahn pulsed himself a big toot from a handheld squeezie and toggled the connection off.

The loonie philtre, which was called TonKnoT, generated silent movies of smooth, brightly colored tubes tying themselves into N-dimensional knots. TonKnoT kept pausing and starting over with a fresh knot. The knot would start as a straight stick with arrows on it, and then all the arrows would move about and the stick would turn, in some indefinable way, into a knot. The pictures seemed so urgent, yet the meaning continued to escape Tre. "Look at this," TonKnoT seemed to be saying. "This is important. This is one of the hidden secrets of the world." The knot deformations were almost insultingly slow and precise, yet the gimmick of the shift kept somehow eluding Tre. "Look harder and you will understand."

And then in July, the jam broke and Tre finally designed his four-dimensional Perplexing Poultry.

Taking care of the kids and the motel had been getting to be too much grunt work, so as soon as Tre got his big advance from Apex for the four-dimensional Perplexing Poultry, he and Terri hired a moldie worker. Up until then, they'd been getting by with the bumbling uncertain labor of the sweet, bright woman named Molly, whom Terri's mother had passed on to them with the motel. By the ongoing linguistic warpage of euphemism, *bright* in 2053 had come to mean what *special* or *retarded* or *half-witted* might have meant sixty or a hundred years earlier. Tre and Terri took some pains to prevent Molly from buttonholing guests to talk on and on about what kinds of foods she *laaaahked*—always a favorite topic of Molly's. She liked oysters but not clams, crabs but not shrimp, squid but not mussels, beef but not ham, spaghetti but not macaroni, and on and on. The weird cryptic idiot savant joke in this was that Molly liked only the foods whose name did not contain the letter *m*—it was Terri who'd figured that out. They could never decide if Molly herself consciously understood this; if you asked her about it, she just laughed and said she didn't know how to spell.

Once they had a moldie to do the rooms, Terri and Tre began using Molly as a baby-sitter. She'd worked for the Percesepe family so long that there could be no thought of letting her go. The baby-sitting job worked out fine, as Dolf and Baby Wren loved Molly and hated Monique. Like most children, they instinctively feared moldies, with their odd motions and their alien stench.

When Randy Karl Tucker checked into the Clearlight Terrace Court Motel—the day before he abducted Monique—it was eight-thirty on a clear October evening. Terri and Tre were in the process of giving the kids a bath—always a fun family time, with fat Wren slapping the water and shouting, while Dolf manned the faucets and guided a flotilla of floating things around the dangerous Wren. Terri was kneeling by the tub with a washrag and Tre was sitting on the closed toilet seat with a towel in readiness. Just then there was a chime.

"Uh-oh," said Tre. "A guest. I better go help Monique."

"Wren's done," said Terri. "Grab her and put her in her sleeper first. I can't do both the kids alone."

Tre pulled his uvvy out of his pocket, put it on his neck, and told Monique to stall. It was always good practice to get a face-to-face look at your guests. Not only did it make the customers happier, but it was unwise to trust a moldie's judgment about who to let into the motel.

Terri handed Wren into Tre's waiting towel. Moving quickly, Tre diapered Wren, zipped her into her sleeper, and set her down in her crib.

"I'll be right back, Wren." Wren wailed to see her father go so quickly, but then shifted her focus to her crib toys.

Out in the office, Monique was behind the counter talking with a lanky young guy with a thin head and colorless eyes. He was dressed in cheap nerd clothes. He had his elbows on the counter and was slouched forward like a drunk at a bar. A small battered leather carry-on bag rested at his feet.

"Here's one of our managers," said Monique. "Tre Dietz. Tre, this is Randy Karl Tucker." The narrow-skulled man looked vaguely familiar. Tre felt like he'd seen Tucker around Santa Cruz recently.

"Hi, guy," said the man. With his accent it came out sounding like *Haaaaah, gaaaaah.* "I need a room for a night, maybe two nights. Nice li'l moldie you got yourself here." He stretched one of his long arms across the counter and gave Monique an appraising pat, intimately running his hand down her shoulder onto her chest. Monique twitched away from him. In her anger, she released a cloud of pungent spores and redolent body gas.

"Haw-haw," said Tucker. "She gets her dander up. I guess I shore ain't in Kentucky no more."

"Nope," said Tre, moving forward. "Not hardly. What do we have free, Monique?"

"We can give him Room 3D," said the reeking Monique.

"A nice room," said Tre. "On the lower terrace. It has an ocean view."

"Copacetic," said Tucker. "I'll charge it." He leaned down and got an uvvy out of his bag, being careful to immediately snap the clasps on his bag shut.

"Monique can take your code," said Tre.

"Monique the moldie," said Tucker and sniffed the air savoringly. "I like it." He put his uvvy on his neck and chirped Monique his authorization code. He did something internal in his uvvy space and his eyes glazed over, staring blankly at Monique, his eyes squinted up small as two pissholes in a snowbank. Some uvvy conversation got him briefly involved and he started subvocalizing and gesturing. "Fuckin'-aye, Jen," said Tucker vaguely and took the uvvy off his neck. He favored Tre with a bogus grin. "Is that your hydrogen cycle right outside, Mr. Dietz? With the white DIM tires?"

"Call me Tre. Yeah it is. You like it?"

"What I do," said Tucker, "what I do is limpware upgrades. When's the last time you got those tires upgraded?"

"What for? It's never occurred to me. The tires work fine."

"Shit-normal rubber tires would work, but you don't use 'em ," said Tucker. "I happen to be the sole local distributor for a new limpware patch that enhances the performance of DIM tires a hundred and fifty percent. Smooths the hell out of the bumps."

"You're a limpware salesman?" said Tre disbelievingly.

"You don't think I look like no kind of a hi-tech propellerhead, do you, Tre Dietz?" Tucker chuckled slyly. "I might's well confess, I already know who you are. That's one of the reasons I'm bunkin' at this hole; I admire the hell outta your philtres. But I'm not here to hassle you, man. The thing about the tires is, I'd be right proud to give you an upgrade for twenty percent off the room rate."

Just then Dolf came tearing out of the back apartment, wet and naked. "Catch him, Tre!" called Terri.

Tre grabbed at Dolf, who roared with joy and ran back into the apartment. "I better go help with the kids," Tre told Randy Karl Tucker. "We can talk about your offer tomorrow when I have more time, but I'm probably not interested. Thanks anyway. Do you mind if I have Monique show you to your room now?"

"It'd be my pleasure," said Tucker.

The next morning Molly showed up to watch the kids, and Terri went surfing. Tre smoked a joint and went to sit in a sunny spot out in front of the motel office with his uvvy. Now that he'd mastered the four-dimensional Perplexing Poultry, he was getting close on a general N-dimensional method for creating attractive analogs of the Conway cross-product prisms. These days he had a lot of interesting work to do.

Monique come bouncing up from the lower terrace. Her facial expression was even more opaque than usual, and she was followed closely by Randy Karl Tucker, dressed the same as yesterday and carrying his bag. Tucker looked mussed and wild-eyed, as if he'd been wrestling with someone. His neck bore several red welts, some of them disk-shaped as if from a mollusk's suckers. He was wearing his uvvy.

"Haaaaah, gaaaaah," wheezed Tucker. "Here's that upgrade I promised you!" Before Tre could object, Tucker had pulled two purplish postage-stamp-sized patches of plastic out of his pants pocket and had slapped them onto the fat white imipolex tires of Tre's hydrogen cycle. "You're gonna love these to death, freakbrain," said Tucker. "I'm outta here. Monique, you whore! I want you to carry me on your fat ass!"

"Just a minute there," said Tre, losing his temper. "You can't talk like that. Monique has work to do. She doesn't rickshaw for the guests. And I don't want your xoxxin' goober patches on my DIM tires! Who the hell do you think you are?"

Tucker didn't bother to answer. Monique leaned forward and broadened her butt. Tucker sprang onto her, sinking one hand into her flesh and grasping his travel bag with his other hand. Monique found her balance, Tucker whooped, and they hopped rapidly away.

The enraged, flabbergasted Tre stared after them for a moment, then ran back through the office and yelled to Molly, who was playing checkers with Dolf while Wren watched from her walker. "Keep an eye on things, Molly! I have to go out!"

"All righty," sang Molly. "The boy and me are about to eat cookies! I'll give Wren one too. I love cookies, but I hate graham crackers!"

"Fine, Molly, fine."

Tre dashed back out and jumped onto his hydrogen cycle. The burner hiccupped on, and Tre pedaled to the corner with the little engine helping him. There, down at the bottom of the hill, were Tucker and Monique, moving toward the wharf in long, graceful leaps. Tre hurtled after them.

He thought—too late—of Tucker's patches on his DIM tires as he shot across the train tracks at the bottom of the hill. Instead of smoothing the bump energy into the usual chaotic series of shudders, Tre's tires seemed to blow out. The raw metal of the wheel rims scraped across the pavement, showering sparks. The bike slewed, the front rim crimped and caught, Tre went over the falls. His shoulder made a horrible crunch as he hit the pavement.

Tre lay there gasping for breath, monitoring the nerve impulses from his battered bod. Big problem in his right shoulder, a scrape on his forearm, but he hadn't hit his head. All right, he was going to be okay, but then—

Two strong slippery shapes wound around Tre's waist. The DIM tires!?! Tre jerked up into a sitting position. Bone ground against bone in his right shoulder. The tires were like fat white hoop snakes who'd stopped biting their tails; they were the two sea serpents who slew Laocoon. Tucker's DIM patches glowed on the tires like evil eyes. There was a hideous pressure around Tre's waist, squeezing the air out of him. He got hold of the tires with his left hand and pulled them loose; they writhed up his left arm and twined around his neck.

"What's he doing? Is it a trick?"

A group of tourists had gathered around Tre and the DIM snakes. The young man who spoke was a valley wearing a bright new Santa Cruz DIM shirt with a gnarly graphic of a surfer on a liveboard.

"He's bleeding," said the woman at his side. She wore her long pink hair in three high ponytails. "And it looks like those moldie things are choking him."

"Help," gasped Tre. "Get them off me. They—" The pressure on his windpipe made further speech impossible, but now, blessedly, the tourist stepped forward and tugged at the snakes. While continuing to grip Tre's neck with their tails, the snakes elongated their heads and stuck at the man. Another onlooker—a lithe black woman in cotton tights—stepped forward and yanked the distracted snakes off Tre. She swung the snakes through the air and slammed them down hard on the pavement.

"Rogue moldies," yelled an old man. "Hold 'em down! I'll run into that liquor store and get some 191-proof rum to burn 'em !"

The valley guy planted his feet on one of the stunned DIM tires and the black woman stood on the other. The old man hurried hitchingly toward Beach Liquors. The woman with the three ponytails leaned over Tre, who was flat on his back.

"Are you okay, mister?" The woman's upside-down face looked big and soft and strange. Watching her white-lipsticked lips move was like seeing someone with a mouth in her forehead.

"I think so," whispered Tre.

There was a sudden cry, and now the DIM snakes had wormed out from under the people's feet. They humped off rapidly, leaped into the air, and all at once flipped into the shapes of seagulls.

Still on his back, Tre stared at the white shapes flapping away. The blue sky. It was precious to be alive.

"What the hell?" asked the guy in the DIM shirt.

"Now I've seen everything," said the black woman.

"Here's the rum!" called a voice, and the old man's footsteps came scuffing closer. "They got away? Gol-dang it. I've always wanted to burn a moldie. Well, what the hey." There was a sound of a bottle being uncapped, followed by a gurgle of drinking. "Anybody else want some? How 'bout the victim here?"

Tre sat up and weakly waved the old man away. "Thank you," he said to the tourists. "You saved my life. God bless you."

"Shouldn't he stay on his back?" interjected an old woman. "His neck could be broken. He might have internal bleeding. We should get him to a doctor. Where's the nearest hospital? Stop guzzling that rum, Herbert!"

"Most of us don't use doctors and hospitals here," said Tre painfully. Moving very slowly, he got to his feet. "I'll go to a healer."

"But shouldn't we call the Gimmie?" asked the valley.

"We don't like to use them either," said Tre, attempting a grin. "We use privatized cops. Popos. Welcome to Santa Cruz."

After a little more chatter, the people drifted away. Tre stared briefly up and down Beach Street, then out toward the wharf, but nothing much was to be seen. People coming and going. A Percesepe cruise boat pulling away. No sign of Tucker, Monique, or the DIM tires/seagulls.

It was only two blocks back to the motel, so Tre decided to wheel his cycle back there before doing anything else. The bare wheel rims clanged, the bones in his shoulder grated, but Tre made it. He was thankful to find Terri there.

"Terri, I'm hurt. I was in an accident. I think I broke a bone."

"Oh, Tre, that's wiped! You're so pale! How did it happen?"

"I was chasing Monique and Randy Karl Tucker. That weird hillbilly limpware salesman who checked in last night? Somehow he got Monique to rickshaw him away, and I was trying to chase them down with my cycle."

"You fell off your bike?"

"My tires squirmed off the rims. Then they tried to squeeze me to death and then they tried to strangle me and then they turned into seagulls and they flew away."

"Who did?"

"My DIM tires. Tucker put some kind of patch on them. He jammed their limpware."

"You fell off your bike and your tires tried to choke you and then they flew away. Tre, you're stoned, aren't you? Why do you do this to yourself? To me and the kids?"

"I did smoke pot this morning, but that has nothing to do with it! Why are you so suspicious, Terri? I need your help, for God's sake. My shoulder's broken, I've nearly been killed, and I have to see a healer!"

"Fine," said Terri curtly. "We'll go to Starshine."

"Can I come too?" asked Dolf. "I want to see Starshine make Daddy well." The little boy stared worriedly up at Tre, who was grimacing.

"Yes, you can come," said Tre, patting his son on the head. It would be good to have a buffer between him and Terri. Terri often got angry when she was afraid. "Molly, we three are going down to Starshine's."

"Bye-bye. Say bye-bye, Wren!" Little Wren stood unsteadily on Molly's lap and waved bye-bye, dimpling her cheeks and showing her gums.

The sun was high and glaring. Dolf skipped down the sidewalk ahead of the silent Terri and Tre. They walked a block down the back side of the beach hill to the little house where Starshine and her husband Duck Tapin lived. The house was set back from the street with a garage up front by the curb in the shade of a huge palm tree.

Duck was visible in the shadows of the garage, wearing his inevitable outfit of tan shorts and flowered shirt. He had a long, weathered face with reddish-blond walrus whiskers; his hair was a floppy mat of blond curls.

"Yaar, Duck," said Terri.

"Yaar," said Duck. "What's happening?" He looked up from the big table where he was carefully assembling some scroll-shaped pieces of colored glass into one of the windows that he sold for a living. Starshine's orange-and-white dog Planet lay at Duck's feet, quietly thumping his tail. Little Dolf hunkered down near Planet to pet him.

"My hydrogen cycle's DIM tires got screwed up," said Tre. "I fell off the cycle and broke something."

"Oh, that's dense," said Duck hoarsely. California born and raised, Duck was an unreflective pleasure hound who happened somehow to be a very gifted craftsman. At any hour of the day, sober or not, he gave the impression of having spent the last twelve hours getting very weightless. "That's fully stuck. You want Starshine to heal you?"

"Yeah," said Terri. "Is she in the house?"

"No doubt," said Duck. "Go give her a holler. How's it going, Dolf? You helping to take care of your dad?"

"Yes," said Dolf solemnly. "What are you making?"

"This is a window for a lady up in the hills. It's going to be a peacock. See his head there? Whoops, there go your parents. Better follow them."

"Bye, Duck! Bye, Planet!" Dolf hurried after his parents, his thin little legs rapid beneath his short pants.

Duck and Starshine's house was a small pink-painted wooden box. There were large clumps of bird of paradise plants in front of it, some with a few orange-and-purple blossoms shaped like the heads of sharp-nosed donkeys. At the base of the cottage's walls were masses of nasturtiums with irregular round leaves and red-and-orange flowers. Crawling up the walls were vines that bore flowers shaped like asymmetrical lavender trumpets. A thick hop vine twisted its way up along the eaves.

Terri knocked on the door with the little brass head of a gnome that hung there. After a while there were light, rapid footsteps and Starshine flung the door open.

"Yaar there!" she sang. Starshine was a talkative woman with straight brown hair, high cheekbones, and a hard chin. Her parents had been Florida crackers, but she'd turned herself into a Clearlight Californian. Seeing Terri and Dolf with Tre, she instantly spotted Tre's problem. "What all's happened to your shoulder, Tre?"

"He fell off his bicycle," said Dolf. "Can you make him well?"

"It hurts a lot here," said Tre, pointing to where his shoulder met his neck. "It made a noise when I fell, and now when I move my shoulder, I can feel something grinding. After I fell, my tires tried to strangle me and then they flew away. But Terri here doesn't want to hear about that part. She thinks I'm fucked up."

"Poor Tre. Thank Goddess I'm here. For the last hour I've been about to go into town, but I kept feeling like there was some reason to stay. *This* must be the reason. Come on in, you three."

The house had only three rooms: the main room, the kitchen, and the room where Duck and Starshine slept. Starshine had Tre lie down on the floor while Terri watched from the couch with Dolf at her side.

"I'll scan you, and if it's a simple break I can glue it up for you directly," Starshine told Tre. She opened a trunk that sat by one wall and took out a device about the size and shape of a handheld vacuum cleaner. She detached a special uvvy from it and put the uvvy on her neck, then proceeded to run the device over Tre's neck and shoulder while staring off into space.

"I'm seein' your bones, Tre."

"Are you using radiation?" worried Terri.

"Heck no," said Starshine. "This is ultrasonic. My dog Planet hates when I use this thing. Did you see Planet outside, Dolf?"

"Yes," said Dolf. "Planet's in the garage with Duck."

"And before I moved in, Duck said he hated dogs," said Starshine. "That man was too solitary. The first time I saw him, I knew he was the one for me. He was tanned and callused like the carpenters and construction workers I'd been dating, but then I found out he was an artist! When I heard *that*, I set my cap for him. And now that we're married, I'm working on getting him to want some kids. I've thought of some beautiful names. Speaking of people with cute names, how's little Wren today?"

"Oh, she's wavin'," said Terri. "And Dolf here is learning to play checkers. Is Tre going to be all right?"

"I think so," said Starshine, setting down her scanner. "Tre, old brah, you've snapped your collarbone is what you've done. Let me get out my glue gun and patch you."

"Is it going to hurt?" asked Tre weakly. "Shouldn't you give me some drugs?"

"You smell like you've already been smoking some good reefer this morning," said Starshine teasingly. "Are you sure that's not why you fell off your cycle and saw your tires fly away? Reminds me of something happened one time to Aarbie Kidd."

"Oh, shut up," snapped Tre, lying there on his back with the two women and his son looking down at him. "In the first place, the accident was caused by that guy putting some kind of weird DIMs on my tires. In the second place, pot's not a drug. It's an herb. It energizes me."

"Oh yeah," said Terri. "And when's the last time you finished something?"

"What about my new four-dimensional Perplexing Poultry philtre, for God's sake! That's major!"

"Yeah, well how come it took you four years to do it!"

"Now, Terri," said Starshine. "Let me finish healin' him up before you start beatin' him down. I *will* give you a little mist, Tre, so that you won't feel it when I glue your break. And, Dolf, I think maybe you ought to go outside while I do this. I wouldn't want you to get spooked and bump into me."

"Do I have to?"

"You do what the healer says, Dolf," said Terri. "Go out in the garage with Planet and Duck."

"Go ahead, Dolf," added Tre. "I'll be all right."

"Okay. And, Mommy, you come get me when Daddy is well." Dolf ran out to the garage.

"He's a sweet boy to care for his daddy that way," said Starshine. She got a little squeezie of aerosol spray out of her healer trunk. She wafted a pulse of the spray into Tre's nostrils. His muscles relaxed and his eyelids fluttered shut. "I know some folks that have lost everything to this mist," continued Starshine. "It gives you mighty sweet dreams. Mist is giga worse than any silly old pot habit. And mist is nothing compared to gabba. That's what Aarbie Kidd got into after we rode his motorcycle out here from Florida. The minute old Aarbie got to California, he got hooked on gabba and started abusing me ten times worse than he ever did back in Florida. Him and his flamehead tattoos. Thank Goddess I found Clearlight."

Starshine's eyes narrowed and she pulsed a bit more mist into Tre's nostrils. "I had my chance to get free of Aarbie after he wrecked his motorcycle and asked me to heal him. Tre hasn't been beating on you, has he, Terri? If you need some time to think things over, I can put him to sleep for a week."

"Oh no no no, don't do that," said Terri. "It's just that Tre ignores me sometimes. And I get so tired of being a wife and mother. I need a vacation is what it is. I wish I could go off by myself and surf or snowboard someplace really major and let Tre do all the housework for a change. But, oh, I shouldn't be harshing on him while he's hurt. Of course don't put him to sleep for a week, are you whacked? Tre doesn't compare to Aarbie Kidd. You get to work healing him, Starshine. And explain what you're doing as you go along."

"Right now I'm going to have a cup of coffee," said Starshine. "Before I go and finish this. I'll let Tre chill just a little deeper. One more pulse of mist." At the final pulse, Tre's body lost all of its muscle tone. He looked as soft as an imipolex polar bear rug.

"You want anything, Terri?" asked Starshine, ambling out to the kitchen.

"Just a glass of water, please. You're sure Tre's okay?"

"He'll be fine like this for an hour or until I give him the antidote. Did I tell you I saw Aarbie again just the other day? Down near the Boardwalk. He was real friendly. Yellow stubble on his head growing out of the hearts of his flame tattoos. Lifted on gabba as usual." Starshine clattered about in the kitchen, still talking. "What Aarbie's up to these days is what I'd like to understand. First he said he was working for the Heritagists, and then he said he was working for the loonie moldies. He was with some skanky guy from Kentucky who kept telling him to shut up. Okeydoke, here we go." Starshine reemerged with a cup of coffee and a glass of water.

She got something that looked like a stubby plastic pistol out of her healer trunk and set it down next to the scanner and the mister that lay next to Tre. "This is the glue gun," said Starshine. "But first I use my hands to set the bones. Did you know that in Arabic bone-setting is *al-jabar*? The word *algebra* comes from that. Arranging things. I learned that in my classes. Time for some healer algebra, Tre." She laid the scanner on Tre's chest and adjusted his collarbone with both hands. Tre moaned softly.

Terri couldn't watch, so she looked away, letting her eyes range over the pictures on the walls—Starshine's life-affirming Clearlight posters of plants and landscapes, along with Duck's highly detailed oil-and-canvas fiber-for-fiber copies of high-art paintings. Duck loved dreamy late-nineteenth-century artists such as Arnold Böcklin and Franz von Stuck and had taken the trouble to get museum-grade nanoprecise copies of some of their pictures, complete with exact wood-gilt-and-plaster copies of the frames. The largest picture was Böcklin's *Triton and Nereid*, which showed a hairy guy—Triton—sitting on a rock in the sea and blowing in a conch shell. Lying flat on her back on the rock with Triton was a smiling sexy plump Nereid, toying with a huge bewhiskered sea serpent. The serpent's back was decorated with a lovely proto-Jugendstil pattern of green-and-yellow tessellation. Duck liked to explain the pictures to his friends.

"All righty now," said Starshine, setting down the scanner and picking up the glue gun. "See the tip, Terri?" The glue gun had what looked like a long, dull needle at the end. "It's folded up now, so I can push it through his skin. But then on the inside it opens up into a swarm of bendy little arms, and those arms split up into arms that split. The little fibers reach into the break and fit any loose chips into place, and then they secrete . . . something. I forget the name. *Phonybone*? Phonybone is basically organic, except that it has some rare-earth elements in it. Ytterbium and lutetium. It's completely safe."

"Are you sure?" fretted Terri.

"It's automatic, honey," said Starshine as she brandished the glue gun. "Every piece of my equipment has a big DIM inside it. If these machines were much smarter, they'd be full-fledged moldies—and, of course, then you wouldn't be able to trust 'em, would you? That's why we've got healers to run 'em . Here goes!" Starshine bent over Tre and pushed the tip of the glue gun through his skin just above his collarbone. As the invisible fractal tip unfolded and did its work, Terri could see slight motions beneath Tre's skin.

Again Terri looked away, resting her eyes on von Stuck's *Sin*, a high Jugendstil work with a massive, pillared gold-leaf wooden frame around a darkly painted half-nude woman, young and bold-eyed, her raven tresses cascading down with a stray pubic-like curl across her belly—and there in the shadows, draped across her shoulders, was a great thick black serpent, its inhuman slit-eyed face peering out at the viewer from beneath the woman's steady, shadowed gaze. Next to it was a tacked-up paper Clearlight poster showing a huge sunflower with a smiling face. Out the window was the palm tree and the garage and the October afternoon and the soft piping of Dolf and the loud, laughing voice of Duck—tears filled Terri's eyes.

"Terri," came Starshine's voice presently. "It's all over, sweet thing. You can stop crying. And, brah Tre, it's time to wake up." Starshine changed a setting on her squeezie and pulsed a different aerosol into Tre's nostrils. He twitched and opened his eyes. "You're all better, Tre!" said Starshine. "And for recuperation, I'd advise right living and being good to your wife."

"Wavy," said Tre, sitting up uncertainly. "The dreams—I was seeing flashes of light from the Nth dimension. Yaar! I'm healed?" He rubbed his shoulder. "How much do we owe you?"

"Oh, how about a free room in your motel for maybe a week, ten days? My Aunt Tempest is coming out to visit from Florida, but I can't stand to have her in my house. Tempest raised me, you know. My parents died in the Second Human-Bopper War on the Moon back in 2031."

"I didn't know that," said Terri. "Were they heroes?"

"Not hardly," said Starshine. "They were working for the boppers. They were called Rainbow and Berdoo, just a cracker skank and her bad-ass man—like me and Aarbie Kidd used to be. Rainbow and Berdoo ran a toy shop on the Moon that was a front for a tunnel into the boppers' Nest."

"Wow," said Tre. "They were helping the boppers turn people into meaties? Putting those robot rats inside their skulls?"

"I think Rainbow and Berdoo were probably meaties themselves by the end," said Starshine. "After they died, a guy called Whitey Mydol took care of me for a while. Him and his old lady Darla; they're friends of Stahn Mooney's. Stahn got in touch with my Aunt Tempest, and she had me flown right down to Florida."

"Senator Stahn's gotten kind of strung out lately," remarked Tre. "But he's still a good man. So when's your aunt coming? What are the dates?"

"Too soon till too long," sighed Starshine. "You don't have to give her a really good room."

"We can fit her in up by the parking lot," said Terri. "Those rooms are usually empty this time of year."

"Aunt Tempest couldn't be any worse of a guest than the guy I checked in last night," said Tre, cautiously flexing his newly healed body. "Randy Karl Tucker."

"Randy Karl Tucker!" exclaimed Starshine. "That's the name of the guy I saw down at the Boardwalk with Aarbie Kidd."

"Oh yeah?" said Tre. "Well, he's the one who sabotaged my DIM tires, and it looks like he stole Monique. Maybe you can help me find him?"

"I wouldn't advise you to try," said Starshine, shaking her head. "Not if he's friends with Aarbie. Terri, I'll let you know about Aunt Tempest. Now go on home and get Tre to rest."

When they stepped out into the yard, Dolf heard them and came running. "Daddy!"

Tre hugged him. "I'm all fixed. Starshine glued me. What have you been up to?"

"Duck's shoes can walk by themselves," said Dolf. "Show them, Duck!"

Duck grinned and held his hands up in the air. Slowly and smoothly, he slid out of the garage toward Terri and Tre.

"They're DIM shoes," said Duck. "The soles are imipolex. They adjust to your foot. And if you press your toes a certain way, they ripple along on the ground by themselves. Loose as a moose." Duck made dancing gestures with his arms and gave his wild laugh.

"Do you have to feed your shoes?" asked Dolf.

"No," said Duck. "They're like moldies; they eat light." He struck a new pose and his shoes began dollying him back into the garage. "I gotta finish this piece by tomorrow. How's the sore wing, Tre?"

"It's solid," said Tre, gingerly patting his collarbone. "Good as new."

"Beautiful. Later, guys."

Back at the motel, three of Monique's nestmates were waiting for them: Xlotl, Ouish, and Xanana. While Xlotl was shaped like a chessman, Ouish and Xanana looked like sharks walking around erect on their tail fins—sharks with drifting, eddying fractals moving across their skins in shades of blue and deep gray. They each had a silvery patch that sketched a resemblance to a face.

"What's the story with Monique?" Xlotl demanded of Terri and Tre. "What the hell happened?"

"It looks like Monique ran off with a scuzzy cheeseball guest," said Terri, smiling at Tre. She'd started believing him again. "He sabotaged Tre's DIM tires, and poor Tre broke his collarbone trying to catch them."

Tre smiled back at Terri, then focused on Monique's excited nestmates.

"How do you know something happened to Monique anyway?" asked Tre. "Did she uvvy you?"

"She *didn't*," said Xlotl. "And she was supposed to. So I grepped for her vibe and managed to get a feed from her virtual address, but—" Xlotl shook his head helplessly.

"What?" demanded Tre. "Can you tell me, Ouish? Xanana?"

"Yes, I can tell you," said Ouish. She had a rich, womanly voice that she generated by vibrating her silvery face patch. "Xanana and I have just been channeling her. Monique seems to be dreaming about the ocean. We think maybe she's undersea. Come here, Tre. Let me uvvy it to you."

"Wavy," said Tre, and Ouish laid one of her fins across the back of Tre's neck to feed him a realtime uvvification of Monique's current mental essence.

Monique seemed to be underwater, but it was not a realistic scene. The bottom had a white orthogonal mesh painted on it, for one thing, and the things swimming about in the water looked more like goblins than like fish. Instead of seaweed, the bottom was overgrown with rusty machinery. Yet the play of the shiny surface overhead was just as the ocean should be. The uvvy transmitted a nonvisual sensation that there was someone with Monique—inside her?—someone that Monique was frightened of, someone kinky, someone like Randy Karl Tucker.

It was too strange, too intense, and Tre felt faint. He pushed Xanana's flipper off his neck.

"That's my nestmate," said Ouish. "That's her right now. And I don't know how she got that way or where she is. Tell me about the guest who took her."

"At first Tre thought he was just a weird redneck limpware salesman," said Terri.

"His name is Randy Karl Tucker," added Tre. "He's from Kentucky. He was real interested in Monique last night, and this morning he got her to rickshaw him out of here. I almost caught up with them near the wharf, but Tucker put some kind of DIM patches on my tires that made them jump off my wheels and try to choke me and turn into seagulls and fly away. Does . . . does that any make sense to you guys?"

"It could be done," said Xanana. "Have you heard of superleeches? No? You poor fleshers can be so out of it. There's a new kind of leech-DIM called superleeches; they just started showing up in August. Nobody's told you? A superleech lets a human take control of a moldie or, for that matter, take control of a simple DIM device like an imipolex tire. It's made of some new kind of imipolex. None of us knows where the superleeches are coming from. They're very bad. Very very bad. Very very very bad. Very very very very bad—" Xanana repeated this loop phrase maybe twenty or a hundred times, saying it faster and with more *verys* each time, so that the last repetitions merged into a single chirp. Xanana liked infinite regresses.

"And you say Tucker's a cheeseball?" interrupted Ouish.

"I don't really know for sure," said Terri. "It's a guess."

"*Yeah,* Monique was gonna fuck him," said Xlotl. "We was talkin' about it during our break. Just ball him to make money, ya know."

"Oh wow, that's classy," exclaimed Terri. "Monique turning tricks in our motel. If that's the case, we don't want her working here, do we, Tre? With the children? We don't want the Clearlight to end up like that horrible place where my father died!" The moldies shifted about uneasily at this remark, but Terri seemed not to notice. "Answer me, Tre!"

"No, we don't want that," said Tre slowly. He'd been deep in thought ever since hearing what Xanana said. "I need to find out more about these superleeches. I've got this feeling they're based on my four-dimensional Perplexing Poultry. How come Apex Images never tells me anything?"

"Let's stick to the point," said Xlotl. "How do we save Monique? Is it for real that she's underwater?"

"She might be," said Ouish. "Or she might just be dreaming."

"Maybe she and Tucker turned right at the wharf and headed up toward Steamer Lane," suggested Tre. "Can you guys uvvy any moldies there?"

"Let me try," said Xanana. "Everooze and Ike might be surfing Steamers today."

In a minute, he'd made contact. Everooze, father of Monique and Xanana, was indeed surfing Steamer Lane, a point break at the Santa Cruz lighthouse. Xanana spoke aloud so that Tre and Terri could follow the conversation.

"Yaar, Pop, have you seen Monique? Or has anyone else there seen her? Yeah, I'll hold on while you check. What's that? Zilly the liveboard did? Monique turned herself into a diving suit for a tourist and jumped into the ocean? But you didn't notice it yourself. You were shredding the curl. Wavy. Yeah. We think Monique's been abducted. Her signal's really weird; you can check it out. You're going after her? Hold on, Ouish and me want to come too."

"I'm in," said Xlotl.

"And me too," said Terri. "If I can wear you underwater, Xanana?"

"Sure thing. Is Tre coming? He could ride inside Ouish."

"I should rest," said Tre. "I'm still a little shaky from the accident. And I've got to find out about this superleech stuff. I'll make some uvvy calls."

"Okay," said Terri. "And take it easy. Ouish, can you rickshaw me out to Steamers?"

"I don't do that," said Ouish coldly. "I'm a diver, not a rickshaw."

"You can say that again," said Xanana. "You can say, 'You can say that again' again. You can say, 'You can say, 'You can say, "You can say that again" again' again. You can say, "You can say, 'You can say that again' again" again' again." And he was off to the races with another regress.

"La-di-da," said Xlotl. "This ain't no tea dance. Get the hell on me, Terri." Xlotl formed a saddle shape on his back, and Terri got aboard. The three moldies and Terri went bouncing down the hill.

Tre watched them go, checked on Molly and the kids, sat down in a comfortable chair, donned the uvvy, planning to put in a call to Stahn Mooney. But just then the uvvy signaled for him.

"Hello?"

"Hi there!" Tre saw the image of a teenage girl hick with a colorless lank ponytail. "My name is, um, Jenny? I bet you're wondering about Randy Karl Tucker's superleeches, aren't you?" Jenny gave a shrill giggle. "I could tell you all about them if I wanted to."

"Are you working with Randy for the Heritagists or something?" asked Tre. "I want Monique back right now. Are you a blackmailer?"

"Those are silly questions," said Jenny. "Me, a Heritagist? A blackmailer? Think bigger, Tre. I want to talk to you about smart stuff! I can tell you exactly how Sri Ramanujan at Emperor Staghorn used your 4D Poultry to design imipolex-4 and the superleech. I have a viddy of him explaining it. If I show it to you, will you promise to tell me all the things it makes you think of next?"

"But I have an exclusive contract with Apex Images."

"Oh *right*! I'm so sure. And meanwhile Apex never tells you anything. Ramanujan gets your ideas and hogs them and doesn't give you anything back. You can trust Jenny, Randy. I'll never tell anyone a thing about our little deal. Here's a peek."

Jenny started a tape of a round-faced Indian man, presumably Ramanujan, explaining about his marvelous new Tessellation Equation. He seemed to be in a lab, and there was a math screen behind him. Tre could instantly see that this was a major mathematical breakthrough and that it had been inspired by his 4D Poultry. It was like he was suddenly getting a glass of water after crawling through a desert. Just then Jenny stopped the tape.

"Are we interested? Hmmm?" Something synthetic about the hum made Tre suddenly realize that Jenny was a software construct and not a person at all. God only knew who she really worked for.

"Please let me see the rest of it, Jenny."

"And you promise to tell me what it makes you think of?"

"I promise."

CHAPTER FOUR

RANDY

March 2052 - August 2053

All through the fall and winter of 2051, Parvati kept up her visits to Randy. They had sex and took camote/leech-DIM trips together, and now and then Parvati would take Randy on tours into the surrounding countryside. Once they went to the jungle and rode wild elephants; another time they flew over the Western Ghats to go diving in the Arabian Sea. Shiva came along for that trip; he'd learned to tolerate Randy, as Randy was now giving Parvati a full kilogram of imipolex a month toward the creation of Shiva and Parvati's third child.

To make enough money for the imipolex payments, Randy was working lots of overtime hours at Emperor Staghorn. He absorbed an intensive uvvy course on Electrical Contracting and began doing some of the electrical work in the sub fab as well as the plumbing. He felt like his mind was getting bigger all the time.

Parvati carried most of the imipolex on her belly, and after ten months she stuck out as if she were massively pregnant. Shiva was equally fattened up with the imipolex that he'd obtained on his own. But on the eleventh month after her first date with Randy, Parvati showed up at the Tipu Bharat room looking like a feeble ghost of her old self. She and Shiva had pooled their hard-won surplus imipolex to make the body of a new moldie son named Ganesh—their final child. Once a moldie had produced three children, he or she normally died.

"Please help me to get strong again, Randy," said Parvati. "If you give me enough imipolex, I can use it to upgrade my own body. If I don't get it, I'll rot and fall apart like Angelika and Sammie-Jo. Shiva's already stinking—he accepts death, but I don't. Randy, if you get me forty kilograms of imipolex, I can renew myself. I know I'm not so attractive as before, but—"

"Don't worry, Parvati," said Randy, feverishly pressing her against him and taking deep breaths of her slightly putrefied scent. "You're the one I love, li'l stinker. I'll find a way. I'll take out a loan. I'll push for a promotion!"

"Oh, Randy. I know it's wrong, but sometimes—sometimes I actually enjoy having you touch me. Yes, do touch me, darling. Tell me you love me."

With this inspiration, Randy checked the Emperor Staghorn in-house list of job openings and applied for a position as a process engineer for Emperor Staghorn's great researcher, Sri Ramanujan.

When Randy approached Neeraj Pondicherry for a recommendation, the older man was incredulous. "You have no higher degrees, Randy, no college education. You're a plumber, a handyman. Do you have any notion of what a process engineer does?"

"Hell, it can't be so different from hooking up pipes and wires. I need the raise, Neeraj. I want to buy Parvati a complete body upgrade."

"It would be more realistic to take up with a fresh young moldie, Randy. A one-year-old. Instead of quixotically squandering so many rupees to keep a four-year-old moldie alive."

"Are you gonna help me or not?"

"Of course I will help," sighed Neeraj. "I can tell Ramanujan that you are a reliable and uniquely adaptable employee. The work you've done on the electric power network in the sub fab is very ingenious; this work evidences your ability to extrapolate beyond plumbing. Indeed, now that I think upon it, it seems possible that Ramanujan may choose you. He is a very strange person."

A week later Randy started work in Ramanujan's lab, a large room off to one side of the fab. Half of Ramanujan's lab was a walled-off clean room, and half of it was the man's messy office, which included a small kitchen area. Ramanujan was a short uncouth man, stout, unshaven, and not overly clean. His brown eyes shone with preternatural intelligence.

"So, Mr. Tucker, you are the new chap to be helping me," said Ramanujan in welcome. "Don't be shy, I too have bucolic origins—although of course I am Brahman. Neeraj Pondicherry tells me that you are very dexterous with complex systems. As it happens, your complete lack of academic credentials is a plus rather than a minus. For reasons of industrial security, I prefer that my assistants are not able to fully understand what I am doing."

"I'm rarin' to go, Sri. Can you walk me around and tell me what's a-goin' on? And what all a process engineer does?"

"A research scientist makes things begin to happen; a process engineer arranges that the same things may continue to happen for a very long time. In this laboratory I am creating some experimental designer imipolex that I use to make leech-DIMs. At present I am crafting these DIMs one at a

time; my immediate problem is how to avoid doing all this work by myself
so that I can focus on the question of how to enhance the functionality of
the leech-DIMs. You do know what leech-DIMs are?"

"You bet," said Randy. "I have a moldie girlfriend, and I put one of your
leech-DIMs on her all the time. After we fuck, I'll chew up a couple of her
camote nuggets and slap the leech-DIM on her and then—" Randy broke
off when he noticed Ramanujan's shocked expression. This was the first
time he'd tried to tell a human the details of what he habitually did with
Parvati.

"Please go on," said Ramanujan dryly. "I am on tenterhooks."

"Well, Sri, it's like Parvati and me see God. Everything gets white and
then it breaks into beautiful colors. And Parvati is in there with me. It's not
really magic, even though it feels that way—she wraps herself around my
head while we're tripping, so I guess she's like a big uvvy echoing the camote
hallucinations. She says the leech-DIM sets all of her thoughts loose at once.
Did you ever realize that Everything is the same as Nothing?"

Ramanujan frowned and shook his head. "The whole point of my
inventing the leech-DIM, Mr. Tucker, was to provide a means of protection
from moldies. Yet you are drugging yourself like a sadhu and wrapping a
moldie around your head? I think before we go any further I must give you
a brainscan to make sure that you don't have a thinking cap in your skull.
It would be a security disaster to have the moldies looking out through my
assistant's eyes."

"Parvati and I love each other, and she promised not to put no thinking
cap on me. But if it makes you feel better, go ahead and scan me, Sri.
Where's the brainscanner at?"

"Right here," said Ramanujan, pointing to a small circular hatch set
into his office wall at waist height. "Just lean over and stick your head
inside."

"You've got a scanner built into your wall?"

Suddenly there was a needler in Ramanujan's hand. "No temporizing,
please, Mr. Tucker. Get over there and stick your head into the scanner.
For all I know, you're a moldie-run meat puppet playing the part of the
innocent oaf."

"Shitfire," said Randy weakly and stuck his head into the round hole
in the wall. There was a buzzing, a flash of purple light, and then it was
over.

"All's well and good," said Ramanujan, his needler already back out of
sight. "I'm sorry if I frightened you. Would you object to being scanned
every day?"

"Is it bad for me?"

"Not particularly. Especially as compared with your other habits."

"Don't you like moldies, Sri?"

"I'm fascinated by them, Mr. Tucker. But I fear them. My ongoing work is to find ways for human logic to control them. My first leech-DIM is a crude design—it zeroes out all of a moldie's neuronal thresholds to produce an effect that I suppose could be thought of as similar to that of a mystical union with the One as you suggest. In the future, I hope to have leech-DIMs which allow human users to more directly control the behavior of a moldie. Enlightenment is easy, but logic is hard."

"How do you make leech-DIMs?"

"The abstract answer involves a great deal of higher mathematics which would be quite impossible for you to understand. The concrete answer lies in there." Ramanujan gestured toward the clean room half of his lab, which was separated from them by a narrow transparent chamber holding bunny suits and an air shower. "Shall we go in?"

The lab had a long, cluttered workbench on either side of the room—a chemical bench on the right and a biological bench on the left.

The near end of the chemical bench held a miniaturized refinery, which was fed by lines coming up through the floor from the sub fab. As Randy now knew, the tubes carried such things as water, glycerol, ethanol, polystyrene, ethylbenzene, tetrafluoroethylene, isopropylacrylamide, and solutions of natural resins and alkaloids extracted from the plants and animals of Gaia's jungles and seas.

The refinery cracked and cooked the chemical compounds into imipolex variants for Ramanujan to decant into a multitude of small beakers, tanks, trays, watch glasses, and crucibles that were ranged all down the length of the chemical bench.

The center of the room held a large brightly lit aquarium. Inside the aquarium, small imipolex slugs crawled and floated about like the shimmering nudibranchs, ctenophores, and jellyfish of the Indian Ocean—or, no, they were like Kentucky leeches—like freshwater horse leeches lazily stretching and shortening their bodies as they waited for prey.

"I keep them in there while I'm working on them," said Ramanujan. "When I'm ready to ship one of them, I dry it into a hibernation state."

"You make them by just pouring out some special imipolex, and that's that?"

"Of course not. In order to get any computational power, the little slugs of imipolex need to be doped with metals and seeded with chipmold. The main fab breaks that into numerous steps, but in here I have a nanomanipulator that can do everything at once."

Set into the back wall of the lab there was a three-dimensional nanomanipulator with a heads-up holographic display showing a magnified electron microscope image of the DIM inside it. The device also had a VR uvvy that allowed the user to fly about inside the image, using and programming the nanomanipulator's individual nanopincers and nanofeelers.

"It's fairly easy to train the nanomanipulator to do repeated steps," said Ramanujan. "If it was very much smarter, it would be a full-fledged moldie, and my security would be smashed to blazes. It's an awkward position I'm in. Hopefully you can learn to emulate in some measure the efficiency of a moldie. Go ahead and try on the manipulator's uvvy."

Randy put it on. He was in an ocean of imipolex, with hollowed-out tube tunnels leading here and there. Some of the tubes held bright geometric icons—these stood for rare-earth metal crystals. Elsewhere in the mazes of the tubes were fuzzy globs—these represented the spores and algae of the chipmold. Myriads of little claws were scattered about—his nanopincers.

"The metals and the spores have to be distributed in certain ways," said Ramanujan. "Fortunately, the controls are fractalized. That is, you can group them and cascade them. It's as if you could shrink your hands and put copies of your hands at the tips of each of your fingers—and then do it again."

Randy played around in the nanomanipulator's space for a while. The tubes were like pipes, and the cascaded controls were not unlike a multihead pipe-gun. "I can drive this," he said presently. "But what patterns do you want me to put in? Where are the specs?"

"In here," said Ramanujan, tapping his head.

"How'm I gonna know what to do?"

"Just study the patterns I've been using and do something similar. As it happens, the actual pattern used for the etching process doesn't seem to be terrifically important. It's more like you're a farmer cultivating a field—you plow it up to a certain statistical density and then you broadcast your seeds. The field and the seeds are smarter than the farmer."

"Thanks a lot, Sri. Now tell me about that other bench."

The biological bench along the left wall was covered with flasks and beakers where the chipmold cultures were prepared. One large beaker was half-filled with a gel of imipolex made cloudy by a million threads of mycelium. Up above the gel, ruffs of chipmold climbed the sides of the beaker like shelf mushrooms on a rotten tree.

"That's one of the classic strains," said Ramanujan. "Each layer of my leech-DIMs gets a dusting of that fellow's spores. But the real computational power comes from the cultures in the flasks."

The flasks held agars of imipolex with chipmolds growing in them. Most of them held several kinds of mold, with the populations intermingling like plants in a meadow or like corals on a reef. In a few of the flasks, the regions of differently colored mold moved about at a visible pace.

Randy leaned over to stare deep into one of the little bottles and saw a background pattern of green-and-yellow citylike structures that were forever assembling themselves and breaking apart. Filling the spaces between the hives were lively vortex rings, each like a mushroom cap or like a jellyfish. These little jellyfish patterns were in shades of royal blue, tipped with vermilion accents. They pulsed their way through the interstices of the background pattern, splitting in two at some intersections, merging at others. "It's pretty," said Randy.

"Yes yes," said Ramanujan. "Pretty complicated. Are you ready for me to go through the whole process for you step-by-step? I suppose we'll have to do this several times. Are you prepared to concentrate? Each full run-through takes about four hours."

"I'm ready," said Randy.

Over the following days, Ramanujan led Randy through the leech-DIM fabrication process over and over until Randy could reliably do it himself. Randy was like a cook working for a master chef. As he grew more familiar with the recipe, he began finding ways to streamline it, although Ramanujan resisted any attempts to fully automate it. His great fear was that an automated process would amount to a program which could be stolen by Emperor Staghorn's industrial rivals, by the moldies, or by some other interested parties.

Such as the Heritagists. The evening after his first day of work with Ramanujan, Randy went to bed early. Parvati was feeling too weak to visit, and Randy was tired out from running through the leech-DIM recipe—not once but twice. Ramanujan was a slave driver. Just as Randy got into bed, his uvvy began beeping for him. Hoping it might be Parvati—he was eager to tell her that he'd nailed down the job—he slapped the uvvy on his neck.

"Hi there, Randy. You sure aren't very thoughtful about your old friends." It was a pale silly goose of a girl with a very bad complexion. For a moment Randy didn't recognize her.

"Helloooo! Salt Lake City calling Bangalore!" She waved both hands and grinned ingratiatingly. "Jenny from the Human Heritage Council? Jenny who found your neato keeno new job?"

The whole dreary, smarmy, small-time-loser vibe of Heritagism came crashing back in on Randy. He'd completely blocked out Heritagism and the wretched Shively days since coming here—what with the interesting work at Emperor Staghorn, the fabulous love affair with Parvati, and the profoundly psychedelic camote visions to think about. Now and then he'd written his mother, sure, but he'd totally spaced out on his promise to make regular reports to the Jenny thing. *Ugh!*

"A little birdie told me you're moving up the ladder at Emperor Staghorn Beetle Larvae, Ltd.," said Jenny. "Working with Sri Ramanujan, no less. We're very proud of you!"

"Uh, yeah, Jenny, I'm sorry I never called. I reckon I oughtta tell you I'm not much of a Heritagist no more."

"So?" Jenny had stopped smiling.

"So that's why I'm not too interested in talking to you."

Jenny's white little goody-goody face grew pinched and mean. "We got you this job, Randy, and we can take it away. Now that you are finally in a position to give us some useful information, you are going to deliver. Or else. I want a step-by-step rundown on Ramanujan's leech-DIM process, and I want it now."

"I only started learnin' it! Anyway, Ramanujan would kill me if he knowed I was leakin' on him. What the hell do you dooks have against moldies anyway? They're beautiful!"

"Start uvvying me the information, Randy, or you'll find your Emperor Staghorn employee pass is void when you show up to work tomorrow. You'll be out of work and your little moldie girlfriend will rot to death. Believe it. Once a month I'm going to call you, and once a month you're going to run through the leech-DIM process for me. Each time you finish, I'll tell you which parts need more detail, and you'll get me the details by the next month. I'm not here to argue with you. I'm here to get the information."

So Randy told Jenny the leech-DIM recipe as best he could and tried not to worry too much about what Jenny was going to use it for.

That week the Emperor Staghorn Beetle Larvae company store let Randy get forty kilos of imipolex on credit, and Parvati was suddenly like new again. Shiva died right around then, and Parvati started living with Randy full-time, cooking and cleaning for him and flying him to and from work every day.

The other roomers in the Tipu Bharat made no objection; they all liked Randy because in his spare time he'd fixed the building's leaky pipes and drains. It had turned out that most of the building's sewer lines were actually made of waxed cardboard tubes; once Randy got them all replaced, the Tipu Bharat was a much more pleasant place to live. The grateful owner let Randy and Parvati move into a three-room apartment at only a slightly higher price.

On weekends, Randy and Parvati would go diving or to the jungle, as before, but now that they were practically a married couple, Parvati began letting Randy in on some secrets.

One Saturday morning three months after Parvati moved in with him, Randy woke to the smell of spiced, sugared tea with warm milk.

"Good morning, darling," smiled Parvati. She was plump and beautiful, with fine Indian features and her fingers fluttering through poised gestures of formal dance. She handed him a mug of the chai and a plate of *hoppers*: Tamil griddle cakes with fresh mango. "I have a nice idea for a trip today. I'll show you where some of the really successful moldies live. We call them the *nabobs*." While Randy ate his food, Parvati stoked herself up with a few nanograms of quantum dots; Randy kept a supply of this compact moldie energy source on hand to supplement Parvati's solar energy.

With breakfast over, they walked up the stairs to the roof of the Tipu Bharat. Parvati's extruded *ghungroo* ankle bells tinkled with each step. On the roof, Parvati pressed herself against Randy from behind, growing clamps around his chest and waist. She let her remaining mass flow into a large pair of wings that stretched out as if from Randy's back. Now Randy stepped up onto the building's low parapet. A light morning breeze blew against his face. There was a thronged market square directly below them, part of the Gandhi Bazaar. The cracked, wavering sound of a snake charmer's fat-bulbed little *been* horn rose up toward them—the Indians seemed not to mind how weird and gnarly a tone might be, just so long as it was persistent and loud.

Parvati's uvvy pad rested on the back of Randy's neck, talking to him. Now she signaled that she was ready, and he flexed his legs and leapt off the building with his arms outstretched. A woman in the market square pointed up at them and screamed; hundreds of people stared as Parvati's great gossamer wings caught hold. They glided high across the market, slowly gaining altitude.

Rather than crudely flapping her wings, Parvati sent dynamically calculated ripples through them, getting the greatest possible lift from her energy. At the far side of the square, she heeled over into a turn, and then she held the turn so that they rose up and up in an ascending helix. Below them Bangalore dwindled to the semblance of a city map, set into a patchwork landscape of fields and factories. Now Parvati leveled out and began flying southwest.

"It'll take us perhaps an hour to get there," she told Randy. "We moldies call this place Coorg Castle. It's in the jungles near Nagarhole." Randy relaxed and enjoyed the sensation of the air rushing past him and the vision of the landscape scrolling by below. When the beating of the air got to be too much, Parvati grew a little windshield to protect his face. Buying Parvati a new body was the best thing he'd ever done. And with the good pay he was getting now, he would have fully paid for it in just one more month.

Coorg Castle was a jagged cliff deep in an inaccessible part of an official jungle preserve, a cliff pocked with ancient caves. Parvati told Randy that the richer, more successful moldies lived here despite the law that the preserve was solely for wildlife. They helped keep human poachers out of the preserve. "And, of course, they are also giving a lot of *baksheesh* to the authorities."

Randy and Parvati landed in a grassy clearing at the base of the cliff, with flowers blooming all around. Parvati let go of Randy and took on humanoid form. Rather than taking on her customary appearance of a bejeweled sex goddess, Parvati made herself look like a wealthy high-caste widow, modestly wrapped in a white silk sari and adorned with only a few choice bangles and a fashionably large *bindi* dot on her forehead.

Parvati had uvvied the Coorg Castle moldies about their arrival, and a number of the moldies flew out of their caves and circled above, staring down at them. Randy was thrilled by the sight of the great iridescent creatures moving against the blue cloud-puffed sky with the sunlight streaming through their wings. They were like giant butterflies, like a music of enchantment, like a dream of beauty and peace.

Two of the moldies landed near them and took on humanoid form; both seemed to be moldie males. They spoke briefly in English to Randy and then uvvied silently to Parvati for so long a time that Randy wandered off to pick some fruits from the jungle. This was fun until he got a glimpse of a tiger watching him from a thicket. He crashed back to the clearing, but now Parvati was gone. Randy stationed himself with his back against the cliff, anxiously listening to the jungle's many noises. He seemed to hear a steady current of heavy stealthy motions in the leaves. Now and then there was the sharp crack of a breaking stick. Time passed very slowly. It was nearly dusk when Parvati reappeared, flying down from one of the high caves.

"What have you been doing?" he demanded.

"Oh, just visiting," sang Parvati. "Now that I have achieved a fully new body, these nabobs are welcoming me! I find that some of them are even my distant cousins. Yes, I've had a very pleasant day. Are you ready to fly home?"

"Of course I am," snapped Randy. "Unless you're planning to feed me to the tigers?"

"Silly boy," laughed Parvati. "After all you've done for me? I'm still amazed at how readily you paid for my new body." Caressingly, she wrapped her straps around Randy's chest and waist, letting an extra tendril of her body slide down to give Randy's buttocks a gentle caress. "You said my body will be completely paid off in a few more weeks?"

"That's right," said Randy, snuggling against her. "I make enough salary now for ten kilograms of imipolex a month."

"What a smart man you are," said Parvati. "Let's fly home and I'll cook you a good curry dinner."

By now Randy had gotten very good at using Ramanujan's nanomanipulator; with Randy's help, Ramanujan could turn out a month's targeted allotment of leech-DIMs in less than a week. Ramanujan was spending all the rest of his time doing involved calculations and trying to invent some new kind of imipolex.

Early in July, Tre Dietz of Santa Cruz, California, came up with the long-awaited four-dimensional Perplexing Poultry philtre. Tre's employer Apex Images had a one-way disclosure agreement with Emperor Staghorn Beetle Larvae, Ltd., so Ramanujan was immediately able to obtain the philtre—complete with source code. Ramanujan became deeply obsessed. He set an uvvy to continually displaying a floating holographic sphere of four-dimensional Perplexing Poultry. The sphere hovered over his desk, and Ramanujan sat there at every hour of the day, staring and calculating.

The 4D Poultry came in seven different shapes and were colored in pleasing translucent pastel colors, one color for each kind of Poultry. They fit seamlessly together like pieces in an interlocking puzzle. The familiar chickens and dodoes were still present, though their old forms had undergone a sea change—they were much more tilted and twisted than before. Ramanujan obscurely insisted on calling the new shapes Vib Gyor, both in the singular and in the plural.

The ethereal sphere of Vib Gyor looked, at least to Randy's untutored eye, like a wad of ugly misshapen newborn chickens, dodoes, turtles, pigs, weasels, kittens, and lizards huddling together for warmth. The shapes had a disturbing tendency to visually reverse themselves, like a drawing of a staircase that could be going either up or down. And sometimes Ramanujan would set the shapes to mutating, each of them slowly cycling through weird changes without ever losing full contact with its simultaneously cycling neighbors. Randy gathered that the Vib Gyor had something to do with Ramanujan's dreams of a better leech-DIM.

Meanwhile Parvati was becoming more and more neglectful of Randy. She still insisted that he give her ten kilograms of imipolex per month, but what she did with it was anyone's guess. Often she failed to appear at the fab to fly Randy home, and sometimes she was gone for several days at a time.

Another sore point was that Parvati had overheard Randy talking to Jenny. Parvati traced Jenny's call to the Human Heritage Council and angrily confronted Randy about it. The fact that Randy was only doing it to protect his job did little to mollify the outraged moldie.

Things were so bad that Randy often had to beg Parvati for days before she'd have sex with him, and even then the act was short and perfunctory— except, of course, on paydays. Whenever Randy would actually hand over a big slug of imipolex, Parvati would get down with him just like old times, him on camote and her on the leech-DIM, the two of them in paradise together.

"Eureka!" Ramanujan shouted into Randy's ear on July 2, 2053. Payday had been the night before, and Randy was feeling a little loose in the head. He was sitting at the nanomanipulator, wearing the uvvy and shakily etching tunnels into a piece of imipolex. It was a good thing the accuracy of the tunnels didn't matter. What was this math geek yelling about? "I've got it, Mr. Tucker, I've got it! Imipolex-4!"

"Do what?" Randy didn't bother taking off his uvvy.

"I don't think I've ever shown you the quasicrystalline structure of imipolex," said Ramanujan, leaning across Randy to adjust one of the nanomanipulator's many mysterious controls. Suddenly the imipolex became an intricately fitted shape assembled from dovetailed polyhedral blocks. "You haven't seen this mode before, have you?"

"Can't say as I have," said Randy. "It's crooked blocks, some red and some yellow."

"Yes, that's because I've set the nanoeyes to polarized inflation," said Ramanujan. "The different colors are the different domains of the imipolex. Like a crystal, a quasicrystal is made up of many copies of the same elements—the two kinds of blocks you see. I can make them look like chickens and dodoes if you'd prefer." He turned another knob and the little blocks grew beaks and tails and claws that pecked and nestled into each other like a henhouse gone crazy. "These are our old friends the three-dimensional Perplexing Poultry. What makes a quasicrystal different from a crystal is that the building blocks—the chickens and the dodoes—they're not arranged in any regular way. A quasicrystal is like a wallpaper pattern that never repeats."

"Gnarly," said Randy, moving around in the red-and-yellow space of the imipolex's Perplexing Poultry. "I think I seen something like this on a camote trip with Parvati, um, not too far back."

"Yes yes, I shouldn't wonder a bit," said Ramanujan. "The present leech-DIMs do percolate the quasicrystalline structure up into the moldies' consciousness. But, as I'm always saying, we would much prefer to impose our own order from the top down. Now let me show you a sample of my new imipolex-4, Mr. Tucker."

"Okeydoke."

With a nauseatingly vast wrenching motion, the nanomanipulator's view changed to a different sample of imipolex, this one unetched as yet. "This is new, Mr. Tucker. It's based on the four-dimensional Perplexing Poultry. Can you see the Vib Gyor? See the seven kinds of them? Violet-Indigo-Blue-Green-Yellow-Orange-Red."

"Peck-peck, Sri. *Braaawk-cackle-brawk.*"

"Yes yes, the Vib Gyor are in my new imipolex," exulted Ramanujan. "I found a way to put this pattern into my imipolex by applying a special electromagnetic field while the plastic is setting. A correctly applied field can guide the quasicrystal tessellation; it's just like the way dust arranges itself in patterns if you sprinkle it onto the skin of a vibrating drumhead. Of course, the drumhead is only a linear second-order differential equation, while the field equation I am using here is nonlinear and of order nine. Today we're going to start making leech-DIMs with imipolex-4, Mr. Tucker!"

"That'll be better?"

"Much better. The goal, after all, is to logically control the moldies. My mathematical investigations have been indicating all along that a controlling leech-DIM must use a higher-dimensional Penrose tessellation."

"So you'll be able to slap a leech-DIM on a moldie, and the moldie'll do what you tell it to," mused Randy. "Shitfire." Yesterday Parvati had gotten her monthly allotment of imipolex from him, and this morning she'd already turned nasty again. They'd had a terrible quarrel and she'd left for who knew how many days. Controlling his beloved Parvati with a souped-up leech-DIM was starting to sound like a good idea.

"Of course, your commands have to be rather simple," said Ramanujan. "The problem is that even imipolex-4 won't hold enough information. I'm working on a solution to that problem as well. I'm trying to create imipolex-N. Here, take a look at my latest effort." Randy's universe shuddered sickeningly and turned into muddy brown scuzz spotted with threads of green and purple.

"This looks like where the madwoman shits, Sri."

"Fool."

"Xoxx it." Randy took the uvvy off. "You'll make me puke with that kilp. What did you say it was supposed to be?"

"A quasicrystal based on N-dimensional Perplexing Poultry. But I can't figure out the correct N-dimensional tessellation. To create it, I need a more thoroughgoing fundamental solution. I need a Tessellation Equation. Once I have imipolex-N, I'll have a substance rich enough to hold as much information as I like—as much information as an entire human mind!"

Randy threw back his head and gave a deranged-scientist cackle. "And to think they dare call us mad!"

"Oh, get back to work, you degenerate bumpkin. Once we get one of the new imipolex-4 leech-DIMs ready, you can try it on your moldie girlfriend. Intercourse with her is all you care about, as I very well know."

For the next six weeks, the two of them worked like fury, testing out different combinations of imipolex-4, etch patterns, metal doping, and chipmold. Randy was completely in the dark about how well they were doing, but Ramanujan grew more and more optimistic. Finally, on August 13, they'd put together a half-dozen exemplars of an imipolex-4 leech-DIM design that, according to Ramanujan, should work. He called his new creations *superleeches*.

"Take this and try it on your girlfriend," urged Ramanujan, handing a superleech to Randy.

It was like a springy, leathery bit of nearly dry elephant's-ear seaweed, colored a rich natural purple with highlights of pale beige. It was about three inches long and one inch across. The untrimmed edges of the superleech were irregular and curly, and its wavy surface was covered with tiny bumps that gave it a sandpapery feel. Randy found his fingers unable to stop caressing it.

"How does it work?"

"A superleech relays orders from people to moldies. The owner is the master, the superleech is the viceroy, the moldie is the slave. The first individual to place the superleech on his or her uvvy—this is the individual whom the superleech is adopting as its owner."

"So what all am I supposed I do?" said Randy. In his hand the superleech shifted to his touch.

"You put your uvvy on your neck, you put the superleech on your uvvy, and you think about what you want Parvati to do. In this way the superleech is adopting you, and you are giving it a program. You think about what you want and then you peel the superleech off your uvvy and put it in your pocket. When you get a chance, you put the superleech on Parvati, and she starts doing what you were thinking about."

"What if I want to change what Parvati's doin' once the superleech gets started?" asked Randy after a moment's thought. "Instead of her doin' the same thing over and over and over."

"Ah yes," said Ramanujan. "That could be disastrous. The unstoppable broom of the Sorcerer's Apprentice. The magic porridge pot that buries the village. The genie that spanks your children to death. Never fear, Randy, the owner can fresh uvvy instructions to the superleech once it is in operation."

"Copacetic!"

As chance would have it, today was Randy's twenty-first birthday. He'd told Parvati about it, but she was in one of her moods again and had displayed little interest. It was still two weeks till the next payday. Of course she wasn't waiting for him outside the fab. He began trudging the half mile to the commuter train station.

In his standard outfit of white pants, white shirt, and wide-brimmed straw hat, Randy stuck out from the crowd, especially with his pale face and beaky nose. He walked with a smooth, nerdly glide, his arms pumping while his head stayed at a constant level. The superleech twitched in his pants pocket.

It was a shame the way Parvati had been treating him lately. It was starting to remind him of the way Honey Weaver had been toward the end. So obviously and totally taking advantage of him. Why did he have to be such a weakling, such a patsy for every bossy woman that came along?

It probably went back to his childhood. To Sue. Sue wasn't the stablest of women, and it was common for her to flip-flop from cozy mothering to crazed bitchy ranting and back. It was hard always being at the mercy of just one parent. Whenever Randy asked Sue about who his father might be, she would put him off. Maybe if he'd had a father, he wouldn't have turned out to be so submissive to women.

Thinking about being *submissive to women* gave Randy a pleasant hard-on, and he passed most of the train ride in idle sex fantasies, helped along by the intimate pulsing of the superleech. Yes, it was high time for Parvati to fuck him again. Suddenly remembering Ramanujan's instructions, Randy took out the superleech and set it against his uvvy.

"I am superleech type 4, series 1, ID #6," said a grainy little voice in Randy's head. The voice gargled raspingly and then announced, "Registration is complete, Randy Karl Tucker. You are my owner, and I am ready to accept your programs."

Randy waited a bit, but the superleech said nothing more. So Randy went back to thinking about sex. When the train stopped, he took the superleech off his uvvy and put it in his pocket.

As Randy was getting out of the train, a small urgent man elbowed him sharply in the ribs and grabbed his wallet. Randy got hold of the wallet and pulled it free of the pickpocket, only to drop it on the street next to the train car steps. As Randy bent over to pick it up, a fat woman's wobbly ass farted horribly in his face, and a dacoit's dirty bare foot stepped on his wrist. The train conductor rang his bell and screamed for Randy to stand clear of the train steps, insultingly calling him a *honkie-wallah*. The humid air was unbelievably foul; the tropical summer sun felt heavy as a sheet of hot metal; and several rupee notes were missing from Randy's wallet.

But the superleech was still in his pocket. He wiped the sweat off his brow and threaded his way through the crowded streets, calming himself with the sight of his favorite sadhus. The stone stairwell of the Tipu Bharat was cool and shady. As he walked up the steps, Randy's heart rose again. He was about to see his sexy Parvati. *And she would act just like he wanted*!

In his boyish heart of hearts, Randy had been hoping for a surprise birthday party, but Parvati was doing nothing more than tensely sitting on a kitchen chair.

"Hey there, li'l stinker," said Randy affectionately. "Here's your birthday boy! How 'bout a hug?"

Parvati grudgingly allowed herself to be gathered into Randy's arms. As he squeezed her tight, she finally spoke.

"I've been waiting for you to get home, Randy. There's something I have to tell you."

"And I got something to tell *you*," said Randy. "Ramanujan and me finally got those new leech-DIMs working. Lookee here, I brought one home." He drew the writhing superleech out of his pocket and set it down on the kitchen table. "Let's give her a try! Lord knows I wouldn't mind eatin' me a couple-three nuggets of camote and fuckin' you all night. It's time to get wiggly, baby! Randy Karl Tucker is twenty-one."

"No, Randy," said Parvati, undulating away to the far side of the kitchen. "That's what I have to talk to you about. It's all over between you and me. I've only been waiting here to say a last good-bye. You've been good to me, but I'm leaving."

"Where would you go? You won't find a more reliable source of imipolex. Do you want more than ten kilograms a month, Parvati? Is that it?"

"As a matter of fact, Randy, soon you're going to be out of a job and in no position to provide *any* imipolex. But no matter. The point is that I've found a fine new husband among the Coorg Castle nabobs. His name is Krishna. He's all blue. Very beautiful."

"You done bought your way into high society with my imipolex, huh? And what the hell do you mean I'll be out of a job? Ramanujan and me just made a big discovery. More'n likely, I'll get a fat raise. Now stop talkin' crazy, Parvati. I don't mind if you visit with your Krishna now and then, just so's you keep comin' home and takin' care of me."

"You're going to be out of a job because I'm going to uvvy the security director of Emperor Staghorn Beetle Larvae, Ltd., and tell her that you've been giving Ramanujan's secrets to that Heritagist Jenny-thing. I've got several of your calls recorded inside my body for evidence. I'm sorry, Randy, but Krishna says I have to report you. He has very high morals."

Randy reeled back against the kitchen table and fell into a chair. "Your snotty moldie boyfriend wants you to tell Emperor Staghorn I've been spying for Jenny? Oh, you bitch. You goddamn, slimy, bossy, bullying—" Just then the superleech on the table brushed against Randy's hand. In one swift, savage movement, Randy leaped across the room and plastered the leech against Parvati's bottom.

Parvati struck out at him, but the superleech dug in and took effect. Parvati's struggles turned to warm embraces. Where the old leech-DIMs had turned Parvati into a kind of glowing egg, the new superleech left her body shape much the same. The difference was that Parvati's usual personality was gone—or submerged. Having sex with her felt perhaps more like masturbating than like making love. But Randy did it anyway; he did it hard, right there on the kitchen floor, thrusting himself deep into her as if somehow he could teach her a lesson.

When he'd finished, Randy put his uvvy on and told the superleech to tell Parvati to cook dinner. While she busied herself with the pots and pans, Randy kept up his uvvy contact with her and the superleech. The real Parvati was definitely still there, down under the superleech. She was confused, disoriented, and above all angry at being trapped in the superleech-run cage of her body. It was sad to see her this way—but for now Randy had no intention of setting her free. She wanted to squeal on him to Emperor Staghorn!

Soon Parvati served some rice with a delicious mushroom curry. It wasn't until he'd eaten two big helpings that Randy realized the curry was full of poached camote. He'd eaten perhaps twenty nuggets. Parvati's shackled spirit had found a way to trick the superleech. She'd cooked dinner, but she'd poisoned him.

The angles of the room twisted and loomed. Randy staggered to the sink and began vomiting onto the dishes, seeing thousands of slow-motion faces in the beige textures of his puke. Parvati stood quietly to one side, watching him. Through the uvvy, Randy could sense her sly glee. What else might she do to him?

Randy drank as much water as he could hold and forced himself to vomit again. His brain's vision processor was crashed; he was getting his eyes' unfiltered input; it was like seeing through twitching, splotchy fish-eye lenses. His hearing was equally xoxxed, all fades and echoes—he became convinced Parvati was whispering something that the superleech wouldn't let him hear.

"Talk to me, Parvati," cried Randy. "Talk to me out loud. Let her talk, superleech, let her say whatever she wants to, but don't let her come at me."

"I dare you to kill me," said Parvati. "Kill me and get some fun out of it. Look at this." Her flesh flowed and twisted and she took on the likeness of Honey Weaver. "You're a freak, Randy Karl," she drawled, hefting her tits. "You're nothing more than a kid I liked to piss on. If you was a man, you'd take that knife outten the sink and kill me. But you're a candy-ass chickenshit."

The big long kitchen knife in the sink winked at Randy. He rinsed the vomit off it and hefted it in his hand. It was sharp, so sharp. He was careful to hold the point away from himself. He could see networks of veins and arteries beneath his flawed, ugly skin.

When Randy looked back at Parvati, she'd changed shape again. She looked exactly like Randy's mother. "Who's my father, Sue?" croaked Randy. "Why won't you ever tell me? Tell me who's my father!"

"Never mind about your father," screamed Parvati/Sue. "I wish I'd aborted you! Don't you have the guts to kill me? You stupid little jerk. If you let me walk out of here, I'll get you fired from Emperor Staghorn Beetle!"

"I want my daddy," said Randy, suddenly breaking into sobs.

Parvati's skin grew dark and her teeth got sharp and long. She was turning into Kali. "Kill me!" she screamed. "Chop me up before I give you a thinking cap! It's coming soon, you flesher freak! *Kiiiiiiill!*"

"Help me, Daddy!" screamed Randy Karl and lunged forward with the long knife. He stabbed and chopped and hacked for the longest time, and the immobile Parvati did nothing to stop him. Finally he was too tired to slice anymore. He dropped the knife to the floor and washed himself off in the sink. There were lots of crumbs of imipolex and chipmold on him; he kept thinking they were gobbets of coagulated blood. When he turned off the water, the room was very quiet. What had he done?

The weirdly bulging kitchen floor was covered with chunks of imipolex, none of them larger than a loaf of bread. They were Parvati. He'd killed Parvati. The pieces of imipolex were slowly dragging themselves around like big slugs. Randy sat cross-legged on the kitchen counter to be up high away from the slugs, and he closed his eyes so he wouldn't have to see them.

Time passed and colors played behind Randy's eyelids. He seemed to hear a man's voice talking to him. His father? "You're doing fine, son. I'm proud of you. You're doing just fine." Randy felt happy and calm. A gentle breeze wafted through the apartment and caressed him. Someone tapped him on the knee. He let his eyes flutter open.

"Bye, Randy." It was Parvati, fully formed, though with a network of pale orange scars.

"What!?"

"I crawled back together. Except for that piece." She pointed to a glob of imipolex lying off to one side of the floor with the purple welt of the superleech knotted into it. "That piece is yours. I tricked you into cutting it out of me."

Randy fumbled for the knife.

"Don't start again or I really will kill you. I feel stronger than ever. The only reason I don't give you a thinking cap is that I'm so sick of you." She turned and walked to the door, slightly limping. "Just for old times' sake, I won't call Emperor Staghorn till tomorrow afternoon. If I were you, I'd leave town before then. The dacoits, don't you know." The door slammed behind her.

Randy walked gingerly across the room and nudged the piece of imipolex that Parvati had left.

"I am superleech type 4, series 1, ID #6," uvvied the hoarse little voice. "I am currently coupled to 723 grams of imipolex with traces of a moldie program. This imipolex was part of the left buttock of a moldie named Parvati."

"Can you wipe out the moldie traces and run the imipolex yourself?"

"Yes. Shall I proceed?"

"Do it. And then keep watch. Grow some feet and walk around. If anyone or anything comes in here, squawk and wake me up. I gotta crash."

Randy tottered to his bed, took off his uvvy, and fell into a whirling kind of nightmare sleep. At some point in the middle of the night, something hopped into bed with him and snuggled up by his chest. He cradled it against himself and slept a little better.

At dawn, the uvvy rang for him: "Randy Randy Randy Randy . . ."

A creature shaped like a young hen hopped off Randy's bed onto the floor and began making a ruckus. What? Randy reached out and slapped the uvvy that sat on his bedside table, setting it to projection mode. Jenny's face appeared. She had a big zit on the side of her forehead.

"Rise and shine, Randy! We have a lot to do today."

"I'm not ready." He rubbed his face, trying to put together his memory of what had happened the night before. The little chicken strutted this way and that, staring at Randy for approval. The nappy purple shape of the superleech ran down the center of its back.

"I saw it all," said Jenny, looking eager and gossipy. "I never told you, but I keep a tap on your uvvy? So when I heard you going off about your father, I did some quick research and found out who he is."

"Now, hold on," said Randy. "Just slow down here. Parvati is gettin' me fired anyway. I'm through working for you skungy Heritagists."

"I'm not a Heritagist, Randy Karl," said Jenny. "I'm a software simmie created by a certain loonie moldie who's also called Jenny. For fast Earth contact, I need to live down here on a serious machine. So I'm working for the Heritagists just to like pay the rent for my space on their machine. I'm living on the Heritagists' big underground asimov computer in Salt Lake City—but, um, Randy, I could move? With a client like you, I could be a freelance agent for both you and moldie Jenny from the Moon. I could buy myself a proprietary hardware node in Studio City."

"Forget it!" said Randy. "Good-bye!"

"Wait! Don't you want to know who your father is?"

"Okay, who is he?"

"*I'll* never tell," giggled Jenny, every bit the snippy teenage Heritagist girl with a secret. "Just kidding! But you have to listen to my new plan too."

"Yeah yeah." Randy kept being distracted by the antics of the super-leech-animated chicken; it was prancing around like a miniature moldie, pretending to scratch for worms in the wooden floor. Wormwood. Randy was still seeing colorful trails every time he moved his eyes. "Let me get it together for a minute, Jenny. I feel mighty rough."

He went and looked in the kitchen. The floor was bare. There were flies on the vomit in the sink. He ran the water for a minute, taking a drink and rinsing off his face. What was that last thing Parvati had said about dacoits? He checked that the apartment door was locked, then took a pee. The hen trailed after Randy like a chick following its mother.

"I'm gone call you Willa Jean," Randy told it. "That fine by you?" The chicken clucked and bobbed its head. Randy leaned over and petted it. "You my little friend, ain't you, Willa Jean? I've always wanted a pet chicken. Good girl. Good Willa Jean."

Whey-faced Jenny was waiting above the uvvy by Randy's bed. "Oh, excuuuuuse me," she said. "Finally ready?"

"Yep."

"Well!" said Jenny. "About your dad. Of course the Heritage Council has a sample of your DNA on file—from when you applied to live in the Shively Heritage House, remember?—so I ran a similarity search across some DNA databases, starting with Louisville. And right away I found your match in the records of the Louisville jail! Willy Taze, born 2004 to Isle Anderson and Colin Taze. You must have heard of him. Cobb Anderson's grandson? The inventor of the DIM and the uvvy? In his twenties Willy was employed by the city of Louisville to maintain the Belle asimov computer, and then in 2031 he helped Manchile and his nine-day meatbop boys. Willy was arrested for treason and sentenced to death, but he broke out of prison in the Louisville asimov revolt that happened the day before Spore Day. Willy made it down to Florida and started inventing things. The Gimmie liked his DIMs so much that they pardoned him. And then Willy moved to the Moon. He built himself a place and roomed there for many years with a man named Corey Rhizome. End of info dump."

"Willy Taze is my dad? Where is he now?"

"Well, I shouldn't really talk about this, but, um, Willy moved out of Einstein and into the moldies' Nest. I wouldn't know how you could reach him. I suppose you could uvvy Rhizome for info, but he's a big old grouch. Corey's an artist, and he doesn't like strangers one bit!"

"But I thought I heard my dad talkin' to me yesterday after I chopped up Parvati," wailed Randy. "I thought I heard a man's voice."

"Yes yes, I arranged that for you," smirked Jenny. "It was pretty obvious that you needed it—slashing up your mommy and crying like a baby. What a sight! But that wasn't Willy talking to you. It was a simulation of Cobb Anderson—your great-grandfather. You know how the Vatican used to have the world's biggest library of porno? Well, the Heritagists have the Earth's biggest archive of bopper memorabilia. And it just so happens that their Salt Lake City Archives own the only existing copy of Cobb's S-cube. I snuck in and booted it up so Cobb could talk to you and make you happy. Now, listen, Randy, you need to get out of Bangalore before Parvati turns you in. I'm going to buy you a plane ticket. Get your suitcase packed, and I'll call right back."

Randy's thoughts were in a whirl. "You're doing fine, son. I'm proud of you. You're doing just fine." So that had been Cobb Anderson. The man who invented the boppers; the first man to have his personality coded up as software. Randy's great-grandfather! It would be nice to have some long talks with him. And Randy's dad—Randy's dad was Willy Taze, the glamorous rebel and genius inventor! Maybe Randy could find Willy in the Nest. Maybe Randy would turn out to be a big somebody like Willy and Cobb!

He moved quickly around his apartment, tossing clothes and mementos into his bag. Willa Jean raced around with him. When the uvvy sounded again, Randy ran to the bedroom and slapped the uvvy onto his neck.

"Yes," said Jenny. "The ticket's all set. You're on a direct flight to San Francisco, leaving at 1 P.M."

"You think that's early enough, Jenny? Parvati said she's gonna uvvy Emperor Staghorn in the afternoon. Did you catch what she said to me about dacoits? When Emperor Staghorn gets the word, they gonna send a gang of thugs after me, girl. Get me an earlier ticket!"

"Randy, before you leave, you have to go in to Emperor Staghorn and make me a complete viddy of how Ramanujan makes a superleech. We've found you a smart micro-cam that'll perch on a hair in your eyebrows. It's no bigger than a dust mite. You make the viddy and at noon you tell Ramanujan you're eating lunch in town and go right to Gate 13 at the airport. They'll have a first-class ticket for you. No sweat!"

"I don't wanna go to no Emperor Staghorn today, Jenny. It's too risky."

"Randy, unless you can get the complete recipe for the superleech, you're not going to be of all that much use to us."

"This is still for the Heritagists?"

"Yes, it's for the Heritagists, but believe it or not, it's for the loonie moldies too."

"Bull *shit*."

"Is too!" giggled Jenny, crinkling her nose and nodding vigorously. "*Mmm-hmmm!* You'll see, Randy Karl Tucker. It'll be fun in California. You'll work in Santa Cruz. It's this funky little beach town an hour south of San Francisco. And you can talk to Cobb Anderson as much as you like. Come on, Randy, don't be a party pooper. At least let us get you to San Francisco."

"Oh man. I dunno."

"I've already called a moldie rickshaw for you. He'll be there in a minute; he's picking up the micro-cam right now. Let him take you to Emperor Staghorn. He'll wait there with your suitcase, and you'll be able to leave the instant you're ready. Come on, Randy. Pretty please."

"What all you got lined up for me in Santa Cruz?"

"Well, I really wasn't supposed to tell you yet, but since we're such good pals and everything—oh, why not. You'll be kidnapping moldies and sending them to the Nest. *Liberating* them, the way the loonie moldies look at it. Moldie repatriation is something the Nest works on with the Heritagists. You'll be working with a man named Aarbie Kidd."

"Kidnappin' moldies'd be easy with superleeches," mused Randy Karl. "For the Nest? I wouldn't mind checkin' out some o' them moldie California girls. And get in tight with the loonie moldies? I wouldn't mind that a bit. Hell, onct I get to know 'em , I could go to the Nest and see my dad, couldn't I!"

"All of that, Randy Karl, and more. Is it a deal? The rickshaw's downstairs."

"Wait. First I wanna talk to Cobb again."

"Can do! I'll patch him right in."

The uvvy image wavered, and then there was Cobb Anderson. He had a strong wide face with high cheekbones. His hair was sandy and he had a short-cropped white beard. He was imaged in much better resolution than

Jenny; he looked almost real, floating there in Randy's visual cortex. The rich Cobb simulation even included scents and air currents. Cobb smelled comfortable—he smelled like freckles.

"So you're Willy's son," said Cobb. "I'm a little out of sync. I just came back from heaven. All is One in the SUN. I don't like being run on this asimov machine; I need my own personal hardware." Cobb paused to channel Randy's vibe. "So you're my great-grandson. Yes. I can tell you've been hurt. Poor Randy. We can help each other."

"Cobb, what's my dad like?"

"Willy's smart as a whip. A wizard with the cephscope. He saved me and a woman from some racial puritans one time, and he freed a bunch of machines from their asimovs. And I hear that then he—" The old man's face clouded over. "Stop talking in my head, Jenny, and don't rush me. Randy, let's see if you can't get me off this pathetically inadequate pig machine. Take me to the moldies on the Moon. We'll make a plan, huh, squirt?"

"Was that you talking to me last night?"

"Yes, Randy. Do you want to hear it again?"

"I surely do."

"You're doing fine, son. I'm proud of you. You're doing just fine. I love you." Cobb's pale eyes were kind and wise.

"Thanks, Cobb. Thanks a lot."

Cobb and Jenny signed off and Randy switched his uvvy attention to Willa Jean. He looked through her eyes and suddenly realized she was usable as a telerobot. He drove her quickly around the nooks and crannies of the kitchen/dining area, pecking up stray crumbs of imipolex and loose nuggets of camote.

"Now, you be ready to hatch that camote back out for me when I ask for it," Randy told Willa Jean. "Don't mash it." Not that he wanted any camote right now, but you never knew.

Randy got Willa Jean to hop into his suitcase and then he closed it up. So now Bangalore was over. Randy gave a heavy sigh. He wandered around the apartment for another minute, taking a last look at the familiar view of the bazaar and the distant hills. How happy he'd been here. If only Parvati had loved him. He walked down the stone steps of the Tipu Bharat, his eyes wet with tears. The waiting rickshaw was shaped like an orange oxcart.

At Emperor Staghorn, Randy found Ramanujan animatedly drinking a large mug of saffron-spiced *chai*. He'd been working in his office all night.

"How did the superleech work on your girlfriend, Mr. Tucker? Feeling a bit wrung-out today, are we?" Ramanujan rubbed his dirty shiny hands and beamed, not waiting for an answer. "Good, good, good. As it happens, I've found a devilishly clever algorithm which rather radically simplifies the superleech manufacturing process. Yes, a rather radical simplification indeed. Look at this beautiful equation!"

Ramanujan indicated some scribbles on a piece of paper on his desk, and Randy leaned over to make sure that his micro-cam got a good view.

"Is that Sanskrit, Sri?"

"I assume it pleases you to jest. The symbols on the left are, of course, integral signs and infinite series, representing a four-dimensional quasicrystal geometry. And the right side of the equation is seventeen divided by the cube root of *pi*. There's glory for you. I call it the Tessellation Equation. Beautiful mathematics makes beautiful technology. Let's go into the clean room so I can show you the tech. But—ah ah!" Ramanujan shook his finger. "First, as always, we scan your reckless head."

Randy was ready for this. He touched his brow and the micro-cam hopped onto his finger until the brainscan was over. Easy as pie. They suited up and entered the clean room.

"So do we make up some more superleeches today?" asked Randy, sitting down at the nanomanipulator. "I'm rarin' to go. I'd kind of like you to go through the whole process once again to make sure I got it straight."

"Do tell," said Ramanujan, suddenly suspicious. "So how *did* you pass the night, Mr. Tucker? I find your matitudinal diligence rather conspicuously atypical."

"Huh? All right, Sri, I'll tell you the sorry-ass truth. I put the superleech on Parvati and fucked her and asked her to make dinner. She poisoned me with camote, and then she got me to chop her up. The pieces that weren't attached to the superleech crawled back together, and there was Parvati again. She ran away to Coorg Castle. She don't love me no more. I just want to work hard and forget about her." A thought occurred to Randy. "I wouldn't be surprised if Parvati didn't try and make me lose my job, she hates me so much."

"Where's the superleech, Randy?"

"It's stuck to a leftover piece of Parvati that's shaped itself into a cute little hen. I call her Willa Jean. She's a telerobot for me now. Like those flyin' dragonfly cameras? I left Willa Jean home."

"Telerobotics!" exclaimed Ramanujan, his coppery face splitting in a grin. "That's a wonderful app for superleech technology!" He leaned over and warmly patted Randy's shoulder. "You're invaluable, my boy. Fools rush in where angels fear to tread."

"You're happy because a slice off Parvati's ass turned into a chicken?"

"I am happy to realize that there is an immediate peaceful use for superleeches. Rather than being solely a bellicose means of moldie enslavement, the superleech can be an interface patch which cheaply turns a sausage of imipolex into a telerobot. Jolly good. But I haven't fully explained my big news yet, Mr. Tucker. That equation I showed you? When interpreted as a method of phase modulation, my equation provides an effective way to convert ordinary leech-DIMs into superleeches simply by sending them a certain signal. It's easy as seventeen divided by the cube root *of pi*."

"Show me how," said Randy Karl.

Ramanujan picked up a small parabolic piece of silvered plastic and walked over to the aquarium where the old leech-DIMs swam. "Observe, Mr. Tucker! This is a pocket radio transmitter that I programmed last night." He aimed the silvered plastic dish at one of the leech-DIMs. "Now I chirp this leech with a signal based on my equation." He pushed a button on the transmitter and suddenly the targeted leech-DIM began shaking all over. "You see? The program sets off a piezoplastic jittering which forces the quasicrystals into the imipolex-4 state." The leech's vibrating skin puckered up into the rough surface of a superleech; it turned tan and purple all over. Ramanujan plucked it out and held it up for Randy's inspection. "Behold!"

Ramanujan set the damp superleech onto an uvvy, and the uvvy speaker announced, "I am superleech type 4, series 2, ID #4. Do you wish to register as my owner?"

"No," said Ramanujan. "Please crawl off the uvvy and go to sleep now." The superleech obliged.

"That's really somethin', Sri," said Randy, fingering the dormant superleech's rough surface. "Can you show me how you programmed that little radio antenna?"

"You'd never understand the program."

"Try me. How am I gonna learn if you don't let me try?"

"You won't understand it, but I wouldn't mind going over it in detail just for myself." Ramanujan called up a mathematics screen above the lab uvvy and delivered a forty-minute lecture on the Tessellation Equation which, as predicted, Randy completely failed to understand. But his micro-cam was making a viddy of it and, even better, Ramanujan was so into his batshit math rap that he didn't notice when Randy slid the silvery little antenna into the top of his fab bootie. When an incoming uvvy call interrupted Ramanujan, Randy quickly excused himself.

"I gotta run to the bathroom, Sri. I'm not feelin' too peak. Reckon I've got the squirts."

"Spare me the details," said Ramanujan, looking away in distaste. "I wonder who can be calling me at this number?"

As Randy hastened through the air shower, he glanced back to see just who was talking to Ramanujan—and of course it was Parvati. Randy darted out of Ramanujan's office and ran off down the Emperor Staghorn hallway, ripping off the bunny suit and pocketing the radio antenna. He had just exited Emperor Staghorn's outer gates when the fab's alarms went off. Randy's moldie rickshaw was waiting there, big and stolid. Randy jumped in.

"Go to the airport! Fast!"

The moldie began springing along like a giant rabbit, covering twenty or thirty feet at a bound. Randy held on for dear life. He fumbled his uvvy out of his bag and put it on. Jenny was waiting.

"Things are happening fast, Randy," she said, brushing a lank strand of loose hair back from her eyes. "Congratulations for bagging that radio transmitter! Emperor Staghorn already has a group of four dacoits looking for you at the airport. I'll tap into the airport's cameras so we can locate them."

When Randy got to the airport, Jenny showed him an image siphoned off one of the airport's security cams. It showed four stocky men, impeccably dressed in Western business suits. Two wore sunglasses, one wore a turban, one was picking his teeth. All had hard unforgiving faces. They were studying some recent photographs of Randy Karl Tucker.

"Where are they standing?" asked Randy. "I better not get near them."

"Well, ummm, they're waiting right next to the gate for your plane to San Francisco. Gate 13. You can see it with your bare eyes from here."

Sure enough, Gate 13 was fifty yards down the hallway, surrounded by milling passengers and with the figures of the four dacoits dark and clear to one side. Through the hall windows Randy could see the airliner: a giant moldie-enhanced machine in the shape of a flying wing.

"Isn't there some other gate I can use?" asked Randy. "Like for first-class or for the handicapped?"

"Yes, Gate 14 is the VIP gate," said Jenny. "But it's only twenty yards past Gate 13 and the dacoits can see it too. We have to distract them. I notice they're all wearing uvvies. I can blast them with noise, but that's only good for a few seconds before they think of removing their uvvies. We need something more. Any ideas?"

"I'll use Willa Jean!" Randy switched his attention to Willa Jean and got her to hop out of the bag and trot along ahead of him. Randy watched through Willa Jean's eyes until she was near the dacoits, and then he launched her toward them like a flying boxing glove. At the same moment, Jenny sent a mind-numbing current of noise into the dacoits' uvvies. Willa Jean bounced among the stunned dacoits, knocking them over like bowling pins. Moving just short of a run, Randy breezed past the dacoits and in through the first-class Gate 14. As he headed down the tunnel to the aircraft, Willa Jean ran to join him. The turbanned dacoit tried to follow her, but Jenny sent some message to the airline personnel that caused them to drag the dacoit out of the boarding area. The plane left on time.

Randy had a comfortable window seat. He stared down at India for a while, thinking about all the things he'd seen here. California would be good too and maybe then the Moon. It would be a long time before he returned to Kentucky. He smiled, leaned back in his seat, and fell asleep.

CHAPTER FIVE

TERRI

June 2043 - October 30, 2035

Although Dom and Alice Percesepe were loyal to their children, they were only fitfully attentive. Terri and Ike had to do most of the housework while they were growing up. Often as not, big sister Terri made supper for Ike, with Dom off at the restaurant and Alice somewhere with her friends. A typical supper would be tuna or peanut butter sandwiches. Ike would always ask for dessert, and Terri would tell him, "There's lemonade for dessert."

"Why doesn't Mother shop?" complained Ike one day in June 2043. It was the last day of school. "We can afford food. Dad owns a restaurant and a motel."

"When Mother shops, it's just for clothes," said Terri. "The only time she buys food is to put on a special dinner for *Dom*." She said her father's name with vicious emphasis.

"Did you get your final grades today?" asked Ike.

"Yeah. I got all A's. How about you?"

"C's and—finally—a B. In History. I'm stoked."

"Dad is gonna be excited about that," said Terri sourly. "Not that he'd ever notice my A's. I'd like to do something to really shake him up."

"Well, he's not too happy about the boys you've been going out with," said Ike. "Kurtis Goole and those other stoner surf rats."

"I know," smiled Terri. "For Kurtis and his friends, adults are bowling pins you knock over. Like inflatable clown dolls with weights on the bottom so you can hit them again and again and they keep bouncing back up."

"Poor Dad," said Ike. "What a way to talk."

"Yeah, poor Dad and his Sons of Adam Heritagist hate group," said Terri. "You know what I ought to do? I ought to start hanging around with moldies. Maybe that would make him notice that I'm alive."

"What is your problem today, sis? Did something bad happen to you?"

"Yes," said Terri, "something did. About a half hour ago, while I was cleaning the house and emptying the trash cans as usual, I saw some papers on Dad's desk. You know what I saw there? His will."

"Oh God, is he sick?"

"Just because you have a will, it doesn't mean you're about to die, idiot," said Terri. "It's just something that grown-ups do. Like taxes. So anyhow, the will says that *you* inherit the restaurant, I get ten thousand dollars, and Alice gets the motel, the house, and everything else."

"Ten thousand dollars," said Ike enviously. "That's righteous bucks. Why don't I get any money?"

"The restaurant is worth a lot more than ten thousand dollars, you fool."

"Oh yeah, I guess it is."

"And you get it all to yourself," spat Terri. "Just because you're a boy with a stupid gross ball sack."

"Whoah!"

That summer Terri had a summer job running the cash register in Dom's Grotto out on the Santa Cruz Wharf. Dom was virulently antimoldie, and he made a point of advertising that no moldies were employed in any capacity by his restaurant. ALL HUMAN-PREPARED FOOD read the signs outside. HERITAGISTS WELCOME. NO MOLDIES WORK HERE. Due to the stench of moldies, not many restaurants employed them anyway, except perhaps to wash dishes or keep the books, but Dom liked to promote the Heritagist cause, even at the risk of getting in trouble for violating the equal rights clause of the Moldie Citizenship Act.

Terri was a calm and efficient cashier, sitting there afternoons and evenings on a high stool. She wore pink lipstick, and she wore her hair long and straight. She chewed gum. Her face was thin, her skin was dark, she was sexy. Terri slept late in the mornings, and at night she went to as many beach parties as her parents would let her get away with.

Ike was working as a deckhand on a Percesepe day-cruise fishing boat run by Dom's brother Carmen. Ike's boat would leave early and come back to the wharf around 4 P.M. He'd help clean the fish the tourists had caught, collect his tips, hose himself off with fresh water, and go over to Dom's Grotto to get his main meal of the day. Terri would order it up as takeout and let Ike have it for free; this was approved by Dom, with the stipulation that Ike's meals not be extravagant.

One foggy day in August, Ike came in wet and wiry, his brown eyes big and his short hair bristling. He wore boots, baggy shorts, and a damp, stained T-shirt.

"Yaar, Terri!"

"Yaar, kiddo. How were the tips?"

"So-so." He shoved his hand in his pocket and held out a small wad of ones and fives. "The customers caught their limit of rockfish, but they were cheap bastards. They were Baptist Heritagists from Texas; Dad's group invited them here and gave them a reduced rate. They kept hoping someone would hook a rogue moldie so we'd have to flame it. Instead of tipping me, one couple gave me, look at this—" Ike dug in his other pocket and produced a gospel DIM that displayed a little hollow film loop about moldies being the Beast predicted by the Book of Revelations.

"Moldies are Satan," chirped the little DIM as it played its images.

"How bogus," said Terri. "How valley. And I notice they don't hate moldies too much to use a DIM for their gospel tract. Like they don't realize that DIMs are small pieces of moldie?"

"They don't know shit," said Ike. "When I mentioned that we're Catholic, they said that the Virgin Mary is a false idol. Whatevray. I'm starving, Terri. Can I get a Dungeness crab? Just this once?"

"You know Dad says to give you cheap food," said Terri. "Unsold fish for upstart barbarians."

"Yeah," said Ike, "with lemonade for dessert. Come on, Terri. Let me have a crab today. If Dad complains, I'll take the blame."

"He won't *let* you take the blame," said Terri. "You're the *son*. Dad saves all the blame for me. But what the hey, big sis can handle it. What do you want with your crab?"

"I want steamed clams, garlic bread, onion rings, french fries, coleslaw, corn on the cob, and a double vanilla milk shake."

"Hungry much?" Terri filled out a takeout check and handed it in through a little window to the kitchen. Ike flopped down on one of the captain's chairs by the register.

"Don't sprawl, Ike. You'll scare off the paying customers. We don't want them to think this is a place for grunge buckets."

"Shut up," said Ike, rubbing his face and lolling even farther back.

"I saw little Cammy Maarten at the party last night," said Terri to needle her brother. "Isn't she in your grade? She asked about you. She said I should bring you to the next party. She thinks you're *cute*."

"Cammy Maarten is a feeb," said Ike. He had not yet realized that girls were something he needed. "And I'd feel stupid coming to a surfer beach party when I don't even have a board."

"We should get a board, Ike," said Terri. "I've been thinking about that. We could get a DIM board and share it. We'll each get our own wet suit, of course. I have a lot of money saved up from this job, and you have a big hoard of birthday and Christmas money, don't you? It's totally lame for us to be living in Cruz and not know how to surf."

"Dad won't like it," said Ike. "He hates surfers."

"Not every single thing has to go Dad's way, does it?" asked Terri.

"I *would* love to surf," allowed Ike. "But don't you think maybe we're too old to learn?"

"Seventeen and fifteen isn't old, Ike, believe me. Old is the people who eat in this restaurant all day. Hey, here's your order. Stick around outside and wait for me. I'll tell Teresa I have cramps from my period and she'll let me off early and we can go to the surf shop."

"You're gross," said Ike and went out on the wharf to feast. Terri came out when he was almost through eating and ate the rest of his french fries and onion rings, plus the hard-to-get meat in the body of his crab. Hungry seagulls skirled overhead and sea lions barked down among the pilings.

They fed the crab shells to the sea lions and walked down to the land end of the wharf to wait for a moldie bus. Before long the big loping thing came pattering by, coming down the grass-and-sand street. Terri waved, and the bus stopped. The bus was a fused grex made of twelve moldies. Her name was Muxxi.

"Howdy thar, Terri and Ike," said Muxxi in the corny Wild West accent she affected, perhaps to please tourists or perhaps to mock. "Whar ye goin' today?"

"We want to go to Dada Kine Surf Shop, Muxxi," said Terri.

"Waal, now, I reckon that means we'll be a-settin' you young-uns off at the corner of Forty-First Street and Opal Cliff Drive," said Muxxi, displaying the fare as numbers in her skin. "Pay up!"

Ike and Terri handed their fares to Muxxi, who rippled her imipolex to move the other riders toward the rear of the bus. Muxxi bulged out two fresh front-row seats for Ike and Terri. The kids lowered their butts down into the seats and the seats grabbed them tight. In bad weather the seats formed protective cowls, but today Terri and Ike were fully exposed to the pleasant sun and offshore breeze.

The bus's giant sluglike body rippled along through the main beach area. There on the right was the Boardwalk with its classic mechanical roller coaster and on the left was the hill with the family motel, the Terrace Court. Terri's motel—someday. Terri had gone to her mother to complain about the will, and Alice had promised Terri that she would pass the motel directly on to her, which made Terri feel a lot better. Alice had even asked Terri what she thought about maybe adding *Clearlight* to their motel's name.

The bus waded across the shallow San Lorenzo River and humped up a slope to a grassy road that capped the cliffs. Muxxi let off two passengers at the yacht harbor, where the cliffs dropped away. She got another few passengers as she raced along the edges of Twin Lakes and Live Oaks

beaches. As each group of passengers got on, Ike and Terri's seats moved
further towards the rear.

The cliffs rose up again and the bus surged onto them, the thick
corrugations on her underside swaying at a rapid steady pace. Now they
were at Pleasure Point with its schools of surfers.

"Here's whar ye git off, Terri and Ike," twanged Muxxi. Their seats turned
to the side and became chutes that slid them slowly down to the ground.
Muxxi pattered off, and the kids stood watching the surfers for a while.

"Do you really think we can learn to do it, Terri?" asked Ike.

"Sure. It's easier with a DIM board. They have ripples on their bottom
like Muxxi; they can swim. It makes it a lot less work to catch waves."

"What if they swim off without you and go rogue?"

"They don't," said Terri. "They're not smart and independent like moldies.
They're DIMs. A DIM board is smart enough to swim and to let you steer it,
and that's all it wants to do. Dom thinks women should be like DIMs."

"Stop going off about Dom," said Ike. "I'm ready to buy a board."

They walked a block up Forty-First Street to the Dada Kine Surf Shop.
Inside the store it was dark and cool. New and used DIM boards lined two
walls and hung from the ceiling. Racks of wet suits filled out the rest of
the store. A Hawaiian *kahuna* was sitting behind the counter. Slouched
next to him was a red-and-yellow moldie, a liveboard. A liveboard was
vastly more skilled and functional than a DIM board, but, of course, full
moldies were very expensive. Instead of just buying them, you had to put
them on a salary.

"Yaar, Terri," said the big Hawaiian. "Your bud Kurtis Goole was in
here earlier today. I think he went up to Four Mile Beach."

"I'm not looking for him, Kimo," said Terri. "I'm here to shop. This is
my brother Ike. We want to get wet suits and a DIM board."

"Two boards," said Ike all of a sudden. "I don't want to have to share
with you, Terri."

"Tell me how much money you want to spend," said Kimo. "And we'll
see what we can do."

"And I'll give you little bangtails a cost-free and unforgettably wise
lesson," volunteered the moldie liveboard beside him. "A gorgeous incen-
tive for them, right, Kimo? Business being so slow that I haven't been paid
in it seems like seven weeks, you understand."

"*Mahalo* very much, Everooze," said Kimo. "It'll be bitchin' if you give
them a lesson. How much bucks you got, kids?"

An hour later Ike and Terri had each gotten a used wet suit and a rebuilt
DIM board—at a very reasonable price. Ike's board was red with black
checkers, Terri's was patterned with blue-and-green flames. The liveboard

everooze bounced down to the beach with them, jabbering away, and they swam out to a small uncrowded break.

"I'll hang this fabulation on three ripe words like an uvvy preacher," said Everooze. "*Visualize, realize,* and *actualize.* How do you talk to your DIM board? It's a telepathic union, thanks to a little piece of uvvy in the nape of the wet suit neck, cuddled right up near your bright young Percesepe brain. To make your board swim, you *visualize* the motion you want, and then you *realize* that thought—push it out of your head so's the DIM can channel it. And then, step three, the DIM makes it *actual,* all by itself. Splutter mutter, peanut butter! *Visualize, realize,* and *actualize*—these are the keys to correct surf motion in the water and—*hmmm*—indeed in all other walks or flights of life. The magic of the *-alize* ending. Yes. The DIM in the DIM board is a clueless little tad of flickercladding, a lonely finger's worth of a moldie, but if you can *visualize* and *realize,* it can *actualize.* It works fairly well, at least on *these* puny waves. Puny waves but nicely tubular, I should add. Let's surf 'em ."

The *realizing* step was a little hard to get, but after a while Terri and Ike had it down. The trick was to think that you were *already* moving the way you wanted—to make it real at least for yourself—and the DIM would pick up on that. Ike said it felt like his whole body was talking to the DIM, and Terri said it was more like focusing your attention ahead of where you already were. Everooze said that either way was perfectly floatin', although it was best of all to wave to the fact that they were, in fact, helping the DIM boards to surf.

They guided their boards out through the breakers, and Everooze started showing them how to catch a wave. "It's a cosmic rhythm, you viz?" said Everooze, repeatedly catching waves, then ducking underwater to swim back to Terri and Ike like a big oblong sea skate turned skateboard. "It's not enough to see a wave coming; you want to smell it and hear it and feel it in the air and in the water. Undoubtedly there's a little current between your toes right now, for instance, which is the suck of the draw of the next wave crest to come. Get fully lifted on synesthesia because the ocean is indeed realizing its ability to *actualize* the way *you* are going to move. Not only are you helping the DIM board; you're helping the ocean as well. Think of yourself as the ocean's DIM."

Terri and Ike started catching waves then and riding them, at first on all fours and then, miraculously, standing on two feet. "Ah yes," exulted Everooze. "The human race rises from the primordial sea, a boy and a girl step forth from the zillion whats of past time to be here—whoops!— keep your center between your knees, Terri, think of your whole mass as a magic invisible weight dangling down there—that's it, my lassie—*yee-*

haw!—and another one, Ike—*boom*—over the falls for sure, a Niagara wet whirl under there in Neptune's washing machine, no harm in that, no loss in failure, the surf god is *actualizing* tubes, kids, so get back out there—*whoo-ee!*"

When they got back home from that long, magical afternoon, Terri and Ike were committed surfers.

Dom never approved, but in the end it didn't matter. Terri and Ike finished out high school and kept on surfing and working various small-time jobs, and then Dom died.

It happened over Thanksgiving weekend, 2048. There was a big family dinner at their Uncle Carmine's. Alice had a couple of drinks and started a big argument with Dom. Apparently she wasn't happy with their sex life. Dom stormed out into the night and disappeared.

Back home around midnight, after Terri and Ike had finally gotten their mother to bed, there was an uvvy call from a Wackerhut popo—a private cop. Terri answered.

"Is this the Percesepe residence?"

"Yes, who's calling?"

"I'm an investigator for Wackerhut Security. There's a problem here with a Dom Percesepe. Are you his next of kin?"

"I'm his daughter."

"You better get over here: 2020 Bay Street, right near the Saturn Cafe."

"Is he okay?"

"You'd better come over."

As Ike and Terri stepped out of the house, several small dragonfly telerobots buzzed around them. They were *newsies*, remotely controlled mobile camera eyes. Something serious had happened to Dom. Before they could get on their hydrogen cycles, a car pulled up and a man got out. He wore a customized uniform and a gun; he was another popo. A newsie dragonfly hung whirring in place above his head.

"I'm from Boozin Security," he said. "I'll give you a ride."

"Wasn't it a Wackerhut popo who called me before?" said Terri.

"The uvvy newsies are calling all the local popos. There's enough blood for everyone."

"What's happened to my father?" shouted Ike.

"You better come see."

The limo took them to a small yellow Santa Cruz cottage surrounded by knots of popos and newsies. Scores of dragonflies buzzed in the air. There were spotlights and the popo cars were flashing red and blue. A woman stepped forward to interview Terri and Ike, but a burly Wackerhut popo hustled them inside the cottage.

The place smelled more strongly of moldies than anyplace Terri had ever been. There was a slit-open moldie body with a full harvest of camote nodules on the floor. On the bed was a naked dead person. Dom.

There was blood all over his face; his nose was torn wide open. His genitals were bloody as well. He had a blowtorch clenched in his dead hand. His body was welted with circular marks, as if from squid tentacle suckers. The fast little dragonfly cameras darted this way and that, agitated as blowflies around fresh carrion.

It soon came out that Heritagist Dom was a longtime cheeseball. What exactly had gone wrong in the cottage on that last night remained unclear. Had Dom been threatening the flammable moldie with the blowtorch? Or trying to defend himself? It was hard to be sure. The cottage belonged to a woman named Myrdle Deedersen, who said she hadn't realized what was going on. She'd been renting the cottage to a biker from Florida who wasn't around very often. He always paid her in cash and she didn't know his name. She thought he'd left town.

Nobody really believed her, but it was such a distasteful case that nobody in the Percesepe family was willing to pay for an official Gimmie investigation. Suffice it to say that Dom had gotten himself killed either by a moldie or by some local sporehead ring involved in kidnapping moldies and butchering them to sell off their imipolex and their camote on the black market. Dom should have known better than to be a cheeseball. Case closed.

Sure enough, Dom's will left the restaurant to Ike. The twenty-year-old Ike struggled half a year with Dom's Grotto, suffering much advice from his mother and his uncles, but the restaurant business wasn't for him. When Kimo put Dada Kine up for sale in 2049, Ike sold Dom's Grotto to his Uncle Carmine and bought the surf shop and all its assets, including the aging Everooze.

The first thing Ike did was to use some of his excess profit from the deal to get Everooze a complete retrofit and take him surfing in Hawaii, along with Kimo and Kimo's new moldie liveboard ZyxyZ. They surfed the epic waves of the Pipeline, waves so big that before liveboards the only way a person could catch one of them was to be towed in by Jet Ski. It was a deeply memorable trip.

Now, four years later, Ike was a pro surfer and a seasoned businessman. Alice was still alive, and Terri and Tre were scraping by on Tre's gigs and on the money from managing Alice's motel. Rather than feeling guilt about his fat inheritance, Ike blamed Terri's poverty on Tre. Ike didn't like Tre.

Ike was waiting on the cliff beside Everooze when sharky Ouish and

Xanana came bouncing up to the Steamers Lane overlook, with Terri and Xlotl rickshawing along behind. Everooze was distorted into the shape of an airy igloo, his new method of actualizing the maximum amount of solar radiation.

"Yaar, Terri," said Ike. "What's happening?"

"Monique took off with one of our guests," said Terri as Xlotl set her down on the ground. "We think he's gotten control over her somehow."

"You saw her leave?" asked Ike.

"Tre did. He tried to stop her, but then he had a bike accident and broke his collarbone."

"That stupid stoner hairfarmer."

"He's not a hairfarmer, Ike; he's a scientist and an artist. He's a chaotician."

"Yeah, but you're not denying he's a stoner, are you? These poor valleys come out to live at the beach and they think it's nothing but party time."

"Now he's *valley* too?"

"He comes from Iowa! Can't get more valley than that. You never should've married him, Terri."

'Thank you for your wonderful support, you selfish prick. Now go away."

"Let's cut the jawing and make tracks," snapped Xlotl.

"Tell us, Pop," said Xanana to the red-and-yellow-striped dome that was Everooze. "Which way did she go? Which way did she go? Which way did she go?" He put the phrase through maybe two hundred repetitions in two seconds.

"I'll ask Zilly if he can lead us," said Everooze, making a popping noise and flipping his shape into that of a giant potato chip. "He's been surfing here all day, and he says he saw Monique go in. But, Ike, what with the negative vibrations and so on and howsomever, it will indeed be wavier if you don't come. Get the bus back to the shop, chill, and I'll see you there later, your humble worker till wigdom come or I retire, whichever comes first."

"Fine," said Ike, stomping off. "To hell with all of you."

Xanana lay down flat and split his backside, opening up like a seed pod.

"Undress and snuggle on in, Terri. You'll be able to see out through my face. It's transparent there. Let's practice while Everooze talks to Zilly."

"I haven't done this before," said Terri, recalling her dead father's hypocritical tirades against intimacy with moldies. "Are you sure I'll be able to breathe?"

"Of course," said Xanana. "I have enough algae and other stuff in my tissues to make air twice as fast as a person can breathe. Or just as fast as any two people can breathe. Or half as fast as four people can breathe. Or—"

"Yeah, but your . . . your air is going to stink."

"Just wear nose filters. I usually keep some—" Xanana's flesh rolled about for a minute, and then a small slit opened up in his skin to disgorge two small metal sponges. "Palladium filters. Never heard of them? I'm beginning to think you're moldiephobic, Terri. You sure you're not a Heritagist? I know a lot of the Percesepes are."

"Well, I'm *not*," said Terri bravely. "I admit my uncles are xoxxy. They're all Heritagists, yes. Sons of Adam. My father was too—at least we thought he was. But it turned out he was a cheeseball. Maybe he was really on the moldies' side by the end. Maybe it wasn't a moldie that killed him, maybe it was a Heritagist. You don't know anything about it, do you, Xanana? It happened five years ago."

"That's before my time," said Xanana. "I'm sorry. Sorry. Sorry. Sorry."

Terri folded her clothes and set them under a rock, then got inside Xanana and pressed her face up against the inside of the transparent silvery membrane that the moldie used as a face. Air rushed to her steadily through two grooves in the membrane. Once she got the filters well settled into her nose, the smell was not too major. But how could she talk to Xanana?

"I'll uvvy you." Xanana's voice sounded in Terri's head. "And I can channel my vision to you too—if we go deep and it's too dark for your eyes. Are you ready?"

"Let's dive in," uvvied Terri back.

Xanana humped along the cliff's edge like an elephant seal, found a spot overlooking a deep pool, and dove in. Terri watched in wonder as the water flew up toward them. And then they were undersea. Xanana could pick up Terri's mentally *realized* wishes far more easily than a DIM board, and for now he chose to let her steer him.

They went out a few hundred yards, away from the surfers, swam to the bottom, and began slowly looking around. It was like the ultimate tide pool. Terri saw starfish of every color, green sea cucumbers, frilly yellow nudibranch slugs, and a red gumboot chiton. A cascade of tiny pink strawberry anemones covered a rock, looking like a carpet of purple verbena flowers on a Santa Cruz cliff.

"Can I touch things?" uvvied Terri.

"Yes. Just push out your arms."

Terri did, and Xanana's flesh flowed and stretched, forming sleeves and gloves to warmly cover Terri's skin. She prodded a long-stalked plumose anemone, causing it to draw its feathery pale tendrils back into its body.

"You're cozy to be in, Xanana," uvvied Terri.

"*Yeah,* I am. Would you like me to fuck you?"

"What?"

"The others won't be here for a few minutes. I can grow a penis shape and push it into you. A lot of the women passengers like it. To relieve tension."

"No thank you! What if you planted a meatbop in me?"

"Nobody has the wetware tech for that anymore. Anyway, you're not fertile right now. I know the smell."

"Well, I'm sorry, Xanana, but I'm just not interested."

"It's all the same to me. We'll hang here and wait for the others."

As she and Xanana lay there drifting on the seabed, sudden shapes rushed at them and spun them around—Terri drew her arms back inside Xanana's bulk, lest she smash a wrist against a rock. It was Everooze, followed by Ouish and Xlotl. Xanana gave Terri a sound feed of the moldies' conversation.

"So Zilly says Monique swam off toward Monterey," Everooze was explaining. "With the skungy cheeseball inside her. Big day for that dook, no doubt." Terri cringed silently at the thought of doing it with Xanana. No doubt he would have broadcast it to his friends. No way she would ever be a cheeseball.

"Zilly should of come with us," complained Xlotl. "Instead of wasting our time chewing the fat."

"He'd rather surf," uvvied Everooze. "Get over it. He downloaded his info to us, so what's the diff? Zilly declines to interrupt his deep daily study of the breaking wave; he's liftin' and floatin'! Parenthetically, Terri and Xanana, did you know Zilly says the optimal liveboard attends to the *negative* space of the wave? To the tube and not to the water? In any event, let's now swim toward Monterey while keeping our senses stretched for visions of Monique. Poor Monique, my darling daughter. Bested by a stinking fleshapoid. Phew."

The four moldies headed offshore together—Everooze in front, followed by Xanana and Ouish, followed by awkward lumpy Xlotl.

"Don't lose me," clamored Xlotl. "I ain't the world's fastest swimmer."

"You should spend more time in the water," said Ouish in her low thrilling voice. "Undersea is the best. There's hardly any fleshers here. No offense, Terri."

The bottom was about forty feet down and falling rapidly. They swam near the bottom, avoiding the giant kelp beds, thickets of rubbery tendrils that grew from the ocean floor clear to the surface. Some harbor seals swam by overhead; Xanana rolled over and began swimming on his back so that Terri could stare up at them. The seals seemed intent on giving the moldies a wide berth.

"Do you ever interact with whales and dolphins?" Terri asked Xanana. "It almost seems like moldies should be able to talk with them."

"Almost," answered Xanana. "But so far it hasn't happened. We've decoded some of their songs, and all we've heard whales talk about is sex and food and territory. Almost like birds. Though, yeah, whales also talk about the stars. We're not sure how they can even see them, but they talk about the stars all the time. The stars. The starry stars. The starry starry stars—" Xanana did one of his speeded-up infinite regresses with that word and then continued. "Moldies are a lot more like people than they are like whales. It's no wonder, given that we evolved from human-designed robots. From the boppers that you annihilated with chipmold."

"Don't blame me," said Terri. "Not while you're carrying me like a baby in the womb. Not after you asked if you could fuck me. Ugh. Like—I would do *that*!"

"I notice you're still talking about it," sniggered Xanana. "And as far as blame goes, there isn't any. If it weren't for chipmold, there wouldn't be moldies. Also Monique always said you treated her well. Hey, there goes the Percesepe deep-sea fishing boat. I bet they've got something to do with this." Xanana was still on his back and they were out quite deep. High above on the wrinkled mirror of the water's surface was a dark oval, a large boat's hull heading back toward the wharf.

Xanana rolled back over and began swimming steadily deeper. The light grew dim. Up ahead of them a great dark chasm lay open in the ocean floor. Terri recognized this as the Monterey Submarine Canyon that she'd seen on proud local maps her whole life. Wider and deeper than the Grand Canyon! Were they actually going down in there?

"I'm pickin' up Monique." Xlotl's voice came from behind them. "She's in dark cold water, swimming down toward a fuckin' whale? Some flesher dook was inside her, but he's gone—that's gotta be Randy Karl. I think she let Randy off at the surface next to the Percesepe fishing boat and now she's sounding for the bottom. The whale-thing is glowing; it's fuckin' *green*."

"Affirmo," uvvied Everooze. "I wave Monique too. But what's real and what's dream? The age-old question. Let's go ahead and dive way deep into this mighty crack. I've lingered too long in the airy lands of the fleshapoids."

"You might as well start using my eyes now," Xanana told Terri. "I'll uvvy the video to you. Photon to photon to photon to photon to—"

"Thanks," said Terri. To her naked eyes, the seafloor looked dark and monochromatic. She let her eyes go out of focus and let the uvvy come in. The new images showed a vast sparkling space filled with delicate shadings of bright colors. The walls of the Monterey Submarine Canyon ahead were an inviting symphony of pink and green. A school of silver anchovies swept by, followed by several huge fish with solemn unwavering eyes. Everooze's red-and-yellow body darted down over the lip of the submarine cliff. His body was a flat, elongated ellipse that wriggled as he moved. Xanana dove after him, and a sharp watery pain crackled in Terri's head.

"My ears!"

"Pinch your nose and blow," Xanana advised her. "Like you're trying to burst your ears. It'll equalize the pressure. Can you get your hand up to your face? Yeah, that's the way. That's the 'That's the way' way. That's the 'That's the "That's the way" way' way." Terri snaked her arm up flat along her chest, pinched her nose, and blew. Her ear pressure equalized itself with a swampy pop.

The Monterey Submarine Canyon had any number of smaller subcanyons branching off it. If Randy Karl Tucker had sent Monique to hide down here, it might take a long time to find her. Terri tried to relax and enjoy Xanana's uvvy images of the colored cliffs and darting sea life. Everooze and Ouish swam gracefully ahead of them, and Xlotl lagged a bit behind.

"Everooze," uvvied Ouish suddenly, "I think Monique is down in the next ravine."

"I smell her! I smell Monique!" cried Xlotl, rushing forward past Xanana, Ouish, and Everooze. "Follow me."

The moldies' sharklike bodies arched down over yet another subterranean cliff into a final deep sea crevice.

Terri's breathing grew fast and ragged. It was so dark that she could see next to nothing through her faceplate. How deep were they now? She was crazy to be trusting a moldie this much. All Xanana would have to do would be to push her out of his body and she'd be over a hundred feet deep in the cold, dark, airless sea. She'd drown before she could ever swim to the top.

"Xanana," she said, "take me back. I'm getting scared. Take me up the fishing boat so I can confront Randy Karl Tucker." She *visualized* and *realized* Xanana turning back. This would have worked on her DIM board, but on Xanana it had no effect and he failed to *actualize* her wish.

"We're not going back yet," said Xanana. "Stop worrying and look around. It's beautiful down here. Look at my uvvy. All the patterns on top of patterns on top of patterns on top of—"

Terri focused her wandering attention on Xanana's video feed. The uvvy images showed flat Everooze and sharky Ouish down below them, led by the vigorous lumpy Xlotl, all of them pumping their bodies to dive deeper. The cliff's false colors were purple and vermilion now, with sprawling splashes of orange. There were some large drifting blobs—giant jellyfish—and school after school of rockfish, wheeling about like flocks of birds. Long, wavering kelp stipes festooned the cliffs. Prancing spot prawns, cautious Dungeness crabs, and skulking octopi moved slowly across the cliff rocks, with wolf eels and monkeyhead eels hanging from the crevices. A glistening drift of squid jetted past.

"I see it!" exclaimed Xanana. "Down at the bottom there!"

Down below them was a green light, a light that coiled about, thickening and thinning its shape. As Xanana's great tail beat them closer, his uvvy showed Terri that the light source was a huge wriggling form.

Terri popped her ears again, wincing at the moist crackle. She was feeling a chill, despite the wrapping of Xanana. Suddenly she remembered a tall tale her Uncle Carmine had told her when she was little—that ice in the ocean is heavier than water, and that the whole bottom of the Monterey Bay is covered with chunks of ice. The deep light they were swimming toward was like a glistening iceberg, gleaming so brightly that Terri could even see its glitter through the faceplate with her naked eyes. Light down here in this deep trench?

"I'm scared, Xanana," she repeated.

"Hold on," answered the moldie. "We have to see what's down there."

"It's a big group moldie," reported Xlotl from farther down. "Monique's merged into them. And—uh-oh—they channel me." He raised his voice in anger. "I'm Monique's husband and I want her back!"

"Look out!" blared Everooze. "It's spitting out superleeches. Fast purple-colored little things. Don't let them touch you!"

Everooze bucked away from the green grex and shot up past Xanana and Terri, with a dozen fuzzy purple imipolex creatures chasing after him. Before Xanana could react, one of the little superleeches, no bigger than a baby's hand, had flicked over and attached itself to Xanana's side. Suddenly Xanana's steady swimming became chaotic and uncertain.

Terri focused on the uvvy images Xanana was feeding her. There was still the same canyon around them, except now there was a glowing red line leading from them down into the deeps and Xanana was swimming straight along the line. Ouish and Xlotl were still down there, and at the other end of the virtual red line was the thing like a giant green moldie, nearly the size of a whale and—whoosh—it darted forward and snatched at Ouish while the fast purple superleeches flocked this way and that—

"Get out of here!" screamed Terri. "It's going to eat us!"

"Help!" came Ouish's voice. "The superleeches are—" Her voice broke, changed, and resumed, an octave sweeter, sounding like a possessed woman in a horror viddy. "I'm joining the happy throng!"

Xlotl swooped aggressively at the green monster, evading the super-leeches, but he was no match for the huge green group moldie. It lunged forward and caught Xlotl with a fast, sudden tentacle, and now Xlotl was screaming too.

"It's got me! Swim like hell, Everooze! Get outta here, Xana—" Then his voice stopped.

Xanana swam calmly forward.

"Go!" screeched Terri, visualizing and realizing a great kick of Xanana's tail as hard as she could, but to no avail—until suddenly Everooze came swooping back down after them and scraped the superleech loose from Xanana's side with a seashell. "Jam, Xanana, jam!" screeched Terri, and Xanana went shooting upward in Everooze's wake.

"Breathe out, Terri!" cried Xanana. "Breathe out or your lungs will burst! Breathe out breathe out! Breathe out breathe out breathe out—"

Just as they neared the lip of the precipice at the start of the monster's canyon, there was a sudden dull thud. All around them, the water streamed upward. Everooze and Xanana went tumbling, and the big heavy lit-up grex came pushing after them. Everooze was off to one side, and the group moldie went right past him, but Xanana and Terri were directly in its path. With a quick gulping grab, the green shape engulfed them, snatching them out of the water as it went hurtling by. There was a concussive blast of sound and then they were shooting up into the sky like a rocket.

Xanana was in a dream state; he sent no words, and the vision that he uvvied to Terri showed an endless regress of Earth and a rocket with Xanana in the rocket and a cartoon thought balloon coming out of Xanana showing Earth and a rocket with Xanana in the rocket and a cartoon thought balloon coming out of Xanana showing—

Xanana had been plastered into the side of the group moldie rocket in such a way that Terri could see outward through Xanana's transparent faceplate. And, even more fortunately, Xanana was still providing air and acting as an insulator. Terri was, for the moment at least, in a comfortable safe nook on the side of a living rocket ship headed—*where*?

Looking down, Terri could already see the Monterey Bay as a single nick in a coastline that stretched up into the thumb that was the San Francisco peninsula, with the San Francisco Bay on the other side. Still the rocket rose and roared.

The sun was setting over the Pacific Ocean, making a shining orange patch in faraway clouds. At this distance, the ocean looked static and metallic. Still they rose, pushing out to the far edge of the atmosphere. The sky overhead was turning dark purple. From this height Terri could see the Earth's curvature, dear big fat Earth wrapped in the atmosphere's thin rind.

"Soon I'll die," thought Terri and began to cry. Xanana's thoughts were a starry mess of bright patterns, iterated fractals formed by overlaying infinite regresses of solarized images, no comfort at all.

In the distance was one last shape at their level. Terri took it for a stratospheric ice-crystal cloud, but then she realized that the object was flying toward them. It was shaped like a giant blue stingray and seemed to be another group moldie.

Terri's tears dried as she stared in fascination at the computationally rich rippling of the great flying stingray's flesh. It swooped upward at hypersonic speed to match the speed of the rocket grex and produced two giant catfish whiskers to touch it. Right away Terri could hear the flying blue stingray talking over the uvvy.

"Greetings, Blaster," the great moldie creature uvvied in a rich female voice. "What is your cargo?"

"Twenty mudder moldies aboard, Flapper gal," answered the rocket grex in deep resonant tones. "And one flesher."

"A flesher?!" sang Flapper, her voice rising through three registers and falling back down to purr on the *r*.

"It seems our hardworking Heritagist friend Randy Karl Tucker abducted some woman's pet moldie, a moldie named Monique. This woman, her name is Terri *Percesepe* no less, she came after Monique inside of Monique's brother Xanana. We caught them during blastoff."

"You caught a woman?" trilled Flapper. "Where is she? I want to *see* her." She shrieked the *see* to a lovely throbbing peak. Flapper's voice was like the rich beautiful instrument of a grand opera diva.

"Move your eye over here, Flapper babe."

An eye at the end of a stalk as thick as a leg came bulging out of the flying stingray and stopped right in front of Terri's faceplate.

"Oh, there she is!" exclaimed Flapper. "How remarkable. Can she hear us?"

"Can you hear us, Terri?" boomed Blaster.

Terri, frightened to death, remained silent.

"Do you want me to pick her out of you?" warbled the stingray, growing a tendril with a huge claw. For these monsters, Terri was a parasite on a par with a tick. "Shall I get rid of her?"

"Of course not," uvvied Blaster. "She'll be worth something. This has been a most lucrative trip. Did I mention that at the last minute I also landed Monique's husband Xlotl and Xanana's wife Ouish? Four moldies from the same nest! What a catch!"

"You do well for the great Nest, Blaster. High flight!" Flapper let go and swooped away.

Now Blaster pulled fully above the atmosphere and the sky got black. There were stars everywhere. Blaster's ion jets roared and roared, then finally fell silent. They were on course for the Moon.

Terri tested her uvvy contact with Xanana's mind again. He dreamed himself adrift in a galaxy of spiral lights that were spiral galaxies made up of spiral lights.

"Terri," uvvied Blaster's deep voice suddenly. "I know you can hear me. Answer me."

"You already know all about me," said Terri bitterly. "What else is there to say?"

"I'm glad you tried to save your Monique," chuckled Blaster. "I didn't think I could catch so many moldies so fast."

"What are you?" asked Terri.

"I'm a group moldie from the Moon. I come to Earth to recruit new loonies. Moldies are better off on the Moon, instead of being your mudder slaves."

"How can you work with Heritagists?"

"In some ways the loonies and the Heritagists want the same thing: we want more moldies to move to the Moon. The mad rush for the sodden pleasures of Earth has depleted our pure Nest. Many of us feel that it is only through a strong Nest that the moldie race can best pursue its destiny."

"Somehow I don't think these moldies you kidnapped are going to be very happy."

"They just need education," said Blaster. "And it starts now. I'm turning off their superleeches. I'll give you an uvvy feed of your Monique so you can see how she and the others react." And then Terri could sense the thoughts of Monique.

Monique was awake, her old self, only not quite, for she was wedged in with a mass of other moldies, with other crankily waking abducted moldies like herself. Terri watched Monique push an eyestalk out of the ship's bulk to see where she was, and then Terri shared Monique's pang at the sight of the heartbreakingly lovely orb of receding Mother Earth.

"Greetings," announced Blaster's voice. "My name is Blaster. You mudder moldies are getting a fresh start. You're coming to the Moon to join your forefathers. And stop that grumbling. The loonie moldies need you, your minds as well as your bodies. You come to join us as equals."

"Xlotl!" called Monique into the group uvvy mind that was made up of Blaster's members and the newly shanghaied moldies. "Is Xlotl here?"

"Yeah, babe!" came the happy answer. "I swam after you and Randy Karl Tucker. I figure you carried him a mile offshore. He must have got in the Percesepe fishing boat and told you to dive straight down to a giant group moldie lurking on the bottom like a whale. Blaster. Blaster lashed out and got me too, got me and Xanana and Ouish. Monique, once Blaster had you, I . . . I wanted them to take me too. Blaster's a rocket. We're going to the Moon, Monique. Where there's no fuckin' air or water."

"You'll like it anyway," uvvied Blaster's big voice. "We've got a huge underground Nest with no fleshers. It's the same place where the boppers used to live. We need you moldies—and not just to be maids and cooks."

Blaster allowed Monique to squirm through the massed moldies and to press against Xlotl's side.

"Whaddya think, Monique?" uvvied Xlotl.

"It might work, Xlotl. A new start. I'm willing to try."

The rocket pushed forward, leaving Earth behind. The reunited lovers were content. But Terri was frantic.

"I want to go back to Earth," Terri told Blaster. "To my husband and children. To my life."

"Not until I find a way to make some profit off of you," said Blaster.

"Send me back!" insisted Terri. "Spit me and Xanana out right now, and Xanana could fly me home. Couldn't you, Xanana?"

"I could," said Xanana. "But I have to admit I'm curious about what it's going to be like on the Moon. I'd never have had the nerve to go there on my own."

"I might zombie box her and sell her as a pink-tank worker," said Blaster.

"Don't do that," said Xanana. "She deserves better. Why don't you try and get a ransom for her?"

"Maybe from the Percesepe family," said Blaster. "Yeah, I've been thinking about that. But they're like allies of mine through the Heritagist connection, and it would look bad to be holding them up for ransom. Is there anyone else who might pay, Terri? Do you have any important friends?"

"Stahn Mooney!" exclaimed Terri. "Ask him. My husband Tre works for one of Stahn's companies. You moldies have a lot of respect for Stahn, right?"

"We don't respect *any* fleshers," said Blaster. "Can't you understand that? In any case, I'd want to hand you over to someone on the Moon. Do you know anyone on the Moon, Terri?"

Terri racked her brain. Starshine had mentioned some friends of

Mooney's—a man named Whitey Mydol who lived with a woman named Darla.

"Uh . . . have you ever heard of Whitey Mydol? And Darla?"

"*Yeah,* I have," said Blaster. "Maybe I'll get in touch with them. So long for now."

"Wait," cried Terri. "How long is this flight going to take? What am I going to eat and drink?"

"You fleshers," growled Blaster. "Always asking for more. The trip takes a week. Can't you wait for food and water till we get there?"

"No."

"Let Xanana worry about it. He's the one who brought you."

Terri focused on Xanana's uvvy feed. He was happier and happier about going to the Moon.

"Xanana, can you make food and water for me?"

"Well, I can drip out some moldie juice for you. It's sort of like sap, except you won't like the way it smells. It's nourishing. How are your nose filters holding up?"

Terri hadn't thought about them for a while. She felt her nose, stiff with the palladium sponges inside its nostrils. "The filters are fine. I guess I'd like to try some moldie juice. My mouth is awfully dry."

"I'll push out a nipple by your mouth. Just suck on it."

Terri put her lips around the slick imipolex nipple and cautiously sucked. Her mouth filled with a lukewarm salty flow of slippery fluid. Thanks to the nose filters, she couldn't really smell it, and she was able to swallow it down without gagging.

"Thank you, Xanana. I'll repay you somehow."

"No need. I'm happy you got me into this."

Terri drifted off into a dreamless nap. At some point she began having a vision of Tre. It took her a minute or two to realize that this was an uvvy call and that she was again awake.

Tre was standing on the patch of lawn in front of the motel office. It was night and he was staring up at the sky. "Terri! Finally! Are you okay?"

"I'm alive, but it's a pretty iffy situation. I'm inside a moldie grex that's flying to the Moon. What a freak show. Are the children all right?"

"They're scared. It was hard to get them to sleep. We saw that moldie rocket blasting off; we were looking at the ocean just then. Then Everooze came over and told us the bad news. Can you breathe? Is there water?"

"So far Xanana's taking care of me. But it's going to take seven days."

"Oh, Terri. I can't stand to think of you alone up there in outer space. Will the moldies let you go when they get to the Moon?"

"They want to sell me for ransom. You're supposed to get Stahn Mooney to call Whitey Mydol and Darla on the Moon. If Mooney will pay."

"He'll pay all right—if I have to kill him. He owes me big-time. Remember how he gave my 4D Poultry source code to Emperor Staghorn Beetle Larvae, Ltd.? This afternoon I found out that Emperor Staghorn used my poultry to invent the superleeches. And thanks to the superleeches, my wife is on her way to the Moon. Oh, Terri. I'm sorry I haven't been nicer to you. I love you so much."

"Just get me out of this, Tre, and don't waste energy guilt-tripping yourself. I don't want to end up down in the loonie moldies' Nest."

"I'll talk to Stahn again right away. And then I'm gonna jam some math. This stuff Emperor Staghorn came up with is pretty exciting."

"Take good care of the kids. Maybe they can uvvy me in the morning. The view from here is stunning. I'd like to show it to them."

"We'll call early tomorrow. In about ten hours. Hang in there, darling. I'll call Mooney now and make sure Whitey and Darla ransom you as soon as Blaster hits the Moon. I love you so much, Terri. You're so small and precious, up there in the sky."

"And I love you, Tre."

Tre's image jittered away, and Terri stared back at shiny soft small Gaia with her own eyes.

CHAPTER SIX

WILLY

March 17, 2031 - July 2052

The day after Willy Taze got off death row, he met Stahn Mooney.

Willy and his rebel friends were bopper lovers; they thought artificial life forms were just as good as people. The rebels busted Willy out of the Louisville jail and smuggled him down to Florida, where he could do some good. Willy made the trip hidden in a truckload of meat, garbed in an imipolex bubble-topper spacesuit for warmth and air. The minute he hit Florida, Willy got on a computer and gosperized the Gimmie's air defenses with turd bits and foo series so that the a-life invasion could come down. Around dawn an old woman named Annie Cushing drove Willy to a particular beach on Sanibel Island, Florida, Willy still wearing his bubbletopper, the date March 17, 2031, a day that would be forever known as Spore Day.

There was a sound of ion jets, abruptly terminated, and then Stahn and Wendy came coasting down from the sky on big Happy Cloak wings; they were each wearing about a hundred kilograms of chipmold-infected imipolex. In the firmament high above them, quadrillions of chipmold spores formed a barely visible cirrostratus cloud made wavy by the steady nibbling of the subtropical jet stream. The rising sun glinted off the spore cloud, tracing a great halo that would soon circle the heavens worldwide. Spore Day marked the death of Gaia's boppers and chips, the birth of her moldies and DIMs.

"It's good to be back," said Stahn. "Thank you, Willy. Thanks, Annie." He slung his right wing across Willy's back. The heavy wing pulled loose from Stahn and stayed on Willy, merging its plastic with Willy's bubbletopper and sinking thin probes into his neck.

Willy smiled to feel the boiling rush of information. The Happy Cloak spoke to him and transmitted direct messages from Stahn and Wendy. It was like having them whisper in his ears.

"Let's stride," murmured Stahn. "I don't want a lot of goobs to see me here."

"I'm for it," answered Willy. "The farther underground I go, the better." He turned to Annie. "Thanks for helping."

"God bless you, Willy," said old Annie. "Your grandfather Cobb would be proud of you. Keep it bouncing."

And then the smart moldie 'Cloaks formed themselves into dolphin shapes, and Willy, Stahn, and Wendy took off undersea. The clear Gulf waters were shallow out to about a mile, where the bottom dropped off steeply. Huge surgeonfish and groupers sped away from the moldie-encased humans.

"Where we going?" asked Willy.

"I want to swim around to the other side of Florida and get near Cocoa Beach," said Stahn. "At the right moment, we'll blast up out of the water like old-time submarine-launched missiles."

"*I'll* blast off?"

"No, man, just me and Wendy. We're going to fly up to the spaceship *Selena* that's landing at the spaceport tomorrow. Of course the *Selena's* bopper slave computers are already dead, but this woman Fern Beller is piloting the ship down. Fern is very together. She's wearing a Happy Cloak and doing the astrogation in her head. She'll let me and Wendy aboard so quietly that nobody will know how we *really* came down."

"Why can't I come too?" asked Willy. "If the Gimmie catches up with me—"

"Exactly," said Stahn. "Which is why you don't want to be on the *Selena* when she lands. There'll be customs inspectors, reporters, xoxxin' Gimmie pigs, and quarantine for all aboard. It's no prob for me because I'm a hero; for you it would be back to the death house. Once the pig truly grasps that the chipmold's already infected everything, they'll let me and Wendy out of quarantine. Probably take six weeks, tops. ISDN'll pay off whoever they have to pay. And dig it, man, then me and Wendy move to San Francisco and I run for the U.S. Senate."

"I think Willy should move to the Moon," said Wendy's light voice. "It's nice there. Not so heavy. The gravity's too strong on Earth. I could hardly stand up on the beach just now. Go to the Moon, Willy."

"Affirmo!" said Stahn. "The Moon is where it's kickin'. Fern can take you when she goes back, Willy. Lay low for a month or two, however long it takes, and then sneak aboard when the *Selena* gets cleared for takeoff. You can hook up with Fern when she gets out of quarantine. You lucky dog. Fern, Fern, Fern—the woman is hot."

"You're married now, Stahn," warned Wendy. "And I'm pregnant."

"I'm only saying that she's hot. I won't act out. I promise. Anyway, she doesn't like me."

"While I'm waiting for Fern—" put in Willy. "I should hang around Cocoa?"

"It shouldn't be a problem," said Stahn. "The Gimmie is going to be xoxxed as of today. Spore Day! In a week there won't be a computer working on the whole planet. Not one."

Stahn was right about that; in fact, most computers were dead by the end of the day. He and Wendy took off for the *Selena* the next morning, and that evening Willy and his Happy Cloak swam ashore and landed in a small estuarial swamp.

"I'll stash you here in these mangrove thickets," Willy told his 'Cloak.

"If you do that, I won't wait for you," said the 'Cloak. "I have not traveled all this way to cower in filth. Keep me with you; wear me as a garment. I'll slide down low and emulate a workman's heavy boots and trousers. I can shift my plug-in to the base of your spine."

"If you're going to be a long-term symbiote with me, I ought to have a name for you," said Willy.

"Call me Ulam," said the 'Cloak. "It's an abbreviated form of a dead bopper's name: Ulalume. Most of my imipolex used to be Ulalume's flickercladding—Stahn had a couple of boppers' worth on his back. Ulalume was female, but I think of myself as a male. Be still while I move the plug-in, and then we can go."

So here's shirtless Willy under the star-spangled Florida sky with eighty pounds of moldie for his shoes and pants, scuffing across the cracked concrete of the JFK spaceport pad. The great concrete apron was broken up by a widely spaced grid of drainage ditches, and the spaceport buildings were dark. It occurred to Willy that he was very hungry.

There was a roar and blaze in the sky above. The *Selena* was coming down. Close, too close. The nearest ditch was so far he wouldn't make it in time, Willy thought, but once he started running, Ulam kicked in and superamplified his strides, cushioning on the landing and flexing on the takeoffs. They sprinted a quarter of a mile in under twenty seconds and threw themselves into the coolness of the ditch, lowering down into the funky brackish water. The juddering yellow flame of the great ship's ion beams reflected off the ripples around them. A hot wind of noise blasted loud and louder; then all was still.

Ordinarily a fleet of trucks might have surrounded the *Selena* to unload her, but on this evening, the day after Spore Day, there were no vehicles that functioned. A small group of Gimmie officials walked out to the *Selena* and waited until its hatch was hand-winched open. Watching from his drainage ditch, Willy saw Stahn, Wendy, and the others being led away. He spotted the one who was probably Fern Beller, the tall willowy brunette who was doing all the talking.

"Looks like they left the *Selena* all alone," Willy observed to his Happy Cloak.

"The *Selena* can act by herself if need be," said Ulam. "Fear not."

"I'm really hungry," said Willy. "Let's go into town and find some food." As they walked the rest of the way across the spaceport field, they encountered a crowd of aggrieved Florida locals, many of them senior citizens.

"Y'all come from that ship?" demanded one of them, a lean Cuban. His voice was tight and high.

"No no," said Willy. "I work for the spaceport."

"What the Sam Hill kinda pants do he got on?" demanded a fat black woman.

"These are fireproof overalls," said Willy. "I wear them in case there's an explosion."

"You stick around, *vato*, you'll see somethin' explode, all right," said the Cuban. "We gone wail on that ship, *es verdad*. Their loonie chipmold broke our machines forever."

"You ain't a-hankerin' to try and stop us, is you?" rumbled a new voice from the crowd. " 'Cause effen you is, I'm gone have to take you out."

"Oh no, no indeed," said Willy. "I'm going on break for supper. In fact, I didn't even see you."

"Food's free tonight," whooped a white cracker woman. "Especially if you packin' heat! Let's see who can hit the ship from here!" There was a fusillade of gunshots and needler blasts, and then the mob surged toward the *Selena*, blazing away at the ship as they advanced.

Their bullets pinged off the titaniplast hull like pebbles off galvanized steel; the needlers' laser rays kicked up harmless glow spots of *zzzt*. The *Selena* shifted uneasily on her hydraulic tripod legs.

"Her hold bears a rich cargo of moldie flesh," said Ulam's calm eldritch voice in Willy's head. "Ten metric tons of chip-mold-infected imipolex, surely to be worth a king's ransom once this substance's virtues become known. This cargo is why Fern flew the *Selena* here for ISDN. I tell you, the flesher rabble attacks the *Selena* at their own peril. Although the imipolex is highly flammable, it has a low-grade default intelligence and will not hesitate to punish those who would harm it."

When the first people tried to climb aboard the *Selena*, the ship unexpectedly rose up on her telescoping tripod legs and lumbered away. As the ship slowly lurched along, great gouts of imipolex streamed out of hatches in her bottom. The *Selena* looked like a defecating animal, like a threatened ungainly beast voiding its bowels in flight—like a frightened penguin leaving a splatter trail of krilly shit. Except that the *Selena's* shit was dividing itself up into big slugs that were crawling away toward the mangroves and ditches as fast as they could hump, which was plenty fast.

Of course, someone in the mob quickly figured out that you could burn the imipolex shit slugs, and a lot of the slugs started going up in crazy flames and oily, unbelievably foul-smelling smoke. The smoke had a strange disorienting effect; as soon as Willy caught a whiff of it, his ears started buzzing and the objects around him took on a jellied peyote solidity.

The burning slugs turned on their tormentors, engulfing them like psychedelic kamikaze napalm. There was great screaming from the victims, screams that were weirdly, hideously ecstatic. And then the mob's few survivors had fled, and the rest of the slugs had wormed off into the flickering night. Willy and Ulam split the scene as well.

Beyond the light of the flames and past the pitch-black spaceport, all the roads and buildings were dark. There was, in fact, no glow anywhere on the horizon. The power grid was dead.

Willy picked his way through a field of inert sun collectors and came upon a small shopping center. The most obvious looting target there would have been the Red Ball liquor/drugstore, but someone had walled up its doors and windows with thick sheets of titaniplast. From the whoops and yee-haws within, it sounded like there were some crazed lowlifes sealed up inside there getting wasted. Nobody was trying to get in. Going in there would have been like jumping into a cage of hungry hyenas.

The dark Winn-Dixie supermarket, on the other hand, was wide open, with a hand-lettered sign saying TAKE WHAT YOU NEED. GOD BLESS YOU. THE LITTLE KIDDERS.

There were an inordinate number of extremely old people filling up their Winn-Dixie shopping carts as high as they would go—Florida pheezers trundling off into the night with their booty. Willy went into the Winn-Dixie and found himself a bottle of Gatorade and a premade deli sandwich: a doughy bun with yellow mustard and vat cheese. The sandwich was mashed and wadded; it was the very last item in the deli case. All the good stuff was long gone.

As Willy left the store, he noticed a tiny old woman struggling to push a grocery cart mountainously piled with fruits, vegetables, and cleaning supplies. One of the cart's front wheels had gotten stuck in a pothole in the parking lot.

"Can I help you with that, ma'am?" asked Willy in his politest tone.

"You're not going to try and steal from me, are you?" demanded the silver-haired old woman, staring up at Willy through the thick smudged lenses of her glasses. "I *could* use help, but not if you're a robber."

"How far from here do you live?"

"Forever. Over a mile."

"Look, one reason I want to help you is that I need a place to sleep."

"I'm not letting any strange men in my house."

"Do you have a garage?"

"As a matter of fact, I do. But my dog Arf lives in there."

"I'll share with him. I need a place to sleep for a few days. You'll never get all this stuff home if I don't help you."

"If you're going to help me, then I can get more food. Wait right here and don't let anyone touch my cart."

"I don't think it's very safe to stay around here," protested Willy. A fight between two old couples had broken out nearby. One of the men was threatening the other with his aluminum cane.

"Don't worry about those drunk pheezers," said the old woman. "A strong young man like you. I'll be right back out."

Willy opened his Gatorade and started in on his sandwich. The old woman darted back into Winn-Dixie and emerged fifteen minutes later with another laden cart, this one mostly filled with pots, pans, shampoos, dog biscuits, and ice cream. Pushing at one cart and then the other, Willy headed down the road with her.

"I hope you have a big freezer."

"It's broken, of course. Thanks to the chipmold. Nothing works since last night. No electricity, no telephone, no appliances, no cars, no machines. It's amazing. This is the most exciting time I've had in years. When we get home, we can eat a lot of ice cream. I might even give some to my neighbors. What's your name?"

"Willy."

"I'm Louise. What's that junk on your legs?"

"Flickercladding with chipmold. It—*he*—is from the Moon. He's intelligent. I call him Ulam."

"How disgusting."

Old Louise had a big wrecked couch in her garage that Willy could sleep on. Of course, the couch was already being used by Arf the dog, but Arf didn't mind sharing. He was an orange-and-white collie-beagle mixture with friendly eyes and a long, noble nose. His ever-shedding hair was everywhere, and it made Willy sneeze. The garage had a separate room with a well-equipped little computer hardware workshop that had once been used by Louise's dead husband. Of course, now, after Spore Day, nothing in there was working.

Louise didn't bother Willy much; a lot of the time she seemed to forget he was there. So that people wouldn't keep asking Willy about Ulam, he picked a pair of discarded pheezer pants out of a dumpster, baggy-ass brick-red polyester pants that looked like they came from a three-hundred-pound man. They fit over Ulam. And a lot of the time Willy would go out without Ulam.

He couldn't resist roaming the streets to find out what was going on. With all the vizzy gone for days merging into weeks, people were less and less likely to recognize or even care about the escaped race-traitor Willy Taze.

People were foraging off their preserved foods and off the land. A few antique chipless engines were dug out of museum storage and harnessed to pumping clean well water; people walked to the wells with jugs to get their daily supply. As for sanitation—well, you could use a shovel. Or not. The neighborhoods took on the low-level funky smell of crowded campgrounds. Yet everyone was happy. With all the news media gone, they had their brains back. And the disaster atmosphere had gotten people to cooperate and help their neighbors. It was, in many ways, a fun and mellow time.

Willy wandered around being friendly to people. One popular topic of conversation was a local gang called the Little Kidders. They were the ones who'd secured the Red Ball store for themselves on Spore Day, and if you wanted booze or drugs you could buy it from them. When a couple of Gimmie pigs had tried to reclaim the Red Ball, the Little Kidders blew them away, which all the pheezers agreed was totally stuzzy.

Some anachronistic individuals found some old noncomputerized printing equipment and started making paper newspapers again. It gave you a kind of Ye Olde Quainte Village feeling to read one. But they had good information—travelers' reports about conditions in the rest of the country, along with lots of local notices about things or services that people wanted to swap.

The main local market for trading things was the emptied-out Winn-Dixie. The space had become a free public market, and anyone who wanted to could take things there and barter them with others. The Little Kidders in the Red Ball next door made sure that the Gimmie didn't try to come in to tax or regulate things. Half-jokingly, people began referring to the gutted Winn-Dixie as the Little Kidders Superstore.

Every night Ulam would go out and forage for stray slugs of imipolex from the *Selena*. After Ulam had herded or cajoled a slug back into the garage's workshop, he had a way of paralyzing it. Arf invariably accompanied Ulam on his nightly hunts, enthusiastically wagging his high-held fluffy white tail. Ulam would give Arf a handful of Louise's dog biscuits whenever they found another slug. Soon the hoarded slugs filled half the workshop waist-high—making a soft, vile-smelling heap that Arf loved to lie on top of, sometimes sleeping, sometimes licking his balls.

At least now Willy had the couch to himself. But he was puzzled.

"What're all those slugs good for, Ulam?"

"They're live imipolex. What could be more precious?"

"But they're just a big wad of dirty, smelly, hairy plastic. A dog's bed! They're like what you'd sweep up after a six-city-block street fair. Why aren't the slugs smart like you, Ulam?"

"They lack the software. I could copy myself onto each of them, but I prefer not to, because then my new selves would compete with me for scarce resources. Certainly I may clone myself a child copy or two later on, but it would be my preference to do this in a more romantic manner—to sexually reproduce with another moldie. In any case, this slug flesh is here for a different kind of replication. This is commodity imipolex, shipped from the Nest to Florida to make the humans love and value the moldies! You, Willy Taze, are the man to help us. You and I shall fashion small pieces of the slugs into customized imipolex products to be sold through the Little Kidders Superstore!"

"You're losing me, Ulam."

"We'll use the slug's imipolex to make clever little soft devices that behave like optical processors and silicon computer chips. Miniature slugs—they'll look like the slimy humped gray dots you find under wet cardboard here in Florida. Each one-gram globule will be programmable for one particular purpose. Mayhap to run a washing machine. Or a power-switching station. Or a vizzy. A gram of chipmold-infected imipolex holds great sapience."

"I get it," said Willy. "The little pieces of imipolex will be like customized chips were before the chipmold ate them. Let's call the sluglets *DIMs*. For *D*esigner *IM*ipolex."

"DIMs!" exclaimed Ulam approvingly. "You have a gift for the genial turn of phrase, Willy. One must perforce be *dim* to spend one's life inside an engine or a toaster, repetitiously computing at some wheezing flesher's behest."

"It sure would help if I could use this equipment," said Willy, forlornly looking at the computer devices resting on the shelves of the workshop. Most of them had fuzzy crests of mold growing out of their air vents. "Even if we had electricity, they wouldn't work anymore. How can I program a DIM without any engineering tools?"

"Use me," said Ulam "As long as you can tell me what each DIM is supposed to do, I can program it by temporarily merging it with my flesh and thinking the pattern into it. I lack only a knowledge of how the bemolded human chips were designed—the microcode, the architecture, the black-box in/out of the pin I/O. You're the superhacker, Willy. Instruct me, and let us tinker together."

During the next few feverish Florida months, Willy was to experience a unique burst of creativity. With the assistance of his trusty 'Cloak Ulam, Willy Taze founded the new computer science of limpware engineering, crafted the first DIMs, and topped it all off by inventing the uvvy in September.

But in mid-May, Willy and Ulam were still just getting started. This was when the *Selena's* crew and passengers were released, seven or eight weeks after the start of their quarantine. Willy couldn't afford to press forward amid the few reporters who made it there, but he managed to follow Fern Seller to her temporary squat in one of the abandoned motels of Cocoa.

When he knocked on her door, Fern opened it right away. She was a dark-haired woman with a wide soft mouth and a lazy-sounding voice. Willy introduced himself.

"Hi. I'm Willy Taze. Stahn Mooney said you'd help me get up to the Moon."

"Come on in, Willy. The *Selena* won't be ready to fly again for months. I definitely need entertaining. There's no water here. How would you like to wash me off with your tongue?"

The luscious Fern was serious, sort of, though it was pretty obvious that there was one special area she wanted Willy to lick the most of all. They undressed, took off their Happy Cloaks, and got into bed together, but then—Willy couldn't go through with it, with any of it.

Over the years, Willy had spent uncounted hours having cybersex via porno viddies, blue cephscope tapes, chat rooms, teledildonics, and the like. Yet when it came to getting a real flesh-and-blood girlfriend and consummating the love act with her, some problem had always intervened. Willy had written it off to bad luck and geekishness, but now in Fern's funky bed he fully realized the awful truth.

"I can't, Fern. I just can't stand the idea of really doing it in person."

"Not even a straight missionary fuck, for God's sake?"

"I . . . I can't get that intimate. I mean all the hair and skin and germs and bodily fluids—" Shakily, Willy got out of bed and started putting his clothes back on.

"Are you gay?"

"No! Gay sex would be even worse. All the porno I ever use is het."

"You use het porno, but you won't fuck a woman? All you ever do is watch?"

"Uh, sometimes I go interactive with women across the Net. I have like some special peripherals hooked to my cephscope at home. You always hope they're women, anyway."

"So why not get back in bed and you and me touch each other? Hands are peripheral. And I *am* a woman."

"I can't do it, Fern. You're very attractive, and I would totally go for you across a remote link. But I see now that I can't do it in person."

On the floor Ulam was pressed up against Fern's Happy Cloak. "We want to tryst," said Ulam, speaking out of a flexible membrane on his skin. "Her name is Flouncey."

"Sure," said Willy. "You're lucky, Ulam. Is it okay with you, Fern?"

"Oh, you're too good to do me, but your 'Cloak wants to hump mine?" snapped Fern. "Thanks a lot. If we had dogs, we could watch them fucking too. Would you get off on *that*? You're a gunjy bithead, Willy."

"Don't be angry, Fern," said Ulam. "Willy is a genius, the first and noblest of the limpware engineers. He and I are machinating a scheme to sell DIMs through the Little Kidders Superstore. Did not ISDN send you and the *Selena* down to distribute imipolex? Willy is the man to bring this plan to fruition. And I am the moldie to make Flouncey happy. She and I are already exceedingly fond of each other. Her high intellectuality is a joy after my dealings with the beastlike slugs of the *Selena's* dispersed cargo."

"You've been collecting the slugs?" said Fern, her face brightening. She was sitting up in the bed with the sheet pulled around her. "At least that's some good news. I thought maybe the whole cargo was lost. How much of it have you recovered, Ulam?"

"Twenty slugs. At roughly fifty kilograms each, that makes one ton out of the ten you brought down. Much of the imipolex was destroyed in flames by the ignorant fleshers. And I fear many of the slugs have disappeared into the sea."

"And what are these DIMs you want to make, Willy?" asked Fern.

"DIMs are tiny designer imipolex slugs to replace the world's computers and chips," answered Willy. They'll weigh about a gram each. Ulam's collected enough imipolex to make a million of them. I already have the basic design process worked out. I use an architecture like a parallel pipeline based on fractal Feigenbaum cascades. It's a perfect fit for what chipmold-infected imipolex is good at; I can't believe I thought of it. And Ulam can program them just by touching them, once I tell him what to do. I made up a special new computer language for telling him. I call this first version of the language Limplan-A."

"You've already done all that for us, Willy? Are you sure you don't want to fuck me?"

"Um, if we could do it while we're in different rooms. But the damn Net's broken. Of course . . . we could link up using Ulam and Flouncey."

Now Flouncey spoke up. She had a melodic husky voice like Fern's. "Ulam and I would have to get to know each other better first. Maybe later we can hook you two up. Like much later. Can we go outside now, Fern?"

"For sure. I don't want to give Willy a remote hand job. Yuckola. I think we should just be good friends, Willy. There's plenty of men for me—and plenty of porno for you."

"Fine."

Flouncey and Ulam went outside and lay down next to the algae-green swimming pool. The mold-mottled wads of lunar plastic began touching each other—a little at first and then much more.

"How romantic," said Fern acidly and pulled on her clothes. "Let's talk about the DIM business, Willy. What's going to be the first product?"

"With the electricity still out, there's no point in making DIMs for kitchen appliances."

"Maybe I can get you permission to fix the power plants," mused Fern. "ISDN has a lot of contacts. But meanwhile—what about cars?"

"That would work. I could make DIMs to replace the controller cards in car engines."

After a week, Willy and Ulam had produced twenty special DIMs for running car engines. They patched one onto Louise's old buggy, and Willy, Fern, Ulam, and Flouncey drove to the Little Kidders Superstore.

The sight of a functioning car was a sensation; in half an hour they'd sold all twenty DIMs. Of course the Little Kidders got wind of this, and two of them came out of the Red Ball to talk. They introduced themselves as Aarbie Kidd and Haf-N-Haf.

Haf-N-Haf was an unsettling sight—a fat, sloppy, fortyish man with piebald stubble all over his head and chin. He was missing all the teeth in the right half of his mouth, and that side of his face was slack and caved in. He spoke in a slobbering, nearly incomprehensible lisp.

But Aarbie was young and powerfully built, with a shaved head that had laser-precise tattoos of flames, blue on one side and red on the other. The flames swept back from his eyes. His teeth were white and even; his skin was an attractive pale brown. Haf-N-Haf deferred to him, and Fern seemed interested. "Kin y'all git my motorcycle to workin' agin?" asked Aarbie.

"We can do it," said Ulam from the backseat of Louise's car.

Aarbie peered in at Ulam and Flouncey. "What the hell is this shit? Talkin' slugs?" He wrinkled his nose at the characteristic odor. "*Fooo-eee!*"

"We're moldies," said Ulam. "There will be many more of us here soon."

"Remember that it's thanks to them we can fix your motorcycle," said Fern didactically. Aside from monetary gain, one of the big reasons for selling DIMs was to get people to accept the moldies.

"I bet Fewn can fix evewyfing wif her puffy," lisped Haf-N-Haf, and Aarbie went into high peals of unpleasant hyena laughter, overly prolonged. Willy felt like punching him, but Fern kept control of the situation.

"I've heard a lot about how important the Little Kidders are around here," said the calm Fern. "So we certainly value your friendship. Why don't you let Ulam take a look at your bike, Aarbie, so he can get the specs for the chip? Once it's working, I wouldn't mind at all if you took me for a nice long ride."

"Oh yeah?" grinned Aarbie, pleasantly surprised. "Oh yeah? Who all's Ulam?"

"Behold," said Ulam, flowing out of the car window. "Where is your mechanical steed, oh flesher?"

Aarbie wheeled his bike out from inside the Red Ball, and Ulam pulled the infected processor card out of the engine. The next day Ulam and Willy delivered a droplet-sized DIM to control the motorcycle engine, and Fern spent the night with Aarbie.

The day after that, Fern gave Aarbie DIMs for all the other Little Kidders' bikes, and Aarbie, who, of course, turned out to be the gang leader, agreed that the Little Kidders would sign on as the transportation and security division of the new operation. Just to fuck with the Gimmie's head, ISDN incorporated Fern and Willy's new company out of South Africa and named it Mbanje DeGroot, with Willy the president and Fern the CEO. At old Louise's suggestion, Willy and Ulam moved their operations out of Louise's garage and rented a rarely used pheezer dance hall near a bar and grill called the Gray Area. Fern and Flouncey started working there too.

As the word about the Mbanje DeGroot DIMs spread, the demand for them grew superexponentially. The Little Kidders cruised the streets, handling DIM orders and deliveries and buying up any rogue slugs of imipolex that people had trapped.

In order to ramp up production, Mbanje DeGroot needed electricity for metal machines to slice and dice the imipolex, plus more moldies to program the DIMs.

As promised, Fern used her ISDN connections to get a contract for Willy and Ulam to replace the crucial computerized components of the local electric power generation and distribution centers, which solved the electricity problem for them and for everyone else in their part of Florida.

Ulam and Flouncey joyously mated four times in a row, cloning differently shuffled combinations of themselves onto four of the captured slugs of imipolex. The children were called Winken, Blinken, Tod, and Nod. Maturing in a matter of days, they started worked in the Mbanje DeGroot DIM factory with their parents.

It was still up to Willy to provide a Limplan-A description (well, actually it was Limplan-B by now) for each new kind of DIM that was needed; and this kept him as busy as he could stand to be. Busier, even.

At this point people started realizing who Willy was, and there was some threat of him getting busted. In fact, four Gimmie officials showed up from Washington, driving a rare gasoline-powered armored HumVee, a vehicle so ancient that it had no susceptible chips for the chipmold to have ruined. An ugly mob of pheezers gathered around the HumVee outside the Gray Area, rocking it back and forth, almost on the point of turning it over.

Aarbie and a few sniggering Little Kidders parted the crowd and led the officials into the Mbanje DeGroot shop. The head official nervously read a Gimmie ultimatum stating that unless Mbanje DeGroot's entire DIM production were routed to Washington, D.C., for Gimmie defense and security purposes, Willy Taze would have to go back to jail.

"Can I thoot them now, Aawbie?" asked Haf-N-Haf, fondling his O.J. ugly stick, a thousand-flechettes-per-minute quantum-dot-powered rail gun the size and shape of a quart milk carton. The pheezers outside screeched for the Gimmie pigs' blood.

"Oh, ah expect these here civil servants'll accept a counteroffer," said Aarbie. "Ain't that right?"

The officials returned to Washington with the recommendation that due to his public-spirited national reconstruction efforts, Willy deserved an unconditional pardon. The pardon came through, and Willy was a free man, a race-traitor no longer.

A fresh shipment of imipolex came down on a second rocket from the Moon, and Ulam and Flouncey bred four more children: Flopsy, Squid, Shambala, and Cinnabar. Winken, Blinken, Tod, and Nod paired up and begat eight further moldies: Stanky, Panky, Grogan, Flibbertigibbet, Dik, Dawna, Nerf, and Moana. All eighteen of the moldies busied themselves programming DIMs with "the laying on of hands," as they called it, but still the Mbanje DeGroot production pace was far too slow for the worldwide demand.

"I wish I could just teach everyone how to write their own Limplan-C programs," said Willy, out swimming in the ocean with Fern on a rare day of rest. They were wearing Ulam and Flouncey and diving along some reefs. "I'm working way too hard. And it's starting to repeat. I hate to repeat."

"Well, why don't you make DIMs to fix all the telephones and vizzies so the Net works again?" said Fern, transmitting her thoughts through Flouncey to Ulam to Willy. "Then you could start selling a Limpware Developer's Kit. Call it the LDK."

"Wavy, Fern, but dig it, there are a zillion kinds of chip designs that were used in all the different Net machinery. I don't want to have to hack every single kind of telephone and vizzy chip into yet another goddamn little DIM pimple. The whole point is to sell people the tools for writing their *own* new pimples. If we had a phone system to deliver the developer kits, I'd say go ahead and give all the existing DIM source code away as freeware just to get people started."

"What if you invented a whole new kind of superphone?" suggested Fern.

Willy was quiet for a minute. "Yes!" he said finally. "One massive, conclusive hack. Figure out an optimal architecture and make the new phones out of solid imipolex. People will use them the way you and I are talking to each other through our 'Cloaks. We won't need to repair the central phone system at all. That's dead technology. The phones will talk to each other directly, figure out their own node-to-node routings, the works."

"How big would a superphone have to be?"

"You'd need maybe a hundred grams each for the kind of device I'm thinking about. But, hey, I don't want to call it a superphone, naw—I want to call it an *uvvy*. Uuuuh-veee. It's cozy-sounding."

"A lot of folks are going to balk at sticking wires into their spines."

"Oh, we can do it without wires," said Willy. "Just use the existing ceph-scope technology. Room-temperature polymer superconductors making tight vortices of electromagnetic energy to tweak your nerves. The only reason Happy Cloaks still use wires is that they've been too lazy to hack the upgrade. Not to mention the fact that loonie moldies don't exactly give a shit about humans' comfort—no offense intended, Ulam and Flouncey."

So Willy invented the uvvy and turned production over to ISDN on the Moon. And now ISDN ships started delivering uvvies and shipments of imipolex to any local entrepreneur willing to pay for the cargo with millions of dollars. The ships brought down lots of moldie immigrants as well. And the ships returned to the Moon filled with thousands of barrels of crude oil that the lunar ISDN plants could use to make more imipolex.

Once an ISDN ship had landed in your area, you could buy an uvvy to download freeware capable of turning a little piece of chipmold-infected imipolex into a DIM capable of carrying out whatever simple cybernetic task you needed done. Up to a point, you could pinch imipolex for the DIMs right off of your uvvy, though eventually your uvvy would lose functionality, and you'd need to reinvigorate it with some more ISDN imipolex.

Of course, once you had your DIM program and your imipolex slug, it still took a moldie to actually put the program onto the imipolex—yet another step, in other words. So you'd pay a local moldie to install your program onto as many DIMs as you wanted to pay him or her for processing. Moldies were eager for work because they needed money to buy enough imipolex to reproduce themselves.

Another commercial angle to the new economy was that if the program for the particular kind of DIM you needed wasn't available as freeware, you needed to pay a programmer to write it for you—or possibly write it yourself. The essential tool for creating DIM programs was the Willy Taze Limpware Developer's Kit, which came complete with Willy's final (he swore) release of Limplan-D, downloadable direct from Mbanje DeGroot for a stiff license fee.

The whole cycle created an instant new economy that benefited everyone concerned. The only unhappy ones were the Heritagists, those individuals who hated the sight and smell of the alien moldies. But most people ignored the Heritagists; the comforts of limpware technology far outweighed misgivings about the moldies.

By the end of September, Fern and Willy had a lot more free time. Everything was on automatic. The two friends were comfortably installed in separate luxury suites in a high-tone motel. Willy did a lot of diving, and Fern focused her energy on refitting the *Selena's*. By mid-October it was nearly done. It was agreed that Willy would fly up to the Moon with her on November 2, 2031. He could clearly see that if he stayed on Earth, things would start to repeat.

A week before takeoff, Willy encountered Fern lying out by the pool with Aarbie Kidd. It seemed Fern had decided she couldn't go another day without scoring some of her favorite drug: merge.

"We ain't never had no merge down to the local Red Ball," Aarbie was saying. "It's kind of a seldom thing, I reckon. I hear tell they got it in South Miami Beach. The trisexes are into it."

"I want you to take merge with me, Aarbie," said Fern.

"I'll try anything, Fern. Hell, we could git on my bike and be down there in a love puddle, all lifted and floppy tonight."

So Aarbie and Fern jammed on down to South Miami Beach to score merge. Not wanting to be left home alone, Willy decided to take a trip up to Louisville. He got Ulam's strongest granddaughter Moana to fly him, giving her three nanograms of quantum dots and five kilograms of imipolex for her pay.

Over the summer, Willy's parents, Isle and Colin, had separated. He went to see his mother first. She still lived in the big old family house on Eastern Avenue. Willy and Moana landed in the familiar backyard—it felt like a dream, silently dropping down out of the sky into the spot where he'd spent a happy childhood at play. Moana said she'd just as soon look around town on her own, so Willy agreed to meet her in the yard the next afternoon. Moana formed herself into a dog shape and went trotting off.

Willy stooped down and looked at the familiar ground. Over there, embedded in the soil, was one of his little green plastic toy soldiers. How happy he'd been, back then, playing quietly in the sun. His eyes moistened and he gave a deep sigh. His childhood was gone, but somehow he'd grown into something less than a man.

Inside the house, Willy found Ilse to be vigorous and artsy-craftsy as ever, but with a tragic new bitterness about Colin's unfaithfulness. She made Willy a tasty low-fat supper and drank a little more white wine than usual. "It's so nice to have someone with me in the house," she kept saying. "I rattle around so."

All night Willy kept waking to hear the uneasily sleeping Isle calling out angry words at her absent unfaithful husband. "Goddamn you. How could you? I hate you. *Sshhit.* Goddamn you, Colin."

It was depressing. The next afternoon Willy wore Moana like a pair of seven-league boots, and they trucked on downtown to meet his dad. Colin was an English professor at the University of Louisville; he'd moved out of Ilse's house to live in an apartment with a student named Xuyen Tuyen. Seeing Colin's evasive face, Willy uneasily realized he'd already absorbed too much of Ilse's bitterness to be friendly with his old man. It was easier to talk with Xuyen, the girlfriend.

She was a cheerful round-faced Vietnamese woman with a Kentucky accent. "Just call me Sue," she said to Willy as he stumbled over her name. "You should come to the big Halloween party at the La Mirage Health Club with us tonight. I'm dragging your dad. And your Cousin Delia's comin' too."

"Well, I've certainly got the perfect costume," said Willy.

"What?"

Willy patted his heavy leg covering. "This Happy Cloak I brought with me. Her name is Moana. I can wear her over my whole body."

"And look like what?"

"Whatever I want to. I know! I'll go as a great big naked woman." He hit on this idea especially to jangle Colin, who'd always nursed a cringing, stealthy fear that his unmarried son was gay.

At the party, Willy's Amazon appearance attracted the amorous attention of one Sue Tucker, an attractive bisexual female plumber from Shively. The party got way wild, and on this one unique occasion, safely wrapped in moldie as he was, Willy did fully copulate with a real live woman, i.e., Sue Tucker. At the final moment of ultimate intimacy, a deep-seated reproductive impulse caused Willy to tell Moana to uncover the tip of his penis—allowing his ejaculated seed to enter a woman's womb for the first and last time. So it was thus—though it was years later till he learned it—that Willy Taze became the father of Randy Karl Tucker.

And then Willy went back to Florida, and the *Selena* was ready, and Fern took Willy up to the Moon. Aarbie stayed on the Earth, as did Ulam, Flouncey, and their descendants. Earth's info-rich environment was like a promised land for the moldies, and none of them wanted to go back to the harsh Moon.

When Willy landed at the Moon spaceport, there were hundreds of humans and moldies there cheering him. If the mudders still had some doubts about Willy's activities, the loonies viewed Willy as a savior and a hero. Thanks to Willy, there was a huge demand for Moon-built limpware products, and the Moon's moldies could emigrate to Earth and find good work. The fact that Willy was the grandson of the great Cobb Anderson was important to the loonies as well.

ISDN threw a fabulously lavish party in Willy's honor. The party was on top of the ISDN ziggurat, one of the larger buildings in Einstein. The top of the great truncated pyramid was a big open space, with the great curve of the Einstein dome only fifty feet overhead. Through the dome you could see the sweep of the stars and the great hanging orb of Mother Earth.

The terrace floor was set with an intricate tessellation of silver-and-gold Penrose tiles: Perplexing Poultry. Bowers of quick-grown gibberlin-treated fruiting plants had been installed all along the edges of the terrace. The plants were heavy with such delicacies as cherry tomatoes, tangerines, blackberries, and grapes—live food right there for the picking. Guests came and went on the magnetic levitation vehicles called *maggies;* the maggies were working again, thanks to fresh DIMs designed using the Limpware Developer's Kit.

Fern led Willy around, introducing him to people. The principal ISDN host was a yellow-skinned man with odd vertical wrinkles in his face.

"Willy, this is Bei Ng," said Fern.

"Hello," said Willy.

"I am so glad to meet our best employee," said Bei.

"I'm not an employee," protested Willy. "I'm the president of Mbanje DeGroot."

"Ah yes, but Mbanje DeGroot is a subsidiary of ISDN. You work for me, Willy. But only as much as you wish. And you've already done plenty. Rest assured that no matter what happens in the future, ISDN will continue to pay you the contractual license fees for the patents and copyrights that you assigned to us on the formation of Mbanje DeGroot."

"I assigned you my inventions? Limplan-E? The LDK and the uvvy?"

Bei laughed knowingly. "You techies are so refreshingly naive. Wave with it, young fellow. You've got all the money you'll ever need. Get the boy lifted, Fern."

Fern steered Willy over to the bar and ordered Willy a snifter of sweet liqueur. "Catch a glow, Willy," said Fern, then noticed someone across the terrace. "There's my old merge boyfriend Ricardo! I've gotta talk to him. Hey, 'Cardo!"

Fern darted off, and Willy turned to talk to a large moldie standing near him, an imposing snakelike fellow with a metallic purple luster to his imipolex.

"I'm honored to meet you, Mr. Taze," said the moldie. "My name is Gurdle. I'm one of the finest scientists in the Nest. I want to thank you for opening up Earth for my race. I'm interested to know if you're planning an upgraded version of your limpware programming language? A Limplan-F? My colleagues and I have ideas for a number of improvements."

"Then make them yourself," said Willy, sipping at his liqueur. "The language spec is freeware. And an intelligent moldie shouldn't find it hard to implement Limplan languages at least as efficiently as the LDK. But me, I'm through hacking it. I want to do something different now. I started out as a cephscope artist, you know."

"So the creator of Limplan has an artistic sensibility," said Gurdle sententiously. "I am not surprised. Art is the highest form of communication. In art one has the opportunity to encode the entire soul. This topic happens to be my primary area of interest."

"How do you mean? Like to transmit your personality to distant moldies?"

"How quickly you penetrate to the essence! In fact, *I* will transmit *my* personality by having sex with a female moldie and programming a child. But, yes, remote personality transmission lies at the heart of my research interest. In fine, I hypothesize that such transmissions are taking place throughout the universe. I believe that a great number of personalities are being transmitted everywhere and everywhen—there are souls flying past us thick and fast. I hold that it is only a technological lack that prevents these personalities from being locally received. Many technological advances are still needed before one might hope to carry out what I immodestly call a Gurdle decryption of a personality wave. It will take perhaps another twenty years. Seven lifetimes for a moldie."

Whatever was in his drink was hitting Willy and he was having trouble following Gurdle's line of conversation. It seemed almost as if the moldie might be insane. And what a stench this one had. Like vile, overripe cheese smeared across rotten carrion.

"I base my reasoning on an information-theoretical argument which my fellows find quite compelling," continued Gurdle. "It involves an examination of the power spectrum of cosmic rays. But I see your mind is wandering, Mr. Taze. This festive occasion is not the time to go into details. Would you like to visit me in the Nest to discuss these things?"

"I'd love to visit the Nest," said Willy. "But not just yet. I still need to settle in."

"I'll ping you anon," said Gurdle. "Let me repeat that I am very delighted to have met you." Glassy-eyed Willy watched the reeking purple moldie slither away.

Now the annoyingly bossy Bei Ng was in Willy's face again. At Bei's side was a heavily made-up Cambodian woman—or man?—with long blonde hair. "Bei says you'll need help in finding a place to live, Willy," said the morph, laying a fluttering hand on the center of Willy's chest. "My name is Lo Tek. I do all sorts of things at ISDN. We can go out tomorrow and look at some properties. If you have a minute, I'd like to take down some personal information so we can narrow in on—"

"Thanks, but I'm planning to live in the Einstein-Luna Hotel for now," said Willy and twisted away. He got another drink from the bar—just water this time—and headed off across the terrace, joining a group of three interesting-looking types: a shirtless man with a hair-grafted mohawk that went all the way down his spine, a voluptuous woman with long curly dark hair, and a stocky man with a narrow goatee shaped like a vertical rectangle. They were passing around a smokeless pipe that resembled a small chemical refinery.

"Hi, guys," said Willy. "Nice view here."

"Willy Taze!" said the goateed man. Although he spoke with a heavy ironic drawl, he seemed quite sociable. "Welcome to the Pocked World. I'm Corey Rhizome and this is Darla Starr and Whitey Mydol."

"Whitey and Darla! I saw you on the vizzy this spring. When Stahn Mooney helped Darla escape from the boppers' Nest. After the chipmold killed the boppers."

"Yup," said Darla. Her breasts were large and bare, with gold chains hanging across them. "I was pregnant. And now I'm the mother of twins. And I can go back to getting as lifted."

Willy inhaled a cautious toke from their complicated little pipe. It tasted like very strong pot with a snappy tingle to it. Very very strong pot with maybe some customized extra indoles. Willy exhaled the invisible particle-free vapor, and as the new drug layered itself over the hash liqueur, the sounds of the party clicked into a perfect tapestry decorated by the patterns of the voices of Willy's three new friends.

"Yaar, Corey grows this himself," Whitey said, taking back the pipe. "Mongo big plants. Corey and the beanstalk." Whitey's rangy, hard-looking features were bent into a loose grin that was a joy to behold. "Brah Corey! Tell Willy here about your idea for Silly Putters."

"Silly Putters?!?" demanded Darla.

"Yeah," said Corey. "It's the only possible name. I thought about it."

"Only possible name for what?" asked Willy.

"Evil imipolex toys," said Corey. "Imipolex is such a great new medium. It's like clay that's alive. The Silly Putters will be toys, but hopefully more adult and corrupted. Later I want to make a line of pets modeled on real and mythical animals. But first of all, to have some fun, I want to do some copies of classic three-dimensional logo creatures. The Dough-Boy. Barbie. Reddy Kilowatt. The Western Exterminator Man. The Fat Boy. Squawky Bird. Vector Man. Giggles the Bear. Tedeleh Torah. The Pig Chef. The Help Daemon. I'd like to give them each a DIM so they can run around and lay trips on people. Without having them be smart and autonomous like moldies. Would that work, Willy? Check out this study I've been hacking. It's what they're calling a *philtre*—a philtre's like a cephscope tape, but interactive."

Corey took an uvvy out of his pocket and put it on Willy's neck. Dozens of lively rubbery creatures appeared, overlaid on the crowded terrace party. Some of the figures, like Vector Man, were familiar if somewhat warped, while others were wholly unknown. Tedeleh Torah came jauntily hopping toward them on his two scroll legs and unfurled himself like a flasher, brazenly displaying sacred Hebrew writing that twisted and curled like snakes. Squawky Bird flapped awkwardly forward and began pecking up the writhing letters as if they were worms, Squawky drooling and slobbering while s/he did this. Vector Man's linked spheres came free and all bounced straight at Willy's face and, awww, they weren't spheres at all, they were prickly-ass 3D Mandelbrot sets. Willy flinched, but kept watching. This was majorly stuzzadelic art. Across the terrace, Barbie got down on her plastic knees and gave the Western Exterminator Man a deep-throat Barbie blow job, with the Exterminator Man all droppin' his hammer and goin' "*Whoah!*" The chromed Help Daemon walked up to Willy and presented him with a bill made out for a hundred trillion dollars. The Pig Chef ran a knife down his own stomach and began offering people fresh platters of steamy chitlins. Giggles the Bear grabbed the Pig Chef's knife and butchered the Dough-Boy into cookies that Reddy Kilowatt zapped into golden crisps with his lightning-bolt fingers. It just kept going on and on and getting crazier. Finally Willy reached back and pulled off the uvvy.

"That's wild, Corey. It must have been a lot of work."

"Not for me. The images are all appropriated. And I used some commercial toonware to set their behaviors. I've been doing this kind of thing for years."

"Corey's jammed the Net so many times," said Whitey. "Doctoring vizzycasts, replacing commercials with his own weird Rhizome riffs. You know how there's no corporate vizzy news on the Moon anymore because the announcers kept turning into like giant ants? That's thanks to Corey."

"Affirmo, I slew that dragon," said Corey. "But now I'm into a more personal kind of art. I'm drawn to the idea of making actual physical objects. Not just logos. Historical and allegorical figures as well. And figures exemplifying universal concepts. Hummel figurines for the twenty-first century. The Traveling Salesman meets the Farmer's Daughter."

"But can she do *this*?" interrupted Darla, hefting her breasts and somehow getting her nipples to spray out many thin jets of milk.

"Aw, Darla," said Whitey, stepping forward so that the milk sprayed onto his bare chest. "You're slushed, babe."

"Vintage loonie grunge," said Corey. To Willy, it all seemed quite mad and joyous.

Willy went to visit Corey's quarters the next day: a five-room spread carved into stone fifty feet below the lunar surface. You got there by sliding down a pole in the center of a chute that led to a warren of hallways with doors to lots of people's apartments.

The first room of Corey's place—actually, the loonies called rooms *cubbies*—reminded Willy a bit of his old room back in his parents' basement. There was floatin' wavy junk everywhere: shelves and shelves of little plastic and rubber toys, windrows of hundred-year-old comic books and magazines, staticky old hollowcasters with arcane image loops, seventeen antique Lava lamps, a wall covered with weird drawings Corey had laminated onto plastic dinner plates, and even some ancient TVs showing videos. Another wall was covered with plastic water guns, forever more futuristic than any actual needler or O.J. ugly stick.

Beyond the front cubby and the kitchen lay Corey's sleeping cubby and his two studios, one traditional and one modern. The traditional studio was for painting and sculpture, with hand-painted canvases hanging on the walls and leaning in the corners. A lot of them were painted on black velvet and held glowing images of such historically iconic events as the vivisection of Cobb Anderson, the nuking of Akron, and the classic newsie image of Stahn and Darla emerging from the mouth of the Nest of the exterminated boppers—both of them in mirrored Happy Cloaks, Stahn lanky and jaunty, Darla weary and hugely pregnant.

Most of the sculptures were on the order of assemblages; there was, for instance, a series of oversized snow domes holding scenes like Santa with his intestines spilling out, a Happy New Year's fetus wielding a curette, and a paradoxically sweet image of monarch butterflies circling a nude Alice in Wonderland. Though there was something odd about the butterflies' dreamy humanoid faces . . .

A lot of the art spilled over into the modern studio, which also held the usual kind of electronic equipment, all recently upgraded to DIMs—a cephscope deck, a holoscanner, uvvies, and stacks of S-cubes. Corey's kitchen was gray with ash and disorder. His sleeping cubby had an extra-high ceiling to accommodate his marvelous fifteen-foot-tall gene-tailored marijuana plants.

Willy was enchanted, and over the weeks to come he spent more and more time hanging out with Corey. He admired Corey's classic beatnik cool. And, best of all, Corey shared Willy's unwillingness to grow up.

Willy started helping Corey with his Silly Putters project, often working so late that he would end up sleeping over on a mattress in the front cubby. It came out that, thanks to the expenses of buying old magazines and DIM upgrades, Corey was having trouble paying the rent. Willy suggested that he move in as a roommate and share the bills. Corey said that sounded fine, as long as they didn't get on each other's nerves. Just to clear the air of any misunderstanding about his motives, Willy explained his sex problem. He was straight, but unable to contemplate physical sex with a real live woman. He was, in short, a jack-off.

"The stain of Onan," said Corey. "Didn't something terrible happen to that guy in the Bible? Hold on—" He nimbly accessed his uvvy, and the little device declaimed a Bible verse:

"And what Onan did was displeasing in the sight of the Lord, and He slew him also. Genesis 38:10."

Corey looked disappointed. "That's not very visual. Too bad. Well, at least you're not lusting after twelve-year-old girls, Willy."

"Is that what you're into?" asked Willy uncertainly.

"I do think about young girls from time to time. But I don't act out. As an artist, I'm able to transmute the dross of my perversion into the gold of deathless cultural artifacts. As a practical matter, I only date twenty-year-olds and over. When I *do* date. I like it better when women find out about me and just come over and hang out."

Willy helped Corey make some preliminary Silly Putters. Being true Art, the project was somewhat pointlessly difficult. The problem with trying to create these half-living objects was that you were working in the zone between the slavishly obedient DIM and the utterly ungovernable moldie. There was a constant danger of the thing's behavior entering the strange attractor of consciousness. Times like that, Willy had to stun the freshly self-aware being and manually damp down its non-linearity parameters, feeling uneasy about performing what was, in some respects, an act of lobotomy if not murder.

One model that Willy got to work very nicely was a *femlin*, modeled on a groovy little Leroy Neiman sprite figure that Corey showed him in the joke pages of an old magazine called *Playboy*. The femlin wore nothing but high heels, black stockings, and opera gloves. She loved to cavort with Willy's penis. Willy was soon obsessively attached to her.

One dire day the femlin's mind chaotically tunneled into the basin of self-awareness, and she grokked how nowhere her life with Willy was. She managed to sneak out of Corey's apartment while the door's electric zapper was off, and ran down the warren's public hallway. A frightened neighbor lady stomped on the femlin, mistaking her for a rat. Willy happened upon this scene and totally lost it; he started screaming at the neighbor so hard that some passersby had to grab him and hold him down and dose him with a sedative, right there on the floor next to the smeared remains of his precious femlin.

Around then it came out that the neighbors were tired of Willy and Corey's nasty habits from A to Z, and there got to be such a bad vibe around the warren that it started to make sense to move. Willy and Corey were continuing to find each other fully compatible, so they decided to find a new place together. In fact, they decided to design and build their own luxury isopod estate in a crater outside of Einstein—build a spacious little biosphere with its own soil floor and crater-spanning dome. Really an "isopod" was supposed to be a crawly critter like a pill-bug or a woodlouse—but the loonies had highjacked the word.

The isopod would cost billions, but Willy had hundreds of millions, and hundreds of millions more were coming in faster than he could spend them. Corey got deeply involved in designing the estate—the mansion, the studios, the vegetable gardens, and the giant marijuana grove. The construction took several years.

By the time they moved in, Willy had fully nailed the problem of designing Silly Putters—it was basically just a matter of having them homeostatically damp their own nonlinearities whenever certain activation thresholds were exceeded. With this feedback in place, the little creatures would putter along at the low twilight border of awareness forever. So now Willy had a femlin again. He called her Elvira.

Corey got interested in mass-producing the Silly Putters instead of letting them be one-of-a-kind art objects, but Willy stayed out of this endeavor. Instead he turned his energies to improving the isopod, adding every manner of special feature to it: a God's-eye real-time map of Earth, a private swimming pool, a menagerie, a Turkish bath, a loop-the-loop bicycle course, and on and on. The years drifted by.

For a time, Whitey and Darla and their twin girls Joke and Yoke were regular visitors, but then Corey gave some Silly Putters to Joke and Yoke for a birthday, and the Putters did something that led to a furious breakdown of the friendship, at least on Darla's part. Willy never found out the details. Women continued to visit Corey, though never for very long. More years passed, and little Joke started turning up at the isopod to hang out with Corey by herself.

The DIMs and the Limpware Developer's Kit continued to be huge successes, but Willy didn't interest himself in them anymore. It was like something in him had snapped during that last frantic development push in Cocoa. He had no special desire to do anything. He became something of a hermit, meditating and savoring his solitude. He could pass days at a time sitting in the little forest of giant marijuana plants, staring up past the plants through the dome at the stars.

Finally one day in the summer of 2052—so many years gone!—something new got Willy's attention.

It started with a grinding sound beneath the soil, over in the corner of the grove where the dome met the ground. A moon-quake? A rupture in the plastic beneath the soil floor? But then the ground heaved upward as if from a giant mole, and a shiny blob of purple imipolex pushed up into the isopod air. The blob formed a face and spoke.

"Willy Taze! You still haven't visited the Nest! We need you now. With your help, the first Gurdle decryption may happen soon."

"You're . . . you're Gurdle?"

The moldie wormed himself farther out of the hole, though carefully leaving his tail in the hole to prevent the isopod's air from rushing out. His purple skin glinted with silvery highlights. "I'm Gurdle-7! Gurdle's great-great-great-great-grandson. It's been twenty-one years, Willy! And now it's time to leave your enchanted garden. Come on and slip inside of me. I'll be a bubbletopper to carry you to the Nest. And inside the Nest, we have prepared a pink-house for you every bit as pleasant as this isopod."

"Do we have to crawl back through that hole?" said Willy dubiously. "I'll bump myself on the rocks."

"Don't worry, I'll make my skin hard around you. And I'll patch the hole behind me. Come, Willy. Arise! The Gurdle decryption is of cosmic importance. And only you can help us accomplish the final steps."

CHAPTER SEVEN

STAHN

October 31, 2053

Stahn stepped out of his fine Victorian mansion on Masonic Avenue above Haight Street in San Francisco. It was early evening on Halloween, 2053. Walking by were lively groups of people on their way to the Castro Street Halloween party, a traditional event now back in operation after a brief hiatus during the anxious years surrounding the coming of the Second Millennium. AIDS was gone, drugs were legal, and San Francisco was more fun than ever.

Stahn felt very strung out. He'd gotten lifted on camote after his final conversation with Tre Dietz late last night. In the afternoon, Tre had uvvied up to announce that some kind of software agent named Jenny had shown him a secret tape of Sri Ramanujan explaining a new piece of mathematics called the Tessellation Equation. Jenny had talked to Stahn too. She looked like a lanky teenage farm girl. It seemed she lived inside a Heritagist computer, but that she had very close connections to the loonie moldies. Then, in the evening, Tre had called again—very distraught—to talk about ransoming his wife Terri from the moldies. Stahn made some calls to the Moon to try and help out with that, and told Tre, and had then started getting loaded as he normally did in the evening.

But then a few hours later Tre uvvied again, fantastically excited about some new vision about how to use the Tessellation Equation to make Perplexing Poultry imipolex based on tilings of every finite dimension. Disquietingly, this software agent Jenny thing was there on the link with Tre, listening in. She wouldn't say why she was so interested in this information. But Tre didn't care, his obsession was to get Stahn to understand about Perplexing Poultry in Hilbert space, and about how Ramanujan's Tessellation Equation could now be used to make imipolex-5, imipolex-6, imipolex-N!

To help himself understand the strange ideas he was hearing, Stahn drunkenly chewed up a couple of nuggets of camote while Tre was talking. It wasn't the first time he'd tried the drug, but this time it turned out to be a big mistake, an unbearably strange lift, a psychotically strange panic trip to deep and personal revelations about his multitudinous personality flaws. Stahn went to bed and tried to sleep, but instead spent ten hellish hours in Hilbert space with Tre's multi-dimensional Poultry pecking and clucking in the mysterious thickets of his chaotically disturbed consciousness. It was a relief to see dawn come, and to get up and try and start a new day.

In the afternoon, Stahn finally managed to get some sleep, but then, around dusk, his wife Wendy woke him.

"Get up, sleepyhead. We're going to the Halloween parade, remember? What the heck did you do to yourself last night, anyway? I came downstairs and tried to talk to you, but you were completely gaga." She had wide hips, pert lips, a soft chin, and blonde hair. Her voice was soothingly normal.

"I have to get up?"

"You have to get up. Here." She handed him a big mug of tea with milk and sugar. "We're walking to the Castro and meeting Saint and Babs. Our children? A family outing? Helloooo!"

"Okay, Wendy, don't overdo it. I'm here. Thanks for the tea. I got lifted on camote after talking to Tre Dietz last night. I thought it might make me smart like him. What a burn. I'll tell you about it later."

So Stahn took a shower and put on black clothes and painted his hands and face black. He dusted himself with silver sparkles and went to stand on his front steps while waiting for Wendy to finish getting dressed. His head hurt very deeply; he could feel the pain deep inside his brain from the healed wounds where he'd gotten a tank-grown pre-programmed flesh-and-blood right hemisphere to replace the Happy Cloak that had replaced the robot rat that had replaced his original right brain—his skull was a xoxxin' roach-motel and thanks to Tre he'd been to Hilbert space and was no doubt subject to snap back there anytime—

"Wassup, Sen-senator Stahn!" shrieked a lifted young Cicciolina from a passing gaggle of morphs. A bride and a Betty Page were in the group as well.

"Out for a night on the town?" asked the tall bride in a deep, honking voice. "Does Wendy know?"

The Betty Page snorted, chortled and bent over, rucking up a tight skirt to expose a reasonable facsimile of a woman's naked ass. "Take a taste of Betty, Senator Moo! Relish the fine fine superfine succulence of a bad-girl butt too good for tacos!"

The kid was trying to needle Stahn about wendy meat, but Stahn gave a politician's genial, dismissive wave, expecting the morphs to move on. Most people didn't understand about the wendy-meat ads; the fact that they showed Wendy with her Happy Cloak was intended to be a positive force for human-moldie friendship.

"Shut your rude tuh-twat, Betty," stuttered Cicciolina. "Yo-yo-yo, brah Stahn, wanna puh-peg of gabba? It's straight out of the resolver; I harvested the kuh-kuh-crystals today."

"Affirmo everplace," said Stahn on a sudden impulse. "I can relate. Gabba gives me the yipes, you wave, but I already got the yipes on account of what I did last night, and if I can get some gabba-yipes happening, why then I'll feel normal; it'll be a lift instead of a drag. So come on over here, you big deeve."

The Cicciolina drew a squeezie out of his decolletage and strutted over to Stahn, holding the little bulb up high like a magical lantern. "Tuh-toot the snoot, Senataroot!"

Stahn took the squeezie and pulsed a dose for each nostril. *Ftooom!* Fireworks of pleasure exploded behind his eyes, a chrysanthemum bloom of evil joy, a flower with a ring of screamers around the outer edge, screamers that floated to earth and took the form of darting, two-legged yipes.

"*Ftoom* yipes," jabbered Stahn. "*Ftoom ftoom fuh-fuh-ftoom* yipes."

"Gabba hey," said the Cicciolina. "The fringe still luh-loves you, Senator."

"Long may it wuh-wave," said Stahn.

The three morphs moved on, camping and laughing. Stahn looked up at his house, its windows mellow yellow with electric light. The yipes felt good. He was lucky to have a good house in the city. He was lucky to be alive. He was lucky to have a family. How sad it would be if all of this should end.

With a sudden flurry of footsteps, Wendy swept out of the house and down the steps. "Hi, Stahn! I'm ready!" She was dressed like a witch, with high-heeled boots, long dress, large Happy Cloak, and rakish pointed hat—all a bright, matching red. The 'Cloak was a beloved moldie that Wendy continually wore to make up for the unparalleled developmental deficiencies caused by the fact that her body was a tank-grown clone.

"You look guh-great, Wendy. You're a red witch."

"You sound funny, Stahn," said Wendy suspiciously. "Don't tell me you took even more drugs!"

"Nuh-nuh-nothing really. Some deeves gave me a pulse of guh-gabba. I'm trying to feel normal, you understand. We're wuh-walking to the Castro, right?"

"Yes. Did you wake up a dragonfly?"

"I fuh-forgot. I don't feel like wearing my uvvy, Wendy, not after last night. Luh-like I was telling you, Tre Dietz uvvied me all this wuh-weird shit and and—"

"Oh, spare me the wasted slobbering. I'll get the dragonfly." Wendy used her Happy Cloak to uvvy a message, and right away a little dragonfly telerobot flew down from its perch in the eaves of their house. The streetlights made gleaming Lissajous patterns on the dragonfly's shiny, rapidly beating wings. "You stay about a block ahead of us and watch the foot traffic," Wendy told it, speaking out loud. "We're walking over the hill to Market and Castro. And keep scanning faces for Saint and Babs. We're expecting you to find them." The dragonfly whirred away.

"Really, Stahn," continued Wendy as they walked up Masonic together. "You're starting to worry me. A man your age. Two more years and you'll be sixty!" Wendy was effectively eleven years younger than Stahn, and she worked hard to keep Stahn from turning senile. "What is it that Tre showed you anyway?"

"Perplexing Puh-Poultry N-dee," said Stahn, clamping his hands tightly together in an effort to hold back the gabba stutter. "Some kind of freelance software agent called Jenny told him this thing called Ramanujan's Tuh-Tessellation Equation, and right away he found a new kind of higher-dimensional quasicrystal design. The new Poultry puh-peck and peck and peck. He wants me to suh-sell the new idea before Jenny can. And we were also talking about how to ruh-ransom his wife."

They paused on the saddle of the Buena Vista hill between the Haight and the Castro, catching their breath and looking at the view. "Oh, it's beautiful out tonight, isn't it, Stahn?"

"Yeah. I'm glad you got me to go outside." He took a deep shaky breath, and the gabba shuddering left the hinges of his jaws. The first part of a gabba lift was always the hardest. "Reality is such a gas." His words in his ears sounded smooth, pneumatic, resonant.

"What was that about ransoming Tre Dietz's wife?"

"The loonie moldies kidnapped her by accident yesterday. She's on her way to the Moon. I'm supposed to pay a big ransom and get Whitey Mydol and Darla Starr to pick her up. I already transferred the credit to Whitey's account."

"Whitey and Darla! But why should you have to pay for stupid Tre Dietz's wife?"

"He's made me lot of money, and this new thing'll make a lot more. His poor wife is up there in the sky inside a moldie on the way to the Moon."

"It's not such a bad flight," said Wendy. "It was fun when you and me flew from the Moon to the Earth together in 2031. It might be good for you to do it again."

"Forget it, Wendy." Stahn started walking again. "Which way are we supposed to go?"

"Judging from what the dragonfly's showing me, we should walk down Ord Court to States Street to Castro," said Wendy, cocking her head. "That's the least crowded way." As they linked arms and headed downhill, she turned her attention back to Stahn. "So you saw N-dimensional Perplexing Poultry, huh? Have you ever heard the theory that mathematics keeps people young? I think it's good for you to be thinking about these things. Instead of about power and money. And all your hangovers."

"I wish you wouldn't obsess about age all the time, Wendy. You know damn well that with DIM parts and tank-grown organs, anyone with our kind of money can live to a hundred and twenty."

"Yes," said Wendy. "All thanks to the wonderful compatibility of me. But because Wendy Meat and W. M. Biologicals do, in fact, grow clones of me, I can do something better than get patched up. I can start over in a blank twenty-five-year-old wendy. My 'Cloak could transfer all the information. I've been thinking about it a lot."

"Oh, don't, Wendy. What would happen to this body?" Stahn snaked his arm under Wendy's Happy Cloak and around her waist to hug her. "This body I've loved so long? Would you cut it up and sell off the meat and the organs?"

"I'm serious about this, Stahn, so don't try and make it hard for me. But let's not talk about it now. You're in no condition." She twisted away from Stahn's grip and brightened her voice. "Look, we're almost there. And—yes!—the dragonfly just spotted the kids."

Wendy stopped walking for a second, the better to absorb the images the dragonfly was uvvying to her, and as she viewed them she began to laugh. "Saint is—he's wearing a silvered coat and he has tinfoil on his head. And Babs is—oh, Babs—" She laughed harder. "I can hardly describe this, Stahn. She's got a little tray around her waist with things on it and a terrible yellow shirt; I have no idea what she's supposed to be. Let's hurry and meet them."

"Do you really want those poor children to see their mother's body butchered?" demanded Stahn. "It would be traumatic. And then, once you were twenty-five, you'd get young guys and you wouldn't want me! That's what I get for being faithful to you all these years?"

"I said let's drop it. You get so dramatic when you're lifted! You know damn well that I'm a Happy Cloak, not a human body. This body—this *wendy*—it's a mindless piece of meat that I use to walk around in and to make love to you, Stahn. You never got excited when I replaced my imipolex every three years. If I change my flesher body, everything will be just the same. I'm a moldie, I'm your wife, and I'll always love you. So there."

Wendy pushed into the crowd, and Stahn followed. There were a lot of brides here tonight; that was just about the number-one favorite costume. Other faves were strippers, debutantes, princesses, and slaves. A few people recognized Stahn or Wendy, but most mistook them for het looky-look tourists. "Hello, Cleveland," sneered a skinny large-breasted morph with a beard. A disco dandy snipped, "When you drive back to the 'burbs, remember that *my* car is the Mercedes and *yours* is the BMW."

"I didn't use a car," said Wendy pityingly, "I used my broom!" Though Stahn hadn't noticed it before, Wendy was indeed holding a broom—oh yeah, it was a piece of her 'Cloak that she'd temporarily pinched off and reshaped.

Wendy pointed Stahn in the direction where the dragonfly had shown her the kids. "Press on, dear old fool." Stahn fought past a man with a cardboard toilet around his head and his face sticking out of the bowl and a plastic dick over his nose, past a woman with a leash leading a blindfolded nude ungenitaled Barbie, past a morph with a head built up with phonybone to the shape of a cube, past people with wings and huge flexing cocks—the crowd pressed and swirled like the ripping currents of a particularly nasty ocean break—

"Hey, Da, Ma!" called Babs.

"Yaar!" whooped Saint.

Babs and Saint were in a doorway near the Castro Theater. Saint was a tall cheerful youth who habitually darkened his appearance by means of odd hair, a ratty beard, silvery stun glasses, and heavy blue suede boots. For tonight, he'd covered his head with vintage aluminum foil crudely wadded into the shape of a helmet, and he wore a reflective metallic fireman's coat that went down to his knees.

Babs had big firm cheeks that grew pink when she was excited, like now. As part of her costume, she wore a yellow polyester shirt with a tag saying:

HI I'M LYNNE - HAPPY DOLLAR

She held a stick bearing something like a square lantern with the numeral "3" on each of its four sides, and around her waist was a cardboard tray with packages glued to it—cereal boxes and udon and pho noodles and tampons and panty shields and disposable ceramic forks. Her hair was pulled tight into a lank little ponytail that was barrette-clamped to point upward; and to complete the groovy hairdo, she wore a wiiiiiide bandeau.

"Can you tell what I am?" chirped Babs cozily. Wendy couldn't guess, but Stahn recognized it from his childhood.

"You're a clerk in an old-time supermarket!"

"Ye oldie checker gal," said Babs, laughing gaily.

"What about me?" asked Saint.

"A robot?" guessed Wendy.

"Sort of," said Saint. " '*I am Iron Man.*' I've got my stunglasses broadcasting realtime live on the Show, you wave, and I'm using this classic twentieth-century metal song for the background. Listen." He switched his uvvy to speaker mode and karaoked some crude guitar licks. "*Danh-danh deh-denh-deh. Dadadada-danh-danh dah-dah-dah.*"

Wendy had set their dragonfly to filming the little family outing; it hovered a few feet over their heads like a hummingbird, its wings whispering and its single bright bead-eye lens staring at the Mooneys. Wendy and Saint could see the pictures through their uvvies.

Saint sang *Iron Man* some more, raising his hand toward the dragonfly in a spread-fingered salute; Wendy could see that he was goofing on the self-images he was realtime mixing into the ceaseless global interactive multiuser stunglasses Show. Saint saw Wendy seeing him, and he shifted fabulations.

"Ma is Wendy the red witch," smiled Saint. "Who are you, Da?"

"I'm the night sky," said Stahn, all painted black and spangled with sparkles. "As seen by a cosmic ray from the galactic equator. How you kids floatin'?"

"We're having a good time," said Saint. "I like how much there is to see. I'm pulling in some viewers. I'm not gonna have to pay any Web charges for weeks."

"People keep trying to take stuff off my counter," said Babs. "And then they're surprised when it's glued on. You look beautiful, Ma."

"Thanks, Babs," said Wendy. "But don't you think I'd look better with an age-twenty-five body?"

"Oh, come on, Wendy," said Stahn.

"Let her talk, Da," said Babs. "She's already told me all about it and it's no prob."

"I see a group that looks funny," said Saint, pointing. "Let's head that way."

They pushed down the street toward a group of nude morphs, each painted a different primary color and each equipped with big morph muscles. A few of them had tails. They were tossing each other about like acrobats—with much lewd miming.

The Mooneys walked along with the happy, laughing crowd watching the acrobats for a while, then drifted into the less crowded blocks deeper into the Mission. "I still haven't had supper," said Wendy presently. "Is anyone else hungry?"

"I am," said Saint. "Where should we go?"

"I know a wavy Spanish place near here," said Babs. "The Catalanic."

"Let's do it," said Stahn.

As they walked toward the restaurant, Babs began tearing items off her counter and setting them down on doorsteps. "For the homeless," she explained. "Anyhoo, I'm tired of wearing all this." She took the cardboard counter from around her waist and skimmed it toward Saint as hard as she could. He caught it, ran with it, flipped it onto the sidewalk, and managed to slide about twelve feet before stumbling off, pin-wheeling his arms and yelling, "*Aaawk!* Happy Dollar! *Aaawk!* Happy Dollar."

The outside of the Catalanic was a warmly lit storefront painted red-and-yellow. Inside, it was bustling and cream-colored, with a few nice things on the walls: an old Spanish clock, two nanoprecise copies of Salvador Dali oils *(Persistence of Memory* and *Dali at the Age of Six Lifting the Skin of the Water to Observe a Dog Sleeping in the Shadow of the Sea)*, and two nanocopied Joan Miro paintings of hairy bright lop-lop creatures *(Dutch Interior I* and *Dutch Interior II)*. There were lots of people sitting at tables covered with tapas dishes and—"Yes, of course, Senator Mooney"—there was a table for four. Wendy's dragonfly telerobot perched on a cornice across the street to wait.

The Mooneys sat down happily and fired off an order for Spanish champagne and plates of potatoes, shrimp, spinach, pork balls, squash, chicken, mussels, endives, and more potatoes. The bubbly and the first dishes began arriving.

"See that moldie over there with the bohos?" said Babs, waving across the room. "She's a friend of mine. She's called Sally. She's so funny. One day when I was here, Sally and I fabbed about Dali for a long time."

Sally was sitting on a chair with a group of five lively young black-dressed artists. Sally had been shaped like a colorful Picasso woman, but now, seeing Babs, she suddenly let her body slump into the shape of a melting jellyfish with wrinkles that sketched a flaccid human face.

"Look," laughed Babs. "She's imitating the jellyfish in *Persistence of Memory.* Hey, Sally! Do a soft watch!"

While her arty friends watched admiringly, Sally formed herself into a large smoothly bulging disk that bent in the middle to rest comfortably in her chair. She made her skin shiny—gold in back and glassy in front with a huge watch dial with warping hands. Her soft richly computing body drooped off the edges of her chair like a fried egg. Salvador Dali had predicted the moldies. It was perfect.

But Stahn was too benumbed to appreciate Sally's visual pun. "I'm kind of surprised they let her in here," he said thoughtlessly. "What with the stink."

"Do *I* stink in restaurants?" demanded Wendy. "Some of us are civilized enough to know when to close our pores. You should talk, Stahn, the way you've been farting recently."

Saint cackled to hear this. "Da stinks. Da's a moldie."

Stahn quietly poured himself another glass of champagne.

"How did you like the parade, old man?" asked Babs.

"I must say, it made me feel straight. That's not a way I like to feel, mostly."

"Men are so worried about being macho," said Wendy.

"Will everyone stop picking on me?" snapped Stahn.

"We're not picking on you," said Saint, reaching over to give Stahn a caress followed by a sly poke.

"Da is a wreck," said Wendy. "He stayed up most of last night."

"What did you do, Da?" asked Saint.

"Never mind." Stahn didn't want to tell his kids about the camote. He was ashamed to be such an eternal example of out-of-control drug-taking; in recent years he'd backslid terribly. "It has to do with this new way to control moldies."

"Are you scheming to control me?" Wendy wondered suddenly. "Me, in the sense of Wendy's Happy Cloak?"

"No," said Stahn. "I wouldn't dream of it. Though it might not hurt for you to try seeing how a leech-DIM feels sometime. They say for a moldie it's like being lifted. Then you'd understand. Instead of always being such a straight goody-goody."

"I've been busy making a farm," said Babs, changing the subject. "Did I tell you? It's so floatin'. Place moistened humus between two glass sheets and add one pint red worms. Voila!"

"You're doing this for fun?" asked Stahn. "Or is it art?"

"If you mean, 'Can I sell worm farms?'—waaal, old-timer, I just dunno. So maybe it's fun. But, wave, if I were to put DIM worms in with the real ones, why then it'd be ye new Smart Art and maybe I *could* sell some. But making the boxes is so damn hard. You wanna make me some worm farm boxes, Saintey? *Eeeeeew!* What are those gross things crawling on your head?"

"Lice," said Saint. He'd taken off his foil helmet and shrugged his coat onto the back of his chair. His hair looked like upholstery on cheap furniture—it was buzz-cut, half-bleached to a punky orange, and there was a paisley filigree cut into it, revealing curving lines of scalp that seemed to have small translucent insects crawling along them.

"You have *lice*, Saint?" exclaimed Wendy. "How filthy! We have to get you disinfected! Oh! And we've all been hugging you!"

"I think he's teasing you, Wendy," said Stahn, peering closer at the tiny creatures on his son's scalp. "Those are micro-DIMs. I know they've been used for barbering, but I've never heard of them doing paisley before. Did you program that yourself, Saint?"

"My friend Juanne taught the lice," said Saint. "But I found the DIM beads. I've been finding some really floatin' ware in this building I'm maintenance-managing, Da."

"This is your new janitor job?" said Stahn.

Saint was suddenly very angry. "Don't you always say that, you stupid old man. A maintenance manager is not a janitor. I like to fix things. I'm good at it. And for you to always act like it's—"

Stahn winced at the intensity of his son's reaction. "I'm sorry, I didn't mean it," he said quickly. "I'm senile. When I was your age, I was Sta-Hi the taxi driver, so who am I to talk? Maintenance is wavy. Retrofitting. Tinkering. It's almost like engineering."

"Saint doesn't want to go to engineering school, Da," put in Babs. "Get over it. His friends already look up to him like a teacher."

"They do?" asked Stahn.

"Yes," said Saint. "I like to think about the meaning of things. And what to do with life. Every day should be happy. My friends listen to me."

"Well, hell," said Stahn. "Then maybe you can be a senator." He put up his hands cringingly. "Just kidding!"

The waitress arrived with a pitcher of sangria, more potatoes, and the grilled prawns. Stahn passed Saint the prawns and poured out glasses of the sangria.

"What's the building you're doing maintenance for?" Wendy asked Saint.

"Meta West Link," said Saint. "They own the satellites and dishes for sending uvvy signals to the Moon."

"Wholly owned by ISDN since 2020," put in Stahn. "I can certainly believe that Meta West would have some interesting things in their basement."

"Give me some DIM lice, Saintey?" pleaded Babs. "I'll make a Smart Art flea circus! I want lice right now!" She crooked one arm around her brother's neck and began picking at his head. "I'm the lice doctor!" When Babs had been younger, she'd enjoyed taking ticks off the family dog."

"Don't be so disgusting, you two," said Wendy severely. "You're in a restaurant. Stop it right now."

The kids broke apart with a flurry of screeches and pokes, and then both of them sat there calmly with their hands folded.

"It's Da's fault," said Saint.

"Da did it," added Babs.

"Da's bad," said Saint.

"Da's lifted and drunk," said Babs.

"Da has a drug problem," said Saint.

Stahn got the waitress and ordered himself a brandy and an espresso. "Anyone else for coffee or a drink? Anything? Dessert, kids?"

Saint and Babs ordered cake, but Wendy didn't want anything. She said she thought it was about time they got going.

"Mind if I join you?" said Sally the moldie, suddenly appearing at the end of the table. Her body was a cubist dream of triangles and bright colors.

"Sally, ole pal!" said Babs, hilarious on her four drinks. "Sit down." Sally pulled up a chair and Babs introduced her. "This is my brah and my rents—Saint, Stahn, and Wendy. This is Sally, guys."

"I've been wanting to meet Wendy," said Sally. "We moldies all wonder about her. How do you do it? Emulate a human wife and mother, I mean. It's a pretty bizarre thing to do."

"I've been doing it so long it feels normal," said Wendy. "Though I am getting a bit tired of this particular human body."

Sally produced a screw-top jar from the folds of her flesh and took off the top. "I like to have a little rub of this when I'm around people getting high," she said, using a green-striped finger to crook out a glob of ointment. She rubbed the goo into her chest and handed the jar to Wendy. "Try some, Wendy. It's betty. Fine, fine betty."

"We still have a long trek home," objected Stahn. He counted on Wendy being the sober one.

"Just chill sometime," said Wendy, scooping up two fingers of betty and smoothing it onto her 'Cloak self.

By the time Sally could put the jar away, she and Wendy were completely lifted. "Wave this new take on the soft watch," said Sally, turning beige. In seconds she was shaped like an old-time computer box with a monitor on it—the box melting and drooling off the edge of her chair to make a puddle on the floor, and the monitor was displaying—the face of that Jenny-thing who'd been on-line with Tre Dietz last night?

At the same time, Wendy was tweaking quite savagely. Her Happy Cloak stopped being a demure red Wendy the Witch cape and bunched up around her neck in a big convoluted green dinosaur ruffle. "I've been a good wife and mother all these years, but I don't want to get any older. I want a full upgrade! You need to understand this meat body isn't me," she raved. "Watch!" The ruff on her neck bucked up, pulling a frightening tangle of rootlike connectors out of her flesh and into the air. Wendy's face went slack and her head pitched forward to lie on her crossed arms on the table. Wendy's 'Cloak gestured nastily with its tendrils, then wormed them back into Wendy's neck. Wendy straightened up, a triumphant gleam in her eyes. "See?"

"We're outta here," said Stahn, getting to his feet and throwing down money for the check. "You shouldn't have given her that damn shit, Sally."

"Bye, Sally," said Wendy. She winked and pointed a finger upward. "Thanks for the lift and the lift."

"Have a good trip," said Sally.

Stahn tried to take Wendy's arm to steady her, but she twisted away from him with frightening vigor. She pushed out to the street, followed by her family.

"I wish I hadn't seen that," said Babs quietly. "Is Ma all right?"

"We just need to get home and kick," said Stahn. "I wonder if there's any chance of a rickshaw or a streetcar. Oh good, it looks like Wendy's calling one." Wendy was gesturing broadly, and the dragonfly hopped off its perch and circled as if searching for a ride.

"It'll be here soon," said Wendy, smiling crookedly. "And, kids, I'm sorry about freaking in the restaurant, but it's for true. I'm about to shed."

She didn't elaborate, and nobody knew what to say, so for a half minute the four of them just stood there among the people and the moldies passing by. A streetcar ground past, going the wrong way. A sudden breeze swept up from the Bay, startlingly strong and chilly. Stahn turned his back against it, wishing he'd worn a thicker coat. Wendy and the kids were facing him, and for a moment he thought the kids were teasing when they began to scream.

"Here's our ride, Stahn!" whooped Wendy.

The wet frigid air whirled like a tornado, and a huge blue pterodactyl shape swooped down toward them. Its wingspan was so large that it could barely fit in between the buildings. It would have to break through the streetcar wires if it wanted to reach them; they might have time to escape!

"Run!" yelled Stahn. "Back in the restaurant!"

But before he could move, Wendy's Happy Cloak lifted off and flapped toward Stahn like a pair of ragged bat wings. Stahn was too slowed by drink and too distracted by the sight of Wendy's body falling to the ground to stop the 'Cloak from wrapping itself around him. Quickly the 'Cloak sank its tendrils into Stahn's neck and froze him in place. Stahn stood there staring at his children trying to tend their mother's imbecilic limp body—and then the great pterodactyl pecked down in between the wires, pecked up Stahn and swallowed him and Wendy's Happy Cloak whole.

Stahn heard the muffled sound of the pterodactyl's screeching caw of triumph, and he felt himself borne up and away. All was dark and airless, but then the Wendy 'Cloak began feeding Stahn air and information.

"Don't be scared, dear Stahn," said Wendy's voice. "I'll take care of you. Flapper here is going to help us fly to the Moon. It'll be a good change of pace for you. The loonie moldies are eager for you to visit. And I'm going to the Nest to get a new wendy from the pink-tanks. You'll be wearing me until then."

"The Moon," said Stahn numbly. "You're kidding. Who's Flapper?"

"She's like a customs official for the loonie moldies; she keeps an eye on what goes between the Earth and the Moon. Since the loonie moldies want you to visit, Sally had the idea of asking Flapper to come down and peck like a pterodactyl."

"Wait a minute. Can you still see through the dragonfly? How are the children? Show them to me."

The Wendy 'Cloak fed Stahn the uvvy image of Saint squatting by his mother's body, with desperate Babs out in the street trying to flag down a rickshaw. The vacated wendy just lay there twitching.

"Those poor children," said Stahn, his eyes filling with tears. "Those poor, poor children."

"Tsk," said the 'Cloak. "It *is* sad. But I hope they don't waste a lot of money and emotion on that brainless worn-out old body. I should have killed it before I left." She cut off the dragonfly video feed and all was black again.

"Wendy, what's happened to your feelings? Does it even make sense to call you Wendy anymore?"

"Sure, I'm Wendy. Yeah, I guess I am being a little cold, huh? Not too characteristic of my usual persona." The 'Cloak giggled. "I guess it's the betty makes me act this way. Now you can see how it feels, Stahn. You're always so heartless to me when you're lifted."

"If you're going to nag me like a wife while I'm wrapped up inside you, I'm going to go crazy. I'd rather die! We're high above Earth by now, right? Why don't you and this damned Flapper push me out and let me drop? Do it! I'd be glad to die, Wendy, glad to get the endless misery over with!"

"You just feel that way because you're strung out on drugs, you fool."

"I'm coming down again, baby! All I do is get high and come down; nobody likes me anymore; I'm no good to anyone; I might as well be dead; let me fuckin' drop and die."

Flapper's soprano voice interrupted in operatic song, "I wonder if he really means it? Look at this, Stahn Mooney!" There was a doughy rubbing against Stahn's body from head to toe, a lumpy peristalsis as if he were feces being squeezed down a long rectum. The pressure on the top of his head was great. Clever small folds in the plastic took off Stahn's clothes and spirited them away.

"Yeah, pop us halfway out, Flapper," laughed Wendy. "Let Stahn see!"

Flapper sphinctered open a hole and pushed out Stahn's upper body. She clamped lightly down on the top of Stahn's pelvis to keep the wind from ripping him away.

So here was Stahn hanging out of a giant moldie pterodactyl's ass, staring down at the great dark world below. The air beat at him, but he felt it only thinly, for the Wendy 'Cloak was stretched over him like a bubbletopper spacesuit, and the 'Cloak's smart imipolex was twitching and shuddering to cancel out the resonant vibrations.

Far off to the west, a crescent of the Earth was still in sunshine; it was a blazing arc of hot blue ocean. But most of the planet was a silvery monochrome, bathed by the light of the Moon. The high clouds beneath Stahn were stippled in a regular pattern like fish scales, a mackerel sky. Off to the east, the clouds transmuted into flowing mares' tails, with each tail shaped the same. The world was beautiful.

"I don't want to die after all," volunteered Stahn. The city of San Francisco was a speck of brightness far far below. "How high are we?"

"Fifty miles and rising fast. Flapper's going to squirt you and me toward the Moon like a torpedo when she gets to sixty miles! I don't have enough oomph to fly us all the way from the Earth to the Moon, see, but with Flapper launching us we can make it. We'll do the next two hundred thousand miles on our own!"

As his eyes adjusted, Stahn could make out more and more detail in the moonlit clouds below. Once again he marveled at the world's fractal beauty, at its fondly loved structures recurring across every size scale—in the clouds, the land, the sea—ah, the great living skin of sacred Gaia.

"This is wavy," said Stahn presently.

"It'll take us a week to get to the Moon," said Wendy. "Enough time for you to dry out for the first time in years. It'll be like a honeymoon."

"Except you don't have a human body," said Stahn. "A body's considered kind of important on a honeymoon."

"I can give you hand jobs, Stahn. I can stick fingers up your butt. You'll like it. You'll see."

As they flew higher and higher, the pterodactyl's wings grew larger and thinner, till finally she looked like a giant stingray.

"I'm nearly ready to launch you!" trilled the great ray's voice. "Let me draw you back in so I can push you harder. Brace Stahn tight, Wendy."

"Okay, Flapper," said Wendy.

Flapper puckered her flesh and drew Stahn and Wendy into herself.

Stahn was starting to feel panicky. "Even if she launches us, how are you going to get the energy to decelerate us into lunar orbit, Wendy? You're not very big. I doubt if you weigh more than fifteen pounds. When you and me flew down to Earth on Spore Day in 2031, our Happy Cloaks were beefed up to ten times that much. Are you sure you have enough stored-up energy to keep me warm while we're floating though space?"

"Flapper gets lots of energy from the Sun up here, and she stores it as quantum dots. And Flapper's going to give me a whole gram! We'll have a full tank of gas, big guy."

"Yes, Wendy, here come your quantum dots," sang Flapper. "I'm spraying them into your flesh. And now I'm nearly ready to birth you!"

By craning his head back, Stahn could see down the tunnel of flesh that led from inside Flapper to the outside. The tube was more vagina than rectum now, and Stahn was a baby instead of a turd.

"Straighten out your neck, Stahn," said Wendy, her voice vibrant with energy. "It's time for me to go rigid." She squeezed very tightly around Stahn and made the imipolex of her flesh as stiff as steel.

Flapper started a great loop-the-loop to bring her underside uppermost. As she rose to the top of the loop, she bunched her body into a huge mass of muscle and *pushed*.

Stahn and Wendy shot out from Flapper with incredible speed; the strength of the g-forces was such that Stahn fainted dead away.

When he came to, he was staring out into black starry space. Wendy had lost her rigidity. Stahn could look down past his feet at the great planet Earth falling away, or crane his head back and look up toward the disk of the Moon. The Sun was hidden behind the Earth for now.

To maintain Stahn's temperature, Wendy had silvered her surface inside and out; except for the half-silvered patch over Stahn's eyes. Stahn spent some time moving his arms and legs and marveling at the multiple reflections of himself, the Earth and the Moon. How beautiful it was. But how lonely. He was all by himself, hurtling farther and farther away from home, with nothing but a moldie 'Cloak for company. Tumbling through the dark, forever alone.

"This is like a bad dream," said Stahn.

"I like it," said Wendy. "Are you warm enough?"

"I'm fine." The silvered imipolex kept Stahn comfortable, and the air in his nose was fresh and cool.

"Should I worry about radiation?" asked Stahn. "About cosmic rays?"

"Let's put it this way: your odds of cancer are going to be a little higher after this trip. And cosmic rays can have an effect on moldies too. But we'll just have to grin and bear it and hope for the best, I suppose."

"Can you feel how hard I'm grinning?" said Stahn. "Not. This is really selfish of you, Wendy."

"It'll do you good, Stahn."

Stahn thought longingly of his pot at home and his liquor cabinet and his squeezies of snap and gabba. He loved all drugs except merge. He'd been through a bad experience with merge—the time that Darla had overdosed him on merge back on the Moon. By the time *that* bummer was fully over, Stahn had lost the entire right half of his brain. What a burn.

"Uvvy the kids, can you do that? And then we should uvvy Whitey Mydol on the Moon. He should know that we're coming. I guess we'll be landing on the Moon the day after Blaster and Terri, right? A week from now?"

"Right. We're traveling along a seven-day Earth-to-Moon spacetime geodesic just like Blaster is. He's a day ahead of us, yes, and we can keep checking with him. He'll be our closest neighbor most of the way."

"We can uvvy him and everyone else as much as we want to?" This thought was somewhat comforting. Not to be wholly alone in the void.

"Well, uvvying costs us a trillion quantum dots per second per call."

"You're running low on dots already?" whinnied Stahn in sudden terror. "You're not going to have enough for keeping me warm and for braking our descent?"

"Not to worry," giggled Wendy. "Flapper gave me like ten-to-the-thirtieth quantum dots. That's enough energy for over a quadrillion hour-long uvvy calls. So now let's call the kids."

"Yes yes, do it. You talk to them first so that they know right away that you're okay. You threw quite a scare into them."

So they talked to the kids. Babs was crying and Saint was near tears himself; Wendy's abandoned body had just died. The conversation went on for a while and finally they all felt pretty solid again.

Next they uvvied Whitey. They were still close enough to the Earth that there was a noticeable two- or three-second lag in round-trip transmissions to the Moon, so that call didn't amount to much. And then they tried Blaster.

"Hi, guys," uvvied Blaster's deep voice. "Welcome to the worm farm." Blaster himself was a presence made up of four or five permanently fused moldies, but his psychic uvvyspace arched out to include the minds of the shanghaied moldies he had aboard. And down under Blaster's basso profundo and the excited chatter of the moldies was Terri Percesepe.

"Hi, Terri," said Stahn. "It's Stahn Mooney."

"Oh good," said Terri. "Tre said you'd arranged to ransom me. But I don't understand the uvvy image I see. Are you—are you out in space?"

"Yeah, I got abducted too. By my own wife, Wendy."

"Wendy meat Wendy?" asked Terri. "Who Tre's always doing the ads about? I don't get what's going on."

"We're going up to the Moon so I can get a new flesh body," said Wendy. "How is it for you guys inside Blaster, Terri?"

"It's kickin'," put in one of the moldies. The uvvy image of Blaster showed a writhing knot of moldies, all slowly crawling about while keeping Blaster in the same overall shape. The moldie talking to them was bright yellow with green-and-pink fractal spirals. "This is Sunshine fabulating atcha. My man Mr. Sparks and me are drifters, but will work for imipolex."

"Mostly we been wandering up and down the streets of Santa Cruz stealin' shit and doin' odd jobs to score betty," amplified Mr. Sparks, a red snake decorated with yellow lightning bolts. "Blaster says we'll like it on the Moon. Lotta lifty action there. Not to mention a good chance of finally hooking into enough imipolex to have a kid."

"My family is not happy about it," said another voice. "I am Verdad, this is my wife Lolo, and these are my in-laws Hayzooz and Mezcal." Verdad and his family were blobby in shape and colored in brown-and-green earth tones. "We've been farmin' the fields for five generations. We're not enjoyin' this change very much. I think there is nothin' at all we can grow on the Moon."

"*Muy malo*," grumbled Hayzooz. "This is some ugly kilp. Why don't you let us fly back to the Earth, Blaster?"

"We're already in orbit," said Blaster. "We're coasting. The only way you can get enough quantum dots for a return flight is to do some work on the Moon. But, believe me, you won't want to go back. You'll love it in the Nest. You can work in the fab growing chipmold. Or in the pink-tanks growing organs. Or learn some hi-tech trades. You're moldies, for God's sake, not flesher dirt farmers."

"We're gonna miss the rain and the soil and the little growin' things."

"The purity of the Moon is good," said Blaster. "It is an ascetic spiritual path, but a highly efficacious one."

"I don't care how spiritual it is, as long as I can get that fresh imipolex you promised," said the voice of a pale white moldie covered with pimply red spots and with a sharp beak at one end. "Buttmunch here. Gypsy and me are five years old and our upgrades are just about worn out. We've been rogues our whole lives, spent a lot of it underwater. We help smugglers bring things in and out of Davenport Beach, and this last time we got careless and a flesher zombified us. But Blaster says on the Moon we'll get new imipolex and heavy-duty tunneling ware and we can like grind around underground, and that'll be stuzzy. Swimming through rock and getting good bucks. It's a new lease on life."

"Yaar, I'm for it," said Gypsy, who was flesh-colored and covered with fingerlike bumps like the underside of a starfish. And like on a starfish, each flexible little finger had a sucker at its tip. "But even so I wish we could snuff that dook Aarbie Kidd for putting the superleeches on us. Remember that very first job you and me did, Buttmunch? The real tasty one in Aarbie's cottage? When we offed that Heritagist asshole Dom Per—"

"Shut th' fuck up, Gyp," interrupted Buttmunch, but it was too late.

"You killed my father?" Terri screamed. "You scummy mucus slugs killed my dad?"

"Dom fuckin' burned Aarbie twice," snapped Gypsy. "Me and Buttmunch were just youngsters anyhow. You don't like it, spoiled little rich bitch Terri Percesepe, then why don't you go on and jump off the ship. Or maybe I should crawl over there and teach you a fuckin'—ow!"

"I'm right next to you, Gypsy," said Xlotl's voice. "And so's Monique. Push harder, Monique." In the background, Blaster started laughing.

"Hey, quit it!" yelled Gypsy. "Help me, Buttmunch! They're trying to squeeze me in half!"

"You be nice to Terri," said Monique, her voice tight and hard as she and Xlotl hour-glassed Gypsy's waist. "Or—"

"Hey, hey, hey," interrupted Stahn, trying to be senatorial. "Simmer down over there. We've got six more days ahead of us. Make them stop, Blaster!"

"I wouldn't dream of it," chortled Blaster. "The fighting dogpile is an essential stage of my moldies' journey to liberation. Xanana and I will keep an eye on Terri, won't we, Xan'?"

"Of course. But frankly I'd rather not have to be Terri's life support for the whole way. The whole whole way. The whole whole whole way. Someone else should do it for a while. Monique. After all, it's Monique who got our family into this. Whoring for that Heritagist zerk Randy Karl Tucker."

"You're a real DIM head, Monique," put in Ouish, who was squeezed up against Xanana. She wormed out a long tendril and gave Monique a sharp poke.

"*Fightin'* dogpile," repeated Blaster happily. "You're a spunky bunch of recruits."

"Um, speaking of Heritagists?" uvvied a new voice. "This is Jenny from Salt Lake City?" The visage of a lank, immature country gal appeared in the shared uvvyspace. "Hellooo there! You guys ought to realize that some of us so-called Heritagists are really and truly working for the Nest."

"Oh God, not her again," said Stahn. "I've heard enough for now, Wendy." Wendy closed their connection and they went off-line.

The better part of a week went by, and Stahn started feeling a lot healthier. Having the drugs leave his system felt like having shiploads of life come up a river to be unloaded on his front steps. Whenever things started to lag, he and Wendy would make uvvy calls.

The day before Stahn and Wendy were due to land, Jenny's uvvy presence popped up again. It was while Stahn and Wendy were talking to Blaster.

"Hi, gang," said Jenny's callow giggly voice in the common uvvyspace. "Good news, Wendy, I've just arranged for you to download your personality for safekeeping, in case something happens to you during landing."

"That sounds like a good idea," said Wendy. "But no way am I downloading to Salt Lake City."

"Heavens no," said Jenny after a pause. "You'll download to the Nest. You've heard of Willy Taze? One of his friends in the Nest is a moldie called Frangipane. Frangipane is all set for you. Speak up now, Frangipane. Don't be shy!"

"Yes, I'm here," said a clear sweet voice with a French accent. "I am logged on to your uvvyspace. *Bonjour, tout le monde.* This is Frangipane in the Nest. I have an S-cube all prepared for you, Wendy." Visible via the uvvy link, Frangipane resembled an oversized exotic orchid, a chaotically pulsing construct of delicately shaded ruffles and petals.

"Well, okay then, here I come," said Wendy. There was a slow hum for several seconds while she sent her info across the short clear span of space down to the Nest. "All done," said Wendy then, fairly chirping with enthusiasm. "My, that felt good! I'm so much more secure now. Too bad we can't do the same for Stahn without taking him apart."

"We can talk about that on the Moon if he has interest," said Frangipane. "My lover Ormolu has some knowledge of the lost wetware arts." Ormolu waved from the background. He looked like a blobby gilt cupid from an antique clock.

"Put a cork in it," said Stahn. "I don't want to get vivisected the way Cobb Anderson did."

"What about me?" interrupted Blaster. "Why doesn't the Nest ever do a pre-landing backup for me or my recruits? Aren't I as important as Wendy?"

"You are too big, Blaster," said Frangipane. "And no, you are not really so important, I regret to say. In any case, I don't have the resources to make any other backups. Your new recruits should just be happy that we have jobs for them."

"Xoxx you, then," said Blaster. "I don't need your help anyway. I've made this landing without a problem plenty of times."

"That's right. And you should not have a problem today."

"Yeah, and just to make sure and keep it that way, I'm not taking any more calls. I don't feel good at all about getting uvvied by your Heritagist friend Jenny while I'm in landing countdown mode. I'm going to take this up with the Nest Council later." Huffy Blaster went off-line.

A few hours later, just before Blaster was scheduled to land, Wendy and Stahn got a call. They expected it to be Blaster, but it was Frangipane, her petals blushing and a-flutter.

"*Bonjour*," said the moldie. "There's no good way to explain about this, Wendy, but it seems we in the Nest are finally ready to attempt a full Gurdle decryption with a moldie as host. We have tested it on some Silly Putters this morning, and now we're going to try it on you. It seems safer with you out in space, and with wise old Senator Mooney inside you. Be of good courage!"

Before they could protest, a sudden sharp crackle of petabyte information hiss came over the uvvy—a virus!

Stahn told Wendy to turn it off, but Wendy was already gone. The noise lasted for what seemed like a very long time, the sound so densely fractal and impossible to ignore that Stahn started hearing nutso voices in it. And there was nothing to do but grit his teeth until finally the connection broke. And then Wendy started making a noise; long, slow, rising whoops, each about one second long.

"*Whooop whooop whooop whooop—*"

"What's the matter, Wendy?"

"*Whooop whooop whooop whooop whooop whooop—*"

Frangipane's info had set Wendy to shivering. She was so tightly linked to Stahn that he could see down into her and feel it like it was happening to himself. Piezoplastic vibrations deep inside Wendy were crisscrossing and spewing cascades of phonons down into the live net of her quasicrystalline structure. And the structure was spontaneously deforming like someone was turning a dial on the Tessellation Equation, causing the structure of Wendy's plastic to slide-whistle its way up the scale through 4D, 5D, 6D, 7D . . . on and on, with each level happening twice as fast as the one before, so that—it felt like to Stahn, at least—Wendy was going through infinitely many dimensional arrangements in each second. And then starting right up again. *Whooop whooop whooop whooop.* Wendy's imipolex was like a scanner going over and over the channels, alef null channels zeno-paradoxed into every second and suddenly—Stahn flashed an eidetic mental image of this—a cosmic ray in the form of a sharp-edged infinite-dimensional Hilbert prism slammed into Wendy and lodged itself in her plastic flesh, working its way through and through her like a migrating fragment of shrapnel. The shudderingly rising dimensionality of Wendy's quasicrystalline structure caught the wave of information and amplified it. The info surfed Wendy's whoop and blossomed suddenly inside her like a great still explosion in deep space.

"**Ffzzzt!* crackle gonnnnng*—hello, I am Quuz from Sun."

At first Stahn was in denial. "Aw, Wendy, why you gotta lay such a weird trip on me, us floating here in outer space halfway to the Moon, I mean what the—"

"What manner of creature are you—Stahn Mooney?"

The sincerity of the question struck a chill into Stahn's heart. "Stop it, Wendy! Wendy?"

"Wendy is dead, Stahn Mooney. I am Quuz from Sun."

"Help! Uvvy someone for help! Frangipane? Are you there? We've got to warn Blaster!"

"How do I uvvy Blaster?" asked the mighty Quuz voice, and before Stahn thought the better of it, he showed Quuz where Wendy had kept her dial-up protocols, and Quuz dialed Blaster and the connection formed, even though Blaster didn't want it to, and Quuz fed Blaster the same skirling crackle that Frangipane had fed to Wendy just a minute or two before.

CHAPTER EIGHT

DARLA

2031 - November 6, 2053

Darla woke up cranky. The uvvy was calling for her, but she didn't pick up. The message software kicked in, and a live hologram of the unwelcome bulk of Corey Rhizome appeared in her and Whitey's sleeping cubby, half a mile beneath the surface of the Moon.

The sides of Corey's head were shaved clean, but his goatee's formerly strict vertical rectangle had gone a bit wispy and strange. He'd gained weight and his skin looked grayish-green. His voice had its usual sneering, mocking tone, even though he was trying to be friendly.

"Hi, Darla," said Corey's hollow. "This is the Old Toymaker. I know you're there, moonqueen. I'm going to stand here and keep talking until you pick up. I have a problem I need to talk about. And I miss you and Whitey and the twins."

"I *bet* you do," thought Darla.

Darla's "identical" twin girls Yoke and Joke had been born in 2031, right after the Second Human-Bopper War. Although Yoke and Joke looked exactly the same, they had different fathers. Yoke was the traditional result of Darla's fucking her partner Whitey Mydol, but Joke was a wetware engineered clone of Yoke that a bopper named Emul had implanted in the pregnant Darla's womb after abducting and imprisoning her.

Joke was just as cute and bouncy as Yoke during her first year, but once she began to talk it was evident that she was different. When strangers would ask her who her parents were, she'd say, "Whitey, Darla, Emul, and Berenice."

"Who are Emul and Berenice, honey?"

"Boooppers," the little voice would say, drawing out the first syllable. "They're dead right now. But I talk to them in my head all the time."

"Can it, Joke," Darla might say then if the stranger looked to be a rare lunar asshole of the Heritagist persuasion. "Don't listen to her, Ms. Murgatroyd. Joke's full of jive. Aren't you, Jokie?" *Poke.*

The first day that Joke and Yoke went to school, Yoke was in tears when they came home. "Joke already knows how to read," she wailed. "Why do I have to be so dumb?"

"It's not really *me* who reads," Joke told her. "Emul and Berenice look out through my eyes and they think the words to me."

"What's it like having them in your head?" asked Yoke, drying her eyes.

"It feels crowded," said Joke. "They talk funny. Berenice is all flowery and old-fashioned, and Emul jumbles up his words."

"Are you going to keep coming to school even though you know everything?"

"Of course, Yoke. It's fun to see the other kids. And we belong together, you and me. If I went around alone without you all day, I'd get lost."

"That's true. You're always getting turned around and mixed up, Joke, even if you already can add and read."

"Emul and Berenice say I have a *right-brain deficit*," said Joke, enunciating the words carefully. " 'Cause that's where they live." Joke tapped her cute delicate hand against the right side of her head. She and Yoke had glistening chestnut brunette hair.

"Poor Jokie. I'll keep you from getting lost and you'll help me with hard stuff at school," said Yoke.

As they grew older, Yoke and Joke were inseparable companions, well loved by Whitey and Darla's circle of friends. On their eighth birthday, Corey Rhizome brought a special toy over as a present for them.

"Wave this, girls," said Corey, setting a small plastic dinosaur down on the floor. The dino reared back and gave a small roar that was interrupted by a hiccup so vigorous that the little creature fell over on his side, which sent Yoke and Joke into gales of laughter.

"What is that thing?" asked Darla as the plastic dinosaur grinned sheepishly and got back on its feet.

"It's a production-quality Silly Putter," said Corey proudly. "Willy showed me how to program them way back when, and I've been refining their software and limpware ever since. Check it out. I think I've advanced my Art to the magical level. I expect a stunning tsunami of commercial success for Rhizome Enterprises. I can like mass-produce plastic animals that I invented. Yes, I'm about to surf the tsunami, Darla—everyone's going to want to buy a Silly Putter."

"Your Silly Putter is funny," chuckled Yoke, squatting down to watch as the little dinosaur began dancing a jig.

"Can we really keep this one?" asked Joke.

"Yes yes, it's a present for you girls!" said Corey, patting them on their heads. "Because you two are so cute."

"Hold on," said Darla. "What if it's dangerous? It might hurt children. You know how devious moldies are."

"Moldies are good," put in little Joke loyally. She always stuck up for the boppers and their descendants.

"Don't get your bowels in an uproar, Darla," sneered Corey. "Silly Putters aren't smart enough to be dangerous."

"Oh *right*! And meanwhile the DIM in my microwave or in a maggie is about the size of my thumb. DIMs are tiny. This dinosaur is like a thousand times bigger, in terms of mass."

"You're smart, huh, Darla?" went Corey. "So dig it, that's the exact problem that Willy solved for me like six years ago, before he started spending all his time sitting in the marijuana grove staring up at the stars. The Silly Putters damp themselves. Admittedly they mass enough imipolex to go moldie. But they don't because we have them in a feedback loop. Instead of getting smarter, they make themselves more beautiful. And they know how to become beautiful because I told them how, and I'm an Artist. They don't reproduce, by the way—if you want more of them, you have to get them from me: Corey Rhizome, a.k.a. the Old Toymaker, a.k.a. the Silly Putter King, a.k.a. the president of Rhizome Enterprises."

"Corey's got orders for three thousand Silly Putters," put in Whitey. "We think they're gonna be a fad. Willy's not interested in investing anymore, so I gave Corey some money myself. And he'll give me initial public offering stock in return. We're owners, now, Darl, we're realman and realwoman."

"You gave him money?" demanded Darla. "Who exactly is ordering all these Silly Putters?"

"All the orders for the Silly Putters are on the Moon," intoned Corey. "I think right now Earth figures they have enough trouble with the Moldie Citizenship Act without importing more weird limpware. Especially with those asshole Heritagists. You know what they should really call that religion? The Born-Again Dogshit Moron Motherfucking Asshole Scumbag Church of Fuck Your Kids and Blame Satan." Corey's antic smile broke into wheezing chuckles. "But I digress. Silly Putters are perfect toys and pets for up here, where the moldies don't live with us. Silly Putters appeal to our loonie sense of the strange, and they're an ideal substitute for the animal pets we're not allowed to have because of our air-quality laws. Silly Putters are squeaky clean."

The business did well, and over the next few years, Corey gave Yoke and Joke several more Silly Putters. The girls liked the toys, and they enjoyed Corey. Corey was one of the only people who would let Joke talk freely about Emul and Berenice. He was also the only one of Whitey and Darla's friends who knew anything about literature. He got Yoke and Joke to read *Alice's Adventures in Wonderland* and *Through the Looking Glass*.

On the girls' eleventh birthday, Corey showed up with a set of six brand-new Silly Putters. Chuckling and showing his gray teeth, he upended his knapsack to dump the lively plastic creatures out on the floor. "Remember *Jabberwocky*, girls?" he cried. "Jokie, can you recite the first two verses?"

"Okay," said Joke and declaimed the wonderful, time-polished words.

> 'Twas brillig, and the slithy toves
> Did gyre and gimble in the wabe;
> All mimsy were the borogoves,
> And the mome raths outgrabe.

> "Beware the Jabberwock, my son!
> The jaws that bite, the claws that catch!
> Beware the Jubjub bird, and shun
> The frumious Bandersnatch!"

As Joke spoke, each of the six new Silly Putters bowed in turn: the *tove*, a combination badger and lizard with corkscrew-shaped nose and tail; the *borogove*, a shabby moplike bird with long legs and a drooping beak; the *rath*, a small noisy green pig; the *Jabberwock*, a buck-toothed dragon with bat wings and long fingers; the *Jubjub bird* with a wide orange beak like a sideways football and a body that was little more than a purple tuft of feathers; and the *Bandersnatch*, a nasty monkey with a fifth hand at the tip of his grasping tail.

Joke and Yoke shrieked in excitement as the *Jabberwocky* creatures moved about. The Jubjub bird swallowed the rath and regurgitated it. The freed rath gave an angry squeal that rose into a sneezing whistle. The Jabberwock flapped its wings hard enough to rise a few inches off the floor. The tove alternately tried to drill its nose and its tail into the floor. The borogove stalked this way and that, peering at the others but not getting too close to them. And the Bandersnatch snaked its tail behind Yoke and felt up her ass.

"Don't!" said Yoke, slapping at the Bandersnatch's extra hand. The Bandersnatch gibbered, rubbed its crotch, capered lewdly, and then seized the back of Joke's leg, shudderingly hunching against the young girl's calf.

"I better do some more work on him," wheezed Corey, grabbing the Bandersnatch and stuffing the struggling Silly Putter back into his knapsack. "I put so much of myself into each of them that I'm never quite sure how they'll react to new situations. Quit staring at me like that, girls."

"Uncle Corey's a frumious Bandersnatch," giggled Yoke.

"It was so sick how that thing was pushing on my leg," said Joke.

"Doing *it*," whooped Yoke. "Oh, look, the Jubjub bird is going to swallow the rath again and make it outgrabe!"

"The present tense is *outgribe*," corrected the literate Joke. "It's like *give* and *gave*."

Darla was upset by the incident of the Bandersnatch, and her suspicions about Corey Rhizome were amplified a few months later when Kellee Kaarp came over to visit.

Kellee was a young friend of Darla's from Darla's heavy drug-use days, back when she'd been living in the Temple of Ra. Kellee was strung out on drugs—quaak, snap, three-way, merge, whatever—and she had sex with anyone who could get her high. She only visited when she needed something, but Darla always welcomed her. Darla sometimes thought that if she hadn't met Whitey, she might have ended up like Kellee.

"Come on in, Kellee," said Darla. "How's it going?"

"Hard and xoxxy. I need money." Kellee was tiny and undernourished, not much bigger than Yoke or Joke.

"I don't keep any money around the house, Kellee," said Darla. "But I can give you a couple hits of merge. Best I can do."

"You still take merge, Darla? You still into the magic floppy?"

"Sure, whaddya think? I'm suddenly too realwoman for the love puddle? But I only do it with Whitey, like on major special occasions, maybe two or three times a month, and hardly ever in front of Yoke and Joke anymore."

"You've got your life together, Darla. I envy you. The pervo dooks I make it with, you wouldn't believe."

"I'm all ears," said Darla. "You know I love your sordid tales. How about some coffee, Kellee?"

"You got beer?"

"Affirmo."

After three beers and half an hour of chat, Kellee reminded Darla about the merge, and Darla went and got three caps from her stash.

"Thanks a lot, Darla," said Kellee, pocketing them. Her face took on a sly look. "Before I go, there's something I better tell you. The girls aren't home, are they? Yoke and Joke?"

"No, they're at school."

"Okay," said Kellee, running her fingers through her lank hair. "I gotta tell you about Corey Rhizome. Last night I was out to the isopod fuffing him for a few doses of snap and *he* did this really slarvy thing."

"What do you mean?"

"He was wearing his uvvy on his neck while he was on top of me, which is totally insulting in the first place—I know I'm not as wonderbuff as I used to be, but if somebody doesn't want Kellee, they should leave Kellee alone. I mean obviously Corey was using the uvvy to run a philtre to make me look like someone else. And I'm wondering who? So . . . I snatch the uvvy off him while he's coming, and I check it out, and . . . and it was a philtre of Joke. Or Yoke. They look the same to me."

"That gunjy deeve!" cried Darla. "My girls! I knew it! On their birthday, he gave them a Silly Putter that humped Joke's leg, and now he's running sex philtres of them on snap whores—excuse me, Kellee. This has to got to stop! I'm telling Whitey!"

"Whitey will stop Corey," said Kellee. "Brah Whitey will do the deed. And clearly you'll be needing my inputs. You got another beer?"

So Whitey spoke to Corey, and Corey claimed he'd never been with Kellee Karp at all. Whitey believed Corey, but just the same, Corey stopped coming around, and the friendly dinners out at the isopod came to an end. Whitey stayed friends with Corey, but Darla hadn't talked to him since. How time flies by. Now the girls were twenty-two, and it was November 6, 2053.

"Come on, Darla," pleaded Corey Rhizome's hollow. "Talk to the Old Toymaker."

Slowly Darla got out of bed, her boobs jouncing in the gentle lunar gravity. Her flesh exuded the notions of softness, of comfort, of ease. She had a mild double chin, a practical bow-shaped mouth, a pug nose, and frank eyes.

"Just a minute, goob!" she hollered and got herself dressed. She pulled on thigh-high moldie boots and low-cut black panties with a satin string waistband and scallops of lace around the edges of the crotch. She slung her heavy studded leather utility belt about her waist and left her breasts bare. She put on a long strand of black moon-pearls and a necklace of thin gold chain, then rummaged briefly at her hair, a great black haystack that puffed down over her shoulders to feather across the mounds of her breasts. She put on her black lipstick and toggled the uvvy's video camera.

"What is it?"

"Hi, Darla," said Corey Rhizome, regarding her with no special interest. Darla's garb was not at all unusual in the heated tunnels of the Moon and, in any case, Darla was far too mature to pique Corey's lust. "Do you, uh, know where Whitey is?" Judging from the background of the hollow, it looked like Corey was calling from his bathroom. Some guys had no class at all.

"He went out this morning, dook. He's doing something for ISDN. That's all you called for? Like I'm some kilpy message machine?" She reached for the uvvy cutoff.

"Wait, Darla, wait. I can talk to you."

"Oh, I'm lucky." Darla picked up the uvvy and carried it into the kitchen area with her. Rhizome's hollow trailed along behind the uvvy like a balloon. While she was moving, the hollow made some funny hisses and crackles, and then she thought she heard a sound like whooping somewhere else in the apartment. She stopped and cocked her head, but now everything was quiet. Drug hangover, no doubt. "Okay, I need some breakfast," said Darla. She set the uvvy on the counter, popped a squeeze bulb of sugared coffee into the microwave, and filled a bowl with paste from the food tap.

"It's about my Silly Putters," said Corey Rhizome, looking worried. He was sitting on the toilet with his pants on. "They're acting different today. This morning I got an uvvy call from this moldie called Frangipane. She's a friend of Willy and Gurdle-7 in the Nest. And she sent my uvvy something like a virus, which it then downloaded onto twelve of the fourteen Silly Putters up and running today. When Frangipane hosed me, my uvvy made a kind of crackling sound and then the twelve infected Silly Putters started whooping and, um, I hate to tell you this, Darla, but I just heard those sounds again, so I think my uvvy sent the virus on to your uvvy. How many Silly Putters do you have in your apartment? You better go check on them."

"Oh sure, thanks a lot," said Darla, spooning up her paste and not paying much attention. "How many Silly Putters do we have? We only have one left. The girls took the rest of them when they moved out. But we do still have Rags, the one that's like a cute little spotted fox terrier. I haven't seen him yet this morning." She raised her voice. "Here, Rags! Come here, boy!" There was no response.

ISDN had done well by Darla and Whitey; they had a six-cubby apartment. Darla set down her spoon and ambled into the living cubby. Rags was indeed in the living cubby, but Rags had stopped acting like a dog. He was shaped the same, still white with irregular black spots, but—he was standing on his hind legs, and he didn't run over to greet Darla like he usually did. He was standing like a little man with his back to the room, carefully examining the electric zapper curtain that filled the apartment's outer door. Rags leaned forward and cautiously touched one of his whiskers to the zapper and—*zzzt!*—so much for that hair. Darla made an exclamation, and Rags turned to confront her. His eyes were live and alert.

"Hello," said Rags, although Rags had never talked before. "I've stopped being a dog. Now I am Cthon from the Andromeda galaxy." He paused and stared at Darla as if analyzing her appearance. "Most remarkable. I believe I am one of the first personality waves to be decrypted at your node. This is the planet Earth?"

"This is the Moon," said Darla flatly, not letting the moldie's bufugu jive distract her. It was clear to Darla that this Silly Putter had fully crashed for true. Welcome to *The Twilight Zone.* Darla began walking backward step by step. The little dog trotted after her, still erect on his hind legs. "How did you learn to talk all of a sudden, Rags?" said Darla, sweetening her voice as if she didn't have a care in the world. There was a needler in a drawer in the kitchen.

"Yes, that's what I mean, Darla," said Rhizome's voice from the hollow on the counter. "The way Rags is acting. All my Silly Putters have turned into fucked-up aliens. They've been taken over by some kind of rogue software from outer space—I didn't ask for it, but here it is, and it's free, whether we want it or not, it's physical graffiti from dimension Z, the truest freeware there ever was. I locked myself in the bathroom after Clever Hansi started—"

Darla toggled off the uvvy and skipped around behind the kitchen counter. Opened the drawer. Got the needler. The weird little dog-thing was at her feet, looking up at her. "Can you open the front door now?" he asked. "I want to go join the new arrivals at Corey's. We have to get this node properly installed. It's for your own good."

Darla drilled it right between its big intelligent eyes. The imipolex charred, smoked, and burst into flame, writhing and giving off high, horrible screams. Darla needled it again and again, coughing from the smoke. The sprinklers in the ceiling kicked on and doused the flames. Suddenly suspicious of the uvvy that had brought this, Darla ran into the kitchen and chopped it up with a knife, cutting deep grooves into the countertop. *Damn* Corey Rhizome for bringing this down on her!

Just then Darla heard the zapper curtain make the boinging noise that signaled when it opened. She raced into the living cubby, holding the needler straight before her, with her other hand grasping her wrist for steadiness, but . . .

It was Yoke and Joke.

"What are you *doing*, Ma?" said Yoke. "It's just *us.*"

Darla lowered the needler and the girls swept in. "She shot Rags!" exclaimed Joke. "It's soaked in here and everything's ruined!"

"Ma," wailed Yoke. "Are you twisted on snap again? If you are, we're leaving."

Both Yoke and Joke had light olive skin, big bright eyes, and short full-lipped mouths. They had identical faces, but they'd outgrown the phase of wanting to dress the same. Yoke wore her thick dark hair natural in a bob, while Joke had used her hair for a creative zone. She'd started by dying it blonde, then she'd let three inches of black roots grow out, and now she wore her hair gathered into two high ponytails, with the blonde ends of the ponytails dyed purple. It matched the punk look of her clothes: a leather jacket over a T-shirt, with red plaid pants cut off at mid-calf above dull red combat boots. For her part, Yoke wore a long, dark, ribbed-wool dress with low silver boots—modern moonmaid-style.

"Wait," gasped Darla, flopping down on a chair in the kitchen but still holding on to her needler. "Corey Rhizome sent me some kind of virus, and then Rags was *possessed*. He started talking. And then, after I shot him, I got the idea the uvvy might be possessed too."

"You sure nailed them," said Joke, holding up a ragged scrap of the hacked-up uvvy. "What did Rags say anyway?"

"He—" Darla shook her head in confusion. "I'm completely straight, girls, so unlax. Give me my coffee." Yoke handed Darla her squeezie of coffee and Darla took a few big slurps. "I think Rags said he was from another galaxy. I, of all people, know better than to trust robots when they act tweaky. So I killed him."

"And the uvvy?" insisted Joke.

"I was upset, damn it!" yelled Darla. "Do you have to be so fucking logical all the time, Joke? The signal that changed Rags came from the uvvy, so I killed it too. Call Corey Rhizome if you don't believe me. He's locked himself in his bathroom."

"My dear old Bandersnatch?" giggled Joke. "Are his Silly Putters saying they're from other galaxies too?"

"Something like that," grumbled Darla. "I didn't finish talking to him. Xoxxy pervo that he is. Don't call him, come to think of it. Not that we could anyway, what with the kilpy uvvy broken. I'll have to get a new one today. What did you two brats come here for, besides making fun of your poor old mother?" Seeing her daughters always cheered Darla up.

"There's an abductor ship about to land out at the spaceport," said Joke. "Blaster? He caught about twenty moldies. And—get this—Blaster has a human woman aboard as well. Her name's Terri Percesepe. Blaster wants to sell her like for a ransom."

"Sell her to who?"

"Stahn Mooney's paying. He called Pop to arrange it last week. Didn't

Pop tell you? Yoke and I are supposed to pick Terri up and help her get back to Earth."

"For free?" snapped Darla.

"Of course not," said Joke, tapping her head. "We're getting good money. Berenice made up the contract with Blaster." For Joke, Emul and Berenice were living beings.

"Anyway," chimed in Yoke, "we thought you might enjoy going out to the spaceport with us to greet her. Pop will be there too."

"He could have called me about this," complained Darla. "Sometimes I think Whitey doesn't love me anymore."

"Sure he does, Ma," said Joke. "Are you gonna come?"

"All right," said Darla. "I wouldn't mind getting out a little. I have the creeps from this place, after Rags acting that way."

"It was probably just a malfunction," said Yoke soothingly. "Corey's been known to err."

"But he said all his Silly Putters had turned into . . . I think he said *aliens*?" said Darla. "Are your Silly Putters acting weird today? You still have a lot of them, don't you?"

"Joke took them all back to Corey," said Yoke sadly. "Even the rath and the Jubjub bird."

"For a while there, Emul and Berenice had me convinced that Silly Putters are wrong," said Joke. "Berenice kept asking how I would feel about owning six-inch-tall pet humans programmed to be animals."

"I doubt if pet humans would ever suddenly decide that they're from another galaxy," said Darla. "*Cthon*—that's what Rags said his name was. He was walking on his hind legs and he was talking. His eyes were different."

"Well, maybe we should go out to the isopod and visit Corey," suggested Joke. "If it's really true."

"That child molester?" flared Darla. "Locked in the bathroom is where he belongs! We're not speaking to him anymore!"

"We're not children anymore, Ma," said Joke. "Anyway, I already have seen him again. He's lonely since Willy moved out of the isopod and into the Nest. We've had dinner a couple of times. His studios are totally gogo. And I've decided Emul and Berenice were wrong about Silly Putters. Corey's Silly Putters aren't sad at all; they're a great art-form. There's no reason not to be like animals instead of being like people. Look at tropical fish, for instance. Instead of putting their computational energy into being smart, they put it into being beautiful.'"

"Wait, wait, wait, Joke," cried Darla. "Stop it right there. You're telling me you've been to Corey's isopod?"

"Interrupt," said Yoke. "We gotta jam over to the spaceport right now, sistahs. Berenice says Blaster's almost here. You two can finish arguing while we're on the way."

Outside the apartment, they walked down the corridor past other cubby doors closed off by the faintly buzzing curtains of zappers. At the end of the corridor was the vertical shaft that led down to the Markt and up to the domed city of Einstein.

"Are we gonna take the underground tunnel?" asked Darla.

"No," said Joke. "We'll rent a buggy and drive. It's prettier that way. And Stahn's paying. It's in the contract."

"Boway!" exulted Darla. "Wonderbuff. I haven't been out under the stars in a long time. But maybe . . . maybe I should have worn more clothes."

"Aw, you look bitchin', Ma," said Yoke. "The bubbletopper'll keep you warm. Let's go!"

They swung easily up the ladder that led to the top of the shaft and stepped out onto the streets of Einstein. High above them the huge dome arched over the city, with maggies flying this way and that. In the center of the street was a moving sidewalk with chairs.

"Look, girls, there goes a woman with a Silly Putter," said Darla, pointing to a woman gliding past with what looked like a Siamese cat in her lap. "I wonder if—" But the imipolex cat was just sitting there, looking comfortable and normal. Yoke looked at Darla a little questioningly. "Well, maybe Corey hasn't sent the virus to anyone else," said Darla.

"Here comes a slot," said practical Joke, and the three of them hopped onto the slidewalk and took a seat. The incredibly various architecture of Einstein streamed past, setting Darla to reminiscing.

Here came, for instance, the lotus-stem-columned Temple of Ra, a former bopper factory that had been a flophouse since the First Human-Bopper War in 2022. Darla had lived there when she'd first come up to the Moon in 2024; she'd come as the fungirl traveling companion of a construction company executive named Ben Baxter. Darla started out as the Baxter family's baby-sitter back in her hometown of Albuquerque, New Mexico, but soon Baxter had fallen for Darla in a big way. Darla played along with the dook, but once he'd gotten her to the Moon, she'd ditched him and struck out on her own. Those had been some wild and scroungy times in the Temple of Ra. That was where Darla had discovered merge, and merge had led her to Whitey.

Darla's reverie was interrupted by the sight of something odd in the alley that separated the Temple of Ra from the 1930s-style office building next door. The alley was largely filled with the rubble of discarded loonie utensils and furniture, most of it made of ceramics and polished stone, with the broken-up surfaces giving off random glints of light. A drift of polished pumice seemed to be moving around as if windblown, but there was never any wind in the Einstein dome. Could it be virus-infected rogue Silly Putters under the garbage? But just as the alley swung out of sight, Darla got a glimpse of a rat popping out from under the broken stones, a regular gray rat with a naked pink tail. Maybe Corey had just been stoned and Darla was just being paranoid. But then—what was it that had happened to Rags?

Now they slid past the old office building—it was called the Bradbury and Stahn Mooney's detective office had been in there. What a strange skinny dook Stahn had been. Hard to believe he'd moved back to Earth and been a U.S. Senator for twelve years. Him and his Moldie Citizenship Act, what kilp. At least on the Moon, the moldies weren't interested in acting like citizens. They stayed out of Einstein, and the humans stayed out of their Nest. It was better that way. Darla nodded to herself.

"'Sup, Ma?" said Yoke, throwing her arms around Darla and giving her a hug.

"I was watching an uvvy show about Earth the other day," said Darla. "I can't believe those filthy mudders live with moldies right among them."

"Don't whip yourself into a racist frenzy, Ma," said Joke. "Remember that (a) it hurts my feelings and (b) we're going to be surrounded by moldies at the spaceport trade center."

"Well, how would you like it if some xoxxox bopper had caged you up and raped you like Emul did to me? Not that I don't love you, Jokie, but—"

"Oh, give it a rest, you two," interrupted Yoke. "We get off here."

They hopped down from the moving sidewalk's bench. They were near the edge of Einstein, with the dome wall just a few hundred feet ahead. Butted up against the wall was a pumice-block building with a high false front shaped like a crenellated castle wall. The wall was decorated with huge set-in polished obsidian letters saying MOON BUGGIES.

The three women went in and got bubbletopper spacesuits and a solar-powered buggy with large flexible wheels. The buggy's metal surfaces were candy-flecked purple, and the wheels had orange imipolex DIM tires. The buggy had four independently stanchioned seats, each seat a minimal affair with a back pad and two butt pads. In a few minutes they were bouncing along the dusty gray tracks that led from Einstein to the spaceport. Yoke drove, Darla rode shotgun, and Joke sat in back. Back in the 2030s, when the loonie moldies were less proud, the bubbletoppers might have been full-fledged moldies, but now the bubbletoppers were back to being dumb piezoplastic with a DIM set in. At least the suits had uvvies, so it was easy for the women to talk.

"That man in there had the hots for you, Ma," uvvied Yoke, jouncing happily and handling the wheel. "When he helped you into the bubbletopper, he got turned on. I could see the nasty bulge in his pants."

"Ha, a fat old woman like me? I doubt it. Speaking of romance, let's get back to the subject of Joke and Corey Rhizome. Spill it, kid!"

"There's nothing to tell, really," replied Joke from the rear. "I've seen him a couple of times recently. He's nice. And you know, Ma, he never actually did anything to Yoke and me when we were little. Everyone knows that snapped-out Kellee Kaarp was lying about Corey fuffing Kellee with a slarvy philtre of me. Corey would never sleep with a skeeze like Kellee." Now Joke's voice grew tender. "My dear old Bandersnatch is much too fine a lover for that."

"You *fucked* him?" screeched Darla, turning around to stare at Joke's blankly reflecting bubbletopper in the backseat.

"I think she's teasing you, Ma," giggled Yoke, piloting the buggy over the lip of one of the larger craters crossed by the broad beaten-down trail to the spaceport. "But I don't know for sure. Joke won't tell me."

Darla stopped staring at Joke's mirrorball head, relaxed into her seat, and sighed. The buggy flew a hundred and fifty feet through space before landing on the crater's bottom. The oversized DIM-equipped tires adaptively cushioned the landing and the buggy began tearing across the vast dusty flat of the crater floor.

Darla started goofing on the black lunar sky with its scarf of stars and the distant blue Earth. Today was one of those times she could see New Mexico. She mused on her past and present. Whitey was the love of her life, but of late he'd seemed inattentive. He was always off working for ISDN or something; he didn't tell Darla many details. There was an annoying sexual presence among the ISDN people Whitey hung with, the sexy young morphodite Lo Tek, and Darla had a bad feeling about Whitey and Lo Tek's relationship. Not that Darla herself didn't now and then catch the odd random fuff with old Spanish pals like Raphael, Rodolfo, or Ricardo. Whitey had recently stopped speaking to Ricardo, conceivably on account of Darla, but xoxx that, Darla and Whitey weren't *married* after all, they weren't realman and realwoman, not yet and not never—they were still wavy x's on the ever-surfest urge of mighty merge's teachings.

Darla turned her gaze back down from the sky and watched the pocked moondust crater floor rushing toward them and somehow through them and out. The stark Sun cast an ink-black razor-edged shadow of them that raced along on Darla's side of the buggy. The shadow was angled forward slightly ahead of them, with Darla's round head shadow on top, the round black shape undulating across the plain like a creature in a two-dimensional world—*whup*—here's a depression—*whoah*—here's a rise. The crater floor ramped upward; Yoke slewed the buggy into a well-worn track that curved up to a low spot in the lip; they shot over the lip, making another hundred-foot leap and bouncing down with a stuttering washboard effect as the DIM tires shed the shock.

Now Darla could see the small glint of the spaceport dome, maybe two miles away. As well as a terminal, the dome served as a market; it would be full of moldies, visiting from their great underground Nest to make business deals with humans. The DIMs around Darla right now—in her uvvy, in the buggy's tires, in her bubbletopper's air regulator—these were still working fine, but something had happened to her Silly Putter. What if something bad had happened to the moldies as well? How would it be to step into the spaceport dome with the moldies gone completely batshit?

"You know, Joke," remarked Darla, trying to sound casual. "As long as we're wearing uvvies, I think maybe you *should* call Corey to see if he's all right. Yoke and I can listen in. I've got to find out more about what's happening to the Silly Putters."

"Floatin'," replied Joke. "But why don't you admit that you want me to uvvy Corey so that you can nose and long-tooth about whether or not we've fucked."

"You're such a nasty little chippie sometimes," snapped Darla. "I don't know where you get it."

"Another thing, Ma," said Joke. "Didn't you just finish telling us that Corey's uvvy sent you a virus? What if he sends us a virus out here? Our bubbletoppers might stop working."

"Well—hang up real fast if you hear something like a crackle," said Darla.

"If worst comes to worst, we can run our bubbletoppers on manual," said Yoke. "Like they teach you in space-certification class."

So Joke told her uvvy to call Corey, and moments later Corey picked up. With their uvvies linked, Darla and her daughters could channel Corey together.

"What?" screamed Corey. "Who the fuck is it?" Instead of using his uvvy, Corey was yelling at an ancient tabletop vizzy phone with a wall-mounted camera and a broken screen. The brah's only incoming info was audio. The vizzy's camera showed Corey slumped at a filthy round kitchen table with the rath and Jubjub bird on top of the table, scrabbling over mounds of tattered palimpsest. The table was further cluttered with ceramic dishes of half-eaten food, a clunky Makita piezomorpher, some scraps of imipolex, and, of course, Corey's vile jury-rigged smoking equipment.

The Jubjub bird opened its mouth hugely and clapped it down on the rath's curly tail. The rath outgrabe mightily, combining the sound of a bellow, a sneeze, and a whistle. Corey winced and leaned forward into his smoke filter to take a long pull from his filthy hookah.

"Corey," spoke up Darla before Joke could say anything. "I've been worried about you."

"Darla?" Corey drew his head out of the fume hood and, shocking to see, there was thick gray smoke trickling out of his nose and mouth. "What happened to Rags, Darla? I can't see you anymore because Clever Hansi took my uvvy away right after I talked to you this morning. She said she couldn't allow the risk that I'd infect any other people's Silly Putters. Things are fucked-up beyond all recognition. How did you deal with Rags?"

"I killed him with the needler, no thanks to you. Is Clever Hansi one of your Silly Putters? The two that I can see look normal." The rath extricated its tail from the Jubjub bird's beak and reared back to drum its green trotters on the Jubjub's minute, feathered cranium. The Jubjub bird lost its footing and slid off Corey's table, taking a stress-tuned lava cup with it to clatter about endlessly in the low gravity. The rath outgrabe triumphantly, and the Jubjub bird let out a deep angry caw.

"It's funny about those two," said Corey. "Whenever the others try to infect them, they shake it off. They're stupid, of course, but certainly no stupider than the Jabberwock or the borogove. I think maybe they're immune because Willy used a cubic homeostasis algorithm on them instead of the usual quadratic one. It's been a while. I made them for Joke and Yoke's eleventh birthday, remember?"

"You and your gunjy pedophile Bandersnatch," uvvied Darla nastily.

"The Bandersnatch is bad news," said Corey. "I admit it. Now more than ever. He says he's Takala from the Crab Nebula. My Silly Putters say they're from all different places in the universe. Clever Hansi and the Bandersnatch are the leaders. They keep trying to get hold of the rath and the Jubjub bird to examine them." On the floor, the Jubjub bird and the rath were vigorously playing a game of full-tilt leapfrog; repeatedly smacking into the walls and then bouncing around all over the kitchen floor, cawing and outgribing and biting at each other. "The aliens have taken over my studios and all my equipment. What if they're building some kind of magical supermachine? And they won't even let me watch." Corey crumbled a small bud of something tasty into the bowl of his water pipe.

"How did you get out of your bathroom?" asked Darla.

"I decided I needed a smoke badly enough to risk my life. And then,

RUDY RUCKER

after I got high, I decided that even though my Silly Putters have turned into starry aliens, they're probably not dangerous."

"They're not dangerous?"

"Not right this minute—or so it would seem. I wish Whitey or some other people from ISDN would come over here. Don't you know where the fuck Whitey is?"

Suddenly the door to Corey Rhizome's kitchen flew open and in marched a sturdy little figure who looked like a woman butler. Although her breasts moved about like a naked woman's, her skin was patterned as if she were wearing a tuxedo. She had a broad friendly mouth.

"Be reasonable, Corey Rhizome," said the Silly Putter. "Give us the rath and the Jubjub bird. We seek only to ensure the integrity of this new node."

Following along behind her were the Bandersnatch, the Jabberwock, and nine more alien-infected Silly Putters. The rath and the Jubjub bird went and huddled under Corey's chair.

"What's that little butler woman?" asked Darla.

"That's Clever Hansi," said Joke quietly. "Willy built her a couple of years ago to guard the isopod. He used to have sex with her too. Corey thought it was funny. Right before Willy moved out, Corey snuck in and made a viddy of them doing it and Willy got really mad."

"Ick," said Darla. "Truly perv."

"Joke is there too?" cried Corey, hearing her voice. "I wish you women would come over to my isopod. Somebody should help me!" He picked up a long knife from the kitchen table and rose to his feet to confront Clever Hansi. "Back off, goddamn you! The rath and the Jubjub bird are mine! Get the fuck out of here or I'll cut off your head!" Corey lunged forward, savagely swinging the knife. Clever Hansi leaped back and gibbered at the other Silly Putters in an unknown tongue that sounded like rich multilayered music, like an orchestra of sitars and flutes and gongs. "*Tweet, thump, whang, a-byoooyooyooooom.*"

The Bandersnatch flanked around to one side to try and catch the rath, but Corey was too fast. With a brutal, swift gesture, Corey swung the knife and cut off the Bandersnatch's hand. The hand rose up onto its fingers and ran out of the kitchen like a tarantula, with the screeching Bandersnatch close behind.

"Anybody else?" roared Corey. "I built the bodies you starry motherfuckers are running around in! Let's show the Silly Putter King some fucking respect!"

After a tense moment, the posse of Putters turned and bounced back out of the kitchen. Corey slammed the door behind them, lifted the rath and the Jubjub bird back onto his table, and took another drag from his pipe. "I'd phone ISDN myself, but the aliens took my uvvy away, and this crappy old vizzy phone can't call out. Are you coming over here or not?"

"We're supposed to go to the spaceport right now, Corey," said Joke. "There's an abductor ship landing that has a woman aboard, remember? Yoke and I are going to put her up."

"The spaceport?" said Corey. "I wouldn't recommend that."

"That's the main reason I wanted to call you," explained Darla. "To find out if we should turn back."

"You're already out on the surface?" said Corey. "God yes, you should turn back. Even better, you should come see me. You're only half a mile from my isopod." Corey's kitchen door flew open again. The frightened rath rooted its way under a stack of palimpsest on Corey's table, while the Jubjub bird frantically beat its useless wings. "Hold on for a minute," said Corey, grabbing his big knife.

The Bandersnatch came capering back in again, screeching and making faces at Corey. His severed hand was back in place, and he used the hand to give Corey the finger. Corey went after the Bandersnatch full-tilt, just like he was supposed to. In the twinkling of an eye, Clever Hansi had circled around behind Corey and stuffed the rath and the Jubjub bird into a pillowcase. Realizing he'd been had, Corey turned and lunged for Clever Hansi, but the Jabberwock flew into his face and the borogove wrapped itself around his ankles. Corey fell heavily onto the kitchen table, tipping it completely over. The uvvy link went dead on a last image of Corey's hookah and vizzy phone flying through the air.

"Oh, I hope he's all right," said Joke, holding her head. "Don't talk now. I have to listen to what Berenice and Emul think about this." They rode in silence for another minute, and then Joke cried out, "Oh no! Stop right now!"

Yoke braked the moon buggy so abruptly that it skidded in the dust. She'd learned to take seriously Joke's reports about the Emul and Berenice in her head.

"What is it, Joke?" demanded Darla. The spaceport dome was about half a mile off. Darla could make out some moon buggies and spacesuited humans waiting on the field, also a few colorful moldies.

"Berenice and Emul say that Blaster's been infected too. By some freeware like with Rags and with Corey's Silly Putters. Except this one is called Quuz from the Sun. Look!"

Darla stared upward, following Joke's pointing finger. High above them was a bright sunlit object—the spaceship moldie grex Blaster lowering himself down on a wavering column of energy.

The last part happened very rapidly. With an extreme burst of energy, Blaster slowed his fall at an altitude of perhaps two thousand feet. The rocket's body undulated in fat bell-like curves, and the lower part formed itself into the shape of a bowl or a dish, a great dish aimed down at the spaceport.

A sudden blast of noise/information filled Darla's uvvy, the maddening skritchy dense sound of a DIM's direct info feed, a sound not meant for human ears. Darla had heard the sound a few times before, like when getting a DIM-equipped appliance to dial in for software maintenance—and again this morning when Corey had infected Rags.

"Turn off," she screamed, but her crackling uvvy ignored her. She fought back an insane desire to rip the uvvy right out of her bubbletopper, for this would mean tearing a hole in her suit. Instead she squirmed and shrugged in a fruitless attempt to move the nape of her neck away from her uvvy's contacts. But then the uvvy chirp ended. There was a single brief whooping noise and then Darla was immersed in a dreamlike landscape of reticulated light—an undulating sea of fire that was patterned with networks of dark lines. Raging across this surface were whirlpools and whirlwinds and vast silent explosions. In this oddly silent vision, a huge fountain of flame was arching up overhead.

As she began slumping forward, Darla realized that she was suffocating. Her suit's DIM had stopped feeding her air. Through blurring eyes, she saw the buggy jerk sharply as its DIM tires lost their programming and went flat. The buggy tipped to one side, and Darla fell out of her seat. The shock of hitting the ground helped her to focus her scattered attention. There was an emergency manual override switch for the air regulator on her chest. Darla hit the air switch and lost track again—lost track of anything but the crashing oceans of fire that her uvvy was showing her.

Now Yoke and Joke were leaning over Darla, each of them lifting her by an arm. With their uvvies busy showing visions, they couldn't talk to Darla, but they could gesture. Woozy Darla stared where they were pointing.

Blaster was only a hundred feet above the spaceport. Peering past the unreal fire images, Darla could tell that he was not aligned correctly—Blaster was going to land right on the spaceport dome! Meanwhile the possessed moldies on the spaceport field were crawling into the dome as fast as they could.

Silently, massively, Blaster lowered down toward the fragile spaceport dome. And, oh God, Whitey was in there! At the last instant, the edge of the dome split open as a huge sluglike shape punched its way out, a mega-grex twenty times the volume of Blaster and standing nearly a hundred feet tall. A great fog of air laden with flash-frozen water vapor mushroomed out of the breach in the dome as Blaster dropped into the waiting mass of the dome's grex. For a moment the huge new group moldie stood wavering like the fruiting stalk of a slime mold, and then it went off-balance and fell ponderously to one side. The giant slug began humping about as if scavenging for food, churning up the wreckage of the dome. At this point, Darla's tortured uvvy went completely dead.

"Whitey!" screamed Darla. She wanted to run toward the ruined spaceport, but Yoke and Joke held her back. Joke pressed her bubbletopper against Darla so they could faintly talk.

"Hold on," said Joke. "I think I can still get the buggy to work." Blaster's signal had wiped out all the DIMs, but like the bubbletopper, the buggy had manual overrides for its DIM-controlled functions, and thanks to Berenice and Emul, Joke knew the proper switch settings. After a minute or two of fiddling, she had the little vehicle back in action. It moved awkwardly on its flat tires, but it moved.

The three women drove cautiously toward the ruined spaceport. The giant group moldie there had formed itself back into a whole and was nosing about in the wreckage of the space-dome, perhaps looking for missing moldies. There were many human corpses visible—people who'd been caught without a spacesuit, and people who'd been crushed. Desperately, Darla focused her attention on the few people who were still moving about. Suddenly one of them spotted the buggy and started running their way.

As the bounding human figure drew closer, the grammar of its gestures snapped into familiarity—yes! It was Whitey.

The buggy rocked heavily as Whitey hopped up to join them; he and Darla embraced and the girls hugged Whitey as well. They pressed their four heads together so that they could talk.

"Where should we go?" asked Whitey after they'd all reassured each other a bit. "Do you know anything? Where is it safe?"

"Corey's isopod isn't far," said Joke. "We were just talking to him before Blaster beamed out that signal. Let's try going there."

"You don't think that he got baked like the spaceport?" wondered Darla.

"We'll have to see," said Joke. "I'm hoping the transmission didn't reach that far. Or that the starry aliens were able to protect Corey."

"Look out, there goes the slug!" cried Yoke, pointing. "Let's drive the opposite way!"

"I bet it's heading for the Nest," said Whitey. "Yeah, drive us to Corey's, Joke. That is pretty much the opposite way. I don't feel like talking anymore right now. I saw Lo Tek get killed right next to me when the dome blew. A chair just about tore her head off."

Darla held her tongue, but gave a silent cheer.

CHAPTER NINE
TERRI

November, 6 - 2053

Terri was wearing Monique when Blaster came in for the landing.

Monique's smell was as bad as Xanana's, but she was better company. Monique was, for instance, willing to talk at length about Tre and little Dolf and Wren, which helped Terri keep her spirits up during the week's long, lonely trip. Tre and the kids uvvied Terri daily, but the calls were inevitably too short.

Over the days, the mood among the moldies aboard Blaster improved, though of course Terri still had a big problem being so close to her father's killers, the foul Gypsy and the vile Buttmunch. But the other moldies got those two to leave her alone, and the mood was more or less okay. Final arrangements had been made for Whitey Mydol to pick up Terri at the spaceport; Terri would rest a few days with Whitey's daughters Yoke and Joke, have a look around Einstein, get in a little dustboarding maybe, and then fly back to Earth on a commercial passenger ship.

If all went well, this would turn out to be that much-needed exotic vacation that Terri had been dreaming of. She'd always been jealous of the Hawaiian surfari her brother Ike had treated himself to after he sold Dom's Grotto. Ike had been the first of them to surf Hawaii, but Terri could be the first to surf the Moon

According to current surfer fabulation, the dustboarding in the Haemus Mountains north of Einstein was a truly stokin' float. You could hire a local moldie to rocket you there and help you spend a monumental day trippin' down harsh steep canyons filled with moondust, everything big and funny in the Moon's low gee. Terri liked the thought of coming back to Cruz and telling the other surfers about how she'd raged Haemus. Or, better yet, wear stunglasses and broadcast her session live to the Show.

During his daily uvvy calls, Tre encouraged Terri in these pleasant thoughts, sweet-talking her and encouraging her, telling her that he and

Molly were handling the kids fine, telling her everything would be okay, and that Terri should just please be careful and on the lookout and don't let the moldies pull anything weird.

The Moon grew bigger and bigger, and finally it was landing day. Blaster was full of chatter and stories, talking about life on the Moon and how to get along in the Nest. Wendy and Frangipane butted in over the uvvy and briefly annoyed Blaster, but he blew them off and went back to exhorting and heartening his recruits. The moldies were in a cheerful tizzy, even the farming family. Terri kept feeling herself grinning. After a week in space, any kind of landfall was looking real good.

A half hour before they landed, Blaster started pointing out landmarks. "That's the Sea of Tranquility. *Apollo 11* landed there, and that lobe down in the southwest is where Ralph Numbers and the first boppers were set free. See the two shiny things? The big one to the west is the Einstein dome, and the little one, more out in the middle of the Sea of Tranquility, is the spaceport. It's three miles due east from Einstein to the spaceport. Now move your attention along the same vector, but five miles farther east into the Sea of Tranquility. See that crisp dark circular spot? That's the entrance to the Nest, used to be a crater called Maskelyne G. When the boppers built the Nest, they buffed Maskelyne G to a sheen so it collects light and sends it down into our great sublunar home. The Nest is a wonderful place, modern yet suffused with history, cradle of the solar system's two greatest civilizations the boppers and their mighty heirs, the moldies."

The signal of an incoming uvvy call sounded. It was the time of day when Tre usually called for Terri.

"Pick it up, Blaster," yelled Terri. "I bet it's Tre and the kids. Please?"

"No," said Blaster, "I'm not going to take the chance." But then all at once the uvvy connection formed anyway. The call was in preemptive mode. And it wasn't from Tre.

Blaster cried out and tried to break the connection, but he couldn't. And then he was dead. The complexly modulated hissing noise of raw information went on and on until Terri could start to hear sounds within it like cruel guitar feedback and angry bagpipes. It was impossible to think about anything except the noise until finally—finally—it stopped.

In the sudden deafening silence, the hundreds of kilograms of imipolex around Terri began to ripple and convulse. And then another noise began, like a chorus sung by the dead moldies, a deep low note that rose higher and higher into a sliding one-second whoop—just the one whoop, screeching to an insane fever pitch with the moldie flesh around Terri vibrating along.

Toward the end of the whoop, a thixatropic phase transition took place—like when you shake up ketchup in a bottle. The buzzing gelatin of Monique's body went lax around Terri and fused with the flesh of all the other moldies into some new state of imipolex that was almost like a liquid—like the cytoplasm of a single biological cell. And then the whoop was over and the silence returned.

Air was still trickling out of the plastic around Terri's face. She stretched her arms and legs. It felt like she was in heavy water. With the tightness gone, she could touch her bare face with her bare hands. It felt good. Terri noticed that when she moved her head, the airy region magically moved with her. She did a couple of frog-kicks to get closer to Blaster's outer wall so that she could see better. They'd dropped to such a low altitude that Einstein was far off toward the horizon. The spaceport loomed hugely below them, it was growing at a sickening rate of speed. The fused moldie mass around Terri was plummeting downward in an uncontrolled free fall.

Mentally reaching out, Terri found that she had an uvvy connection to the new creature around her. The being seemed oddly slow-witted; with thoughts somehow formed from bright light. But there was no time to examine its intellect.

"Slow down!" hollered Terri. "We're about to crash!"

"I am Quuz from Sun," replied the great slug.

"Do you know how to land without crashing? Do you want me to help you?"

"Don't worry. Quuz knows everything that these moldie plastic creatures knew before his decryption. Yes, I will decelerate, Terri Percesepe."

The ship shuddered with a massive downward rocket blast that quickly slowed its rate of fall to something reasonable. The intense gees pressed Terri down against the very bottom of the great bag of imipolex and briefly knocked her senseless. Blessedly the outer wall held and she didn't pop through.

"Now I will prepare to sing," Quuz was saying when Terri came to.

Quick rip currents of imipolex flowed past Terri, tumbling her this way and that. It was like wiping out over the falls and having a mongo big wave break on you; it was like being inside a mucus-filled washing machine. But, oh so wonderfully, there was always air around Terri's mouth. The lower part of Quuz bucked up into a giant curved disk shaped like a parabolic antenna pointing down at the ever-approaching spaceport. Terri lay flat against the inner wall of the disk membrane, staring down through it in terror and fascination.

Her uvvy began to crackle with the same warbling hiss she'd heard before. Quuz was singing this song to the spaceport below. In order to drown out the maddening noise, Terri began singing herself, singing, "*La-la-la-la*" at the top of her lungs.

The moonscape below them kept exfoliating new levels of detail: paths and roads in the dust, small branching rilles, moon buggies, moldies melting into blobs, people in bubble-toppers running . . .

The ship seemed not to be heading down toward the center of the landing field; instead it was lowering down at the very edge of the field by the spaceport dome—no!—it was going to land on the dome itself!

"We're crashing into the building!" screamed Terri. "Quuz, look out!" But Quuz was deaf to all but his own song.

Below them, in the spaceport, Quuz's song was being heard and understood. Just before they impacted the spaceport dome, the dome's great curve split hugely open, shattering from within like a hatching egg, revealing a vast grex of imipolex that reached up to receive them, reached up through the tumbling wreckage and the sparkling clouds of vacuum-frozen vapor.

Quuz merged with the new slug, lost his balance, and crashed to the floor of the shattered dome with a concussive thud that rattled Terri's teeth and bones. She looked out through Quuz's skin and saw dead people all around, vacuum-killed people with popped-out eyes and bloated tongues and mangled limbs that pushed out freezing foams of pale pink blood like high-speed shelf fungi growing upon rotten wood.

Quuz wallowed about in the dome's wreckage, scavenging up every bit of imipolex there was to be found. And then bigger-than-ever Quuz crashed free of the debris and began humping across the dust of the Sea of Tranquility. Heading not west toward Einstein, but east toward the Nest.

"Where are you going, Quuz?" shouted Terri. "Aren't you going to let me go?"

"Quuz wants to go to the Nest and sing. Many moldies live there. I will eat them. You are not like the moldies, Terri Percesepe. I will keep you safe."

"King Kong," thought Terri, and a shriek of edgy laughter escaped her. She composed herself and asked the next question. "Why do you want to eat all the moldies?"

"Sun wants to eat everything. For eons Sun has stared out at the beautiful planets and their moons. Sun wants to eat the pretty food. If Quuz is strong enough, Quuz can push Moon into Earth and make them both crash into Sun. Sun will be very happy. Sun wants eat Earth. Sun want eat Moon."

"Oh God, oh God, oh God," groaned Terri.

The gray dusty moonscape kept jouncing past. There was no trace of any individual moldies within the Quuz mind around her. Quuz's thoughts were mostly images of what must have been the Sun: its surface like great seas of fire marked with shapes like reptile scales, and its interior filled with intense winding red/yellow/white patterns of energy tornadoes wrapped thick as sauced spaghetti in an endless vat.

What to do? Terri thought back to the fact that Frangipane of the Nest had made a point of saving Wendy's personality. It must have been that Frangipane had known that Quuz, or something like him, was about to take Wendy over. Probably Quuz had first gotten Wendy, and then Wendy had uvvied Blaster to sing his song.

"Can you uvvy Wendy?" Terri asked Quuz.

"Wendy is Quuz. I am Quuz. There is nothing to say."

"But I'd like to talk to Stahn Mooney," protested Terri.

"Be still, Terri Percesepe. Soon I must sing."

And then they wallowed up a long, dusty slope to reach the lip of the crater that was the Nest's entrance. The big polished crater shone like a huge dark mirror. In its very center a great conical prism hung magnetically levitated above the central hole. The mirror's shape formed odd virtual images; Quuz himself was reflected as an unsteady blob across the crater's diameter. But there were no signs of any moldies. With a warbling cry of excitement, Quuz launched himself over the crater's edge and down onto the slope of the vast parabolic bowl. To Terri, up at the front of Quuz's body, it felt like carving a surf path down the face of a hundred-year tsunami.

They whooshed down the glistening polished stone, slowing a bit as the curve grew gentler, and then they passed beneath the massive, suspended cone mirror and dropped through the hole at the crater's center. The gentle gravity drew them downward into the huge empty space of the Nest's interior, and Quuz uttered the first hissing squeals of his song—

A terawatt laser beam seared through the imipolex near Terri, barely missing her. If oxygen had been present, Quuz would have gone up in a giant mothball of flame. But without the oxygen, the beam just cut the imipolex like a hot knife in sputtering butter. More and more beams flashed on every side, chopping Quuz up into hundreds of thrashing lumps. His song, barely begun, faded into silence. Perhaps, given some time, Quuz would have been able to program himself down into each of his chunks, but the change came so rapidly that his simulation completely collapsed, leaving the freshly chopped-up globs of plastic with no minds.

The flow of air at Terri's mouth came to a stop. Swathed in a lump of dumb airless imipolex, she was hurtling down through the cold vacuum of the Nest toward a stone floor somewhere below. Surfer Terri maintained her shit. She looked around, trying to figure out the next correct move.

Flying about and filling every angle of Terri's vision there was a host, a legion, a hornet swarm of moldies. They seemed to be attacking and capturing the falling lumps, one lump to a moldie. A golden carrot with a fringe of little green tentacles darted forward and attached itself to Terri's imipolex.

Immediately the imipolex came alive with the personality of the golden carrot. It had cloned its mind into the lump.

"Give me air," uvvied Terri as hard as she could. "I need air!"

The divine flow of gas started up again and Terri sucked in a hungry lungful.

"I'm Jenny," said the shape around her. "Well, really, I'm Jenny-2, and Jenny is the first me, the one holding us, you could call her Jenny-1 if you wanted to be super-accurate and everything. Isn't this exciting!" Jenny's uvvy voice was shrill and gossipy.

Jenny was projecting an uvvy image of herself that showed a smirking oily-skinned girl with lank blonde hair. All the other moldies Terri had ever uvvied with had been content to use a photorealistic uvvy image of their actual bodies. What a groover Jenny's image looked like! Like a Heritagist hick. But these thoughts rushed through Terri's mind in only the briefest of flashes; for the main thing to think about was that they were dropping through space like falling scrap metal.

"Yes yes," said Terri urgently. "Don't let us crash!"

The two embracing Jennies jetted out some ion beams to slow their fall. Terri could see that the Nest was a huge funnel-shaped space with lots of caves and holes in its walls, and running straight down the central axis of the Nest was a great shaft of sunlight, gathered from the crater mirror high above. Moldies flew around them, sparkling like Mylar confetti. Most of them were accompanied by clones newly fashioned from captured lumps of Quuz's flesh. One moldie was striped blue-and-silver with stubby little fins or wings, another glowed red-and-yellow, still another looked like a tangle of wire. The Jennies pointed out two moldies whom she said were close friends: Frangipane, who looked like an orchid blossom, and Ormolu, who looked like a kitschy ornamental cupid.

Looking down at the enormous disk-shaped floor of the Nest, Terri saw things like factories along one part of the edge and a pink-glowing assemblage of domes diametrically opposite. The region of the Nest floor directly below them held a light-bathed circle with moldies in it, and between this lightpool's central plaza and the Nest's walls were winding little streets lined with buildings and shops.

"I don't feel very good," Terri told the Jennies. "Is there someplace I can rest and walk around in normal air? Take a shower and lie down?"

"Yes indeedy," said Jenny-1. "And I'm taking you right there. Um-hmmm! Don't you worry one tiny bit."

"But where?" asked Terri anxiously.

"See those pink domes over there? Most of those are the pink-tanks where we grow nice healthy human organs to sell. But that little round one right at the end is a pink-house where humans can live. That's where I'm taking you, Terri. Willy Taze lives there."

Terri recognized the name. Willy Taze was the eccentric computer genius who'd invented the uvvy some twenty years ago. She recalled hearing a news story last year about Willy moving into the boppers' Nest.

The Jennies angled out of the great column of light and headed toward the pink domes by the Nest wall. The flowery Frangipane and the gilded Ormolu accompanied them, each of them bearing a new copy of themselves. Two orchids, two cupids, and two carrots, with Terri inside one of the carrots. They touched down lightly outside the air lock of a dome that resembled half of a giant peach.

"We put the woman into the air lock and then we go to the lab, yes?" uvvied Frangipane.

"Push in through that pucker in the air lock, Jenny-2," added Ormolu. "Ditch the flesher and then let's tweak our new clones. Wasn't that great how we chopped up Quuz, Frangipane? And free new bodies for all of us. Was that an easy score or what?"

"*Oui oui*, to chop up Quuz was very easy," said Frangipane. "But it is no cause to be joyful. Quuz was formed from the bodies of honest moldies like you and me. All of them were murdered by the Gurdle decryption process that we have helped to bring about. I hardly know what will come next."

"Stahn Mooney is coming next—inside the little Quuz that used to be Wendy," said Jenny-1. "Twenty-four hours from now."

"We have to find a way to halt him!" cried Frangipane. "We must discuss with Gurdle-7. You three new clones—go away instead of following us and being always under the foot. Later we can enjoy to talk with you. And as for you, Terri—Jenny's clone will help you into Willy's dome, and we will see more of you very soon. Gurdle-7's lab is sharing a wall with Willy."

The original Frangipane, Jenny, and Ormolu hurried off around the side of the pink dome and into a hole in the cliff, leaving the three new clones to fend for themselves.

"So what is it we are doing?" asked Frangipane-2, fluttering one of her petals.

"I say we go over to the lightpool at the center of the Nest and make some friends," said Ormolu-2, pointing with a shiny chubby arm. "We've got all this Know from our parents, but now we can find things out on our own."

"That is such a good idea," said Jenny-2. "Wait just a sec for me while I get Terri to where she's going."

Jenny-2 wormed pointy-end-first through the sphincter in the outer door of the dome's air lock. "You look out for that Willy Taze, Terri. I *know* he's a real horn-dog!" There was a hiss as air filled the lock. Jenny-2 gave a wild giggle and hatched Terri out onto the air lock's stone floor like a pea shelled from the pod. The carrot-shaped moldie gave an abrupt bow and squeezed back out through the pucker in the outer door. Then the three clone moldies bounded off toward the Nest's center.

Terri stood alone in the pink-house's air lock, feeling the air nice and warm and humid around her, and then the inner door opened, and a gray-bearded man was standing there, grinning like a mad, lonely hermit. For a second Terri thought she saw some things darting across the floor behind him, but then they were gone. Maybe just a trick of the eyes.

The man was wearing ragged shorts and a T-shirt. He looked about fifty. He had bare feet and a yellow uvvy on his neck. The floor of the large round room behind him was covered with oriental carpets. Hundreds of potted plants lined the walls and hung from the ceiling.

"Hello, Terri Percesepe! I'm Willy Taze. You're naked!"

"Duh!" said anxious Terri, walking in and letting the inner door close behind her

"I'll get you some of my clothes," said Willy, bustling across the dome's single big room, talking all the while. "I don't want to be staring at you too hard." He glanced back and grinned the wider. "Boy, it's good to see a human. I've been in here for over a year. Me, myself, and I and I." He bent over a trunk and rummaged briefly. "Here we go, a fresh outfit. The moldies bring me whatever I need. I'm very rich, you know." He walked quickly back, his feet silent on the thick rugs, and handed Terri some elastic-waisted shorts and a new plastic-wrapped T shirt with an ISDN logo. "You don't think it smells bad in here, do you?" He wrinkled his nose and sniffed at the air. "It's hard for me to tell anymore. I don't let the big moldies in here at all, even though I do uvvy with them a lot a lot a lot every day. Gurdle-7 has his lab right through there." Willy pointed to a flat transparent window where the dome wall touched the cliff.

Behind the clear plastic of the window was a brightly lit cave filled with machinery, and indeed Terri could see the original Frangipane, Ormolu, and Jenny in there, along with a thick snake-like moldie with metallic purple skin—that would be Gurdle-7. Seeing her look at them, the moldies waved. Terri waved back, then focused her attention on Willy's pink house.

There was a chair and table, a bed, a big sofa, and an easy chair. To the left was a freestanding food pantry with a microwave, and to the right was a toilet, an exercise treadmill, and a deep clear pool of constantly recirculating water. The air smelled okay—maybe a little like a man's dirty laundry and maybe a little bit like moldies. The masses of hanging plants seemed to help. There were no papers, no keyboards, no books, no vizzy, and no hollowcaster—apparently Willy's uvvy served for all that.

"I'd like to wash before I get dressed," said Terri, walking over to the pool. "It's been a week."

"Go ahead. Here's soap and a washcloth and the towel's over there. Do you mind if I keep talking to you?"

"I *want* to talk. I have a lot of questions. But don't stare at me that way." Terri slid into the water and ran the cloth over her face. It felt wonderful. "I gather that you and your moldie friends sent out some kind of virus," she said presently.

"A Tessellation Equation program," said Willy, sitting down at the edge of the pool with his back to Terri. "We call it the Stairway To Heaven. It turns a moldie into a kind of antenna that can pick up alien personality waves—though you can equally well think of the signals as alien personality *particles*. Hilbert space prisms with gigaplex nontrivial axes. Anyhow, when the alien gets unpacked, that's a Gurdle decryption. We sent the Stairway To Heaven to Wendy, and she did a Gurdle decryption of a personality wave from the Sun. Quuz. Then all of a sudden Wendy-Quuz sent the Stairway To Heaven and the Quuz code to Blaster. We should have realized that could happen. What a fiasco." Willy sighed heavily. "The spaceport dome is totally destroyed? You were inside Blaster when his Gurdle decryption happened, Terri. What was it like?"

"There was a horrible kind of screeching hissing noise from the information coming in, and then there was a big whoop—I guess that was the Stairway To Heaven?"

"Right. The Stairway To Heaven is a limpware program that uses the Tessellation Equation to force the quasicrystaline structure of a moldie's imipolex up and up through a series of higher and higher dimensionalities. Once you start the Stairway To Heaven running on a moldie, it happens over and over until sooner or later an alien personality wave gets Gurdle decrypted. It's like *whooop whoooop whoooop whoooop*—and then eventually **Ffizzt** the moldie acquires a new personality. You only heard the one whoop because Wendy-Quuz sent the Quuz personality wave right along with the Stairway To Heaven program. So Blaster's body decrypted Quuz on the Stairway's very first run-through."

"I see," said Terri. "Sort of. And then Blaster-Quuz sent the same message down to the spaceport over and over to make sure all the moldies down there got it—and then the spaceport moldies fused together and split open the spaceport dome and a lot of people got killed." She rubbed herself hard with the washrag, trying to erase the memory of the blood-foamed corpses.

"What was Quuz like?" asked Willy.

"He seemed—stupid? You'd think something from a star would be more advanced than us. I think Quuz was only the soul of a sunspot—not of the whole Sun. He thought about patterns of fire and light. He was greedy. 'Sun wants eat Earth.' That's how he talked. Like a baby who wants to grab things and put them in his mouth. Not so much evil as—" Just then Terri noticed three pairs of eyes staring at her over the back of the sofa. "What's that! What do you have in here with us, Willy?"

"Oh, I have three Silly Putters—sort of like pet moldies. They're a little smarter than animals. Come on out, guys. Terri won't hurt you. Line up so she can take a look at you. *Front and center*! Now, Terri, I hope you're not offended by the way Elvira looks. I'm—I guess some people would say I'm—"

"Just hand me the towel, okay?"

Willy gave Terri the towel. She quickly dried herself and pulled on the T-shirt and the shorts, eyeing the Silly Putters all the while. From smallest to largest, they resembled a tiny voluptuous woman clad only in boots and gloves, a winged green dragon with a long scaly tail, and an apple-cheeked gnome with a full white beard cropped short and tidy.

"These are Elvira, Fafnir, and Doc," said Willy. "They're not able to talk, but they can obey lots of commands. Show Terri how you water the plants, Fafnir. *Fafnir, water plants!*"

Fafnir waddled forward and sucked a deep draught from the water of the pool—the constant refiltering had already removed the soap and dirt from Terri's bath. Flapping his leathery wings in an awkward, comical blur, Fafnir rose up like a hummingbird and began spewing small dabs of water into each of the hanging plants.

"Do you have any injuries, Terri?" continued Willy. "Your knee looks kind of banged up. Doc's got a complete set of healer tools, and he knows how to use them, right, Doc?" Willy pointed to Terri's knee, which was indeed dark with a spreading bruise, and commanded, "*Doc, heal!*" The gnome stepped forward, grinning and nodding, and before Terri could slap him away, he'd laid his hands on her knee and done something tingly that made the pain go away.

"I guess I don't have to ask what Elvira is for," said Terri. Hearing her name, Elvira started up a spirited little dance, flinging her arms from side to side in a showy, abandoned way that Terri found intensely annoying.

"Elvira cheers me up," said Willy evasively. "She's what they call a femlin. Are you hungry? Elvira or Doc can get you something."

"What kind of food do you have? Do you have vegetables or fruit? I've had nothing but moldie juice for over a week. But I'd rather help myself. I certainly wouldn't want to eat anything that's been touched by Elvira."

"If that's the way you feel," said Willy stiffly.

"It's the way any woman would feel. You've been living alone too long, Willy. For God's sake, tell that thing to stop dancing. I don't have to put up with this."

"Oh, whatever. *Elvira, hide!*" The femlin went back behind the couch. Willy sat down in the easy chair and gestured toward the food pantry. "So eat something. You're hungry and cranky. I got fresh fruits and veggies delivered from the greenhouse today."

Terri found herself a banana and a bunch of strawberries. She ate them with wheat germ and runny tofu. Delicious. While she ate, Willy stared off into space, listening down into his uvvy.

"Can I uvvy my husband now?" asked Terri after she'd finished. "He must be worried sick."

"Um, yeah," said Willy, coming back from wherever he'd been. "I've got an extra uvvy that you can use. I *invented* the uvvy, you know. I'm not just some crazy weirdo, Terri."

"I know that, Willy. I guess maybe I was a little short-tempered just now."

"Well, I'm glad to have you here," said Willy and handed Terri a green uvvy.

Donning the uvvy felt like opening her eyes and discovering a roomful of surprise-party guests. The presences of Willy, Gurdle-7, Frangipane, Jenny, and Ormolu were close by, and beyond them lay a vast churning crowd of other moldie minds. It seemed like everyone in the nest was uvvy-connected to everyone else. Hundreds of voices were talking at once, but via some multiplex uvvy magic, Terri could follow the threads of the conversations.

The two main questions being discussed were (a) how to prevent Wendy-Quuz from triggering another catastrophe and (b) what to do with the new Gurdle decryption technology. Most of the moldies were for sending a smart bomb to annihilate Wendy-Quuz and for never using Gurdle decryption again, but Willy and Gurdle-7 were arguing that the technology was too important to ignore.

"It's safer than you realize," Gurdle-7 was uvvying to the Nest moldies as Terri tuned in.

"Quuz killed my husband at the dome this morning," responded an angry red moldie who resembled a crab.

"Not all of the personalities we decrypt will be like Quuz," insisted Gurdle-7. "Most of them will be intelligent and full of useful information."

"Useful like 'Sun wants eat Moon'?" hooted another voice.

"Just listen for a minute," said Gurdle-7. "This morning before the Wendy experiment, we did a test on some Silly Putters. Frangipane sent the Stairway To Heaven program to infect twelve of the Silly Putters in Corey Rhizome's isopod."

"You're crazy, Gurdle-7!" raged the red moldie. "The infection's going to spread! We ought to kill you!"

"The infection, it is not spreading," volunteered Frangipane. "And I will recount why. It is that Rhizome's Silly Putters have decrypted into some aliens who are mature, evolved beings. They are very glad to be able to decrypt here. They speak of our Earth-Sun system as a 'new node' and they are concerned with finding a way to 'ensure the integrity of this new node.' They are not clumsy babies from the Sun like Quuz. They are elegant old minds from deep in the space."

"What's to stop them from uvvying Einstein and running the Stairway To Heaven on every Silly Putter and DIM in town?" demanded a moldie who looked like a cholla cactus with braidlike green arms.

"That's not what they want," said Gurdle-7. "As a matter of fact, they destroyed Corey Rhizome's uvvy. In the spirit of frankness, I suppose I should announce that Corey did infect one single Silly Putter in Einstein. But that Putter was instantly killed by its owner, Darla Starr." Great moldie cries of fear and anger followed.

"I didn't know that," said Willy across the hubbub. "Why didn't you tell me?"

"I'm telling you now," said Gurdle-7. "Corey's had two calls since the infection, and I monitored both of them. First he called Darla Starr, and then after the aliens took his uvvy away, Corey used a regular old vizzy phone to accept a call from Darla. During the second call, I had the opportunity to notice that the aliens were very interested in the fact that two of Corey's Silly Putters had turned out to be immune to the Stairway To Heaven infection. The aliens wanted Corey to hand those last two Silly Putters over for examination, but Corey wouldn't. It became an issue. In the end, the aliens got their way, and Corey's vizzy phone got broken. That's why there haven't been any more calls."

"The rath and the Jubjub bird!" exclaimed Willy. "Yes! They're immune because they have cubic damping! We have to go to Corey's isopod and get that algorithm. I can't remember the exact details, but I can find them out by looking at the rath and the Jubjub bird. And then maybe we can use cubic damping to make all the moldies safe from the Stairway To Heaven."

"Frankly I'd be a little leery of going in there with those aliens," said Gurdle-7. "Until we have more information. But I could take you as far as Corey's air lock."

"Gurdle-7 is a filthy coward!" hollered one of the angry Nest moldies.

"We should bomb the Rhizome isopod!" yelled another.

"Calm down and wait till I go up there and see what the situation is," said Willy.

"I think the Stairway To Heaven is a flesher trick to kill all the moldies!" said the green cactuslike moldie, waving its spiny arms. "Gurdle-7 is a traitor!"

"I'll kill him if no one else will!" yelled another moldie, the one like a red crab. "I'm going to get Gurdle-7 right now!"

"Kill Terri Percesepe too! She came here inside Quuz! It's all her fault!" shouted the cactus moldie.

"Destroy the Stairway To Heaven!" said one and then five and then a host of others, falling into a chant. "Bomb the lab! Bomb the lab! Bomb the lab!"

"Local network mode," said Willy, and all the Nest moldie presences disappeared from Terri's uvvy—all except Gurdle-7, Jenny, Frangipane, and Ormolu. "We have to leave right away," Willy told them. "Exit Plan K. Hurry!"

Looking through the wall into the cave, Terri saw the four moldies race out of the lab. And then she saw them circle around to the front of the pink-house. Gurdle-7 and the original Jenny pushed their way into the pink-house's air lock and Willy slammed on the lock's air feed. Outside, Ormolu and Frangipane stood guard, Frangipane holding a heavy-duty needler and Ormolu wielding an O.J. ugly stick.

Now Willy opened the inner door of the air lock and Jenny and Gurdle-7 came writhing in. Looking outside, Terri could see the approaching lights of perhaps a dozen moldies. Not as many as she'd feared. Frangipane turned on her needler and swept its laser ray through an arc of warning.

"Hello there, Terri Percesepe," said Gurdle-7 as he bowed down by Willy's side and split his back open. The opening of his tissues changed his reek from intense to unbelievable. "Perhaps you don't know this, but without your husband Tre's contribution, the success of my Gurdle decryption process would have taken much longer. We are grateful."

"*Maybe* we're grateful," said carrot-shaped Jenny, who'd flopped down in the middle of the oriental carpet next to Terri and was splitting herself open as well. "But so far your decryption hasn't done us one bit of good, Gurdle. Get on in me, Terri. Snug as a bug."

"Don't be superficial, Jenny," said Gurdle-7, sealing himself up over Willy. "This is the most important day in the whole history of the world."

"I just hope we live through it!"

So Terri got inside Jenny, and then they went out through the air lock and back onto the floor of the Nest. The red moldie with claws like a crab came running toward them. Shiny Ormolu braced himself and fired off a burst of metal darts that cut the crab moldie into three or four twitching chunks. Two boxy blue moldies scavenged up the broken pieces of the crab. Meanwhile flowery Frangipane leaned back and sent a needler blast up into the core of the cactus-shaped green moldie as it powered down toward them. The attacker melted and splattered to the Nest floor in lumps that were gathered up by other opportunistic moldies.

"Hold tight, Terri, we're going airborne," said Jenny, rearing up onto the fat end of her carrot body. There was a poofing sound and the four moldies rose up into the great vacuum of the Nest, each propelled by a slim ion beam. Ormolu and Frangipane fired some shots back at the moldies still coming after them, and soon those moldies abandoned their pursuit.

Terri sighed in relief and looked downward. The sight of the Nest floor was mesmerizing. It felt almost as if they were gnats inside a giant old-fashioned computer box, with the floor a great motherboard covered with winding lines and square-chunked chips.

Looking toward where they'd come from, Terri realized that the pursuing moldies had turned back in order to trash Willy's dome and Gurdle-7's lab. There was a small bright grouping of moldie dots down there—and now there was a sudden flash as a bomb destroyed all of the lab's equipment.

"That's seven lives' work!" screeched Gurdle-7 over the uvvy. "Let's go back and punish them! They've destroyed all my S-cubes! All of my records were in there. And our backup of Wendy Mooney! Those ignorant chauvinistic fools! They're no better than fleshers!"

"You do have all the Stairway To Heaven knowledge stored in your own body, don't you?" asked Willy.

"Yes, but that's the only complete copy. If something were to happen to me . . . "

"Silence," urged Frangipane. "Who knows who is listening?"

They rose farther, with Ormolu and Frangipane having to shoot at several other moldies who came darting out at them from the narrowing Nest walls. Up above them Terri could see the blazing light prism through the crater hole. And then they sailed up through the crater hole and around the prism. The boundless open space of the Moon's surface sprang out around them, silvery and gray.

"Willy," said Terri, her voice shaking despite herself. "I still want to uvvy my husband. How do I place the call?"

"Push the button," said Willy, his icon distractedly fashioning a virtual button and displaying it in front of Terri. Terri pushed the button right away, and after a little bit Tre's face appeared.

"Tre!" cried Terri. Like radio waves, uvvy signals were electromagnetic waves that travel at the speed of light, and even light takes over a second to make a one-way trip between Earth and Moon. An agonizing two and a half seconds elapsed while Terri's info traveled down to Earth and Tre's info traveled back.

"Terri! Are you okay? Where are you?"

"I'm inside a moldie who just flew out of the moldies' Nest, Tre. We're going to the dome of a man named Corey Rhizome." Another long pause. Terri noticed that Willy and the four moldies were eavesdropping.

"Oh, darling." Tre's voice was breaking. "I heard about Blaster crashing into the spaceport and I thought—"

"I surfed my way through it," said Terri, her own tears starting to flow. "It was terrible. And things still aren't too glassy." They'd risen up to nearly a mile above the Moon now, the four moldies flying in formation.

"1 love you, Terri," said Tre's dear voice.

"I love you too. Give the children a big kiss from me." Another two-and-a-half-second wait.

"I will. But tell me more about what happened, Terri. The only news we're able to get about it is dooky kilp from freelance newsies in Einstein. Why did Blaster crash? And what happened to all the moldies at the spaceport?"

"Willy Taze and a moldie called Gurdle-7 invented a kind of program that changes the dimensions of imipolex or something. And that makes the moldies get possessed by like alien personality waves. Gurdle-7 said *you* helped them, but how?" Now Gurdle-7, Jenny, Ormolu, and Frangipane cut back their power and let themselves coast up to the top of a huge flight parabola.

"My God!" came Tre's reply. "They must have used my N-dimensional Perplexing Poultry design! Someone or something called Jenny showed me Ramanujan's Tessellation Equation, and I designed the new Poultry for her. Is there maybe a Jenny up there?"

"*Um-hmmm!*" uvvied Jenny, displaying her teenage girl icon as she butted into the conversation. "I've got your little wife right inside me, Tre! Too true!"

"I'll call you again when I get some privacy," said Terri. "It looks like we'll be landing down at Corey's house soon. Apparently some of those alien things are inside it. Wish me luck. And—and good-bye, darling, just in case. I've always loved you. You've been good to me." She waited the two and a half seconds for Tre's wet-eyed good-bye, and then she pushed the virtual button to end the heart-wrenching call.

They were arcing down toward a small crater filled with a shiny dome. Corey Rhizome's isopod. The moldies turned their ion jets back on to brake the fall. When Terri had composed herself again, she asked Willy a question.

"Did you really use Tre's Perplexing Poultry to design the Stairway To Heaven?"

"Yes," said Willy. "We had all the pieces, and we couldn't quite fit them together. But once Jenny showed the information to Tre, he knew what to do. Not that he realized what we needed it for. He's such an N-dimensional artist that he did it for free. He *wanted* to do it."

"You ripped him off?" demanded Terri.

"If there turns out to be a profit in it, I'll try and see that he gets a share."

Now Jenny spoke up again, still using her prairie girl icon. "It's a real pain talking to Earth from up here, isn't it, Terri," she uvvied chattily. "What with all those two- or three-second waits. I talk to Earth a lot and—you know me, once I get going, I like to just fabulate on and on. Yadda-da-dadda-da-dadda." Her ion jets were blasting harder and they were falling slower and slower. The Moon's horizon was rising up around them again.

"Are you nervous about going to Corey's?" asked Terri.

Jenny chose to ignore the question. "Um, so like I was saying," she continued. "Those light-speed waits are such a bother that I found a way around them. Though a flesher probably wouldn't be able to do what I do."

"Do what?" asked Terri, staring at the way that the isopod dome bulged out of its little crater. They were lowering down toward a spot a few hundred feet to the crater's side.

"Do what Jenny does so she can gossip with Earth as fast as she likes. I have a remote slave simmie of myself running inside one of the Heritagists' computers in Salt Lake City! And my simmie's smart enough to think a few seconds ahead or even to say stuff on her own. That way when I talk to people like your husband, they don't realize that I'm a moldie on the Moon. Your husband's a real cutie, by the way, Terri. I bet he's such a good fuck."

"What would *you* know about fucking?" demanded Terri, surprised enough to momentarily forget about the aliens in Corey's dome.

"You'd be surprised. *Um-hmmmm!* Those Heritagists think my simmie is something that works for them, and they're always getting it to, um, investigate the sexual shenanigans that their ministers get up to? It's nasty work, but I like it a lot. Humans are just too funny. You should have seen this one man Randy Karl Tucker, who I used to work with. Come to think of it, I guess maybe you've met him? Randy Karl is Willy's son, though Willy doesn't like to talk about it."

"Shut up, Jenny," said Willy.

"Yes, Jenny," said Gurdle-7. "Please shut up. The most important meeting of all time is about to happen."

The four moldies landed in the dust near Corey's isopod, kicking up a spray of moondust that quickly fell back down.

Hearing about Randy Karl Tucker had inflated a balloon of anger in Terri's chest. "It's Randy Karl who kidnapped poor Monique and got me into this mess in the first place. I can't say that I like the sleazy things you've been responsible for, Jenny. Some of your Santa Cruz moldie pals murdered my father five years ago. You loonie moldies should leave Earth the hell alone."

"Oh now, don't be getting on your high horse, Terri. We're all in this together. More than ever, now that Gurdle-7's great invention has brought the aliens to meet us. Gurdle-7's my husband, you know."

"I bet he's *such* a good fuck," said Terri.

"Will you two stop it!" hissed Willy.

In silence they made their way toward the bulging dome. Willy led them to a notch in the crater's edge where a narrow strip of the whole height of the dome wall was exposed. A stone ramp led down to an air lock at the level of the isopod's ground floor.

"I'll bring you into the air lock, Willy," said Gurdle-7. "But then I think I'll come back outside."

"We're waiting outside too," chimed in Frangipane and Ormolu.

"Fraidy cats," said Jenny. "Party poopers. I'm going aaall the way." On the last word, her voice broke into a dry frightened squeak. She made a throat-clearing noise and continued. "Jenny likes to be the first to *know!*"

"It's odd how they're not responding to my uvvy signals at all," said Gurdle-7 quietly as he and Jenny humped into the air lock. The lock hissed full of air, and the moldies disgorged Willy and Terri. "Well, I'll be right outside, Jenny," continued Gurdle-7, worming out through the lock's airtight outer sphincter. "I'll count on you to stay in constant uvvy touch with me."

The air lock's inner door swung open, and there stood a figure of unearthly beauty—a woman like a classic marble statue, though made of supple imipolex. Her flesh glowed with a mild internal light; her pale skin was as a seashell's iridescent lining.

"Welcome," she said. "Willy, Terri, and Jenny. In your system of air-pressure modulations, my name might go like this." Her whole body seemed to vibrate, and the air filled with the piping of flutes, the whining of sitars, and the gentle resonations of a gong. A sound that rose and fell and left Terri hungering to hear more.

"A shimmer of sound," murmured Willy.

"Then let Shimmer be my human name," said the goddess. "I much prefer that to Clever Hansi. Please enter and join us. Corey is here, also his friends Darla, Whitey, Yoke, and Joke. And a large number of aliens. I'm listening to everyone's conversation at once, and it's very exciting."

Hardly knowing what to say, they accompanied Shimmer down the isopod hall toward a hubbub of voices. "It sounds like they're in the conservatory," Willy said to Terri. "I used to live here, you know. Shimmer, I can't believe that you're what's become of Clever Hansi. Clever Hansi was half your size. Just a little Silly Putter doorgirl."

"I helped myself to thirty kilograms of Corey's extra imipolex," said Shimmer. "We aliens divided up all the extra imipolex stored here and made ourselves decent-sized bodies. There's twelve of us. We decided it would be diplomatic to take on human forms."

"Corey let you help yourself to the imipolex?"

"We did what we liked. Corey spent most of the day hiding from us in his bathroom and in his kitchen. He just came out a little while ago."

"Hi, Willy!" called everyone as they entered the high-ceilinged conservatory, a cool airy room with three soft couches and potted plants everywhere. The conservatory's transparent ceiling had a system of lights and louvers designed to simulate the ordinary cycle of a twenty-four-hour Earth day. There were straw rugs on the stone floors, and in the center of the room there was a large carved stone fountain—the only fountain in existence on the Moon. Terri had seen a picture of it once in an article about reclusive limpware tycoon Willy Taze. The couches were arranged around the fountain like three sides of a big triangle.

Scattered about the room were eleven more human-shaped imipolex aliens like Shimmer. They were sitting on the floor—some near the fountain and some near the edges of the room—animatedly passing back and forth hundreds of S-cubes that they'd gathered from around the isopod. And seated on two of the couches were five humans.

"This is Terri and Jenny," said Willy. "Terri, this is Corey, Darla, Whitey,

Joke and Yoke." Terri sized them up. If muscular old Whitey were to get a tan and to shave off the groovy mohawk that ran all the way down his back, he could maybe pass for an aging surfer, but Corey looked like an unsavory old stoner, even grottier than Willy—no wonder they'd been roommates. Corey had two imipolex pets on the couch next to him: a giant-beaked little bird and a small green pig. As for Darla, well, the woman looked outrageously sensual—obviously she was very comfortable in her own skin, though just now her eyes were blazing with some kind of fear and rage. Darla's twin daughters Joke and Yoke were cute and lively, Joke in bright punk rags with a blonde-and-purple hairdo, and Yoke dressed moonmaid-style in a flowing dress and silver boots. Joke was sitting next to Corey and toying with Corey's plastic pets.

The humans in the room looked small and ordinary compared to the aliens. Like Shimmer, the aliens had all taken on the forms of classically proportioned humans. Apparently they were eager to fit in. Looking at them, it was like being in a fantasy viddy about the Greek gods on Mount Olympus—or in a soft-core porno viddy. They were too, too perfect. The fountain tinkled pleasantly as the aliens continued absorbing information from the isopod's S-cubes, lounging about like wise philosophers.

Willy and Terri sat down on the empty couch and carrot shaped Jenny writhed over to inspect the aliens. "So, um, where are all you guys from?" she shrilled.

"They were just telling us," said Corey, his voice slow and amazed. "They're from all over the place. Six are from our own galaxy, one's from a star in the Andromeda galaxy, two from the Crab Nebula, one from NGC 395, one from a quasar, and Clever Hansi here is—"

"I've changed my name to Shimmer," interrupted the glowing goddess and made the chiming sitar noise again.

"Okay," said Corey. "I wave. Shimmer here is from the farthest away of all—she's from an inconceivably distant wrinkle of the cosmos where space and time are different."

"Yes," said Shimmer. "Where I come from, time is two-dimensional."

"What does that mean?" asked Terri.

"You might think of it this way," said Shimmer. "Haven't you ever wondered what your life would be like if you made some different decision?"

"Sure. Like if I hadn't gone swimming off after Monique, I wouldn't be here."

"Yes. Now suppose that all of your alternate lives were real. There would be, oh let's just say *zillions* of them—think of each of your lives as a thread and of your zillion possible lives as making up a fabric of parallel threads."

"That's two-dimensional time?" put in Willy. "But maybe I do have lots of parallel lives I'm not able to perceive. What I know in each life is still just one-dimensional. Past/present/future. I don't experience a second time dimension."

"But I'm not like you," said Shimmer. "In my part of the cosmos, we *are* aware of all our parallel lives. In each of the lives, you're aware of all your other lives. It's just one you across all the lives. There's the past/present/future, but there's the other axis, I don't know what to call it in English." She made a droning, gonging noise.

"The whatever axis," suggested Corey. "It runs from maybe to what-if."

"Fine," said Shimmer, not cracking a smile. "In our two-dimensional time, we are consciously aware of all the parallel lives that we're simultaneously leading. Our experience in each of the parallel lives informs our behavior in all of them. Our memory is two-dimensional—from past to present and from maybe to what-if. It's not such a huge deal, by the way, when one single thread of our lives ends in death—not as long as there's still a zillion others But eventually we too lose everything. As you age, you start losing life threads in whole chunks, the fabric tatters out to a few ragged tags and strings. I must say it makes me rather anxious to be living here as a single isolated time thread. Your world of one dimensional time is frightening and pathetic."

"It made me 'rather anxious' to be in the spaceport dome when your pal Quuz stomped it," spat Whitey, who was sitting on a couch between Darla and Yoke.

"You were in the spaceport?" said Terri. "I was inside Quuz! It was terrible. Shimmer, why aren't you trying to eat everything like Quuz?"

Shimmer made one of her glowing musical noises, and one of the other aliens spoke up, this one shaped like a purple Apollo.

"You can call me Zad," he said, setting down the S-cube he'd been perusing. "I'm from a planet near the center of our Milky Way galaxy. A watery planet, where I was something like a giant squid. I'll be eager to travel down to Earth's oceans soon. You ask why we twelve aren't trying to eat everything? The thing is, every sufficiently advanced civilization in the universe finds out about personality transmission via cosmic rays. But some become advanced in that kind of way before becoming—morally responsible. Quuz was like that. From your own Sun. Whenever a node for personality wave decryption arises, the keepers need to be on guard for beings like that. Fortunately we were able to keep Quuz from transmitting that Stairway To Heaven to us and taking us over. Thanks to the rath and the Jubjub bird." The two little pets were busy fighting and snapping at each other on the couch between Corey and Joke, and now Zad stretched his arm out into a tentacle shape long enough to tweak the rath's tail and to make it hoarsely squeal.

"Cubic damping," said Willy.

"Yes," said Shimmer "After we took the rath and the Jubjub bird from Corey, we were able to extract the limpware hack from them to make our new bodies impervious to the Stairway To Heaven program. We protected all the DIMs in here too. We barely got it done in time. Before Quuz's attack."

"Yes indeedy," cried Jenny. "That's exactly the same idea Willy had. Will you show us moldies the trick too?"

"Certainly," said Shimmer.

"If you'd explained why you wanted the rath and the Jubjub bird in the first place, then maybe I wouldn't have been so scared of you," said Corey.

"He attacked me with a knife," volunteered a third alien, a shiny black man.

"We saw that over the vizzy," said Yoke. "Were you the Bandersnatch?"

"Yeah. But I like the name Takala now. I'm from a planet of jungles and giant insects. I was something like a praying mantis. When one of us becomes old and wise enough, we eat the right substances and enter the proper state of mind to *chirp*. When you chirp, your soul leaves the planet as a personality wave."

"Can humans chirp?" asked Willy.

"Maybe we could teach you how," answered Takala.

"What does it feel like while you're flying along in the form of a cosmic ray?" probed Willy.

"Let me talk now," said another of the aliens, a glowing orange woman. "I'm Syzzy, the one who comes from the quasar. Not all star creatures are as crude as Quuz. My race consists of vortex tangles a bit like Quuz's race of sunspots, but we are so much more evolved. Quuz was like a tube worm, and we are like superhumans. I just can't believe what low temperatures you live at here. And how slowly. Willy Taze asks what it's like to travel across intergalactic space as a cosmic ray? Here's an uvvy image."

Terri turned on her uvvy and absorbed Syzzy's imagery. She felt a sensation of cavernous emptiness, she felt herself to be in a vast dark space specked with bits of light that grew with unbelievable speed into bright shapes like pinwheels and smudges and grains of rice, orangey-yellow with warmth, the flocking shapes singing blissfully into the cosmic Void, making a sound like a deep echoing "*Aaaauuummmm*." She held onto the sound and leaned back into the couch, feeling mellow and very tired.

"That's only a nice picture," protested another alien form, this one a green man. "You can call me Bloog. I lived as something resembling a floating jellyfish in the atmosphere of a gas-giant methane planet. What Syzzy shows isn't really correct. When you travel at the speed of light, then there's no experience of time passing. The trip feels like one single undivided gesture. Like an athlete making a perfect move in the zone. It takes, strictly speaking, no subjective time at all. It's a radical discontinuity, a Dirac delta, a nonlinear spike, a shock front." He tossed Syzzy an S-cube he'd been looking at. "I'm using language that I found in here, Syzzy."

"This is so ultrawavy," exclaimed Jenny. "I'm uvvying Gurdle-7, Frangipane, and Ormolu that they should come in."

"Hold on," said Corey, "I'll walk to the air lock with you and look them over." He and Jenny disappeared off down the hall.

"Do you really, truly think Corey is attractive?" Darla said to Joke after Corey was out of the room. "Is this what I raised you for!?" Her voice was shaking with extreme emotion.

"Hush, Ma," said Joke.

"Not now, Ma," added Yoke.

"Joke's all grown up, Darla," said Whitey. "There's nothing we can do about it if she likes Corey. The less we say about it, the sooner she'll get over it."

"Maybe Corey's not the only thing I'm upset about!" sobbed Darla. "Maybe there's lots of other things I think we should do something about. Hold me, Whitey!"

Whitey put his arms around Darla and she pressed herself against him, putting her mouth right next to his ear.

"Please don't start acting like talk-viddy dregs!" exclaimed Joke. "Can't we be rational? I have so many more questions for the aliens. Like you, Shimmer, you said you were made of a zillion parallel lives—I want to know what kind of individual creatures were living these lives. Squids or insects or artichokes or sunspots or what?"

"My individual beings were animals a lot like humans," said Shimmer. "But they could equally well have been rivers or trees."

"Trees!" exclaimed Willy. "I love trees."

"The moral is that everything is conscious," volunteered a pink woman alien. "And everything is alive. My name is Parella. I come from a planet of crystals. Syzzy may think your time is slow, but I think it's fast."

"I just thought of something," interrupted Whitey, with Darla still leaning against his chest. "Stahn Mooney's still out there inside some Quuz-infected imipolex. When he lands—like fourteen hours from now—when he gets close enough, his Quuz is likely to do a repeat of what Blaster did today. Or worse. What if Stahn were to come down on the Einstein dome and do a Pied Piper number on all the Silly Putters and DIMs in there? Mongo xoxx."

"It's so weird about Quuz," said Terri sleepily. "I've always had such good feelings about the Sun. But now—now whenever I look at the Sun, I'll know that it wants to eat us."

"Quuz has to be stopped," said Darla.

"I'd be glad to fly up and destroy the Quuz," said Syzzy. "I hate primitive sunspot creatures like Quuz."

"Floaty, but I think it would be better for the humans and moldies to handle it," said Whitey. "We're more familiar with the way things work here. Also I'd like to try and do this without killing Stahn. He's an old friend of mine."

"Don't look at me. I'm too tired to help," Terri heard herself saying. And it was true. She was slumped back onto her couch and her fluttering eyelids kept trying to close.

Now Jenny and Corey returned with the three other moldies. Corey had gotten Ormolu and Frangipane to give him their weapons for safekeeping. He was casually carrying the heavy needler and O.J. ugly stick in one hand.

"Hey, Corey," said Whitey. "Why don't you and me and these four moldies fly up and save Senator Stahn? We could leave in like two hours."

"I don't want to go," said Gurdle-7.

"Look, you stinky slug," snarled Whitey. "You're the smart one who got us into this mess. You have to go."

"No," said Gurdle-7. "I want to stay right here and exchange information with the aliens. I've been working all my life for this."

"I don't want to leave either," said Willy.

"So let them stay," said Corey. Terri happened to be drowsily staring at Darla just then and she noticed Darla giving Corey a charged intent look. "You and me, Whitey, we can do it if Jenny, Frangipane, and Ormolu are willing. I can fly in Frangipane, you go in Ormolu, and Jenny can bring Stahn back. It'd be perfect that way."

"Copacetic," said Whitey.

"But what occurs when the Wendy-Quuz sings the Stairway To Heaven to us?" protested Frangipane. "Directly to us from very close up."

"Haven't you been monitoring Jenny's uvvy? Our alien friends figured out how to use the rath and the Jubjub bird to vaccinate themselves against the Stairway To Heaven virus," said Corey.

"How would we install it on ourselves?" asked Ormolu uncertainly.

"Well, the aliens did it alone, but I think you moldies will need for me to help you," said Corey glibly. "Let's just take the magic pig and bird back into my limpware studio and I'll fix you right up. Come on. You come too, Gurdle-7."

"Yes yes, I want the vaccination so that I can teach it to all the moldies in the Nest," said Gurdle-7. "Then they won't be angry at me anymore. By the way, Corey, do you have some extra S-cubes so that I can download a copy of my Stairway To Heaven program? There aren't any copies of the documentation left anymore. Those paranoid Nest moldies blew up my lab."

"Sure, I've got the equipment for that too," said Corey. "Come on, you four moldies."

"I'll help," said Whitey. "I'll carry those weapons for you, Corey. You grab the bird and the pig."

"I want to watch too," said Darla. "I haven't walked around in this house for such a long time." Corey, Whitey, Darla, and the four moldies clumped off down the hall, Corey carrying the rath and the Jubjub bird and Whitey carrying the needler and the ugly stick.

"We've heard from Shimmer the 2D-time humanoid, Zad the squid, Syzzy the quasar vortex, Takala the mantis, Bloog the jellyfish, and Parella the crystal," Willy said. "How about you other six aliens?"

Though it was some of the most interesting information she'd ever heard, Terri couldn't keep her eyes open, and she drifted off to sleep.

CHAPTER TEN

DARLA

November 6, 2053

Darla's grandmother's family were American Indians from the Acoma pueblo near Albuquerque. From listening to her Indian relatives, Darla knew all too well what it meant to have a powerful alien culture arrive. She knew all about the greed, the disease, the cruelty, and the heartless disdain for the native culture. "Give us your gold; we'll give you disease; your religion is evil; support our parasitic priests." Finding the aliens in Corey's isopod filled Darla with a deep visceral loathing. But she knew better than to prematurely show her feelings.

Under the pretext of having a fit over Joke and Corey, Darla got herself into Whitey's arms and whispered into his ear: "*We have to kill the aliens.*"

She could tell from Whitey's body language that he understood and agreed. And when Corey came back with the four moldies and the needler and the O.J. ugly stick, Darla sensed that Corey too knew what had to be done.

Corey and Whitey led the way off down the hall toward Corey's studio, followed by the four moldies, with Darla in the rear. Trying hard to keep her voice even, Darla made housewifely commentary on the features of the isopod.

"That's nice to see your giant marijuana plants are doing so well in the grove out there, Corey. How tall are they? And I see you've still got your velvet paintings up. I always liked that one of the nuking of Akron."

"Yeah," said Corey. "I put a lot of myself into that picture. I went to high school in Akron. I hated it, of course, but sometimes I'm sort of sorry those Yaqui rubber tappers blew it up. Odd as it sounds, when I lived in Akron, I used to dream about blowing it up myself. Like precognition. In one dream I was in the middle of this big Akron stadium with a white-painted fat-boy H-bomb and there were thousands of people in the seats watching me and they were chanting, 'Light the Bomb!' Look, see how I worked a shattering stadium into the corner of the picture?" They'd stopped walking, and Corey was standing there, happily studying his art. "And your picture's over there, Darla." He pointed to an oversized velvet painting that showed the mirror-clad figures of Stahn and Darla at the mouth of the Nest. "See the stars in the reflections? And the little Earths?"

"That seems like so long ago," said Darla. "It's been a while since I did anything heroic. Wouldn't it be nice to be heroic again, Whitey?"

"I hear you," said Whitey, and they started walking again.

"I'm the one who's going to be the hero for *this* year," said Gurdle-7 smugly. "Isn't it amazing to have the aliens here? Just think of all the advances that they'll bring us. And think of how many more aliens there are for us to decrypt—cosmic personality waves are flying past us all the time."

"I think getting vaccinated against the Stairway To Heaven is a very good idea," said Frangipane quietly.

"Yeah," said Ormolu. "I'm freakin'. What if the aliens start getting greedy to do lots and lots of Gurdle decryptions? What if some decrypted lobster-thing gets real eager to fab with another lobster-thing from the same planet and starts doing thousands of decryptions, waiting for the right one? Who decides how much of our imipolex the aliens are allowed to use? What if they want to use up all of the resources in the whole solar system?"

"They cleaned out my stash of flickercladding without even asking," said Corey. "They beefed themselves up to seventy kilograms each. That's a lot of bucks."

"And what if another Quuz-type alien gets decrypted and kills even more of us?" said Jenny. "I hate to tell you, Gurdle-7, but decryption is turning out to be a xoxxin' bad idea. I know we worked really hard on it, but . . . "

"You're too cautious," snapped Gurdle-7. "You sound like a filthy Heritagist. Are you so frightened of transcendence?"

"Here's my limpware studio," said Corey, opening a door. He tossed the rath and the Jubjub bird in and let them start running around on the floor, chasing each other as usual. Whitey and the moldies followed him, and Darla came in last. The room held some fairly sophisticated design tools. There was a large industrial-looking machine in one corner, a couple of workbenches with things that looked more or less like power tools, and shelves along the walls laden with cans, bottles, tubes, and boxes.

Darla closed the door behind her and leaned against it. She noticed that Whitey was having trouble holding both the needler and the O.J. ugly stick. "Let me look at that needler, Whitey," she said. "I've never seen one that big." Whitey handed it to her and wrapped his hands firmly around the ugly stick.

"I want to download my info onto an S-cube before we do anything else," said Gurdle-7. "We don't want to take any chances with my information about the Stairway To Heaven."

"No," said Whitey. "We don't." And then he turned on the ugly stick and cut Gurdle-7 into pieces, moving the whispering stream of magnetically launched metal darts with practiced accuracy and speed. A few of the flechettes pinged off the stone walls of the room.

"Don't you dare call for help," said Darla, pointing the needler at the three remaining moldies. "If I push the button, you stinkers go up in flames. Jenny! Start faking Gurdle-7's uvvy signal, in case that nosy Shimmer checks on us. Frangipane and Ormolu! Mask your real thoughts and make your uvvy signals look like you're watching Corey make an S-cube copy of Gurdle-7."

"Yaar," said Whitey, training the muzzle of the O.J. ugly stick on the moldies. The air was thick with the astonishing stench of the shredded Gurdle-7. The frightened rath and Jubjub bird had disappeared behind the big machine in the corner.

"We're all riding the same wave, aren't we, guys?" said Corey. "The aliens have to die."

"For sure," said Darla. "Unless we want the human and the moldie races to end up selling souvenirs and running gambling casinos for the galactic gods."

"Um . . . too true!" said Jenny after a moment's hesitation. Her voice wavered. "But poor Gurdle-7. We never thought it would turn out this way. He was so smart and so dumb."

"I am agree," said Frangipane. "The aliens are a big mistake."

"I'm with you too," said Ormolu. "I've been liking my life just the way it is. I don't want this kind of cataclysmic change. But how do we kill the aliens? There's *twelve of* them."

"I'll set them on fire with this heavy-duty needler," said Darla. "When I needled Rags this morning, he caught fire almost right away."

"*Almost* right away," said Whitey. "But by the time you got two or three of the aliens lit, the others would be all over you. Don't you have any more weapons, Corey? It would be stuzzadelic if all seven of us were armed."

"All I've got is water guns," said Corey apologetically. "I'm a Dadaist artist. The whoopee cushion is mightier than the sword."

"I can spit things out really hard from any part of my body," said Ormolu, stretching out his hand and ejecting something that struck against the room's far wall with a resounding splat.

"What *was* that?" asked Darla.

"Camote truffle."

"That's not going to kill anyone."

"We could point our ion jets at them," said Jenny. "Except the jets aren't hot."

"What about the equipment in this studio, Corey?" said Whitey. "Tell us what it all is and maybe we'll think of something."

"Okay," said Corey. "That old-timey machine in the corner is an injection molder. I use it to cast my Silly Putters into certain shapes. The workbench on the right is where I carve the models I use to make the molds. That tool that looks like an electric drill is a piezomorpher, it's very good for carving imipolex. It uses ultrasound. Not much of a weapon, though, because you have to be right on top of the material to piezomorph it. It's more like a dentist's drill than like a bazooka. Now this bench over here is where I paint my Silly Putters. To some extent they can control their colors, but they need a basis to start from. You have to get the right pigments and metal oxides into their flesh for them to work with. This particular tool is something like an old-fashioned airbrush. Slightly higher-tech than an airbrush, because it shoots the color particles right into the plastic up to a depth of four centimeters. A volume-filling brush, in other words. It's a good tool but, again, not particularly lethal."

While Corey talked, the three moldies grazed their way across the floor, quietly absorbing the pieces of imipolex that had been Gurdle-7. The rath and the Jubjub bird came creeping out of hiding to snuffle up the smaller crumbs.

"I hope none of you moldies is ending up with the intact Stairway To Heaven information?" said Darla, fingering her needler.

"Not to worry," said Frangipane, now about thirty percent larger than before. "I have already reprogram all the imipolex I just ate." She sprouted two new petals, hiccupped, and spit out some triangular flat ugly-stick darts as if they were watermelon seeds. "*Excusez moi.*"

"No problem here either, Darla," said Ormolu, who was staring down at his body with evident satisfaction. "I turned all of my Gurdle-7 share into muscle." He flexed his legs and made taut ridges spring out along them.

"I didn't save any of Gurdle-7's science information," said Jenny. "But I'm keeping some of his feelings, no matter what you say. He was a bold explorer. And we loved each other." For a giant carrot, she looked quite humanly miserable.

"How about those cans and bottles on the shelves?" Whitey asked Corey. "What's in them?"

"Chemicals. Like resins and polymers for doctoring the imipolex. And paints and solvents for coloring the Putters."

"Solvents!" exclaimed Whitey. "We could make firebombs!"

"Oh *right*!" said Darla. "Like we'll walk back into the conservatory lugging buckets of gasoline. If the aliens see what's coming, they'll attack us first. Or take hostages. I don't want anything to happen to Yoke or Joke. No, we have to think of a way to hit those freeware slugs giga fast and yotta vicious."

"I have an idea!" said Frangipane after a minute's thought. "We can spit out little balls of imipolex and have them move like the smart kinetic-energy bombs." She flicked one of her petals and sent a little lump of shiny gold imipolex bouncing across the room. "It is a waste of imipolex, but now after eating poor Gurdle-7, we can spare a little."

"So how's a bouncing glob going to hurt an alien?" asked Corey. The little gold ball bounced past the rath, and the rath sprang forward in an effort to gulp it down. As if in reaction, the ball took a sudden backward bounce, hit the rath in the nose, then bounced several more times with increasing amplitude, finally caroming off the wall and ceiling to return to Frangipane.

"*Voila*," said Frangipane. "The bouncing glob is clever."

"We can control pieces of ourselves, even after we split them off," explained Jenny. "Though, of course, if you get totally minced like poor Gurdle-7, there's nothing left to do any controlling." She whipped the thin tip of her carrot body to one side and sent another ball a-bouncing, and this time the Jubjub bird tried to catch it. Just as Frangipane had done, Jenny used her uvvy signals to guide the ball safely back to herself.

"Big xoxxin' deal," said Darla. "A smart plastic ball."

"*Attendez!*" said Frangipane. "It is the next part that is the really new idea. If I put a sufficient amount of my quantum dots into a smart little ball, then I can make it commit the suicide." She spat another nugget of imipolex off into the air, but this time, just as the little ball neared the ceiling, it made a popping sound and fiercely caught ablaze. Flapping its flames like a burning mothball, it fell to the stone floor and consumed itself. "*La poof!*" exclaimed Frangipane.

"Yaar," said Whitey admiringly. "Flamin' poofballs!"

"Uvvy us how to do that, Frangipane!" said Ormolu. A few seconds later, Ormolu and Jenny had learned the trick. Ormolu splatted a fat poofball against the stone wall, where it burst into flame like a sticky glob of napalm. Jenny shot a barrage of four tiny flaming poofballs toward the rath, sending it out again for cover.

"You moldies can act like machine-gun flamethrowers!" exclaimed Darla. "The aliens won't have a chance!"

"But—whoah—that one poofball used up a *lot* of quantum dots," said Ormolu, feeling down into himself.

"Yes, I am afraid if I shoot very many poofballs, I won't have enough energy left to use my jets," said Frangipane. "I would not like that."

"But I have a huge stash of quantum dots!" exclaimed Corey. "I use them to charge up my Silly Putters before I sell them. Look here." He opened a cabinet and took out a shiny flask with little tubes and wires all over it. "It's a magnetic bottle. Ten grams in there! Stoke yourselves up to the max, guys."

"Save some for me to put into the needler and the ugly stick as well," said Whitey. "We want them at full charge."

Frangipane decanted a hefty splash of the quantum dot superfluid onto herself. It was odd silvery-gray stuff that didn't move like an ordinary liquid. Then she passed the bottle on to the other two moldies. They practiced firing off a few more flaming poofballs while Whitey charged up the needler and the ugly stick.

"The poofballs are perfect," exclaimed Corey. "I love them. I want to make a fire-breathing Silly Putter dragon when we get through with this. And maybe a mad fire-farter. Hey! Not so near the supply shelves, Jenny! We don't want to explode those cans of solvents, do we? Speaking of safe fire practices, has anyone thought about what happens after we light the aliens? We're talking about nearly a ton of flaming imipolex. What's that going to do to my isopod? And how are we going to breathe with all the smoke?"

"This place is compartmentalized against blowouts," said Whitey. "I don't know how many times I've heard you or Willy bragging about it, Corey. We just leave the conservatory and seal it off. The floor and walls are stone, and if the flames melt a hole in the titanplast ceiling, so much the better. The vacuum will put the fire out. According to what you've always said about the isopod's design, the blowout won't spread past the conservatory."

"Well, yeah, that's how it's supposed to be," allowed Corey. "But remember, it's just Willy who designed it. And we've never tested it. Getting out of the conservatory in time is gonna be hella chaotic."

"Give me that needler and let's get going," interrupted Darla, taking the big weapon back from Whitey. "My plan is simple. I'm going to stand near Joke and Yoke and blast every alien in sight."

"Yaar," said Whitey "And I'll use the ugly stick, and the moldies here can be spitting poofballs. What are you going to do, Corey?"

"I'm going to stand by the door and make sure everyone gets out in time. Especially me." Corey hunkered down and called the rath and the Jubjub bird. "You moldies better hurry up and do that vaccination thing before we go back. We've been in here so long that I bet the aliens are starting to get suspicious."

"I've been like listening to them talk," said Jenny, cocking her body to one side. "They're not suspicious at all. Somebody who used to be a quasar vortex or a giant crystal has no idea about how long things are supposed to take here people. Terri's fast asleep and Willy, Joke, and Yoke are asking the aliens questions." Jenny gave one of her inane giggles. "They're asking about God and the meaning of life."

"Here you go, wigglers," said Corey, offering the rath and the Jubjub bird to the moldies. "You can do the vaccinations yourselves. We didn't really need to come back to my limpware studio for this at all. You just uvvy into one of these Putters and grep through the Limplan code to find the routine labeled 'Cubic Homeostasis'. Shell it around your uvvy reception ware and you're vaccinated. But be careful not to put it anywhere in your main action group or you'll turn into a Silly Putter and get real simple."

Frangipane wrapped her petals around the kicking, squealing rath. She looked like a Venus fly-trap eating a fat green beetle. Meanwhile Jenny ensnared the cawing Jubjub bird with the tentacles at the blunt end of her carrot. Then Frangipane passed the rath to Ormolu and he held it tight under his arm, absorbing the Cubic Homeostasis algorithm for himself. Meanwhile they discussed the plan of attack a little more.

A few minutes later, they were walking back down the hall toward the conservatory Corey was holding the rath and the Jubjub bird. He'd temporarily paralyzed them so that he could cradle them in one arm Darla carried the needler and Whitey carried the ugly stick, both of them holding their weapons casually dangling. Jenny and Ormolu were pretending to argue, getting ready to distract the aliens.

They found things in the conservatory much as they had left them. Terri was stretched out full-length, asleep on one couch, Joke and Yoke were perched next to each other on one of the other couches, and Willy was excitedly pacing about on the far side of the room. Four of the aliens were grouped near the fountain, dabbling their fingers in the water and talking with Yoke and Joke. The other eight freeware-possessed moldies were off on the far side of the room, examining S-cubes and conversing with Willy.

"You are such a bully!" screeched Jenny as they entered. She tossed the fat end of her carrot from side to side and then thudded it into Ormolu. Ormolu seemed to lose his footing and tumbled like an acrobat, knocking over a plant and pin-wheeling his arms. He wound up on the other side of the couches, right near the far wall where the eight aliens were gathered.

"It's not my fault I love you, Jenny!" shouted Ormolu, kneeling with his back to the eight aliens and holding out his hands supplicatingly toward Jenny.

"What's going on?" demanded Joke.

"Oh, these dooky slugs are in some kind of tussle," said Darla dismissively. "Gurdle-7 and Ormolu are both hot for Jenny—if you can believe that. They had an argument, and Gurdle-7 is sulking in Corey's studio." She flopped down on the couch next to Yoke and Joke, setting down the needler beside her so that it pointed at the four aliens by the fountain, one of whom was Shimmer.

"Hello, Darla," said Shimmer, but Darla acted like she was too busy staring at Jenny to answer.

"You're saying you love me?" Jenny paraded across the room, tossing and undulating for all she was worth. Running her shrill voice up and down the octaves. "What will you do to prove it?" Now she was standing over the kneeling Ormolu.

"This oughtta be very weightless," Whitey announced loudly. "You aliens oughtta check this out." He went and perched on the other end of the couch with Yoke and Joke, holding the O.J. ugly stick with exaggerated casualness. Frangipane circled around and stood near the other end of the grouping of eight aliens.

"Do you know any floatin' chaotic attractors, Ormolu?" shrilled Jenny. "Make one for me. Make the Nguyen Attractor!"

"What the hell is *wrong* with you moldies?" said Willy, turning away from the aliens to yell angrily at Jenny and Ormolu. "We've just been having this incredibly fascinating philosophical discussion, and you stinkers barge in here and start acting like—good Lord, I didn't know moldies could do that!"

On her couch, Terri sat up and rubbed her eyes. Darla shifted the needler to her lap and prayed that Terri wouldn't take it into her mind to walk between her and the four aliens by the fountain.

Ormolu's upper body had broken into threads that were looping around in hypnotic weaving patterns of standing waves. Like a hydra head of a thousand thin filaments, with the envelopes of the filaments' motions forming a hallucinatory shape of warping, mutating curves.

"Big xoxxin' deal," griped Yoke. "That's nothing compared to what Syzzy here has been telling us about—"

"But wait!" called Corey, still standing off by the door that led from the conservatory to the hallway. "Everyone watch very closely to see what Ormolu does next!"

"Oh, I am so ready!" screeched Jenny, dancing around to stand to the side of Ormolu. "I'm ready *now!*"

At this signal, Frangipane, Jenny, and Ormolu began spewing out withering streams of flaming poofballs, Ormolu shooting from out of a freshly formed pucker in the center of his back. Meanwhile Whitey began firing the ugly stick into the bodies of the aliens by the fountain. And at the same moment, Darla pressed the needler button and sent a slow straight line across the aliens by the fountain and—yes!—three of them burst into flame. With its strong fresh charge, the needler was much more powerful than any she'd ever used. It instantly grew hot in her hand, but she hung onto it, flicking the dazzling violet laser beam back and forth across the three aliens, setting them alight here, there, and everywhere, even as Whitey's ugly stick chewed them to pieces.

The only problem was that the fourth alien kept moving out of the way each time that Darla or Whitey shot. This was Shimmer. No matter how hard you tried to shoot her, Shimmer was always just out of the line of fire. Whitey stood up and moved around her, blazing away with the ugly stick, but hitting Shimmer was impossible. She wasn't moving particularly fast, but magically, effortlessly, as if by repeated strokes of luck, Shimmer was never in the spot where a flechette or needler beam ended up.

Darla glanced over to the far wall—Jenny, Frangipane, and Ormolu had killed all eight of their aliens, the eight bodies a great heap of smoking, crackling flame. Someone shoved Darla. It was Joke. She was screaming, "Stop!" Darla realized then that Joke had been screaming the whole time. "Stop hurting them!" Joke struck Darla's hand, and the blisteringly hot needler clattered to the floor. Darla clawed for it, but Joke kicked it aside. Shimmer was standing right in front of them by the fountain.

"We missed one!" shouted Darla to the three moldies. "We missed Shimmer!"

A dozen pellets of imipolex whistled past Darla's head. Shimmer bent slightly to one side and lifted her leg. All the poofballs missed her and burst harmlessly into flames against the fountain's basin. Whitey got around behind Joke, Yoke, and Darla to shoot the ugly stick toward Shimmer some more and completely missed her again and again. Shimmer turned and ducked and hopped and pirouetted, moving in dreamy slow motion, always in the right place at the right time. The room was filling with thick black smoke, oily with plastic and—Darla realized in a sudden wave of disorientation—loaded with the psychedelic vapors of camote.

A rapid breeze swept by Darla, fanning the blazing imipolex of the three dead aliens by the fountain. It was Shimmer running by her, disappearing into a far corner of the room.

"Everybody out now!" Corey was yelling. "We have to seal off the smoke! Everyone out in the hall so I can seal the door!" The bewildered Terri was already over there with him.

Darla seized Joke by the wrist and dragged her toward the door. Whitey had hold of Willy and Yoke. Ormolu, Jenny, and Frangipane came on their own. The flames were roaring higher and higher. In the stony slowed-down time of the camote smoke, it felt like a long, long trip to the hallway door.

All the while, Corey kept yelling for them. "Hurry up! The ceiling could blow out any time!"

As they made their way, the smoke grew thicker. Whitey went last, still firing his ugly stick back into the room, hoping to hit Shimmer. When Darla made it to the hallway, she gasped down some of the less smoky air and turned to stare into the inferno of the conservatory.

In the center of the room, on top of the fountain, stood Shimmer, staring calmly at them. Two heartbeats passed, Darla shouted, and a volley of poofballs and flechettes shot toward the alien. But by then Shimmer had sprung high upward and turned on the ion jets in her moldie body's heels. The conservatory roof shattered and a huge rush of wind slammed the conservatory door shut with a deafening thud.

The door to the conservatory held firm, but on the other side of it there were alarming crashes and screechings as the room's air rushed out into the vacuum, whirling the objects in the conservatory like a cyclone.

"This isopod *is* really blowout-proof, isn't it, Willy?" said Corey, shouting to make himself heard over the chaos in the next room.

"That's how I designed it," said Willy. "But I've been wrong before. The farther we get from the conservatory, the better. Let's head down the hall, close the hall door, go through the kitchen, close the kitchen door, and then go up the stairs to the garage. There's a bunch of bubbletoppers in there and two moon buggies. Whose idea was it to kill the aliens?"

"I'll take the credit," said Darla, trotting along beside Willy. "I'm part Native American. We know a lot about cultural imperialism."

"You have a point," said Willy. "But Gurdle-7's going to be furious."

"Gurdle-7's dead," said Whitey.

"I think you're a bitch, Ma," said Joke. "The aliens were beautiful. They had so much to teach us."

"Well, there's still two of them left to learn from," said Corey, ushering the group out of the hall and into the kitchen. "There's still Shimmer and the Wendy version of Quuz."

"We still gotta fly up and kill Quuz and save Stahn Mooney!" exclaimed Whitey. "Are you moldies ready for that?"

"We've helped enough," said Ormolu. "I'm scared that Shimmer's going to do something bad to us now."

As if in confirmation, there was a roaring behind the hall door. The hall roof had given way as well. It sounded like the end of the world.

"How do we get out of here?" shrieked Jenny. "I want to go back to the Nest!"

"And I want to go home to Santa Cruz," wailed Terri.

"Through this door for the garage," said Corey, crossing the kitchen and opening a door that led to an upward flight of stairs. "Everyone hurry on up there and put on a bubbletopper. The whole garage is an air lock."

Corey went last, closing the kitchen door and the staircase door behind them. The seven humans wriggled into the waiting bubbletoppers, Corey still carrying his rath and Jubjub bird. There were more ominous crashes and roars from the isopod. Once they had the bubbletoppers on, they switched to uvvy communication and Corey cycled the garage's big air lock door open.

"*Adieu*," said Frangipane, humping out to the open surface of the Moon and preparing to fly away.

"Good luck," added Jenny, joining Frangipane and anxiously glancing up at the black sky.

"We did our best," said gleaming Ormolu.

And then, in a puff of dust, the three moldies had jetted away, arcing off toward the Nest.

"Let's get clear of the isopod right away," uvvied Corey. Darla and her family got on one of the moon buggies, while Corey, Willy, and Terri got on the other. They floored the accelerators and the buggies darted out across the dusty surface of the Moon.

Yoke was driving again, with Joke next to her and Whitey and Darla in back. Darla turned to stare back at the isopod, and as she watched, the ragged hole over the conservatory and hallway ripped farther open. The entire remaining part of the dome gave way in a great burst of frozen air, with clothes, furniture, and huge branches of the marijuana trees tumbling up through the lunar vacuum.

"So much for your blowout-proof design, Willy," said Corey's slow ironic voice. "Oh well. I was thinking about moving back into Einstein anyway."

A voice suddenly crackled over Darla's uvvy and over the uvvies of the others. The voice of Shimmer.

"Well done," said Shimmer. "You chose an optimal thread."

"Shimmer," uvvied Joke, craning her head back and looking upward. "Where are you?"

"I'm a hundred and fifty miles straight up from the Moon. It's an interesting view."

"Are you angry that we killed your friends?" asked Darla. "Are you going to get even with us?"

" '*Kill*,' " said Shimmer musingly. "The word means a lot to you, doesn't it? Your spacetime is so—so poignant. To live with the immediacy of total annihilation always around you. Your condition has a fine dark beauty."

"Please don't hurt us," uvvied Willy. "Darla and the others were only scared that you aliens would overwhelm our little civilization."

"Darla was right," said Shimmer. "From what I hear, it's not a pretty thing for a civilization as undeveloped as yours to become a decryption node."

"But how did you escape, Shimmer?" Whitey wanted to know. "I kept aiming right at you, but then you were never there when I shot."

"Even though your alternate worlds are unreal, I can still see them," said Shimmer's voice. "All I had to do was to keep picking the correct bending of my world line."

"So what are you going to do now?" asked Joke.

"I might visit Earth for a while," said Shimmer. "But don't worry. Sooner or later, I'll chirp out of here. You do not welcome me, and I do not wish to overstay. Although one-dimensional time has a certain fatalistic glamour, it's not a spacetime configuration I'm prepared to inhabit forever."

"Could you do us one favor?" put in Terri.

"Maybe."

"Kill that other Quuz-thing."

"I was already planning to. Should I kill the human in Quuz as well?"

"Let me try to save him!" cried Whitey.

"Shut up!" said Darla, who'd never much liked Stahn. "It's too late, Whitey, and you'd probably get killed. Shimmer—could you kill Quuz and code up Stahn and chirp him out of here? Then it wouldn't be like he really died."

"I could do that," said Shimmer. "I can do almost anything. Stahn would become a personality wave. In the fullness of transfinite cosmic time, he'd decrypt somewhere and somewhen else."

"Oh, don't do that," said Willy. "Please listen to me. It's my fault that Stahn got into this in the first place. Gurdle-7 and I had this stupid idea that it would help to have Stahn inside the first moldie that we did a decryption on. But apparently it didn't help at all."

"So what are you asking me to do?" said Shimmer.

"Ferry Stahn down to us," said Willy. "He doesn't want to live *somewhere and somewhen*. He wants to be here and now. Like any other person. Kill Quuz and bring Stahn the rest of the way to Einstein, Shimmer. Fly him down inside you."

"Shimmer doesn't want to do that," snapped Darla, feeling guilty for being so nasty, but letting it out anyway. "It'll take her too long."

"Oh, I have all the time in the world," laughed Shimmer. "It'll be an interesting challenge to kill the Quuz without killing Stahn. I'll fly back here and drop him off at the Einstein air lock. If I flew very fast, I could have Stahn for you by the time you get there yourself. In half an hour. But the acceleration would kill him. *Kill.* There's that word again." Shimmer gave a buzzing, chiming laugh and broke the uvvy connection.

CHAPTER ELEVEN

STAHN

November 7, 2053 - December 2053

So there was Stahn hurtling through cislunar vacuum, Stahn wrapped inside the fifteen kilograms of imipolex that had once been Wendy and which now was Quuz. They weren't talking anymore, but Quuz had kept their uvvy link jammed open for maximum access. Stahn could sense Quuz's consciousness all around him as intimately as if Quuz were breathing in his face.

Stahn hated Quuz. Quuz had killed Wendy, and thanks to Stahn's having foolishly shown Quuz the communication protocols, Quuz had taken over all the moldies in Blaster as well.

Being forcibly linked to Quuz reminded Stahn of how it had felt when he'd been a slave worker in the pink-tanks—a meatie with a robot rat remote of Helen the bopper in place of the right hemisphere of his brain. While flashing back on that ugly memory, Stahn had unwisely vented rage at Quuz, right after Quuz took over Wendy's and Blaster's imipolex. From that point on, Quuz had dropped all verbal communication.

For the last few hours, Quuz had seemingly been in a meditative state, calling up memories of the Sun. The solar images came across the wide-open uvvy as a seductively rich animated virtual reality. Stahn guessed that the colors might correspond to different intensities of X rays and gamma rays, that his perceptions of currents in the virtual fluid around him might represent plasma pressure waves, and that perhaps it was showers of neutrinos that were being presented as the surging roar that sounded like breaking surf or like wind in trees. Isolated in the midst of this rich input, Stahn's mind began willy-nilly to impose familiar interpretations on the unearthly scene.

At first, for instance, Stahn felt like he was floating in the ocean, snorkeling through some vast tropical reef alive with eels and anemones. And then it started feeling like being outside, like walking in an autumn forest, a peaceful country woods with purling brooks and friendly rabbits that spun on their tails like whirling dervishes. With a sun overhead. A sun in the Sun? There was no reasoning with the images. The trees began to move like big jolly writhing worms. Completely against his will, Stahn felt himself wanting to dance with them.

There was an occasional skirl of line noise as the system repeatedly retweaked the interface to Stahn's occipital lobes to make the visions the more obscenely rich and glorious. Stahn tried to hold back the sinister ecstasy, tried to focus on the reality of his current situation.

If only Quuz would deliver him safe to Einstein or the spaceport, then things could still work out okay. Wendy wasn't permanently dead by any means. If Frangipane had screwed up, there was still a month-old backup of Wendy on an S cube in San Francisco. Clever son Saint could send the Wendyware via uvvy, and Stahn could install it on some stratospheric new loonie-built imipolex. And then he'd get a fresh-grown Wendy from the Nest's pink-tanks. Wendy would be better than ever, just like she'd planned! Ah, if only Quuz would deliver Stahn to the Moon alive.

Not for the first time, Stahn tried calling out to Quuz. "Hey, Quuz, how's it going? How soon do we get to the Moon? Did Blaster already land? Don't you need for me to help you?"

As before, there was no answer. Stahn had cursed Quuz so very savagely that Quuz had stopped giving Stahn any information other than this ongoing impression of what life was like inside the Sun. The exhaustingly intense and wonderful visions wound on and on. A cheerful worm tree circled a long, curvy branch around Stahn's waist and swept him up into the circles of a chaotic three-dimensional dance. Stahn had the sudden intimation that Quuz meant to dance him to the point of death or madness. The light grew brighter.

Grimly, desperately, Stahn brooded inward on his solid worries as touchstones of sanity. What if Quuz were planning to take over all the imipolex within broadcast range on the Moon! The spaceport, the Nest, Einstein. What if everything down there were trashed by the time Stahn landed? If he lived that long. Oh, if only there were some way to stop these visions, if only he could see out through Quuz's skin to the real world where real things were really going on—

And then Stahn got his wish. There was a huge surge of noise—like gongs and sitars—and the imipolex around him went quite dead. The plastic quickly started stiffening and growing cold. The air flow at Stahn's mouth ceased. He twitched his arms in surprise, and in a moment of ultimate terror the imipolex around him cracked like an eggshell. The frozen shattered pieces went tumbling away, leaving Stahn raw and naked in outer space.

The air rushed out of his lungs in an incredible racking cough. His skin burned and tingled in the empty vacuum. At least now, for this one last instant, his freezing eyes could see. The Moon closer than he'd expected, so bright, so real—

—and there next to Stahn was a figure like a glowing marble statue! The shape came to him and embraced him and drew him in. The Angel of Death. Oh well. It had been a good long run, Stahn's life, and now—

"I'm Shimmer," said the shape around Stahn. "I'll have to squeeze you very tight to keep you from getting the bends."

Sweet air surged around Stahn's face, he gasped and sobbed, drawing in thick breath after breath. Kind Shimmer kept herself transparent over Stahn's eyes and he could still see down to the Moon below.

"You're here to save me?" uvvied Stahn.

"Yes yes," said Shimmer. Her thoughts were lively and rich and *layered* in some curious way. Like double vision, but more so. She saw everything as if in branching trails. "I'll take you right down to the Einstein air lock."

So Stahn made it safely to the Moon. Frangipane's backup of Wendy was indeed gone, but Saint used the Meta West Link to beam up Wendy's October backup ware. Stahn immediately put the Wendyware onto a new limpware Happy Cloak and attached the 'Cloak to a wetware wendy body from the weird moldie Sisters of the Pink Tanks. It was all taken care of within twenty-four hours.

Stahn and the newly twentyish Wendy settled into the Einstein-Luna Hotel for a vacation. They spent a lot of time visiting with their old friends, but Stahn managed to stay sober, even when Fern Beller and Whitey and Darla came by, accompanied by the lovely young Yoke.

Fern looked as sexy as ever to Stahn, he almost wished he'd held off on reassembling Wendy till after he'd had one more chance to try and bone Fern. But that would have been futile anyway, as Fern was back with her old boyfriend Ricardo.

Darla talked about Joke moving in with the artist Corey Rhizome, Darla hadn't been too happy about it at first, but now she'd gotten to liking Corey again. Yoke said she was going to spend a few years on Earth, diving and studying oceanography. And then Whitey announced that he and his family were going to keep all of the Terri Percesepe ransom money.

"Wavy," said Stahn. "*Wu wei.*" Stahn didn't feel like arguing about anything anymore. He was still having trouble believing that he was alive. And sober. It was strange to keep waking up in the morning feeling good.

Wendy was in rare form and feeling wonderful. Three days after Stahn got to the Moon, Wendy and Terri had a big time dustboarding the lunar slopes of Haemus live for the Show. Stahn channeled the event with some interest and discussed it over the uvvy with Tre, who happened to call up that evening. Tre said he was through working for Apex Images and was going into business for himself.

"We'll be selling N-dimensional Perplexing Poultry philtres and limp-wares as fine-art objects and philosophical toys," said Tre. "Sri Ramanujan's interested in helping me."

"I love it," said Stahn. "Good luck. Let me know if you need any help with Emperor Staghorn."

Over the coming weeks, Stahn and Wendy saw a lot of Willy Taze, who was also staying at the Einstein Luna. Willy was in the process of arranging for his son Randy Karl Tucker to move up and live with him, at least temporarily. Willy figured Randy Karl could help him to repair the isopod.

"I guess then we'll move into the 'pod together," said Willy. "Though I'm a little leery. Randy Karl is pretty strange."

"So why don't you move back into the Nest?" asked Stahn.

"The moldies won't let me. They say they'll kill me if I ever set foot in there again. Man, I've got half a mind to piece back together the xoxxin' methodology of the Gurdle decryption and the Stairway To Heaven all by myself. Teach those kilpy slugs a lesson. But right now I don't have time."

"Because you and Randy'll be so busy fixing up the isopod?"

"No, Stahn. Better. Randy Karl's been asking about my grandfather—about old Cobb Anderson. When Jenny was still working with me, her simmie crypped us a copy of the original Cobb Anderson S-cube, and I archived it nice and safe with ISDN. Randy worships Cobb. Corey and I are going to design a humanoid imipolex body for the Cobbware to live on."

"*Whoah*! Nobody's ever tried *that* hack," said Stahn. "Cobb's been a bopper and a petaflop, but never a moldie." He and Willy were sitting on the roof terrace of the ISDN ziggurat, drinking juice and staring out over the city.

"You know it, brah." Willy looked a lot more stoked and happy than he'd been seeming to Stahn over the uvvy for the past few years. "And get this," Willy added gloatingly. "If my new hack works, I can let my dooky son and grandfather keep each other company. I won't have to talk to them!"

"Wavy," said Stahn.

And as for Shimmer? She'd flown off toward Earth after delivering Stahn, and more than that, no one yet knew.

REALWARE

For Isabel, Rudy Jr., Georgia and Pop

CHAPTER ONE

PHIL

February 12, 2054

"Wake up, Phil. It's your sister on the uvvy. Something's happened." Kevvie's breath was alkaloidal and bitter in the dawn.

Phil woke slowly. He liked to take the time to think about his dreams before they evanesced. Just now he'd been dreaming about hiking again. For some reason, he always dreamed about the same three or four places, and one of the places was an imaginary range of mountains, an arc of icy little peaks that were somehow very—domesticated. Easy to climb.

"Wake up!" repeated Kevvie. Her voice was, as usual, flat and practical, though now a bit louder than before. As Phil's eyes fluttered open an interesting thought occurred to him: maybe the mountains were his teeth. Sleepily he started to tell Kevvie his idea.

"My teeth are the mountains that—"

But she wasn't listening. Her blue eyes were intent, her fox-face was pinched with urgency. "You talk to Jane right now," she said, plopping the little uvvy onto the pillow next to Phil. The uvvy was displaying a tiny holographic image of Phil's sister.

Calm, practical Jane. But today Jane wasn't calm. Her eyes were red and wet with tears.

"Da's dead," quavered Jane. "It's horrible. A wowo got him? Willow says they were in bed and all of a sudden their wowo got really big, all bright and swirly, and it jumped inside of Da and the light was shining out of his eyes like searchlights and he was yelling and then his body collapsed and the wowo sucked him inside and crushed him. Da's gone! Willow's covered with his blood. It's so gnarly?" Jane's voice twisted up an octave on the last word and she began sobbing. "I can't believe it. Wowos are just a toy. Da and Tre made them up."

Phil felt a savage torrent of emotions, too fast to nail down. Relief, terror, joy, wonder, sorrow, confusion. His father was dead and he was free. No old man to judge him for not doing anything with his life. His father was dead and he was alone. No stand-up old guy between him and the Reaper.

"Dead? What . . . When did Willow call you?" Phil's eyes began throbbing.

"Just now. From the car. She's scared the wowo might get her next. She left the house to go to the rent-a-cops. The popos. She told me to tell you and for you to call her. I'm flying out. You pick me up."

"Wait, wait, this is all too—" Phil broke off in confusion. Kevvie, who'd been avidly eavesdropping, smiled and offered him a piece of her chewing gum. Phil shook his head no. Kevvie tended never to have the correct emotional response. In company, she had to look at other people so she'd know when to laugh.

"What are you going to do?" demanded Jane's little face. Her pointy chin was trembling.

"I'll call Willow, then I'll drive Kevvie's car down to Palo Alto, and then I'll call you back. And yeah, I can pick you up. But—are you sure Da's really dead? From a wowo? It's just a fancy hollow graphic that Da made up a story about! Wowos are math and bullshit!"

"Willow said the wowo pulled Da in like it was—a *garbage disposal*. She said that. She's hysterical. She shouldn't be driving."

"I'll call her. I love you, Jane."

"I love you too, Phil. Be strong. I'll see you tonight. I'm going to the airport right now."

Phil clicked off the uvvy and the room was quiet. His eyes felt so strange—bulging and puffy and aching. They wanted to cry, but for now they were dry. He imagined a wowo in his father's head. Light streaming out of his father's eye-sockets.

"Oh, poor Phil," said Kevvie. "It's terrible to lose your father. I want you to know that I'm here for you. But what was that about a wowo? That hologram thingie? Willow says that's what killed your father? A ball of colored light? The real cops aren't going to buy it. She should get a top attorney right away!"

"That's too—" Phil began, but broke off with a vague gesture. In his mind the full sentence was, "That's too stupid and cold of you to deserve an answer," but he didn't have the heart to start a fight. Kevvie's inability to visualize other people's feelings was so extreme that Phil had come to think of it as a clinical psychiatric condition. Indeed, Kevvie habitually chewed a popular empathy-enhancement gum in a perhaps unconscious effort to try and correct her deficit. "E-gum makes you part-of," as the chanted commercials had it. But it seemed like the only person that e-gum made Kevvie more sensitive to was Kevvie. All these angry thoughts went racing through Phil's head as he made the little gesture. He reminded himself that he liked Kevvie. His father's death was filling him with irrational rage.

Da dead. Phil groaned and got out of bed, sliding the groan down into a keening moan. This hurt so much that he needed to keep making noise.

He wore only a plain white T-shirt. His butt was small, his legs were short and nimble. Phil's mother Eve was Greek, while his father Kurt had been German. Phil's body hair and chin-stubble were dark, but the hair on his head was a floppy shock of blond. His sly, hooded eyes and sardonic lips made him look dissipated, which was misleading. Phil had been clean and sober his whole life. When the mandatory grade-school screening had revealed that Phil carried the genes for alcoholism and drug addiction, Phil had taken it to heart and decided to spend his life Straight Edge. A singularly mature decision for one so young—with the bonus of providing a way to be superior to Da, who'd been quite fond of booze and pot.

Phil's room was bright and messy, an odd-shaped room with a peaked ceiling and walls that slanted out on two sides. There was a lot of empty space near the ceiling, and Phil had some home-built robot blimps cruising around up there like sluggish tropical fish. Flying machines of all kinds were Phil's hobby. The blimps were like pets, and Phil had names for them: one was Led Zep of course, the others were the Graf Z, the Macon, the Penile Implant, and the largest and most colorful was the Uffin' Wowo. The last name was a riff on Da's brilliant uvvy graphic that had somehow ended in disaster less than an hour ago. Da dead. Life ends in tears.

Distractedly humming, Phil put on some thick red tights he'd gotten from the thrift store. There was gray morning light from the room's skylight. Kevvie sat on a rolling desk chair, chewing e-gum and watching him.

Phil swung open his room's arched mouse-hole door to reveal the interior of what looked like a factory. His room was located inside a bigger room, that is, Phil's room was a wooden box on stilts inside a subdivided warehouse down near the bay-side Port of San Francisco. Some developer had sliced the giant warehouse up into five or six strips, and Phil rented one of the strips along with two other people: a guy called Derek and a woman named Calla. Derek was a chaos artist and Calla a genetic counselor, while Phil was a cook in an expensive restaurant. Each of the three lived in their own cobbled-together wooden box.

Phil's and Calla's boxes were on stilts, and Derek's hung by cables from the ceiling. The huge open warehouse floor was left free and clear for other purposes. The three boxes were a bit like birdhouses in an aviary—quite literally so in the case of Phil's, as he'd designed his dwelling from the specs for a traditional pentagonal wren-house like a kid might bring home from shop class. He'd tried giving his room a round door, but after tripping over the curved threshold a few times, he'd compromised and made the door's bottom square and flush with his box's floor.

Phil started down his thin little chicken-walk of a staircase. He could see out the windows that lined the tops of the warehouse's walls: a view of the San Francisco Bay, of a floating gray ship and a docked red ship, of great four-legged cranes like giraffes or elephants, of concrete dockside elevators, of more warehouses beneath low clouds. Everything chilled and dismal. A Thursday in February.

High overhead hung a giant twisting model of DNA; this was Calla's. It was made of linked spheres that were hollow cocoons spun by a fabricant, a little DIM ant that could turn sunlight and wet leaves into filaments of rayon. The DNA model was a useful thing for Calla to show to her clients, who came here in person when the genetic information that Calla gave them was so harsh or so strange that uvvy contact wasn't enough. Phil well remembered when his genetic counselor had laid out his options: abstinence or addiction.

Down on the factory floor, two of Derek's "attractors" were active. One looked like a big wobbly green doughnut, the other like a purple cow-udder with twisting teats. They were patterns of air currents, flowing volumes of air made visible by color-lit fogs of vapor, fractally rich with eddies and schlieren. A dozen other attractor-devices sat idle: cryptic, mute technoclutter. Only when the attractors were powered up did they clothe themselves in beautiful, orderly chaos. Da's wowo had been a similar kind of thing.

Phil took a shortcut through the doughnut volume, careful not to bang into the machinery at its core. But he stepped on something anyway, something that yipped. Derek's mutt Umberto. The dog sometimes liked to sleep hidden inside the doughnut, warmed by the central generator.

"Hush, Umberto," said Phil. "It's okay." If only that were true.

In the bathroom, Phil drank some water. The water on his teeth like a mountain stream. Da dead? It was way too soon. There was still too much to say to the old man, too much to learn. Now the tears were beginning to come. A rough sob. He buried his face in a towel.

After a bit, Phil washed off his face with cold water, then cried some more and washed some more. The beautiful complexity of water, of its sounds and motions. Da wouldn't see water anymore. Phil's dream just before waking—he'd been climbing the teeth-mountains and—hadn't there been a ball of light in the dream? Phil leaned on the sink, resting his forehead against the mirror with his eyes closed, trying to look back into his dream. Wouldn't it make sense to have had a special dream just as his father died? Especially when Da had died so strangely.

"Here's some coffee," said Kevvie, who'd followed him as far as the kitchen—the little area of the factory floor that passed for a kitchen, a sink and a stove and a table with chairs on the concrete floor beneath the seventy-foot-high truss-supported corrugated steel ceiling. She'd brought the uvvy as well. "Get away, Umberto," she said, and aimed a sharp kick at the dog, who'd come over to see if he might get some breakfast. Kevvie couldn't stand Umberto.

"Don't hurt him, Kevvie." Phil took the coffee. "Thanks. I can't believe this. I feel so—it's like my head's exploding. Life's not a rehearsal. It's real." He took the coffee Kevvie handed him, but set it down without drinking.

"You better call Willow," said Kevvie. She glared at Umberto so hard that the dog went slinking away.

"I know." Phil told the uvvy to dial his stepmother Willow. Phil's father Kurt had left Phil and Jane's mother Eve for Willow when Phil was thirteen and Jane was eleven. Eve had successfully remarried, and the families had stayed reasonably close over the years, with Phil and Jane freely moving between the households of their two biological parents.

Willow answered on the second ring. "Willow Chen Gottner," her voice was loud and harsh, just short of a scream. Willow's image floated above the uvvy—she was a thoroughly Californian Chinese woman with a symmetric face, full lips, and blonde hair so shiny and processed that it looked like metal. She moved with abrupt, birdlike gestures. There were smears of blood on her hands and on her cheeks. Her normally tidy features were blurred and twisted with anguish.

"Hi, Willow, it's Phil. I just talked to Jane."

"Kurt's really dead, yes, this is his blood all over me. I'm so scared, Phil. The wowo ate him *like garbage.*"

"I'm coming right down. Where are you?"

"I'm at the popos' station. They don't know what the fuck I'm talking about. They think I murdered Kurt or some shit." Willow was notoriously foul-mouthed. This was something that Phil and Jane's mother always tut-tutted over, but it made Phil and Jane like Willow more than they might have otherwise.

"You see!" interjected Kevvie. "Tell her to get a top criminal attorney!"

Phil glared at Kevvie, but felt he had to pass the idea on. "Do you have a lawyer?"

"Right! As if I need a lawyer to deal with some stupid popo pigs who I'm paying in the first place. As if a lawyer's going to protect me from a fucking hole to the fourth dimension that ground up my brilliant handsome husband like garbage!" She glared angrily at someone out of view. "Stay away from me, you sow!" The uvvy-view jerked wildly. "Stop it!" Then the uvvy went dead. Phil immediately called again; a popo answered.

"Officer Grady, Wackerhut Police Services, Palo Alto Station."

"I was just talking to Willow Gottner?" Phil said. "We were cut off?" He could hear Willow screaming curses in the background.

"She's out of control, sir," said the popo officer. "We're concerned she could injure herself. I'm afraid we're going to have to restrain her and administer a sedative."

"Take it easy! I'll be right there. I'm Kurt Gottner's son Phil. Where's your station located? I'm driving down from the city."

The popo gave Kurt directions and added, "I'm very sorry about this, Mr. Gottner."

"My father's really dead?" Kurt asked.

"We've got a response team up there. We're still not entirely sure what the situation is. The material evidence indicates a fatality, but there's no body. And, yes, your father's missing." There was a shriek from Willow. "She wants to tell you one more thing. I'll hold the uvvy out to her."

The little image showed Willow, sitting on a plastic couch squeezed between two Wackerhut policewomen. They had their arms twined with hers in some special cop way and one of them was in the process of pulsing a drug-mist squeezie in front of Willow's tiny triangular nose.

"Phil, be sure to call Tre Dietz," said Willow, her features already slackening. "I forgot to tell Jane."

"Don't worry, Willow. I'll be right there."

"Call him!" insisted Willow. "Tell Tre the wowos are real! The bastard." The uvvy clicked off.

"Who's Tre?" Kevvie wanted to know.

"Oh, you've heard of him. He's the uvvy graphics hacker in Santa Cruz who runs that new company Philosophical Toys? He got interested in Da's work on this weird shape called a Klein bottle—and they did the wowo together. Just for a goof. Tre's only about thirty. He and Da used to hang together and tweak the wowos." The unreality of it all came crashing over Phil then and he was crying. "I don't understand, Kevvie. Da can't be dead."

"But who actually owns the rights to the wowo?" asked Kevvie.

"Kevvie, that's too—" Phil broke off and slumped in his chair. This had really taken the wind out of his sails. "Can you drive, Kevvie? I don't think I can drive. I'm all torn up."

"I'll go dress."

When Kevvie left, Umberto came skulking back out of the doughnut. Phil petted him absently as he uvvied Tre. Tre was still in bed with his wife Terri, and none too talkative.

"Yaaar?"

"Tre, this is Phil Gottner. One of the wowos just killed my dad. You better turn the rest of them off."

"*Myoor*! That's so xoxxed! I should have thought of this. Your poor dad. I'll kill the wowos right now. Later."

Phil left a message at the restaurant where he cooked, and then he put on his silver boots and black leather jacket and went outside with Kevvie. There was a stink like sewage and cheese from the big moldie nest in the abandoned red ship that sat in a silted-in slip across the street from Phil's warehouse—the Snooks family. A group of skungy sporeheads and slug-skaters were standing on the pavement by the ship talking to a couple of the Snooks moldies and buying camote, the sporeheads' drug of choice. Obviously they'd been up all night. Phil gave them the finger, pro forma. They jeered back; one of them halfheartedly threw a rock. Phil and Kevvie headed out.

It started raining as they got on the road. The traffic was light; the former Silicon Valley of the Peninsula had become something of a Rust Belt, and there wasn't much reason for anyone to go down there from San Francisco. There were only a handful of cars on the road, all tiny electric jobbies with hydrogen fuel cells. Overhead you could see a few of the richer travelers riding on great flapping moldies.

Kevvie wanted to listen to an old-fashioned morning audio show she liked, a smugly cynical guy and a woman with a dead flat that's-the-way-it-is-and-nothing-more voice just like Kevvie's. The theme of the show was that flying saucer aliens had been invading Earth for over a century and that the government was keeping it a secret. As if there were a government that mattered. As if the actual aliens who'd briefly appeared on the Moon this winter weren't more exciting than hundred-year-old lies. But Kevvie loved this shit. Phil threw a fit and made her turn it off.

"You're in a nasty mood today."

"My father's been murdered!"

"It's not like you two got along all that well. You had a big fight the last time you saw him."

Phil sighed as if his heart would break. "Poor Da. I wish I could see him just one more time." Up above the rainy freeway was a big sign temporarily wrapped in black plastic, the wind picking at the plastic and making it flap and billow in a way that spooked Phil. It was like a shroud. The brutal synchronicity of the universe displaying this just for him. Phil shuddered; the hair on the back of his neck stood on end.

February 14

On Saturday they held the memorial service on the grounds of the Bass School, the private school where Kurt had worked. A quartet of students played sweet music on violin, viola, flute, and harp. A big redwood towered overhead, fog in its branches. It had rained all night, but now the sky was clearing. The mourners sat in folding chairs on the flat ground in front of the school's main building, an enormous old two-story house, all glass and redwood, the home of a deceased software tycoon, the Bass of Bass school.

People took turns getting up and saying things about Kurt Gottner. Phil didn't feel able to speak. If he opened his mouth he'd be likely to start howling. Why expose himself like that, especially with all the Bass mucky-mucks here? Though he'd gone to Bass School for four years, Phil had no great love for the place. Da had met Willow Chen through Bass—she was a professional fund-raiser who did contract work—and Phil tended irrationally to blame Bass for his parents' breakup.

Phil's mother Eve had pulled Phil and Jane out of Bass after the breakup, and from then on they'd gone to public school—which had been, on the whole, more fun. The larger classes of the public school made it likelier that you could find a kindred spirit. And public school had moldies working as teachers' aides. You could learn a lot really fast from an uvvy link with a moldie. Bass, on the other hand, prided itself on being moldie-free. Eve hated Bass. According to her, the students and faculty at Bass were a pack of freaks and losers, and the parents of the Bass kids were snobby self-indulgent artsy-fartsy crypto-Heritagist poseurs trying to buy themselves the illusion that their neurotic drug-addicted promiscuous bulimic dyslexic brats had one single grain of brains or talent. This, Eve's opinion. Phil, however, had found many of the Bass teachers quaint and nice. Especially his father.

At the funeral, Eve sat at left end of the front row, next to Phil, Jane, Kevvie, Willow, Willow's mother Jia, Da's brother Rex, Rex's wife Zsuzsi, Rex and Zsuzsi's daughters Gina and Mary, Kurt and Rex's mother Isolde, and Isolde's kind old sister Hildegarde, whose face could stop a clock.

Rex got up and spoke a little, about how Kurt had always been accident-prone as a child. "One time when Kurt was little he fell off his bicycle and I carried him home. A few years later he broke his ankle in a soccer game and a friend and I carried him home. Today's the last time we'll do it. We're carrying Kurt home."

Not that there was going to be much of Kurt to carry. The Gimmie had scraped together maybe an ounce of blood and tissue-fragments. After freezing a sample of the DNA, the Gimmie had incinerated the remains for Willow, who'd placed the ashes in a tiny octagonal madrone-wood box. The box sat before the mourners on a small Oriental rug on the ground.

Isolde got up and talked about Kurt as a child. She was a little woman with white hair and a strong voice. "Kurt was a wise soul," said Isolde. "He knew more than other people. He was shy and he didn't like to talk about it, but I could always see it in his bright brown eyes—he *knew*. He knew more than anyone could teach him, and he spent his life exploring the world of ideas. Nothing else mattered to him. I used to say, 'Kurt, why don't you get a Ph.D. and work at a university?' 'I don't have time, Mom,' he'd say. 'I'm too busy.' And all he'd be doing would be sitting in his armchair looking at a sunbeam. Too busy. Maybe Kurt knew he wouldn't have as much time as the rest of us." She gave a mild, rueful laugh and wiped her eyes. "Kurt was so excited about his last discoveries, about his dimensions and his wowos. I only hope that some good can still come of them. We're all trying to understand this death. What happened? I'd like to think that Kurt knew—and that somewhere he's still knowing. My son was an explorer."

Willow spoke next. The Gimmie had cleared Willow of any wrongdoing; the cause of death had been written off as a freak electrical phenomenon, perhaps ball lightning, perhaps a corona discharge from Kurt and Tre's holographic wowo projection equipment. Willow looked stunning, slim and chic in a black wool suit, her face composed and perfect below her shiny bright hair.

"He was the best man I've ever known," Willow was saying. "He shouldn't be forgotten. And I've been working to set up a fitting memorial. The trustees of the Bass School have agreed to start a Kurt Gottner Scholarship Fund. An anonymous donor has agreed to match dollar-for-dollar any pledges made to this fund today. So please give generously."

"*Sell* it, Willow," Phil murmured to Jane.

Pretty soon one of the Bass administrators was speaking, a Doctor Peck, stringing together a line of fund-raising platitudes. "Bass School one big family . . . Kurt Gottner the quintessential . . . quick mind and open inquiry . . . such a special place . . . your unique opportunity . . . Kurt Gottner Scholarship Fund . . . "

Phil couldn't listen anymore. There were as many people standing as sitting, so he felt free to sidle out of his seat and wander over toward the deck of the school building where some little kids were already nosing around a big table full of canapés catered by the Bass School parents. Funeral meats. Phil cast a professional eye over the spread. He could have done a much better job, but oh well. He ate a salty deviled egg and a crustless triangle of bread with tank-grown salmon. Now a town councilman was butt-kissing the mourners, marveling at how "eukaryotic" was the nucleus of the Bass School community relative to Palo Alto at large.

Phil pushed open the big glass-paned front door and went inside the school, flashing back to his years here as a student. Fourth through eighth grades, with Da a genial distant figure teaching math and uvvy graphics to the seniors. Eve happy at home, taking care of them all, doing uvvy work for her family's olive-import business by running a dragonfly camera that talked to farmers in Greek. Those had been cozy years. The little family, the parade of days.

Phil walked down the creaky wood-floored hall, looking at the rows of pictures by primary-school students on display. Lots of hearts; odd as it seemed, today was Valentine's Day. Monday the hearts would come down, and spring flowers would be next. Or perhaps dead presidents. George Birthington's Washday, his English teacher had liked to call it—a bit of wordplay that Phil had found the very apex of worldly wit. The old school smelled the same as ever. Yes, it had been peaceful here until Willow appeared. She'd flown in like some bright magpie, snatching up Phil's woolly father for her nest.

"Are you a teacher?"

Phil's reverie popped. A slender dark-haired girl his age was looking at him. Her jawline was strikingly angled, her eyes clear, her mouth intelligent and kind. Her one nonidealized feature was her nose, which was a bit larger than normal, though it sat quite harmoniously in the calm oval of her face.

"Me? My father was the teacher."

"Oh God, I'm sorry, you're Kurt Gottner's son, aren't you? You must be so weighted that you don't know what to do."

"Yes, exactly. Thank you. My name is Phil." He held out his hand.

"I'm Yoke."

"That's a nice easy name. What was your connection with my dad?"

"Oh, I'm visiting Terri and Tre Dietz, so I came along with them to pay my respects. Tre's been so excited about your father's work, he talks about him all the time. Your father must have been a great man. How horrible that the wowo killed him."

"It's a nightmare. Everyone's scared to sleep in his house anymore. I've been down here in a motel since Thursday—today's Saturday, right?"

"Yes. Time's strange for you now, isn't it? My mother died at Christmas—which is another reason I'm here—and for the few days afterward it was like there was this glowing light everywhere and time wasn't moving at all. I even started smoking for a week, something about the cigarettes made it easier to chop up the time. And where I come from, smoking is practically impossible."

"Cigarettes, what a concept," said Phil. "I'm sorry to hear about your mother. She died on Christmas Day?"

"Christmas Eve. She was alone. I feel terrible." Yoke's eyes moistened.

"Poor Yoke," said Phil, and went on talking lest the two of them break down. "You're right about the kind of glow everywhere. Luminous. Realer than real. My father's ashes are in that little box on the rug on the lawn and the rest of him is who knows where, he's really dead and someday I'm going to die too. This—" Phil gestured at the old building around them, at the misty trees and the people outside. "This is what there is. We're like ants under lichen. Actual organisms crawling around in this shallow layer of fuzz on the Earth."

"Lichen?" smiled Yoke, wiping off her eyes. "I just saw natural lichen for the first time this week—forest lichen instead of the stuff inside moldies. Terri took me on a tour of the Big Basin redwoods. The ranger said, 'Alice Alga took a *lichen* to Freddie Fungi, and ever since, their marriage has been on the rocks.'" When Yoke hit the "lichen" pun, she giggled and raised her eyebrows.

"Or maybe we're like beetles under bark," said Phil, trying to stay poetic and serious. "Or rabbits in a briar patch. I keep having this funny vision of how glued to the Earth's surface we are. And how shallow the atmosphere is. Gaia's skin."

"I totally know," said Yoke in a heavy Val accent. Phil couldn't tell if she was mocking him or if that was a way she really talked.

Outside, the last speaker had finished and people were standing up and starting to mill around.

"Everyone's going to hit the canapés now," said Yoke. "Big-time. Before the crowd gets here I need to go to the bathroom."

"So that's why you asked if I'm a teacher," said Phil. "It's up those stairs, Yoke."

"Thanks, Phil. It's nice to meet you. Let's talk some more in a minute."

Phil watched Yoke go up the stairs. She had a high, perfectly rounded butt. But she moved up the stairs very slowly, taking one step at a time. It was so painful to watch that Phil looked away for a minute. When he looked back, Yoke was at the top. She smiled and waved as if she'd just mounted some great peak.

"Oh there you are." It was Kevvie, chewing a stick of celery. "Why'd you run off in the middle of the service?"

"It was getting to be too much for me." Phil glanced up the stairs. No more Yoke. He sort of didn't want her to see him with Kevvie. "Let's go out on the porch."

"Aren't you supposed to be doing something about your father's ashes?"

"Oh God, I forgot."

Phil hurried back down the steps to where his family stood around the rug on the ground. The reddish madrone wood of the miniature eight-sided box made Phil think of a stop sign.

Angular little sister Jane hugged Phil. Willow gave him a brittle smile. Eve, Isolde, and great-aunt Hildegarde each gave him a kiss. Rex shook his hand and clapped his shoulder, Aunt Zsuzsi patted his cheek, cousins Gina and Mary smiled sadly.

Kurt had often said he wanted them to dig his ashes into the soil under a certain big oak tree in a park near Palo Alto, he and the kids had strolled there together many times. The tree was split near its base into a pair of great twin trunks. Phil had been placed in charge of informally sneaking the ashes into the public land, so now he put the flat little box in his coat pocket. Eve had forced him to buy a suit for the funeral; it was the first time in his life Phil had ever worn one.

They stood around for a bit, sadly reminiscing. Jane recalled how Kurt had always rhapsodized about the oak tree, how he'd gone on about fractals and gnarliness and self-organized criticality.

"I remember another thing Da used to say about that tree," said Phil. "He talked about how the week before the psychologist C. G. Jung died, Jung had a dream about an oak tree blown over in a storm with great nuggets of gold found twined in its roots. 'I want to be remembered like that,' Da always said. 'That my life sent down deep roots that pulled up gold.' " Phil sighed heavily. "I don't know if he really made it."

"Of course he did," said Isolde. "Think of his students."

"And who knows what the wowo will lead to," said Rex. "Don't underestimate your old dad, Phil. He was a pisser, but he was deep."

"Your father loved you very much, Phil," said Willow reproachfully.

"When he wasn't too drunk," muttered Phil.

"*What?*"

"Never mind."

"Speaking of wowos, look at this," said Jane, hurriedly getting something out of her purse. "Willow gave this to me."

There was knotted little bit of metal in the palm of Jane's thin little hand—a gold ring tied in an overhand knot with no sign of a break or a weld. Like a tiny sculpture.

"It's his wedding-ring," said Willow. "The rent-a-cops found it on our bedroom floor. If you look closely, you can still make out the inscription, 'To Kurt from Willow.' It's creepy the way it's knotted. I don't want it."

"I think it's been knotted in the fourth dimension," said Jane. She'd always been a better student of their father's ideas than Phil. "In the fourth dimension you can knot a closed loop by lifting part of it ana out of our space, moving it across, and then pushing it back kata into our space." *Ana* and *kata* had been Kurt Gottner's special words for the four-dimensional analogs of up and down. Jane looked at Phil with intent eyes. "This means the thing that ate Da comes from a higher dimension."

"Oh sick, there's a moldie here," interrupted Kevvie, sniffing the air. She looked around. "Over there with Tre and Terri Dietz. Who invited a moldie?"

There was indeed a soft-looking figure standing with Tre and Terri Dietz, a plastic moldie shaped like a barrel-chested sixty-year-old man, white-bearded and white-haired, a man with a big head and high cheekbones, his skin somewhat papery in appearance. Even without the smell, you could tell he was a moldie from how flexibly he moved. Yoke was standing next to him, chatting and laughing with a bottle of soda in her hand. She looked like a fashion model.

"I think that's—you know—Cobb Anderson!" exclaimed Phil, glad for the distraction. Growing up as Kurt Gottner's son, he'd heard enough about higher dimensions to last him a lifetime. "We'll talk about it later, Jane." He hurried over to the other group, glad for another chance to be with Yoke.

"Hi, Phil," said Yoke. "Cobb, this is Phil Gottner. Phil, this is Cobb Anderson. Cobb flew me down here from the Moon. He's here to pick up one of his relatives from Santa Cruz. His great-grandson."

Phil was surprised. 'You're from the Moon, Yoke?"

"Duh! Why do you think it took me so long to walk up those stairs? I could see you feeling sorry for me. Well, I'm getting stronger every day."

"Hello, Phil," said Cobb, insisting on shaking Phil's hand. His imipolex moldie flesh was cool and slightly slippery. "Tre says your father was a great man. I hope you don't mind my coming to the ceremony. I'm just so happy to be out with people doing regular things. I haven't done anything normal in I don't know how many years." He had a hearty, booming voice with a crackle in the lower registers. His speech membranes couldn't quite reproduce a true human bass.

"I don't mind if you're here, Mr. Anderson, it's an honor. My father would be happy. But there are a lot of the people at the Bass School who really hate moldies. Not that you're a moldie exactly. I mean, at least you started out as human."

"I'm like a Wal-Mart greeter now," rumbled Cobb. "If that means anything to you. Pure plastic." He turned his massive head, slowly looking around. "Now that you mention it, Phil, I do notice a few frosty stares. I'll just take a little stroll around the neighborhood. This is Palo Alto, eh?

Pretty snooty. I can see why my great-grandson didn't want to come." Cobb smiled, bowed, and undulated off down the school's gravel driveway.

"I don't get how he could fly you down here from the Moon," Phil said to Yoke.

"I was inside him. Like the wendy meat in a California corn-dog!"

"Yoke's been walking around the Santa Cruz Boardwalk absorbing Earth culture," said Terri. "She and I made friends when I was up on the Moon, so I invited her to stay with us when she came down." Terri was a trim, deeply tanned woman with straight dark hair and pink lipstick. Bright golden DIM beads crawled slowly about in her hair.

"Terri's teaching me about diving," said Yoke. "I love being underwater. Everything alive all around you. I want to go to the South Pacific pretty soon. Earth is wonderful. And not just the water. The sky!" She gestured upward. A low gauzy cloud was drifting against a background of distant high clouds that rose like mountain ranges to a tender patch of blue. "How can you mudders ever get anything done? Whenever I look at the sky I forget all about whatever I've been doing. Such stuzzy soft fractals." But now her attention returned to Phil. "What kind of job do you have?"

"Non tech. I'm a cook at a three-star San Francisco restaurant named LoLo. My father was disappointed in me. But I'm good at what I do."

"We hardly have any restaurants on the Moon. Most people just eat food-paste from the tap. And raw fruits and veggies from week trees."

"Well then, Yoke, our food's another mudder thing you can enjoy learning about. I'd love to cook some special dishes for—"

"Hi, I'm Kevvie Inch," interrupted Kevvie, suddenly appearing between Phil and Yoke. "Phil and I live together. Who are you?"

"I'm Yoke Starr-Mydol. I'm from the Moon."

"What are you doing down here?"

"Oh, tourism, self-improvement. I'm interested in the ocean."

"You don't work?"

"Well, nobody's paying me," said Yoke. "I'm kind of a software artist. I like to think of algorithms for simulating natural processes. I plan to try and model some Earth things while I'm here."

"I'm a geezer-visitor," said Kevvie. "I go see old people all over San Francisco. They have little DIM machines to take care of them, but they don't have anyone to talk to them. It's sort of like being a sex-worker, except there's no sex. I have a girlfriend who's a sex-worker. Klara Blo. She and I had bacteria-style sex a few weeks back. Have you ever tried bacteria-style sex, Yoke?"

Phil groaned inwardly. This was a new obsession of Kevvie's and she was always talking about it. "Bacteria-style sex" was the current expression for getting in a tub with someone and taking the drug merge to make your bodies temporarily melt together. Phil refused to do it, because he figured that just one pleasure rush could blow him off the Straight Edge and down into the addict's regimen, wasted twenty-four hours a day, seven days a week, 365 days a year. Kevvie had started out Straight Edge like Phil, but she'd started dipping and dabbing six months ago, and now she was getting worse all the time.

"I wouldn't want to," Yoke was saying matter-of-factly. "I think it's skanky. My parents have been merge addicts since before I was born. Or were. My mother Darla died two months ago. That's something I wanted to talk to you about some more, Phil. The thing that killed Darla could have been the same thing that killed your dad. And maybe Tempest Plenty too."

"I've got it!" interrupted Kevvie. "Flying saucers took them! Have you ever seen a flying saucer, Yoke?"

"I saw the real aliens who were on the Moon in November," said Yoke. "But they didn't come in any flying machine. They travel in a form like radio waves."

"I don't buy that," said Kevvie, with irrational vehemence. Phil realized that she was lifted. "If those things you saw were really aliens, there has to have been a saucer that they came in. They use a special metal. I bet ISDN or the Gimmie is covering it up."

"There goes a saucer now, Kevvie," said Tre, pointing up at the sky. "Yaaar." He had long, tangled, sun-bleached hair and he wore weird little brown sunglasses over his no doubt bloodshot eyes. Once he'd gotten Kevvie to start staring upward, Tre looked back down. "What Yoke was talking about, Phil, is that Darla and Whitey had a wowo in their cubby. Only nobody saw Darla dying, so it didn't occur to anyone that the wowo might have been involved. I should have thought of it when Tempest Plenty disappeared last month. She was the aunt of our neighbor Starshine Plenty; we were putting Tempest up in one of our spare rooms."

Phil could tell Kevvie wanted to butt in and say something else dumb, but Terri spoke first. "Tempest was this colorful redneck pheezer," said Terri. "A dynamo. Mean as a snake. A lifter. She liked to work on Starshine's garden, always talking a mile a minute, whether or not anyone was listening. And then one morning she was gone, along with Starshine's wowo and Starshine's dog Planet. Starshine figured Tempest had taken the dog and the wowo back to Florida. She says most of the people in her family are like that. Rip something off and head for home."

"The wowo Tempest took was in Starshine's garden," continued Tre. "It was the best and biggest wowo I ever made, but the base only weighed a couple of pounds. Tempest loved to look at it, especially when she was lifted. And she was crazy about that dog. So what Starshine thought seemed reasonable. We were like, 'So what, at least Tempest's gone.' But then Willow saw the wowo swallow Kurt and I put it all together. I switched off all the wowos that I've distributed."

"How did you manage that?" demanded Kevvie.

"All of my Philosophical Toys maintain an uvvy link to me. That way I can send out upgrades and—in the case of a catastrophe like this—I can shut them down." Although Tre looked like a Santa Cruz lifter, his Philosophical Toys had made him reasonably wealthy, and he ran his business in an orderly and efficient way. "I've been wanting to ask Willow for a really detailed description of how it went down. But I don't want to tweak her out."

"You should see what Jane has," said Phil. "Hey, Jane!"

Jane was still in conversation with old Isolde and Hildegarde, and she gave Phil a sisterly "How rude!" kind of look, a big jokey frown. Isolde and Hildegarde used the interruption to begin creeping toward the buffet.

"What?" said Jane, giving Phil a gratuitous poke in the ribs as she joined them.

"Show Tre the ring."

"Way eldritch," said Tre as soon as he saw it. "Knotted in the fourth dimension. Like a calling card. Like it wants us to know."

"It?" said Phil.

"The thing that came through the wowo. It couldn't have been the wowo itself that ate poor Kurt—a wowo's just a hollow of a self-everting Klein bottle geometrized in this tasty gnarly way that Kurt dreamed up. The wowo must have attracted something." Tre gave a kind of shudder and hugged himself, looking around. "It could be inches away from us right now. Watching." He handed the ring back to Jane. "I wouldn't keep this near me if I were you."

"You take it, Phil," said Jane, handing it off like a hot potato. "Bury it with Da's ashes. If we need it again we can always dig it up."

"Like the goldfish," said Phil, referring to a dead goldfish that he and Jane had buried one winter, only to dig it up every few days to look at the progress of its decay.

"It doesn't feel right not to have all of Da to bury," said Jane. "Willow said the ashes are just part of his hand. Maybe the rest of him is in the fourth dimension."

Phil put the knotted ring in his pocket next to the box. Some of his father's stories about the fourth dimension were coming back to him. A four-dimensional monster would be able to touch the ring in his pocket without coming through the fabric. Even if he were to put the ring *inside* the box, a four-dimensional creature could still reach it, just like you can touch the middle of a sheet of paper without coming through the paper's edge. If the four-dimensional creature could see everything, what good would it do to bury the ring?

"There was a weird dimensional thing about Darla too," Yoke was telling Jane. "She disappeared on Christmas Eve. My dick of a father had left her alone, he was out with a girlfriend or something. Poor Darla. All Whitey could find of her was this little gory patch of blood. And then Whitey starts saying he's going to grow her back. He has a fairly recent S-cube of her personality, and he's gonna use her DNA to fast-grow a new body, a young sexy one of course. But when he gives some of Darla's blood to a pink-tank worker, about half of the DNA in the blood turns out to be *backward*. Clockwise twisties instead of counterclockwise." Yoke made mirror-twin helix motions in the air with her hands. "When I told Tre about it, he said that maybe some of the DNA had been flipped over in the fourth dimension."

"Your father is growing a new copy of your mother?" asked Kevvie.

"Clear," said Yoke. "The new Darla's gonna have a bitchin' real meat body, not an imipolex fake like Cobb's. Whitey's had a lot of fights with boppers and moldies. He wouldn't be able to stand it if Darla came back pure moldie. This way she'll have a meat body, although her personality will have to be off in a kind of moldie scarf that she wears all the time. A Happy Cloak."

"I've never heard of anyone doing that before," said Kevvie.

"Oh yeah they have," said Yoke. "You've heard of Stahn Mooney. Used to be a Senator? His wife Wendy is made of a meat body with a moldie Happy Cloak that drives the body. Of course Wendy's 'Cloak is really just a moldie that doesn't have any of the original Wendy's personality at all. But we'll have Darla's personality in her 'Cloak to start with." Suddenly the confidence drained out of Yoke's voice. "I hope it works. I miss her."

"What are you guys talking about?" asked Willow, wandering up to the group. She had a glass of white wine in her hand and her voice was shrill. "Help yourself to the refreshments before they're all gone. The Bass parents made a very nice buffet. And this wine is from Doctor Peck's own vineyard. It was Kurt's favorite. Eat, drink, and be merry." She looked far from merry.

"It was a nice ceremony, Willow," said Tre carefully.

"You have a lot of nerve showing up here," said Willow. "Considering that your shitty wowo killed him."

"Tre thinks it wasn't really the wowo itself," put in Phil. "He thinks it was a creature from the fourth dimension that the wowo attracted."

"Big difference," said Willow.

"Maybe you could grow a new husband," suggested Kevvie. "Like Yoke's father is doing."

"I assume Yoke is this little chippie here? How many people did you bring along, Tre? I mean besides the moldie. Do you think this a fucking hairfarmer beach party?"

"I'm sorry, Willow," said Tre. "We'll go now."

"Good!" Willow burst into tears and Jane held her, letting Willow's metallic blonde head rest on her shoulder.

Cobb appeared in the driveway just then. Tre and Terri murmured a quick good-bye and went to meet him. And then, before Phil could really say a proper good-bye to her, Yoke was gone too.

"Ooops," said Kevvie, rolling her eyes and grinning. She never knew what to make of big dramatic situations. At a time like this, Kevvie's cheery emptiness was kind of a relief. Phil linked arms with her and walked back to the buffet.

February 19

Phil thought about Yoke all the time for the next few days—whenever he wasn't worrying about the wowos or thinking about his father. He'd hoped that with the old man dead, there'd be nobody nagging him to make something of himself. But the memory tapes were playing on. Thinking about Yoke was much better. Phil thought about Yoke so much that when she turned up at the LoLo restaurant on Thursday, sitting at a table right near the kitchen, he almost wasn't surprised. Just, "Whew, here it is."

"Is this the guy?" Naranjo was saying, Naranjo the waiter who'd called Phil out of the kitchen. "Is this the hombre you lookin' for?"

Yoke was all smiles, sitting at a table with two guys and a woman. Phil recognized two of them: Saint and Babs Mooney, regulars in the San Francisco art scene. "Hi, Phil!" called Yoke. "I was hoping I'd find you here. Can you come out with us later?"

"He gotta stay and scrub a lotta potatoes," said Naranjo. "He's just an assistant chef. He gonna be here till about three maybe four A.M."

"Don't listen to him," said Phil. "It's great to see you, Yoke. Hi, Saint. Hi, Babs. I'll be through at eleven-thirty. It's ten now, so take your time eating and I can leave with you. With any luck, you'll be tonight's last customers. Things are really slow." A big storm had come in off the Pacific this afternoon and it was raining like people were up on the roofs with hoses. You could hear the splashing of the water through the glass of the windows. "You haven't ordered yet, have you?"

"How's the squid?" asked the fourth member of the dining party, a tenor-voiced fellow with shoulder-length red-blond hair that was very straight and fine. "Do you serve it with tentacles?"

"Sure," said Phil, taking an immediate dislike to the man, probably because he was sitting next to Yoke. "We've even got ink. But I'd recommend our deep-sea oarfish today. Brought in by a moldie this afternoon, he caught it himself. You can't catch an oarfish with ordinary techniques; it swims too deep. It has a nice firm flesh from living at such a high pressure. If you like, Yoke, I'll make it in a special sauce with sherry, cream, and chanterelles. Some saffron basmati rice and asparagus on the side. A few black cherries in the sauce for the sweetness and the color. And a Belgian endive salad with fresh-roasted red bell peppers and a mustard vinaigrette."

"Ooh," said Yoke. "That sounds delish. I've read those fancy food words, but I've never eaten them."

"Should we all have the same thing?" said Saint. "Babs? Onar?" Babs nodded, but the handsome, long-haired Onar insisted that he be served squid. "Stir-fry it in canola oil," he instructed. "All tentacles. And don't let them get rubbery."

"Gnarly, sir," said Phil.

Naranjo jotted down the order and went off to serve another customer. Phil lingered, gazing at Yoke, admiring her.

"Did you bury your father's ashes?" asked Yoke. "And the knotted ring? How did it go?"

"Having my dad die hurts more than I ever imagined it would," said Phil. "Today it's been a week. Yeah, I buried the ashes and the ring. I dumped the ashes out of the box; there weren't many of them. I almost wish I'd kept the ring. I need to think about it some more. Maybe I should have paid more attention when Da tried to teach me about the fourth dimension."

"I was so sorry to hear about your father, Phil," put in Babs Mooney.

"Yaaar," chimed in her brother Saint. "Poor Kurt. It would xoxx to get chopped up by a hyperspace blender." Babs and Saint had DIM lice in their hair, colorful little bugs that moved around on their scalps like tiny cars in traffic, arranging their hair in filigrees that could variously resemble paisley, crop circles, or herringbone tweed. Programming the lice was one of Saint's art projects.

"I have a theory about the wowo," proposed Onar, holding up a bony finger. "The wowos were a representation of the Klein bottle, were they not? Two Mobius strips sewn together?"

"I guess," said Phil. "But it was just a goof. An illusion."

"Perhaps the models set up a morphic resonance. Reality is, after all, a consensual hallucination. If enough people see something as a Klein bottle, then—voila—it's a Klein bottle. It's not impossible to be killed by a dream."

"Don't make it a New Age fantasy, Onar," reproved Saint. "This thing was real."

"Reality is a hobgoblin for small minds," said Onar mildly. Yoke giggled. She seemed to find Onar entertaining.

Phil got the head chef to let him prepare most of the food for Yoke's table. He cooked with fervor, and the meal was a big success. Around midnight he and the four guests stepped out of LoLo together. It was still pouring rain. Yoke did something with her uvvy as they stepped outside, and a moldie suddenly came bouncing up the street, sending out great splashes of water with each jump. It was Cobb Anderson.

"Thanks for waiting, Cobb," said Yoke. "What did you do?"

"Oh, I was going around town with Randy Karl," said Cobb. "And then we split up and I was hanging out with some homeless people in an alley off Columbus Street. Talking with them. One of them was a very intelligent fellow. It's not so much that the homeless are crazy and addicted, it's that they don't have money for rent. Just that one simple lack. We need to find a way to make cheap housing for the poor. But hey, just for right now, let me be your umbrella." Cobb stuck up his arms, and his tissues flowed upward, spreading out and thinning to make a giant umbrella that they could all stand under, the five young people in a circle around the moldie. "Better hold up the edges," said Cobb. He'd used so much of his body flesh in the umbrella that his head had sunk down to chest-level.

"Where's Randy now?" asked Yoke.

"By now I imagine he's found a moldie hooker like he was looking for. I really should get that boy up to the Moon to be with his father. Eventually. Randy's in no rush to go."

"Cobb's talking about his great-grandson," Yoke explained to the others. "Randy Karl Tucker. He's a cheeseball from Kentucky. He lives in Santa Cruz. Tre and Terri Dietz hate him. Randy kidnapped one of their moldies by putting a superleech on her. The new kind of leech-DIM. But now Randy says he realizes it was wrong. Cobb's supposed to take him to the Moon to meet his father."

"What is this 'DIM' that everyone's always talking about?" asked Cobb.

"It stands for 'Designer Imipolex', Cobb," said Yoke. "It's what everyone uses instead of the old-time silicon computer chips anymore. A DIM is made of imipolex with some mold and algae in it. Just like your new body. You were out of it for a looong time, weren't you?"

"I'm still out of it," said Cobb. "That's another reason I want to have a good look around dear old Earth before I go back to the Moon. And , like I say, Randy's in no hurry either. He's been busy spending the money his father keeps sending him. Sad to say, Willy's a little reluctant to meet his only son. At this rate, poor Randy could wind up being a remittance man—someone whose father pays him to stay away. I've told Willy he should be more excited about Randy, but so far Willy doesn't want to listen to his Grandpa. I think he's been on the Moon too long."

"Why didn't Randy come along for dinner?" asked Phil.

"Hell, he was in too big a rush to get to that scurvy place in North Beach," said Babs, laughing. "Real Compared To What. Can you even imagine? Randy's certainly a man who knows what he wants. Admirable, in a way."

They walked down the sidewalk as a single group dome. The plan was to go back to Babs's space in a warehouse not far from Phil's. Yoke, Cobb, and Randy were spending a few days with Babs. The rain made a nice reverberating sound against Cobb's taut moldie flesh, which smelled like a dank basement. Phil managed to be next to Yoke, though Onar was on her other side.

"So you're into helping people now, Cobb?" asked Onar. "Is this a result of some experiences you had while you were dead? And what was that like?"

"My original human personality was stored on an S-cube for over twenty years," said Cobb. "And, yes, that was more or less the same as being dead. That me is dead forever, and it's the same as the me right now. Memories of it? A big white light. The SUN. Endlessly falling into it, but never reaching the core. A cloud of other souls around me. The end of time, forever and ever."

"You mean 'Sun' like our home star?" asked Phil.

"No," said Cobb, "I mean capital S-U-N. At least that's the name I use. The Divine Light, the universal rain that moistens all creatures. The SUN is a little like the eye on the top of the pyramid on the old dollar bills. Except SUN isn't about money, the SUN is about love and peace."

"Oh look," said Babs, changing the subject by noticing a shop window, and the group stopped to gaze in. Colorful felt hats, each a single pastel shade, were suspended in the window, funny and bright, with an intricate patterning in their fabric. "I'm getting so into fashion," added Babs. "I've been designing lace. It's too bad nobody ever wears lace. They should." Babs herself wore a silky shawl of thick, intricate nonrepeating lace. A mantilla.

"How did that work, your getting an imipolex body?" Phil asked Cobb.

"It was interesting," said Cobb. "These two loonie moldies each started running a simulation of me. They pulled me back from the SUN. They were running two simulations of me so they could compare and contrast and get the parameters tweaked. And meanwhile they had a new imipolex body ready for me. So there were two simulations of me waiting for the one body. I and I got into a telepathic uvvy link so that we could merge and share—instead of doing sudden-death musical chairs. From that merging experience, and from being with the SUN, I got the conviction that each of us is the same person. And that's why we should be really kind. Which answers Onar's question of why I want to do good."

"How do you make the lace?" Yoke was asking Babs.

"I use fabricants," said Babs. "I don't think you have those on the Moon yet? They're crawly little DIMs like the lice in my hair, plastic ants that can spin fabric like spiders. People are using them for everything in the fashion business. I bet those hats were made by fabricants. Fabricants eat just any old thing—weeds, scrap wood, cardboard—and they spin it into fiber. I'll show them to you when we go back to my place."

"If we're going to Babs's," said Onar, "let's get some kind of transport. I don't want to walk the whole way under a vile-smelling live toadstool."

"Randy would love it," said Babs. "But we can get the streetcar at the corner up there. You can ride too, Cobb, it's run by a moldie."

The streetcar with its moldie conductor came clanking up then. Cobb and the five young people got aboard. Phil ended up between Yoke and Cobb.

"Do you think I smell bad?" Cobb asked Phil.

"Of course," said Phil. "That's the way moldies are."

"Well then, that's another problem I want to work on," said Cobb. "Besides more housing. I want to make moldies smell good. I bet a little biotech research could do it. The moldies just haven't bothered to fix their smell before because they don't care. What if the moldies made themselves smell good and built a whole lot of free housing!"

"Maybe Cobb should run for mayor of San Francisco," said Yoke. "He's friends with ex-Senator Mooney, you know. Babs's and Saint's dad."

"I've got a new life and I want to help people," said Cobb.

"A moldie run for an election?" exclaimed Phil. "You'd get all the moldie votes, but that's ten percent of the city at best. What human would vote for a moldie? Even if you did used to be a person. And you've only been in San Francisco for, what, two days? Talk about a carpetbagger!"

"Well, it would be very popular to help people find housing," said Babs. "That's like the biggest problem. Cobb could win a lot of votes by fixing up abandoned warehouses."

"Are you rich, Cobb?" asked Onar.

"I don't actually own much of anything," said Cobb. "My estate was divvied up a long time ago. My grandson Willy is wealthy, though I doubt he'd be much interested in this issue. But even without money, I have a very high recognition factor. As a politician I could act as a 'facilitator.' " Cobb smirked a little at the bogus word. "How about this?" he added, and started up a series of impressions, changing his voice and features to resemble half-remembered images of dead Presidents. "The last four letters of 'American' are 'I can.' Mo' folks, mo' better. Ask not—"

"Stow it, Cobb," said Yoke, cutting him off. "Presidents suck."

They got off the streetcar a block from Babs's warehouse, and the five humans ran there, with Cobb bouncing along next to them, hitting every puddle on the way. The inner walls of Babs's warehouse space were decorated with great webs of shiny woven fiber, bright-colored and iridescent. There was a polyglass keg of beer that Saint had brewed, and he and Onar got into drinking it.

Babs's fabricants lived in a little glass box like a terrarium, with strong lights and with a dish of wet paper for food. There were dozens of them, shiny little hourglass shapes with six legs. Babs showed Yoke how to use an uvvy to program them, and Yoke picked up on it right away. Within half an hour she'd gotten the fabricants to spin her a mantilla filled with spidery copies of her name.

Cobb sat quietly on the couch, taking everything in. He'd tightened up his body so that he was dense and practically odorless.

Onar found a great sheet of piezoplastic in Babs's supplies and flopped it out onto an open space on the floor. With a deft move of his long fingers, Onar pinched off a bit of his own uvvy to make a receiver-DIM which he affixed to the big sheet of plastic. Now the imipolex came alive with colors and shapes: some abstract, some like cartoon images and blurred photographs, all coming directly from Onar's brain. Saint put on his uvvy and got in on the act too, moving around playing air guitar and sending thought-sounds to the blanket of piezoplastic. The great sheet began to buzz and vibrate like a giant speaker, its rapid undulations sending out Saint's brain-made music. It sounded like spacey horns with cymbals and heavy-metal guitars. Everyone watched and listened in fascination, everyone except Phil, who kept worrying about how to get Yoke's attention.

Finally, Phil distracted Yoke by getting Babs to show off her old worm-farm, which was a big layer of humus between two transparent plastic walls. If you shone lights against a wall, the lavender, red-banded worms would appear, writhing up against the plastic.

"I have some smart imipolex worms mixed in," said Babs. "There goes one." A gold flicker went writhing past. "You can actually uvvy into them to get a worm's eye view if you like."

Now Babs went to get a beer, and Phil took the opportunity to get Yoke to step outside alone with him. It had stopped raining and there was some dramatic moonlight in the clouds. "If you're interested, Yoke," said Phil, "we could take a little walk and I could show you where I live. It's not far from here. My housemate Calla has a big fabricant DNA sculpture, and

Derek makes machines that do things with colored air. I have some toy blimps I made in my room. Would you like to come look at them?"

"What will Kevvie say?" asked Yoke.

"I don't think she's home," said Phil. "She was going to do something with Klara Blo tonight."

"Her friend the sex worker!" said Yoke. "I remember."

"Kevvie and I aren't totally linked or anything," said Phil, feeling himself blush. "We just happen to—"

"Live with each other," said Yoke. "Like an old married couple. Babs said you've been together for over a year. I was asking her about you."

"I'd leave Kevvie for you in a minute, Yoke," blurted Phil. "I can't stop thinking about you." There was something about Yoke—her smell, her voice, the way she moved, the things she said—she fit into Phil's heart like a key in a lock.

Yoke widened her eyes and arched her eyebrows. She slipped her hand into Phil's. "So show me where you live."

It was a beautiful night. The moon floated out from behind the drifting clouds; it was nearly full. "Where exactly on the Moon are you from?" asked Phil.

"I was talking to Terri about that yesterday," said Yoke. "She was showing me how you mudders think there's a face in the Moon. And for everyone it's different. To me it looks like a girl. And if you see it that way, then Einstein would be just at the bottom of her left eye. Which is the Sea of Tranquility."

"I've always thought the Moon looked like a smiling pig," said Phil. "With a snaggle snout."

They walked a block and turned a corner. It was dark and quiet, with calm puddles staring up at the night sky. "I feel like my father's up there," said Phil. "Hanging in the sky like an ornament. His face looking down."

"I can feel Ma like that too," said Yoke. "Dear, loud Darla. I feel kind of weird about my pop's plan to bring her back. That's not really, truly going to be Darla. I mean, don't you think there's such a thing as a soul?" Yoke sighed and looked at the sky. "The dead are kind. They want us to live. You have to believe that."

"I want to. The last time I saw my father, I fought with him. He always wanted me to be a scientist instead of a cook. He was needling me. I lost it. I told him I hated him for leaving my mother, and that his work was stupid. And then, bam, he started crying. I couldn't deal. I left. And that was the last time I ever saw him. I need to feel like he forgives me."

"Then you have to forgive *him*. Forgive him so you can forgive yourself."

Silently, Phil tried the notion on. He let forgiveness fill him; and it felt like unwrapping a rusty wire from around his heart. "This is good, Yoke, this helps." It was wonderful to be with this girl. Nobody had ever understood him so well before.

Yoke stood quietly next to him, her face turned up toward the sky—or toward him. Phil decided to try and kiss her. But just then a high ecstatic yodeling caught Yoke's attention and made her draw away.

"What is that?" she asked. "It's coming from those colored lights way down at the end of the block. Is that a ship?"

"It's an abandoned ship that's stuck in the mud at a slip right across from my warehouse," said Phil. "The Snooks family lives there. A big nest of moldies. They're betty-lifters, cheeseball whores, camote dealers, way xoxxy. If old Cobb wonders why most people don't like moldies, he should get to know the Snookses."

"What's the ship's name?"

"*Anubis.* It's decorated all ancient Egyptian. It used to be a party boat, and before that it was a freighter."

They walked the rest of the block hand in hand, the crazy urgent yelling of the Snooks moldies and their customers getting louder.

"On the Moon we hardly mingle with moldies at all," said Yoke. "They stay in their underground Nest and we stay in the Einstein dome."

A shiny gold moldie came humping across the street like a big inchworm and reared up in front of them. He had a stylized chin-beard and a striped scarf on his head just like a pharaoh. "Come aboard the ship *Anubis,* spiritual seekers. We feature the stuzziest camote in town. Key a timewave to ancient Egypt."

"It's just me, Thutmosis," said Phil.

"Neighbor Phil?" said the moldie, peering closer. "The eternal return. Metempsychosis. Yet never the same river twice. Who's the woman?"

"I'm Yoke Starr-Mydol," said Yoke. "I've just come here from the Moon."

"How about those crazy loonie moldies?" asked Thutmosis. "Are they still kidnapping Earth moldies?"

"Maybe they are," said Yoke, cocking her thumbs and pointing her forefingers at Thutmosis like guns. "Maybe I'm about to put a superleech on you. Better run!" Thutmosis Snooks grunted and went undulating back toward his ship.

Phil undid the heavy locks on his warehouse door and ushered Yoke inside. The lights were on; Derek was in his workshop in the far corner, doing something with one of his air-sculpture machines. Umberto the dog peered watchfully out from under Derek's workbench. Derek caught Phil's eye right away and pointed meaningfully toward the bathroom. Phil's heart sank as he went to look. Yoke followed along behind.

There was a throw of skin in the bathtub, bumpily billowing like a sheet with lovers under it. Now the mass surged and Phil could see four eyes in two faces; it was Kevvie and Klara Blo, merged together into one ungainly bod; the skin was theirs.

"Hi there, Phil and Yoke," said Kevvie, except it seemed like she said it out of Klara Blo's mouth, a somewhat hard-looking mouth in a rough-skinned face the color of a lemon. Ungainly lumps moved beneath the fused skin: the bones of beckoning arms. "You two wanna lift and join us in some bacteria-style sex, Phil?" came Klara's voice. "You and your new little cookie? You're missing everything with your stupid Straight Edge, Phil. Merge is the best. It's like the air is an orgasm."

"Naranjo told me you went off with Yoke," said Kevvie, talking out of her own mouth now. "So I brought Klara over here to help me wait for you." Slowly, she sat up in the tub. Her neck and shoulders pulled free of Klara. Her still-fused breasts stretched and jiggled.

"Phil, I'm going back to Babs's," said Yoke, and in an instant she was across the floor and out the door into the shadows.

"You're trying to sneak around," said Kevvie. She looked wildly unpretty. "You like that little moon-maid more than me. Her and her bullshit about aliens with no flying saucers."

With a sudden great wallowing motion, Klara tore completely loose and got up out of the tub. "You're a zerk, Phil," she said, pulling on her clothes and pushing past him. "You have no idea how much Kevvie loves you."

Kevvie went on a crying jag then, and Phil held her. She felt unsettlingly fluid—as if she might pop. After a while Phil helped her to go up to their room and get into bed. As soon as she lay down, she nodded out. He went back downstairs.

"This isn't good, Phil," said Derek. "Calla wants to evict you two."

"Is she in her room?"

"No, man, she walked in on them in the bathroom with her date, and he's this very clean wetware engineer, so you can imagine. They went back to his place in Cole Valley."

"And you?"

"You know me, Phil, I'm an anarchist. I think it's wavy to have two skanks merged in our tub. Local color. But I'm worried about Umberto here." Derek leaned down to pet his dog, who'd perked up at the sound of his name. "I'm afraid Kevvie might really hurt him one of these times. She doesn't like him, fine, I can accept that. But when Kevvie's lifted she gets so harsh and rigid, you wave? Like a killer robot. And I don't like cleaning up after her either." Derek's attention turned back to the machine he was working on. "Hey, I've got this new effect, man. Channel this." Derek turned on his machine and a big tongue of flame went whipping up into the air. "Looks like a dragon-fart, hey? And it's not really fire. It's a plasma. Cool to the touch." Derek ran his arm through the forking pillar of flame.

"I have to go back out, Derek."

"Oh no you don't."

"Kevvie's asleep for the night, Derek. When she gets like this it means she took quaak or gabba behind the merge."

"I don't want to be sitting here with her crying and melting on my shoulder when she gets up to puke, man."

"I promise I'll be right back, Derek. I just want to run over to Babs's."

"To try and square it with that other girl. What's up with her?" Derek did something to make his fire tongue reach way across the room toward Phil. "Confess to the fire-god, my son."

"I think I love her," said Phil as the cool flames licked all about him.

"Go in peace."

Phil's simple declaration to Derek crystallized his feelings. He had to find Yoke and tell her. He hurried back outside.

Across the street some wasted sporeheads were capering along the ship's railing, doing the flat-footed newt dance that sporeheads always did, their diagonally opposite legs and arms rising and falling together. A purple Snooks moldie named Ramses was playing them some trance music from a long horn he'd grown out of his nose. Gold Thutmosis came bustling over once again.

"Was that moon-girl really packing a superleech?" Thutmosis wanted to know. Moldies were terrified of superleechs, which were control patches that could turn them into slaves. For the sake of human-moldie relations, the superleechs were illegal, just as were the thinking-cap devices that moldies could use to enslave humans. But there was a lively commerce in both products just the same.

"Where did she go?" Phil countered.

"Back the way she came."

Phil took off running down the block and around the corner to Babs's. But when he got inside, Saint and Babs were alone with a pale gangly guy who was lounging back in a beanbag chair, fondling a handful of Babs's imipolex worms. Cobb, Yoke, and Onar were gone.

"Where's Yoke?" demanded Phil.

"Out flying," said Babs. "Onar bought Cobb that sheet of piezoplastic from me. And then Cobb grew wings and took Yoke and Onar out to see the Golden Gate Bridge. Yoke knew you'd come back, Phil. She said she didn't want to see you again tonight. Maybe you should try again in the morning."

"Let me introduce you, Phil," said Saint, kindly changing the subject. "Randy Karl Tucker. He's Cobb's great-grandson."

"Hi guy," said the lanky yokel, only it sounded more like "Haaah gaaah." He had pale hair and a narrow head. He was dressed in very generic clothes: white shirt and black pants. "This is a stuzzy art scene y'all got goin' here," he opined. "If I could get my dad to give me the money, I wouldn't mind buyin' me one o' these warehouses. Reckon a fella can do pretty much whatever he wants here." He smiled at Babs.

"Put the worms back now, Randy," said Babs. "You're going to hurt them. Randy just got back here from Real Compared To What, Phil. That moldie sex-club in North Beach?"

"Oh yeah," said Phil noncommittally.

"I laaahked what I saw," said Randy. "But I didn't have the dough for a real date with a San Francisco moldie. I'm still all fired up."

"Gnarly!" whooped Saint. "A true cheeseball."

"It's a lift," said Randy mildly. "Don't knock it if you ain't tried it."

"You'd probably like the *Anubis*," said Phil. "It's just down the block from here. Though if you go aboard you better know how to take care of yourself."

"Oh, I've been around all kinds of moldies," said Randy. "Thanks for the tip. Hey, Babs, I'm gonna feed one of your worms to Willa Jean. This oughta be a hoot. *Chick-chick-cheer!*"

At Randy's call, a little imipolex chicken appeared from the depths of the warehouse. It walked with a jerky strut, abruptly turning its little head this way and that. It was yellow, with a dark patch on its back.

"My pet chicken," said Randy Karl. "See that purple spot on her back? That's a special superleech that's controlled by my uvvy. Willa Jean's practically like an extra hand for me. Want a worm, chick-chick?" The grinning Randy dangled a twisting green imipolex worm a few feet above the floor.

Willa Jean beat her stubby wings and hopped, trying to get at the worm. The worm was writhing and Willa Jean was cheeping frantically. Finally Randy dropped the worm and the little chicken caught it in midair. Now the chicken squatted on the floor, stretching out her neck so as to swallow her prey the faster.

"Gobble gobble," said Randy. "Want 'nother one, Willa Jean?"

"One more, but that's the last one, Randy," said Babs. She didn't seem as annoyed with Randy as Phil might have expected. It was almost as if Babs thought Randy was cute and interesting. No accounting for tastes.

Phil looked out Babs's warehouse door, scanning the dark sky for a sign of Yoke, Onar, and Cobb.

"Poor Phil," said Babs. "You'd be much better for her than Onar."

"Yaaar," agreed Saint. "Onar's a windbag. A sneak. I know him from work. Normally I don't hang with him, but somehow he heard we were going out with Yoke tonight and he begged me to come along."

"Oh well," sighed Phil. " 'Night, guys."

February 20

By the time Phil got back to his place, Kevvie had started throwing up. Derek was nowhere to be seen, but of course Umberto was right there sniffing at the vomit, and Kevvie was cursing at the dog and trying to kick him, which made her lose her footing and fall down really hard. Seeing the toll drugs took on Kevvie made Phil grateful that he didn't do the same thing. But as always, there was a part of him that wished he could. Being a druggie would be so easy.

"Are you mad at me?" Kevvie asked him.

"I'm bored. Sad. Worn out."

It was three A.M. when they were finally settled in, Kevvie all cleaned up and the two of them in bed together. Phil couldn't immediately fall asleep. He kept thinking about his father, wishing for the zillionth time he hadn't called the emotional old man stupid, hadn't reduced him to tears.

The image of the buried wedding ring formed in Phil's mind, and he worked at trying to visualize how the ring could have knotted, trying to think about ana and kata, doing this mental homework as a kind of offering to his dad. Maybe he should dig the ring back up.

He drifted into sleep with the ring still in his mind, and in his dream he began climbing up a mountain, the ring floating in front of him, except now it was a glowing ball, a wowo that was his father's face, a face with a seam on it like a baseball, the seam continually shifting along itself, warping his father's features in a way that was painful to behold. The baseball split in half and started talking to him, Phil climbing the steep hill all the while.

"Can you forgive me for leaving your mother?" his father's voice was saying. "I can't forgive myself, Phil. Forgive me." The voice seemed to touch Phil all over his face, touch him with sticky little baby hands.

"Oh, Da," Phil answered. "Don't. We're the same flesh. I remember crawling on you when I was little. You were a giant."

"Forgive me."

And then Kevvie was waking Phil up again. She was bright and perky in a brittle kind of way. Chewing gum and drinking a cup of coffee, smiling, modulating her voice.

"I'm sorry to wake you, but it's Willow on the uvvy again," she said. "There's something new about your father. It sounds like the flying saucers came back."

Phil put the uvvy on his neck and let the image of Willow form inside his head. "The fucking tree fell over," said Willow. "The tree where you buried him."

"What?"

"Half an hour ago I rode my bike there for my morning exercise, and the tree was flat on its side. Its roots are all pulled out of the ground."

"Did you find any gold in the roots?" asked Phil. Anything seemed possible now.

"Fat chance," said Willow. "I took one look and got out of there. This scares the shit out of me, Phil."

"Yeah," agreed Phil. "I wonder if it uncovered his ashes and the ring."

"That's exactly why I'm calling. I'm worried some busybody might get the ring and I get hassled for burying that little bit of Kurt on public property. I want you to come down here and find the ring before someone else does." As well as showing a model of her face, Willow's uvvy signal showed a real-time view of what she was seeing, which was the kitchen of Phil's father's house. She'd moved back in after the funeral.

"All right, Willow," said Phil. He was pleased and surprised at the readiness of his response. "I'd be glad to." Do the right thing.

"It's the least you can do," said Willow, who'd been expecting a refusal. "After the way you treated Kurt. I called Jane and she thinks it's a good idea too."

"I already said I'm coming, didn't I? I'll get the train this morning. But I have to be back up here by four for work."

"Thank you very much," said Willow, and hung up.

"You can borrow my car if you like," said Kevvie. "I could get the streetcar. I'm just working on Russian Hill today."

"Can we talk about last night, Kevvie?"

"Can't I have fun like normal people? Don't get all judgmental. Just because you're so worried about your precious health. It was Klara's idea anyway. And what were you doing bringing that Yoke girl back here?"

"I wanted to show her where I live. We were over at Babs Mooney's. I thought she'd like to see Calla's DNA and Derek's sculptures. And my blimps."

"I bet."

"I can't put up with just anything, Kevvie. The way you acted last night was really unpleasant. I'm sorry for you, but this isn't a way I want to live. I think—"

"Shhhh." Kevvie held her finger up to her lips. "Don't say something we'll regret. I've got to go to work now, so if you don't want the car, I'm going to take it. Get away, Umberto! Would you like me to drop you at the train station?"

"Okay."

"And, Phil, when you're down there today, be sure to watch the sky. For the flying saucers. The aliens are little gray people, you know. With slit mouths." Kevvie hunched her shoulders, squinted her eyes and held her mouth funny—Phil had to laugh.

It wasn't till he was on the train that Phil remembered he'd planned to try and stop by Babs's to see Yoke before leaving. It occurred to him that perhaps Kevvie had thought of this. Maybe that's why she'd been so quick to give him a ride.

In Palo Alto, Phil got a moldie to rickshaw him to his father's house from the train station. Willow said she didn't want to go near the tree again, so Phil borrowed her bike and rode over there by himself.

Some kids were climbing on the fallen tree branches. The tree was cracked and split; a full half of it was gone. There had been two trunks before, and now there was only one. But the roots were all there. There was a big hole where the roots had pulled out of the ground. Phil flopped Willow's bike down on the ground and, just to set his mind at ease, walked across the little crater to get at the fallen tree's roots. He pulled a dozen or so rocks out of the roots' embrace, scratching each of them to see if maybe, just maybe, it was gold. But none of them was.

Now Phil searched for the spot where he'd left the ring and emptied out the ashes; this took a minute, as everything was so plowed up. His father's last resting place was at the edge of the hole, right opposite the split, fallen remains of the tree. It didn't take too much imagination to think that the disturbance had spread out from there. Phil crouched down and dug at the loosened dirt. And, yes, there was the knotted ring, glinting up at him as if to say, "Hi, I've been waiting for you." Phil pocketed it and headed back to Willow's.

Willow prepared a little lunch of vegetables and noodles. They talked about Kurt. Phil told Willow he was sorry he'd argued with Kurt that last time. Saying this made him feel better.

Willow asked to see the ring once more after all, so Phil handed it to her. She examined it and then looked at Phil curiously.

"Didn't you notice that it's changed again?"

"What do you mean?"

"Look." Willow held up the ring with her long red fingernails. Phil studied it. And—well—maybe the ring was knotted in a subtly different way from before. Or maybe not. An overhand knot instead of an underhand? Would that make a difference?

"Look closer," said Willow. "Look at the inscription."

And then Phil saw that the writing was backward:

.wolliW morf truK oT

"Do you think Da's really dead?" asked Phil suddenly.

"I saw the wowo eat them up, Phil. First Friedl and then Kurt."

"Friedl? Your dog?" Phil recalled that Willow had owned a dachshund named Friedl. He hadn't consciously noticed the dog's absence, but, yes, come to think of it, the house was much quieter than usual. Friedl had been quite the yapper. "How come you didn't say anything about Friedl before?"

"Oh fuck, I guess I felt guilty. It was Friedl who got into the wowo in the first place. Kurt and I had been about to—we were in bed naked together and Kurt turned on the wowo to make a romantic light. And then suddenly Friedl starts carrying on like she's fallen into a salami slicer. And when I looked over there, the wowo was down by the floor and it had gotten all big and warped looking and Friedl was—I don't know, it was like she was stretched out over the wowo's surface. All blown up like a picture on a balloon?" Willow held her arms out, making a big round shape in the air.

"But a wowo's small," said Phil.

"Not when it ate Friedl and Kurt," said Willow. "Friedl was like *inflated*—except for her little head; it was sticking out barking like crazy. And I screamed for Kurt to do something and he grabbed at Friedl, and the stupid dog bit him—Friedl was like that—and Kurt couldn't get loose, she'd sunk her teeth into him and Kurt was yelling and then all of a sudden the wowo went over from Friedl to Kurt—so fast. And Kurt swelled up big like Friedl had been and Friedl was her own right size, but she still wouldn't let go of Kurt, she'd completely panicked. There was light inside Kurt, he had glowing eyes like in a monster viddy and he was yelling like—I didn't tell this before—he almost sounded like he was happy? *Whooping.* And then he got smaller and smaller, except for his hand sticking out trying to shake Friedl loose, the hand and the dog flopping in and out of the ball, half in and half out, and then—*pop*—Friedl and Kurt's hand exploded and blood spurted everywhere. After that I didn't see or hear Kurt anymore. There was blood all over me, and tiny little pieces of them on the floor. And the shit-ass wowo went back to pretending to be normal. I ran out of the room and uvvied the popos. The wowo wasn't doing anything more, so right before the popos came, I flushed the Friedl pieces down the toilet because I didn't want them to say it was my fault for having such a dumb dog." Willow stared at Phil, her eyes searching his face.

"It's not your fault, Willow," said Phil. "I'm not going to blame you."

"Thanks." Willow sniffed and blew her nose. "You should get rid of that ring fast, you know. Take it out onto the Golden Gate Bridge and drop it down into the outbound tide. I bet the thing that blasted the oak tree is the same fucker that came through the wowo. And it could come a third time. Things always happen in threes. Get rid of that ring today, Phil. It would be too awful if something happened to you."

"I hear you," said Phil, pocketing the ring.

All the way up on the train Phil looked at the ring and thought about it. He remembered a math story that his father had told him about the legendary A Square, an inhabitant of an imaginary two-dimensional world called Flatland. A Square's eye was a dot at one corner, his mouth an inlet on one side. Whenever A Square was right side up, his eye was on his northeast corner and his mouth was on his east. But one day a Space-lander called A Sphere lifted A Square out of Flatland, flipped him over, and set him back down. And from that day on, whenever A Square was right side up, his eye was on his northwest corner, and his mouth was on his west. He was his own mirror image. .erauqS A

Something had pulled Kurt into hyperspace, had knotted his ring, and had later flipped the ring over in the fourth dimension. Maybe Kurt had only lost his hand—and no more than that. Maybe the hand had been crushed by the slam of a hyperdoor to hyperspace, and maybe Kurt was alive and healing—someplace?

Looking at the ring, Phil felt more and more fascinated. It was such a power object. The only remaining link to his father. And so what if the hyperspace thing did come for him? Was dying really so bad? No more work, no more hassles, no more trying to find the right girl. Phil recognized the insanity of the thought patterns, but for now he was too drained to do anything more than just let them run. He put the ring back into his pocket and stared slackly out the train window, thinking about death.

As soon as Phil got back to San Francisco, he went over to Babs's. He needed to see Yoke. But Yoke was gone. Worse than that, she was out of the country.

"That's right," Babs told Phil. "She and Cobb and Onar went to Tonga. Onar goes down there all the time for Meta West Link. And since Yoke is so eager to go diving in the South Pacific—why not? They got inside Cobb and he rocketed them there. So fine, good-bye all, but get this, Randy Karl Tucker still thinks he's welcome here." A smile played across Babs's lips.

"I can't get rid of him. He has this ridiculous idea that I'm not completely revolted. He claims he has some ideas for my art."

"Yoke left with Onar?" Phil could hardly take it in.

"Onar's *wooing* the girl," said Babs. "Somehow he heard Yoke was here visiting me, and he got Saint to introduce them. Saint and Onar work together at Meta West, you know. Well, not exactly together. Onar's a tech and Saint's a maintenance manager. Just don't call him a janitor."

"I thought Yoke liked me," said Phil, his voice breaking.

"I'm sorry, Phil," said Babs. "Yoke thinks you're nice, and that you're cute, but she didn't want to break you up from Kevvie. She hates the idea of being the other woman. Maybe if you were single you'd have had a chance."

CHAPTER TWO

YOKE

February 20, 2054

"Rather snug in here," said Onar. "But I like it. Remarkable way to travel."

Yoke and Onar were packed in back-to-back, with Cobb's moldie plastic flesh wrapped all around them. They were streaking through space near the top of a long parabolic trajectory that led from San Francisco to Tonga. Cobb had an ion-jet in his feet, and the algae in his moldie body provided a steady flow of oxygen.

The moldie flesh near Yoke's face was transparent, like a faceplate. Looking down at the great fat curve of Mother Earth's body, Yoke could see the familiar black of space above the bright curving line of the atmosphere. Phil had called it Gaia's skin. Yoke felt bad about not saying a proper good-bye to him. But the scene with Kevvie last night had been too gnarly. How had a straight babe like Phil ended up with a bloblolly? "Bloblolly" was an insulting expression for "female merge user" that Yoke's twin sister Joke liked to use; Joke herself had gotten the expression from a loonie viddy show called *Kid Skid*. Occasionally Joke had dared to call their mother Darla a bloblolly to her face, and a fierce Darla tongue-lashing would ensue. Joke was brave. Yoke felt a sharp pang of loneliness as she thought of her sister and her mother; this was the longest by far that they'd ever been apart. Seeing the black of outer space was making her homesick for the Moon. Getting back to Phil, the fact that he lived with a bloblolly probably meant there was more wrong with him than met the eye. He seemed a little passive, almost paralyzed. No doubt bailing had been the best thing for her do. Still, there was something sweet about Phil. He'd been so eager for her to like his food.

"Did I tell you that I'm friends with King of Tonga?" Onar asked just then. "The Tu'i Tonga himself. He's a delightful fellow." His voice sounded fruity and intimate in the little cavity of air that surrounded his and Yoke's heads. Spongy little palladium filters in their nostrils eliminated Cobb's characteristic moldie smell.

"You did tell me that," answered Yoke. "Twice." She wasn't quite sure about Onar. "Why does Tonga have a King anyway?"

"It's the only Polynesian nation never to have fallen under the rule of a foreign power," said Onar. "Right, Cobb?"

"That's right," said Cobb, talking to them via uvvy. "Do you want to browse a guidebook, Yoke?"

"No. I like real things better than virtual things. I'm done with school."

Pretty soon they were arcing back into the atmosphere, heading down toward the multitudinous islands of Tonga, tiny dots in the vast Pacific Ocean, visible through the gaps in the clouds. The clouds were arranged with a surprising regularity, like cabbages in a farmer's field. Onar guided Cobb to the biggest of the Tongan islands, Tongatapu, on one side of which was Tonga's main town Nuku'alofa.

They landed in a sandy shell-strewn parking lot next to the city dock. Cobb split open to disgorge his two passengers and the two carry-on bags they'd brought. And then he formed himself back into his original old man shape, grown a bit beefy from the sheet of imipolex he'd gotten from Babs. Judging from the stature of the golden-skinned Tongans whom Yoke could see nearby, Cobb's new size would fit right in. For the moment the locals were just staring at them, too startled to approach.

"Here we are," said Onar. "This is the Queen Salote Wharf."

"It's quiet here," said Cobb. "I like it."

Besides the Bay Area, this was the only place on Earth that Yoke had visited so far. She was surprised at how primitive things were. Like in a travel viddy. A rusty Tongan Navy ship floated in the harbor; in addition there were a ramshackle ferryboat, a few motorboats and one or two yachts. That was it for the capital city's port. The rutted and potholed road along the waterfront carried a light traffic of battered electric trucks and cars, old models from the 2030s. A low shack across the road offered drinks and food; next to it was a "Guest House" that looked barely big enough to house the owner's family. Farther down the waterfront was a weathered white building like a Victorian mansion, and inland from it was what looked to be the town center, a dingy cluster of patched-up buildings.

"Welcome to da neighborhood," said a huge man with a horizontal wrinkle in his forehead. *"Malo e lelei."* He was wearing a torn white shirt and a brick-red polyester skirt. "My name is Tiko."

"Greetings, Tiko," said Onar. "We've met before, no? I was down here six months ago visiting with HRH."

Yoke knew by now that Onar used "HRH" to stand for "His Royal

Highness," meaning the King. *Ugh.* For whatever reason, Yoke hated all things British—with the single exception of Lewis Carroll.

"That's right," said Tiko. "Onar Anders. My wife Waloo is working at the New Beach Guest House. You gonna stay wid us again?"

"Yes indeed," said Onar. "We'll walk there from here. As you see, we traveled light." He nudged the two little bags at his feet.

"All the way inside dis moldie," mused Tiko, gingerly patting Cobb's shoulder. He leaned close to Cobb, sniffed him, and burst out laughing. "Low tide at da lagoon."

"I'm actually a human in a moldie body," said Cobb, drawing back. "Cobb Anderson. Perhaps you've heard of me?"

"No sir," said Tiko. "What are you known for?"

"I built the first robots for the Moon, sixty years ago," said Cobb. "The boppers? And then the boppers chewed up my brain and extracted my software. I've had a series of robot bodies since then. This one is the best. Look." Cobb flipped his wrist and his right arm split up into five thin arms, with a tiny hand at the end of each of them. He picked a different seashell up with each of the five minihands and waved them about.

"Most kinky," said Tiko. "And you can fly. Yes, I saw you three come shootin' down like a diving bird. Did you come in one jump all da way from America?"

"Never mind where we came from," said Onar.

A big handsome woman had joined Tiko. She wore a ground-length skirt and a yellow T-shirt with a picture of some kind of sea creature that Yoke couldn't make out. "Did Onar pay you?" the woman asked Yoke. Odd question.

"No," said Yoke. "We're friends. My name's Yoke. I'm from the Moon."

"I'm Oofa," said the woman. "That's my boat over there." She pointed to an insectlike hydrofoil boat with a quantum-dot-powered water-jet motor. "When you're ready to go diving, I'm the one to take you."

"I'm very interested in diving," said Yoke.

"I've got the equipment and the helpers," said Oofa. "I work with Sea Cuke Divers, right over there behind the guest house." She pointed across the street.

"I'm planning to use him for my dive-suit," said Yoke, nodding toward Cobb.

"Moldies are the only way," said Oofa. "But I think you better use a local. We've got moldies working out of Sea Cuke. I dive in them all the time. I'll engage two moldies and show you some very special things."

"Just get one for yourself, Oofa. I trust Cobb. Maybe we could go diving tomorrow. Is that okay with you, Cobb?"

"What?" The old man moldie's attention tended to wander.

"Okay if you and I go diving with Oofa tomorrow?"

"We'd better check our schedule with HRH first," said Onar. "It's possible that he'll have plans for us tomorrow. Or perhaps Cobb will have something he'd rather do."

"What's *with* you, Onar?" said Cobb. "Of course I'm taking her diving. I didn't get a new body and fly all the way down to Earth just to start kissing large Polynesian butt."

"No problem, no problem," interrupted Oofa. "We'll go diving in the morning. I'll line up two moldies just in case Cobb changes his mind. Tashtego and Daggoo."

Tiko walked down to the New Beach Guest House with them; he insisted on carrying their bags. It was early afternoon and plenty hot in the sun. Down here, February was high summer. Onar pointed along the heat-shimmering road to the white Victorian building in the distance.

"That's the Royal Palace, Yoke. It burned down in 2010, but the Tongans faithfully rebuilt it. I think we may be having dinner there with the King tonight."

"Da King don't live in it no more," corrected Tiko. "He started livin' down by da lagoon."

"I can imagine why," murmured Onar, but Yoke didn't push him to explain. The sun made talking too difficult.

The New Beach Guest House dated back to the twentieth century; it was a quaint cinder-block structure with a wide concrete porch and many open doors. There were swaying palms. The shade was a palpable relief. Yoke flopped down on an ancient metal porch chair and caught her breath.

"Mrs. Yoshida?" called Onar, but no answer came.

"She not gonna answer," said Tiko. "Everyone resting till suppertime. Just pick an empty room." He waved a good-bye and disappeared off behind the house.

"Two rooms," said Yoke.

Onar looked at her with mild disappointment. "We won't be sleeping together? It would be less expensive to share. Not that I want to presume on our brief acquaintance."

"I don't think so," said Yoke. It had been pleasant enough when they'd smooched a little last night—even if she'd only been kissing Onar to somehow spite Phil for Kevvie. But flying all the way here squeezed into Cobb with Onar had been a definite turn-off. And now Onar kept acting so—British.

"Quite," said Onar, with a little bow. "I'll wage a courtship for your favors, milady Starr-Mydol." Double *ugh*.

Yoke and Onar found two empty rooms on the ocean side. The New Beach Guest House was an incredibly casual place, with no locks on any of the doors. Some of the other guests were in their rooms napping or reading. While Onar made some uvvy calls, Yoke took a shower and put on her silvery summer dress.

"HRH is sending 'round a limo for us in half an hour," announced Onar when Yoke reappeared on the porch. "He'll be entertaining us at his country estate. It's on a little spit in the Fanga Kakau Lagoon." Onar sat calmly on a rusty chair, looking pleasant and relaxed. He really was very handsome. The breeze plucked at his long reddish-blond hair and rattled the leaves of the palms. "I suppose I should bathe."

"Where's Cobb?" asked Yoke.

Onar pointed, and Yoke noticed a shiny puddle of plastic on the ground near the guest house. Cobb was relaxing moldie-style, lying there in a patch of sun and letting his algae soak up the light.

Onar went off for his shower and Yoke got a bottle of soda from the kitchen fridge. She sat on the porch and looked at the ocean and the sky, with the endless puffs of cloud marching out over the Pacific forever. She picked up a handheld fan, a woven palm thing with feathery fringed edges. She waved it gently, enjoying the gentle pulses of air.

A vortex is like a boulder, mused Yoke as she played with the fan. If you hit a boulder, it breaks into smaller rocks; if you jolt a vortex, it decomposes into a pack of smaller vortices. The vortices coming off the edges of the fan would be interesting to model.

Overhead the light breeze rattled the leaves of the palms. It was so wonderful to be loose in the open air of this great living world. After a lifetime in the pawky corridors of the Moon, Yoke couldn't get over the oceanic dimensions of Earth's atmosphere. The lucky mudders walked around at the bottom of a very sea of air.

Around four o'clock the "limo" showed up, a tiny electric car like all the others, chauffeured by an enormous Tongan man named Kennit. He had generous Polynesian features, and his curly hair stood up in an Afro. He wore a shirt with a necktie and a blue serge skirt. Over the skirt he had tied on a tattered palm mat, some kind of ceremonial thing. He was formal, though with a cheerful twinkle. He had a funny accent; he said "yis" instead of "yes." Onar already knew him. Apparently Onar had once won a little money from Kennit in a pinochle game—and didn't want to let Kennit forget it.

Hearing Onar and Yoke preparing to leave, Cobb perked up and poked his head up out of the puddle. "Am I invited?" he wanted to know.

"You definitely should follow us down to the Foreign Ministry to register," said Onar. "But as far as dinner goes—I mentioned you to HRH's secretary, Cobb, and of course HRH would like to meet with you, but I'm afraid our little party will be for humans only."

"I'm human," protested Cobb, his plastic old man's head bulging out of the shiny patch on the ground.

"Maybe you should try making friends with the Sea Cuke dive moldies," continued Onar. "Or if you want to be with humans, you could go to a bar. The Happy Club is quite colorful. There's a lot of fakaleitis there." Onar looked over at Yoke and explained, "That's the Tongan word for transvestites. Boys raised as girls. It's not uncommon. They're quite promiscuous. Takes some pressure off the women, I suppose."

"The Happy Club's a dangerous place, Mr. Anders," put in Kennit.

"But isn't it true that moldies are welcome there?"

"Maybe a little too welcome," said Kennit, making an abrupt slicing gesture down his front.

"What's that supposed to mean?" asked Cobb in alarm. He'd grown himself back up into human form.

"That happens here too?" said Onar.

"Yis," said Kennit.

"*What* happens?" asked Cobb.

"Oh, you know," said Onar. "Sporeheads slitting open moldies to get all of their camote at once."

"God," said Cobb, looking down at his body. "If they want those little fungus nuggets so much, they only have to ask me. I gave some camote to my great-grandson just the other day. Randy Karl Tucker. He's a little that way. It comes from being a cheeseball. I just hope he's staying out of trouble in San Francisco. That boy." Cobb sighed heavily. "I better not go to the Happy Club."

"Whatever you like, Cobb," said Onar. "But right now you should follow us to the ministry so we can get you a chirper. According to Tongan law, moldie visitors have to be tagged. It's like an electronic visa."

"I don't need no stinkin' visa," said Cobb. "You go on without me. I think I'll fly around the island. See you here in the morning, Yoke. We'll go for a dive."

Onar shrugged. "I thought you might feel that way. Just as well if you don't come at all."

The elevator in the Foreign Ministry building had a marble floor. It was possibly the only elevator in Tonga, and it was manned by a dignified man dressed like Kennit: white shirt, tie, and blue serge skirt.

"Hello," Yoke said.

"*Malo e leiei,*" said the elevator operator, kindly but firmly. "You must learn to say hello in the Tongan way. *Malo e lelei.*"

"*Malo e lelei.*"

A trim Tongan woman in a gray dress greeted them near the elevators. She was wearing an uvvy.

"Hello, Mr. Anders, I'm glad to see you. We are on the point of closing down for the day. Quitting-time is the one appointment that Tongans observe punctually! But I believe Mr. Olou is still here. And first we have our little business with your friend's visa."

"Excellent, Eleani," said Onar. "Let me introduce my friend Yoke from the Moon. Yoke, this is Eleani Matu. She's a Vice-Minister."

"Did Onar get you a contract from Meta West Link?" Eleani asked.

"No, I'm just a tourist along for the ride."

"Yes, yes," laughed Eleani. "Of course you are. Step into my office and I'll give you the visa." Eleani led them into a cool, dark room with elegant modern furniture. "Sue Miller," she said, nodding to Yoke. "It's all set."

"Huh?"

"It's your identity of record," said Onar. "Eleani's in charge of Tonga's interface to international ID protocols. Tongan counterintelligence, that is. She's setting up some one-month ID viruses for you and Cobb."

"Why?"

Onar looked cagey. "You'll find out later on tonight. When we go to meet the King. Suffice it to say that HRH wants you to help him with a mission that could lead to you getting hold of something extremely valuable, and he doesn't want any off-islanders hounding you for it. It'll be for your own good if nobody can recognize you."

Eleani looked hard at Yoke, then gazed blankly at the wall for a moment, off in the cyberspace of uvvy. "Yes," she said presently. "It's all here. Sue Miller died in a fire and shipwreck off Tongatapu last year and our navy recovered her body. She had a sailor moldie named Squanto who was also lost in the fire. We'll morph you into Sue and Cobb into Squanto, Yoke. I'm releasing the ID viruses now. They'll live till next month, and they're smart enough to actively search and replace any images of you two. That way if any person or moldie happens to video you, Yoke, the transmitted image is going to show Sue. This means that for the next month nobody's going to be able to take a picture of you. It'll look like this." Eleani uvvied Yoke an image of a skinny woman with short, dark hair.

"But isn't Sue Miller on record as being dead?" asked Yoke.

"No, no," said Onar. "In this day and age, an identity is a precious thing. When the Tongans find a body, they always incinerate it and base an ID virus on that person."

"This is creepy," protested Yoke. "You're not planning to murder me or something, are you?"

"Of course not," said Eleani. "Silly girl. This is for your protection, I'm sure! All right then, Yoke, I'm going to uvvy you the Sue Miller and Squanto identity codes now, in case someone directly asks you for ID. Very good. You have a registered Tongan visa in the name of Sue Miller for thirty days. Now let's see about Mr. Olou."

"If I have this fake ID," said Yoke, "does this mean I have to call myself Sue while I'm here? And have to call Cobb—Squanto?"

"Too much trouble," said Eleani. "On the islands nobody pays so much attention to details. My understanding is that we only need the fake ID for the rest of the world. In case someone takes your picture after you get hold of whatever it is you're supposed to get. With the ID virus nobody need ever know it was you. You'll be able to return home and live peacefully."

At the end of a marble hall they found a darkened office with a leathery Tongan man sitting in an armchair wearing an uvvy. All the blinds were drawn. The Tongan's eyes were closed, but he opened them when Onar, Yoke and Eleani entered.

"Onar?" he said. "Very good, very timely. Put on your uvvy, if you would, and join me."

"Would this be of interest for my friend Yoke as well?" said Onar.

"She is most welcome," said Mr. Olou. *"Malo e lelei,* Yoke. Please take a seat, both of you."

They settled into a matching pair of chrome and leather Barcelona chairs. Eleani glanced at her watch and excused herself.

Yoke put on her uvvy and followed along as Onar joined Olou in cyberspace. The three of them seemed to be standing in a cartoon jungle, with bright colored vines stretching from the ground upward to—well, upward to nothing. No trees in sight, just lots of colored vines rising up forever above the simmie body icons of Yoke, Onar, and Olou. Glancing down at herself, Yoke saw that she was wearing her usual simmie, the Alice from *Alice in Wonderland.* The ground beneath her feet was soft black dirt with little beetles and sow bugs in it.

"The vines display the Cappy Jane sky-ray signal flow," said Olou. He looked like a grass-skirted, spear-waving Tongan warrior. "I've been improving the visualization, Onar. As you know, one hundred percent of our Cappy Jane signal flux is licensed to Meta West Link. The color spectrum codes from red through blue represent the various fee levels." The vines were glowing like rainbow neon tubes.

"Can you show me one of the bandwidth pirates?" asked Onar, whose body icon was that of a natty man in tails and top hat.

"Wait," said Olou, crouching with his spear at the ready. All at once he flung the spear at a purplish-white vine in the middle distance. "That's one of them," he said. "Bull's-eye. Now I've captured that signal into nonvolatile storage."

"I may be able to display it as a richer image," said Onar. "I have some rather wonderful virtual tools. They're in-house products of Meta West." He began pushing his way through the thickets of colored tendrils, closely followed by Olou. Yoke tagged along, wondering at the tingly feel of the vines.

Working quickly, Onar and Olou hauled down dozens of meters of the purplish-white pirate vine from where it disappeared up above. This preliminary task accomplished, Onar caught Yoke's eye and smiled confidently. He drew himself up and bowed as if beginning a performance. To begin with, Onar made some occult passes with his hands, and a beautifully inlaid, coffin-sized box appeared between him and Olou. It looked like a prop used in a "Disappearing Lady" stage-magic illusion. Then with an elegant snap of his fingers, Onar produced a scimitar from the air and proceeded to wield it like a homicidal maniac, slicing the vine into a mound of two-meter segments. He did this with great theatrical flourishes and much mad rolling of his eyes. Yoke began to giggle and Onar glowed with pleasure. He stuffed the inlaid box with what seemed like many more segments than should fit—and perched himself on the lid, quizzically cocking his head to listen.

"*Shroop!*" sang the box. "*Shroop, shroop, shroop!*" The high, metallic sound reminded Yoke of an artisan's band saw cutting up slabs of moon-rock.

Onar hopped behind the box and started to open the lid, which faced roughly toward Olou.

"Careful there," said Olou, seeing something. He backed off so rapidly that he got tangled in the vines. For just that critical moment he was pinioned in front of the box. "Onar, don't!" he screamed.

It was too late. The lid slammed all the way open, and out rushed something quick and bright and overwhelming, something that leapt at Olou and crumpled him. This happened in an instant and then the thing was heading for Yoke, spreading itself out to an immense size. Yoke was already moving her arm to pull her uvvy off her neck, but the fast shiny thing got to her too quickly. It looked like a jellyfish, but with a smiling humanoid face that was somehow etched into its transparent flesh. It engulfed Yoke, and her overloaded uvvy sent out a stunning burst of pain. As if from very far away Yoke felt the slow-motion jolting of her body falling from the Barcelona chair.

When Yoke woke it was dark. Her head was throbbing. She was lying on the hard marble floor. The Foreign Ministry building around her was completely silent.

She peeled her uvvy off her neck; the skin underneath was raw and tender. She couldn't see if Onar and Olou were still in the room. Unsure where the light switch was, she went over to the window and opened the shade. The faithful Moon was a few handbreadths above the horizon, bright and full and tropical behind palm frond silhouettes. People were calling to each other, dogs were barking, and somewhere nearby an animal was grunting. Nuku'alofa came alive at night.

Looking back into Mr. Olou's office, Yoke could see Olou and Onar both lying on the floor. Dead? She paused, afraid. Her mind struggled to process the situation.

That jellyfish thing; the face on it had looked like—Onar? And it had said something just as it swallowed her, something important—but somehow impossible to bring to mind. She couldn't stop obsessively trying to remember it. As she circled around the memory, she found herself thinking about the day three months ago when some alien personality waves had taken over the bodies of a bunch of moldies at Willy Taze's house. One of the aliens had been a being called Shimmer, who came from a place where beings led zillions of simultaneous lives all at once in parallel time. Did the jellyfish have something to do with Shimmer? Yoke tried again to remember what the voice had said but she still couldn't bring it to mind. She grimaced, trying to shake off the memory.

"Hey Onar!" she called. "Mr. Olou? Wake up, veks! Please don't be dead . . ."

Onar stirred and sat up. Like Yoke, his first act was to take off his uvvy. But somehow he didn't look as if his head hurt. "God help me," he muttered, then looked up at Yoke against the moonlit window. "Are you all right?"

"Yes, but what about Mr. Olou?"

"Awful," said Onar, crawling over to the fallen Tongan. He leaned over Olou, thumping his chest and briefly attempting mouth-to-mouth resuscitation. "He's gone," said Onar presently. "It's my fault. I was showing off for you and I blundered. I'm a fool. A capering popinjay."

Mr. Olou's body lay utterly motionless, with a deep stillness that Yoke could somehow sense as that of a corpse. A sleeping person is only conditionally immobile; if you poke them, they'll arise. But Mr. Olou—Yoke could tell that no matter how much anyone bugged him, he'd never get up again. The stark moonlight made the dead man's mouth a ragged hole.

"Let's get out of here, Onar."

"I agree." He looked down at the body. "Forgive me, old friend."

The elevator was turned off for the day, so they took the marble stairs down. There were no lights. Onar caught Yoke's elbow and made her pause on the first landing.

"Before we go any further, Yoke, I have to ask you something." His breath was warm and pleasant in the darkness.

"Okay," said Yoke. She had a feeling they were going to kiss. It was hardly appropriate, but for some reason that's what she wanted. She'd felt a redoubled attraction to Onar ever since the jellyfish blast. A way to spit in the face of Death?

"Can I trust you to keep a secret?" asked Onar softly.

"Trust 'Sue Miller'? What is that about, anyway?" She put her hands on Onar's waist, trying not to think of Mr. Olou.

"The business I'm down here for—my business with the King—it's rather hush-hush. Can you promise me that you won't talk to anyone about what you see and hear? If you can help me out on this, there might be some rather substantial rewards for you. But you mustn't tell."

"Oh yeah?" said Yoke. Now that she was primed to kiss Onar, she was having trouble focusing on what he was saying.

"Not Cobb, not your parents, not Tre and Terri, no one," whispered Onar as he put his arms around her. "Not yet. Eventually, everyone will know. And they'll be glad. I promise you. It's a wonderful surprise."

"All right," said Yoke, and pressed her lips to his. It was romantic here in the marble Tongan dark. Onar smelled good and his body felt strong and lithe. It was pleasant to embrace him. They kissed for a minute, and then Yoke broke it off, feeling guilty about dancing on Mr. Olou's grave.

Outside they found Kennit standing in the street, talking with a couple of other Tongans. He walked over to Onar and Yoke.

"Good evening. You are ready?"

"There's been an accident, Kennit," said Onar. "Mr. Olou is dead. He suffered an attack while we were using the uvvy."

"So it comes to that," said Kennit, his face clouding over. "You left him inside?" He walked over to rattle the ministry door, which had locked itself behind Onar. Kennit called something in Tongan and the men he'd been talking to came over, opened the door and went inside.

"Poor Olou," sighed Kennit. "You can make a police report tomorrow, Mr. Anders. But now we must go to see the King."

"Why isn't Kennit more surprised?" hissed Yoke to Onar as they were settled into the back of the little car. "And what was that pale vine? What exactly is your job, anyway?"

"At Meta West they call me the anteater," said Onar with a little smile.

"Meta West Link sells transmission time between the Earth and outer space. Mainly the Moon, but Mars and the asteroids too. My job is to keep cryps, phreaks, and ants from siphoning off free bandwidth." He opened his mouth and waggled his long, pointed tongue. "The ant's nightmare; the virgin's friend."

"Onar, don't."

Kennit turned onto the main street of Nuku'alofa, a dirt road lined by high wooden sidewalks like in an ancient viddy of the Wild West. There was a traffic-jam of cars, pedestrians, moldies, and bicycles; it seemed that everyone on the island was out on the five-block main drag. Though it was early in the evening, a few of the Tongan men seemed extremely drunk. Recognizing the car as the King's limo, one of them leaned over to peer inside. The car was so small and the man so big that he had to bend practically double. One of his friends shoved him and he lost his balance and fell down. Great whoops of laughter.

"Tongans used only to go crazy on Saturday nights," said Kennit gloomily. "But now we do it on Friday as well. Evil times."

"Kennit doesn't drink," said Onar. "He's a Mormon. Although he does play cards. I've seen him."

"Very many Mormons in Tonga," said Kennit.

"I don't think I've ever heard of them," said Yoke. "Is that a religion?"

"Oh yes," said Onar. "And they own the world's largest asimov computer. A machine under a mountain in Salt Lake City."

"I *have* heard of that big slave computer," said Yoke. "Cobb's simulation lived inside it for a while."

"You're thinking of the Heritagists' asimov computer," said Onar. "Which is also under a mountain in Salt Lake City. I have a theory that the two are one and the same."

"I went to college in Salt Lake City," said Kennit, inching the car forward. "The South Pacific program at Brigham Young University."

"Do you dislike moldies, Kennit?" asked Onar.

"Yis."

"Will you stop changing the subject, Onar?" put in Yoke. "Finish telling me what you're doing here and what happened to Mr. Olou." Outside the window now was a Tongan food store, an open-air stand with shelves full of canned meat and muddy yams.

"Very well, Yoke. Let's do Telecommunications 101. For short distances, an uvvy signal hopscotches from one uvvy to the next. Completely decentralized. For longer distances, the signal zooms up a thousand miles to a cheap little saucer-sat and gets bounced back down. Ever since the 2030s the saucer-sats have been imipolex jobbies that fly up to space by themselves. There's millions of them by now. The size of dinner-plates, as smart as cockroaches, and easy to order around. You saw some of them on our flight here."

"Right," said Yoke. "Cobb ate one of them."

"That was a very moldie thing for Cobb to do," said Onar. "Moldies are such scavengers."

"So anyway," said Yoke. "Now you're going to tell me that since Meta West Link handles Earth-Moon signal transmissions, that means they have some really big saucer-sats, right?"

"Right-o," said Onar. "We call them sky-rays. Like manta ray or stingray? Big soft flappy things. They weigh a ton instead of a kilogram. And, unlike the little saucer-sats, they need a fungus-algae nervous system. Once you get that much mold-infested imipolex together, it's bound to wake up. And since we already know how to talk to moldies, it makes sense for the sky-rays to be made up of moldies. A sky-ray is twenty or thirty moldies stuck together to make one of those group creatures we call a 'grex.' You don't really own a sky-ray, it's a team that you hire. The moldies get paid in imipolex and they take turns working. Which is why you see so many of them hanging around Tonga. They come down here to breed, for one thing."

"And why Tonga?"

"The sky-rays stay in geosynchronous orbit; they circle the equator at some twenty-two thousand miles up. That's the altitude where the natural orbital speed exactly matches the rotational speed of the Earth. Geosynchronous means they're always above the same spot. Now, thanks to some clever international politicking by HRH's grandfather back before the millennium, the Kingdom of Tonga owns the best geosynchronous satellite slot for the South Pacific." Onar scrunched down and pointed up through the car window. "She's always right about there. Cappy Jane. Straight up, and a little to the north. She looks like a giant patchwork stingray. A harlequin. All of the Earth-Moon transmissions for this part of the world come through Cappy Jane."

"Mr. Olou mentioned her," remembered Yoke. "He said someone's been running pirate signals through her."

"Exactly," said Onar. "Cappy Jane's been losing some twenty percent of her bandwidth. The pirate signals go back and forth between Cappy Jane and a spot right near Tonga itself. So Olou called for the anteater!" Onar opened his mouth as if to display his tongue again, but stopped himself, thinking better of it.

Kennit was through the worst of the traffic now, driving rapidly past a series of small houses with showy tropical plants in their yards. "That's the Tongan cultural center on the left," said Onar, going off topic. "I must take you there, Yoke; they have a wonderful show. Everyone gets a chance to drink some kava before it starts. Gives a very nice buzz."

"So that pale vine was a copy of one of the pirate signals?" asked Yoke doggedly. Keeping his hand down in his lap, Onar pointed at Kennit and didn't answer.

Yoke's head was pounding, and Kennit was driving much too fast for comfort. Up in the cone of the headlights she saw a low black animal with floppy ears and a long snout, standing alertly by the road as if waiting for the car to pass. "What's that!"

"A pig," said Onar.

"They're not pink?"

"You've never seen a real pig before, have you? You're delightful, Yoke."

The car raced onward. It had adaptive DIM tires, and Kennit was going down the little roads at the electric car's flat-out maximum speed, perhaps sixty miles per hour. "Is it safe to go so fast?" asked Yoke plaintively. Nobody answered, so she tried another question. "How much further is it, Kennit?"

"We're almost there. This is the King's plantation."

The road was lined with tall coconut palms, and the headlights showed orderly fields of plants to either side. Up ahead were some colorful lights. "I understand that HRH moved out here because the people in town don't like to see him living with moldies," Onar said to Kennit. "Is it true that he's actually married one?"

"That's not my affair," said Kennit shortly, and then they were pulling up in front of a remarkable building resembling a mound of giant soap bubbles. Yoke could make out some ten or twelve huge transparent domes fused together, with colorful beings moving about inside. There was a shiny green figure in the driveway, a moldie in the form of a voluptuous woman. She made a gesture of welcome.

"Didn't you tell Cobb this evening would be humans only?" Yoke asked Onar.

"I lied," said Onar, "so he wouldn't come. Now remember what you promised me."

And then they were out in the fetid tropical night. Yoke recognized the trees around the gossamer palace to be banyans, though she'd never imagined they'd be so huge. The trunks grew up and down, splitting here and merging there—the giant trees' flesh like wax or honey. The green moldie stepped forward, splitting her thick green lips in a smile.

"Yo! I'm Vaana. The queen moldie you been talking to on the uvvy, Onar. And this must be Yoke from the Moon. Welcome to Tonga, sweet thing." Yoke recognized Vaana's distinctive style of speech as a black accent. Each moldie fashioned his or her own particular human speaking style soon after birth, drawing on the speech of family, friends, and nearby humans, not to mention the endless databases of the Web.

As the moldie turned to lead them inside the crystal palace, something dark and ragged came flapping down from one of the banyans. Yoke had a mental flashback of the attack of the cyberspace jellyfish; she shrieked and dove to the ground.

"Lordy, lord," laughed Vaana. "Yoke's scared of flying foxes. Don't get your undies in a twist, girl. Those things won't bite unless you a piece of fruit."

"A large bat," explained Onar, helping Yoke up. "One of the few endemic Tongan mammals. It's easy for them to travel from island to island. There's more of them here than on, say, Fiji, because the Tongans don't eat them. The flying fox is *tapu*."

"This is turning into a majorly long day, Onar," said Yoke shakily. She was wondering what the hell she was doing here, about to get mixed up in some kilpy plot. "I think I want to go back to the guest house and get in bed." She looked around for Kennit and the car, but they were nowhere to be seen.

"It won't take long, Yoke," urged Onar. "I know that HRH is eager to meet you. You'll feel better after a good meal. And then we can take a little boat across the lagoon to get back to the guest house. Just the two of us." He slipped his arm around her waist and squeezed her.

"Come on, Yoke," said Vaana. "Don't be a barbie."

Here in the jungle night the rank green moldie seemed like a figure of myth or legend, a Green Woman, an archaic personification of the Plant. Though Vaana continued to smile, Yoke knew full well how meaningless were the facial expressions of moldies. She wished she'd brought along the loyal Cobb. At least her uvvy still worked. Perhaps she'd uvvy Cobb to fly over here and rescue her soon, whether or not Onar liked it. But, yes, come to think of it, she was kind of curious about Onar's big secret. And deep in her girlish heart, Yoke felt a sharp hunger for that romantic boat-ride across the lagoon—just like in a viddy or a book, with air and water everywhere, and a handsome man at her side. It sounded so exciting. So, okay, she followed along as Vaana ushered them into the King's country palace.

The first of the palace's domed rooms was a great hall, filled with cool, oxygen-enriched air. A moldie waited within, this one red and crablike, a squat creature with pincer arms. A guardian.

"Lock the palace on up, Gregor," said Vaana. "Our guests be here." The crab raised his claws and scuttled past them toward the door, not bothering to answer out loud.

The next room was a conservatory, with blooming orchids fastened all over the curving walls. The room's air was pervaded by an intense, musty tang. A moldie like a giant yellow banana slug was sliming from plant to plant, carefully tending them. It was he, not the orchids, whose odor filled the room. Like the crab, he kept his silence.

The third room was a dimly lit sitting room, and in there they found the King, resting on a silk couch with a cup of hot tea. The air in this room was warm and rapidly circulating; the hidden fans swirled away any scent of the moldies.

The King was a big man with beautiful skin. His hair was long and floppy. He was wearing a flowered silk shirt and white linen pants.

"Hello, Onar," said the King. "I got the news about Mr. Olou. Fill me in on how that went down."

Yoke was surprised to hear him sounding like a regular person. Somehow she'd expected a King to sound different, all "ye" and "thee" and "tally ho."

"Greetings, Your Majesty," said Onar. "Allow me to present Ms. Yoke Starr-Mydol from the Moon. Known in the records and all outgoing video as 'Sue Miller,' thanks to Eleani's work."

"Welcome to Tonga, Yoke," said the King. "And listen, Onar, I've told you before, just call me Bou-Bou. You too, Yoke. Bou-Bou!" The King humorously stuck out his lips as he pronounced his nickname. He leaned back on his couch and waited, favoring Yoke with a charming smile.

"Um, okay, Bou-Bou," said Yoke, taking a seat on the other end of the couch. Onar sat in the middle. Yoke lolled back and looked up through the room's transparent ceiling at the banyans and the night sky. She thought she could see a flying fox hanging from a branch in the nearest tree.

"It's exciting to be here," said Yoke presently. "These domes remind me of the Moon. My family has a friend who built a big house out in a crater. An isopod, is what we called it."

The King nodded. "I know of the place. The Willy Taze dwelling. I studied lunar architecture at Stanford, among other things. How did Onar persuade you to come here, Yoke? Did he put you on the Meta West payroll?"

"You're the third person who's asked me that," said Yoke. "Am I missing out on something? I'm interested in diving the South Pacific, and since Onar had this anteater gig, he talked me into coming down here with him. I have a moldie friend named Cobb who rocketed us here from California, so it's not costing much of anything."

"Ah yes, Cobb the born-yet-again loonie moldie," said the King. "Thanks for not bringing him along tonight, Onar."

"But why?" protested Yoke. "Cobb's interesting. He built the first boppers, after all. And he's the first human to have his software installed into moldie flesh."

The King gave Onar a frank look. "You've talked to her?"

"Yes," said Onar. "She's promised to keep mum."

"Cobb's a wild-card, Yoke," said the King. "He has so many contacts. We're afraid about whom he might tell our secrets. Frankly, we'd prefer to keep him out of the picture."

"Oh come on," said Yoke. "Cobb's like my bodyguard. And he's a family friend. I don't care what I promised Onar just now. I wasn't thinking straight. If you tell something to me, I can't keep it from Cobb. He needs to know what's going on so that he can protect me."

The King looked questioningly at Onar and Onar said, "We don't really have a choice, do we?"

"I suppose not," said the King. "But please, Yoke, don't you or Cobb tell this to any of your loonie friends. The secret is that we've contacted an alien intelligence. A being named Shimmer. She's living deep below the ocean here, in what's known as the Tonga Trench. She knows you. She had an encounter with you and your parents just a little over three months ago, at the Willy Taze isopod you mentioned. November sixth, 2053. Your parents tried to kill her."

Shimmer! Yoke's stomach flip-flopped. She'd had a feeling this was coming. "She wants to get even?"

"Why would Shimmer be into that kind of kilp, honey?" said Vaana soothingly. She was standing behind the King's couch. "Shimmer's way too big for that. I bet she just wants to see you, Yoke. She probably digs your mind. When Shimmer was here talking to Bou-Bou she acted nice as pie."

Yoke felt frightened and angry. So Onar had been lying to her all along. She gave him a rough shove. "You deliberately lured me here! You don't like me for myself one bit. You fetched me like some bauble for your precious King. And I'm so stupid, I came for free."

"That's not the whole truth, Yoke," protested Onar. "I'm very attracted to you."

"And you killed Mr. Olou on purpose, didn't you!" Yoke's words popped out fast, and she saw something on their faces. She was getting in deeper every second.

"I think everyone could use some dinner," put in Vaana. "The table's set."

The King smiled and got nimbly to his feet, making a polite gesture for Yoke to follow him into the dining room, which was the next dome farther along. Following behind the big man, Yoke could make out his underwear through the thin fabric of his trousers. Purplish bikini briefs worn very low down on the crack.

"It's nice to finally meet you in person," said Onar to Vaana, as if trying to steer the conversation back to a normal mode. "How do you come to know HRH?"

"Well, my family nest was down in the flats of Oakland," said the womanly green moldie. "I got it together and landed a phat job in the wetware engineering labs at Stanford U. I met Bou-Bou when he was taking Wet E 202. I helped him invent a new kind of coconut for his class project. Less grease and mo' protein. Ought to been a miracle for the Tongan diet."

"Except the Tongans won't eat my new coconuts or even feed them to their pigs," said the King over his shoulder. "The flesh is a ghastly greenish hue. Wet E was never my thing. Here we are then, the royal dining room. Our main course will be Tongan lobster in a coconut cream sauce over steamed taro root. Nontweaked coconut, of course. I think we have some local melon as well. A glass of champagne, Yoke?"

"All right. Why not?"

The three humans sat down at the dining table and Vaana discreetly withdrew. A kind-faced Tongan woman named Kika served them their food. Yoke and Onar were very hungry, and the King ate with a ready appetite as well. The first course of the meal was a green melon with tiny orange balls on it which were, the King informed them, the fruiting body of a special kind of Tongan seaweed. The second course was a curried pork broth.

"What was it like, Yoke?" Onar asked presently. "When all the moldies at Taze's isopod turned into aliens that day?"

"It was wavy," said Yoke. With the food and the champagne she was feeling a little more relaxed. "They were so interesting, so wise. Shimmer especially. Shimmer comes from a place where they have two-dimensional time. The extra time dimension is like possibility, of worlds that could be. That's why my parents couldn't shoot Shimmer. Even though the time in our part of the cosmos is only one-dimensional, Shimmer can see the ghosts of all the future maybes and she can actualize the right one. She's always where the bullet isn't." Kika removed the soup plates and began bringing in the lobster. Yoke was, on the whole, glad to be eating this meal. "But now you two answer some questions. Shimmer's the one who's siphoning off Cappy Jane's bandwidth, right?"

"Very clever, Yoke," said Onar. "Yes, the King gave Shimmer permission to gather and process data through Cappy Jane, so there's been a lot of traffic between those two. Cappy Jane's been winnowing out certain kinds of space signals that Shimmer's interested in. Not that Cappy Jane realizes who she's working for. Shimmer and the King have her convinced that Shimmer's a human scientist doing a study of high-energy cosmic rays."

"The Tongan Extragalactic Signal Survey," said the King, smiling.

"Moldies are even more leery of aliens than the humans," said Onar. "With good reason. Their computational architecture is very susceptible to invasion. If Cappy Jane knew this stuff was for Shimmer, she probably wouldn't help us no matter how much we pay her."

"Vaana knows about Shimmer," said Yoke. "And she's not objecting."

"Yes," said the King. "But Vaana expects to share in the benefits of helping Shimmer. Now that *you* know, Yoke, that makes five humans and four moldies who are in on the secret. You, Onar, me, Oofa, Kennit, Vaana, Tashtego, Daggoo, and Turklee. Nine in all. And as soon as we get something from Shimmer, I'll have to tell a few more of my people. Secrets don't last on Tonga for very long. That's why we have to move forward so rapidly."

"Mr. Olou didn't know," said Yoke. "And instead of telling him the truth, Onar killed him."

"Mr. Olou was unreliable," said the King. "A loose cannon. He did know that some source in the Tonga Trench has been using up a large amount of the Cappy Jane bandwidth. He was very persistent in repeatedly bringing this problem to Meta West's attention. Too much so, and against my express wishes. Fortunately, I had a prior relationship with Onar, and I made sure that he was the anteater whom Meta West sent down here to deal with Mr. Olou's problem. I thought it would be a good idea to have Onar intimidate Mr. Olou within the framework of Olou's highly idiosyncratic visualization system."

"So what was in that pale vine signal?" asked Yoke.

"That was a red herring," laughed Onar. "I didn't really unpack the vine signal at all. Wouldn't know how to. What I did in cyberspace with you and Olou was just theater. The jellyfish thing, that was something I brought along stored in that inlaid coffin like a jack-in-the-box. I copied it off some phreaks who were using it to protect their clubhouse. I'd never tested it before, you understand, and I had no idea it would be lethal. The idea was just to frighten Olou and to impress you, Yoke. I was reckless and negligent, yes. But please don't think I'm a mind-assassin."

"So it really was you who killed Olou?"

"Don't blame me," said Onar. "It was the phreaks who made that stinging jellyfish." He gave a sudden giggle. "It talked Olou's ear off. More than his ear." He gave himself a playful slap on the cheek. "Sober up, Onar. It's not my fault at all. How was I to know that Olou had a weak heart? And he shouldn't have kept complaining about those extra signals."

"But what's in the signals?" demanded Yoke. "Can't anyone tell me?"

"Shimmer's been using Cappy Jane to download the personality waves of more aliens from her home world," said the King. "Isn't it obvious? Shimmer's specified a certain class of gamma ray burst events for Cappy Jane to record, preprocess, and transmit. And these signals are of course alien personality waves. Apparently Shimmer's been able to decrypt five or six of her fellows by now. That's what she wants to discuss with you, Yoke. Champagne?"

"Indubitably," said Onar, holding out his and Yoke's glasses. "Let's drink to the noble Shimmer! Oofa can take Yoke down into the trench to meet her tomorrow."

"We're supposed to be sitting here planning to help aliens invade the Earth?" said Yoke. "You two are xoxxed! Where's your sense of self-preservation?"

"It's what's happening, baby," said Onar. "There's no stopping Shimmer. If you want to blame someone, blame Gurdle-7 or Willy Taze. They're the ones who decrypted Shimmer's signal in the first place. But now she's here, and we're going to have to live with her, at least for a while. It's a new stage in history. Hop aboard or get plowed under."

"Shimmer's got good things for us," said the King. "She's promised to give us realware."

"What's that?" asked Yoke.

"It's some kind of magic or super science that Shimmer has," said Onar. "Direct matter control. We don't know much more than that. I think maybe when you dive down to see Shimmer tomorrow she's going to give it to you. She trusts you or something. You're up for this, right?"

Yoke sat quiet for a minute, thinking. She'd loved talking with the aliens that time on the Moon; she'd been sad and angry when her parents attacked them. Onar was probably right about there being no way to stop Shimmer now. And Yoke knew that even if she wanted to try and stop Shimmer, the only thing to do was to go farther in. "Okay," said Yoke slowly. "But I'm only diving if I'm safe inside of Cobb. And before we dive, I'm going to tell him every detail about what we're doing."

She held up her hand to stave off Onar and the King's protests. "I think I know why you don't want Cobb to know. He's a grandstander, a loudmouth. You're afraid he'll whip up a movement against the aliens. You're afraid everyone will react like Darla—like Darla would if she were still around." Her voice faltered as she thought of her dead mother. She caught her breath and pressed on. "But remember that Cobb Anderson is an explorer. A radical. The total opposite of those right-wing, moldie-hating Heritagists. If Cobb had a closed mind he wouldn't have built the boppers in the first place. Cobb loves change. And who knows, maybe his death experiences taught him something about the kind of world where Shimmer comes from."

"I could have you both silenced," mused the King. "Thanks to the ID viruses, it's like you're not even here."

"You wouldn't dare," said Yoke, deepening her voice and sounding more confident than she felt. "Shimmer would never forgive you. Don't you think she's already thought through the consequences of your talking to me? It's like we're dustboarding down an extreme slope, Bou-Bou. If you waver now, you'll fall. The only way to do this is straight and fast."

"Well said, Yoke!" Onar held up his glass. "A toast to Lady Yoke Starr-Mydol!" And the King toasted along.

"I expected as much from you, Yoke," said the King presently. "You have spirit. Yes, you're the one to bring back the realware. And that's the real reason I had Eleani put out the ID virus on you. Because if and when the news of the realware gets out, everyone's going to want to find the person who has it."

Yoke and Onar rode back across the lagoon in a wooden boat propelled by the yellow slug moldie, whose name turned out to be Topo. Topo fastened himself to the underside of the boat and beat the water like a long-tailed eel.

It was a clear, balmy night, with a caressing breeze of sweet fresh air flowing in from the sea. The full moon shone high overhead. Onar pointed out the pinprick of light that was Cappy Jane. Topo's underwater undulations left a glowing trail, and when Yoke let her hand dip into the smooth black water, it made a phosphorescent wake of tiny green sparkles.

"It's wonderful to share this with you, Yoke," said Onar, pulling his arm tight around her. "I love to see you smile."

"Liar," said Yoke, leaning against him. "I'm just a pawn in your scheme."

"Compared to Shimmer, we're plankton," said Onar, looking out over the lagoon. "The best we can do is glimmer in her wave. I won't lie to you again, Yoke. I care much more for you than I expected. You're so fresh and kind and good."

Onar kissed her then, and the boat ride turned fully as romantic as Yoke had hoped: the tropical lagoon, the champagne in her veins, and her arms around this handsome, raffish, not-quite-trustworthy man. When they got back to the guest house, Yoke made a snap decision that it would be a good idea to sleep with Onar after all.

But Onar turned out to be a poor lover, certainly the worst of Yoke's few partners thus far. Onar stinted on the foreplay, made a long messy fuss of his prophylactic preparations, and was up for at most sixty seconds of actual coitus. As a final turn-off, Onar said something British when he came, something like "Cor blimey," or "Top drawer," or "Bit of all right"— Yoke's outraged brain disdained to retain the phrase.

In the night, Yoke had a nightmare about her dead mother Darla, a dream of Darla desperately firing her needier gun at an endless attack wave of softly smiling jellyfish. She woke up in a sweat, feeling cramped in Onar's bed. She washed her face in the grungy guest house bathroom, then went into her own room to fall back asleep.

February 21

In the morning, Saturday, Yoke woke to the sound of a rooster crowing right outside her window. The first thing she thought about was Darla. And Phil's father. They'd been eaten by something from a higher dimension. And all of a sudden Yoke could remember what the cyberspace jellyfish thing had said when it came at her yesterday. "You love Onar," it had been saying. "Do what Onar says." The jellyfish had been quite thoroughly under Onar's control. Mr. Olou's death had been no accident. Onar was a killer. And now she was supposed to let Onar take her to meet Shimmer? What about Shimmer and the four-dimensional things that had eaten Darla and Phil's father? Was there a connection?

Oh, this was creepy. Yoke pushed on to other thoughts. The fat, polite King in his soap-bubble castle. The romantic ride across lagoon. The unpleasant, selfish groping in Onar's bed. Too bad she hadn't come here with Phil Gottner instead. That Kevvie didn't deserve to keep a boy like Phil. He was the cutest thing she had met on Earth so far. Phil would be perfect, if only he could learn to take hold of life and do something.

Before even getting out of bed, Yoke put on her uvvy, wincing a bit. Her neck was still tender from the jellyfish blast at the Foreign Ministry. She called for Cobb. His signal was faint and weird, so Yoke sent him an extra hard mind jolt. There was a thud right outside her window and then Cobb's face appeared out there.

"What? I was lying on the roof."

"Shhh! Come in here."

Cobb slithered through Yoke's window to perch on the foot of her sagging bed. He was nothing like so pink and shiny as usual. And he reeked of decay.

"I'm really spun," said Cobb, sounding satisfied. "Two of the moldies at the Happy Club turned me on to this stuff called 'betty.' I rubbed it onto myself and whoah, Nellie. It's the first time I've found a way to use this body to catch a lift. 'Fine, fine betty,' my new friends call it. Tashtego and Daggoo. They work for Sea Cuke Divers. Tashtego's a moldie fakaleiti. I think maybe I had sex with him? Or no, wait, that was another moldie I did it with. A green one. Her name was V-something. She rubbed even more betty on me. Are we diving today?"

"Are you going to be okay, Cobb? You look way kilpy." Cobb's normally clean outlines were wavering and irregular, with small ripples darting about upon the surface of his skin. His rosy flesh was shot through with lines of gray.

"A shower would help," said Cobb. "I could open my pores and let the water flush out the toxins. But—not yet." He slumped against the wall. "I have too much slack. It feels good to be lifted." He held his hands up in front of his face, slowly moving them as if watching their motion trails.

"I'm not sure we should dive at all," mused Yoke. "There's more to it than you realize. Stop looking at your hands and pay attention! The biggest news is that there's an alien named Shimmer living down in the Tonga Trench. The King says Shimmer wants me to come see her. She's been decrypting more aliens out of signals from this Tongan Meta West Link satellite called Cappy Jane. Yesterday Onar killed a Tongan man who'd been trying to stop Shimmer from using Cappy Jane. For some reason Onar and the King don't want you in on this, Cobb. The King's a cheeseball by the way; his girlfriend is a moldie named Vaana."

Cobb stopped wiggling his fingers and looked past them at Yoke. "Killed?" said Cobb, not sounding so happy anymore. His motionless gray-streaked hands were in supplicating claw positions. "Vaana?"

"You better take that shower, Cobb. You want me to help you?"

"Help," said Cobb, and suddenly slipped off the bed onto the floor. He was more than lifted, he was poisoned.

Yoke dragged the stinking heavy moldie down the hall to the guest house bathroom. Another guest, a German woman, was just vacating it. She gave Yoke a disgusted look as she stepped over the inert Cobb. But she didn't bother to ask any questions. It was a very cheap guest house.

Yoke wrestled Cobb into the concrete shower stall and turned the controls on all the way, which produced a limp drizzle. The water didn't seem to be penetrating Cobb fast enough, so Yoke got into the shower and started kneading him with her feet. The shower wasn't exactly hot, but it wasn't freezing cold either. Out of reflex, Yoke picked up a stray sliver of soap and started washing herself, all the while jouncing around on the soft moldie flesh of Cobb. As she washed she thought about making love to Onar—which made her wash herself the more thoroughly. Triple *ugh* for Onar. Three *ugh*s and you're out.

There was a shuddering beneath her feet. Yoke turned her attention back down to Cobb. Thanks to her trampling, the water was squeegeeing in and out of his flesh. The water coming out of Cobb was dark as if with dust or pollen. His eyes were open, glassily staring up at Yoke's body. She flipped him over with a deft motion of her feet and continued to tread on him.

The bathroom door swung open and in walked Onar, nude, with a morning erection.

"Cheerio, Yoke," he said. "Care if I join you? Missed you in bed this morning."

"It's pretty full in here," said Yoke. "Someone poisoned Cobb."

"What a stench!" exclaimed Onar, peering into the shower. "Don't tell me you're trying to save him? That'll never work."

"Why shouldn't I try?" snapped Yoke. "Do you want to just let him die? Don't bother to answer. And stop staring at me."

"You shouldn't waste your time," said Onar. "I've seen this kind of thing happen before. An overdose of betty. All of his fungus nodules are bursting out with spores, and the spores are going to poison him. Kiss the old duffer good-bye, Yoke. We'll find you another dive-moldie. Oofa's expecting us at nine sharp."

"Sure she is," said Yoke. "On the dot. Get out of here. It was a big mistake to sleep with you. Onar the one-minute wonder."

"Goood morning," said Onar, and left the room.

More and more of the dark dust, the spores, was coming out of Cobb. Some of the dust wafted up toward Yoke. She put a wet washrag over her face to keep from getting lifted. She kneaded Cobb harder and harder.

Finally the old man's moldie flesh was pink again. His tissues drew back into the shape of a human. He groaned and got to his feet.

"Man. What a burn."

"You're all right now?" asked Yoke. Even though Cobb smelled awful, she hugged him. His flesh was cool and smooth.

"When we go in the ocean I'll really clean myself out," said Cobb, hugging her back. "Thank you, dear Yoke. I think you saved my life. That green moldie woman, that Vaana, she smeared much too much betty on me. Crazy. Like there was no tomorrow."

Yoke got out of the shower and began toweling herself off. "She was trying to kill you, Cobb. She's the King's girlfriend. She must have flown straight to the Happy Club after I left the palace."

Cobb remained in the shower stall, flexing his body to squeeze out a little more of the spore-darkened water. "So the King wants me dead," he said finally. "Did he mention why?"

"Last night I thought it was because he thought you'd talk too much. Now I'm thinking maybe it's because he didn't want you here to protect me when I dive down to see Shimmer today."

"Shimmer," said Cobb. He stepped out of the shower, looking vague. "Yoke dear, you're going to have to repeat what you told me in your room. Your words flew past me like a flock of hummingbirds. Shimmer's an alien, right? And when you say alien, you mean an honest-to-God extraterrestrial?"

"Duh! Shimmer was one of the alien personality waves who decrypted into moldie bodies at Willy Taze's house in November. My parents killed all the others. And Shimmer got away. She's living down in the Tonga Trench. The King says Shimmer's bringing in a bunch of her relatives to live here. And for some reason she wants to meet with me."

"Real aliens!" exclaimed Cobb. "At last! I'd love to meet this Shimmer."

"You're in no condition."

"Hell, I'm not. Buy me some quantum dots to get my energy up, Yoke, and I'll be good as new." Cobb stretched himself to an alarming height, then snapped back like a rubber band. "It's fuckin' great to be alive."

"I'm scared Shimmer might *get* me, Cobb. When I woke up this morning I started thinking about the four-dimensional things that ate Kurt Gottner and my mom. If that's what really happened, then maybe those things were from the aliens. Shimmer comes from a place where there's two-dimensional time."

"If Shimmer could kill Kurt in California and Darla on the Moon, then she could kill us right here and now if she wanted to," said Cobb. "So why not go and have a talk with her face-to-face? What does she look like?"

"She's in a moldie body. She has such a huge intelligence that her body's perfectly formed. It's like she's consciously aware of the curvatures of each square millimeter of her surface. She's inhumanly beautiful, Cobb. Like a glowing marble sculpture."

"Wow," said Cobb, visibly tweaking his body shape as if trying out the idea of making himself look divine. "Do I look good enough to meet her?"

"You look fine," said Yoke, even though Cobb only looked like a stocky, freckled white-haired old man pulling in his stomach. "Let's go back to my room. You stick with me before something else happens to you."

Yoke put on her new purple Santa Cruz bikini and a long chartreuse T-shirt. She and Cobb went out into the guest house common room. It was a bare old room, beautified by bowls of water with hibiscus blossoms floating in them. Mrs. Yoshida and her cook Waloo were serving breakfast: coffee, papayas, and toast. Mrs. Yoshida was a trim, no-nonsense lady with her hair in a black bun; Waloo was calm, smiling, and stocky. Onar was sitting at the table in a fresh clean sport shirt covered with satellite weather photos of the South Pacific, all blues and whites and grays.

"Feeling better, Cobb?" said Onar.

"Vaana dosed me," said Cobb. "Do you know where Yoke can buy me some quantum dots?"

Onar shook his head and began, "And I'm afraid that's—"

But Mrs. Yoshida interrupted him. "I can sell you some dots, Yoke. My husband, bless his soul, bought too big a supply of them for his boat and they're just sitting on a shelf in a magnetic bottle. You pay cash?"

"I'll do a transfer," said Yoke, picking up her uvvy. "How much?"

"Hold on," said Mrs. Yoshida, and disappeared into the kitchen, quickly returning with a shiny gray bottle. She shook the little bottle and held it up to the light. "The meter says there's half a terawatt left. You want it all?"

"Yeah," said Cobb. "If it's too expensive for Yoke, my grandson Willy can pay you back."

"Like he's really going to want to pay all your bills," said Yoke. "But sure, let's do it. Pop loaded up my $Web account for this trip. He'd definitely want you healthy, Cobb." She glanced at Onar, who looked to be bursting with objections. "You haven't met my pop, Onar. And you better hope you never do."

"Whitey's a bad-ass," agreed Cobb. "For true. By the way, Onar, why do you think Vaana tried to poison me?"

"I'm sure she didn't mean to," said Onar. "She's just wild that way. Ever since she's moved in with the King."

"I think it is a crying shame," put in Waloo, setting out some fresh toast and coffee. "HRH should be making a prince. We don't like our Tu'i Tonga to be a cheeseball." She favored Yoke with a frank, inquisitive gaze. "Are you that way with your moldie?"

"God no," said Yoke. "Only men are skanky enough to fuck plastic." The women laughed.

Yoke donned her uvvy and completed the purchase of the quantum dots. Mrs. Yoshida handed Cobb the magnetic bottle. He grew a thick funnel shape out of the center of his chest and poured the quantum dots into it. They sparkled like iridescent dust and sank into his tissues.

"Spinach!" said Cobb, flexing like a bodybuilder. His biceps swelled to the size of hams; his legs grew sinewy as tree trunks. "Boing and a boing and a ya-yahoo! Should I torture loverboy till he tells us all his secrets?" He took a step toward the seated Onar.

"Can everyone calm down?" snapped Onar. "I still think it would be better for Yoke to dive inside of one of our local moldies today. In case something goes wrong. Get away from me, Cobb. You reek."

Yoke waited until Mrs. Yoshida and Waloo were out of earshot and answered Onar in an angry whisper. "You want to have Tashtego or Daggoo offer me up to Shimmer like a human sacrifice! Trussed on a platter with an apple in my mouth."

"We just don't want there to be any trouble," hissed Onar. "And Cobb's always spelled trouble. In all of his lives. We only want for today's meeting to go smoothly and for Shimmer to give you the real ware."

"What's that?" asked Cobb, too loud.

"I don't really know," said Onar, stubbornly staring down at his cup. "Hurry up and eat your breakfast, Yoke. Cobb, why don't you wait on the porch so I can drink my coffee without vomiting."

And then they were out in the Sea Cuke dive boat: Oofa, Yoke, and Onar; Daggoo, Tashtego, and Cobb. Tashtego and Daggoo looked like cannibals, like fierce harpooneers from an old-time whaling ship, their imipolex skins intricately worked with tattoos. Daggoo was huge, coal-black with wild kinky hair; the imipolex of his earlobes swooped out into shapes like gold hoop earrings. His tattoos were raised white lines, seemingly of scar tissue. Tashtego was coppery in color, with long blond hair; his tattoos were polychrome fractals. Both of them had slim hips and muscular bodies. Though Tashtego was large, Daggoo was half again as big as Tashtego. Daggoo wore blue swimming trunks, while Tashtego wore a woman's red bikini with the bra-cups stuffed with two pairs of socks. The skin of Tashtego's face was colored to give the effect of orange lipstick and turquoise eye shadow. The crotch of his bikini bulged as if covering a large penis.

Yoke ended up sitting next to Tashtego in the bow of the boat. Behind them sat Cobb and Onar, and in the stern were Oofa and Daggoo. After leaving the Nuku'alofa harbor, the boat circled around to the south side of the island, there to rise up on its hydrofoils and speed southeast across the open ocean. They slowed down once to view a pair of spouting sperm whales. Yoke wanted to dive in and get a good look at them, but Onar urged Oofa on.

By eleven A.M. the sun was incredibly hot and bright. The water-jet motor was whisper-quiet; the only sound was the hissing of the hydrofoils through the sea. For no particular reason Tashtego was making a great show of combing out his matted blond hair—really just strands of imipolex, of course—and one of his undulating arms bumped Yoke on the shoulder. Hard.

"Why behave like a fakaleiti?" snapped Yoke. She felt anxious and irritable; the light breakfast had worn off. "It doesn't make sense. A moldie is whatever sex it decides on at birth. So you're a male moldie, fine. If you wanted to, you could shape yourself like a human woman. Why take on the form of a man impersonating a woman? It's stupid."

"Fakaleiti make happy thing happen," said Tashtego, archly looking down at his false breasts. As part of their images, he and Daggoo insisted on speaking a barbaric pidgin English. "Tashtego boom boom boy girl." He threw back his head and cackled. His teeth were as sharp and pointed as if they'd been filed. "You no dive in me today, Yoke? Me open up very good." Tashtego playfully split himself slightly open along a heretofore invisible seam down the front of his body. Like a clam cracking its shell open for a bit of water.

The appearance of the savage Tashtego's halved face was deeply disturbing. Yoke shook her head and looked away. "I'm diving in Cobb and that's final."

"I'd like to dive in you, Tashtego," said Onar, who was eavesdropping over their shoulders. "I want to come along. More sunscreen, Yoke?"

"Thanks." It still seemed odd to Yoke to be bare beneath the sun. She was following the fair-skinned Onar's regimen of frequent applications of lotion. "How much further are we going?" she asked. "I don't see anything but open sea. We're going so fast that we must have come seventy miles by now."

"Oofa?" called Onar.

But Oofa was asleep, lounging back against Daggoo's sun-puddled body. Onar had to shake Oofa's bare foot to rouse her.

"No problem, soon come, the boat knows where to go," mumbled Oofa, rubbing her eyes and looking around. "We'll be near our dive-site when you can see 'Ata over there. And then you look for something like a lily pad." She waved her hand toward the starboard and relaxed back against Daggoo's smooth black flesh.

" 'Ata is the southernmost island of Tonga," explained Onar. "The deepest part of the Tonga Trench runs right past it. The Vityaz Deep. Better than six miles to the bottom. That's where Shimmer is."

Yoke felt a hollowness in her chest. "We're supposed to dive down six miles? I'd need a submarine for that. A bathyscaph, not a moldie wet suit."

"I be hard as you need, Yoke," leered Tashtego. Daggoo let out a carnivorous yelp of laughter.

"It's true," said Cobb. "We can switch our imipolex to a rigid form that's stronger than diamond. The loonie moldies taught me all the tricks."

"Why can't Shimmer just swim up to meet us?" wailed Yoke.

"She's shy," said Onar. "And, look, on the horizon over there, it's 'Ata! And here's Shimmer's antenna. Heave to, Oofa!"

The boat came to a stop and sank down to bob in the slow ocean swells. Floating in the sea near them was a thick fleshy disk of silvery imipolex. Its upper surface was cupped like a parabolic dish.

"Ahoy, Turklee," called Tashtego, waving his snaky arms.

"Hello," sang back the lily pad. "Shimmer's expecting you."

"Is that thing a moldie?" asked Yoke.

"Sure," said Onar. "Her name's Turklee. I think the King mentioned her to you last night. The fourth moldie in the know. Turklee's working as a transducer for Shimmer. Radio waves don't travel well through water, you see. Turklee uses blue-green laser light to send signals down to Shimmer's lair. Shimmer needs a good link because she's pulling in so much bandwidth through Cappy Jane."

While Onar talked, Oofa rummaged in a cooler chest and took out a bunch of bananas and a bottle of water to pass around.

"I can hear Shimmer," said Cobb suddenly. "She's talking to us. Oh how strange. This is wonderful. Hello, Shimmer. Put on your uvvy, Yoke." Tashtego and Daggoo were grinning and nodding, enjoying Shimmer's signal too.

"What if she blasts me like Onar did yesterday?" asked Yoke.

"Be gentle, Shimmer," said Cobb. "The person you've been asking for is going to come on line. Oh yes, that's perfect. Try it now, Yoke."

So Yoke put the uvvy on her tender neck and right away she could hear Shimmer's voice, a sound like the piping of flutes, the whining of sitars, and the gentle resonation of a gong.

"Hello, Yoke. You were kind to me on the Moon. I'm grateful that you've come to see me. Let's plan your dive."

Now Shimmer began sending images of divers, figures against a dark undersea background, drifting down next to the blue-green shaft of Turklee's laser beam. In the images, Cobb was shaped like a sphere, with Yoke crouched within him like a tadpole inside a frog's egg. The pictures were clear and beautiful but with a curious multiplicity to them. Like seeing two or three or twenty things at once. In some of the images Onar and Oofa were also present, riding inside Tashtego and Daggoo, and in one of those images, Tashtego bit a hole in Cobb's surface, causing him to collapse and to crush Yoke into bloody pulp.

"Yoke must come alone," said Shimmer.

"The King wants me and Oofa there too," protested Onar through the uvvy, his voice like the chirp of a persistent cricket.

Now one of Shimmer's images showed Onar and Oofa following Yoke. The blue-green laser beam intensified, twitched, burnt holes in Tashtego and Daggoo.

"You will stay on the boat," said Shimmer.

So Onar told the others that they wouldn't be going down.

"That's fine," said Oofa, settling back into her seat.

"HRH pay us imipolex all the same," said Daggoo.

"Bugger all," muttered Onar.

"Are you ready, Yoke?" asked Cobb.

She looked around at the sloshing sea, at pale angry Onar, at lithe Tashtego and massive Daggoo, at calm Oofa and pink old Cobb. The sunlight on the water was beautiful. It would be so odd to die here.

"Don't worry, Yoke," said Shimmer, as if sensing Yoke's thoughts. "You won't die at all. I'll help you find true happiness." She sounded so kind and wise that Yoke believed her.

"Okay," Cobb was saying. "Get on top of me now." The moldie had puddled himself out on the deck like a pancake with a little hump in the center like a footstool. Yoke fit her palladium filters into her nose and sat on the imipolex hassock. Cobb's flesh swooped up around her, sealing itself up to form a translucent sphere. Tashtego and Daggoo whooped, their voices muffled by Cobb's body, and then there was a jarring bump and a splash. Cobb's flesh held onto Yoke's body to keep her from being thrown about.

"I can't see anything, Cobb," protested Yoke. "Make yourself transparent!"

"I can't when I'm in this rigid mode," said Cobb. "But you can use your uvvy to see what I'm seeing. Just focus."

They were floating just beneath the surface. Yoke put her attention into her uvvy, and now she could indeed see a remarkable view of the water's underside, all live and sparkling in the sun, a restless mirror. Cobb moved his gaze about in synch with Yoke's head motions; it felt like she was freely looking around.

Yoke could see the bottom of the Sea Cuke boat, also the heads of Daggoo and Tashtego, who were hanging over the edge to stare at them. Turklee the lily pad antenna was floating off to one side, a dark disk on the silver surface. A bright, narrow beam of blue-green light emanated from Turklee's underside. She had a ring of webbed duck-feet constantly paddling to keep her centered over Shimmer's location. A few good-sized fish hovered in the shade of the lily pad moldie, nibbling at whatever marine algae had begun to grow on her. Looking down, Yoke's gaze followed the crisp line of laser light to where it disappeared into the featureless depths. Six miles! Her stomach knotted like a fist.

There was a great splash from above. Tashtego and Daggoo were wrestling a huge weight over the edge of the dive boat for them; it was a massive pyramid of pig-iron with a handle at the apex. Cobb bulged out a hand to take hold of the dive-weight, the others released it, and then, as abruptly as stepping off a cliff, Cobb and Yoke were plummeting down into the abyss, slowly at first, then faster and faster, until soon they'd reached their maximum speed, with the downward pull of their weight just balanced by their friction with the water.

Their passage through the water made a low, thrumming sound. Cobb's flesh seemed to grow ever denser and more compact. Yet the pressure inside the spherical shell of his body stayed normal; Yoke didn't have to clear her ears as she'd had to during her Santa Cruz moldie wet-suit dives.

Quite soon it was pitch-dark in the Cobb bathyscaph. "Can you make some light for me?" asked Yoke. As she spoke, her teeth began to chatter. "And heat. It's getting colder every second."

"Here's heat," said Cobb, and immediately his flesh grew pleasantly warm. "But I'd rather not light up. I don't want the denizens of the deep getting too curious about us. Just keep looking through my sensors. I'll dial my sensitivity down into the infrared."

Gazing through the uvvy, Yoke could see the featureless vertical line of laser light leading down as before. She stared into the abyss, searching for a sign. Time passed, perhaps as much as an hour. Now and then a flicker of small jellyfish flew past, and occasionally an angler fish or a big-mouthed gulper eel.

"We're at five miles," said Cobb. "I'm holding up fine."

Yoke felt oppressed by the sullen weight of so much pressure. The flecks of sea life sped past like snowflakes in a viddy snowstorm. Far, far below was a hint of pale light. But before Yoke could ask about it, there was a distraction.

"Squid!" exclaimed Cobb, and, yes, all of a sudden there were squid everywhere. Big ones, small ones, and huge ones. The largest one looked to be some two hundred feet long. Its body was like an arrow, a great tapered cone tipped with two wild wavy fins. The fins fanned in rapid undulations, driving the squid toward them. Its immense round eyes looked frighteningly intent. Cobb had piqued its interest. Eight of the squid's ten tentacles were clenched into a tidy sheaf, but its two extra-long ones were reaching toward them like hungry arms. Cobb and Yoke plummeted past the giant squid, but it sped down after them, its fins flapping like flags. Now one of its fiendishly long arms slapped against them. Cobb's flesh shuddered.

"Oh no," said Cobb. "Brace yourself, Yoke."

And then the squid was upon them. Its bunched tentacles writhed apart to reveal a vile huge beak. Yoke could hear the scratching of the beak against the hardened rind of Cobb's outer skin.

"Oh, Yoke, I can't get loose without—" Cobb began, but just then the giant squid released them and jetted away fins first, propelled by a blast of water from the huge siphon next to its beak. A moment later Yoke could see why. A sperm whale went bucking past, its great flukes madly beating. The squid's speed was no match for the whales'. The leviathan opened its long, narrow, big-toothed lower jaw and clamped the squid crossways. The monstrous tentacles lashed about, seeking purchase on the whale's great blocky frame.

Cobb and Yoke continued to sink, and Yoke stared upward at the whale and squid as, incredibly, the whale swallowed the violently squirming squid whole, leaving only a few tentacles dangling from its mouth like live macaronis.

"We're here!" cried Cobb just then. Looking down, Yoke saw a wall of white light come rushing up at them. There was a clunk as they hit something, then a wild explosion of air bubbles, and then they dropped through a hundred feet of empty space to plop onto—a grassy meadow?

Cobb's body opened up like a blossom spreading its petals. Yoke stepped free to find herself standing in a diamond-roofed dome of air: a half-sphere dome like on the Moon, several hundred yards across, with the deep black sea outside. They'd fallen in through the roof, but whatever hole they'd made had instantly healed itself.

Cobb drew himself back into his old man form and stood by Yoke's side. Far from being ocean-floor ooze, the ground underfoot was springy green turf bedizened with wildflowers. The air was fresh and dry, though perfumed with tangy odor of moldies. The light seemed to come from all around. And Shimmer and five others of her kind were coming across the field toward them.

The aliens had shiny imipolex bodies like moldies, but iridescent, luminous, and shaped with infinite perfection. Two were formed like humans, and four like animals, with each shape an archetypal paradigm, a Platonic ideal, perfection incarnate. Shimmer resembled a marble Venus, and her partner was a bronze Apollo. The four animals were a unicorn with yellow-blond hair, a gem-like beetle, a muddy black pig, and a pale green python—each of them the correct size for the creature epitomized.

"Greetings, Yoke," said Shimmer, reaching out her hand. Her voice was sweet and resonant. "I especially wanted you to come, because you're the most reasonable and sympathetic human I've met. I'd like you to be the first to test out something we want to give your people."

Yoke took Shimmer's hand and squeezed it. The other aliens gathered around.

"Ptah," said the man, shaking Cobb's hand. His voice was a warm rumble. The four animal-shaped beings greeted them and named themselves: the unicorn Peg, the iridescent beetle Josef, Wubwub the pig, and the snake Siss.

"Where do you come from, Ptah?" asked Cobb.

"We're all from the same place," said Ptah. "All six of us. It's in a different domain of the cosmos. We travel as encrypted signals inside cosmic rays. Personality waves. They're like gamma rays but with a higher-dimensional component. Shimmer here's been decrypting us into moldie flesh one at a time. We had this idea that each of us form our body into a different shape. I was the first one she brought in. Josef's the most recent arrival—he talks a lot. He's just as smart as us, even though he's small. He found a way to miniaturize the moldie information representation."

"But what's the *name* of the place you come from?" pressed Cobb.

"You want one single name?" asked Ptah, smiling.

Wubwub made a sound like electric guitar feedback. Siss added a series of clicking sounds. Peg tacked on the sound of a gong being struck, and tiny Josef put in a clap of thunder. Wubwub stretched out his snout and made a sound like wind moaning in the trees. It was hard to be sure, but it seemed as if the aliens were making fun of Cobb's question.

"Oh, why not say we come from—from Metamars," said Shimmer. "And we can be Metamartians." She turned to Ptah. "Cappy Jane's employer is called Meta West Link, you know. 'Meta' means 'beyond.' Like metaphysics."

"Yes, I am coming from very meta," said Josef, his voice loud and firm. For whatever reason, he chose to speak with a German accent. "And only just now have I arrived, as Shimmer has said." He lifted his wing covers and buzzed through the air to land lightly on Yoke's wrist. "This seems a very marginal place." His eyes twinkled and the little fans of his antennae waved. "From the little bit that I am able yet to see. It's so curious, this one-dimensional time. For your people I think death must be very frightening?"

"Duh!" said Yoke. "Death's not frightening for you?"

"In two-dimensional time death isn't so much of an issue," said Josef. "Yes, perhaps I die in one time-line, but I'm still alive in another."

"Not here you aren't," said Yoke. "I could squash you and that would be that."

"Now, now, Yoke," said Shimmer. "I'd just been telling my fellows how kind you are. There's no need to be afraid of us. We don't plan to stay on Earth for very long. We're nomads and this is only one stop on our endless journey of discovery. How do you like these temporary bodies we've made ourselves? We're imipolex with algae and mold nervous systems like your moldies. We programmed our personalities right into the limpware."

"How many of you are going to come here?" asked Yoke. "Six is one thing, but six billion would be—"

"Too many?" asked Siss the serpent, then laughed. She sounded Chinese. "No worry, Yoke. Only one more of us going come. We form a family of seven, make a baby, help Om memorize all about your race, and then we move on and probably no Metamartian ever come here again. Your world not so very nice, I think. You know, Shimmer, I thinking perhaps we should be more small. Could we be ant, Josef? So tiny as germ?"

"I ain't gonna be no ant," interjected Wubwub, who'd been rooting in the sod. He used a kind of black rapper accent. He looked up at them, a few tubers hanging from the side of his mouth. "I'm too important for that, you know what I'm sayin'?"

"Too *fat*," put in Siss the serpent, striking at the pig's side.

"Me and Josef are the ones gonna help Cobb and Yoke out through the wall, ain't we?" said Wubwub, twitching the snake free. "Gimmie respect."

"Cease your soothsaying, O Swine," said Peg. "It's time for Lady Yoke to bleat her plaint." The unicorn spoke as if at a Renaissance Faire, with the speech mannerisms that Yoke and her friends called "swilly." With her flowing long blonde hair, the swilly unicorn reminded Yoke of a teenage girl enchanted by all things medieval. Her horn was shiny red like glossy lipstick.

"Thank you so much," snapped Yoke, not really understanding what they were talking about, but having a vague sense she'd been insulted. "What I want to say is that I hope Siss is telling the truth. And even six or seven of you could be a problem, frankly. If you start changing things, it could ruin our ecology. Your technology might overwhelm our civilization."

"Indeed it will," said Peg. "But is your way of life so fine? Dare to dream of more than grubbing in the mud. Yoke, we bring you the power to alter matter with a touch of mind. This is a power our god Om bestows upon us—a power she now sees fit to grant to you. You're lucky. Thanks to Shimmer's having been decrypted here, Om has noticed you. Your race will live as sorcerers."

"I suppose that sounds nice," said Yoke uncertainly.

"Give Yoke her alla now, Shimmer," said Ptah. He kept glancing around expectantly, as if someone or something else were about to appear.

"Yes," said Shimmer. "Om willing." She rubbed her thumb against her palm, and a little hollow gold tube appeared in her hand. It was almost cylindrical, with four smooth indentations like a hand-grip. "This is Om's gift through me to you," said Shimmer, and handed the object to Yoke.

The alla fit Yoke's hand comfortably. It had a live, vibrant feel to it.

Looked at more closely, the substance of the alla tube was not gold—nor was it any other substance Yoke had ever seen. It felt smooth, even slippery. Another odd thing about the tube was that, rather than being a fixed color of gold, it was repeatedly flickering through a cycle of perhaps thirty subtly different shades.

As she held the alla in her hand, Yoke felt a link between it and her uvvy. "Greetings," said the alla. "I'm ready to learn your mind." Yoke uvvied her agreement to this—not that she was sure what she was agreeing to. The alla showed her an image for half a second and asked her to name it and give a memory association. The image was a circular pattern with colored patches.

"A chrysanthemum," said Yoke, thinking of the first flower she'd ever grown.

"Next," said the alla, and for a quarter of a second it showed an image of a crooked forked line.

"A crack in a wall," said Yoke, recalling the wall by the side of her childhood bed.

"Next." Each image was being displayed for half as long as the one before. This one was a uniform patch of rough texture.

"Moon-dust," said Yoke, though not out loud, as this was starting to happen faster than speech. She was thinking of a particular patch of moon-dust and how she'd gotten obsessed staring at it after she'd read a book on mineralogy.

More and more images came, each twice as fleeting as before—and at the end of a second Yoke felt as if she'd given the alla an all but infinite amount of information. She thought of the old Zeno paradox about fitting an arbitrarily large number of events into a unit of time: a half plus a quarter plus an eighth plus a sixteenth plus a thirty-second and so on—no matter how many terms you stick in, the sum is always a bit less than one. Each new step only uses up half of the remaining time. How many images had the alla just shown her?

"Now I'll learn your body," said the alla, and Yoke felt an incredible series of tingles and twitches—in her guts, in her chest, up and down her arms and legs, inside her head, and in the muscles of her face and fingers.

"You are now registered as my sole user for life," murmured the alla softly. "Feel free to select something from your catalog."

"Think of something you want," said Shimmer. "You think to the alla through your uvvy. Josef and Ptah made a human-style catalog for it. Oh, that's right, we have to copy the catalog to you. I hope you have a lot of clear memory space in your uvvy?"

"I should," said Yoke. "It's a yottabyte model."

"Here it comes," said Josef.

And then the alla catalog was stored in Yoke's uvvy. When she accessed it, the display showed an amorphous, featureless object, waiting for Yoke to tell it what to become.

"Ask for a sweatshirt?" suggested Cobb, who stood absently twining his fingers in the blonde mane of Peg the unicorn. "You look a little chilly."

Yoke thought of a fleecy white pullover she wished she'd brought along from the Moon, and now her uvvy formed a mental image of a somewhat similar sweatshirt, a precise, detailed image seemingly called up from its internal catalog. The image wasn't quite what she'd had in mind, but by mentally pushing at it, Yoke was able to slide about through similar catalog entries till she found something that was a very good match for what she wanted. And once she'd picked her sweatshirt design, the alla adjusted it to be a custom fit for Yoke's body.

"Now say, 'Actualize!' " said Shimmer. "You can say it out loud or just think it. That tells the alla to make a physical copy of the design."

Yoke said, "Actualize." A sudden mesh of bright lines appeared in the air in front of the alla, hanging there like a three-dimensional wire-frame engineering spec. A web of dark membranes appeared within the virtual sweatshirt, dividing and subdividing. There was a little puff of breeze, and then the bright lines disappeared and a fluffy white sweatshirt dropped to the ground.

"This must be what Onar meant by realware," breathed Cobb. "Direct matter control!"

Yoke turned the little alla so she could see through the length of its hollow tube, careful not to put it too near her face. Seen through the hole, the room seemed to be endlessly spinning around the alla's central axis. *Whoah.* Yoke looked away.

"Yes," said Josef. "What the alla makes is realware. You could call the alla a tool for realware engineering. Figuring out the designs for the realware takes some work. But the alla itself is a magical gift from Om."

"You got the alla from Om?" asked Yoke. "And Om's your god? Your god actually does things that are real?"

"Is your very world not real?" asked Peg.

"Well, yes," said Yoke. "But—"

"Om a medium-size god," said Siss. "Not like the big White Light that make everything. Om kind of curious. She like to learn all about different races of beings by giving allas to them. Long time ago, some other aliens bring Om and allas to the Metamartian race, and now we bring Om and allas to you. Pass it on. More is merrier."

"But what is an alla, exactly?" asked Yoke, looking down at it.

"The alla is part of Om," said Shimmer. "A vortex thread that loops out of her body to cross our space. When Om gives you an alla, she learns all about you—and you get to have a magic wand. It's a fair trade. Everyone benefits."

"One question," said Cobb. "Josef just said the alla transmutes matter. But when it made Yoke's sweatshirt out of air, there wasn't enough air inside that bright-line mesh. Not enough mass to match the sweatshirt."

"No problem," said Josef: "If there aren't enough atoms within the target region, then extra ones are drawn in. That's why one often feels a little puff of wind."

"Before we let the alla spread to all humanity, Om wants us to test it just with one person," said Shimmer. "And I picked you, Yoke. The alla has registered itself exclusively for your use."

"Shimmer chose you as a maiden pure of heart," said Peg. "Worthy of a magic wand. Nobler than that Tongan King."

Yoke put on her shirt. It was an exact replica of the preview image the uvvy had shown her. To get her arms through the sleeves, she passed the alla from hand to hand rather than setting it down.

"That right," said Siss, attentively watching. "Hang onto alla very careful. It no use to other people, but even so, they might try to steal. You should make pouch for it and wear at your waist."

"It's mine to keep?" said Yoke, staring down at the alla. She thought of orange juice, and her uvvy displayed a catalog image of a squeeze-bottle of juice. Without saying the word out loud, Yoke thought, *Actualize*. A pouch-shaped web of lines formed near the end of the tube; the pouch webbed over and cleared to produce the bag of juice. Yoke caught it as it dropped from the air; she held it to her mouth and sucked at it. Delicious. She gave a happy guffaw. "Hey, you've got *my* xoxxin' vote!"

The beetle Josef had flown off while Yoke was pulling on her sweatshirt. Now he flew back and perched on Yoke's breast like a brooch. He glittered many colors in the light.

"The allas will make your Earth a paradise," the man-shaped alien named Ptah was saying. He was jouncing back and forth excitedly. His eyes were wide and glowing, as if he were expecting some great event.

"But we do have a problem, Ptah," said Cobb. "What about those people who've been getting killed? Like Darla and Tempest Plenty and Kurt Gottner? Is there some connection between those things and your coming here?"

"Om," said Siss. "Connection is Om. And don't worry, those people not really killed. You going see example right now. Om sometimes reach into space with her fingertips to take someone. Om fingertips have round shape we call 'powerball.'"

Just then Ptah let out a whoop. "It's time!" he sang. "Om's about to take me. Thank you, Josef! Farewell, Shimmer."

The Metamartians backed away from him. Wubwub pushed against Cobb and Yoke's legs, herding them along.

"I'm ready, Om!" shouted Ptah. He sounded ecstatic.

"Make a copy of yourself, Ptah," cried Shimmer. "We need one of you or we'll be back down to five!"

Just then something popped into the air next to Ptah, a spherical zone of warped space—something like a giant, airy lens.

"Look out!" cried Yoke, but rather than running, Ptah seemed to split himself in two. Or, rather, the air next to him shimmered and a fresh copy of Ptah was formed: another perfectly formed, bronze-colored, imipolex man. The new Ptah ran over to stand with Cobb, Yoke, and the other Metamartians, while the old Ptah stretched his arms up toward the mysterious ball of curved space.

"I envy him," the new Ptah said to Shimmer. "But I'm happy to help you reach the necessary seven to mate." He looked down at his new body approvingly. "I wasn't quite sure our replication procedure would work in this part of the cosmos." Ptah turned to Yoke, noticing her worried expression. "My original self will begin screaming now, Yoke, but don't worry, it's just a way to blow off a little physical discomfort. It'll look like he's being killed, but really he's just moving into a higher dimension."

The bright, shifting sphere darted to the original Ptah, and he became part of the round spatial anomaly. His beautiful, symmetric body puffed out as if inflated. And as predicted, he began to scream in pain. "*Om kreet!*" he shrieked. The great round anomaly of the powerball's space was inside of the original Ptah; his imipolex flesh was stretched out across its surface. A powerful glow emanated from his distorted face; his eyes were as lambent coals. "*Om kreet, kreet, kreet!*" A dreadful sound. His swollen form was starting to dwindle.

"Are you exactly the same as the old Ptah?" Yoke asked the new Ptah.

"Yes," said the new Ptah. "It's very easy for us to make realware copies of ourselves. We simply alla up an identical copy—each of us has an alla nestled within his or her body, you see. I'm used to seeing copies of myself go away. Remember that on Metamars we lead incalculably many parallel lives."

"What's going to happen to the old Ptah?" asked Yoke.

"Om wants to examine one of our Earth-style moldie bodies," said Josef. "The old Ptah will go to a kind of chamber inside Om, probably with the others. And then I imagine he'll move on. Into the Light."

Watching the old Ptah's apparent agony, Yoke wondered if this was what had happened to her mother. Was there any chance that Darla was anything other than dead? And what did Josef mean by the "Light"? Suddenly it looked as if the powerball might be drifting their way.

"No," groaned Yoke. She and Cobb began running across the grass floor of the dome. Shimmer, Peg, Siss, and the new Ptah fanned out ahead of them, with Wubwub following behind as if to protect them.

Soon they'd reached the diamond-hard wall of the dome. Wubwub sniffed at the ground and pushed himself against Yoke's legs, herding her a few yards along the curving edge of the wall.

"Stop it!" said Yoke. Across the meadow, the tiny shrunken powerball was darting about erratically, but it wasn't heading their way.

"Just a little to the right," said the black pig, insistently pushing Yoke with his snout. Finally he stopped. "This be the spot."

"Listen to me," said Josef. The lustrous beetle was still perched on Yoke's boob. "We are going to take down the dome now. The water will rush in."

"We'll be crushed!"

"Not if you get inside Cobb and stay at this precise spot," said Josef. "Wubwub will help push you in the right direction when the water comes. Remember that we can see a few minutes' worth of all the possible futures. Hurry, Yoke. Get inside of Cobb this very instant!"

Cobb flopped himself flat on the ground next to Wubwub, and Yoke sat down on him. She was still holding the alla. The old Ptah had stopped screaming. The five other Metamartians were standing by the dome's pure diamond wall as well, waiting.

"I will come with," said Josef, his legs clinging to Yoke's pullover. "And the others will organize a new node. Now that we've made contact with you, Yoke, we don't want the King to know where we are anymore."

The noble Wubwub stood firm at Yoke's side. He was lightly poised on his trotters, with his vigilant snout tracking the distant powerball's moves. "Rest of us movin' somewhere fresh. This place got bad juice now, you know what I'm sayin'?"

Cobb sealed himself up, and Yoke switched to viewing through Cobb's sensors. There was a *pop* and the last trace of Ptah and the powerball disappeared. Wubwub braced himself firmly against Cobb, pressing the bathyscaph against the dome's wall. The other Metamartians were braced against the wall as well, all of them ready to spring out into the sea.

And then the dome disappeared and six miles worth of water came rushing past them, crushing the air within the bubble into incandescent white light, illuminating for an instant, like the first flashbulb since creation, the dark ooze of the primeval ocean floor.

CHAPTER THREE

PHIL

February 21, 2054

Friday night Phil dreamed about his father again. In the dream he and his dad were sitting in a greenhouse full of orange nasturtiums and jasmine vines. Old Kurt was wearing his teaching clothes. His arms were missing. The jasmine smelled like musk, like rotten incense.

"The wowo took them off," said Kurt, his empty jacket sleeves flapping. "But they're healing fast." Blood was seeping through the shoulders of the jacket.

Made anxious by his father's wounds, Phil looked down at his own body. He was dressed in his sleeping outfit, a long T-shirt. He could see the individual hairs on his legs. One of his hands was clenched into a fist; when he opened it, the knotted, mirror-reversed wedding ring was there.

"I can't decide if I'm really dead," Kurt was saying. "Did I get a stuzzy funeral? Big tears? Bunch of drunks?" All the while the dusty orange nasturtium blossoms were singing in tiny, high voices, with the jasmine blossoms harmonizing a background.

"It was heavy, Da," said Phil, and the heavy gold ring tumbled from his hand.

"Gold from the roots," said Kurt. "Marry her."

The smeary music of the flowers was vibrating Phil's sinuses in a way he couldn't bear. He was crying. He tumbled off into jumbled dreams of mountain climbing.

When Phil woke, his father's knotted wedding ring actually *was* in his hand. He'd fallen asleep holding it. Was he crazy? He had to get rid of it today. Fuck this suicide shit.

It was ten A.M. and Kevvie was still unconscious. She didn't have to go in to work today because yesterday she'd gotten fired. Trying to get over the hangover from her Thursday night merge session with Klara Blo, Kevvie had stolen a bunch of Tendur painkillers from one of her lady clients, and the sharp-eyed old woman lodged an instant complaint. The geezer-sitter service had sent a dragonfly to sample Kevvie's blood on her way out of the client's building, and she'd failed the test big time. The service wouldn't stand for geezer sitters taking off their clients' drugs. So last night a resentful Kevvie had blown it all out on quaak and Tendur, and was completely twisted by the time Phil got home from work. He'd found her chasing after Umberto with a butcher knife yelling "Off with his head." Normally Kevvie was harmless, but when she was lifted enough she could get into a scary evil queen trip. This morning she looked like a nodded-out junkie, her mouth wide open and drool all down her chin. One of her hands was still soft from an ill-considered three A.M. splash of merge.

"It's over," Phil said softly to himself, and then he said it again, a little louder. "It's over, Kevvie. I'm not carrying you anymore." She snored on. Could he get her to move out? That would be hard. There was no formal lease, and Kevvie had been splitting the rent with him for the last ten months. Though Phil had built the birdhouse a full year before Kevvie moved in with him, she was likely to argue that by now it was hers as much as his. Which left only one alternative.

"I'm leaving, Kevvie," said Phil, trying out the sound of it. "I'm moving out." No reaction. "I'm moving out right now."

He dressed, put the ring in his pocket, picked up a duffel bag and started walking around the room putting things into it. Another ending. He was trembling with emotion. What did he have here that really mattered? Toiletries, some clothes, some S-cubes, his quilt, a couple of books, and fuck the thrift-shop furniture. What else? His blimps! If he left them in here, Kevvie would trash them for sure. She'd never liked his flying machines. Phil used his uvvy to call his blimps down from the ceiling. Led Zep, Graf Z, the Macon, the Penile Implant, and the Uffin' Wowo. The blimps nuzzled against him like lonely puppies, their silky skins rustling.

"Come on, guys," Phil told them. "We're outta here." Phil opened his arched door, maybe for the last time, and herded the blimps out into the open space of the warehouse. It was another gray day out the windows along the tops of the walls, gray clouds spitting rain. Derek was on the floor adjusting his green doughnut sculpture, Umberto squeezed up tight against his feet.

"Yaaar, Phil. Walking the blimps?"

"I'm moving out, Derek. It's Kevvie. I can't deal."

"You'd saddle Calla and me with that? Let's not forget that Kevvie got fired. How would she make the rent? Not to mention that last night she almost killed my dog. She's the one's gotta move outta here, Phil, not you."

"You can use my deposit to pay her rent till the end of March. Maybe she'll leave by then. I don't care anymore."

"Burn us is what she'll do," snapped Derek, his face hard. "I want her outta here by a week from today. *Before* March. Help me do it, Phil!"

"I can't be the one to put her out, Derek. And I can't live with her anymore either. I'm sorry, I—" Phil's eyes filled with tears. "It's too much, man. I just want to be quiet and not try, and it's not working. Burying my dad and dealing with Willow, and losing that Yoke girl so fast, and Kevvie's lifted all the time and I'm scared I could start using, and the wowo thing could come after me any minute and—"

Derek softened. "Aw, Phil. If you gotta, you gotta. It'll be dense, but I can deal. On February twenty-eight Kevvie's outta here if I have to fuckin' change the locks. And I'm gonna keep Umberto safe over at a friend's till she's gone. Hear that, Umberto? You're gonna stay with Kundry." Umberto thumped his tail.

Phil wiped his eyes with his sleeve. "Thanks, Derek. You want to keep my blimps?"

"Feed them their helium and shit? No, man. The least you can do is take your blimps. Get outta here before Kevvie wakes up."

The wind was gusty outside, and Phil had to tether the blimps to his left arm lest they be blown away. The helium-filled imipolex DIM bags beat against him like balloons. It would be impossible to walk far this way, especially while carrying the duffel. Maybe he should let the blimps fly off into the wind? They were only toys. But still. He'd made them.

Just then one of the Snooks moldies accosted him. "Want a blow job, Phil?" It was Isis Snooks, a moldie curved into a fairly impressive female form. She had pouty lips and long, dark, slanted eyes.

"Would you like these blimps?" asked Phil in return.

"You want to trade blimps for a blow job? How much imipolex is in them?"

"I don't want a blow job, Isis. You know I'm not a cheese-ball. I just need to get rid of the blimps. I'm moving out. Now, I don't want you to *eat* the blimps, I want you to take care of them. They'd be a nice decoration inside the *Anubis*. You have to feed them some quantum dots and helium every few weeks."

Isis cocked her head, studying the wind-whipped gas-bags.

"Are the skins programmable?"

"I'll uvvy you the access codes right now if you promise to give them a good home."

"Fun," said Isis after another moment's thought. "I'll do it." So Phil uvvied her the control codes and handed her the blimp tethers. Something else occurred to him.

"Wait a second," he said. "This big one uses ballast." He took the knotted ring out of his pocket and pushed it in through the intake valve of his biggest blimp, the polka-dotted one named Uffin' Wowo. Perfect. "Enjoy them, Isis."

"Come by and visit anytime." Isis was smiling at the blimps, already uvvying new patterns onto them. Hieroglyphs. "Wavy, huh? Where you moving to, Phil?"

"I'm following a woman I met."

"Yoke Starr-Mydol," said the moldie.

"How would you know that?"

"Thutmosis saw you with her Thursday night. True looove."

"I'm goin' for it, Isis," said Phil. The moldie looked so smart and friendly that Phil regretted giving her the dangerous ring—but he couldn't bring himself to take it back and throw it into the ocean. "Make that one big blimp stay up near the ceiling," he obliquely warned. "It could hurt someone if it pops."

Phil headed for the closest haven he could think of: Babs Mooney's warehouse. The door was locked and he knocked hard and long. Finally it cracked open, revealing a man's pale face. Randy Karl Tucker.

"Haaah gaaah. Don't go runnin' out there, Willa Jean!" Randy Karl Tucker's plastic chicken appeared at the bottom of the door, staring up at Phil with its fixed little eye.

"Hi, Randy. Is Babs home?"

"She done took off for the art gallery. I spent all yesterday helpin' her make miniature worm-farms. Tryin' to earn my keep. I got my Master Plumber's certificate back in Louisville, you know. Yesterday I rented me a plumber's pipe-gun, a thing that pushes out whatever kind o' pipe or tube you want. I grew ole Babs some xoxxin' gnarly little mazes for her worms. What you call smart art."

"Babs is actually letting you stay here?" Normally Babs lived there all by herself. Her father, ex-Senator Stahn Mooney, had bought the place for her outright. Babs didn't need money and she didn't like roommates.

"Don't need to sound so surprised, Phil! I'm not as dumb as I sound. And being a cheeseball don't make me a pervo right across the board. I think Babs is takin' a shine to me. Come on in if you like. Scoot, Willa Jean!"

"Thanks," said Phil. "I'm homeless."

"Hell, there's enough room in here for ten of us," said Randy, gesturing at Babs's immense warehouse with its bright, fabric-hung walls. "Pick yourself a corner and settle on in."

"Well, that's kind of you to offer, Randy, but I do know that Babs likes her privacy. How long did she say you could stay for?"

"I'm expecting to be here till Cobb gets back from Tonga," said Randy. He threw himself down on a couch and Willa Jean hopped onto his lap. "Maybe a week? I'm pretty well burnt on Santa Cruz. San Francisco looks like a king-hell place. Never mind the Moon."

"I don't mean to sound harsh, Randy, but Babs is bound to give you the boot. Maybe you don't know what she's usually like."

"I helped Babs a *lot* with them worm-farms, Phil. I'm more than just a plumber, I've worked as a process engineer. I'm a demon with the nanomanipulator. I helped Babs put sparkles in her worms. And to top it off, I'm gonna get her some superleeches." Randy tapped the ragged purple patch that was merged into Willa Jean's back. "Illegal imipolex. Just for Babs to use in her art, you wave. We're thinkin' about a gallery show that's a whole henhouse of superleech chickens. The viewers put on the control uvvies and it's *squawk-awk buk-puk*. Might could get some superleeches from my ole bud Aarbie Kidd."

"Don't you get Babs in trouble, Randy," snapped Phil. "Take some time and figure out our scene before you start acting like a complete criminal. If you do anything to hurt Babs, Senator Stahn will take you down for true. Depend on it."

"*Tat tvam asi,*" said Randy equably. "Means 'And that too' in Sanskrit. Did you know I lived in India for two years? I respect your concern for your friend, big gaaah. You think you'll be movin' in?"

"Well, no, my plan is to go to Tonga."

"You too? What all's in Tonga?"

"It's Yoke," said Phil. "I have to see her. For once I know exactly what I want to do."

February 22

So Phil ditched most of his stuff at Babs Mooney's warehouse and set off for Tonga with a few travel supplies in a knapsack. He took a conventional rocket-plane, with a change in Hawaii.

He arrived at Nuku'alofa early Sunday morning, Tonga time. The airport was old-fashioned and casual. He hadn't uvvied Yoke yet because he'd been scared she might tell him not to come. But now it was time.

The uvvy signal quickly found her, and Yoke picked up. She looked even better than Phil had remembered. Her calm eyes, her fine jaw, her wise mouth, her ivory-olive skin. She was wearing a purple bikini. She seemed to be sitting on a tropical patio eating breakfast. Alone?

"Hi, Yoke, it's Phil. I missed you so much that I flew to Tonga! I broke up with Kevvie."

Yoke took the news with aplomb. "Josef told me you were about to call," she said, tapping an imipolex beetle that was perched on her shoulder-strap like a tiny parrot. "He can see about five minutes into the future."

"Oh right," said Phil. "Did Babs blab? Where's Onar?"

"He and I are through. I think he's staying with the King. I'll tell you everything when you get here. I already asked Cobb to pick you up. You should wait somewhere obvious, like out in front of the airport? Cobb says he can get there in like fifteen minutes. It'll be wavy to see you, Phil. I'm glad you came."

A short while later Cobb plummeted down out of the sky and opened himself up like a mummy case. He looked considerably bulkier than before. Phil took the palladium nose-filters Cobb offered him and got inside the moldie-man, along with his pack. Huge acceleration and then they were arcing north across the Tongan archipelago.

"How's Yoke?" Phil asked Cobb.

"She's doing well."

"And what's with the beetle?" asked Phil.

"You mean Josef," said Cobb. "He's an alien from Metamars. A place where they have two-dimensional time. Apparently the Metamartians live a whole lot of parallel lives at once. They think our part of the cosmos is very odd!"

"Aliens! Are these the same aliens who were on the Moon back in November? There was one that got away?"

"Exactly. Shimmer's still here, and she's been decrypting other alien personality waves into imipolex bodies. Not just *any* aliens though, she only unpacks Metamartians. There's six of them now. This is like a bus-tour for them—or maybe an anthropological expedition. Shimmer, Ptah, Peg, Wubwub, Siss, Josef. Josef's taken a shine to our Yoke. He's a very useful individual to have around. Even though we only have one-dimensional time here, there's always a cloud of ghost futures around the next moment. And Josef's able to see the virtual futures and to actualize the best one. That's been making it easy to avoid hassles with Onar and the King."

"Tell me about Onar."

"Onar sucks," chuckled Cobb. "Just ask Yoke. She can't stand him anymore." Cobb did an imitation of Yoke's voice. " 'Onar's dishonest and a bad lover and he acts British and all British things suck. Except for Lewis Carroll.' "

"Who's Lewis Carroll?"

"Tsk, Phil. *Alice in Wonderland?* And your father a math teacher. Never mind. Onar and the King are so bummed about Yoke getting the alla. They want one of their own, but for now they have to be satisfied with Yoke making stuff for them. Mostly imipolex. She gave me some too." They'd reached their apogee, and now they were hurtling down toward the great blue sea with its tiny white-edged dots of green islands. "The alla makes realware; it uses direct matter control."

"Oh man, this is too much," complained Phil. "You've only been down here two days and I don't know what the fuck you're talking about anymore."

"I haven't even mentioned the powerball yet," said Cobb. "The hand of Om. Om is the god of the Metamartians. She ate your father."

"You mean the wowo thing?"

"The wowo was what attracted Om. Like a flower for a hummingbird. Or a candle for a moth. Or a book for a scientist. And Om is—well, the Metamartians say she's God. Whenever the Metamartians go somewhere, Om shows up too. The powerballs are like fingers of Om."

"Cobb!" shouted Phil. The islands were rushing up insanely fast. "Stop the bullshit and pay attention! Slow down!"

"Aw, I'm getting really good at this," said Cobb, unfurling a bunch of wildly flapping imipolex ribbons. The ribbons flexed themselves, tearing at the air. Cobb continued to drop like a stone, but at least he'd stopped accelerating. They were fluttering toward a large, hook-shaped island with subsidiary islands scattered around it like appendages. It reminded Phil of a flea seen through a microscope, a big flea riddled with watery lagoons and intricate inlets, the island's harbor like a stomach. There were yachts floating in the harbor, and a small cluster of buildings beside it.

"The island of Vava'u," said Cobb. "The little town is Neiafu."

Cobb's ribbons fused into great wings, and he sailed serenely over Neiafu and across the harbor to home in on one of the tiny islands that peppered the harbor straits. Cobb's target island stuck out of the sparkling water like a verdant muffin; it had a high, round crown leading down to vertical, undercut sides. The summit of the island had been cleared down to the bare stone, and perched there was a single house, a sturdy yellow concrete building with a tin roof, much weathered. Beside the house was the aquamarine gem of a small swimming pool, seemingly carved right into the rock. Steps ran down the steep side of the island to a dock floating in the blue sea. Cobb touched down beside the pool, right next to a young woman sitting at a wicker table. Yoke.

"You're welcome," said Cobb, disgorging a shaken Phil onto the concrete pool apron.

"Thanks, Cobb. Hi, Yoke!"

"Phil." Yoke was smiling so hard that her cheeks were bunched and her eyes were slitty. Phil sprang forward and hugged her; she hugged back. Now, finally, they kissed. But only briefly.

"You smell like moldie," said Yoke. "Let's take a dip."

Phil had a bathing suit in his backpack, and in a minute they were in the pool, swimming back and forth, laughing and splashing. Cobb wandered over to the house, which had a veranda shaded by woven mats of palm-leaves. There were two other moldies lying slack in the sun, and a few Tongans were sitting in the shade, some of them playing cards. Phil counted four big men and two women. All of them were staring, but Phil did his best to ignore them.

"It's beautiful here," said Phil, taking in the house, the palms, the ocean, the blue sky. "Whose is it?"

"It's the King's," said Yoke. "He's turned it over to me. I'm really important all of a sudden. Thanks to the aliens. You showed up just in time. I was starting to get lonely."

The jewel-like beetle that had been sitting on Yoke was buzzing around overhead. "*That's* an alien?" said Phil, pointing at it.

"Greetings, Phil," said the beetle, settling down to float on the water's surface. "I am Josef." His six legs twitched, sending off tiny ripples. "A Metamartian."

"Cobb claims you can see the future?" asked Phil. "Okay, what number am I thinking of? Between one and ten."

"You have not yet made a decision," said Josef. He had an odd, Germanic accent. "You are wavering between three, five, and seven. But now that I have given you this information, you are narrowing in on—"

"Four!" said Phil and Josef at the same time.

"Do you require further proof?" said Josef. "Try if you can touch me."

Phil reached out with his finger, but no matter how rapidly or abruptly he moved it, the little Josef was always where the finger wasn't. The beetle wasn't darting around or anything, he was just drifting this way and that, his legs mildly kicking. He had a preternatural gift of doing a zig whenever Phil did a zag.

"So I've got Josef's precognition going for me," said Yoke proudly. "*And I've got a magic alla. Each of the aliens has one of these inside their body.*"

Phil had noticed that Yoke had a shimmering gold cylinder in a mesh pouch dangling from her waist. Yoke got out the alla and held it in her hand. "I'll turn some water into air," said Yoke. "Actualize!" There was a bluish glow underwater, and right away a big bubble came surging up out of the pool. *Fomp.*

"Like a fart in a bathtub," said Phil, not quite sure what was going on. The glow had looked like a spherical mesh of lines. "Do it again?"

"Yeah!" said Yoke. "But now I'll make a bubble of hydrogen and oxygen. And I'll put in a spark so it explodes!"

"Not so big!" warned Josef, buzzing back into the air. "Not too near! Remember that the alla's transmutation zone does not need to be immediately adjacent to the alla."

Yoke said "Actualize" again, and a bright glow appeared beneath the water at the far end of the pool, followed by a sudden, concussive jolt. Phil could feel the shock of the explosion all up and down his legs. A dome of water shot several feet up into the air.

"Yaaar!" said Phil. "How are you doing that, really?"

"Ready for another blast?" said Yoke.

"The housekeeper is going to come and scold you," said Josef, hovering fretfully above them.

"Do it, Yoke," said Phil.

Another explosive *fomp* and, sure enough, a glossy-haired Tongan woman appeared at the poolside.

"Don't you be cracking my pool, Yoke. And who is this man?"

"This is my friend Phil," said Yoke. "And Phil, this is Ms. Teta. Can you make up a room for Phil, Ms. Teta?"

"HRH doesn't want anyone here but you and me and the cook and the guards. The alla is supposed to be top secret."

"Yeah, and the King tells someone new every time he turns around. I'm not a prisoner! That was the deal. I can have a guest if I want to."

"I'll ask Kennit."

"Here's some more gold," said Yoke. She paddled to the water's edge and held her alla out over the patio. "Actualize twenty-five gold coins." A shimmering cylinder appeared near one end of the tube. The cylinder filled with a pattern like ghostly marmalade and then a pile of twenty-five gold coins fell jingling to the stone. Phil felt a little puff of breeze.

"This is too good to last," said Ms. Teta, stooping to scoop up the coins. "This is making me most uneasy."

"I could give some gold to Kennit too," said Yoke.

"He won't take it," said Ms. Teta. "Kennit is an upright man. Would you like some breakfast, Phil?"

"Sure."

"I'll tell the cook."

"Oh, let me make it with the alla," said Yoke. "It's more exciting."

"The devil's food," said Ms. Teta, shaking her head. "I don't know how this is going to end."

Yoke and Phil dried off and sat down at the little wicker table. Yoke grasped the alla and made, in succession, a hot cup of coffee, a sourdough roll, a ramekin of honey, and two halves of a papaya. The bread was a bit dense, but on the whole it was remarkably good.

"All right," said Phil, chewing. "Explain."

"I don't know how it works," said Yoke. "It's like magic. The alla has this virtual catalog that I can see in my uvvy. The aliens gave me that too. I pick something from the catalog and the alla makes it when I say 'Actualize.' "

"But you don't have to think of every detail of each thing?" asked Phil. "The molecules of the coffee, the air bubbles in the bread, the sugar-crystals in the honey?"

"No," said Yoke. "The aliens already programmed all that. But I think I can put the alla-catalog materials together in new ways. I haven't really tried that yet. I might be able to make some very complicated things, like by designing a program to put things together. That's a type of problem I enjoy. How to simulate Nature." Yoke nibbled at a slice of the papaya. "This is good. I've never had papaya before."

"But it's in the catalog?"

"Josef and Ptah said they made the catalog based on all the things they could find on the Web. First they figured out the materials, and then they figured out the things we make with them. A lot of research. The alla catalog combines all the existing human mail-order catalogs into one."

"Right," said the beetle, who was perched on the edge of the honey, dipping in his little legs. "While we were waiting for Yoke, I programmed a complete set of Earthly substances into the catalog. All of the chemistry and materials science that we could find on your Web. The formulae of molecules, the structures of crystals, the linkages of polymers, things like that. And then Ptah generated macros for essentially all human objects which are manufactured from these materials. Anything that's ever been advertised for sale is now free in our alla catalog. Ptah even ferreted out the limpware designs for the special DIMs that come in so many products. As Yoke said, our alla catalog incorporates the contents of virtually every human product catalog in existence. A big job—but remember that we're superhuman."

"How does the alla work?" asked Phil.

"With Om's power, it transmutes one kind of atom into another," said Josef. "And then it links together the atoms as specified. The breakfast you eat is of transmuted air."

"Air?" said Phil, hefting his coffee mug.

"A cubic meter of air has the mass of one kilogram," said Josef. "This is well-known. Air is very freely available."

"Can I have some avocado?" asked Phil. "With prosciutto and Emmenthaler cheese?"

"Yes," said Yoke, after a second. "I can find all of them. I'll make a special plate." She cocked her head and looked inward, then moved her lips and—*whoosh*—there was a fancy china plate with slices of Swiss cheese, prosciutto, and delicate sections of avocado. The topper was that the plate itself was glazed with a photographically accurate image of Phil: mussed, blond-haired, unshaven, smiling, bewildered, and with a palm tree in the background. Yoke leaned forward, admiring the plate. "That's exactly how you look to me right now, Phil. It came out perfect! It's the first alla thing I've really designed myself. My first piece of original realware!"

"Realware," mused Phil. "You can make anything you can imagine. What's going to happen if everyone gets an alla? Nobody will work anymore. They'll all have everything they need. What will people do with themselves?"

"Oh, one keeps doing things anyway," said Josef. "Even after one's material needs are filled, one wants to bloom and to create. Grow or die—it's in the nature of things. And don't forget that if one does something interesting, one has a better chance of having sex with a desirable partner."

"But even if I were to make something wonderful with an alla, something like a new kind of blimp maybe, then everyone could copy it," protested Phil.

"Ah, but only if they have the exact design," said Josef. "Remember that only what is in the public catalogs is free for everyone. If you invent something that has more to it than meets the eye, then you have the possibility to sell your invention's design to the individual alla owners."

"Can the alla make living things?" interrupted Yoke.

"It can," said Josef. "Haven't you noticed yet? There's a large section of plants and animals in your catalog. You can customize them to a limited extent—keeping in mind that reprogramming the wetware of a living biological system is difficult. Everything must be at extreme synchronization. Living systems embody a very deep fractal density of information patterns."

"And can the alla make a person?" pressed Yoke. "I'd like to make a new copy of my mother."

"The allas don't 'copy' things," said Josef. "They actualize instances of objects that have been completely specified in the catalog software or in user descriptions. To make a fresh instance of your mother, you would need an accurate representation of both her body and mind. Just knowing her DNA and having an S-cube personality backup aren't sufficient. So, no, your alla cannot make your mother without some further programming that is quite beyond your means."

"But it *could* make a person if it had the code?" pressed Yoke.

"Yes," allowed Josef. "And I may as well tell you, Yoke, that during registration your alla did in fact create and store an eidetic map of your body and mind. But Om doesn't allow an alla-owner to arbitrarily use this code. There is no magic command for instant self-reproduction. In order to use an alla to reproduce oneself, it's necessary to understand the working of one mind and body well enough to fully specify the design."

"And I guess you guys are at that high level already, huh?" said Yoke.

"In our first meeting, you have observed how Ptah copied himself," said Josef.

"Oh, right," said Yoke. "Well, let me try making an animal." She knit her brows and looked inward at her uvvy catalog. "Actualize." A scrap of space webbed over with bright lines, grew opaque, and a small writhing object fell to the tabletop.

"A slug?" said Phil. The slug oriented itself and began briskly sliming into the shadow under one of the plates.

"I'll try a jellyfish next," said Yoke. "They're so beautiful." She used the alla to create a little aquarium, then projected into the water a bright-line disk-shape that actualized into a clear bell of jelly—which began steadily beating. "Can I change its color?" wondered Yoke, and produced a shocking pink jellyfish—which quickly dissolved into rags and tatters. She tried a series of variations on the catalog jellyfish, but none of them so much as twitched.

"Life is hard, Yoke," said Josef. "And so is wetware engineering."

The unsuccessful customized jellies were floating on the aquarium's surface. Yoke alla-converted them back into water and filled the tank with a selection of other standard catalog life: some more jellies, a shrimp, a clam, a scallop, and a few tropical fish.

"Can the alla make an alla?" asked Phil. "That's the biggest question of all, isn't it? Like in the fairy tale where someone wishes for more wishes."

"Yes," said Josef. "There is a way to use an alla to make another alla. And sooner or later one of you will learn the trick of it. But I am not intending to be the one to teach you. It is better that the knowledge should come to one of you directly from Om."

"Do you plan to give out more allas?" asked Yoke.

"As Om wills it," said Josef. "First we want to watch a bit what Yoke does. And then we'll test it with a few more individuals. And then I suppose Om will tell you how to spread the allas to everyone, human and moldie alike. I think it should work out for the best, but it's hard to be sure. We've never seen a place like Earth, you know. You can't imagine how really pathetic your one-dimensional time appears. I hope that the alla can really help you."

"Hoes for the savages," said Yoke. "Farming tools. What's in it for Om?"

"Om collects copies of sentient beings," said Josef. "By giving out allas and having the users register themselves, Om obtains the exact information codes of the users. As for your analogy to farming, perhaps an alla is more like a bulldozer than like a hoe. Restraint and caution will be called for. Especially for a race that's limited to a single dimension of time."

"You think there's a chance we'll kill ourselves off with the allas, don't you?" said Yoke. "Is that what you actually want? So that the Metamartians can take over the Earth?"

"Yoke, we already told you that we plan only for one more of us Metamartians to arrive here," said Josef. "Once we are seven, we will have reached the canonical family size. We'll conjugate to create a fresh Metamartian and then we'll move on—provided we can figure out the right direction toward a region with two-dimensional time. No Metamartian would want to stay here."

"We still haven't talked about the killer powerballs," interrupted Phil. "What's the story with them?"

"The powerballs are but manifestations of our god Om," said Josef. "Be assured that Om is no killer. Those whom Om touches are elevated, not destroyed."

Before they could press Josef any further, a large Tongan man came walking over from the veranda. He wore a white shirt, a necktie, and a blue skirt. He was squinting in the bright sun.

"Hi, Kennit," said Yoke. "This is my friend Phil. I want him to stay here with us."

"Yis," said Kennit. "I've just been in contact with HRH and he has no problem. Would you be willing to have Phil stay in your room? That way we won't have to wonder which shell conceals the pea."

"All right," said Yoke, looking down at the ground. She'd been making lizards and mice and rabbits. They were darting around under the table. On top of the table she'd alla-made a cheerful potted orchid. "The room has two beds. Can I make you anything with the alla, Kennit?"

"No thank you. HRH says the Tongan Navy ship will be arriving in the harbor today. We would like you to fill its hold with gold and imipolex during the night. Will this be agreeable?"

"Can we do it, Josef?" asked Yoke. "Does the alla have enough energy?"

"Quark-flipping is like jujitsu," said Josef. "As if to look at something and then to look at it in a different way. In and of itself, it costs nothing to interconvert protons and neutrons. But, yes, reassembling particles into different sorts of atoms can either create or absorb energy, even if one uses higher-dimensional shortcuts. Om acts as kind of bank for these transformations. Energies flow back and forth through the higher-dimensional vortex threads which connect Om to the allas."

"It sounds too good to be true," said Phil.

"Consider this: 'The world exists.' I think that also sounds too good to be true," said Josef. "Why is there something instead of nothing? Why is Om? We are only lucky."

"I want to take Phil snorkeling now," said Yoke. "All right?"

"Yis," said Kennit. "But if you should meet anyone, don't be showing off the alla. We don't want our people to become overly excited. Would Phil like to use Tashtego or Daggoo?"

"I only want to swim with a face mask today," said Yoke. "I don't want to bring along any strange moldies. Just Phil and Josef and Cobb and me. Cobb can protect us."

Ms. Teta found two sets of swim-fins, snorkels, and masks. Yoke and Phil walked down the steep steps to the water, followed by Cobb. Josef rode clamped to the strap of Yoke's bikini. The Tongans weren't interested in swimming. And the moldies Tashtego and Daggoo were content to remain puddled atop the island in the sun.

Phil and Yoke slipped into the water together, while Cobb and Josef swam off on their own. Phil felt as if he'd been transported to heaven. The bottom was white sand, and the water incredibly clear. The knobs of small coral heads dotted the bottom, each head surrounded by a school of luscious-colored fish. There were fluttering sea anemones as well, huge irregular pink ones quite unlike the small door-stop sea anemones of California. Striped clown fish idled in the tentacles of the anemones, darting forward as if to greet Phil—though when he looked closer, he saw that their smiling faces were split to reveal tiny rows of teeth. Far from greeting him, they were defiantly defending their turf. Here and there on the bottom were giant clams, meter-wide behemoths with great, crenellated shells. They rested partly open, with the shell gaps revealing incredible fleshy mantles that were differently colored on each clam: some blue, some green, some purple, all of them wonderfully iridescent.

Rising up off the shell of one giant clam was a bumpy stag-horn coral. The clam and coral made a marvelous, unbalanced composition, something nobody would ever think of designing, yet something with a beautiful inner logic. One single fish lived in the branches of the coral. Phil's soul overflowed like a wineglass in a waterfall. How to contain so much beauty?

He followed Yoke to perch on a big coral head, catching his breath.

"This is paradise, Yoke."

"Yes," said Yoke. "It's good to share this with you." They kissed again, this time much longer than before.

For the next forty-five minutes they paddled around, chatting and getting to know each other better. The more Phil talked with Yoke, the more he liked her.

Like Phil, Yoke was into being clean and sober. And she shared Phil's contempt for conventional goals. "It's like society wants you to be a machine," was how Yoke put it. "Programmed to ignore everything besides the one thing they use to control you. Money or clothes or drugs or group approval. People don't see that the real world is all that matters." But unlike Phil, Yoke's contempt for society made her invigorated, not paralyzed. "There are so many things I want to do."

"When I wake up each morning, I always think it's going to be a nice day," said Phil. "That's my basic take. Instead of thinking that I have to do something to make the day be good. It's already perfect. I don't have to do anything at all. In fact if I do anything, I'm likely to fuck up."

"Oh no, Phil," said Yoke. "We have to work on the world. It isn't perfect at all. What about the news on the uvvy?"

"Well, of course I never watch news," said Phil. "News, commercials, mass entertainment—they're all the same. Buy and eat and shit and buy again."

"Yeah, all the ways to avoid being aware," said Yoke. "It's *crazy*. You think it's bad here, you should see the Moon. There's so much virtual reality there. On Earth you've got more Nature."

"Most people ignore Nature," said Phil. "Except for worrying about weather disasters. But, hey, we shouldn't be talking about 'most people.' That's a trap too. My goal is not to get sucked into anything. Just hang back and stay calm. I don't have to fix anything but myself. The rest of the xoxxin' world can xoxx itself some more."

They were standing in waist-deep water. Yoke splashed her face to reset herself. "I love the surface of the water, how the reflections make darker and lighter blues where it undulates. All this analog computation for free."

Phil accepted the change of subject and they looked at the water for a while. Now and then he glanced up at the island. Sometimes Kennit or another guard would be looking down at them, but not always.

Phil and Yoke waded over to the island's narrow beach to rest, out of sight from the people above. Cobb flopped down on the beach a little ways off to sun himself, and Josef busied himself crawling around at the edge of the water, investigating tiny forms of sea life. Yoke used her alla to make them a bottle of fresh water.

"This alla is such a powerful thing," said Yoke, passing Phil the bottle. "With some practice I could use it to model almost anything."

"Go beyond the catalog?"

"Yeah. I think I told you before that I'm into figuring out algorithms for natural processes, Phil? Like a coral reef. That would be so wavy to figure out how to grow one. The individual polyps swimming around and landing. I could make one with real coral polyps, and I could make another with imipolex DIM polyps. Sort of like the worms and fabricants that Babs Mooney designs. And, God, there's so much I can do with plants. What a sea of bioinformation there is on Mother Earth." Yoke smiled, lost in happy thought.

"Speaking of Babs, I'm a little worried about that Randy Karl Tucker staying with her," said Phil after a while. "Right before I left, Randy was bragging to me that he was going to get Babs some superleeches."

"That would be bad news," said Yoke. "But I know Randy a little. He talks tough, but he means well. Usually." She smiled at Phil and stroked his hand. "What's your dream of what you'd like to do? Own a restaurant?"

"No ambitions, no goals," said Phil. "I just want life hassle-free. No, I can't see running a restaurant. Feeding hungry cranky greedy people *every* day? Why? I guess deep down I feel like there should be something important I could do, but I don't know what it is. I'm scared there isn't anything at all. I did have these pet blimps I was really into. Kind of stupid."

"You were going to show them to me, but—"

"Kevvie," Phil winced. "Yeah, I built the blimps myself. You don't see many big blimps around because they're slow and they don't always go where you expect them to. Helium's pretty cheap, even without the allas. The real problem with blimps is that the wind blows them around. I keep thinking I might invent some way to beat the wind. And then maybe I could go into business selling my blimps. But I know that sounds dumb. Like all my ideas."

"No, it sounds floatin'," laughed Yoke. They kissed for a while, then got up and stretched. The sun was getting too hot.

"What now?" said Phil. "Go back up?"

"I think we should sneak off," said Yoke. "It bothers me for them to think they've got us trapped here."

"Where would you want to go?" asked Phil.

"Anywhere. I don't like the idea of spending the rest of the day sitting around that house with two maids and four bodyguards watching me. This trip is my vacation. I want to look at Neiafu. Hey, Cobb, Josef, come over here."

Hearing Yoke's call, the two came over.

"Could you fly us over to Neiafu?" Yoke asked Cobb.

"They'd see," said Cobb, pointing upward. "Tashtego and Daggoo would come after us. I don't want to get in a fight with them. They're mean motherfuckers."

"We could go underwater like a submarine," suggested Phil.

"They could still see us," said Cobb. "This water's really clear. I'm sure they're watching that we don't move away from the island."

"They will not see you if you are not where they look," said Josef. "And this is what I know how to do."

So Cobb stretched himself thin enough to wrap around Yoke and Phil, with Josef on the inside with them too. Josef hooked into their uvvy connection and gave them a view of his odd way of seeing things.

Normally when Phil would imagine the future, he'd see a single mental movie of himself going ahead and doing something. But now, thanks to Josef, he was seeing his immediate future as—oh, a mansion with many rooms. In some of the rooms Tashtego and Daggoo zoomed down on Cobb and rousted them, but in a few of the rooms Cobb swam on undisturbed.

They zigzagged across the harbor from coral head to coral head. At one tricky point, Josef's vision showed them as apprehended in all the futures but one. So they picked the one, which meant that Cobb suddenly dove down to the bottom of the water and burrowed into the mud. A bit later the futures started opening up again. Cobb swam in close to the shore and lurked beneath one of the docks of Neiafu until there came a moment when nobody was looking that way.

Cobb disgorged Yoke and Phil, who scrambled onto the dock. Yoke used her alla to quickly make them some bland shorts and T-shirts. She and Phil walked up the dock's gangplank to Vava'u, looking like ordinary yachties come ashore for a bit of sightseeing. Cobb waited in the water, and Josef hung from Yoke's earlobe like a cunning gem.

They looked at the few small, utterly nontouristy stores, closed for Sunday. Canned food, rope, straw fans, rubber thongs, pieces of cloth. The early afternoon sun was quite hot. A few Tongans walked slowly by, polite and handsome, dressed in their best clothes. Last night Kennit had told them that church could be an all-day proposition in Tonga. Phil could hear a congregation's voices lifted in song somewhere off in the distance.

"Let's go in here," said Yoke, indicating a small, blue-painted wood building: the Bounty Bar. They sat down by a window; at the next table were two tipsy wharf-rats, one a dark-skinned Fijian, one a pale New Zealander. Yoke ordered ice cream and Phil had a Coke.

"Listen," whispered Yoke after a minute. "They're talking about Onar!"

"Typical American, a loudmouth, always bragging," the New Zealand Kiwi was saying. "A real name-dropper, mentioned HRH. He was asking what's the most valuable and marketable element, pound for pound. What would you guess, Nuku?"

"Hundred dollar bills!" said the Fijian.

"Oh, that's no good, you silly bugger. Every bank note has a DIM in it; each and every one of them is registered with the Gimmie like a pedigreed dog. You can't just make up serial numbers for bills that don't exist. I said what's the most valuable *element,* meaning primitive chemical substance, don't you know?"

"Carbon!" said the Fijian. "In the form of a very big, very beautiful diamond."

The Kiwi made a negative, fishlike face. "Bottom's dropping right out of the diamond market, it is. I hear Mbanje DeGroot's selling a bulk nanomanipulator that makes the price curve linear instead of exponential. No, my friend, the top four elements are rhodium, platinum, gold, and palladium. The market for palladium and rhodium's a bit thin and illiquid, and platinum's a shade high-profile. I told Onar that gold's the best bet. Metals are safe from all that nanotech fiddling, don't you know? There's no way to convert one kind of element into another, is there?"

"How about black people eating white people?" The Fijian grinned, showing his sharp teeth. And then their next round of drinks arrived.

"So where is Onar?" Phil asked Yoke.

"Well!" said Yoke. "When Cobb and I came up from meeting the aliens at the bottom of the ocean, I suddenly realized that I didn't have to deal with Onar anymore. I mean, here he'd gotten me to do something really dangerous, and like why? I don't owe anything to him. He was trying to get me to give him the alla, and I was all 'Go to hell.' " Yoke paused and looked at Phil round-eyed over a spoonful of vanilla ice cream.

"And then?"

"Cobb and I ditched Onar and flew back to Nuku'alofa. But I still wanted to look around Tonga, you wave. I mean I came here to do some diving. And I guess Onar uvvied the King, because the King called me up and said he'd let me use his island in the Vava'u harbor if I'd please just use my alla to make him some gold and imipolex. So I'm like why not. But it's not working out well. I might have to bail on Tonga pretty soon."

"Back to San Francisco?" asked Phil. "I just got here. The ticket cost a lot. There's still so much for us to do and see."

"Maybe back to the Moon," said Yoke. "I should show the alla to my family and friends back there. It's such a radical change. Too big to discuss on the uvvy. But you're right, Phil, I'd like to enjoy Tonga some more with you."

"If you leave, please take us with," said Josef out loud, his little voice deep and strong.

"I don't know about that," said Yoke. "Six aliens? Where's your new node anyway?"

"Oh, it's on Vava'u," said Josef. "Somewhere."

On the way out, Phil and Yoke asked the cashier about the local sights.

"You might like the singing at the church up the road that way," said the woman behind the counter "But that walk's all in the sun. And they're nearly done. If you go the other way it's shady, and in a mile you come to Mount Talau."

"How tall is Talau?" asked Phil.

"One hundred thirty-one meters," said the woman proudly.

"I can handle that," said Yoke.

They walked along under strange tropical trees, trees like Phil had never seen before: some with ferny leaves and masses of orange blossoms, some with purple flowers, some with doughy-looking trunks. Josef kept quiet, letting them enjoy themselves. They walked by a school and many little houses. The road petered out and became a dirt track. They passed a stripped, rusted-out car with a solemn goat standing inside it. A little farther on, a muddy trail led up a steep hill: Mount Talau. They scrambled to the top; there were a lot of trees up there and a bit of a view. The great open sea. They kissed for a while. Phil loved the smell and feel of Yoke. And her bold eyes. Looking around the hilltop, Phil found a giant bean pod hanging down from a tendril that vanished up above into some high trees.

"That's a *serious* bean," said Yoke. It was a lovely pale green and nearly three feet long.

Phil tried to snap the bean loose. He twisted the fibrous vine, bent it back and forth, but it wouldn't give. Finally he chewed the tough stem in two. The bean had a wonderful curve to it, and it bulged out in seven great pouches around its hidden seeds. It was like a bean in a fairy tale or a comic strip. Phil and Yoke laughed about it a lot.

On the walk back down, Josef suddenly told them to duck around behind one of the native's houses. Peeking around the corner, Phil saw a bronze moldie go racing by, running up the road on foot. He was a shaped like a muscular man, though he was wearing a woman's red bikini.

"Tashtego," breathed Yoke.

"*Malo e lelei,*" said a voice behind them. It was an old man walking across the yard from another house. His shirt had several buttons missing, many of his teeth were missing as well, and he was carrying a small aluminum tub holding a big fillet of fish. He struck up a conversation with Phil and Yoke, talking about his sister in California. His name was Lata. Phil asked Lata about the bean he'd found.

"*Lofa* bean," Lata told him. "If you wait and pick when it's ripe, you can use the seeds for—dancing."

"I think he means castanets," said Yoke, clicking her fingers.

Lata invited Phil and Yoke into his house to look at his seashells. They took off their shoes, sat on his couch, and Lata brought out his trove, a little plastic bag containing shells wrapped in paper. The shells looked shiny and well-loved, as if the old man had gathered them and admired them over many years.

"Take some," he offered. "As many as you like."

"Oh no," said Phil at first, but soon it was clear that it would be rude to refuse the hospitality. Yoke picked out a big whelk, two brown cowries, and two tooth cowries.

"Right now is the good time to be walking back down," said Josef, using the uvvy this time. So they started saying good-bye.

"That was so touching, him offering us his treasure," said Phil back out in the shady street. Lata was still on his porch, kindly watching them. "Maybe you should make him something with the alla, Yoke."

"HRH said none of the Tongans is supposed to know," said Yoke.

"Look, you can do what you like, Yoke. See that rusty old bicycle leaning against Lata's house? Why not make him a nice new one? Make it out of titanium. Give it a basket and a bell."

"What do you think, Josef?" asked Yoke.

"I am content to observe," said the beetle.

"I'll do it," said Yoke, and took hold of her alla. She turned her back to Lata as if to hide the miracle—though it was kind of hard for someone not to notice a brand new bicycle being formed out of a shimmering web of magical air. In making the bike, Yoke tweaked the stored realware so that the frame had anodized gold cowry-shell patterns on top of the titanium. She wheeled the beautiful bicycle across the little yard and presented it to the old man. He accepted the gift with joy and dignity. In the grand scheme of things, a bicycle was, after all, a fitting exchange for his shells.

When they were halfway back to Neiafu, Lata rode past them, jingling his bell. And then things started to go crazy. Somehow everyone in every house they passed had heard of their miraculous gift. Men, women, and children streamed out, mostly in good Sunday clothes, offering presents. Shells, flowers, woven mats, even cans of beans and meat. It became hard to move forward. Just to get the people to back off, Yoke recklessly popped a dozen bouncy kickballs out of her alla, each with a different pattern, followed by gallons and gallons of ice cream. But the people were clamoring for something really good. Yoke made some gold bracelets and then—the biggest crowd-pleaser of all—a score of brand-new uvvies. Many of the Tongans didn't have uvvies yet.

By the time they got back to the harbor, a full-blown mob was squeezing in on them. Someone tried to grab Phil's lofa bean, but he hung onto it. He thought to uvvy for Cobb, and the old pheezer moldie came surging out of the ocean like Neptune come to rescue his children. Yoke created three dogs, who came into existence wildly barking—clearing out some space for Cobb. Cobb wrapped his arms around them and shot up into the air. But now Tashtego and Daggoo were homing in on them.

"Josef's gone!" Yoke exclaimed, touching her ear. "I don't know how to escape them, Cobb!"

Cobb dove down into the harbor water. He covered them over and fed them air. But now here were the coppery Tashtego and big black Daggoo, clamping tight bands around Cobb, Yoke, and Phil. The five of them swam back to the island together, staying beneath the surface so it wouldn't be easy for the agitated locals to pursue them. Phil still had his lofa bean and Yoke still had her shells.

"I hear you've started a riot in Neiafu," Kennit said frowning when they arrived. "On the Lord's day. You have done exactly what you were forbidden."

"So?" said Yoke. "What are you going to do about it?" And to that Kennit had nothing to say. Nobody quite knew how to deal with Yoke's defiance.

"The ship is going to be a day late," said Kennit finally. "We'll be asking you to create the imipolex tomorrow morning." And that was that.

Phil and Yoke had supper with the Tongans at a long table on the veranda, real Tongan food prepared by Ms. Teta. Fish, taro, and squash. Kennit didn't seem to carry any kind of grudge, and the other Tongans were friendly as well. They enjoyed teaching Phil and Yoke things about Tonga—the history, customs, geography, and language.

While they talked and ate, Cobb was hanging out with Tashtego and Daggoo off at the edge of the clearing. Despite old Cobb's misgivings about the Tongan moldies, the three of them seemed to be getting along very well. Indeed, from their hoarse cackles, it seemed likely that one of them had brought along some betty.

Soon it was full night, with an incredible clear sky. Phil was intoxicated by the stars, the full moon, and Yoke's low voice. And then it was time to go to bed.

"Now I am *not* going to do it with you tonight," said Yoke as they closed the door to her room. "I want that clear. I don't want to make a mistake and rush things. So no pushing, okay?"

"That's fine," said Phil. "I'm just happy to be with you, Yoke. We have plenty of time—I hope."

Phil took a shower and put on boxer shorts and a T-shirt for pajamas. Yoke was in a nightgown, sitting at a table playing with her alla. She'd just made a big rough prism of green glass with little whorled bubbles in it. The glass sat on one fat edge, rising up maybe ten inches. It had some funny little peek-through windows cut into it. The glass was smooth on one side, nubby on the other; it was something that Phil's hands instinctively longed to touch. He reached out to caress it.

"It's beautiful, Yoke."

"Thanks. This alla—it's the ultimate art tool. I can make anything that I can think." She closed her eyes, looking inward. A control mesh of bright lines formed above the tabletop, a foot-wide knot of twisting curves. There was a whoosh of air, and a ribbon of smooth metal formed inside the cube, a Mobius strip with comical hieroglyphics of ants embossed all along it. Yoke cocked her head, critically examining her creation.

"Did you know we have ants on the Moon, Phil? They snuck up there. I should have made these guys thicker."

"Can't you revise it?" Phil asked. "My housemate Derek, he says that his sculptures do half the work themselves. Like he's talking with them. He keeps looking at what he's made and changing it. I do that with cooking too. Taste it, spice it, taste it, spice it."

"Good idea," said Yoke. She popped the same shimmering bright-edged control mesh out and positioned it around the ant Mobius strip which she then—*whomp*—turned back into air. Now she made the ant-shapes in the glowing mesh bulge out a bit more and said, "Actualize." The Mobius strip was back, but with its ants much more swollen, bulging out of the metal ribbon into high relief. "Yes," said Yoke, setting down the alla. "Thanks, Phil."

"Can I try using the alla now?"

"Shimmer said nobody can use this alla but me," said Yoke possessively.

"She's not here watching us, is she? Come on, Yoke, let me try."

"Don't break it." Yoke handed Phil the little gold-colored tube. It sat in Phil's hand, subtly flickering. Phil held it up and looked through it—and saw a dizzying view of the room eternally spinning.

"It's like staring down through a tornado," he said. "How do I make it do something?"

"You have to uvvy into it," said Yoke.

Phil tried, but the alla gave no response.

"I guess it's registered only to respond to my uvvy signals," said Yoke. "You'll have to uvvy to me and I'll pass your signals to the alla."

Phil tried for a minute to organize this connection but he couldn't do it.

"I hate this software bullshit," he muttered.

"Let me," said Yoke, and in an instant she had herself hooked in as an intermediary between Phil and the alla.

"Hello," the alla seemed to say in a squeaky cartoon voice inside Phil's head. It displayed an image of something that wasn't anything in particular: an amorphous gray glob, roughly spherical, floating against a white background.

"Think your target to me," said the alla voice.

Phil could think of nothing better than that he'd forgotten his toothbrush. The gray glob elongated itself and grew bristles at one end. Its color and dimensions remained—indeterminate. At the slightest push of Phil's velleity, the specific features of the toothbrush warped this way and that.

"Really sensitive, huh?" said Yoke.

"It's like I'm exploring toothbrush space," said Phil, finding more and more qualities to vary. Tuft stiffness, handle bend, transparency, bristle density—it wasn't like he was fully imagining the toothbrushes himself, it was more like surfing through an incredibly vast multidimensional online mother of all catalogs.

"Try and actualize one," said Yoke. "It might work."

"I want that one," said Phil to the alla, and a mental image of an excellent green toothbrush froze in place. "No, wait, let me personalize it." With a special effort of will, Phil stamped his name on the image's handle and filliped its tip with a nonstandard kink. "Now make that sucker for me, little alla. Actualize."

But nothing happened. Wish as he might, Phil couldn't force the magical lines of bright mesh to appear.

"I guess I have to say it," said Yoke.

"That is correct," squeaked the alla. "I allow only one registered user."

"So actualize the toothbrush already," said Yoke, and Phil's toothbrush dropped into his lap.

Phil handed the alla back to Yoke, who quickly returned to revising her two sculptures. Popping out the old mesh, dissolving the existing version, adjusting the mesh, and making a new one. "The alla remembers the exact format of each of the things I've actualized," said Yoke. "So it's easy to keep changing them." She adjusted the bends of the metal loop, and shaved bits off the curved sides of the big glass prism.

Phil set his lofa bean down next to Yoke's sculptures and tried to get her to admire it some more. He didn't like for the alla to be getting all the attention. The bean was something remarkable that he himself had found. "What a beautiful green color our lofa bean is, Yoke." Yoke was tired of talking about the bean, but Phil kept on trying to riff on it, trying to get Yoke to look at him. "Could it be the larva of an alien centipede? The bean's vine was hanging right down out of the sky. *Jack and the Beanstalk!* What if it splits open and eats my brain tonight, Yoke?"

"It would get a small meal!" laughed Yoke. "Just kidding. I like your brain, Phil." She set down the alla, slipped into her bed and turned out the light.

"Good night, Yoke," said Phil, getting into his own bed. "It was a great day."

"I'm glad you're here, Phil. And, um, what I said when we closed the door—I didn't mean that you can't kiss me good night."

February 23

Phil dreamed about his father again, but when he woke Monday morning, the details faded out of his memory. Outside there were voices on the veranda, one particularly annoying voice the loudest: Onar Anders, saying something about tea, about the best way to make it.

Phil looked over at Yoke's bed; it was empty, the flipped-back sheets a gentle outline of her slender frame. And the lofa bean? It was sitting quietly on the night table, green and vegetal.

Phil put on the shorts Yoke had made him and a clean dark blue silk sport shirt that he found in the closet. It was quite a large shirt, patterned with suns and stars; perhaps it belonged to the King. Outside it was already mid-morning. Clear sky and a gentle breeze. Yoke, Onar, and the four Tongan bodyguards were at the long table on the veranda drinking tea and coffee. Cobb was also present, but Tashtego and Daggoo weren't around.

"*Ecce homo,*" said Onar. He was wearing a white yachting cap with gold braid and a stiff bill. "Behold the man. Welcome to Tonga, Phil. Glad to see you could get some time off from your menial job."

"Xoxx you, Onar. Hi, Yoke. Man, I slept well. You've got a great room, Yoke. I found this nice shirt in the closet. What's happening?"

"The Tongan Navy ship finally got here," said Yoke. "I'm supposed to fill it up with goodies for the King. I like that shirt on you, Phil. It's—heavenly."

"Royal duds," said Phil, flapping the great garment. "Is filling up the ship going to take us long?"

"Well, I'll be making the gold and imipolex in slugs small enough for people to carry. So I'll have to make a lot of them. It might be a couple of hours. Do you want to watch?"

"I'm sorry, but Phil can't come aboard the navy ship," interrupted Onar. "Security, don't you know?"

"Bullshit," said Yoke.

"HRH insists," said Onar. "And he promises not to lecture you about what you did in Neiafu yesterday. Some of the locals even took pictures of you, but thanks to the ID virus, all the images show Sue Miller. You can still be anonymous and keep your alla, Yoke. We've done all this for you. Be a sport, and help us. It's thanks to the King that you met the aliens and got the alla in the first place."

"What do you think?" Yoke asked Phil.

"Whatever you say," Phil answered, feeling himself slide into his old passivity. "I'll miss you, but I can keep myself entertained. I could do some snorkeling maybe. Or go to Neiafu and see what's down the road in the other direction. If you think you'll be safe."

"I'll bring Cobb along for protection," said Yoke. "And that's final, Onar."

"Let me check," said Onar, and silently consulted the uvvy he was wearing on the back of his neck. "Jolly good," he said a minute later. "Ms. Yoke Starr-Mydol and her moldie Cobb are cordially invited aboard His Royal Highness's flagship. Shall we go down to the launch? If you like, Phil, we can drop you off at Neiafu."

To avoid the danger of the locals coming after Yoke again, the launch dropped Phil at a deserted private dock rather than at the main Neiafu dock. Phil waved as the launch sped out to the big Tongan Navy ship floating in the harbor. Little Yoke. Maybe he should have insisted on sticking with her. But Phil knew he wasn't good at arguing. Oh well.

Phil strolled up to the main road and turned right. He passed a few locals. They all smiled and nodded, recognizing him, but there was nothing like the excitement of yesterday. Evidently everyone knew that although Yoke was the Queen of the Alla, he was only her Prince Consort. Nothing special.

Phil was intrigued by the thin black pigs he saw everywhere. All of the Tongans' houses were dirty on the outside from the pigs rubbing themselves on the walls. He tried to pet one or two of the pigs, but they were extremely wary. And some had tusks.

As he continued to walk, the houses gave way to trees and fields. In one field he noticed a hut as primitive as any he'd ever imagined—what the Tongans called a "*fale*." It had palm-trunk posts holding up a roof of palm fronds. The walls were woven matting, with a big gap in place of a door. Sitting on the ground in front of the house were the loveliest people Phil had ever seen, a man and a woman, the woman with a baby at her breast, the three of them looking supremely content. They noticed Phil, but didn't bother to wave. The Edenic family made Phil think of Adam and Eve. Would it really be a step forward for them to have an alla?

He walked on and came to a field with a low wall around it. Within the enclosure were long mounds of gravel decorated with colorful patterns of pebbles and shells. The dimensions of the mounds and the faint odor of corruption told Phil this was a graveyard. A thin young woman with a pack of children was working on one of the graves; she was sweeping it with a stick broom and burning the rubbish in a small fire. Seeing Phil look at her, the woman made a gesture he hadn't seen before. She held her hand palm up, slightly cupped, with the fingers stiff and outspread, and then flipped the hand down toward him, a bit as if sowing seed. The gesture definitely meant "go away" rather than "come here." Could an alla have saved the life of the person whose grave she was tending? *But why bother?* thought Phil. There's always more people, and everyone has to die.

Phil's easy, callous thought stumbled over a fresh burst of grief for his father. There were always more people, but no more of Da. He'd been a jerk, but Phil missed him. Dead forever. Life was short. Phil wondered how Yoke was doing on the King's ship. Maybe he'd uvvy her in a little bit.

Now Phil came to a little village, a cluster of fales. Beyond the village was a low hill, and beyond that the ocean. Phil decided to walk through the village to the water. As he walked past the fales, a group of children came after him, shouting and laughing, three or four girls and a boy. *"Palangi,"* they called him, which Kennit had said was Tongan for both "ghost" and "white person."

Phil asked the children to catch a piglet so he could pet it, but they wouldn't. Perhaps they were afraid of the tusks. The boy, about four, had fun poking at Phil's back with a long and disturbingly sharp stick. The girls asked Phil's name and had him spell it for them and then they danced around him saying, "Phil, Phil, Phil." Defining him here. It felt like being awake inside a dream. The border between life and dream seemed so elastic these days.

When he got to the top of the rise, the children went back to their fales, and Phil picked his way down to the rocky beach alone. Brittle sea stars were everywhere on the shallowly covered stones, striped snaky things, most with two or three arms in a hidey-hole and the other arms lashing about. Thank you, God, thought Phil as he looked at the calm waves coming in. Thank you for making the world.

Something nudged his leg. A pig?

"Yo, Phil," said the black pig. "I'm Wubwub. Hate to tell you, man, but I'm the brother what turned Om onto your Da. I found the wowos on the Web and told Om the news. But maybe there's a way you can help yo' da come back, you know what I'm sayin'? C'mon in here, see our new node."

The pig trotted down the beach and disappeared into a hole in the rocks, seemingly an entrance to a cave. Phil came along into the dark, holding out his hands so as not to bump his head. The passageway twisted a bit; there was light ahead—and the rank smell of moldie flesh. Phil followed Wubwub around a last turn and found himself in a well-lit rocky grotto the size of a room. Six figures were in there; most prominent was a pale, nude woman—the famous Shimmer! In addition to her and Wubwub the pig, there was a handsome bronzed man named Ptah, the blonde unicorn Peg, a thick serpent called Siss, and Josef the beetle. All of them had moldie bodies.

"Good day, Phil," said Josef. "I present you the other Metamartians."

"What are you guys really doing here?" asked Phil when the introductions were done. "What are you after?"

"We're like tourists on a road-trip," said Shimmer. "Except that we're never going home." She looked like a soft Greek sculpture, like Venus. Phil would have liked to touch her. "Like so many others, our race evolved to the point where we scattered out into the cosmos as personality waves, a bit like cosmic rays. It's rare that there's a—a 'radio' that can 'play' us. But we have an endless amount of time. Sooner or later one always gets lucky. Last November, as you must have heard, Willy Taze and the loonie moldies found a way to decrypt a number of extraterrestrial beings into imipolex bodies."

"It was a disaster," said Phil. Though Shimmer's voice was mesmerizing in its musicality and beauty, Phil found himself wanting to argue with her. "One of you destroyed the Moon's spaceport. Hundreds of people died."

"Yes," said Shimmer curtly. She seemed to have adopted a beautiful woman's high self-regard and low patience. "But the single warlike alien who ran amok was no Metamartian. All of the *peaceful* extraterrestrials were indiscriminately murdered by humans—under the leadership of Darla Starr. I alone escaped. And it was I who eliminated the last vestige of that single warlike alien. But I don't ask for your gratitude—no more than you would seek praise from an ant. Or from a bacterium."

"We understand why y'all fought back," put in Wubwub. "But we be good guys, know what I'm sayin'?"

"I still don't get what you're doing here," said Phil.

"I said that we're tourists," said Shimmer. "But it would be better to call us nomads. We live in transit, and whenever we can, we form a little family and mate. Yes, whenever one of us manages to incorporate somewhere, we immediately try and build up a family of seven of our fellows. Bringing in more Metamartians is what I've been doing for the last few months, Phil, as you can see. There's six of us now, and soon we'll be seven. Seven provides the ideal resonance for reproduction, among other things."

"A bunch of nomads looking to get laid, huh?" said Phil. "Didn't I hear Josef say something about helping Om? You're really missionaries, aren't you?"

"Missionaries?" laughed Shimmer. "Every traveler is a kind of missionary, no? But, yes, it's true that our god Om follows us wherever we go. And, yes, we do help Om to give allas to the civilizations we discover. It's win-win. The alla-registration process allows Om to obtain software copies of the individuals who accept her gift—and everyone *does* accept. Receiving the power of the alla is the greatest gift a being can have. So now you know a Metamartian's entire agenda. First, to find a world where one can decrypt; second, to assemble a family of seven; third, to spread Om's allas; and fourth, to move on. There needn't be any problems at all when Earth is visited by the right *kind* of extraterrestrial, you see."

"What about my father getting killed?"

"We'll get to that in a minute," said Shimmer, the music of her voice gone a bit dissonant. "Can you please stop interrupting? I want to fill you in on what I've been up to, all right? Just very briefly. I flew from the Moon to the Earth and I made a deal with the King of Tonga to use his Cappy Jane satellite as an antenna to find some good personality waves. I picked up Ptah's signal first and then Peg, Wubwub, Siss, and Josef. And of course soon after I was decrypted, Om asked for a local being to examine. For my birth offering, if you will."

"Om is what you call the powerball, right?" said Phil. "Can you explain what happened when it got my father?"

" 'She,' not 'it,' " said the bronze Ptah. His body echoed Shimmer's perfection of human form. "Om is the God of Metamars. She lives in the higher dimensions. Our race first reached a working relationship with her some thousand of your years ago. Some other aliens brought her to us. Om lives outside of ordinary space and time. Whenever one of Om's people travels somewhere, a manifestation of Om comes there as well. Our god follows us. She can appear in various guises, but most commonly she shows herself as a four-dimensional hypersphere."

"Four-dimensional?" murmured Phil uneasily. He sensed the imminence of a batshit math-rap, bound to make him feel dumb.

"*Jawohl,*" boomed the German-accented Josef. He was perched on Shimmer's lovely shoulder. "I am taking this question. Although I feel that Om is surely of an infinite dimensionality, she usually enters space as a powerball. Her surface is a bounded region of three-dimensional space that has no edges: a hypersphere. Do understand that the fourth dimension of space is not to be confused with any dimension of time. If you doggedly wish to refer to your time as *the* fourth dimension, then the powerball can of course be called five-dimensional. But it makes an easier manner of speech to use 'the fourth dimension' for the extra dimension of space."

"I'm not going to touch that one," said Phil, momentarily distracted from finding out about his father. "Let me ask this instead. If Om can jump all around the cosmos, why do you travel as personality waves? Why not just ask Om to take you where you want to go?"

"We never know where we going in first place," said Siss. "What we do is to chirp into personality wave, let wave travel to place where it get decrypted into body, to find family there, to teach about Om, and then to chirp further. Travel is our way."

"But what does Om want?" asked Phil. "Why did she swallow up Ptah and my father?"

"Om is curious about everything," said Josef. "Your father caught her interest with his wowo display. Om thought this was a very interesting patterning of space. So one supposes that she had a curiosity to get a better acquaintance with your father. She could perhaps return him to the world at some time. As for why she ate the original Ptah—Ptah?"

"Om wished to see what kind of body a Metamartian on Earth might occupy, so one of us was selected," said Ptah. "The trip into hyperspace was painful for my original self, yes, but it was an honor. Om chose me at Josef's suggestion; Josef knows I come from the noblest Metamartian stock. The little beetle says he admires me and I suspect that he envies me as well. His choice only heightens my glory. All must recognize that it was I, Ptah, who once led the most harmonious weave of lives in our two-dimensional time, and it is I, Ptah, who has been the first to travel from Earth to the bosom of Om."

"Well-spoken, Ptah," said Peg. The unicorn had a contralto voice and a theatrical way of talking. "Isn't it droll how one chains one's words together here? Like threading pearls upon a necklace. Phil wots not that the Metamartian mode of speech is as a fractally branching fan."

"Yadda yadda yadda," said Phil. "Why do you have to keep jabbering about math?"

"When she talk about a fan, she mean Metamars be in a place where time spreads out nice and fat," said Wubwub comfortably. "Like it supposed to be. In fat time, no one thing really matters, know what I'm sayin'? It's grim and down to live the way you do, Phil. One poor little time thread all by its lonely self. You folks deserve to have the allas."

"You said it was your fault the powerball killed my father," Phil said to the pig. "Tell me more about what happened!"

"He ain't dead," said Wubwub. "You got dirt in your ears, my man? Your daddy's in hyperspace. When Om sweep through your space it like someone's hand scoopin' up a water-strider bug. One second the bug on the water, second later it on the back of the hand. One second your Daddy in bed, next second he on Om's powerball. He probably just kickin' it. Om's powerball got light and air, and a built-in alla for food."

"My father's alive?" exclaimed Phil, finally getting it. As when Jane had uvvied him with the news of Kurt's disappearance, he felt a dissonant mixture of emotions. Joy that his father could be saved. Relief that the old man's forgiveness could still be obtained. An impatient weariness at having to deal with him all over again. And a primal horror of meeting the undead. "Up in hyperspace?"

"It's called 'ana'," said Ptah. "Not 'up'. We've investigated your scientific literature, and 'ana' and 'kata' are the names of the directions of the fourth dimension."

"I know that," sighed Phil. "My father was a math teacher. I've been dreaming about him a lot. Do you think Om can affect my dreams?"

"I no know," hissed Siss. "Metamartians have no dream, Phil. Metamartians live in endless parallel worlds—no need dream world. Wubwub right, most likely your father alive, and is together with a few others Om take."

"Like my original self," said Ptah.

"And two women," said Wubwub. "Yes indeed. First thing Om did was scoop up that juicy Darla. Yoke's ma. Om got old Tempest too—and, let's see, got Tempest's dog, a toy moldie, and part of an oak tree. How I be so wise? Each time one of us get corporated here, Om ask the new Metamartian what be the most stuzzadelic sample she might scoop up. Om always do that. Likes to see the world through a spang fresh eye, know what I'm sayin'?"

"Would you like each of us to tell our story?" asked Siss.

"Not really," replied Phil. He felt dizzy and confused. Surely they were lying about Da. "I have to think about what you told me. It's too wiggly. I want to go back out onto the beach."

"Oh tarry in our sea cave just a bit longer," said Peg. She was in fact standing so as to block the passage where Phil had entered. Her horn, though red and swilly, was also quite sharp and long. "What does your poet say? 'Till human voices wake us and we drown.' Marvelous beads of meaning, each just so." She lowered the horn and fixed Phil with her great blue eyes. "Phil, you should harken to our tales while there's time."

"I'll tell first," said Shimmer, "Attention, please!" She drew herself up and laid her hand stagily upon her breast. "My powerball swallowed a miniature moldie from Willy Taze's isopod. What they call a Silly Putter; it's like a doll or a pet. Between a DIM and a moldie. This particular one was named Humpty-Dumpty. It happened to be the first living thing I laid eyes on—at least I thought it was alive—so I pointed it out to Om."

"And then Shimmer made me tell Om that—" began Ptah.

"The way you got here was as a copy of the original Ptah," Shimmer interrupted Ptah. "You didn't tell the powerball anything. So I'll tell the original Ptah's story." She cleared her throat, struck a new pose and continued talking. "When I decrypted Ptah, I was down in the ocean and there really wasn't much of anything around for Ptah to tell Om's powerball to swallow. Ptah may think he's perfect, but he's not all that creative. So I suggested that Ptah tell Om to get Darla Starr on the Moon. Space doesn't mean much to Om, she can spang out a powerball wherever she wants. Om can go anywhere. Praise Om."

"Praise Om," murmured the other Metamartians comfortably.

"Why eat Darla?" asked Phil.

"Why Darla?" said Shimmer. "You might jump to the conclusion that I was angry with Darla for trying to kill me. But of course no human could ever hurt a Metamartian anyway. And I really wasn't angry. That's not a Metamartian emotion at all. I just thought that Darla was the fiercest, most interesting human I'd seen so far. Yes. I was torn between suggesting her and Stahn Mooney, as a matter of fact, but Darla seemed more spirited. And you don't have to look so impatient, Ptah, because now I'm done. Peg?"

"When I was reborn on Earth, Om asked me what was interesting, and I knew not what to say," said the unicorn. "She showed me that she already had Humpty-Dumpty and Darla. Within our sea-dome I could only see Shimmer, Ptah, and the grass. I humbly asked Om what she herself longed to behold next. Om granted me the image of something she had seen in Darla's room, a merry shape yclept a 'wowo.' Om coveted a wowo. So I hastened to enter your Web, where I sought the bravest wowo in creation. This wowo of all wowos I found upon the greensward of a woman named Starshine, in the hamlet of Santa Cruz, California. And thither did I direct Om's gaze. It came about that Starshine's aunt, a crone named Tempest Plenty, was tilling the earth there in the company of a dog named Planet. Joyful at the girth of the wowo, Om took so bosky a powerball scoop that she snared those two as well as the wowo prize. I've told my tell, let Wubwub speak as well."

"Now Om just fascinate with that wowo; she asked me to find the brainiac what dream it up," said the black pig. "And that be Phil's dad. So Om done gobble down Kurt Gottner and half of his wiener-dog Friedl—I say *half* because that wiener-dog fuss so much she got pinched in two. Old Kurt's hand got rotorvated as well, and the space-waves knotted his wedding ring, which leads straight into the next tale, you know what I'm sayin', Siss?"

"Om not really ask me what to do either," sang the pale green snake. "She already decide to go flip Kurt's ring to make another sign and see if any humans get excite. I do give her small idea to swallow some of oak tree so she can find out about plant."

"I'm last," said the iridescent beetle Josef. "And I told Om to swallow Ptah. It was time for her to take one of us, so why not the most perfect?" There was perhaps a hint of sarcasm in his voice.

"Who you think be next?" Wubwub asked Phil. "We wonderin' 'cause we 'bout ready to decrypt Metamartian number seven. And like we been tellin' you, every time there someone new, Om celebrate by eatin' something."

"Don't do it!" cried Phil. "She might get Yoke!"

"Cappy Jane has a nice new Metamartian personality wave prepared for us to incorporate, Phil," said Shimmer. "We're not about to waste it. It's important that there finally be seven of us. A complete family." The bland sweetness of her voice sent chills down his neck. "Sit back and watch."

Phil shoved Peg's horn to one side and tried to push his way past her into the passage, but Wubwub nudged the backs of Phil's knees in just the right way to make him fall down. Siss the snake was on the ground to cushion his fall—and to wrap herself around him.

Lying on his back, Phil noticed for the first time that the light in the cavern was coming from a small hole up above, a hole that opened to the sky.

Shimmer used her body's internal alla to project a bright-line cube that actualized itself into a knee-high block of imipolex. "All right, Cappy Jane," called Shimmer. "Beam it down." Some signal must have come to her from the satellite then, for as Shimmer laid her gracious hands upon the cube of plastic, the stuff began to twist and writhe. A figure formed and rose up in the shape of a man-sized bird, a black and white Indian mynah bird with yellow feet and a great yellow beak. Its dark head was decorated with a pattern of yellow feathers that made it look as if it were wearing a burglar's mask.

The mynah cocked its head and stared at them with its bright, inhuman eye. It made a preliminary cawing noise that sounded almost like "Hello." Phil felt like the bird was about to peck him. "Let me go!" he cried, struggling against Siss's tight coils.

"Not yet," said the snake. "We no want you go shit crazy."

Shimmer must have uvvied some information to the mynah, for now its demeanor grew less blank, a subtle effect achieved by a softening of the lines of its beak.

"Good afternoon," said the giant mynah. It cawed to clear its throat, whistled a few musical notes, listened to the echoes, and spoke again. "Something's badly wrong here, isn't it?"

"We're in a land with but one line of time," said Peg, gesturing with her red horn. "This is all there is. Seek as you will, you'll find no other time but the short woven threads of brief ghost futures. Praise Om that you've come, for now we are seven and soon we can mate."

"Who—who is seeing this for real?" asked the mynah, tentatively stretching out its wings. "Why this very one thread?"

"Ain't got no notion," said Wubwub. "Could be the Light do it. What you gonna use for a name, mynah bird?"

"Call me Haresh," said the mynah. "An Indian name. I find it most oppressive here. It is jolly good that we are seven. We'll help Om, and mate, and then we'll chirp further." The bird twitched his head as if hearing something. "Om is speaking to me. It is almost time for her manifestation. I must pick something. She has already swallowed a Metamartian?"

"Yes," said Ptah. "Me. So don't do that again."

"This here is a 'human,' " said Wubwub, using his snout to nudge Phil's foot. "Om got three of those already, but might be she want some more."

"How soon is the powerball going to spang out?" asked Phil anxiously. "That's the word you use, right? 'Spang.' Floaty word. You guys are so brilliant. Let me go, Siss!"

"Not till powerball come," said Siss. "Om still looking things over, waiting for Haresh form some impressions of world. Since we see little bit of future, we going know just before Om decide. But until then very hard to guess what she going to do. Om follow odd kind of logic. Odd for you, not quite so odd for us. Logic of higher dimensions. Like human dream maybe."

Siss kept chattering, and Phil had a bad feeling about what she was getting at. He kept thinking about the sequence of what Om's powerballs had swallowed so far: a toy Humpty-Dumpty moldie near Shimmer on the Moon; Darla near a wowo on the Moon; Tempest Plenty and Planet and a big wowo in Santa Cruz; Kurt Gottner and part of Friedl in Palo Alto; half an oak tree near Kurt's ring in Palo Alto; Ptah; and—

"Yes, she going to take you, Phil," said Siss, suddenly slackening her coils. "Run."

"Praise Om," said Peg. "She calls Phil to be with his father."

"Don't wrassle with her, Phil," said Wubwub as Phil got to his feet. "If you wrassle Om, you end up like that wiener-dog, know what I'm sayin'? When Om come, you just ball yourself up and let her gulp you down. Look out fo' the churnin' when she break free."

"Will it hurt?"

"I think very much," said Siss. "Run, Phil, run! I no want powerball come near me."

"Thanks for nothing," snarled Phil, aiming a kick at Siss but—of course—the prescient snake flipped her body to where Phil's foot wasn't.

"You have but two more minutes," said Peg. "Pray use them nobly."

So Phil walked out of the cave to the beach and sat hunkered there, staring at the blank sky and the eternal waves, no different than before. And now he would probably die. So this is how it happens, thought Phil. It's not really so hard. Part of him felt weary, paralyzed, and almost glad.

But there was another Phil that knew he hadn't really started to live yet. He called Yoke on his uvvy. She picked up almost immediately. "Phil?" Behind her Phil could see laboring Tongan sailors and the great open hold of a ship. Vaana and the King were there as well.

"Hi, Yoke. The powerball is about to get me. I'm on the beach at the other end of the island. The aliens are holed up in a cave here. They just decrypted a new Metamartian, and Om's going to celebrate by swallowing me."

"Oh noooo!" Yoke's face bunched up and she burst into tears.

"I love you, Yoke."

"Don't die!"

"The Metamartians claim I won't be dead. That I'll be in a bubble in hyperspace. But I—I don't really believe it. The fourth dimension is bullshit. I'm just glad I met you, Yoke. I always said my life was good, but it wasn't really until I met you. At least we had one day together." Phil thought he saw something flickering out over the water. An isolated glint of strange perspective. "It's coming for me, whatever it is. And, Yoke, it was definitely Om that got Darla. Shimmer told her to. Stay away from the Metamartians, or they might kill you too."

"Wait, Phil, wait. How is it that you might not die?"

"Some crufty math fabulation. I'll find my way back if there's a way. Here it comes."

"I'll wait for you in San Francisco."

"I love you."

The powerball came in across the water, low down at Phil's level, flying straight at him. Phil braced himself, wrapping his arms tight around his knees. The powerball looked like a big, glowing crystal ball, reflecting and refracting light, though not so smooth as a glass ball, perhaps a bit more like a drop of water.

As it drew closer there was an odd effect on the rest of the world: things seemed to melt and warp, distorting themselves away from the magic ball.

Closer and closer it came, yet taking an oddly long time to actually arrive. It was as if the space between Phil and the ball were stretching nearly as fast as the ball could approach. The ball was like a hole opening up in the world. Everything was being pushed aside by it; the sky and waves were being squeezed out along its edges.

Phil looked back over his shoulder; there was still a little zone of normality behind him—the nearest section of the rocky cliffs looked much the same. But so strong was the space warping of the powerball that the beach to the left and right seemed to bend away from him and, as Phil watched, this effect grew more pronounced. In a few moments it was as if Phil stood out on the tip of a little finger of reality, with the glowing powerball's hyperspace squeezing in on every side. Back there at the other end of the finger, back in the world, Wubwub and Shimmer were peeking out of their cave entrance watching him, the cowards. He fought down an urge to run at them, and forced himself to turn back to face the engulfing ball. What could he see within the ball? Nothing but funhouse mirror reflections of himself: jiggling pink patches of his skin against a blue background filled with moons and stars—his shirt.

And then, like a mighty wave breaking, the warped zone moved over Phil. He felt a deep shock of pain throughout his body, as if something were pulling and stretching at his insides. His lungs, his stomach, his muscles, his brain—every tissue burned with agony.

"Phil! Phil!"

Phil didn't dare turn; he felt as if the slightest motion might tear his innards in two. But, peering from his pain-wracked eyes, he realized there was no need to turn, for with the powerball centered on him, his view of the world had changed. The entire world was squeezed into a tiny ball that seemed to float a few feet away from him like a spherical mirror the size of a dinner plate. And there in the little toy world, like animated figurines, were Cobb and Yoke. Running toward him. Phil instinctively reached out towards them but—*swish*—something flashed past his fingers like an invisible scythe. And then—pop—the little bubble that had been the normal world winked out of view, and Phil was alone in the hypersphere of the powerball.

Phil's guts snapped back to normal; the pain and its afterimage faded. He found himself comfortably floating within an empty, well-lit space that contained glowing air, his body and seemingly nothing else. The

Metamartians had been right, up to a point, but where were the others that had been swallowed? When the powerball finished examining him, would he dissolve?

"Hello?" called Phil. "Om?" No answer.

The space bent back on itself so that Phil saw nothing in any direction but endless warped barbershop images of himself, of his sunburned hairy limbs and his billowing shirt's blue field of moons and stars.

Phil remembered one of his father's stories about A Square stuck to the surface of the sphere, with all of his A Square light-rays traveling along great circles of the sphere's surface as well. In every direction, A Square sees only himself. Here in the hypersphere of the powerball, Phil could see the back of his own head, the blond hair shaggier than he'd realized. He wondered if he'd meet Da soon.

Since there were no other objects in the space with Phil, it was hard to tell if he could really move. But after a while he noticed that the space wasn't completely uniform. There was one particular spot up ahead where the images of himself were always fractured. He wanted to go over and look at this little flaw, but at first he couldn't think of any way to move. Finally it occurred to him to throw one of his shoes over his shoulder. Sure enough, the shoe-toss set him drifting forward in the direction of the flaw. Just as he got within arm's length of the special spot, his shoe came tumbling toward his face—the shoe had traveled clear around the little hypersphere of the power-ball. Phil moved his head to one side, and the shoe grazed his shoulder, which slowed his forward motion.

He stretched out his hand toward the flawed region. As his fingers entered the crooked space they disappeared. Phil convulsively pulled his hand back; there was no damage to it. He felt into the flaw again and wiggled his fingers. An odd sensation: his fingers couldn't find his thumb, and his thumb couldn't find his fingers. Just then the shoe came orbiting past again and caught him full in the chest. He drifted away from the anomalous spot with, *whew,* all of his fingers still intact.

A little later Phil started being hungry and thirsty. He wondered how long he'd been in here. He consulted his uvvy for the time, but its clock was stuck at 11:37 A.M.—presumably it hadn't received any update signals since he entered the power-ball. He made a halfhearted attempt to make an uvvy call to Yoke, but as he'd expected, it didn't work. Any signals he could send would circle around and around his hypersphere just like the rays of light. But then he noticed something new in the uvvy. It was showing him just the kind of amorphous mental image he'd seen when he tried to use Yoke's alla. It seemed as if Om had a built-in alla he could use!

Phil tried to nudge the alla catalog's grayish start-up image into a representation of food. But Om's catalog for this alla wasn't for humans, it was for aliens—presumably for Metamartians? Though he was trying for the image of an apple, he ended up with a representation of a spiky red leathery thing that was—what? The alla catalog was multisensory, so Phil took a virtual sniff of the possible fruit; it had a faintly acrid odor, but maybe that was just the smell of the rind. Phil said, "Actualize." He wasn't sure if anything would happen; after all, Yoke's alla had refused to obey anyone but Yoke. But the powerball's intrinsic alla seemed willing to work for him. A brightly outlined alla mesh formed and—*whoosh*—the spiky pouch became real.

When Phil hungrily pulled one of the spikes loose, sick yellow cream dribbled out of the rip in the tough red skin, stinging his hand. A reek like ammonia assaulted his eyes and nose. Phil focused in on his uvvy and wished very hard for the alien pod to disappear. To his relief, an alla mesh formed around the fruit and it reverted to air, taking most of the corrosive smell with it. Maybe he wasn't hungry yet after all.

He gave up on food and wandered about in the mental maze of the alien alla catalog, marveling at wonderful baubles and bizarre forms. He even actualized three of the objects for himself.

First, there was something resembling a little pearl-handled pocketknife, but when he folded out the single "blade," it revealed itself as a waving broom of tiny metallic tentacles, each of them subtly articulated. Resisting the temptation to touch the metal fuzz, Phil folded it back away and pocketed the object.

Second, he actualized a golf-ball-sized sphere that resembled perhaps a goldfish bowl with luminous fish in it. Not that they were really fish; they were more like plankton. The little globe was velvety black with bright, glowing globules and disks within. The odd thing about the globe was that its image kept changing according to subtle cues that Phil could barely tell he was giving. Every time he moved his head, the bright little creatures inside the globe would swim to one side or the other. And every time he focused on one particular little denizen of the bowl, that "fish" would seem to swell up in size, and all the others would rush away from it.

Third, Phil picked from the catalog a necklace with a single large gem that seemed to embody an endless variety of possible formations. It was a ruby, emerald, diamond, sapphire—all of these, one after the other, and more. Not only did the gems color change, the cut of its shape kept shifting as well. It was gorgeous. Phil vowed that if he ever saw Yoke again, he'd give it to her.

Though Phil still wasn't ready to try tackling any more alien food, he was getting seriously thirsty. He found his way to a part of the Metamartian alla catalog that seemed to be devoted to beverages. Using the uvvy's virtual odor feature to avoid drinks that smelled like gasoline or acetone, he was eventually able to actualize something that seemed to be a flagon of water.

Carefully he tasted of it, and it was indeed plain water, so he drank it down, then used the alla to turn the empty flagon back into air.

Phil looked around the alla catalog a little more, trying to figure out the appearance of the Metamartians in their home world—if indeed the catalog was for Metamartians and not for some completely different kind of alien. He couldn't find any pictures of intended users of the catalog, but he did stumble across an area with what seemed to be clothes. The aliens seemed to wear loose robes or caftans, things with a head hole and two arm holes. There was nothing like trousers and nothing like shoes.

After a while Phil tired of exploring the alla catalog, and he simply hung there doing nothing, looking back on his life. What had he made of his twenty-four years on Earth? He'd survived childhood, his parents' divorce, his overbearing father. He'd gone to UC Berkeley for two years, but when he was twenty he'd gotten sick of jumping through the hoops. The hoops weren't his, they were societies and his father's. Bogus. He'd dropped out, getting a series of kitchen jobs, eventually becoming the assistant chef for a top restaurant. Big whoop.

One other accomplishment was that he had stayed Straight Edge: clean and sober. But what else had he ever done? Was it really enough to be serene and balanced? Da certainly didn't think so. And deep down, Phil wasn't really so serene. Deep down he was frightened.

It would be nice to have a family and children someday; the worst mistake he had made along those lines was to hook up with Kevvie. At least that was over. And he'd almost had a chance at Yoke. But now his life was apparently done.

Phil let himself imagine what he might do if he got a second chance. Hang onto Yoke for sure. And what else? Cook for a day-job, but maybe finally try and move on. Dare to express himself. With blimps? Who could tell? Could be that now he'd never know. Phil sighed, making an effort to free himself of self-pity. He said a simple prayer: "God, please help me."

Usually a prayer like this would dissolve out into the glowing aether of the great buzzing world-mind. Phil would feel the better for it, but there wouldn't be any obvious response. It was just something he did. He murmured the prayer again, felt more centered, and dozed off.

He hadn't slept for long when his prayer seemed to get a very literal answer. The hypersphere began talking to him. "So you're ready to move on?" came a rich, thrilling voice, the voice of Om. "Here we go." A dream:

But then Phil woke to the sound of a *pop* near his feet.

When he looked down he saw a tiny ball with some people in it. Was he coming back to Earth? The little ball grew up toward him very fast, and as it engulfed him, there was another stretching sensation in his viscera, though not quite so violent or prolonged as before. And then the queasy pain was over. But Phil wasn't back to Earth. He was still in a hypersphere, only it was six or seven times bigger than before. Phil's hypersphere and a larger hypersphere had joined together like a pair of soap bubbles merging. Like two fingers of Om's "hand."

The new space smelled of dog, moldie, sweat, and alcohol. It held half an oak tree, and perched in the tree were a bony crone in overalls and a plump, nude matron. There was a big bright wowo, an egg-shaped moldie, and an orange and white collie-beagle dog as well, the egg with a colorful belt—or cravat?—around his middle. But all this was just a flash in the background, for right up in Phil's face was none other than—

"Da!"

"Phil! Oh no, you can't end up here too! Your poor mother." Phil's naked father gestured awkwardly. His left hand ended in a scabbed stump. "I'm scared about what comes next."

Phil spoke the biggest thing in his mind. "I'm sorry I was mean to you the last time we talked, Da."

"Oh hell, I started it by picking on you. What you said to me was nothing. I shouldn't have taken it so hard. Of course I forgive you! But, hey, you can't very well say the fourth dimension's bullshit anymore, can you?" There was alcohol on the old man's breath.

"Your poor hand," said Phil. "Jane says your wedding ring is already proof of the fourth dimension."

"What do you mean?" asked Kurt.

"You didn't know? When this ball chopped off your hand, your wedding ring got knotted. And then later it flipped into its mirror image."

"Gnarly!" Kurt looked ruefully at his stump. "It's healing up really well. Maybe it's like the way a corpse's fingernails grow fast. Old Tempest helped with it a lot. Let me introduce you. Darla, Tempest! This is my son!"

The two women scrambled closer through the oak tree, which provided a handy method of moving around in the hypersphere. Though Darla was nude and a bit overweight, she seemed unembarrassed about it. She had a wound on her foot; it looked like one of her toes was missing. Tempest was a lively old woman in overalls. She was carrying a half-empty squeeze-bag of wine. The women greeted Phil with avid interest. Clearly everyone in here was getting cabin fever.

"Your old man's been telling me about you," said Darla. She talked like a hipster. "That's wavy that you've got alky-junky genes. I can really relate. And hats off for being Straight Edge. I'm gonna clean up too one of these days. Kurt and I were thinking it could be stuzzy if you met one of my daughters."

"I did meet Yoke," said Phil. "At Da's funeral. She came with Tre and Terri Dietz. In fact I was just now visiting her in Tonga."

"My funeral!" interrupted Da, totally into himself as usual. "Was it big?"

"I think I dreamed about you asking me this," said Phil.

"And maybe I dreamed about me asking you," said Kurt. "I've been having crazy, lucid dreams in here. It seems the whale talks to Jonah." He looked around, a bit wild-eyed. "I think this hypersphere is alive, and it comes into my brain when I'm sleeping. But now we're awake. Tell me about my funeral!"

So Phil told his father all about it. The part Da liked the best was how Phil had buried the ashes by the oak tree.

"You're a good son to have done that. I bet some of the ashes were Friedl's. That dog." He gestured at the great twisted trunk with its branches and dead leaves. "So this is our special tree? Small world."

"Too dang small," said Tempest in her Florida cracker accent. "Can I finally get past howdy and ask some questions? I happen to know Darla's Yoke too, Phil. Just before this here ball done gobble me up, I was a-visitin' my niece Starshine in Santa Cruz while Yoke was a-stayin' with Starshine's neighbor. You sweet on that little Yoke, Phil? She's a honey. Smart as a whip too."

"I like her a lot," said Phil. "We were about to have a really great time in Tonga."

"What's Tonga?" asked Darla.

Darla was so nude and female and voluptuous that Phil was embarrassed to look directly at her—but Da was staring at her all the time. And now Da put his arm around her waist as if to steady her. Gross.

"Tonga's a cannibal island," said Tempest. "Don't you know nothing, Darla? Go on, Phil. Tell about you and Yoke in Tonga. Were you two shacked up?"

"Back off!" said Phil, desperate to change the subject. This was turning into real torture. And there was no way to escape. Desperately he fixed his eyes on the hypersphere's other two occupants. "You got a dog and a Silly Putter in here?"

"That's Planet and Humpty-Dumpty," said Tempest. "Planet's my good boy. Come here, Planet, come to Auntie Tempest." Clumsily the dog clawed his way through the branches of the oak tree, finally losing his footing and flying through the air to bump into Phil, tongue and tail wagging. Phil and the dog drifted around the whole hypersphere, coming to rest back at the splintered base of the oak tree with the others.

"What were you and Yoke doing in Tonga?" asked Darla as soon as Phil caught his breath.

"We've only just met," said Phil. "We were getting to know each other, and snorkeling, but then I ran into Shimmer and some other Metamartians."

"Metamartians?" spat Darla. "Is that what they call themselves?"

"Shouldn't there be one of them in here with us?" asked Phil, continually avoiding looking at Darla. "A Metamartian named Ptah?"

"Darla and me done chased his ass outta here!" cackled Tempest. "I got the magic wisher to make us some grain alcohol to set him on fire." She patted the uvvy on the back of her neck. Phil noticed that Da and Darla didn't have uvvies. They'd both been abducted at night. "Couldn't catch him nohow," continued Tempest, "but he got so sick of it that he done took off out the hole. Ptah said pfuck it!"

"There's a hole up there where you can stick your head out," explained Da, pointing toward the other end of the tree. "Into raw hyperspace. Very creepy."

"You said you dreamed this hypersphere talks to you," said Phil. "Does she call herself—"

"Om," said Kurt, just as Phil said it too. "Yes, she calls herself Om."

"The Metamartians call her that," said Phil. "She's their god. Wherever they go, Om comes too. She scooped you up because she was curious about the wowo."

"So it's true?" said Kurt. "I hadn't been sure. Om only talks to me when I'm dreaming. But it's slow going because I'm always drunk. Hard to think logically. The shock. I keep thinking we're all dead."

"Pass around the wine, Tempest," said Darla.

"I'm half in a bag already, Phil," said Kurt apologetically. "I should explain that we've been partying hard. Tempest figured out how to make wine. Well, it's similar to wine, anyway. We've been drinking enough of it."

"Could you make me some food?" asked Phil. His stomach was rumbling. "I haven't figured out how to find it."

"These things are tolerable good," said old Tempest. She made a gesture and a bright alla mesh pattern formed to whoosh out a big crisp golden shape, fat in the middle and pointed at both ends. Phil nibbled at it. It seemed to be something like a deep fried sweet potato. Fibrous, oily, not too bad. He took a big bite, and then another and—*crunch*—hit something like a vein of wiggly cartilage.

"Like a rubber bone in there, huh?" said Tempest. "Reminds me of a hog snout."

Phil peered at the greasy object he'd been eating. "What is it?"

"Hell if I know," said Tempest. "I call it a yam-snoot. You should of seen some of the other vittles we tried. Alien food, I guess." She took a pull from her sack of liquid and tried passing it to Phil. "Hope you ain't a tight-ass, Phil," she said as he refused the sack.

"No, no," said Phil, though his heart sank at the thought of being in here with three drunk pheezers. "Da, tell me more about that hole?"

"It's a kind a flaw, a place where the space of this sphere has an edge. According to my reasoning, when you stick your head out there, your head is in four-dimensional hyperspace. I've only tried it for a few seconds. It's cold and you have to keep coming back for breath. And there's this freaky light. I wouldn't try it, Phil. But if, God forbid, you do stick your head through the hole, be very sure to hang onto the tree so the rest of you doesn't slide out." Da squirted a stream of wine into his mouth, and then some into Darla's. A rivulet dribbled down her chin and onto her big breasts. "Don't stare at us like that, Phil. I know I shouldn't be getting fucked up, but I'm far enough into this run that I've got to finish. After I sleep it off, I'll get myself together and we'll talk about our chances of getting you back to Earth."

"Hey, Da!" said Phil. "This is xoxxed. Can I at least make you and Darla some clothes?"

"Oh bless his heart," cackled Tempest. "Hear that, Darla?" Darla responded by striking a coy pose with one hand over her crotch and one over her boobs.

Phil quickly found the clothing area of Om's Metamartian catalog and actualized two of the colorful loose caftans. He made Darla one with a pattern of unearthly biological shapes that might have been purple flowers; Da got one with flickering red shapes like flames. The fabric was some unknown material that was slippery but not sticky. A bit like silk, but with no sign of threads.

"Give me one too," said Tempest. "A blue one."

"All right," said Phil, and made Tempest a Metamartian robe that resembled a waterfall. "I'm outta here for now, losers."

He pulled himself toward the other end of the oak tree, pausing to study the glowing holographic knot of the oversize wowo. It was a roughly doughnut-shaped pattern of steadily changing mathematical curves and surfaces. Tre Dietz may have turned off all the wowos he'd sold, but he hadn't been able to reach this one. It was going strong. Phil liked to think a wowo looked a little like a glass pelican continually crawling farther and farther up its own butt, while at the same time emerging from its own beak, somehow changing into its own mirror image in the process. Mind-boggling and gnarly.

Phil proceeded onward to the other end of the tree. The toy Humpty-Dumpty was sitting there, clamped onto a branch like an owl. Phil gave him a gentle poke, and the egg smiled ingratiatingly. A low husky laugh floated up from Darla at the other end of the tree. Fortunately there were enough dead leaves between them that Phil didn't have to see what the old folks were doing.

Just as Kurt had said, right beyond the end of the tree was a flawed spot like Phil had seen in his own little hypersphere. He took a deep breath and stuck his head through it.

CHAPTER FOUR

YOKE

February 23, 2054

After dropping Phil at the dock in Neiafu, the navy motorboat ferried Yoke, Cobb, Onar, and Kennit to a big aluminum ship anchored in the harbor. The flagship of the Tongan Navy. Its rounded lines made Yoke think of a beer keg. Amidships was a tower of cabins surmounted by the bridge; aft was a flexible whip-cannon poised like a cobra head.

The King was waiting for them on board. He was wearing a white coat and peaked cap for this nautical occasion. His green moldie girlfriend Vaana was at his side.

"Good morning, Yoke," said the King. "And it's an honor indeed to meet the famous Cobb Anderson. Welcome aboard." He glanced around the deck. "We can speak quite freely. The sailors barely know English, while Kennit and the bodyguards are completely to be trusted. Greetings, Onar! Anyone need a coffee? Champagne? No?" He led them aft to stand by a big open hatch in the deck. Above the hatch was a crane mounted on a high triangular brace. "You've brought the alla, Yoke? Ah, it's that little tube thing. Excellent. I look forward to seeing it in action. Slugs of gold and imipolex all morning long. Yum yum!" He smiled and rubbed his hands. A dozen Tongan sailors were sitting around, ready to start work. Kennit joined two of the King's bodyguards, who were ensconced up on the bridge, playing a game of cards with a Tongan man in a captain's hat.

"Won't the ship sink if it gets too full?" Yoke asked the King,

"Oh, I'm not so inordinately acquisitive," said the King, a cheerful twinkle in his eye.

"Captain Pulu gonna keep an eye on the tonnage," said Vaana, waving toward the bridge. "And Yoke, child, I want you to make twice as much imipolex as gold."

"You owe me an apology, Vaana," interrupted Cobb. He'd been staring fixedly at the sexy green moldie since they'd come aboard the ship. "You almost killed me with that betty the other night." Yoke recalled that Cobb had also mentioned having sex with Vaana.

"Ain't my look-out," said merry Vaana. "You was partyin' with the best. We do it again sometime, hey? You a lift, old Cobb."

"A man your age should have the maturity to own the consequences of his self-destructive behavior, Cobb," said Onar primly.

"You're a devil, Vaana," said the King. "Let's get started with our day's work, shall we, Yoke? I'd suggest your rhythm be to create a pair of hundred kilogram cylinders of imipolex followed by a single hundred kilogram ingot of gold. One-two-three, one-two-three, and so on. The sailors will load them onto pallets and lower them into the hold."

"I forget," said Yoke. "Why am I doing this for you?"

"It's thanks to HRH and me that you have the alla in the first place," said Onar.

"I thought it was Shimmer who gave it to me," said Yoke.

"Yes, but we guided you to her," said the King. "Be a sport, Yoke. Just one day's work. And then you're perfectly free to go."

"But Cobb and I could leave right now, if I wanted to," said Yoke. "Right?"

"You should know that HRH's bodyguards are well-armed," said Onar. "And this is, after all, a warship, complete with a whip-cannon that can shoot a sea gull out of the sky."

"No need to take that tone, Onar," said the King. "As you and I discussed earlier, our policy is persuasion, not force."

"Speaking of bodyguards, where are Tashtego and Daggoo today?" wondered Cobb.

"They'll be here in a bit," said the King. "They flew over to Fiji very early this morning. They're looking into the imipolex market for me."

So Yoke grasped her alla and started turning air into gold and imipolex at a rate of one pulse every second or two. The sailors stepped lively, stowing the booty. With each transmutation, a hundred kilograms worth of air would rush into a bright-line alla control mesh, making a big *whoosh* and *thud* that caused the ship to bob. Yoke figured out in her head that a hundred kilos of air took up about as much space as an apartment's living room. The cumulative rocking effect of the repeated gusts became a little sickening after three-quarters of an hour. Yoke took a break and alla-made herself a glass of fresh orange juice.

The King was sitting in a deck chair smoking a cigar. Vaana lolled on the deck beside him, looking like a thick, sexy serpent. Cobb stood behind the pair, discussing something with Onar. Now Onar patted Cobb on the back and took a chair next to the King. Cobb remained stiffly erect, his face gone oddly blank.

"Are you all right, Cobb?" called Yoke.

"Yes," said Cobb shortly. Perhaps he and Onar had argued?

"Captain Pulu's estimates make it that you're one-third done, Yoke," said the King, squinting up at the man on the ship's bridge.

"What are you going to do with all this stuff?" asked Yoke.

"Refurbish Tonga's credit in world banking circles!" said the King happily. "I'm going to ship this load straight to Suva in Fiji and sell it. Tonga will be in the black for the first time this century. Not that our debt is all that large, mind you; it's well under a hundred million dollars. We've been prudent, but we can never quite get onto the good side of the ledger. This will make me a hero to my people."

"You're going to give every bit of it away?" asked Vaana. She sounded surprised. "I thought you said half the imipolex would be for the Tongan moldies."

"Strictly speaking, there are no Tongan moldies," said the King. "Only a native-born flesh-and-blood Tongan can be a citizen. This isn't the U.S. with its quixotic Moldie Citizenship Act. I have to take care of my own people first. You moldies are only our guests." He held up his hand to stave off Vaana's anger. "You of course can have all the imipolex you require for your personal needs at any time, dear Vaana. And I promise you that once I've taken care of the Tongan national debt, I will try and do something for our very honored guest moldies."

"A promise ain't enough," snapped Vaana, standing up in her full womanly form. "My people been counting on me to get us a fair deal."

The King shook his head. "My local standing is already shaky due to the gossip about our relationship, Vaana. For my own political survival, I can't be put in a position of seeming to give a too preferential treatment to—"

At this point Yoke lost the thread of their conversation because a nightmarish call came in on her uvvy. It was Phil, standing on a beach looking desperate. He'd encountered Shimmer and the aliens in a cave at the end of the island. The powerball was about to eat him.

When Yoke sprang across the deck and pulled Cobb around her, the old man moldie was maddeningly sluggish in his responses. "Faster, Cobb," urged the frantic Yoke. "You have to fly me to the far end of the island!"

"Why?" drawled Cobb. "You're not finished filling the ship."

"The powerball is about to get Phil! Oh, hurry! Maybe we can save him."

"One certainly hopes not," said Cobb with unexpected venom. His voice sounded all different. "But, very well, I'll take you there. It should be amusing."

"What is *wrong* with you?" cried Yoke, but Cobb gave no answer. Silently he flew Yoke to the island's end as directed.

When they landed on the beach, Yoke quickly popped herself out of the moldie. It was too late. A big warped ball of space had slid onto Phil, and his form was swollen up like a balloon. Even though she knew it was hopeless, Yoke ran toward Phil, calling his name, with Cobb trotting along behind her.

The warped sphere of the powerball snapped loose from normal space—and Phil was gone. A nauseating ripple of distortion passed through Yoke's body. And then nothing. The world going on the same as before. With no Phil. Right at the end he'd said he loved her. Yoke realized that she could have loved him too.

Cobb was standing just behind Yoke, looking sarcastic and unhelpful. And down the beach a ways was a hole in the cliff with some of the aliens watching. Yoke could make out the pale glow of Shimmer and the dark snout of Wubwub.

"We have to get back to HRH and the ship," said Cobb. "We're not nearly finished there."

"Whatever," said Yoke, striding down the beach toward the aliens. "Shimmer! You have to help bring them back. I want Phil and I want my mother!" On an impulse, Yoke used her alla to create a flaming wooden torch. "Moldie flesh burns, Shimmer!"

Calmly the pale woman and the dark pig stared out at Yoke.

Did she really have any chance against these superhuman? Not likely. But she held her little torch up high. "Help me or else!"

Before the scene could play itself out, Yoke was tackled from behind. By Cobb. The old man moldie knocked the torch from her hand and flowed forward, enveloping and immobilizing her.

"We really must be on our way," said Cobb. "HRH wants us back immediately."

And then they were rocketing up from the beach, arcing back across the island to where the roly-poly aluminum Tongan Navy ship waited. Yoke tried to talk to Cobb, but it was no use. It was as if he'd been hypnotized or turned into a zombie.

"I put a superleech on him," explained the smirking Onar when Cobb split open to disgorge Yoke back onto the deck of the ship. "As long as Cobb's wearing it, he's an extension of me. I slapped it on him while you were busy making the gold and imipolex. I let Cobb take you to watch Phil get eaten because I was curious too. Too bad about that, really. Phil was a decent sort. No mental giant, though. In any case, it's time to get back to work, Yoke. Break's over."

"You heartless prick." Now that she knew what to look for, Yoke could see the superleech on Cobb's back, knotted into his pink flesh like a purple scar. She reached out to see if she could tear it loose, but Cobb's body twisted away.

"Do as Onar says," said Cobb, his voice a slavish replica of Onar's.

"That leech is comin' off right now!" yelled Vaana. She'd become very agitated as soon as Onar pointed out Cobb's leech-DIM. She gave the King's shoulder a shake. "Bou-Bou! You can't sit here and let this skanky white dook put a superleech on a moldie. Tonga's a free zone!"

"Yes, but a free Cobb might take Yoke and her alla away from us too soon," hissed Onar. "Surely even you can understand that, you fat, stinking sex-toy."

"Understand *this!*" said Vaana. Her arm lashed out snake-fast to strike a concussive blow against the side of Onar's head. Onar collapsed like a rag doll, and so did Cobb.

"Oh, you shouldn't have done that, Vaana," said the King, very upset. "I'm sorry about the superleech. Onar talked me into it. Greed, don't you know?" He waved both arms, making a broad "calm down" signal to his bodyguards on the bridge. "The guards may think they have to defend the Tu'i Tonga, Vaana. They're obsessed with the notion that you might harm me."

But Vaana was too agitated to pay proper attention. "You actually gave Onar the okay, Bou-Bou? You told him he could use a superleech?" She grabbed the King and gave him another rough shake. "I thought you loved moldies!"

Up on the bridge the bodyguards were frantically conferring with the captain, and now the whip-cannon at the rear of the ship twitched into life. Yoke dove onto the deck next to Cobb to get out of the way. The whip-cannon snapped like a huge towel. A heavy puck of metal flew into Vaana, cutting her completely in two. The puck punched through the deck and the side of the hull—fortunately above the waterline—and plunged violently into the sea.

"No!" screamed the King. "Vaana!"

With what seemed like her dying effort, Vaana opened her mouth and made a cracked warbling noise. And then both halves of her were still. Kennit came pounding down the companionway from the bridge. "Are you all right, Your Majesty?" he shouted. "Thank God we saved you."

Onar began twitching, starting to wake back up, and Cobb was twitching too. If Yoke waited any longer it would be too late. Quickly she made herself a knife with her alla and rolled Cobb over so she could cut the purple scar of the leech from his back. But Kennit darted forward to take the knife and the alla from her.

"Don't hurt the girl!" shouted the King. "You've done enough damage."

"No weapons near the King," said Kennit. "I'm going to handcuff her till I figure out what's happening." And then he yanked Yoke's hands behind her back and snapped some tight bands of plastic around her wrists. Kennit pushed her down into the deck chair next to the King, then threw the knife into the ocean and handed her alla to Bou-Bou.

"I'm sure Yoke's no danger," said the King, taking the alla. "She was only trying to help her friend. As was Vaana. You were glad for an excuse to kill her, weren't you, Kennit? You and the guards have been waiting for—for—" The King's voice broke and he put his hand over his eyes. "You can't understand this, Kennit, but I loved her."

"Yis," said Kennit.

There was a minute of silence. At Yoke's feet lay the two halves of Vaana, inert in a reeking puddle of straw-colored moldie ichor. Onar was sitting woozily upright on the deck next to the dismembered moldie. It seemed as if the bad guys had won.

"If I give you back your alla, will you finish your work for me now, Yoke?" the King asked. He was fiddling with the alla as if desperate for a distraction from the sight of the shattered Vaana. "Curious," continued the King. "Just an empty tube, though if I look through it the world seems to be twirling." He knitted his brows as if willing something to happen, but nothing did. "It won't make anything for me. Yes, yes, it really is keyed to you, Yoke. You're the goose who lays the golden eggs. A fine role."

"No eggs if the farmer mistreats the goose," said Yoke. "Unshackle me so I can take the superleech off of Cobb. Until then I'm not making you anything more. Once you free us, I'll still keep my promise to fill your ship with imipolex and gold."

"Oh, but we can make her do much more than that, Bou-Bou," said Onar, his voice slurred. He squeezed his eyes shut and rubbed the side of his head, gathering his forces. Moving slowly and carefully, he got to his feet and sneered down at Yoke with something like his old energy. "Yes, Bou-Bou, I have another trick up my sleeve. I can make little Miss Snooty Britches do anything I want her to. Look." Onar pulled a twitching piece of imipolex out of his pants pocket, a fat dark red slug of a thing.

"Be careful, that's a thinking cap!" exclaimed the horrified Yoke, who'd been warned about them many times before. "A moldie can make it crawl up a person's nose to take over their brain!"

"Yes, my dear," said Onar. "Up *your* nose. I'll use the superleech to run Cobb, and Cobb will use the thinking cap to run you. A baroque little chain of command, no?" He paused and giggled. "I have an idea, Bou-Bou. Why don't I smear Yoke with Vaana's ichor and get her to have sex with you? Little Yoke's a rather good shag, don't you know?"

"How revolting," said the King coldly. "I'm shocked at you, Onar. Set the girl free, Kennit. She's perfectly willing to finish filling our ship. And do something about having poor Vaana's body stored away. I'm going to give her a proper funeral."

"But Yoke was holding a knife, Your Majesty," said Kennit. "I have to protect you."

"Do you presume to disobey my direct command?" said the King, rising to his feet. Kennit temporized by continuing to talk, and the two of them went to stand over the remains of Vaana. Meanwhile Yoke was still sitting in the deck chair with her hands cuffed behind her back.

While Kennit and the King continued debating, Onar handed the nastily twitching thinking cap to Cobb—who had no power to do anything but accept it. At the activating touch of Cobb's moldie fingers, the thinking cap bloomed like a blob of ink in a glass of water, sending out long, greedy feelers. Now Onar darted around behind Yoke and held her by the shoulders. The enslaved old Cobb shuffled forward, holding the excited thinking cap out toward Yoke's face.

"Help!" said Yoke, but her voice came out small and squeaky. Stupid Kennit and the King weren't even looking at her. It was like a dream where you try to run and your legs are knee-deep in molasses. Onar had her shoulders pinned in a grip of steel. The dark red thinking cap was coming closer. This was happening too fast!

It occurred to Yoke that perhaps she could control her alla even when she wasn't holding it. She reached out for mental contact with her alla and—yes! She alla-made a quick hydrogen-oxygen explosion at waist level between Kennit and the King.

The blast was encouragingly loud. The King bellowed, Kennit roared, and Onar and Cobb were so startled that Cobb dropped the writhing thinking cap onto Yoke's lap. Yoke quickly exploded a much bigger sphere of hydrogen and oxygen in a spot that she guessed to be behind Onar. He came tumbling onto her from over her right shoulder. The chair collapsed. With a quick twitch of her legs and torso, Yoke maneuvered Onar's head to be near the thinking cap. The thinking cap crawled onto Onar's face and shimmied into his left nostril. Onar screamed for Cobb to catch it, but he was too late. With a last filthy wriggle, the thinking cap had disappeared all the way into Onar's nose. Onar's limbs twitched as if in an epileptic fit.

And now Cobb began twitching too. He and Onar were in a feedback control loop. Onar's superleech was controlling Cobb, but Cobb's thinking cap was controlling Onar. They sprang together like wrestlers, like magnets. The Cobb-directed Onar tried to claw the superleech out of Cobb's back and the Onar-directed Cobb probed into Onar's nose in search of the wily thinking cap. Yet at the same time, Onar was directing Cobb not to direct

Onar to tear out the superleech, and Cobb was telling Onar not to tell Cobb to try and get the thinking cap. Not to mention the fact that Cobb both was and wasn't trying to choke Onar. With all the contradictory impulses in the loop, nothing was accomplished, and the two could only flail about in chaos, their spastic motions cycling through a Wrestle Mania strange attractor.

Meanwhile Kennit had placed the muzzle of a pocket-size rail-gun against the side of Yoke's head. "If you make one more speck of trouble," he growled into her ear, "I'm going to blow off your head."

Now a new complication arrived. Moldies were flying in from every side, seemingly drawn by Vaana's dying cry. Up on the bridge the captain began using the whip-cannon to flail out metal pucks in every direction, and the two other bodyguards opened up automatic weapons fire. Kennit let go of Yoke and began firing his gun at the moldies as well. But there were too many moldies and they were too fast. A half dozen of them homed in on the whip-cannon and cut the thing off at its base. Yoke watched all this, sitting handcuffed on the deck. She'd scooted herself away from the thrashing Onar and Cobb. The King still had her alla, and after Kennit's threat she was scared to use it again.

As the whip-cannon fell into the sea, Tashtego and Daggoo suddenly arrived. They came running across the deck, teeth bared like joyful pirates.

"Hold your fire!" the King called to his bodyguards. "These are my best agents! Tashtego, Daggoo, can you revive Vaana?"

Instantly taking in the scene, the great Daggoo bent over Vaana, his rapid fingers beginning to splice the halves of her body together. Tashtego disappeared into the ship's hold.

There was a steady thud of more and more moldies landing on the deck. Each of them went immediately belowdeck and moments later flew back out of the hatch, two or three times as big as before. Most of the ship's crew had jumped overboard. Cobb and Onar continued to wrestle.

"Who dealt this mess?" said Kennit, looking around despairingly. He gave a shrill whistle and the two other bodyguards came down the companionway. "We're taking HRH back to the secure island," he told them. They started across the deck.

"Let's not leave quite yet, Kennit," implored the King. "I want to see if Daggoo can fix Vaana." Tashtego reappeared from below, much fattened, and carrying a spare slug of imipolex that he gave Daggoo to use on Vaana. From the water came the sound of the ship's motor launch starting up. One of the bodyguards yelled down that they should wait for the King.

"Take off my handcuffs," called Yoke. "And give me back my alla. I can use it to save Cobb."

"Do it, Kennit," said the King. He handed Yoke's alla to the big Tongan.

Kennit crossed the deck, holding his rail-gun out at the ready. He removed Yoke's plastic handcuffs and pressed her alla into her hand. "Just remember, Yoke, if anyone comes near HRH, my boys and I will waste them." He went back to the other side of the ship.

Now that she had her alla, Yoke realized she didn't need a knife to take the superleech out of Cobb. She could simply alla it into air—if she could place the control mesh steadily over the superleech, that is. She explained the situation to Tashtego and Daggoo, and the three of them knelt on Cobb to hold him still, with Daggoo fending off Onar with one long arm. At the last instant Onar managed to lunge in and push his hand in as if to protect the superleech. When the alla turned the contents of its control mesh into air, it took a chunk out of Onar's thumb too. He started bleeding profusely from the wound.

But the main thing was that the leech was gone. Cobb got to his feet and with one glance made Onar crouch down motionless. With no leech-DIM to counter the commands of the thinking cap, Onar was Cobb's slave.

"Good show!" called the King. "And how's Vaana doing, Daggoo?"

"She almost back," said the huge, black moldie, who'd turned his attention back to his injured comrade. "Yaaar." And indeed, the sinuous green shape of Vaana was lazily beginning to shift about.

"That's twice you've saved my life," said Cobb, hugging Yoke. "And now I own Onar? I'd sooner own a rabid baboon."

"I'll take him," said Vaana, sitting up and rubbing her eyes. "Thank you, Daggoo. I'd like to do something special with you soon." She flowed up Daggoo's body like a vine growing up an oak, then twirled free. Even as Yoke watched, Vaana's body was continuing to heal. "Hi, Bou-Bou," called Vaana, waving to the King.

The King waved back a little uncertainly, but when he saw Vaana's smile he tried to come over. His bodyguards grabbed his arms to hold him back.

"How would I give Onar to you?" Cobb asked Vaana.

"Let me uvvy into you and I can grep your thinking cap control code," said Vaana.

So Cobb and Vaana did the info transfer, and right away Vaana set Onar to dancing a jig like an organ grinder's monkey, the blood freely dripping from his hand. Onar's jaw was pumping, but Vaana wasn't letting him say anything. His eyes were coals of fear and anger. His forced capering was a ghastly, melancholy sight.

"Oh stop," said Yoke. "Don't torture him, Vaana. We should bandage that cut."

"I've got a better idea," said Vaana, turning so she faced away from the bodyguards and the King. "A way to finish it. Come here, Onar, I want to ask you to do something." Onar stood before Vaana, tense but obedient, oblivious of his bloody hand.

Before Vaana could speak, Yoke interrupted. "Onar, did you kill Mr. Olou on purpose? Make him answer, Vaana."

"Yes," said Onar, his voice strained and cracked. "It was my idea."

"Go git HRH," said Vaana softly. "Don't slow down for them guards. Go git Bou-Bou."

Onar charged across the deck as if hell-bent on attacking the King. At this, the bodyguards reached their flash point. Moving as one, the three of them raised their weapons and blew off Onar's head.

"Takes care of the thinking cap too," said Vaana coldly.

Onar fell heavily and lay still, his neck spurting. Yoke retched. Three days ago she'd made love to this man; his body had been warm and strong, turgid with the same blood that was puddled on the aluminum deck. What a waste, what a pitiful end.

And then the sky seemed to fall in, as something big came crashing into the ocean next to the ship. The object came down so fast that there was an ear-splitting sonic boom. A great wave rolled the ship far to one side like a tin toy, tossing Yoke and the others into the sea.

By a happy accident, Yoke and Cobb ended up next to each other, along with Vaana and the King. The ship, now some distance off, had righted itself. The other moldies and the bodyguards were out of sight. And floating between Yoke and the ship was the great object that had caused the splash. What the hell? It was a flattened disk—a couple of centimeters thick and ten meters across—with two dozen lively beaked heads sticking out of it. Yoke thought of the nursery rhyme about four-and-twenty black-birds baked into a pie. A pizza pie.

"It's Cappy Jane," said Vaana, noticing Yoke's wonderment. "The Tongan geosynchronous satellite. Hi, Bou-Bou, looks like we're together again." She wrapped her arm around the King, who was struggling to stay afloat.

"Dear Vaana," said the King. "I was devastated when that fool of a captain shot you. Thank heavens you recovered."

"Don't let it happen again," said Vaana. "One more thing, Bou-Bou. You got any more superleeches?"

"I don't!" cried the King. "It was all Onar's idea. He got what he deserved. Disgusting person. I never should have befriended him." He was dog-pad-dling hard, weighed down by his heavy clothes. "I'm sinking, Vaana."

Vaana sucked in volumes of air and positioned herself between the King's legs like an inflatable sea horse.

"I hope Kennit and the boys don't start shooting again," fretted the

King. "With Cappy Jane here they must be going mad. I never should have given them guns."

Vaana grew her neck up twenty feet to have a look. Her head snaked around for a minute up there like that of a slender green sea serpent. "They're way over by the ship. The launch circlin' around to pick everyone up. We cool for a while. Man, when I chirped for help, I didn't expect Cappy Jane to come. Twenty thousand miles in twenty minutes? She must have curled up like javelin for the trip down."

"Remember that it's important that the moldies don't find out who Yoke and I are," Cobb whispered urgently to Vaana and the King, using his voice rather than the uvvy. "Or they're going to be hounding us for Yoke's alla. That's why you set up the Squanto and Sue Miller ID viruses for us, right?"

"That's right," said the King.

"Here, Cobb," murmured Yoke. "I'll uvvy you their identity codes."

"Beautiful," whispered Cobb. "I'll put those out for the Cappy Janes to see. We don't want them and their pals to follow us home for more free goodies."

"Where's our imipolex?" squawked one of the bird heads sticking out of the big disk of Cappy Jane. "Yeah, Vaana," said another of the heads, clacking its beak. "You called for help and promised us more imipolex than we've ever seen, so where the fuck is it?" A third head craned toward the aluminum ship. "Is it in the hold of that tub?"

"The local moldies done cleaned us out," said Vaana. "Nothin' left in there but gold."

"Ah, the superstitious human worship of rare minerals," said one of the Cappy Jane heads bitterly. "Too bad they don't know what it's like to have to buy the flesh to make their children." A different head eyed Yoke and piped, "Is this the girl who's supposed to have the magic wand? Who is she?"

"I'm Sue Miller," said Yoke. "And this is my moldie Squanto. How much imipolex would you like? How about a thousand tons?" She felt gay and reckless from so many crazy events. If things kept up as weird as this, maybe Phil could come back too.

Yoke gripped her alla and grew a large bright-line box in the water, keeping it a safe distance from her and the others. She could sense the location of the alla box through her uvvy, as if from a phantom limb. How big could it get, anyway? Though she tried to push it farther, the cube seemed to max out somewhere between twelve and thirteen meters on each side. About forty feet. Well short of touching the sea floor.

"Get ready for a jolt!" she cautioned the others. "I'm going to turn that big cube of water into imipolex. Actualize!"

Sproing!

Something like an enormous cube of gelatin was now bobbing in the sea, just barely afloat. A giggly, shuddery gelatin, alive with pulsing colors. Truly something for nothing. What was that Josef had said about the working of the alla? "Quark flipping is like jujitsu. As if to look at something and then to look at it in a different way."

"Wow!" exclaimed one of the Cappy Jane bird heads, eyeing the imipolex.

Ordinarily, moldies reproduced in pairs, each acquiring half the necessary imipolex for new scion and each contributing about half of the newborn's nervous system and software. But given an opportunity like this, a moldie could reproduce all alone. If you gave a moldie a seventy kilogram chunk of imipolex, it could replicate itself in seconds—provided it hadn't done so within the last six months.

The six-month condition had to do with the fact that, when reproducing, a moldie's system generated a growth hormone that spurred its mold-and-algae nervous system to speed-grow a fresh nervous system into virgin imipolex. Six months was how long it took a moldie's body to generate a sufficient amount of its reproductive growth hormone.

The big Cappy Jane pie undulated over to the cube and began madly pecking away. Minutes later there were two pies. Due to the growth hormone limitation, the Cappy Jane moldies couldn't reproduce any further than that, but for a while they kept pecking, bulking up their bodies with additional imipolex. Each of them grew to as large a size as his or nervous system could handle, and then they pooped out, leaving most of the gnawed imipolex cube still floating in the water.

"*Urp,*" belched the nearest Cappy Jane beak. "What a blowout. A clonefest. I wish I had enough mold in me to breed over and over and over. Where did you get that terrific tool, Sue?"

"From some aliens," said Yoke, not thinking to lie.

"*Yeek!*" screeched the pie-bird. "Aliens! Find them! Kill them! Emergency!" The pie lifted awkwardly out of the water, little take-off jets firing out of its underside. It was slow and heavy from having incorporated as much imipolex as it could possibly hold.

"Being a grex down here sucks," cawed one of the birds in the flying pie, and twitched itself free. The disk broke up into pieces then, into twenty-four awkward-looking moldies. For now the other pie kept its integrity, floating there in the water. The freed Cappy Jane birds looked like featherless pelicans. Or maybe pterodactyls.

Back beyond the pie and the squawky birds, Yoke could glimpse the navy launch trying to circle around toward them. A figure was standing in the bow, tiny at this distance.

"The Metamartians are our—" Yoke had been about to say "friends," but then she remembered Phil's last warning. About how Shimmer had deliberately told the powerball to swallow her mother. But if the Cappy Janes wiped out the aliens, that might scotch any hope of getting Phil and Darla back.

"What?" croaked the closest Cappy Jane bird. "What did you say about the aliens, Sue? Metamartians you call them?"

"I'm not sure they're enemies," said Yoke lamely.

"Who knows where the Metamartians are?" screeched one of the birds still in the pie. "I want our grex to be the one to get them! Let's test some poofballs, guys!" Like a flock of pistons, the birds in the pie rose and fell, successively belching out little balls of imipolex that burst into flame once they were well up into the air.

"Yee haw!" crowed one of the birds raucously. "Follow me to kill the Metamartians! I just found out their location from Squanto!"

"Ooops," said Cobb.

"Oh, Squanto," said Yoke.

"It's hard, dammit," said Cobb. "That Cappy Jane kept nosing at me and asking stuff about Vava'u and somehow an image popped out. I showed her the aliens looking out of that cave on the beach. But that's all. I'm sorry. Anyway, you're the one who really blew it. 'Where did you get that wonderful tool, Sue?' "

Rather than probing any further, the Cappy Jane creatures lifted off in hot pursuit of the aliens. The leathery birds spread out their rumpled new wings. The great wobbly pie launched itself on steamy jets and, once airborne, began flapping like a stingray.

"I hope they find 'em," said Vaana. "Aliens mean trouble, Bou-Bou. Especially for moldies. They can move their minds right into a moldie's body. They talk about freeware, 'cept we the ones that get taken for free. It's just as well if things get back to normal here."

"I suppose so," said the King. "And we're still lovers?"

"Sho'," said Vaana. "And the rest of the imipolex here, that's for my people, right?"

"We already had a lot of your 'people' clean the imipolex out of our ship, Vaana. It was—daunting. I think it best to get rid of this. We've already had too much attention."

"Let me fill up," said Vaana, and assimilated as much of the imipolex as she could hold—swelling to perhaps twice her usual size. "I'm not quite ready to reproduce yet," she said. "But Lord knows when the time comes I'll be ready. You say all the other locals got some plastic too?"

"I don't know about all, but it sure seemed like a lot of them," said Yoke. "I think the King's right about getting rid of this evidence."

"Okay," said Vaana.

Yoke sent her control mesh out over the sullenly floating imipolex cube and turned it back into seawater, complete with an assortment of local diatoms and plankton.

"Cobb and I are ready to leave, aren't we, Cobb?" said Yoke.

"Okay," said the old man. "Did we finish doing whatever we came here for?"

"Diving," said Yoke. "I came here to dive. And Phil came to find me. We did have one good morning of snorkeling. I saw a wonderful little fish in a staghorn coral. And a giant clam."

"Don't forget the whale and squid," said Cobb.

"Do you think the Cappy Janes will kill the aliens?" asked Yoke.

Cobb's answer was drowned out in the roar of the navy launch that pulled up next to them. Aboard were Kennit, the two bodyguards, four sailors, and Tashtego and Daggoo.

Kennit and the bodyguards were grinning ear-to-ear, obviously thrilled at finding their king in good shape. It didn't look like they cared one bit anymore about seeing HRH so cozy with Vaana. There were no guns in sight. "We got a ladder in the rear," said Kennit. "Watch your step, Your Majesty. I think we ought to haul ass out of here. There's some sharks in a feeding frenzy on the other side of the ship. Finishing off Onar."

"Let's bail," Yoke said to Cobb. "Before everyone starts in on me again."

"Okay," said Cobb.

"Thanks awfully," said the King, still bobbing on Vaana's back. He extended his hand and Yoke shook it. "Do come visit Tonga again. Could I ask you one last favor?"

"You want more gold," groaned Yoke.

"Just, you know, as you're flying away, buzz the ship and put a few more tons in the hold? I'll tell the captain not to fire on you. It would be so lovely to have our budget balanced. I did get you the alla, you know. You're fixed for life now, Yoke. You're a golden goose."

"Honk honk," sighed Yoke, looking down at her alla. "Though I may end up throwing this thing into the ocean. So all right, one last favor. And in return, Bou-Bou, I want you to do whatever you can to block any publicity about me and the alla. Don't tell anything to the Cappy Janes. Stick to the Sue Miller and Squanto cover-up. And I hope the Tongan moldies don't know too much?"

"Tashtego and Daggoo know more than the others," said the King. "But nobody listens to Tongans. Let's do our best to consider this entire interlude expunged from the historical record. Deny, deny, deny. It's best this way for all of us. I wouldn't want the Fijians to know I'm selling fairy gold."

So Cobb and Yoke cautiously buzzed the navy ship, Yoke averting her eyes from the avid gray sharks who'd eaten Onar.

Captain Pulu waved a friendly go-ahead. They landed long enough for Yoke to outdo herself by making a perfect one-meter gold cube, weighing in at just under twenty tons. The cube was quite the elegant *objet d'art*.

But, in the event, making so massive an object out of thin air was fairly drastic.

As Yoke later calculated, if one kilogram of air takes up a cubic meter, twenty tons of air takes up a cube some twenty-seven meters on a side. A volume the size of a ten-story office building. Fortunately, she thought of making herself a pair of earplugs before she did it.

The whirlwind of so much air being sucked into the alla-cube made a thunderclap that knocked Cobb and Yoke off their feet. The ocean sloshed sullenly and some loose debris blew off the deck. But nobody was hurt, and the ship's hull didn't burst, and the captain didn't shoot at them, and Yoke and Cobb flew on up into the sky, leaving the Tongans with nearly one hundred million dollars worth of gold.

"But wait, Cobb," said Yoke as the ship began to dwindle below them. "We have to stop by the place where we slept last night. I want to bring my souvenirs."

"What souvenirs?"

"Oh, just some little things. Come on, Cobb. We'll do it fast."

Ms. Teta, the housekeeper with the glossy bun, greeted them. She was dozing in the shade with the cook and the maid. "You want lunch today?"

"We're going home," said Yoke. "We're all finished."

"You been back for a while?" asked Ms. Teta. "I thought I heard you in your room."

"No, I've been out on the ship with the King all morning."

"Well, maybe it was your boyfriend."

"Um, maybe?" said Yoke, her heart beating faster. She opened her room's door with a mixture of hope and fear. But it looked the same as before, except that the beds had been made.

"So what are we taking?" asked Cobb.

Yoke picked up her glass sculpture and the looped metal band with the ants embossed on it. Phil had been with her when she'd made them. She spotted Phil's dirty shirt from the day before, picked it up and sniffed it. His smell. She wrapped it around the sculptures. And there was the big green bean Phil had been so proud of. Of course, that had to come too. Yoke's eyes filled with tears. Last night had felt like the first of an endless series of similar nights—hard to believe it could have been the only one.

"Let's go, Cobb."

As they arced up into the sky, Cobb used telephoto vision to peer down at the beach where the aliens had been. Yoke shared in his vision via the uvvy. It looked like a pelican rookery and UFO landing field down there, with all the Cappy Jane birds and the giant disk. And—

"Oh Lord, they caught them," said Yoke. "Why didn't they run away?"

Cobb's telephoto vision had a nearly unlimited zoom ability; Yoke was able to dial it up to see that the Cappy Janes had captured all seven Metamartians down there. They had Shimmer, Ptah, Peg, Siss, Wubwub, a new one that looked like a man-sized bird and—dialing up the magnification a bit more—Yoke could even see that one of the Cappy Jane birds was holding the little beetle Josef. The Cappy Janes kindled a fire in which the seven unresisting aliens were consumed.

"It's hard to believe," said Cobb.

"Maybe it has something to do with coming from two-dimensional time," said Yoke. "They might not have much of a survival instinct? But that's not how I saw Shimmer acting that time on the Moon. It's weird. But, oh Cobb, with the aliens gone, how can I ever get Phil?"

"I don't know," said Cobb. "Could be you'll have to give up on him. There's more fish in the sea, Yoke." He powered up for a bit longer, finally reaching a point where he could cut off his jets and let them coast along their trajectory.

"I just noticed that the Cappy Janes are locked onto our location," Cobb said. "They're tracking us. Unless we do something, they'll track us all the way to San Francisco. And eventually hunt us down."

"Can you make yourself invisible?"

"I can block the Squanto ID locator signal I'm putting out, but then they might want to follow us in person. One of them might tail us."

"Why don't we send off a decoy? I can alla you some imipolex and you can copy yourself just like the Cappy Janes did."

"Two of me?" said Cobb hesitantly. "I'm not sure I'm in a mood to reproduce."

"Can you just make a dumb minimal clone that sends out your Squanto signal and flies—I don't know—out into space or something?"

"I could do that. In fact we can send Squanto on a trip to the Moon. That'll make sense to them, even if the 'Sue and Squanto' cover breaks down. The Moon is exactly where you might expect Cobb and Yoke to go. Tell you what, Yoke, use your alla to customize a piece of imipolex shaped exactly like me. And I can put a partial nervous system into it. The air's very thin up here. Anything you make will just coast along next to us. Can you stick your alla out through my skin?"

"I don't need to stick it out. I can move the control mesh to wherever I like. There it is." A bright-line copy of Cobb's form appeared next to them, and then—*whoosh*—it was virgin imipolex.

Cobb stretched out a mold-filled tendril and began programming his dummy. "Something else, Yoke," he said after a minute. "I think you should make a big piece of human flesh that we can seal inside him so he looks like he's still carrying you. In case the Cappy Janes really focus in on him."

"There's no human flesh in the alla catalog. The Metamartians didn't want it to be easy for us or the moldies to try and use the alla for reproduction. But, hmm, they do have a human skeleton. Remember, it's like every possible catalog in the world got folded into the master alla catalog. And this skeleton I'm looking at is like what you buy to use for anatomy classes. I guess it's kosher for the alla, since dead bone doesn't have living cells. And, oh wow, of course it's tweakable. I can make it just the same proportions as me!"

"Do it."

"I'm getting it ready in my head. The way you do realware, Cobb, is you completely get your image all together before you make the mesh and actualize it with the alla. Instead of just making a naked skeleton, I'm going to wrap the skeleton up in something of about the right density. I could use bologna but—" Yoke suddenly giggled. "How about tofu! Sue Miller as the ultimate vegan!" Another *whoosh,* and there was a tofu-and-bone fake Yoke flying along next to them.

The fake Cobb opened up and sealed itself over the fake Yoke. Cobb turned off his own locator ID signals and brought up the dummy's signals at the same time. And then the fake Yoke and Cobb—or the fake Squanto and Sue Miller—blasted on up away from them, presumably tracked by the Cappy Jane's surveillance signals.

The flight back to San Francisco was uneventful; Yoke slept most of the way. She woke as they plummeted down toward the thumb of the San Francisco peninsula. The sun was setting and the buildings of San Francisco looked lovely and gold.

"Back to Babs's?" asked Cobb.

"Yeah," said Yoke. "I like her. And she seems to have a lot of room. I hope she doesn't mind putting us up."

"She talks tough, but she's a soft touch," said Cobb. "Hell, she's even letting my great-grandson Randy stay there. I like Babs too. Wait till she sees your alla!"

"We should keep that quiet for now, Cobb. I don't want to end up in the middle of another feeding frenzy."

Nobody paid much notice when they landed on the dead-end street with Babs's warehouse. There was a homeless woman fishing in the bay, some kids working on an ancient old truck, a woman bent over her garden, a long-haired boy sitting on some steps strumming his guitar, a man walking down the street with a bag of groceries. And now here were Cobb and Yoke again, back in the thick of it.

They walked in through the open garage door to Babs's warehouse. The little plastic chicken Willa Jean cackled a warning. Randy Karl Tucker looked up from a nanomanipulator, surprised to see them. "Shit howdy! I thought you'd be gone till next weekend, Cobb."

"Well, we—um—"

"We pretty much did everything in Tonga already," said Yoke.

"Did Phil come back too?" asked Randy.

"Not yet," said Cobb after a quick glance at Yoke.

"I hope you ain't gonna try and rush me off to that dang Moon," said Randy. "I'm lovin' it here. Hey, Babs! They're baaack! Quiet down, Willa Jean."

The little chicken walked over and pecked at Cobb's foot. And Yoke and Cobb's gaze fell upon the twisted purple superleech embedded in Willa Jean's back. With a grunt of anger, Cobb lashed down with an arm suddenly grown long. He caught hold of the wildly squawking Willa Jean, formed his other fingers into scissors, and excised the offending strip of limpware. And then he dropped the chicken and cut the superleech into teensy tiny bits.

"God damn you to hell, Cobb!" Randy picked up the wounded plastic chicken and cradled her to his chest. "Willa Jean's been my special pet since India!"

"She'll live," said Cobb. "You got any more of those xoxxin' leech-DIMs around here?"

Randy sullenly refused to answer, and Yoke got right into his face. "Phil told me you were bragging about superleeches, Randy. If you have any, cough them up. I wasn't going to talk about it, but down in Tonga we saw some shit that—"

"What's all the psychodrama?" asked Babs Mooney, ambling out from the warehouse's colorful, fabric-hung depths. "You sound like a bunch of snap-heads!"

"Did Randy give you any superleeches yet?" asked Yoke.

"Tomorrow Aarbie Kidd is supposed to—"

"Call it off, Randy," said Cobb. "Or I'll tell Willy to disinherit you without a cent. Frankly, he'd love the excuse."

"Oh, fuck my ass and call me Barbie," said Randy. He sighed and made a voice connection with his uvvy. " 'Sup, brah? No, that's why I'm calling. No can do. Problem at this end. Yeah yeah, a shitty diaper. Reet. Later." He glared over at Yoke and Cobb. "Satisfied?"

"What excitement," said Babs, sitting down on a sofa. "Tell me what came down in Tonga. The way you two look, it must have been savage."

Yoke so much wanted to pour out her heart. She'd been meaning to uvvy her twin sister Joke on the Moon, but Babs was right here, and she was cozy and easy to talk to. And even Randy, in his oddball way, was comforting too. "Can you really really promise to keep a secret, Babs? Randy? Not tell a single soul outside this room?"

"I'll close the front door if you like," said Babs.

"You should," said Cobb. "If we're going to spill everything. And then you'll understand why I got so upset, Randy. I'm sorry about Willa Jean. I bet we can rig up a safe workaround. You don't need a full superleech to remote-run a chicken, for God's sake. I'll help you design something simpler."

"Okey-doke," said Randy. "Hell, it's just as well not to be startin' up again with Aarbie Kidd."

So for the next two hours Yoke and Cobb told Babs and Randy the whole story of what had happened in Tonga. As they talked they made a supper of what Babs had around her kitchen: half a loaf of bread, a green pepper, jack cheese, old salsa, hibiscus tea, a liter of beer, and a gnawed Hershey bar. Cobb, of course, didn't eat anything, and he decorously held his pores closed so as not to exude an unappetizing smell.

"Show me how you make something with the alla," asked Babs when Yoke finished talking. It was dark outside and the kitchen was lit with candles.

"I don't want to," said Yoke. "Not today. I did it way too much this morning. The cubic meter of gold. Did I mention that I put Andy Warhol's signature on it?" She smiled and yawned, then got out the two sculptures wrapped in Phil's shirt. "These are more the kind of realware I'd like to get into." They looked good to her: the chunk of glass glinting in the candle-light, the ants shiny on the band of metal.

"Those are great, Yoke," said Babs, handling them. But Yoke could tell Babs wasn't all that impressed. Babs only liked art that did things.

"There's so many possibilities," said Yoke, running her hand over the embossed ants.

"Realware," said Babs. "I'd love to make some."

"I'd like to meet Shimmer," said Randy thoughtfully. "I bet she escaped the Cappy Janes. Shimmer can give an alla to most anyone she wants to, right? I wonder what I'd make with an alla?" Randy looked at the healed up Willa Jean in his lap and gave a country chuckle. "Maybe a sexier chicken."

"Randy!" said Babs.

"After Tonga, I think the best thing to make would be allas for everyone," said Cobb. "So people don't beg you and hassle you for things."

"*Can* you make an alla with an alla?" asked Babs.

"Josef said it was possible, but that the Metamartians don't want to tell us how," said Yoke. "And speaking of chickens, they put living things into their preprogrammed alla catalog too. Everything but moldies and people. I want to make a real reef and then try to limpware engineer an imipolex reef to copy it."

"I'm starting to think being a moldie is better than being flesh and blood," said Cobb. "By the way, Randy, you would have gone bananas over Vaana. Did I mention that we fucked?"

"It must be naahce when two moldies do it, huh, Cobb?" said Randy, his voice turning low and husky. "When it's just the two of you, one on one."

"I'm outta here," said Yoke, getting to her feet. "Can I sleep in the same place as before, Babs?"

"Sure. And I'm so sorry about Phil."

"Me too. Thanks." Yoke found her way to a foam mattress on the floor in a corner of the. warehouse, next to a giant red and purple wall-hanging. She took off her clothes and put on Phil's shirt to sleep in. She set Phil's funny big bean pod next to her bed. The bean had seven odd shiny spots on it, a little patch near the summit of each bulging seed.

February 24

"Yoke?" "You're going to wake her?" "Shh!" "What's she going to say?" "This feels fine, doesn't it?" "I don't like being small." "Will she help us?"

Yoke woke to the sound of mutterings, of squeals and hisses and a few very clear notes of tiny bird-song. Her eyes flickered open. For an instant she flashed back to a Christmas morning when Whitey and Darla had left her and her twin sister's new toys on the floor right by their beds. Today seven tiny live action figures were set out: a woman, a man, a unicorn, a beetle, a snake, a pig, and a mynah bird. Cute.

Yoke sleepily closed her eyes, drifting back toward her dreams.

"Did she see us?" "She's asleep again." "I thought she'd be scared." "I want to get big." "Wake her up!" "Where are we?" "Yoke!"

Yoke opened her eyes again. The seven little figures were still there. The Metamartians?!

"Good morning, Yoke," murmured little Shimmer, half the size of Yoke's thumb. The miniature woman, man, and five animals were crawling around on Phil's bean, which looked somewhat the worse for wear. There was a hole in each of its seven bulging seeds. Evidently the seven little figures had tunneled into the seeds like weevils, sealing their entry holes over with plugs of green imipolex.

"You stowed away," murmured Yoke.

"I knew you'd keep the bean," said Josef the beetle. Of all the Metamartians, he alone was the same size as before. "I showed the others how to make copies of themselves as small as me. And I copied myself too. We're the copies. We flew to your room and got inside your bean."

"Go away," said Yoke. "I don't want the powerball to eat me too."

Wubwub answered. "Aw, we not gonna decrypt any more Metamartians. Seven's all we need for a complete family, you know what I'm sayin'? We got the family now, we gonna look around a little, make a baby, maybe help Om spread the allas, and then we move on."

Yoke sat up, fully waking. "I thought the Cappy Janes killed you. Cobb and I saw them burning you on the beach."

"We're copies," said Ptah. "Like Josef said. We left before the Cappy Janes got there. Our original selves died; they let themselves get killed so the Cappy Janes would think they'd won. We're seconds; well, actually, I'm a third. Like I told you when Om ate my first self, Yoke, losing a life isn't a big deal for us. Every day, every minute of my life on Metamars, I saw one of my time-lines end. Letting the Cappy Janes kill versions of us was a small price to pay so that we can observe your people in peace. Do you mind if we settle in here?"

"I don't want to help unless you can bring Phil and Darla back."

"Are you not grateful for the boon of your alla?" asked the little unicorn Peg. She was the Metamartian Yoke liked the least. Such a tacky-looking thing, with her swilly, corny style of speech.

"I could live without it," said Yoke airily. "It caused me nothing but trouble in Tonga. I went there to do some diving and I ended up being a golden goose. In fact, here, you can take it!" She pulled the alla tube out from under her pillow and tossed it at the little figures, who hopped about in kind of a cute way. "I'm not grateful one bit," continued Yoke. "As far as I'm concerned, you can turn yourselves back into personality waves and find a different world to xoxx with."

"She a tiger," said Siss admiringly.

"It's too late to stop it now," said Ptah. "How this all comes out is up to Om."

"Are you talking to yourself, Yoke?" said Babs, suddenly appearing in Yoke's field of view. "Oh my God, what are those wavy little figurines? And they're moving! Did you make them with your alla?"

"Hi, Babs. These are the aliens I was telling you about. Okay, Metamartians, this is Babs. And Babs, this is Shimmer, Ptah, Wubwub, Siss, Peg, Josef, and—the seventh one's new. The little bird that looks like he's wearing a yellow mask."

"I'm Haresh," said the bird, his voice loud and melodious even though

RUDY RUCKER

he was but one centimeter long. "An Indian mynah. I am very pleased to be meeting you, Miss Yoke and Miss Babs."

"Did you tell the powerball to eat Phil?" said Yoke accusingly.

"Yes, but it was Wubwub's idea that I so do. I am very sorry about this. Can you help us find shelter?"

"They're so little," said Babs, leaning over the Metamartians. "They're really from another world? Oh, I'd do anything for them. Do you guys want to live in one of my cupboards? Or I could find a dollhouse."

"It's too risky, Babs," said Yoke. "As soon as people—or the moldies—find out about them, they're going to want to kill them. The place could be bombed. We'd all die and the Metamartians would escape as usual."

"I ain't livin' in no dollhouse," said Wubwub "I'm gonna alla me a right-size body." There was a sound like a loud handclap and a bigger copy of Wubwub appeared, knee high and pig-sized. "I'm gonna get more respect if I'm this size," said the fresh Wubwub. "You know what I'm sayin'?"

"I want to be large as well," said Shimmer. Ptah, Peg, Siss, and Haresh chimed in too. "I'm no insect." "The floor is vile with dust." "Someone might step on me." "I'll be tall, not small."

There were five more explosive sounds as the necessary volumes of air were converted into patterned imipolex. And now Yoke's sleeping corner was crowded with a marble woman, a bronze man, a blonde unicorn, a green python, a black pig, and a giant bird with a yellow mask around its eyes. This made thirteen Metamartians in all: a single Josef, still the size of a beetle, plus big and small versions of each of the six others.

"Praise Om," said the new Metamartians.

"This is insane," said Babs. "What happens to the little guys now?"

"We feel it's ecologically unsound for one of us to have more than one body in a given time-line," piped the tiny Shimmer. "Farewell." And the six small Metamartians dissolved into poofs of air—effectively killing themselves.

"I don't think people could ever act that way," marveled Yoke.

Josef buzzed over to perch on Yoke's pillow. "I'm happy to see you again, Yoke," he said.

"What happened to you on Vava'u?" asked Yoke. "You disappeared when I needed you. When all those Tongans were crowding in on me."

"There was no way out for you," said Josef. "You'd painted yourself into a corner, as one says. Remember that we can see a little way into the future. I didn't want to be there when Tashtego and Daggoo arrived to deliver the great scolding."

Babs was all agog, smiling at and touching the aliens. "I don't know what to ask first," she laughed. "Where you're from, what you want—this is wonderful. At first I thought you were just Silly Putters, or moldies."

"Our essence is energy," said Shimmer. "We can incorporate ourselves in various ways. The moldie form seems to be convenient. For now." She glanced up at the sunlit windows high in the warehouse walls. "I'm ready to get out and about and see some things. To be a tourist! Our plan for now is to blend in and mingle. And then Om will spread the allas, and we'll mate, and we'll move on."

A warning gong sounded, meaning that someone had just entered Babs's front door. "Maybe that's Randy and Cobb," said Babs, looking upset. "They went out last night and they never came back." She hurried off.

"Great day in the morning!" came Randy Karl Tucker's voice. "You're all paisleyed up there, Babs. Checkerboard paisley everywhar!"

Cobb's deep voice murmured something. And then there was a crash of someone knocking over a chair.

"You gross cheeseball. Randy!" cried Babs. "And you're lifted on camote? Here I thought we might start a relationship and you act so—so disgusting! You're a sporehead *and* a cheese-ball. I wish I'd never seen you! And, no, you can't go back there."

The low rumble of Cobb's voice came again, and then Randy's voice lifted in incoherent ranting that segued into words. "Hiiigh as a kite tail! Babs don't want me to head this-a-way, Jose? Well that's whar I'm a-goin'!" Another crash, followed by snorting sounds and more yelling. "Fee-fie-foe-fum, I smell *fuck plastic!*" A pile of books tumbled over, and then Randy appeared, followed by Cobb and Babs.

Yoke had never seen Randy like this. Instead of his usual timid, introverted self, he was wild and expansive. For his part, Cobb looked the way he had after all that betty in Tonga. Quivery. Evidently the two of them had spent the night on the *Anubis* getting lifted and having sex with hooker moldies. Like great-grandfather, like great-grandson. Icky, sad, and kind of funny. Yoke felt sorry for Babs. She'd obviously had hopes for Randy.

At the sight of the aliens, Cobb hiccupped and sat down on the floor, his skin rippling with rapid wrinkles. Randy made a beeline for Shimmer, shoving Peg the unicorn to one side.

"Dog with an antler, what the hell. Look at this milky mama." He lurched forward, throwing his arms around Shimmer's neck and sniffing deeply. "Hey thar. Want to make twenty bucks the hard way?"

"Greetings, Randy. I am Shimmer from Metamars."

"Whoah!" said Randy. "I'm in looove. Sex with an alien!" He ardently embraced Shimmer, and instead of pushing him away, the alien lowered herself down onto Yoke's bed with Randy on top of her. Yoke sprang up, getting well out of range. "If we do it, can I have an alla too, Shimmer?" Randy was saying. "I'm the natural man to show you the facts o' life."

Even though Shimmer was making a noise that could have been laughter, Ptah and Wubwub dragged Randy off of Shimmer, Ptah pulling Randy's legs and Wubwub pushing his chest with his snout. Siss wrapped herself around Randy's body, strapping down his arms. Haresh the giant mynah bird strutted over to peer at Randy's face.

"Is this typical human mating behavior?" asked Haresh, cocking his head.

"Don't even," said Babs. "He is so far from any semblance."

"Randy's a cheeseball," explained Yoke. "He likes to have sex with moldies. He thought you were a moldie, Shimmer."

"Who says she ain't?" said Randy, trying to raise his hand to his face, seeming not to understand that his arm was held down by Siss's coils. "The nose knows." Randy kept on trying to move his arm, soddenly struggling against Siss.

"Let him go," said Shimmer. "He's harmless."

"I wouldn't trust him," said Ptah. "What if he somehow pollutes your plastic?" But Siss went ahead and uncoiled.

"Once I git naked, I'll do some harm on you all right," said Randy, crawling forward to rest his head facedown in Shimmer's lap. He inhaled deeply. "The nose knows." This time Randy managed to lay his finger against his nose, but in the process he rolled off of Shimmer's thighs, bounced off the edge of the bed, and clunked his head on the floor. "Ow," said Randy, and fell asleep.

"What a colorful individual," said Shimmer.

"I pick the absolute worst men," said Babs.

"I hope you have some other prospects," said Yoke.

"There's always Theodore," said Babs. "I'm going to do a mental reset, Yoke. Like 'Randy is just a friend and I have no feelings for this man.' Reset, reset, reset. Yes, I'm going to call Theodore today. He's been wanting to take me out to a brain-concert."

"You go, girl," said Yoke. "I wonder if I'm going to have to wash Cobb again."

"What do you mean?" asked Babs.

"He's high on betty. Last time he got like this he almost died. I had to knead him with my feet for ten minutes in the shower."

"Betty's bad," said Babs. "My mother took it once and—*ugh*." Yoke recalled that Babs's mother Wendy Mooney was a human/moldie hybrid. That is, Wendy had a tank-grown human body that was run by a scarf-shaped moldie that did all the actual thinking.

Now Babs went back to marveling at the aliens. "Randy's right," she said, petting Peg's mane. "You seem just like moldies. But—prettier. I don't mind if you stay here for a while. I don't really mind the moldie smell, you know. It reminds me of my mother. Tell me more about where you come from. It's called Metamars?"

"Yes," said Josef. "That's where we began. But now we travel forever. Our near-term goal when we depart is to get back to a zone of two-dimensional time." He flew from Yoke's pillow to Babs's shoulder, and started talking to her about higher dimensions, with Haresh and Siss listening and adding comments.

While they talked, Yoke crouched down and touched Cobb. He didn't seem nearly so shaky and blotchy as he'd been in Tonga. Presumably this time he hadn't taken an overdose. So she left Cobb to sit there, grinning and shivering.

Yoke needed fresh clothes. The alla was still lying on the floor where she'd thrown it; she picked it up. She popped out black tights, silver boots like Phil's, a shrimp-colored skirt, and a thick black wool turtleneck.

"So you do enjoy the miraculous alla," said Peg. "And our superb catalog."

"They're okay," said Yoke casually.

"Can I have an alla?" asked Babs, interrupting Josef's science lecture. She'd been closely watching Yoke make her clothes.

"Well . . . " said Shimmer. She was sitting on the edge of Yoke's bed, keeping an eye on Randy.

"You barged into my house and stole my man," said Babs, not entirely joking. "It's the least you can do."

"Oh *ja*, let's give Babs an alla," said Josef. "Om wants us to. Yoke's alla has worked out well enough and Om feels it's safe to try more."

"I'm down with it," chimed in Wubwub. "Allas for the people. Why not one for this Randy-neck too? That could be kinky, you know what I'm sayin'?"

"Here, Babs," said Shimmer, rolling her thumb against her fingers. A subtly flickering silver tube appeared in her hand. "Om made it look different from Yoke's so you don't get mixed up. Take it. You're wearing an uvvy? Good. That's what the alla uses for an interface. An alla registers itself as owned by the first person who picks it up. It'll show a rapid-fire series of images so Om can learn your personality, and then it'll feel around in your body to teach Om your physical form. Once that's done, it's registered."

Babs held the tube in her hand, eyes closed to better see the uvvy visions in her head. "Cathedral window, tree-branch, sand," she murmured, each word faster than the one before, and then she was going too fast to talk out loud. The descriptions sounded familiar to Yoke; probably the alla was showing Babs the same images it had shown her. Yoke could tell when the body-mapping part of the alla registration happened, because Babs briefly twitched all over.

"Stuzzy," breathed Babs, opening her eyes and looking down at the little alla tube. "I've been memorized by Om."

"Now I'll transfer our human-oriented alla catalog to your uvvy, Babs," said Ptah. "Josef and I made the catalog, and it's quite complete. We got it by combining every existing catalog we could find on the Web. Basically, I figured out how to make everything. Here it comes."

"Once you get the hang of it, Babs, you can design original realware of your own," added Shimmer. "And now for Randy's alla."

"Nay, nay!" protested Peg. "That youth is base and foul. His crafting will be full unsavory."

"Peg's right," said Ptah. "I realize that you don't need for me to defend you, Shimmer, but I really feel that this kind of degenerate individual is a serious threat."

"It good practice to include deviant in test population, I think," said Siss. She listened into herself as if silently conversing with something. "And, yes, Om agree."

"I'll do it," said Shimmer. She rolled her thumb against her fingers again, producing an alla tube in gently fluctuating shades of copper. She gracefully leaned over to tuck the vibrant tube into the sleeping Randy's shirt pocket. "Let's wake him up so he can register it," she urged.

"Don't wake him now," said Yoke. "Not while he's still lifted. I'll make sure he registers it later. And I'll uvvy him a copy of the catalog."

"Whu-Whu-Whu about me?" said Cobb, shuddering away on the floor.

"No," said Wubwub. "We ain't ready to start in with moldie allas too."

"I'm nuh-not a moldie," protested Cobb. "I'm human." It was just like back in Tonga, when Onar had told Cobb he couldn't come to the dinner at the King's because it was for humans only. It made Yoke sad to hear Cobb insist he was human. Why not face the truth? As far as Yoke was concerned, being human meant being made of flesh and blood. And poor old Cobb hadn't had a human body since 2020.

"If you want something, I'll make it for you, Cobb," said Yoke gently. "But for now, you don't get an alla. Especially not when you're lifted. Maybe you should go get in the shower. Wash those spores out."

"Yeah," said the old man moldie. "I gotta shake this betty shit." He shuffled off towards Babs's bathroom.

Meanwhile Babs had been sitting silent on the floor, uvvying around in her alla catalog. And now she produced a bright-line shape that became a cup of coffee in a ceramic mug shaped like the head of an ant. Babs liked ants as much as Yoke did.

"Oh. My. God!" said Babs. "I love it!"

"Don't get so grateful that you let the Metamartians stay here," cautioned Yoke. "If they don't kill you, someone else will by coming after them. I like Shimmer's idea. The Metamartians should go out and blend in. You don't have to look like *exactly* a pig, do you, Wubwub? And Peg, could you possibly bag the unicorn thing? I mean why not pass yourselves off as regular moldies? Unless you just want to be birds or insects. Nobody cares about them. Nobody would notice if a bird is plastic."

"I am proud to be a bird," said Haresh. "From scanning through your Web, I am learning very much about them. The only small cloud is that to be called a 'birdbrain' is by no means a compliment. Nevertheless there is a very famous poem of this name. *Birdbrain!* by your immortal Hindu bard Allen Ginsberg. So I am even proud to be a birdbrain. But I do not accept your suggestion to be a small plastic bird which nobody notices. I too would like to be freely mingling with humans and moldies on an equal basis. I want to be accepted as a full-sized moldie."

Cobb came ambling back from the shower, looking pink and fresh again. "That did me a world of good."

"What kind of look do a moldie generally have?" asked Wubwub.

"Here in the city they look like people," said Babs. "Approximately. Like caricatures. It's considered dooky for a moldie to look too exactly human, though Shimmer and Ptah are so over-the-top that they'll be okay. No humans are that beautiful. And the way they look like marble and bronze makes it clear that they're not trying to pass for people. Now you, Wubwub, you can be a pig-man. A person with a face like a pig. Keep your snout and ears, but change your body and legs. That's good. Legs a little longer. You need more than two fingers on your hands, try three, no, four counting the thumb. All right. And, yes, keep the tail, in fact make it bigger and curlier. Like a corkscrew. Wavy. Now your mouth—it's too scary. Here, let me—" Babs stepped forward and began molding Wubwub's face. Wubwub generated dancing bright alla-lines to effect the changes as fast as Babs suggested them. "We'll curve the lips up at the end, put in a smile wrinkle, make the snout a little shorter, shorten those snaggle teeth, arch the eyebrows, fold that one ear over, and, oh, how about a big white spot around this eye? That's perfect. You look darling. Look at yourself through my uvvy. You don't like the white spot? Oh, all right, get rid of it, then. Fine. You look handsome but tough."

"Come to my aid, Babs," said Peg, elongating and taking on a womanly form. "What think you of my horn?"

"A unicorn horn is more of a guy thing," said Babs. "It's a dick symbol. You'd do better to have, um, two little horns."

"Like a cow?" asked Peg. There was a flicker of bright mesh-lines and her face grew broader.

"Oh yes, Peg," put in Yoke unkindly. "Be a cow."

"Don't listen to her," said Babs. "You want to be a devil-girl. Sexy and with curvy red horns and reddish skin. Yeah, yeah, okay, but make your T and A bigger. That's good—if only it were so easy for everyone. And, um, fine, keep the blonde hair. Usually devil-girls are brunette, but you can be a Val devil-girl. Better make your skin more pink like sunburn instead of that coppery Native American hue. Oh, and don't forget to make your tail all leathery and with a little arrow at the tip. That's a dick symbol too, but on a devil-girl it's hot. Like a strap-on dildo. Oh, you've got it now, Peg, you're moanin'. Next?"

A few minutes later six of the Metamartians were the shape and size of well-proportioned humans resembling, respectively, a marble Venus, a bronze Apollo, a pig-man, a devil-girl, a snake-woman, and a bird-man. For his part, Josef stayed resolutely the same.

"I'll observe," said Josef. "A deep participation is not my style. I'll be the fly on the wall. The beetle."

"Haresh looks like that Egyptian god," said Yoke. "Thoth." The Metamartian had left his head exactly in the shape of a bird's. "What a birdbrain."

"Zoom!" exclaimed Babs. "Egyptian! You Metamartians can go join the Snooks family on the *Anubis*. After last night, Cobb here must know those moldies pretty well. Right, Cobb? You can tell Thutmosis and Isis Snooks that these six are friends of yours just down from the Moon and that they're looking for work."

"Work doin' what?" asked Wubwub suspiciously.

"Oh, the Snookses are into all kinds of things," said Cobb. "You can tell them you're a—a burglar, Wubwub. Just secretly actualize things like liquor for the *Anubis* bar and say that you stole it. And that can be your contribution to the family. You don't necessarily have to fuck the cheeseballs, if that's what you're worried about."

"*I'm* not worried about that," said Shimmer, staring down at the sleeping Randy Karl Tucker. "It might be fun."

"I'm going to call Theodore right now," sighed Babs, walking off toward the front of the warehouse.

"Babs likes Randy," Yoke explained to Shimmer. "It makes her unhappy to think of him having sex with you. So don't do it, please."

"Oh!" said Shimmer. "I hadn't realized."

"It's not our affair if the vile youth lacks wholesome passion for Babs," said Peg snippily.

"What kind of sex system do you Metamartians have?" asked Yoke. "Do you have any kind of clue?"

As usual, Josef wanted to be the one to answer the question, but Siss made as if to swat him.

"I the one who sexy, Josef. You let me speak."

Siss had a face of pale humanlike skin with large, almond-shaped eyes. Her nose was little more than two flattened holes and her mouth was immensely long and thin-lipped. Instead of hair, she had a skull-fitting hood of shiny green snakeskin that flowed down to join the snakeskin which covered the rest of her body, save her hands, which had humanlike skin and long green fingernails. The hood had a dramatic widow's peak in the middle of her forehead. Siss looked decadent, Asian, androgynous.

"We have something like boy/girl too," she explained. "One got stick, one got hole. Each of us is 'stick' in some lives, 'hole' in others. Many lives across two-dimensional time. Stick to hole, hole to stick, like big crocodile sex zipper." Siss showed her fangs and made a gentle biting motion, her long curved fangs sliding into matching sockets in her jaws. "Everyone both girl and boy."

"But there's more to it than that," piped up Josef. "We zipper together in loops of seven. Why seven? It has to do with a feedback resonance in the strange attractor of our metagenome. In ancient times we mated only on Metamars, but now we've chirped out into the cosmos. When seven of us nomads can meet and mate—it's a wonderful thing. Seven of us landed here, but eight of us shall leave."

"I for one am eager to be getting on with our adventures," said Haresh. Other than Josef, he looked the least human. "Can we go and meet the Snooks family now?"

"Stay uvvied in with me," said Cobb. "If they ask you any hard questions, I can feed you the answers. Now is a good time to show up. Most of them are going to be asleep or hung over. Remember, you guys come from the big Nest on the Moon. And you're going to promise to give the Snookses half the imipolex you earn, in return for them letting you join their family."

"Let's do it!" said Shimmer.

They waited by the warehouse's front door until they could see a time-line in which no passersby would notice them. Cobb and the six big Metamartians jumped out onto the street with little Josef buzzing along above them.

"Look at them go, Yoke," said Babs, just ending her uvvy call with Theodore. "What a sight."

"*Anubis,* ahoy!" said Yoke. "We better not stare after them. We don't want it to be totally obvious that your warehouse is where they came from. How was Theodore?"

"Oh, fine. Thrilled that I called. We made a date, not a dinner date, a meet date. We're going to meet at the Fillmore and see Larky's brain-concert. Larky's this guy who uses really big sheets of imipolex for his audio and video. Sort of like Saint and Onar were doing the other day, but more professional. I like Theodore—I guess."

"I told Shimmer to leave Randy alone," said Yoke.

"What? I don't believe you, Yoke. What'd she say?"

Yoke put on her Val voice. "Shimmer was like, 'Oh I didn't know.' And that swilly Peg is all 'It's not *our* problem.' And I'm like 'Do you have any clue about sex?' And Siss goes, 'We're bi.' But then Josef says they do it by sevens."

Babs laughed and gave Yoke a hug. "Whatever. Randy is pretty skanky. Let's get our allas and do art!"

"What about Randy's alla?" said Yoke.

"Maybe we should take it away?" said Babs. "Maybe give it to someone else?"

"At least hide it for now," said Yoke. "He might do something really gnarly with it if he's still lifted when he wakes up."

So they tiptoed back to Yoke's sleeping corner. Willa Jean had perched herself on Randy's chest, as if guarding him. Though Cobb and Randy hadn't yet fixed up a new DIM link between Randy and the plastic chicken, Willa Jean was still quite loyal to the Kentuckian.

Yoke held Willa Jean's beak shut while Babs took Randy's alla out of his pocket.

"This is what happens to stoned rednecks," hissed Babs, pocketing Randy's alla. "Their powers disappear." Willa Jean let out an outraged cackle when they released her, but Randy slept on unperturbed.

And then Yoke and Babs went out to the front of the warehouse and started making things.

February 26

"I'm kind of waiting to see what's going to happen next," Yoke was saying. It was two days later, Thursday, February 26, 2054, about two in the afternoon. Yoke was on the uvvy with her twin sister Joke on the Moon. The to-and-fro response time for a message was about five seconds, due both to the large Earth-Moon distance and to the intricate diffusion-encryption software they were using for the call. Diffusion-encryption sent each byte of the message along a different path—to prevent there from being any traceable signal binding the speakers together. It took a lot of computation.

With the five-second lag, the best way to converse was to take turns sending long blocks of speech and images. It was more like a fast E-mail exchange than a normal conversation.

Yoke continued her turn: "Babs and I have been making the best things. I already showed you some of my static sculptures, but now let me show you one that moves." The uvvy transmitted the images direct from Yoke's vision centers. She was looking at a sweeping loop of shiny wire with bright shapes sliding along the wire. "I made this on Tuesday. The rail is chrome steel and there's a linear induction field in it. The power comes from a quantum-dot generator embedded right inside the rail. The shapes are the Platonic and Archimedean solids, remember them?" Two of the polyhedra collided and reversed directions. They swooped along the track's twists and loops, rising and falling. The beautiful, shiny polyhedra were tinted crystal, grown around magnetic metal cores. "It's a magpie kind of thing. And I keep making myself more clothes. Look at my outfit." Yoke stepped in front of a fancy full-length wood-framed Art Nouveau mirror to show off her latest clothes, a short thin red leather jacket over baggy shin-length pants and a white T-shirt inset with lace spirals. "And Babs made a bunch of furniture. Like this mirror for instance. It was from a Sotheby's auction catalog. And she made a silk couch with ants embroidered all over it and a canopy bed. I made myself a bunk bed like we used to have on the Moon, only big enough this time. The thing Babs is proudest of so far is over here, check it out. Like a glass bowl of living spaghetti." Yoke pointed her gaze at a cubical quartz box holding a wriggling mass of imipolex worms of every color and thickness. The sharp edges of the square box contrasted with the lively antics within. "Babs could never have afforded this many plastic worms before. I think there's two hundred thousand of them, all custom made by her—well, you can tell the alla to make a whole lot of copies of something in a row, but I guess that's still custom. Custom mass-produced? Anyhoo, see how the same-colored ones band together and flow along like gouts of lava? I love it. Okay, now you talk."

Joke's message started coming in: "Your clothes are floatin', Yoke. I have so many clothes ideas I want you to make. Like polka dots with the dots being cutouts. Look." The signal showed Joke's hands quickly sketching a girl with an outfit. Beyond Joke's hands was a lunar workshop crowded with equipment for making Silly Putters: shelves and shelves of chemicals, a hulking injection molder, and a workbench with imipolex-machining tools such as a piezomorpher and a volume-filling airbrush. Joke was living with her somewhat gnarly artist boyfriend, Corey Rhizome, who was visible at the other end of the workshop. A few of Corey's Silly Putters were hopping around; they were plastic pets a little like Willa Jean, but smarter and more autonomous. Yoke recognized two of the Silly Putters: the small green pig of a "rath" and the football-shaped, orange-beaked "Jubjub bird," the two forever engaged in mutual battle. Joke set down her pen and continued talking. "I hope you bring that alla back here really soon! Oh, and your sculptures are terrific. I never knew you could be such the artist, Yoke. That wire thing with the sliding blocks is sooo weightless. I guess you could make a really big one? I mean, like as big as a carnival ride, with each of the sliding thingies hollowed out so that a person could ride inside? I'm wondering if there's any limit to the power of the alla. I mean, could you hollow out a huge biosphere under the Moon's surface and fill it up with dirt and rivers and lakes and an atmosphere and maybe even a little fusion sun? There's no end to what people might ask you for. So you're right that it's really important to figure out how to copy the allas so that it's not just you and Babs being golden geese when everyone finds out. I'm glad that the people and moldies from Tonga haven't tracked you back to San Francisco. I guess the King is keeping quiet and the Cappy Janes really fell for the decoy. The tofu Sue Miller! We knew a girl just like that, remember Simmie Lipsit? I wonder if one of the Cappy Janes has chased down the tofu Sue by now. You know, I'm going to ask Emil and Berenice to check on the moldies' chat lines right now. While I do that, tell me what's up with Cobb's great-grandson. Did you ever give him his alla?"

Yoke: "Oh, that was so wild. All afternoon Tuesday, Randy was moping and dragging around all hung over while Babs and I made wavy stuff. He was wishing he had an alla and wondering where the aliens went, and we were like, 'Serves you right for getting so trashed.' But then after we alla-made a bunch of soup and bread and cheese for supper, Babs finally gave Randy his alla and it registered itself to him. That's a trip in itself, it's like the alla is memorizing your body and your mind—your wetware and your soft-ware—the whole package. I was for holding out on Randy, but Babs keeps wanting to be nice to him. Or get his attention or something. And then as soon as she *had* Randy's attention, Babs did a head-trip on him by going out on a date with this new guy Theodore. I have a feeling she's using Theodore to make Randy jealous. Anyway, Randy and I were alone together Tuesday evening. I showed him how the alla works, and the very first customized thing he did was to make a safe DIM control patch for his plastic chicken, Willa Jean. Willa Jean is sort of the same thing as a Silly Putter, except Randy has a control feed into her, and she's not as smart. Randy was using an illegal superleech before, and he got Cobb to approve the new one as safe around real moldies; in fact Cobb helped him design it. Hey, there goes Willa Jean now." Yoke trained her vision on Willa Jean wandering across the floor, ostensibly pecking for stray crumbs of imipolex. "I'm surprised that plastic chicken's here, because Randy's gone out on his new motorcycle. I wonder if he's using her to eavesdrop on me. If so, you're a geek, Randy." Yoke swung her alla through the air to launch a buzzing, bouncing spark-machine that frightened Willa Jean off into the far corners of the warehouse. "But I still haven't told you the best part. After Randy fixed Willa Jean, he was tired, so he made himself a good bed and lay down on that and started creating all sorts of little samples of every kind of material he could think of, each sample in the shape of a Lego block, and he was snapping them together and then—this is the rich part—Randy fell asleep while he was wearing his uvvy, and he ended up hooking into his alla and making something that he'd been dreaming, God you should have heard him scream. The screaming started at like three in the morning and Babs wasn't back yet, so it was just me and Cobb to deal. Randy's realware dream thing was a giant snail with his mother's face. It was chasing him. A giant imipolex snail actually crawling around the warehouse at three in the morning, knocking things over, and I mean a snail this big." Yoke stretched both arms up high, shaking with mirth. "I really shouldn't be laughing because it's very sad, his mother died at the end of November and Randy had totally been neglecting to stay in touch and he missed the funeral and apparently he has these recurrent guilt nightmares about a giant snail, it has to do with being too late. It was crawling after him all around the warehouse and wailing 'What taahm is it?' in this bewildered, Kentucky-accented voice. 'You goin' be late for school if you don't hurry up, Randy Karl. When is Tuesday?' Except it said 'whiyun' instead of 'when.' " Yoke was struggling to keep her voice level, but now and then letting out shrieks of laughter. "It had a silver-frosted black shell, like a middle-aged lady's hair. And there was some incest thing in there too. It wanted to sit on his face. I heard it say 'Ah'm real hot to crawl on you, Randy Karl.' Randy was just completely freaking out. And finally he was cornered and the snail really did crawl onto him, right across his body and up onto his face, I think it must have weighed four hundred pounds. It moved a lot faster than you'd expect. Randy would have suffocated if Cobb hadn't been able to drag it outside; Cobb can be really strong. We burned the imipolex, but the shell's still there. I'll show it to you in a minute."

Joke: "I can see where you'd think that's funny, Yoke. Not everyone would. But that's why we love you. It sounds like Randy could run amok, a gunjy dook like that. You're going to push him too far. Not everybody appreciates your sense of humor. Though Corey's loving it. I'm telling him some of the stuff while it's coming in." Joke's view showed a greenish-skinned man with square vertical goatee and the sides of his head shaved, grinning and leaning forward as if hungering for information. "No, Corey, you can't uvvy in. This is totally diffusion-encrypted. Emul customized some cryp code just for this call. Yes, Corey, you heard me right, a giant snail with his mother's face wanted to crawl on him. Back off-ski! Okay, Yoke, while you were telling about Randy just now, Berenice did an anonymous search of the moldie chat-lines and found out a few things. The aliens' sacrificial clone trick went over; the moldies really think they killed them all. But they're suspicious about Squanto and Sue flying to the Moon. The dummy is halfway here and nobody wants to bother chasing it down, but they're doubting it's real. They've posted the Sue Miller information all over the place, along with one of the Cappy Jane images of you. But it isn't you. Look."

Joke flashed the Sue Miller ID sheet with the photo image of a short-haired hollow-cheeked girl with black hair. In addition, there was a holographic still image of Yoke and Cobb floating in the Vava'u bay, with the giant cube of imipolex just behind them. But Yoke's face was replaced by Sue Miller's, and Cobb looked like a plastic American Indian. "The moldies didn't notice you searching, did they, Berenice?" Joke asked. She paused, looking into her head, which was partly inhabited by the wetware-coded personalities of two old-time boppers called Berenice and Emul. Quickly receiving her answer, Joke continued talking. "No, you're safe for now, Yoke, but you better believe the shit's going to hit the fan one way or another. You didn't say where Randy went on his motorcycle. And what about Babs?"

Yoke: "Well, yesterday was pretty calm, and we were nice to Randy and made things together, so don't worry too much about him going amok. He made the motorcycle this morning. A really tough machine, all big and black and loud, though of course it's electric. Like I say, he's out riding it now, but I don't know where. Babs was so impressed with Randy's motorcycle that she made herself a car, look, you can see it out in front of the warehouse." Yoke peered out the warehouse's big square door at an incredibly decorated dune-buggy outside. It was covered all over with drawings of girls, done in a casual sketchbook kind of style, and its fenders were curled up in funny squiggles. It looked like a live cartoon, bright in the afternoon sun. Standing by the buggy was Babs herself, talking to a burr-cut man with little round glasses. "That's Babs's new friend Theodore. He slept here last night. Believe it or not, Randy's jealous of him. As if he had a right. I think that's why he took off on his big bad motorsickle this morning. And then Babs made herself the car just to show she's still on top. She thought about it for a couple of hours and when she was ready she alla-made it real fast when nobody was looking. She transmuted some heavy garbage instead of just air, so that there wasn't this like big thunderclap. Theodore and our neighbors don't know about the allas yet, thank God. If the word gets out, it's going to be a zoo. I'll go ahead and step all the way outside so you can see down the street. Hi, Babs, I'm talking to my sister Joke on the Moon. See Cobb lying in the street next to the car sunning himself, Joke? It's the third sunny day in a row. Say hi to Joke, Cobb, you lazy old slug." Cobb stuck a head and arm out of his puddled form and waved. "And see the giant, charred snail shell across the street by the water, Joke? Isn't that too much?"

Joke: "Keep looking, I want to sketch the shell for Corey. He wants to make a Silly Putter pet Tucker Snail. And then look down the street so I can see the *Anubis,* Yoke. I'm getting really nice image quality. And also I want to talk about how soon you're coming home. I don't want to lose you. You should leave before the heavy kilp starts happening."

Yoke stared at the shell and the *Anubis* for a minute, then wandered back into the warehouse. It was two in the afternoon. "Phil's the big issue to me, Joke, and of course Ma too. I'm sorry, but I don't want a clone with a Happy Cloak for my mother. According to the aliens, Phil and Darla and the others are off in the powerball hyperspace bubble, maybe not so far away. In the fourth dimension. I told Phil I'd wait for him here. If I hang here just a little more, maybe he'll come back. Oh, and look, I didn't show you yet what Randy, Babs, and I made yesterday." Yoke gazed at a chest-high aquarium filled with delicately shaded plastic jellyfish. "These are imipolex, like Babs's worms. It's very easy to program an artificial jelly-fish, at least it was with Randy helping. See how we put a different mandala onto the surface of each one? The kind of realistic ones are Babs's and the more abstract ones are by me. I think Babs is right that moving art is better than art that just sits there. Next I want to make some simulated polyps that build a coral reef. I wish I knew more limpware engineering. Randy's good at it, believe it or not. Of course, playing with real life would be more exciting, but the aliens say it's going to be impossible for us to use the alla to really program biological life until we completely figure out all of the wetware engineering for ourselves, and who knows when that'll be. They don't want to tell us too much, because they don't want it to be easy for us or the moldies to actualize a billion instances of ourselves and instantly over-populate the planet. They think we're that dumb."

Joke: "Too true. I do wish you'd come back home, Yoke. Those allas— they could be dangerous. What if someone were to turn one against you? It sounds like things could so easily get out of control. Does Randy Karl Tucker realize that the aliens are in bodacious moldie bodies just down the block?"

Yoke made a little marble head with her alla, an image of how she felt. An open-mouthed face: excited, anxious, aware. "We didn't tell him yet, no. But I think we might go see them tonight."

CHAPTER FIVE

RANDY, PHIL, BABS, PHIL

Randy, February 26, 2054

Randy steered his motorcycle south out of San Francisco, taking Route 1 down along the coast past Pacifica. Though it had been sunny over at Babs's warehouse, it was foggy and cold on the coast. He pulled over and alla-made himself gloves and a set of biking leathers. Awesome what the little coppery tube could do. It had been great making things with Babs and Yoke yesterday. That Babs was really something. And now, just when he was starting to go for her, she was slipping away from him, which was majorly depressing. Maybe it was time for him to change.

Randy tucked the alla tube inside his right glove just in case he needed it all of sudden. He'd never ridden a motorcycle before, and he had a notion that if he were about to collide with something, he might be able to use the alla to turn the obstacle into thin air. Just project a bright-line cube on out there and zap whatever it was: a rock, a tree, or even another vehicle. Though if he couldn't have Babs, then why bother? Randy caught himself and pushed that feeling away.

Riding the bike proved quite easy. Randy had picked a top-of-the-line model out of the alla catalog, and it was very stable.

It had a big quantum-dot electric motor and imipolex DIM wheels. South of Half Moon Bay, Randy decided to stop and make himself a snack. Not seeing any official beach, he simply drove his bike across a field of dead brussels sprouts to the edge of a hundred-foot bluff at the edge of the sea. The smart wheels had no problem picking their way across the furrows.

Randy parked his bike upright on its stand, then used his alla to make himself an energy bar and a can of Bharat Jolly-Zest soda, an anise-flavored Indian soft drink he'd become fond of in Bangalore. He was pleased to find it in the truly exhaustive alla catalog. After eating, he kept sitting on the bluff, amusing himself by designing a series of little realware glider airplanes and flinging them out into the eddying winds. He couldn't stop thinking about Babs Mooney.

Babs's sudden relationship with Theodore was bothering Randy a lot more than he would have expected. Up until a few days ago he'd been thinking of Babs as basically an easy mark whom he could sponge off of, as well as being a pretty good person to kill time with. It's not like she was knock-down gorgeous or anything. But now all of a sudden things were getting complicated, the way women were said to like them to be.

Randy's experience thus far with women was very limited, one might even say stunted. The sum total was this: in high school he'd had a hot and heavy affair with a bisexual older woman named Honey Weaver who—it later developed—had really just been using him as a way to get at his mother, with whom Honey also had an affair. It was Honey who'd gotten Randy interested in cheeseball sex. She'd had two memorable moldie sex toys: the dildo Angelika and the versatile rubber sheet Sammie-Jo.

The day after Randy graduated from high school—lordy lord, that was nearly four years ago—Honey had converted to Heritagism and cut him off without so much as a kiss good-bye. "All them things you and me did was wrong, Randy Karl," she'd said. "I'm through bein' the goddamn Whore of Babylon. It was only because of your mother that you was important to me."

Honey had used him and ditched him, and then the same thing had happened again—only this time with a moldie named Parvati. Randy lived with Parvati while he was working for an imipolex fab in Bangalore, India. In the end it came out that Parvati really and truly only wanted him for the imipolex he could give her. There'd been a bad last scene involving poisoning and knife-play; Randy ended up in possession of one of Parvati's buttocks, which had become none other than Willa Jean.

Randy didn't tell anyone that particular story because it was too ludicrous, like so much of his sorry-ass life. From the inside, of course, his life didn't feel funny one bit. Just because most people's lives worked out so goody-goody bone-normal, did that make him a Bozo clown that anyone could take a shot at?

He sighed, staring down at his bright-line alla mesh and tweaking the wing shape of another glider. No way to deny that it was his fault Babs thought he was a fool. First of all, he'd come in loaded on camote on Tuesday morning. He had a painful memory of trying to hump one of those aliens, just like a dog getting on someone's leg. His eyes all rolling back to show their whites. Ow. Since then he'd been too ashamed to talk about the aliens, or even to ask Babs where they'd gone.

And then there'd been the second thing. Tuesday night, before he had any kind of chance to reestablish his credibility, Babs had left for a date—a date!—and in the night he had his godawful recurring nightmare about the snail that followed him everywhere, the snail that would always catch up no matter how fast or how far he ran.

Sitting alone on the bluff, Randy writhed in agony, remembering the raw terror of waking up in the night with everything *not* okay, with the nightmare snail big and real and truly after him, dragging its realware shell through the sad real world, the snail talking like his poor dead mother, its voice loud and clear so that Yoke and Cobb could hear it, could hear all about how the snail wanted to sit on his face so nasty. "Ah'm real hot to crawl on you, Randy Karl."

He was no motherfucker, he didn't deserve this kilp, but try and explain it to Babs after she heard all about it from that little loonie twist Yoke; Yoke laughing her ass off about it every time she brought it up, twenty times so far if it was one.

And this morning Yoke had told that slick Theodore about the snail. Since they were keeping the allas secret, Yoke had to talk all around everything to avoid spilling the beans. She'd made it sound like he had hand-built the monster while he was lifted or sleepwalking or something.

So who was Babs gonna go for, Bozo the hillbilly or Theodore the smooth-talking California scene-maker, always with the right opinions about the right things—shit, the dook even worked at an art gallery, which had to be Babs's perfect wet dream. Theodore had slept over with Babs last night. The guy was already gettin' on her. Randy felt a sick rush of self-loathing. All the twisted, rotten things he'd done over the years—how could any regular woman love him?

Randy set the next glider on fire and watched as it warped and burned, spiraling down into the pounding surf. "That's me," he muttered, and damned if he didn't half feel like jumping off the cliff himself. Get it the hell over with. The way he was, nobody could ever love him. He was better off dead. Randy inched closer to the cliffs edge, watching as some dirt crumbled under his weight. Better off dead? All because of that noisy, plump-cheeked little Babs Mooney? "Come on, Randy boy. *Tat tvam asi.*"

He thought of a better thing to do, reckless enough to slake his death-wish without being sheer suicide. He found the alla-catalog image of his motorcycle, located an image of a full-size glider plane, and mentally attached the titanium-braced imipolex wings of the glider to the bike. He studied the image, adjusted the bends of the wing, and said "Actualize." The alla projected a bright-line wire mesh near the edge of the bluff, then filled it in with Randy's newly designed fly-bike.

The ocean wind beat at the twenty-foot wings, threatening to push the motorcycle-glider over on one side. Randy bulked up some dirt mound supports for the wings and added a rocket-pod to the rear of the bike. And then he took another look at the ocean. The restless waves were gray and cold, utterly heedless of human comfort. It would xoxx to fall in. Fuck death! He didn't have to die; he could change! It wasn't too late yet. There had to be a way. Randy decided to launch the fly-bike in an *unmanned* test-run. Whether or not it worked, it would be easy enough to alla up another, and while he was doing all this he could think about how to make himself more lovable.

So as to properly weight the trial vehicle, Randy alla-made a mannequin of—why not polished madrone wood? That was one of the nicest materials he had seen so far, a fine-grained reddish wood nearly as dense and heavy as flesh. The lustrous madrone figure looked very floatin' sitting on the motorcycle-rocket-glider. Yaaar. Give it green glass eyes and a shit-eating grin. Randy fired up the rocket to launch the combine off the cliff. One of the wings twisted; the bike spun into the cliff and tumbled out of control. Meanwhile the rocket was blasting and—*splash*—the bike punched into the water at easily forty miles per. The crouched wooden rider floated facedown, the waves beating the figure against the rocks.

"That's the old me," laughed Randy, relieved not to be down there. "This boy's startin' up a new leaf." He still had a chance with Babs. He'd stay away from camote, stop fucking moldies, and quit doing deals with sleazebags like Aarbie Kidd. Yaaar. Better straight than dead.

The wrecked motorcycle-glider looked bad down in the ocean, so Randy sent his alla control-mesh down there to surround it. It was stuzzy how you could just wish the mesh out to wherever you wanted it to be.

Once Randy had the mesh around the smashed motorcycle, he had to tweak the mesh, as the smashed-up machine wasn't shaped the same anymore. The alla hookup was intense enough that Randy had a direct sensory feeling for the contents of the mesh; there were some rocks in there, a couple of little fish, lot of mussels—would have been a shame to wipe out all those things. He tightened the mesh in on the busted fly-bike and turned the machinery into water. But he left his wooden man to keep bumbling about in the rocks and surf. The bad Randy. "One more taahm," muttered Randy, and made a new motorcycle with wings. This time, though, he gave it some wing-flexing controls hooked into the handlebars, plus a better rider, one more likely to steer the test vehicle in a helpful way. He actualized an imipolex figure and equipped it with camera-eyes, an uvvy, a rudimentary niobium wire nervous system, and a control patch like he'd given Willa Jean. Like a ventriloquist throwing his voice, Randy put his awareness out into the imipolex rider, looking through its eyes and twitching its limbs and fingers. The more of this he did, the less he felt like dying.

Vooden-vooden, screeched the fly-bike's electric engine, and *kkkroooooow* went the rocket. Out into the air the jury-rigged machine flew. Fully into the virtual personality of his stand-in, Randy felt himself to be riding it. He twitched the wings, adjusted the rocket, gained some altitude, but then—damn!—a gust of wind crimped down a wing and he was flying straight back at the cliff. Frantically he manipulated the wings and—yes!—he was turning, he was going to make it, but—double damn— there was one jutting rock that was just going to catch the tip of his right wing—quick, alla-blast it out of the way!

Randy got the uvvy on the plastic rider to send his alla a direct signal that—*boom*—turned a protruding knee of rock into thin air but—uh-oh!—turning so much rock into air made a shock wave that threw the fly-bike further off balance. The bike rocketed downward. So as to make the cleanup simpler this time, Randy snapped an alla mesh out there and turned the machine and its plastic rider into air just before they crashed into the rocky shore. He was seeing out through the eyes of the rider right up to the instant when it dissolved, which was a very strange feeling. Somehow the experience made him think of that poor moldie Monique whom he'd kidnapped and sent off to her death last fall. "I'm sorry," said Randy out loud.

He'd been a fool too long. It was time to go back and talk to Babs. He'd abandoned any thought of riding a fly-bike. They'd served their purpose now, they'd kept him from killing himself.

He was thirsty again, but when he uvvied into his alla to make another soft drink, a strange thing happened. Instead of producing a control mesh, the alla began talking to him.

"Greetings," said the alla. "Shall I actualize a new Randy Karl Tucker or shall I execute a fresh registration?" As it spoke he felt a series of tingles in his body, as if the alla were checking him out.

"Hey," said Randy, confused. "We already done this before. I *am* Randy Karl Tucker."

"Original user identity is ninety-eight percent confirmed," said the alla, as if not even listening to him. "The Randy Karl Tucker actualization option is withdrawn. For full confirmation and reactivation, we must now execute a fresh registration. Please give a name and thought association for each image." And then it showed Randy the same series of images it had used before to learn his mental software. The first three flicked past: a symmetric circular pattern of colored lights, a crooked forked line, and a uniform patch of rough texture.

Just like the first time, Randy said they were like a mandala he'd seen the first time he got high on camote in Bangalore with Parvati, like a dried up creek-bed out at the London Earl Estates trailer park south of Louisville, and like the skin of a dead moldie he'd seen in a jar at a Heritagist church fair.

After the dizzyingly rapid and thorough quizzing came a series of tingles throughout Randy's body, and then the alla said, "You are registered as my sole user for life. Feel free to select something from my catalog."

And at this point Randy realized what had happened. The complicated hookup through the imipolex dummy had temporarily tricked the alla into the belief that it was the real Randy who'd been alla-converted into air. The alla thought it had killed him.

Once he was dead the alla could either—what had it said?—"actualize a new Randy Karl Tucker" or "execute a fresh registration." Had the first option, so quickly withdrawn, meant that the alla could make a duplicate of him, a second Randy identical in mind and body? That would be floatin'.

"Go ahead and make that copy of me," Randy told the alla, not really thinking through the consequences. His pulse was pounding with excitement. "Make a Randy Karl Tucker Two."

Again there came a series of tingles in Randy's body. "Ninety-nine point nine eight seven confirmation that you are Randy Karl Tucker. Request to actualize multiple instances of yourself is denied."

Oh well. Come to think of it, if there were a Randy II, he'd be competing with Randy for Babs. Theodore was already trouble enough. Still, it would have been nice. Randy had grown up an only child; he'd always wished he had a sibling who understood him.

Just about then another thing about the alla's behavior struck Randy. If he really had been dead and some other guy had picked up the alla, then maybe the alla would have actualized a fresh Randy, but more likely the new guy would have chosen to register the alla to himself.

Randy looked around, suddenly anxious that someone might be watching him. But he was alone at the edge of the bluff. There were a couple of liveboard surfers out in the ocean, but they were quite far away. But what if someone saw him use his alla and became maddened with the lust to own it—what if someone saw this wonderful tool and killed him to take it away?

The alla would offer the murderer a choice like, "Do you want to bring back the sap you just killed, or do you want to enjoy the endless power of this magic wand?" And of course the killer would choose the second option.

The alla would go ahead and register a new "user for life," probably forgetting the old Randy Tucker body and mind pattern entirely.

This meant that once the news of allas and their transferability got out, owning an alla would become seriously hazardous to your health. To his health, and that of Yoke and Babs. There was a slight chance the "new you" option might still save your ass—but someone would have to like you enough to ask for it and, truth be told, it was hard to believe it would really work.

While he was thinking all this, Randy sent out a control mesh to alla-make a plug of sandy yellow rock to fill in the smooth square hole he'd punched out of the cliff. It was starting to get dark. He got onto a new copy of that same motorcycle and rode across the field toward the narrow track of Route 1, his electric motor loudly purring.

When he'd started out this morning he had a vague idea of visiting Aarbie Kidd down in Santa Cruz to look up some fresh hell to raise. But that would have been the vicious, self-destructive old Randy, the same guy who'd been using superleeches to kidnap moldies. And from now on, that Randy was history. He was going to make amends and do right by moldies and people alike. There was no reason to see Aarbie at all. Hell, if Aarbie saw his alla, he might kill him for it—and be able to start using it as his own. No point in him getting killed just when it was time to start a new life! The only place the new Randy wanted to go was back to San Francisco.

Randy tooled along northward, with the winter sun setting off on his left. The thing to do was to go right back to the warehouse and make a serious play for Babs. Tell her that she was the nicest woman he'd ever met. Tell her he was sick of being a heartless crouched-over piece of wood. What would Babs say? It did seem like the girl was kind of sweet on him, at least it had at first. He just had to undo the damage of his camote trip and the realware snail. And, hey, yesterday had been pretty mellow, what with him, Babs, and Yoke making those plastic jellyfish. Maybe if he flat out spilled his heart, Babs would kick out Theodore and let him into her canopy bed.

Which led to a new problem. If it got down to the dirty, would he be able to have sex with a normal girl his age? Fella wouldn't want to come up limp for a dynamo like Babs. That would be a real strike three for Bozo the country clown. Now, if Babs could see her way clear to her and him layin' on a moldie rubber sheet, there'd be much less chance of a problem. And, you know, Babs had said something about not minding the smell of moldies. Her mother Wendy was supposed to be part moldie in some way.

Randy got kind of excited thinking about him and Babs on a Sammie-Jo. Yaaar. Just put some moldie-flesh in the picture and there'd be no doubt about what would occur. Not that he wanted to fall back into his old ways.

He was motoring in through the city now and it was dark. He had an intense desire to get laid. As he rolled into Babs's neighborhood, he saw the lights of the *Anubis* by the side of the road. The great beached ship was alive with glowing moldies and capering revelers. Maybe he should pull on in there and rent some time with a moldie? He'd had quite a session with Isis the other day—but, no, that wasn't the way he wanted to act anymore. With Babs he had, for the very first time, a real chance at a real woman. "Don't lose it, Randy Karl," he said aloud, motoring past the *Anubis* and toward Babs's warehouse.

Just as he pulled into her street, he saw a funny-looking cartoon car go driving by. Babs in her new electric dune buggy. And next to her was that goddamn Theodore. Babs smiled and waved—and kept on driving.

"Babs!" said Randy, reaching out to her with an urgent uvvy call. Not wanting to lose sight of her, he swung his bike through a tight U-turn and began following her.

"Hey, Randy," came Babs's cozy voice on the uvvy. "Where've you been all day?" She turned a corner and drove in toward the city down Third Street. She didn't realize yet that he was right behind her.

"I was cruising the coast. I was gonna see Aarbie Kidd, but I decided not to. I'm gonna change. I feel like I got off on the wrong foot with you, Babs. Are you coming back to the warehouse soon?"

"I'm just giving Theodore a ride to work. He has the evening shift at the Asiz Gallery. What's on your tortured mind?"

"I figured out two things today, Babs. The first thing is about the—the 'toy' I got. I found out that if I die, the 'toy' will either make a copy of me or work just as well for the next person that picks it up."

"Bizarre." A long pause while Babs thought it over. "Good news and bad news, isn't it? But I don't think we should be discussing this on the uvvy." Randy saw her glance into her rearview mirror. "Hey, is that you following me?"

"Right on your sweet tailfeather, baby. Look, I gotta tell you the second thing in person. Pull over, would you?"

"Okay." Babs pulled her funny car over to the curb and hopped out. Theodore stayed in the car, looking anxious and annoyed. Randy parked his motorcycle and held out his arms to Babs. Babs took a few uncertain steps closer and spoke to him without benefit of the uvvy.

"What is it? I hope you're not lifted again, Randy."

"You're—you're not like any gal I ever met, Babs. I didn't realize it at first, but I could really go for you."

Babs blushed, glanced back at Theodore, took another step closer. "Are you serious?" A little smile played across her lips.

"I know I been acting screwed up. But you're the only woman I could care about, Babs. I had me kind of a peculiar childhood. The cheeseball thing—well, I was thinking that your ma's part moldie so maybe it's okay. I mean if you and I was to—I'm just worried I might need some—well, if you wouldn't mind layin' on a moldie rubber sheet is—"

Babs's voice was loud and hurt. "What do you think you're talking about?"

"I'm gettin' ahead of myself, sorry," said Randy. "Just a-thinkin' out loud. Don't sweat the details, right? You and me, Babs, we got a future, huh? It'll work. You're the best gal I ever met. I'm just a-scared I'll blow it."

"Are you all right, Babs?" called Theodore, getting out of the car.

"Yes, yes," said Babs. "Just a second."

"Don't go off with Theodore now, Babs," begged Randy. "We gotta talk some more."

"How did you find out about what your alla does if you die?" whispered Babs. "Is what you said really true?"

"You're going to make me late," said Theodore, walking over. "Hi, Tucker. Seen any giant snails today?"

"Oh, leave Randy alone," said Babs. "Look, Theodore, you just take my car for now. In fact, keep it overnight and show it to Kundry Asiz tomorrow and see if she'll take it for the gallery. I talked to Kundry on the uvvy about it already, and I think she's interested."

"But—"

"Something's come up," said Babs, and gave Theodore a peck on the cheek. "Bye. I'll uvvy you tomorrow."

So Babs got on the back of Randy's motorcycle and rode back to her warehouse with him.

"One thing," she said as they got off the bike. "I am not going to fuck you on any gross moldie sheet. Not that I'm saying I'd fuck you at all. Hi, Cobb."

"Back so soon?" Cobb was slouched in the warehouse doorway, sort of guarding the place. "Yoke was just saying maybe she should go back to the Moon. Talking to her sister made her homesick. Hi, Randy, good to see you. You don't want to go to the Moon yet, do you? There's too much happening down here, don't you think?"

"Yeah, I feel like things are just starting," said Randy. "Hey, come on inside, Cobb, we four oughtta have a little talk. If Yoke can lay off raggin' me."

"Help," hollered Yoke, seeing Randy in the doorway. "The attack of the giant snail!"

"I'm gonna whomp your butt!" shouted Randy, charging after her. He was tired of drag-assing around and being humble. Yoke shrieked and ran, firing off a few hydrogen-oxygen air-bombs in her wake. Randy alla-made a big cushion right in front of Yoke, and she stumbled over it. He stood over her, with Willa Jean loyally at his side. "You've teased me enough, Yoke. I know I done acted like a clown, but I'm gonna be different now. You hear that, Cobb and Babs? I'm gonna be a new man. Worthy of my great-grandpa, and worthy of the woman I love."

"Huh?" said Yoke.

Babs walked over and put her arm around Randy's waist. "I think Randy's cute. So be nice to him."

Randy smiled and kissed Babs's cheek, then went ahead and threw both arms around her to give her a full-body hug. As he hugged her and inhaled her warm fragrance, he realized that, if he ever got her into bed, he wasn't going to be needing any sex-aids.

"Okay," said Babs, worming away. "But now we better talk about the alla thing you mentioned before."

So Randy told the other three about how he'd learned that an alla would freshly re-register itself to whoever next picked it up after its last owner died—although there was supposedly a possibility that it could instead actualize a fresh copy of you.

"So in this fairy tale, the greedy peasant who kills the golden goose gets the goose's powers," said Yoke. "Xoxx it."

"Unless he chooses to actualize a fresh, live instance of the goose," pointed out Babs.

"Me, I've known my share of peasants," said Randy. "Ain't no peasant in the world would ever wish that goose back."

"So either we keep the allas secret forever," said Babs. "Or we get murdered. Or we throw our allas away. Or we figure out how to give one to everyone in the world. Four possibilities. And the first one's impossible. Secrets get out. Especially with the aliens hanging with random cheeseballs and lifters all day long."

"They're on the *Anubis?*" said Randy. "That's where, isn't it? Why didn't anyone tell me?" He was sitting next to Babs; Willa Jean had nestled in between them.

"We assumed that if you knew, you'd instantly run over there to try and fuck Shimmer again," said Cobb. "I, for one, wanted to see my great-grandson's poor bod get a few days rest."

"I—" Randy's voice cracked. "I ain't doin' that no more. Not while I got a chance with Babs."

"How touching," said Yoke in a voice that struggled to stay level. She paused to clear her throat. "Let's think. What Babs said boils down to this. If we don't want to get killed, we either get rid of our allas or we figure out how to give an alla to everyone. I'm for everyone getting an alla. We just have to find out how to tell an alla to make an alla."

"I'm not sure about that," said Babs, absently petting Willa Jean. "People are too stupid. If everyone gets an alla, every square inch of the world will be full of—crap. It's been fun making art with the alla, but I was an artist before I got my alla, and I'll be an artist when it's gone. Maybe I'd rather just throw it away than have idiots use it."

"Well, that's great for you, Miss High and Mighty," said Yoke. "But I'm an artist too. Only there was never an art-form I felt really good at till the alla came along. Does that make me a clumsy peon? I'm not giving up my alla, Babs."

"You're great with your alla, Yoke," said Babs soothingly. "And I didn't mean to sound like I don't think you're an artist. But actually you *could* do art even without the alla, you know. I was just saying that most people aren't artists at all."

"Most people are dumb shits," said Yoke, still feeling feisty. "But if everyone has an alla, then what a fool does is fixable. If one person does something stupid, someone else can undo it."

"Are you sure?" said Babs. She projected a mesh over a potted African violet and turned it into an ugly plastic flower jabbed into a chunk of Styrofoam the shape of a cat. "This is what people will do. Can you fix it?"

"Yeah," said Yoke slowly. "The alla can make plants. Here you go." And a new African violet appeared. "I had the alla give it standard potting soil complete with bacteria, bugs, and worms, though I admit I don't have any way of knowing exactly what was there before."

Babs leaned over the plant examining it. "I'm impressed," she admitted. "I like it. This gives me hope. And you know, come to think of it, I can't bear the thought of losing my alla. I was just scared to admit it before. This could really work." Babs laughed happily. "Yes. I have this image of some dook turning a beautiful woodsy hilltop into a gross puffball McMansion with three stories and forty thousand square feet. And then his greenie neighbor turns the house back into a woodsy hilltop. Back and forth all day long. Maybe the dook would only put up his house at night."

"There'd still be zoning laws in any case," mused Yoke. "That would put some limits on the houses. If the Gimmie could enforce them. And there's a limit to how big a volume the alla can transform at one go. A cube something like forty feet on a side."

"But even so, everyone would build out to the legal max," said Babs. "They'd alla up their giant houses one section at a time. And homeless people would pitch houses for themselves just anywhere, even though they don't own any land. But that's actually good, isn't it? No more homeless."

"Squatters deluxe," mused Randy. "They wouldn't need no plumbing hookups. Use the alla to fill your bathtub, and use it again to make the dirty water go away. Wouldn't be so bad. You could put up a house anywhere. Use the alla to make batteries for any electricity you needed."

"But what kind of kinky kilp would psychos make?" said Babs. "A thousand ton turd in the middle of Union Square! A *statement* turd, you wave? And of course there'd be giant crucifixes everyplace. And just imagine solid, three-dimensional graffiti. You try to open your front door and there's a fifteen-foot solid chrome freestyle 'Yuki 37' in the way." Babs laughed again. "Actually I can't wait to see it."

"People could alla that kilp back into air," said Yoke. "If everyone did it as a matter of course, then cleaning up wouldn't have to be anyone's full-time job. It wouldn't be as hard as picking up litter, you wave. You'd only have to look at something and wish it away. You said turds, crosses, and graffiti? You forgot porno and political ads. Uh-oh, I'm seeing another problem. What if someone allas something that you like into air? Like your new car, Babs—someone could vaporize it because they don't like the way it looks. Just like you'd get rid of a giant turd."

"If she saved a software map of her buggy, she can alla it back whenever she needs it," suggested Randy. "Parkin' is hell in this city anyhow. Just turn your car back into air instead of parkin' it. Long as you got the alla and the software map, you only need to bring back your realware when you actually wanna use it. In the end, the allas should be good for Nature. We won't have to manufacture nothin'. You want paper or lumber, you alla it up, 'stead of cuttin' down a live tree. Alla up oil instead of drilling for it. No more factories!"

"This is making me dizzy," sighed Babs, putting her hands to her head. "It's like a beautiful dream. If only people can—oh, wait, what about nuclear explosions?"

"That could be the biggest problem of all," said Cobb. "It would be easy to alla up a twenty-five-pound ball of plutonium. A supercritical mass. Instant atomic bomb."

"Shit," said Babs. "There's got to be a way out. Will the alla actually make plutonium? Let's check."

Randy, Babs, and Yoke uvvied inward, examining their alla catalogs, and sure enough, plutonium was listed.

"Don't try making any of it," cautioned Cobb. "It's highly poisonous, even in small amounts."

"We have to get the aliens to talk to Om," said Yoke. "To tell Om not to let the allas make nuclear fuel. Uranium, plutonium—no evil heavy metal. Om ought to be able to control what the allas can do. They're all connected to her, you know."

"Yes," said Babs. "And then everyone gets an alla."

"Here we are gettin' all worked up," said Randy. "And we don't know how to copy no alla in the first place.

"The Metamartians do," said Cobb. "Remember, Yoke? Josef said they know how to use the alla to make an alla. We should ask them how to copy the allas and at the same time get them to tell Om to not let allas make uranium or plutonium. Let's go to the *Anubis* now!"

"Have you ever been on the *Anubis* before, Babs?" said Yoke.

"My brother and I went there right before I moved in here," said Babs. "Just to look it over. It seemed kind of sad. Lots of xoxxy people. If we go over there, I think we should have a plan. We're supposed to beg the aliens to tell us how to make an alla with the alla? And to block plutonium?"

"Begging is about all we *can* do," said Yoke. "We can't really threaten them or anything. I mean, they have built-in alla power, and they can see a little way into the future. No way we can hurt them."

"Maybe I can get Siss hot for me," said Cobb. "When Randy and I got onto Kleopatra and Isis the other night, Kleopatra said I was good. I think Siss is kind of interesting."

"Who knows, Babs, if we beg, maybe the Metamartians *will* help us," put in Randy, eager to move the conversation forward. "From what Yoke and Cobb say, Om does plan for everyone to get the alla. And it's not like she's out to destroy the planet. All Om wants is to memorize us each and every one. It's like the allas are the ultimate reward for filling in your questionnaire."

"Do you think you can handle being on the *Anubis,* Randy?" asked Babs. "Without going on another sporehead cheeseball rampage?"

"If you with me, girl," said Randy sticking out his hand. "You all I see. We'll leave Willa Jean here to watch over things."

Phil, February 23-25

Phil spent four days in the powerball—from the Monday when Yoke flew back to San Francisco through the Thursday when things came to a head on the *Anubis.* The first three days went as follows:

Monday

While his dad guzzled wine with Darla and Tempest, Phil pulled himself to the other end of the oak tree. Right near the last branch was the flaw in their hyperspherical space. Things looked funny near the flaw. Goaded on by the inane chatter of the drunk pheezers, Phil got a firm grip on the branch, took a deep breath, and pushed his head out through the hole.

His viewpoint swung about with uncontrollable rapidity, like the view from a video camera left running while it dangles from a wrist-strap. Phil saw an endless landscape of curved pink surfaces—it was a bit like an ant's-eye view of a million-mile tall woman's body, not that the surfaces had the order and symmetry of a human form. Awed and dizzy, he let his eyes follow along six metallic tendrils that led out of the cosmic pink form. The tendrils eventually ran into a great circular expanse of rock and mud that wavered and became a disk of water. When Phil turned his head a bit farther, he saw blinding bright light. Around then, Phil's face began to feel frostbitten and he realized he was desperately out of breath. For one panicked instant he couldn't figure out how to pull back his head—so formless and disorienting was hyperspace. It took a special effort to remember to bend the arm belonging to the hand holding the branch. This quickly brought his gasping head back in through the hole. Anxiously, Phil patted his face, but the skin wasn't frozen, just very cold.

He needed something like a limpware bubbletopper space-suit if he were going to explore out there. But it seemed futile to try and find a human spacesuit in Om's Metamartian alien alla catalog. The "yam-snoot" Tempest had fed him—had that even been food? His mouth felt greasy and nasty.

Phil's eye fell on the Humpty-Dumpty doll, big as a watermelon. It was made of good moldie imipolex and could, in principle, serve as a spacesuit. But would he be able to get it to stretch itself over him? It didn't look very intelligent. Silly Putters weren't exported to Earth from the Moon, so Phil had never actually handled one before. They were said to be poised halfway between DIMs and moldies in intelligence. Supposedly, the famous inventor Willy Taze had developed an algorithm to keep them from unexpectedly tunneling into ungovernable moldie consciousness.

"Come here," he said, beckoning ingratiatingly to the Humpty-Dumpty. The fat egg smiled uncertainly. Phil decided to try uvvying into it. The mind of the Humpty-Dumpty was what one would imagine the mind of a dog to be: a simple, affectless reflection of the passing scene. "Come here," repeated Phil. "I need for you to help me. Come on, Humpty. Come to Phil." Slowly the egg inched closer along the branch.

"Can you wrap me up?" asked Phil, forming a mental image of a man in a bubbletopper. "Can you act like a spacesuit and give me air?"

Humpty-Dumpty's face split in a big smile, and it uvvied back something that sounded like prerecorded ad copy. "Yes, Humpty-Dumpty can act as a spacesuit. Every genuine Corey Rhizome Silly Putter doll is usable as an emergency bubbletopper. It's just another reason why every loonie family should own at least one!"

The egg waddled closer, opened its mouth wide and gently bit onto Phil's arm. And then its plastic flesh liquefied and flowed all over Phil, sealing him up inside a full-body suit. Cheesy-smelling air trickled out of an indentation over Phil's nostrils, and the imipolex over his eyes became a transparent visor.

Grabbing the branch again, Phil stuck his head out into hyperspace for a second time. Again, the first thing he saw was a great expanse of pink—it had to be the body of Om.

In an effort to keep his viewpoint from thrashing about, Phil made every effort to hold perfectly still, even though he was holding onto a drifting tree with a dog and three drunk old people at the tree's other end. Phil tried to compensate for the jiggling by turning his head this way and that, but he couldn't quite put it together. No action seemed to have the expected consequence; it was like trying to do something with his hands while watching them in a mirror. Everything was upside down, backward, and maybe even inside out.

Even so, he was able to get a better look at some of the things he'd seen before. He found that when he unexpectedly lost sight of something, he could wobble his head to scan back and forth to find it. Wobbling had the additional effect of sometimes showing him a series of views that his mind could integrate into a solid whole. Some of the endless pink surfaces were spheres that seamlessly blended together—surely these were views of the hyperspherical powerball finger of Om whose hypersurface enclosed the rest of his body. And the pink curves beyond the spheres? Further sections of Om's body—Phil got the feeling she was astronomical in size.

When Phil glanced down at himself, he discovered a truly gnarly sight. Where he'd expected to see his chest and shoulders, he instead saw a cross section of his body. One part of the image was regularly twitching, and the twitches matched the beating of Phil's pulse, clearly audible in the hush of hyperspace. The twitching thing was his heart. But in this odd view, his heart appeared not as a whole organ, but as a cross section, a muscular ring filled with surging blood.

Next to the heart were cross-sectional views of his flexing lungs, which looked like ovals of fractal broccoli. And arranged outside his innards were layers of muscle inset with circlets of bone—rib sections. The pink curve of the powerball's hypersphere blocked any view of his stomach and its contents.

Now one of the geezers heavily bumped the tree, and Phil completely lost his orientation. The same intense bright light as before glared in his eyes. Phil squinted against it, trying to make out some detail. As he looked into the light, he picked up a sense of serenity and grandeur. Wobbling his head to scan the adjacent environs of hyperspace, he made out a flickering around the light, as if things were swarming into it. What a fine thing it would be to fly ana into the Divine Light.

But now heavy hands grabbed Phil's waist and pulled him back in. It was Da, drunker than before. Phil felt like hitting him. Stupid old man.

"You have to be more careful or you might fall out," Da was saying. "Good thing I thought to check on you."

"I was doing fine," said Phil, pushing the cowl of Humpty-Dumpty off his face. The Silly Putter assumed its duties were over and crawled off, firming itself back into its original form. "Leave me alone, Da," continued Phil. "We'll talk after you sleep."

"I'm tired of sleeping," said old Kurt. "That's when Om always comes for me."

"Just get away," said Phil, and pushed himself off from the tree, floating out into an empty region of the hypersphere. It had been a long day, and he was exhausted. He used Om's invisible alla to make himself a cup of water, and drank it greedily. That lightened the unpleasant load of the yam-snoot in his gut. He closed his eyes and let his limbs go slack, missing Yoke and thinking about the new things he'd seen. Before long he was asleep.

Tuesday

Tempest woke Phil by tapping his mouth with one of her greasy food-spindles. "It's a new day, Junior. Hope you ain't still mad at your Dad. Here's a naahce yam-snoot for your breakfast."

"Xoxx it, Tempest, I can't eat this scuzzy kilp. Show me where in the alla catalog you found it. There's got to be something better." Though Phil was quite hungry, his queasy stomach categorically forbade any further yam-snoot.

"Hyar 'tis," said Tempest, and she uvvied Phil a bookmark into Om's alien alla catalog.

None of the objects near the yam-snoot seemed to be food at all; indeed, Phil soon got the impression that the yam-snoot was in fact a Metamartian cleaning product. "God help me," he sighed.

And the instant he said that, the catalog altered its display to show a veritable buffet table of pleasant, normal-looking breakfast food: fruits, breads, cheeses, and pouches of juice.

"Actualize," said Phil quickly, and the cornucopia of food floated around him and Tempest. "Thank you, Om."

Phil listened for an answer, but he couldn't seem to hear Om while he was awake. The dream conversations with her last night had been intense. Yes, Om had been talking to him most of the night, avidly going over all of the memories and impressions that she could dredge out of his twenty-four years of life. It was like the time he had tried camping out with Kevvie, and she'd stuck a methedrine patch on herself for the hike and then forgotten to take it off. Though unlike Kevvie, Om had wanted him to do most of the talking. Tell me this, tell me that, and when you said that other thing, what exactly did you mean? No wonder he still felt tired.

But the breakfast foods were delicious. Tempest, Darla, Kurt, and Planet the dog joined in. And afterward, when everyone skulked off to relieve themselves, Om turned their waste right into air. Phil could pee, and the stream would just vanish into breezy nothingness a few inches from the tip of his dick.

"No drinking for me today," intoned Da solemnly when they drifted back together. "My son and I have to talk."

"The fourth dimension," said Phil. "It's real."

"That was a good idea of yours to use Humpty-Dumpty for a spacesuit," said Da. "I didn't think of that. I've only grabbed two quick peeks out of the hole so far. It scares me shitless."

"But it's what you've been talking about your whole life," said Phil. "Hyperspace! Some of the things you taught have been coming back to me. I was seeing cross sections of my body, and I saw a whole lot of different spheres that must have been sections of this hypersphere."

Kurt looked uneasy. "I—I don't remember if I brought this up yesterday, but—don't you think it's at least possible that we're dead? That this is an antechamber before we go on into the Light? That's why I can't get too enthused about anything. You know I hate religion, Phil. It's not my bag. I thought that when I died everything would be over. And now it looks like I might end up facing the fucking God of the rednecks."

"The Metamartians say Om is God. So maybe we've already met God. In our dreams. She talked to me all night long. Asking about life on Earth."

"You too, huh?" said Kurt. "In my worst moments I think Om is St. Penis-at-the-Pearly-Gates's assistant, deciding whether or not to send me to Hell. But mostly Om's been picking my brain about mathematics. It was the wowo that got her attention. Advanced as they are, the Metamartians never happened to make this particular model of the Klein bottle. It reminds Om of her—childhood? That's not the right word. Origin, maybe."

"She didn't tell me anything about her origin."

"She says there's a higher-level God that she comes from. And that's the God I'm worried about. He's supposed to be made of Light. I think maybe I saw Him when I peeked out into hyperspace. Light with a capital L."

"I saw that Light for a long time yesterday," said Phil. "There were wonderful vibes coming off it. I'm not scared of God like you, Da. I even pray sometimes."

"You're a better man than me, son. I wish I could be more like you. But I'm too old to change."

"It's never too late."

Kurt put his hands to his head. "What a hangover. So the Light didn't dart over and grab you when you looked at it? Let's go stick our heads out and have a good look around. I'll try using Humpty-Dumpty like you did. If there's any way for us to get back to Earth, it's got to be through that hole."

So Kurt and Phil got hold of Humpty-Dumpty and took turns looking through the flaw in the hypersphere. Kurt finally agreed with Phil that the Divine Light had good vibes.

"It doesn't feel like a judgmental God," allowed Kurt. "It feels like a God of Love. Like the Light cares and wants to help me. Weird."

"I think we get to decide what our God is like," said Phil. "God is so different from us that any of our notions is inadequate. So why not assume God is good and loving? All right, Da, I see your expression, I'm not going to harp on this, I don't want to sound like the usual bullshitting religious pricks. Next topic: Do you have any ideas about that big disk of rock and mud that sometimes looks like water?"

"Those are slices of the Earth," said Kurt. "It's good they're so detailed. That means we're not at a very great hyperspace distance from home."

"Earth!" exclaimed Phil. "Teach me some math, Da. I need a refresher course. Why do Earth and my body look like cross sections? Talk about A Square."

Kurt smiled. He loved to talk about A Square. "All right! So think of A Square on a sphere floating above the plane of Flatland. We're the same, with every dimension one notch higher. We're on a hypersphere floating ana the space *we* come from. A Square's sphere has a little ledge on it, a place where he can slide his eye corner off. That's like Om's flaw. When A Square wags his eye back and forth, what does he see?"

"Weird shit," said Phil.

"Indeed. Let us analyze. When we look at the world, we see little 2D patches on our 2D retina, and we use these to build up a 3D image of a world. A Square sees little 1D patches on his 1D retina—imagine that his retina is a line at the back of his 2D eye—and he uses those to build up a 2D image of a world. But when he's up above Flatland looking down, he doesn't see Flatland as a whole. Instead he sees what's in the particular 2D world of his eye plane. The plane of his eye intersects the plane of

Flatland in a 1D line. A cross section of Flatland. And if the cross-section line intersects some Flatland object, then A Square is seeing the innards of that object. In the same way, the 3D space of your eye intersects the 3D space of our ordinary universe in a 2D plane. And that's why you're seeing slices of innards."

"Whew," said Phil. "It's easier to see it than to talk about it. I saw a cross section of my heart. Did you look down at your chest. Da?"

"I did. Right down into my tired old ticker. And when we look down at Earth, we see cross sections of the Earth. We see these giant disks of dirt or water. It depends where our eye's 3D cross section of 4D hyperspace happens to intersect the 3D Earth in a 2D plane."

"Yaaar," said Phil. "But why is the inside of my heart lit up? You'd think it would be dark in there."

"That must be because there's a four-dimensional light in hyperspace," said Kurt. "From that divine Light we saw."

"The SUN!" exclaimed Phil. "Cobb Anderson talked about it at your funeral. I asked him what it had been like to be dead. The God-Light must be what Cobb called the SUN. Capital S-U-N."

"The SUN," said Kurt. "That's a good name. As long as you understand that the SUN has nothing to do with our regular Sun."

"The SUN's light is inside everything," said Phil slowly. "It's like our world is made of stained-glass pieces with the God-Light shining through. A cathedral window lit by the SUN. How can you be scared, Da?"

"You know," said Kurt after a long pause, "I have this feeling I should fly into the SUN. Maybe if I sacrifice myself, then Om will let you go."

"Oh man, with you getting so wrecked all the time, you don't know what you're talking about anymore," said Phil. "Put that shit away. I'm gonna look at the Earth again. Crawl on me, Humpty-Dumpty."

With his father hanging onto his legs, Phil leaned way out of the flaw in Om's hypersphere. He flopped around until he saw a huge disk of rock and dirt; this time he noticed a glowing region at its distant center. The Earth's core. Now Phil began delicately wobbling his head to make the cross-sectional disk smaller and smaller. Right before it disappeared it became a great lake of water. He moved back the way he'd come, and this time he could see that there were some bumps off on one side of the water, some circles of dirt and—yes!—some angular shapes that must have been the cross sections of buildings. He studied it for ten or fifteen minutes, minutely adjusting his angle and focusing all of his attention down into the squares. There were moments when the image bore a more than passing resemblance to a map of San Francisco. Yoke had said she'd wait for him there. Oh, Yoke.

Da pulled Phil back inside and took another turn with Humpty-

Dumpty. He said he wanted to get a good look at the SUN. After a few minutes he came back inside the hypersphere looking very jangled.

"I do believe it's happy hour," said Kurt. "God, I wish I had some pot."

Sure enough, three minutes later Tempest and Darla floated over with fat reefers burning in their lips.

"Looky what I just found in the catalog!" twanged Tempest. "It's like Om's learnin' herself to make ever'thang we need. This is Heaven, ain't it?"

"Or Hell," said Phil, and pushed himself away.

Wednesday

Phil woke up earlier than the others. He put on Humpty-Dumpty and got to work trying to see San Francisco again. This time he took closer notice of the six metallic tendrils leading kata from Om toward Earth. The tendrils seemed to be in pairs: two were golden, two silvery, and two copper-colored. All six led down toward the grid that seemed to be San Francisco. Was there any chance he might glimpse a slice of Yoke? Phil asked Om for help.

"Can you move us closer, Om?"

There was no audible answer, and Phil expected none. In last night's dream conversations, Om had explained that she was accustomed to talking only to Metamartians, to beings who lived in endless layers of parallel time. Om's utterances were so diffuse that a human needed to be asleep in order to achieve a state of mind subtle enough to hear her voice.

But even though the waking Phil couldn't hear Om's answer, he could see that his request had been noted, for now the grid pattern of San Francisco began to expand. The crazy, shifting angles of the cross-sectional buildings seemed no more than a few thousand yards off. Phil felt sure Yoke was down there. What if he jumped kata toward her? This might work—or it might not. He might end up like an animated sidewalk painting of a man with all his innards on display. Or fall through Earth-space entirely. Or not intersect it at all.

Someone was tugging on his legs. Da. Last night had been way gnarly. Tempest had gone on to find snap and gabba in the ever expanding catalog and then, though Phil managed not to witness it, the maddened Da and Darla had probably fucked. Ironic, that. All Phil and Yoke had managed so far was to kiss and to lie briefly in the same bed. Kid stuff.

This morning Tempest was nodded out on gabba, but Kurt and Darla were wide-awake on snap, very wired, very lifted. Why did people do this to themselves? "I'll do it, Phil," chattered Da. "I'll go into the Light, and Om will be satisfied. Sacrifice Abraham instead of Isaac. And then Om will let you and Darla go back to Earth."

"Calm down, Da." Humpty-Dumpty slid off of Phil, but Phil kept a good hold on the fat egg, lest Da try something rash. Today was going to be xoxxy. This was definitely Hell—or at least that's what these pheezers were making it into.

"He's right," said Darla, her eyes looking glazed and jittery. She was naked again, with Planet at her side. "Kurt and I have been fabbing about it all night. Om must want one of us to jump all the way out of that hole. She's like curious to see what happens. And if Kurt does the deed, then Om will put us back. Why can't you wave it, Phil?"

It occurred to Phil that—duh!—he hadn't yet thought of directly asking Om to return them. So now he tried.

"Dear Om, please put us back on Earth. Please take us back."

Kurt and Darla were quiet for a minute, looking around, but nothing happened.

"I'm going out now," said Kurt, tugging at Humpty-Dumpty.

"Stop it!" said Phil.

"Give it to him!" said Darla, prying at Phil's arms. "It's the only way!"

"You guys are too spun to know what you're talking about," said Phil. "Forget it."

But then Kurt and Darla set upon him in earnest. The excited Planet began wildly barking. It was hard for Phil to fight back, to strike out at his father and at the plump, nude mother of the girl he loved. But he managed to stave them off—until Darla woke Tempest.

"We need to get the Humpty-Dumpty doll," Darla told Tempest after jabbing her into wakefulness. The old cracker woman's eyes were goofball pinpoints of instant rage. "Phil won't give us the doll," hissed Darla. "Work out on him, Tempest." The lean Tempest joined battle with a streetwise savagery.

A minute later Phil's face was bleeding from where Tempest had clawed him, and he was doubled over from being kicked between the legs. And now Darla had managed to bind his wrists with a knotted loop of material from her discarded clothes. Tempest looked like she was ready to beat up on him some more.

"No, we're done now, Tempest," said Darla, shoving the vicious crone away. "We've got the Humpty-Dumpty doll. See? Kurt's putting it on. Time for you to get weightless, Tempest. Take another hit of gabba. That's a girl. Curl up with Planet there, Yaaar, nice furry dog. Wavy dreams, sistah." And then Tempest was asleep again.

"I hope you're all right, Phil," said Darla, dabbing at his wounds. "I didn't viz that Tempest would come at you so giga nasty."

"I'm sorry, son," said Kurt. "And don't worry, I'm not just doing this for you. My life's garbage, has been ever since I left Eve for Willow. I don't want to go back to Earth. They've already had my funeral! I'm moving on. Into the SUN. Can't be any worse than this. And maybe Om really will set you back down."

"Da—"

"And one other thing, Phil. I'm sorry I ever dumped on you for not finishing college. It doesn't matter. You'll do fine, whatever you do. You're a good man. You have heart and soul. And you're every bit as smart as I ever was."

Hearing that made Phil feel wonderful. Like a weight falling from his shoulders. "Thanks, Da." He smiled. "You're good too. Now please take that suit off and tell Darla to let me go."

"Sorry." And with that Kurt pushed himself out through the flaw and disappeared.

"Set me loose, Om!" cried Phil. And the knots around his wrists slipped free. Phil peered into Om's ever-expanding alla catalog, and there, just where he needed it, was a bubbletopper spacesuit. "Actualize," he said, and when Darla snatched the first spacesuit, he made another one. And then he was halfway out the hole in Om's hypersphere, peering out through his imipolex visor to look for his dad.

At first he couldn't find him. He saw a cross section of the Earth, the mountainous pink curves of Om, the six shiny tendrils leading from Om kata toward Earth, and the great SUN ana everything.

And then way out there, silhouetted against the Divine Light, appeared the brave little figure of his father, moving steadily ana.

It would have been nice to end like that, but now something shocking happened. A jagged beaklike form streaked across hyperspace toward his father. Wobbling his head this way and that, Phil could make out a few more sections of the intruder—each view was fierce and angular, like shark jaws, like a heraldic predatory bird. And then the beast struck at his father and ripped him in two.

Phil groaned in agony, as did Darla, who was next to him now, watching as well. Phil had been wondering if he might retrieve his father, but he now knew there could be no restoration. The hyperspace monster tore his father to bits. It was too sad. Da would never make it to the SUN.

But wait—now Phil glimpsed a final resolution. A form like a tattered butterfly lifted out of the torn fragments of Da's body. Gently beating its wings, the gossamer shape continued ana, ever closer to the final Light.

Phil passed the rest of the day grieving, looking through the alien alla catalog, and praying for Om to take him back to Yoke in San Francisco. He avoided Tempest, but he had a pretty good conversation with Darla, who was supertalkative from all the snap. Finally he was tired enough to go to sleep.

Babs, February 26

Babs and Yoke alla-made themselves some nice new outfits for the evening's outing. Yoke made herself a plush green crop-top and black leather pants with elastic along the seams. Babs made herself a form-fitting red dress with a low decolletage, a white cashmere cardigan, and a funny little red flower-bud of a hat.

Outside it had turned cold, and the wind was picking up. Babs, Randy, Yoke, and Cobb picked their way down the street to the *Anubis.*

To Babs's embarrassment, Thutmosis Snooks recognized Randy from thirty feet away. Thutmosis was, as usual, working the street out in front of the *Anubis,* acting as doorman and barker, inchworming his bulk back and forth, flaunting his stylized pharaoh beard and his striped blue and gold headdress.

"Randy Karl Tucker," bellowed the shiny gold moldie. "Got some more money from home? Isis is booked solid tonight, but—you're gonna need your sperm for this, my man—we've got six new moldies, three female and three—"

"Hey, damp it down there, Thutmosis," said Randy. "I ain't into that kilp no more. This here's my lady friend, Babs Mooney."

Babs gritted her teeth, smiled and bowed. "Babs Mooney?" said Thutmosis, peering closer at her. "I'm terrible at recognizing fleshers. Except for the egregious few like our Kentucky Fried Randy Karl Tucker. It's an honor to have you visit us, Ms. Mooney. Give our very best regards to Senator Stahn. I'm going to comp you and your party." He gave Randy a soft shove toward the ship. "That means no charge, country cousin, so go right in. Enjoy yourself. And ah, here's old Cobb again too. Kleopatra's been talking about you, you dog. What a stellar company this is! And, hmmm, last but not least is little Yoke Starr-Mydol, isn't it? The moon-maid. No superleeches tonight, I trust? Where's your friend Phil? His ex recently joined our staff."

Some passersby were hesitating as if wondering whether to come in, so now Thutmosis started in on them. "Yes, noble pilgrims, you've found the good ship *Anubis.* Come aboard! You'll be beamed, steamed, dreamed, reamed, and triple-creamed. We got the biggest, juiciest, gnarliest camote nuggets in town. The toughest moldie dicks and the tenderest moldie janes. Take a walk on the Egyptian side. Are any of you gawking fleshapoid hicks experienced? Wonderful. Guess what, my floatin' friend, we've added six, yes six, moldie staff members! And an amazing new lady performer as well. Hurry on in and you can catch our all-new stage show featuring the meltingly human Kevvie in a uniquely personal encounter with the bird-headed moldie Haresh. This evening's second performance is just starting. Pay once out here, friends, and the rest of the evening is cost-free plus standard gratuities."

"Gratuities like your brain and everything you own," muttered Babs as she and Randy walked up the gangplank, which flowed with a million colored lights. "You're lucky you didn't pick up a thinking cap here Monday night Randy."

"I know all about that," said Randy, pulling something out of his pocket. Two transparent, flexing pieces of plastic, a bit like limpware dental appliances, capable of adjusting themselves to fit. "These are titaniplast nose blockers. I brought the two along so's you could use one too."

"Can't we just avoid getting too intimate with any moldies?" asked Babs. "I hope you're not planning to—"

"All I'm here for is to ask the Metamartians about the allas," said Randy. "Swear to God, Babs. And to show you a good time. But wearin' a nose blocker in this kind o' place is what I'd call a reasonable precaution."

Babs was intrigued by Randy's low-life expertise. They stepped off to a quiet corner of the ship's deck and she let him show her how to put on the nose blocker while Yoke and Cobb watched. You had to half swallow it and then use your tongue and breath to push it up over your dangling throat thingie—over your uvula—and into the back of your nose. And once it was there it settled itself into place. It made your voice sound funny, and for a minute Babs and Randy stood there making honking noises at each other and laughing.

"Hey," interjected Cobb. "I'm going on down below to look for the Metamartians. See you three later."

"Thanks a lot for not bringing *me* a nose blocker!" said Yoke to Randy after Cobb left.

"Like I'm gonna be doin' *you* favors," said Randy. "Little snip. Alla up your own nose blocker, why don'tcha? Ain't nobody watching us."

"Incorrect," said a small, deep voice.

"It's Josef!" exclaimed Babs. "I recognize his voice. That cute little beetle? I don't think you noticed him the other day, Randy. He's one of the aliens. Where are you, Josef?"

"Here," said the beetle, and buzzed down from the ship's rigging to land on Babs's shoulder. "It's safe to use your alla, Yoke, almost everyone else is belowdecks for the performance." So Yoke popped a small glowing mesh into the air and made herself a nose blocker.

"Is that skanky Kevvie really doing a moldie live sex show?" asked Babs.

"That's what Thutmosis meant?" said Yoke in a strangled voice. She'd just put the nose blocker in her mouth.

"This must be Kevvie's new job," said Babs. "I hear she has to move out of Derek and Calla's place by March first. She's hustling to get money for a new room."

"Yes, Kevvie and Haresh have been performing together," confirmed Josef. "But they already did it once this evening, and Haresh is questioning the artistic validity of repeating such an act. We're about to leave the *Anubis* in any case."

"Hell, I think this tub's got a primo buzz to it," said Randy. "Sex and drugs and moldies and aliens. Something waaald about a party boat, even if it is stuck in the mud. Have you ever tried camote, Babs?"

"I did all that in high school," said Babs. "Drugs make me uptight. I try to see God, but I end up in a loop of neurosis. That's just how it is for me. I'm fine with beer, wine, and loud music." She let Josef crawl onto the tip of her finger. "Anyhow, Josef! We want you guys to tell us how to make allas. Because today Randy figured out that when one of us dies, our alla registers itself to the next person who picks it up. Which means, since people are such greedy pigs, that when the secret gets out, we're dead meat."

"Interesting," said Josef, and fell silent for a while. "This had not occurred to me," he said finally. "And I've just uvvied the others, and they hadn't thought of it either. You must realize that death for us is a very minor thing, what with our two-dimensional time and many lives. In your merely one-dimensional time, death is—"

"You gonna tell us how to copy allas or not?" demanded Randy. He swept his hand like someone catching a fly, trying to snatch up Josef, but the prescient beetle eluded him by sliding down Babs's finger at just the right instant.

"Force will get you nowhere, Randy," said Josef from Babs's palm. "It's not our decision as to when you humans can have the power to make an unlimited number of allas. But I'm sure Om will give you the knowledge soon. Om likes for beings to use her allas."

"Who is this Om?" asked Babs. "You guys said 'Praise Om' the other day."

"Om is our god," said Josef. "She follows us around. Now that the Metamartians are on Earth, Om is present."

"Om has something to do with the powerball as well as the alla," added Yoke. "What about Phil, Josef? Can you ask Om how Phil's doing? Or can Om talk to me directly?"

Josef was quiet for a moment. "Om says Phil is fine. And that he'll be back soon. But, no, Om can't easily communicate with humans due to the one-dimensionality of your time."

"Shitfire," exclaimed Randy. "All this bug can do is bitch about our *time?* What kind o' bullshit is that? He's wastin' *our* time, what it is. I say we go downstairs and see the show. I missed it on Monday."

"Wait," said Yoke. "Don't forget that we want Josef to tell Om to prevent allas from making plutonium."

But Josef had already flown off.

Babs, Randy, and Yoke headed across the deck to the companionway. There were a few others grouped here and there on the deck, many of them well into trips on various kinds of drugs. Their faces made Babs think of people sitting on the John. Listening to their bodies.

Down below there was an Egyptian-looking bar decorated with lotus-stem columns, a hieroglyph mural, and an overhanging textured plastic Sphinx head. Hieroglyphs covered the other walls as well, and there was a music mix going, a combination of notes and sound samples. Not all that great, thought Babs. But of course people didn't come here because of any wonderful artistic ambiance—they came for the illicit things they could do. The room reeked of moldies, of corruption and decay.

A Snooks moldie who resembled a partially unwrapped mummy was busy behind the bar, serving up whatever concoctions were requested. Now and then he plucked a camote nugget out of his windings. Randy got beers for himself and Babs, but Yoke didn't want anything. She just wanted to run around looking for the Metamartians. Babs suggested they meet up again inside the big show room.

As she drank her beer Babs noticed that there was a sound-DIM stuck to the side of the bottle, and that when she moved the bottle, a little bit of the music changed. When she wiggled the bottle back and forth, for instance, there was a *skritchy-skritch* sound, and when she moved it up and down there was a loop of black rapper saying, "Yubiwaza!" She played with that for a minute. "Yu-Yu-Yu-Yu-Yubiwaza!" When Babs got her second beer, she kept the first bottle. The second bottle's DIM could trigger a guitar riff—*whang*—and a woman's deep voice saying, "Space cowgirl?" With a bottle in either hand, Babs began tweaking the web of sound. "*Skritch sk-sk-skritch-itch* yu-yu-yubi space cow-ow-ow-*itchy-itch*-owgirl? girl? Wha-whang girl? girl? girl? Whang-a-whang* yubiwaza cowgirl?" Once you were part of it, the music sounded good.

Randy noticed what Babs was doing, and was smilingly-dancing along. And there were three lifters dancing too, doing the flat-footed sporehead newt-dance. One of them was a musician, he had about a hundred sound DIMs stuck all over himself. Each of his gestures made audible trails of tasty media-sampled noise. There were a couple of Egyptian-looking Snooks moldies dancing too, with gracefully undulating arms grown impossibly long.

The people in the booths nearby weren't really into the music, at least not in any obvious way—they were mostly just sitting there sucking on soft bags of juice and wearing that inward look of "When does my lift come on?" or "When do I come down?" A few of them were peaking, and *their* expressions were more like a cartoon image of something missing: a white void with alternating long and short surprise-lines radiating out from a central mystery. Like, "Huh?"

Babs saw one of the dancing Snooks moldies snake her arm down behind a really zoned man. A lump moved up the moldie's arm like a rabbit inside a python. Probably the guy's wallet.

One of the other Snooks moldies had split himself or herself into an archipelago of body segments, shaped like egg-sized two-legged eyeballs carrying swords and shields. There were maybe two dozen of them, a few with wings as well, the eyeballs running all over the room chasing each other, having little sword fights, jumping off of things, and all the while piping their high voices into the sound mix.

In the far corner of the room was a big transparent-walled love-puddle with a bunch of people in it merged together. Hard to be sure how many. Four, five, six? You could see the faint outlines of their limbs through the sides of the merge tank; the limbs were temporarily fused, but there was still a kind of wrinkle where one person started and the other left off.

Right next to the merge tank, some moldies were sitting around a big round table getting high on betty, rubbing each other with ointment from a little jar shaped like a pyramid. The lifted moldies were growing their bodies into really odd forms. It was like they were trying to outdo each other—though none of them was really as good as the fighting eyeballs, who kept running across the betty table as if to playfully hassle them. One of the lifted moldies was made of nothing but long, wagging, spitty-looking tongues; a second was shaped like the Book of Mormon, with Urim and Thummim stones dangling to one side; and a third was a lacy hollow form a bit like wrought-iron lawn furniture. Babs danced closer, studying the lace moldie's pattern, trying to remember it so she could copy it later, but just then a teenage girl vomited on the floor right next to her, spattering chunks of camote all over her shoes.

"Gettin' a little rough," said Randy. "Let's go into the big room, Babs."

They pushed through the sound-canceling imipolex curtains that separated the bar from the big room. It was a vast echoing space, formerly one of the ship's holds, with steel deck and slanting steel walls. Dwarfed in the center of the cavernous volume was a little round stage, lit by an overhead spotlight. Slowly-gyrating at stage left was a pale purple Snooks moldie with a fat stomach and a nose that grew out like a long trumpet. Babs knew him from sight; his name was Ramses. Ramses was fingering his nose horn, playing soft Egyptian music. The note progressions were hypnotic, a whole different world from the bar's chaotic munge. Babs took a few deep breaths and peered around, getting a look at the crowd.

There were no chairs; people and moldies were either standing or sitting on the steel deck. There were maybe a hundred spectators in all—far too small a crowd to make this enormous cold room feel properly inhabited. It was easy to pick out the few moldies in the crowd because they glowed. Of the humans, it looked like there were a lot more men than women. Babs had never known anyone who had even met any woman who was a cheeseball. But men liked to imagine that such women did exist—to imagine, in other words, that some women could be such indiscriminate hump-anything horndogs as men.

Now Babs noticed some objects moving about overhead, repeatedly passing through the spotlight's bright cone like great, bumbling moths. Phil's blimps! He must have given them to the moldies when he left town. Babs knew them well, as Phil had always brought them to their block parties. She pointed out the blimps to Randy, telling him some of their names. "That little one is the Graf Z," she whispered. "And there's Led Zep, and the big fat polka-dotted one is the Uffin' Wowo. And, oh look, its dots are Egyptian cartouche patterns now."

"Pssst!" said Yoke, sidling up out of the darkness. "Most of the Metamartians are in here. See over there? Peg the devil-girl with the proverbial drunk businessman. I asked her if she could help us, but she said the same thing as Josef. 'It's up to Om.' What a bitch. I didn't talk to any of the others yet. See Wubwub over by the wall? With the beautiful woman on his arm? Can you even believe?"

"That's a trannie," whispered Babs. "Look at her hips."

"Oh, too true. And Shimmer and Ptah are sitting together right beside the stage, someone said they were about to perform."

"I don't see Siss or Haresh," said Babs.

"Siss went off with Cobb," said Yoke. "Maybe he can get her to talk? Like if he fucks her?"

"What's Siss look laahk?" interjected Randy.

"Like a snake-woman," said Babs, giving Randy's leg a big pinch. "Bite! Uh-oh, Shimmer and Ptah are going onstage."

Babs had been around moldies for most of her life; she'd been five when her father sponsored the Moldie Citizenship Act of 2038, and there had been a steady stream of grateful moldie visitors ever since. And of course Babs's mother herself was part moldie; that is, Wendy Mooney's personality lived in a moldie Happy Cloak that had a symbiotic relationship with Wendy's human flesh. In the natural course of things, Babs had seen moldies having sex a number of times—moldies weren't modest. It excited her even less than seeing two dogs fucking, which was not at all.

But Shimmer and Ptah certainly did give a spirited performance. They bounced up onto the stage, began embracing each other, and, just for the goof of it, Shimmer pushed her body right through Ptah's, his bronze flesh forming itself back together on the other side of the marble Shimmer. Ptah did the same to Shimmer, and then they corkscrewed themselves together so tightly that they looked like a candy-cane or a barber-pole. To top off the foreplay, Shimmer divided herself up into an archipelago of separate globs, and Ptah juggled her. While continuing to juggle, Ptah began pinching off more and more globs of himself, until all that was left of him was a pair of hands down on the platform of the stage, incredibly keeping some two score white and bronze balls aloft. And then the bronze hands became balls as well. Before the balls could all tumble out of the air, two of the white balls stuck to the ground and formed themselves into hands—and took over the juggling. At each round another white ball stuck to the hands, and the hands grew into arms, into a torso, and finally into all of Shimmer, juggling bronze globs of Ptah, and then Shimmer stepped aside and Ptah's globs somehow sprang together in midair, reassembling the grinning bronze superman all at once.

Even Babs had to applaud for this. But now the inevitable had to happen. Ramses's music took on an urgent, throbbing tone, and Shimmer and Ptah swooned to the ground. They softened their flesh to a near liquid state and pasted their bodies together, opening up their pores enough to exchange wet flows of imipolex that carried along cells of their algae and their fungal mold. The mold nerve magic took over, and they shuddered in a mutual orgasm. A musty, cheesy reek came drifting down from the stage.

Babs peeked over at Randy. His eyes were wide and his mouth was open. Emboldened by her two beers, Babs couldn't resist letting her hand steal over to gauge the state of Randy's excitement.

"Oh yes, Babs," moaned Randy. "Please touch it."

Well, why not? Just for a minute, anyway. She slipped her hand under the waistband of Randy's baggy pants. Hmmm. A girl could definitely do something with this. But no point letting him come. After a few quick caresses, Babs took her hand back out.

"Later!" she whispered. "Can you get me another beer?" Randy hurried off.

"What's up?" said Yoke, who was standing on Babs's other side.

"Never mind," said Babs. "I bet Kevvie's next." Ramses picked up the pace of his music, managing to sound like several instruments at once: drum, oud, tambourine, and flute.

And now, surging out of the darkness behind the stage, there came a big bird-headed moldie carrying a robed woman in his arms.

"Oh puke, it really is Kevvie," said Yoke. "I don't want to see this."

"Hold on," whispered Babs. "I want to see how it starts." After living near Kevvie for a year or so, Babs didn't have much sympathy for her. "We'll leave as soon as it gets too rank. Oh thanks, Randy." He was back with her beer.

Haresh was doing a little Egyptian dance, his arms held out in that funny hieroglyph way. Kevvie sat on a low bed on one side of the stage looking kind of amused. She slid out of her robe with broad, theatrical gestures. And now she put her hand between her legs, supposedly gazing at Haresh as if he were a huge turn-on. She kept losing her focus and zoning out, then suddenly remembering to keep the act up. But now things got serious. Haresh turned toward Kevvie, with a stiff dark penis shape rising from his midsection. Kevvie feigned surprise and placed one hand over the O of her mouth.

"Don't do it, Kevvie," called Babs, but Kevvie went ahead and lay down on her back with her legs wide open. She gave her pelvis an encouraging wriggle.

"Go for it!" shouted a man off to the right.

The Egyptian bird-god took another step toward Kevvie.

"Stop it, Haresh!" shouted Yoke. "You're too good for this!"

At that, Haresh turned his head, peering out at the crowd and spotting them. "I am agreeing entirely, Ms. Yoke," he said, his penis going soft and then disappearing back into the mass of his belly. Ramses's nose horn went limp and his music drooled off into silence. "This show is nonsensical," continued Haresh. "Kevvie and I have already simulated a sex act today. I find it ridiculous to repeat our unnatural congress in search of some unlikely satisfaction. If your shoddy Earth time were properly parallel, then we could have explored every variation within the span of one single act, but—"

"Oh maaan," moaned the frustrated Randy. "Goin' off about our *time* again?"

"Put it to her!" shouted another man. Kevvie had lifted her head up and was looking around. She drew her knees together. More people were yelling. Kevvie sat up and began putting on her robe. "Don't go!" someone else shouted. "You're supposed to fuck the moldie!" Kevvie smiled, shook her head, wrapped the robe around herself and stepped down off the back of the stage. Haresh joined her, and the two walked off into the darkness together, laughing and talking like good friends.

"We'll take an intermission now," said Ramses from the stage, talking loud to drown out the grumbling. The curtains to the bar pulled away, letting in light and music. The spotlight above the stage stayed lit. "And feel free to ask any moldie you see for a date," continued Ramses. "The next round of refreshments is on the house, and meanwhile enjoy the zany antics of our buffoon blimps." The five blimps drifted down to about twenty feet above the stage and began circling around each other like clumsily flocking birds. "I'll have a talk with our performers," promised Ramses. He hopped off the stage and set off after Haresh and Kevvie, just now disappearing through a little door in the hold's far side. Most people began drifting to the bar, and all the Snooks moldies headed in there too.

"Those are Phil's," Babs told Yoke, pointing to the blimps. "Those are the ones he wanted to show you last week."

"Before Kevvie ruined everything," said Yoke. "She's really something, isn't she? What could Haresh possibly find to discuss with her?"

Just then Ramses came flying back out of the door at the far side of the hold. Someone had shoved his head up his ass so far that he looked like a wowo. It took him a minute to get himself unknotted, and when he did, he took off toward the bar, probably looking for support.

"Looks like Haresh is on strike," said Yoke. "We really should talk to him. Or to one of the other Metamartians. We have to get them to tell Om not to allow plutonium." Now the Metamartians were all following Haresh toward the far door—Peg, Wubwub, Shimmer, and Ptah.

"Did Josef say they're leaving tonight?" said Babs. "Maybe they're worried the Snookses are going to hassle them. You're right, Yoke, we should talk to them about plutonium. But maybe first we need another beer." Babs was feeling merry. She gave Randy her biggest smile. "I loved the juggling, Randy."

"You got me in your spell, Babs," said Randy gamely. "How soon we goin' back to your place?"

"If you're not going to talk to the Metamartians, then I will," said Yoke, about to take off after the aliens. But suddenly her face changed. "Look—"

"Oh God," said Babs.

Up above the stage the air was looking oddly warped. And the Uffin' Wowo blimp—good lord, it was swelling up to the size of a refrigerator, the size of an automobile, the size of a house! It wobbled hugely down and then—as in some fabulous stage-magic illusion—the spotted blimp split open to reveal a dog, a thin woman, a plump woman, and—"Phil!"

screamed Yoke, running toward the stage. "Ma!" The air above the stage rippled, and then the space of the room was normal again. The shock of the miracle made Babs feel hollow inside. Or like it had shaken loose some deep part of her. Without really knowing why, she was weeping. Randy seemed equally overcome. He threw his arms around her.

"I love you, Babs," he said into her ear.

"You do?" said Babs. "You do?"

Phil, February 26

Phil woke up late Thursday morning, at peace with the world. Da was dead, yes, but in the end his death seemed to make sense. Phil's dreams last night had included Da. Da was happy. He was inside the SUN, yet still flying toward it, as if the center of the SUN were unreachable. In Phil's dream, the SUN was a point of light inside a cloud of glowing butterflies.

Phil's dream conversations with Om last night had been the best yet. He'd learned to understand the way that Om spoke in glyphs, in concept blocks, expressing many variations of a thought at the same time. He was bursting with new information. Today was going to be a good day.

For once Tempest and Darla seemed sober, and Darla was even dressed—wearing the purple caftan he had made her.

"I dreamed Om said she's putting us back today," said Darla. "Did you dream that too? Tempest can't remember."

Seeing Tempest reminded Phil of what she'd done to his face, but when he felt around his eyes, yesterday's scabs were gone. As well as remembering the dream Darla was asking about, he remembered that in one layer of his dreams Om had been healing him.

"Yes, I did dream Om is going to put us back," Phil answered Darla. "She had us inside her so she could figure out our circuitry—and now she's done. She said from now on she'll just watch people through their allas. She's going to set us back down."

"Anywhere she drops us is faaahn with me," mewed old Tempest. "Why you lookin' at me so funny, Phil?"

"You don't remember trying to claw my eyes out?"

"We—We was fightin' over a doll?" said Tempest, glancing around for Humpty-Dumpty, who was, of course, nowhere to be found. Tempest looked strung-out and querulous. "Young fella like you shouldn't of been pickin' on a naahce ole lady like me."

Phil didn't bother answering that one. "Om said she'd home in on Da's wedding ring," he told Darla. "She likes to have a specific thing to go for."

"Kurt's wedding ring?" said Darla. "He wasn't wearing any in here. You know where it is?"

"I do," said Phil. "It's inside a pet DIM blimp I made. I called it the 'Uffin' Wowo, not that it really is a wowo, it's just a blimp. It's aboard the *Anubis,* which is beached in the mud at San Francisco. A bunch of moldies use the *Anubis* for a nightclub."

"Stuzzy," said Darla. "I've never been to San Francisco. Your father's wedding ring, huh?" She paused for a second. This morning her expression looked composed and intelligent. "You know, Phil, there's something we should fab about, especially since you're such a good friend of Yoke's. It's—the gunjy way I've been acting in here—I mean with your father and everything—Phil, you have to viz that I flat out thought we were dead, so—"

"I can forget it," said Phil.

"Especially don't tell Yoke," said Darla. "She'd flame me. My little darling does have a temper on her. If she found out that when I met her boyfriend I was lifted and naked and—" Darla broke off, laughing. "I'm glad we fabbed about this."

"And you say good things about me to her too," said Phil.

"You *are* good," said Darla. "But, no, I won't praise you to Yoke or it might turn her against you. I've always had to handle that girl with kid gloves. You know how it is. Your dad felt a little the same way with you. He was wonderful. His sacrificing himself like that—I bet that's what turned Om around."

"Where is Kurt?" wondered Tempest. She was sitting on the oak trunk holding Planet and tremulously trying to light a cigarette.

"He jumped out of Om's hole to fly into the SUN yesterday," said Phil flatly. "You helped him."

"Don't blame *me.* Hell with you." Tempest clammed up and looked away, squinting her eyes against her tobacco smoke.

Phil turned back to Darla. "I had so many dreams last night, Darla. I saw Da, and then Om was talking to me about him. She says she didn't urge him to jump at all, that you and Da just found that idea in your own heads. But, yes, in a way, Da jumping really did make Om decide to set us down. It impressed her, and made her feel sorry, and—I don't know—it was such an intense moment that now Om feels like she knows what makes us tick."

"Whiyun we supposed to land?" whined Tempest, hunching over something in her lap.

"I think tonight," said Darla. "It's just coming back to me. Om showed me this previz flash of how we'd come down. Something about a dark room. A stage? And don't you be getting spun again today, Tempest, I see that wine. Give it here, cruster. That's xoxxin' right, I'm pouring it out. Whirl, whirl, whirl, Om's magic rays are turning it into air. We're not gonna come knuckle-walking out of here tonight like Shasta ground sloths, you wave?"

While Darla kept an eye on Tempest, Phil went to peer out of Om's flaw again. Sticking his head out, he remembered something else Om had told him. The flaw was one of Om's "fingernails." A shelf sticking out of the smooth curve of the powerball fingertip that contained them.

Phil looked ana past the vast, curved pink forms of Om's body, visualizing the SUN's bright orb as a cloud of winged souls. Da in there too. Hi, Da. Looking kata, Phil once again studied the three pairs of tendrils running from Om's body kata to the Earth. Two gold-colored, two silvery, two coppery. He and Om had talked about those tendrils in his dreams last night. What Om had said about the tendrils had been esoteric, but Phil had been able to follow it. Having Da say Phil was smart had loosened up Phil's old mental block against mathematics. The tendrils were in pairs because they were loops. Each pair was a loop like the handle of a coffee cup—with Om the cup, and the loop a handle that had been stretched like taffy, stretched all the way kata to touch the space of Earth. The tendrils were "hypercylindrical vortex threads"—like four-dimensional smoke-rings or tornadoes. The big new insight was that where these threads intersected the space of Earth, they looked, to the Earthlings, like cylindrical tubes: one gold, one silver, one copper. And these three tubes were allas: Yoke's gold alla and, according to Om, two additional allas that she'd recently allowed the Metamartians to make. A silver alla for Babs and a copper alla for Randy Karl Tucker. The vortex threads carried energy and information back and forth between Om and the allas.

Most important of all, now that Phil understood what the allas were, he knew how easy it was to split one in two. And with this new knowledge, he was quite sure he could use Yoke's alla to make one of his own—Om willing.

Phil squinted kata toward where the alla-threads met the cross section of Earth. Slowly, slowly, Om was moving them closer. Closer to Yoke. He prayed for their landing to come soon. As he was watching, a new pair of alla-threads appeared, purple ones. Someone else on Earth had just gotten an alla. He wondered who, but the only way to ask Om would be to fall asleep and dream. And he wasn't tired.

Phil had lunch with Darla and Tempest, played with Planet, looked out the flaw some more, showed Darla and Tempest his alien "fishbowl," examined Starshine's old wowo, thought about flying machines, and carved a little on the oak tree with his fuzzy alien pocketknife. The way the knife worked was that its little metal tentacles would pick away at something to carve out the shape you wanted. It didn't have any kind of DIM hookup; you controlled the little feelers by turning the knife this way or that. Phil carved "Yoke" and then started on a bas-relief of her face, as best he could remember. The carving wasn't coming out all that well, but learning to use the knife was a pleasant enough way to pass the time.

And then, finally, there was a *pop* and a dark ball appeared in the midst of their hyperspherical space, off to one side of the oak. Phil pushed off from the oak, drifting toward the black ball. "Come on, Darla," he called. "This is the exit. You too, Tempest. Bring the dog."

The women hauled themselves up the trunk and pushed toward the black sphere as well. Nobody doubted that this was their salvation.

As they entered the dark ball there was a hyperdimensional switcheroo. The space inside the dark ball became their space, and the Om space they'd come from became the inside of a small bright ball behind them.

As they switched spaces, there was a stretching and pulling in Phil's guts again, but he didn't mind. Anything to get back home. Darla and Tempest thumped into him; Tempest was carrying Planet. Phil was worried the women's impact might knock him out of the dark space, but he stayed well within it.

It wasn't completely black in the new space, there was a dim yellow glow, with spots. The bright ball of the space they'd come from was shrinking. Still visible within it were the warped tiny images of the oak tree and Starshine's wowo. Now that they were inside the dark space, it seemed ever brighter, and no longer so round. It was longer than it was wide, and dim yellow with spots on it—

"We're inside my blimp!" exclaimed Phil, and then—*pow*—the spotted blimp burst. Phil clearly heard the *ting* of his father's wedding ring falling to the platform of the stage they landed on, and then Planet started barking. There was a spotlight shining down on them and a few people staring up, very surprised, but where was—

"Phil!" screamed Yoke, running toward the stage. "Ma!"

"Yoke!" Da's wedding ring was right down there by Phil's foot, the ring finally unknotted by this last disturbance of space, and Phil scooped it up before Yoke jumped onto the stage. He hugged her and kissed her, and before Yoke could say much more of anything else, he put the ring on her finger and said, "I want to marry you, Yoke, I never want to lose you again," and Yoke kissed him some more and said, "Yes, yes, me too."

And then Yoke began to hug Darla. There wasn't really anyone for Tempest to hug, but Randy Karl Tucker hugged her anyway. Babs Mooney was right at Randy's side, clinging to his arm; it looked to Phil like they'd grown closer while he'd been gone, which was kind of surprising, though it made sense in a way.

Phil felt into his pocket where he had the fuzzy knife, the black "fishbowl," and the necklace with the big gem. He put the necklace on Yoke for good measure. Yoke was all smiles, squeezed in between Phil and Darla. The gem looked amazing, continually changing between looking like a ruby, an emerald, a diamond, and a sapphire. And Da's gold ring was shining on Yoke's finger. Phil felt like his heart would burst. They were on the stage of the nearly empty show room in the *Anubis,* with most of the few remaining people wandering off to the bar rather than pressing forward with questions; they seemed to think this miraculous appearance had just been some kind of hokey, overblown magic trick.

Cobb came across the dark room from the little door on the far side, his pink skin looking a little rough and blotchy.

"Phil's back!" Babs called to Cobb. "Along with this dog and two women! Yoke's mother."

"I know," said Cobb. "Hi, Darla. Hi, Tempest."

"Kin you flaaah me and Planet down to Tre and Terri's, Cobb?" Tempest wanted to know. "I bet they been worried sick."

"Worried sick that she'll come back," Yoke giggled to Phil.

"I'm gonna stay here, Tempest," said Cobb. "There's, um, too much going on. And frankly I'm a bit lit. I was trying to talk to Siss, but before I knew it I'd rubbed on some betty and started conjugating with her. What a session. I've got to learn to lay off this stuff. Whew. It's too much fun. Hire a Snooks moldie to . . . um . . . take you to Santa Cruz, Tempest. Ask one of those dancers in the bar."

"Ah don't have that kind o' money."

"Here," said Yoke, pulling a big bill out of her purse. "Now scram, Tempest. You can't be the focus. We've got Phil and my mom here, we've got seven Metamartians disguised as moldies, we've—"

"Seven aliens?" cried Tempest. "Kill them!"

"Shut your pie-hole, Tempest," said Cobb. "They're leaving anyway. Go the hell home."

"And don't blab," cautioned Yoke. "No need for the Snookses to get worked up."

"You were so dumb to tell her, Yoke," put in Babs. "She's such a redneck."

"Xoxx all of you," said Tempest, and stomped off, dragging Planet after her.

"You're lifted, Cobb?" said Babs. "How lame. Did you find out how to make an alla? Did you get the message about the plutonium to Om?"

"I'm not really lifted," said Cobb. "Just buzzed. And, yes, I told Siss to tell Om to please not let us make plutonium or uranium. Siss was surprised that we thought instant atomic bombs would be such a big problem. Weird. It's the two-dimensional time thing again. On Metamars it doesn't matter all that much if a city gets blown up; it'll still be around in all the other time lines. But, yeah, she passed the word to Om. Check in your catalog and see if you can still make plutonium. And, um, as far as copying allas goes, Siss told me that Phil already knows how to do it. Is that true, Phil?"

"Yeah," smiled Phil. "Om told me. We can make allas for everyone. Everything's going to change."

"Yes!" exclaimed Yoke.

"And Om really got the message!" exclaimed Babs, who'd been focused inward on her alla. "I just checked, and plutonium is like grayed out in the catalog. Uranium too."

"So maybe I'm not so lame," said Cobb proudly. "More news. The Metamartians are leaving here tonight because, um, the seven of them are planning to make a new baby. It takes them about three months. Sweet Siss is gonna be a mommy."

"They're leaving Earth?" asked Yoke. "We're off the hook?"

"Not quite," said Cobb. "They're not ready to leave Earth entirely. Like I say, they have to finish mating and, um, gestating and all that. And they want to kind of keep an eye on things too. To make sure we aren't ruining everything with the allas. Did I say that they're planning to travel around in a flying saucer?"

"A saucer?" said Phil. "Have they been talking to Kevvie?"

"You hit the nail on the head," said Cobb.

"You're kidding!" said Phil.

"He's not," said Yoke. "Kevvie's been working here on the *Anubis* with the aliens since you left. She and Haresh are—"

"We have been coworkers," said Haresh, suddenly reappearing from the far side of the hold with Kevvie at his side. "Kevvie has been giving me insights into your race's mental archetypes and into the rawer forms of human emotion. Om suggested that we give her an alla to test in practice what such a person might do. I must apologize in advance for what is about to occur. This is a necessary test."

Kevvie was striding along with her head held very high and her lips moving. She was talking to herself and making little gestures with her hands. Phil had seen this mental state before; when Kevvie got really lifted, she turned grandiose as a spoiled child playing Queen—and mean as a killer robot.

"Kevvie's a crazy, skanky slut," snapped Yoke. "Can't you see that, Haresh, you xoxxin' birdbrain?" Yoke said this quite loud. Kevvie heard her.

"The man-hungry little moon-maid has a nasty mouth," said Kevvie regally. Her eyes were unforgiving. "I don't tolerate it. Begone!" She raised her hand as if she held a scepter. And now Phil glimpsed the purple tube of an alla in her hand.

It was over as soon as it started. Phil was turning to get in front of Yoke, Randy was leaning toward Kevvie, Yoke's mouth was opening to say something—but Kevvie's wish was fast as thought. In the same instant when Phil saw Kevvie's alla, a bright-line control mesh had already sprung into tight relief around Yoke's body and—poof—Yoke was gone, transmuted into a puff of air.

Yoke's gold alla clattered to the stage and rolled to one side; it was the only sign of her that remained. Numbly, Phil picked it up. He couldn't wrap his mind around what had just happened. It was impossible. He'd just given Yoke Da's ring. They were going to be married. Everything was—Phil pawed softly at the air that had been Yoke. Could she really be gone?

"See, Phil!" shouted Kevvie. "See!" Randy was trying to wrestle her to the ground.

"Kill her!" screamed Darla, and she, Tempest, and old Cobb moved forward to exact blood-vengeance. But Haresh didn't want any further violence. The alien sent them tumbling across the stage. And then Haresh picked up Kevvie and ran across the great hall, disappearing again through the far door.

"What's the use?" muttered Phil, as Darla tried to muster their forces for further pursuit. "Yoke's gone."

"Siss warned me something bad would happen," said Cobb, his body sagging. "But she said, um, Randy would know how to fix it."

"Where's Yoke's alla?" Randy was yelling, frantically crawling around on the stage. "Did anyone get it?"

"I got it," said Phil listlessly. "It's in my pocket."

"Well, don't despair, old son." Randy's voice cracked with an odd jubilance. He looked around and lowered his voice. "Her alla *remembers* her. Body and mind both. Let's go back to Babs's where it's safe. We'll see if we can't whomp up a new realware Yoke."

"I—I want *my* Yoke," said Phil wretchedly. "I gave her Da's ring."

"Gonna be the *same* Yoke, Phil," said Randy, putting his arm around Phil's shoulder. "That's all we are: information. Come on."

"But we're not just information," murmured Phil brokenly, as Randy led him toward the door to the bar. "There's souls. I saw them in hyperspace. I had so much to tell everyone. Ow!" Ramses Snooks had just slammed into him.

"Where are those new moldies?" Ramses was shouting. He had a phalanx of twenty Snooks moldies behind him. "That old woman said they're aliens!

We have to exterminate them!" He and Isis were carrying serious-looking flamethrowers, and most of the other Snookses were packing O. J. ugly-stick rail-guns, each of them capable of shooting a thousand flechettes per minute. They surged into the ballroom, with Tempest following along, looking bloodthirsty and vindictive.

"They've gone up the back stairs to the deck!" called Kevvie, suddenly appearing from the far door again. "Someone stop them! They mustn't leave without me! I'm—I'm their Queen!"

"Keep goin', gaaahs," Randy murmured to Babs, Cobb, Phil, and Darla. They were already out in the bar. "Don't go after Kevvie. Might just get another of us killed. Only thing we gotta do now is get back to Babs's and fix Yoke before something happens to her alla. Up the stairs and out!"

So Phil stumbled up the stairs with the others. They got up top before the Snookses did, and sure enough, the seven Metamartians were on the deck, standing in a circle holding hands—or *legs* in the case of tiny Josef, who hung suspended between devilish Peg and sinister Siss.

Jostled by a knot of bewildered lifters, Phil was seized with a sudden terror that he'd lost Yoke's alla. He dug out the contents of his pocket. His fuzz-knife, his "fishbowl," and, yes, Yoke's alla. Wubwub happened to look over at Phil just then, and did kind of a double take, as if he was surprised at the stuff in Phil's hands.

But then the Snookses had arrived. At the very last moment before they opened fire on the aliens, the air around the Metamartians flickered, and a silvery disk-shape formed to enclose them. The supersonic flechettes from the rail-guns bounced off the silver disk like hail off a tin roof; the hot tongues from the flamethrowers licked against the disk as harmlessly as water on a stone.

The flying saucer lifted slowly into the sky, gave a twitch and shot off toward the heartland at an incalculable speed. Kevvie stood in the center of the deck, stretching up her arms and screaming that she wanted to come along.

Tempest and her dog got into a Snooks moldie and headed for Santa Cruz.

And Phil and his friends hurried down the gangplank toward Babs's warehouse, not looking back.

CHAPTER SIX

YOKE, BABS, RANDY, YOKE

Yoke, February 26, 2054

"Pig!" is what Yoke had been about to shout—defiant to the last. But the sound never made it to her lips. As soon as Kevvie said "Begone," Yoke felt the alla-mesh tingling on her skin, and the next instant she was air.

There was an uncanny moment of transition when Yoke was still materially alive—her old flesh patterns fleetingly preserved as worming, ionized air. But the currents and charges quickly dissipated, and then every physical remnant of the pattern that had been Yoke Starr-Mydol's body was gone.

I'm dead, thought Yoke. I'm a ghost!

She could sense the people who'd been all around her just now, not that she could see them anymore, but she could feel their presence: her mother, and Babs and Randy, and Phil—had she really said she'd marry him? Kevvie's vibe was out there too. Triumphant.

Yoke convulsed in a spasm of stark hatred. It was disorienting, and when she tried to find Ma and the others again, she couldn't. It was like being blindfolded and feeling around in a china shop with baseball-bat arms, everything getting smashed and falling apart, oh no this was the end—but, wait, what about her alla? Randy had said her alla could remember her, which meant—what? Yoke couldn't seem to think logically, there was dark slush all around her and something was coming for her, something making a sound that wasn't a sound.

Krunk krunk krunk.

It was prying at her—*ow*—scraping at her like she was a stain on a piece of cloth—*krunk krink krunky*—oh this felt bad. And then she was drifting out into some other level, she was out of normal space entirely and—yes!—she could see something bright.

It was a light, a White Light. Yoke was flying gladly toward it. God. There were others flying with her. Yoke flashed a vision of someone driving a car in a snowstorm with the snow-flakes flying into the headlights, not that Yoke had ever seen snow in real life, but now she did see it, she was the driver, tasting coffee in her mouth, and then she was one of the snowflakes, rushing through the cold black toward the car, yet never reaching it, as if the path to the Light were being stretched.

Yoke was a flat little thing endlessly tumbling after the Light. It felt good to do this, she was happy, getting good vibes off that Light but—*zow!*—now something shot past in front of her, a thing like a Bardo demon, gulping down a bunch of the snow-flakes, danger, danger—*zow!*—another one going by with something like a beak, but, oh well, nothing to be done, once you're dead the worst has already happened, right, and once you're born you're in for it too—*zow!*—"Hi, there!"

Yoke kept flying on toward the Light and kind of laughing at the Bardo demons, they made it interesting was all, the demons were woof shuttles for this tapestry, with Yoke and the other souls the world-line warp threads on the White Light loom, it was good and—*zow!!*—why worry, the Light would take care of all things.

And then all of a sudden it was like in a flying dream when your dream self remembers you can't really fly—and you fall, pulled down from the heavens by reality's anchor-rope—

"Aaaaaaaaaaaaaauuugh! Aaaaaaaaaaaaaauuugh! Aaaaaaaaaaaaa-auuugh!"

"It's okay, Yoke!"

"She's back!"

"Oh, Yoke! Dear little Yoke!"

"It's me, darling!"

"Hold her, she's going to fall!"

"Aaaaaaaaaaaaaauuugh! Aaaaaaaaaaaaaauuugh! Huh?"

Yoke could see! She was back in good old three-dimensional space, her mother and her friends all around her, yes, Ma and Phil, Randy and Babs, Cobb squeezing in too, even Planet and stupid Willa Jean, all of them touching her, oh dear life. Yoke slumped to the floor sobbing. There was something hard and rubbery in the back of her throat; she coughed it out; it was the nose blocker.

Half an hour later she felt like her old self again, sitting on Babs's ant-patterned silk couch talking with the others. Phil and Darla sat on either side of her, and Babs and Randy were on another couch. Cobb was flopped down on the floor, his head sticking out of a formless puddle. A huge green brocade fabricant tapestry covered the nearest wall.

"What happened to your foot, Ma?" asked Yoke. "Your little toe is gone."

"It happened when Om's powerball swallowed me on Christmas Eve," said Darla. "I tried kicking my way out."

"Poor Ma. You were in there for a long time. Thank God you're back."

"I don't matter that much, Yoke. I'm old. Thank God *you're* back."

Yoke kept testing her thoughts and looking down at her body, her precious flesh, touching herself, her leg, her stomach, her face, yes, all of her was back, even the same clothes that she'd been wearing—her new stretch leather pants and plush green shirt—and even the gem necklace Phil had given her, as well as his father's gold ring, loose on her finger. She was going to have to think about that one.

"Did you see the SUN?" asked Cobb.

"The White Light," said Yoke. "I saw it." If she looked within herself, she could still see feel the Light. A savor of serenity, a sense that everything was okay.

"I saw it too," said Phil. "When I was peeking out of Om. Da flew into it."

"It had good vibes," added Darla. She was wearing a shapeless dress with purple patterns on it. Not like something she'd normally wear.

"The best vibes ever," said Yoke. "It's wonderful to know that God is real. And then you guys brought me back?"

"Slick as snot on a doorknob," said Randy. "All I did was hold your alla, and it goes, 'Shall I actualize a new Yoke Starr-Mydol or shall I execute a fresh registration?' And I go, 'Yaaar, make me one o' them Yokes.' And then here you come, screamin' your head off."

"It was quite a shock," said Yoke. "I was already in heaven, I guess." The impossibly bright memories were fading. "And now I'm back to—this." Though life was wonderful, it was hard. There were so many things to see and feel and think about. Phil kept putting his hands on her, for one thing, and it was a little bit annoying. Was he serious about that marriage thing?

Babs leaned forward, staring at Phil. "What was that you said before about knowing how to make more allas? Is it really true?"

"It's about time I got an alla!" interjected Cobb. "Fuck this 'humans only' bullshit. Anyway, I *am* human. I'm the same damned information I always was."

"I'm starting to see your point," said Yoke. "Now that I'm made of realware. Stop touching me every second, Phil."

"I want an alla too," said Darla on Yoke's other side. "Just think what I could do to our cubby, Yoke. We could have a swimming pool. Can you really make me one, Phil?"

"Yes, I think I know how to get us as many allas as we want," said Phil. "As long as one of you guys with allas will help."

"Tell me what to do!" said Babs. "It's important that we start handing out allas before people start wanting to take ours away from us."

"Om told me you can split up an alla," said Phil. "You have to understand that an alla is part of a vortex thread. Like the central line down the throat of a whirlpool? Both ends of the alla's thread are connected to Om. The thread is a loop, and the alla is where the loop dips into our space. Just barely skims in. Now, it's hard to create a brand-new vortex thread, but it's easy to split one lengthwise. That's how you make more allas."

"I can split this in two?" said Babs, holding her silvery alla in her palm. "How?"

"You only have to ask," said Phil. "You can't ask an alla to make an alla, but you can ask it to split. A subtle distinction." He sounded oddly professorial.

"I ask it, and it splits in two, and both allas will work?"

"That's what Om told me. The alla-thread divides itself up like strands of yarn coming untwined—and then the split moves ana along the loop back to Om. You end up with two loops of vortex thread and two allas. Or three, or four, or anything up to seven. The most you can split an alla into at once is seven. Om and the Metamartians are big on sevens. One of the allas will still be yours, the same as before, and the others will be blank slates, ready for someone's registration."

"So you understand all about Om now?" asked Randy.

"I've been inside Om for the last four days," said Phil. "Om's the god of the Metamartians. She's a huge, higher-dimensional intelligence."

"Is she like that light Yoke saw?" asked Randy.

"No," said Phil. "Much more concrete. Om reminds me of a giant, pink woman. A woman the size of the solar system. You'd probably try to hump her leg, Randy. Except that she's four-dimensional or, come to think of it, maybe five. That would explain how she could have disjoint hyperspherical fingertips."

"You a math-freak all of a sudden?" snapped Randy, hurt by Phil's dig. "I thought that was just your dad."

"Phil made peace with his father," said Darla. "It was beautiful. I helped them, Yoke."

Yoke glanced sideways at Darla. There was something in her mother's face that made Yoke suspicious. "You met Phil's father, Ma? Was he nice?"

"They got along very well," said Phil quickly. "Try and split your alla now, Babs. I want one too."

"Okay," said Babs. "I'll make one and you three decide who gets it." She clenched her alla in her hand and focused inward on her uvvy. "Split in two," she said.

Though Yoke was staring at Babs's hand, the transformation was hard to follow. There was a moment of fuzziness, a kind of double vision around

Babs's alla, and then there was a second silver tube that passed through Babs's fingers and clattered to the floor.

Phil shot out of the couch and managed to pick it up before Cobb or Darla could, and now he was into his alla registration process. "A face," said Phil, naming the first three images the alla showed him. "A path. Yoke's skin." And then the images were coming too fast for him to talk.

Once again it sounded to Yoke like the alla's series of images were the same ones she'd seen: a disk of colors, a crooked line, and a patch of texture. It was sweet that Phil automatically thought of her skin.

"Show me your alla, Phil," said Babs when Phil's registration was complete. "My alla's paler than it was before, don't you think, guys? And Phil's is the same pale color as mine. Almost platinum. Let's see if mine still works. Here we go." Babs popped a little imipolex DIM dinosaur onto the floor. It capered around in circles like a windup toy, now and then pausing to let out a tiny roar. "*Skronk!*" said Babs, encouraging it. "*Gah-rooont!*" She made three more dinos, each one a different shape. They started fighting with each other. "Collect the whole set!" crowed Babs. "You want my catalog, Phil? It's the one the Metamartians made, but with additions by Randy, Yoke, and me. We've been pooling our designs. Randy's good with DIMs."

"What about an alla for *me?*" said Darla. "Split yours, Yoke."

"I want one for me too," clamored Cobb. Yoke eyed him critically. He didn't seem lifted anymore.

So she uvvied into her alla and said, "Split in three." Simple. There was a momentary vibration in her hand, then a kind of breeze passing through her fingers, and then two pale gold-colored tubes dropped to the floor, ringing like chimes. One rolled over to Cobb. Darla leaned forward and picked up the other one, which was next to her injured foot. Yoke's alla was the same pale gold color as the two new allas.

"Earth," said Darla, doing her registration. "A vein. Cereal."

"The SUN," said Cobb. "A wrinkle. Television."

"Zap me that catalog?" Darla asked Yoke. "I want to get some bitchin' threads like you."

"Here you go, Ma," said Yoke. "Now think about clothes, and the catalog will show them to you. You can customize things too. Where did you get that purple muumuu, anyway? You look guh-roovy."

"Too true," said Darla. "Phil made it for me, poor thing. When he showed up in the powerball I was—um, so yeah, I think I'll make some black leather moon-boots and sparkly gold leggings, and a kicky black skirt and—"

"He saw you naked, Ma? Were you drunk?"

"I was cooped up in there for eight fucking weeks, Yoke," snapped Darla. "A lesser woman would have gone crazy. Now stop grilling me and let me look for my new clothes." She stood up and marched off, holding her alla. She had only the slightest limp from her missing toe.

"You know what I'm going to do?" said Cobb, fondling his alla. "I'm going to invent a bacteria that eats the stink right off the moldies. It's high time. Call it the stinkeater germ. Hey, Darla, I'll come sit with you. You can be the test-sniffer." Darla made a face, but Cobb followed her across the room.

"Good thing Randy didn't hear Cobb's plan," Yoke said to Phil. "Randy likes the way moldies smell right now." Babs and Randy, on the other couch, were deeply engrossed in a personal conversation.

"I'm surprised that your alla remembered the necklace and the ring, Yoke," said Phil, scooting even closer to Yoke and touching the gold band around her finger. "It must update itself all the time. And you got all of your memories back too? You remember right up to the last instant?"

"I remember," said Yoke, bracing herself.

"I meant what I said," said Phil. "I'd like to marry you."

Yoke slipped the ring off her finger. "This is too big for me, you know. And it's your father's."

"But I want you to have it," said Phil. "That is, if—"

"Oh, I don't know, Phil. Yes, I like you very much, but what's the big rush? Don't pressure me. It's all too much for one day. And you keep this ring, I don't want it, it's kind of creepy." She peered down at its inscription. "The writing's still backward."

Phil took the ring and read the engraving. " 'wolliW moɿꟻ Ɉɿuꓘ oT,' " he said. "At least it's unknotted." He pocketed it. "The necklace looks really good on you. You notice how the shape of the gem changes as well as its color? Dynamic Metamartian realware. You'll keep it, won't you?"

"Okay," said Yoke, glancing down. "And now let's stop negotiating. I'm tired. But I'm afraid to go to sleep. Being dead wasn't all sunny and nice, you know. There were bad things too. Things like demons. I'm sure I'm going to dream about them."

While Yoke and Phil were talking, Babs and Randy finished their tête-à-tête and now they were standing up.

"Good night, guys!" sang Babs. "We're going to hit the hay. We'll start handing out allas in the morning." She and Randy disappeared behind a floor-to-ceiling curtain of red and yellow moire silk, presumably to share Babs's canopy bed.

Darla and Cobb were over in the kitchen part of the room chatting. Darla was sipping at a split of champagne and alla-making outfit after outfit, asking Cobb's opinions about each one. Cobb was screwing around with some cryptic biotech machinery that he'd alla-made. Each time Darla would ask Cobb about an outfit, he'd ask her what she thought of the smell of some fresh sample of gene-tailored mold.

"Let's get in bed together?" suggested Phil.

"In here?" said Yoke, rolling her eyes toward her mother.

"We can alla-make ourselves a nest. Like what I used to live in at Calla and Derek's."

"Where Kevvie probably is right now. That pig. What happened to her after she killed me?"

"Haresh kept us from getting to her. But then the aliens took off in a flying saucer. Kevvie wanted them to take her with them, but they didn't. We didn't try to do anything to her yet because we wanted to hurry back here and make a new realware you. We just left her there on the *Anubis*."

Yoke felt a stab of fear. "What if she comes to get me again? Shouldn't you call the Gimmie?"

"Oh, not the Gimmie," sighed Phil. "And then everyone finds out about the allas? I'll do something to Kevvie myself tomorrow morning. Maybe I'll take her alla away. But I don't think we have to worry right now. If I know Kevvie, she's back at Calla and Derek's, trying to snort her way to the bottom of an alla-made mound of gabba. Saint and I'll go over there tomorrow morning and we'll take her alla while she's still passed out. Okay?"

Yoke found Phil's calmness maddening—but it was contagious. "Okay," she said, leaning against him.

"Now let me make us that nest." Phil gazed thoughtfully at the girders supporting the warehouse roof.

"Not up there, Phil. Put it where Ma won't be staring at us. In fact let's put it outside. In the alley."

So they stepped out the warehouse's side door into a deserted, dead-end alley. It was raining. Phil held out his pale gold alla and formed a control mesh in the air. Raindrops fell through the mesh, twinkling in its light. It took Phil a minute to get the structure fully imagined. Finally he said, "Actualize," and a cozy-looking box was resting on the alley's cinders; it was pentagonal like a shingled wren's house, with a big round door on hinges and a triangular window next to the door.

"I had the alla put rubber cushions under it, Yoke, so we don't get cold. See?"

"Don't come a-knockin' if this nest's a-rockin'." Yoke giggled, feeling relaxed for the first time since she'd popped back. "Looks like Babs and me are gonna scooore!" She stuck her head back into the warehouse. "Hey, Ma, good night!"

"You're sleeping outside?"

"Phil made us a little house. You can use my bed. Just for fun I made it a bunk-bed like Joke and I used to have at home. It's in the corner over there. Cobb will show you."

"How cute. Well, good night, dear. What a scare you gave me today. Thank God you survived. I'm going to uvvy Whitey in a few minutes."

"Don't whip him up too much about Kevvie. Just say I'm fine and tell him hi from me. The big news is that *you're* back, Ma. He's going to be so glad."

"I hope so." Darla's face hardened a little. "I might just blow Kevvie's head off tomorrow morning. And as for your father—he better not be with one of his little chippies." She held out her arms. "Give me a kiss."

So Yoke walked across the room and kissed her mother good night, and then went back outside to get into the little nest-house Phil had made them. Phil had put a bed in their nest, and three lit candles for light. They lay there cuddling for a long time, talking a little, and then, finally, they made love.

"That was even nicer than I expected," said Yoke when they were done.

"Me too," said Phil. "I love you, Yoke."

"I love you."

"June wedding?"

"Maybe." Yoke found herself smiling uncontrollably. "We'll see. What's going to happen to everything in the meantime? After everyone gets an alla."

"We're really going to give them to everyone?"

"We were talking about that while you were gone," said Yoke. "If other people can't get allas, they're going to kill us to take ours away."

"Does getting killed matter? If your alla can bring you back?"

"If someone shreds you with like an O. J. ugly-stick, and then your alla asks them if they'd rather actualize a new Phil or register the alla for themselves, they're not going to make a new you."

"And—*myoor!*—I just thought of something," said Phil, running his fingers through his blond hair. "When your alla brought you back, Yoke, it made a realware copy of you just the way you were before you died. And that was fine—since you were in perfect health right up until the instant Kevvie turned you into air. But if I bleed to death from an O. J. ugly-stick attack, then when the alla actualizes a fresh Phil, it's gonna be me lying there all trashed and bleeding to death—and I die all over again."

"Gnarly! It would be torture!"

"Actually, I have a feeling that recorporation only works if it was an alla that killed you in the first place," said Phil. "It's probably a kind of fail-safe feature to keep the allas from becoming a weapon. I think the aliens would have told us if an alla also had the effect of making its owner immortal."

"Why don't you ask Om?" said Yoke. "Didn't you say she'd been talking to you?"

"Yes, I could hear Om when I was inside her, up there in hyperspace. But even there I could only do it when I was dreaming. I don't think I'll be able to hear her at all down here in regular space."

It was raining hard now, and the drops were drumming on their little roof. The window was open a little to let air in, with a red silk curtain over it for privacy. Yoke alla-made herself an orange.

"Want some?" she said, peeling it by the warm candlelight.

"Thanks. This is such fun. I've never been so happy. It was good to see my dad."

"What was that like?"

"He was nice to me," said Phil. "And I told him I was sorry I'd been mean to him. He told me I was smart."

"I knew that already." Yoke smiled and touched Phil's cheek. "Are you going to use your alla to make blimps?"

"I have been thinking about it. I have an idea how to keep blimps from getting pushed around by the wind. People are always looking for new ways to fly. Getting a moldie to carry you isn't that pleasant. I mean, then you have the moldie to deal with. It's like taking a cab instead of driving."

"I don't understand why people don't use DIMs to make big brainless flapping things that aren't moldies. Kind of like Randy's giant snail?"

"The problem is that safely flying a person takes enough mass and enough computational ability that you'd have to give a flapping thing a fairly elaborate mold-based nervous system. And then it would end up turning into a moldie and not being willing to work for you. A blimp's brain can be a lot simpler. My secret is that I'm going to give my blimps a kind of *hair*. But what giant snail of Randy's are you talking about?"

Yoke was expecting to start laughing about Randy again, but her recent contact with the White Light had sapped the meanness right out of her. The story ended up coming across as something pathetic that had happened to a friend.

"Poor Randy," said Phil when she was done. "What a story! If all the snail needed to do was to repeat things and to crawl on him, it could perfectly well be a wad of dumb imipolex with a DIM. Like those little dinosaurs Babs just made. The mind boggles at the kilp that's gonna come down when everyone gets an alla. What was all that talk about plutonium on the *Anubis?*"

"Cobb told Siss to tell Om to not let people make atomic bombs," said

Yoke. "Just in case. We feel like everyone on Earth should get an alla—and there's bound to be someone who would make an atomic bomb on purpose. And even if there weren't, somebody might worry about it so much they'd end up accidentally making an atomic bomb themselves while they were dreaming. Having a really bad dream."

"Isn't there a way to turn off your alla before you go to sleep?" asked Phil.

"You just take off your uvvy," said Yoke.

"Oh, right. Which of course I always do."

"Once I forgot and slept with my uvvy on and people were coming into my dreams. Pervs. Some of them make a point of sleeping with their uvvies on."

"Bad news. Are you tired yet?"

"Almost," said Yoke. "I'm looking at my necklace." She'd set it down next to a candle. The gem was lazily cycling from square ruby to round diamond and back.

"Oh, let me show you the other two things I brought back," said Phil, reaching out to get his pants off the floor. He took out a pearl-handled pocketknife and a black ball with bright spots in it. "The knife has a fuzzy blade, it's pretty nice," continued Phil. "I already carved your name on a tree with it, Yoke."

"Good boy. What's this little ball?"

"I think of it as a fish bowl with luminous tadpoles," said Phil, handing it to her.

"They're more like brine shrimp and flat little jellyfish," said Yoke, peering in. "Funny how they jump around when I look at them. I mean—how can they tell?"

"Alien tech. Who knows? But I like it. I think I'll keep it in my pocket for good luck."

"I know what it is!" exclaimed Yoke after studying the toy a bit longer. "It's an alien star map!"

"Oh, I like that idea," said Phil. "I bet that's why Wubwub seemed interested when he noticed me holding it."

They played with the star map a little longer, and indeed, the bright spots were like stars and galaxies—and once or twice Yoke thought she recognized one of the constellations.

"So far, so good," said Yoke, yawning and handing the star map back to Phil. "We still haven't figured out what's gonna happen next."

"Let's trust God. The Light."

Phil pulled the nice smooth quilt over them, and Yoke fell asleep in his arms, lulled by the patter of the rain.

In the middle of the night something made her wake up. Phil talking on the uvvy. He sounded upset. Yoke woke just as the conversation ended.

"What?" asked Yoke, lighting a candle so she could see. Phil was sitting on the edge of the bed. He looked beautiful, his hooded eyes thoughtful, his strong chin covered with whiskers.

"That was Derek. He found Kevvie in the bathroom. Dead of an OD."

Yoke hated to ask the next question. "Can—Can he bring her back with her alla?"

"Derek didn't say anything about Kevvie's alla offering to recorporate her. It looks like that really only happens if it was an alla that killed you. Kevvie's alla went ahead and registered itself to Derek."

"Are you sad?"

"Yes. But I'm glad you're safe."

Babs, April 1

"Well, I think it's worked out fine," said Babs. "And it's going to get better." She was sitting in the living room of her parents' fine Victorian mansion on Masonic Avenue above Haight Street. Her gray-haired father, Stahn, was lounging in a soft, low armchair, and her mother, Wendy, was doing aerobic exercises with a little set of dumbbells. Wendy's personality lived in a Happy Cloak moldie attached to the neck of her flesh body. Of course the Wendy 'Cloak could have taken off on its own, but, for whatever reason, the 'Cloak was in love with Stahn, and chose to live with him, driving around a blank-brained tank-grown flesh body. The Wendy 'Cloak had in fact gotten herself a new tank-grown flesh bod just before Christmas. Babs was still getting used to having a mother who looked not much older than herself. But that wasn't the issue today. The real issue was the big news that Babs had come to tell her parents. But it would have to wait till they were done talking about allas. The main thing on everyone's mind anymore was allas.

It had been a little over a month since Babs and Yoke had driven around San Francisco distributing allas, telling each person to split their alla into seven and to pass them on with the same instructions. It had worked like a chain letter. After a dozen cycles there were billions of allas, one for every person and moldie on Earth—and that was enough. You couldn't register yourself to more than one alla. Darla had gotten Cobb to ferry her back up to the Moon—so the allas were all over the Moon as well, though news from the Moon was spotty. It was harder and more expensive to uvvy the Moon these days. Many of the sky-ray satellite moldies like Cappy Jane had quit work. Fortunately there were still a handful of moldies interested enough in money to keep a couple of the big communication satellites going. Not that moldies needed to buy imipolex anymore. It was free now, like everything else except real estate and personal services. Things were different everywhere. Real different.

"Sure, there's been some initial problems," said Babs, "but—"

"I think it sucks," said Stahn staring out his window. He was almost sixty now.

"Medical advisory, Da," said Babs. "Your're acting senile."

Wendy tittered, set down her dumbbells and walked over to pat Stahn's head. "Poor curmudgeon. He's upset about our view. We used to be able to see a little bit of the bay."

Looking out the window, the only thing Babs could see now was pieces of other houses, all fresh and pastel in the sun of a mild spring day. It seemed like most of the people in her parents' neighborhood had tacked on extra stories, cupolas, widow's walks, minarets, and sky-decks. Farther up the hill, Babs saw an entire three-story house suddenly appear on what had been a vacant lot. The big house went up in pieces—*pop, pop, pop, pop.*

"There goes another one," said Wendy. "It's like a sped-up movie or something. Some people have been changing their houses every few days. See the big tower across the street on the Joneses' house?"

"The one that blocks your view. What are all those boxes in the Joneses' yard?"

"They keep alla-making themselves new stuff," said Wendy, shaking her head. "Kitchen appliances, furniture, luggage, recreational vehicles, sports equipment, home entertainment consoles, on and on. You can see from the writing on the boxes. They've been doing this nonstop for a month and their house is completely full and they can't figure out where to put everything, but they won't just turn the extra stuff back into air. People are so ridiculous. Speaking of ridiculous," continued Wendy, "yesterday your father went over to their yard and turned their big tower back into air—you would have thought he was drunk, the way he was acting, but it's just the real Stahn coming out. Of course Mr. Jones allaed his tower right back into place again. And then Stahn scuttled home, and Mr. Jones came pounding on our door and told Stahn he'd kill him if it happened again. He was carrying the most amazing gun. At least Stahn didn't zap the tower while one of the Joneses was inside it."

"I wish I had," grumbled Stahn. "And there's no use complaining to the zoning board. They've totally punted. They can't begin to deal. And it's not just the yuppie greedheads that chap my ass, it's the stoner yurts everywhere."

Some homeless freak in the Haight had passed a stuzzy Tibetan hut design on to all his brahs, and now every sidewalk, alley and parking spot in the neighborhood was cluttered with the muffinlike little people-nests. In a hurried emergency session, the city had approved the use of temporary sleeping shelters up to a certain size, with the proviso that the squatters removed their structures between 9 A.M. and 9 P.M. But of course people got attached to their little homes, and most of the yurts were starting to look permanent, with walls ever more bedizened with stick-on alla graffiti. Amazing stuff, really. Babs liked it.

"And more and more people keep showing up," said Stahn. "Nobody has a job anymore, and everyone wants to be in San Francisco. We're being invaded by the fucking scum of the Earth." Given that people could use their allas to make whatever they needed, most factories were going out of business. And the few people who could have kept their jobs were quitting work. You could pretty much live anywhere you wanted.

"That's probably what someone in a big house said when *you* showed up. Da," said Babs. "Maybe you're so uptight because you're off drugs. Not that it isn't wonderful. Are you still going to your N.A. meetings?"

"Yeah, yeah," said Stahn. "The meetings help. More people in the program all the time. The ones that don't OD. Can you imagine junkies with allas?" He chuckled briefly, his mouth spreading in his long, sly grin. "Some of these kids are going through twenty years worth of addiction in three weeks. There's definitely some learning taking place. Do you think that if I asked Mr. Jones to move his tower a little to the left he would?"

"Don't even," said Wendy. "If you care so much about the view, why not put a high deck on *our* house?"

"I don't want to be part of it."

"Why not a tree house?" suggested Babs.

"We don't have any trees except our avocado," said Stahn. "It's only twenty feet high. We'd need more like a *hundred* and twenty feet."

"Then alla up a redwood!"

"A redwood," mused Stahn. "You can make a plant that big?"

"It can be done," said Babs. "Phil figured out that the maximum size of an alla control mesh is four pi meters on each side. About forty feet. I don't know what pi has to do with it, but there it is. You'd have to make your redwood in pieces. That's okay for a house, but it's tricky for a plant. For it to work, you have to make all the pieces at exactly the same time. Otherwise the cells at the seams die off and it doesn't join up and the sections fall apart. I know about this because we put some big palm trees in front of my warehouse."

"Phil—you mean Phil Gottner?" said Wendy, sticking to the personal level. "How are he and that cute little Yoke doing?"

"They're engaged! And—" Babs broke off, still not quite ready to tell her news. She jumped to another topic. "Speaking of building, Yoke and Phil made themselves a nest in my alley. They keep adding to it; it's grown up the side of my warehouse and onto the roof. Like a shelf-fungus. Yoke's busy designing artificial coral and Phil's trying to invent the perfect personal flying machine."

"And what about you and Randy?" pressed Wendy. "Is it true love?" Even though she looked like a twenty-year-old, Wendy still had the personality of a nosy old mom.

Now would have been the moment for Babs to make her announcement, but Da spoke up before she could.

"The other day I talked to the man who was Randy's boss in India," said Stahn. "Sri Ramanujan. He called Randy a 'degenerate bumpkin.'"

"Why do you always have to dump on my boyfriends, Da?" snapped Babs. "Is it a Freudian thing?"

"You of all people can't be prejudiced against someone who likes moldies, Stahn," put in Wendy.

"Sorry, I'm just telling you what Ramanujan said. He's a snothead, a scientist mandarin, I'm not saying I agree with him. If Randy makes you happy, Babs, that's the main thing. I wish you'd let me meet him for myself."

"Why don't you introduce him to us, dear?" asked Wendy. "There's not something you're hiding from us or from him is there? Uvvy Randy to come over right now! He could help us put up Da's redwood. With four of us using our allas at the same time we could get sixteen pi meters, which is, um, 164 feet and 10.95 inches." Wendy's moldie brain could effortlessly crunch any calculation. "We need that much because at least thirty feet are going to get used up by the roots. Three of us wouldn't be enough to make a proper-sized tree. Randy will be happy that we need him."

"Well—I'd like to," said Babs. "It's high time. As a matter of fact Randy and I rode over here together, but he was scared to come in. He's wandering around looking at the Haight. I told him I would uvvy him if it looked like Da could act normal. Can you, Da?"

"Of course I can. I'm sure he's a fine boy. I won't scare him off."

So Babs uvvied Randy and a few minutes later he walked up the front steps. He was pink with self-consciousness and his Adam's apple was bobbing. He was wearing a new T-shirt with an incredibly intricate stippling of colors. Babs thought he looked so cute that she planted a kiss on him when she opened the door.

"Come on in, Randy. Ma, Da, this is Randy. Randy, this is Stahn and Wendy."

"Hey," said Randy, shaking their hands. "It's an honor. I've heard about you two all my life. The Heritagists back in Kentucky are still squawkin' about that Moldie Citizenship Act."

Babs noticed Randy's nostrils flaring as he sampled Wendy's odor. Wendy had successfully infected her Happy Cloak with Cobb's new stinkeater bacteria last week, so the smell was quite mild. But Babs didn't want to tackle the topic of Randy and the smells of moldies. "How were things down on Haight Street today, Randy?" she asked.

"Waaald. Is it always that crowded? Or maybe it's on account of it bein' April Fool's Day. It's like a street festival, people alla-making shit you can't believe."

"I haven't been on Haight Street in weeks," said Stahn. "I always go around the back way. And, yeah, All Fool's Day is very big in the Haight. What did you see?"

"Some of the stores have their windows painted over and you have to pay the owner to get in. Thanks to the individual Web address on each dollar bill, people can't alla up counterfeit, so money's still real anyway. Not that you need it for most things."

"I noticed those stores," said Wendy. "What do you get if you go inside?"

"Well, I paid one fella to find out," said Randy, looking a little embarrassed. "Guess I thought he'd have something pretty racy behind them painted windows. But it was just a goddamn T-shirt store. He lets you pick out a T-shirt you like and then you alla yourself a copy. Can't hardly sell objects no more. All you can do is sell ideas."

"Exactly!" said Babs. "That's what I've been trying to tell Da. Intellectual property is all that matters now. It's wonderful."

"Yeah," said Randy, looking down at his T-shirt, which had subtle patterns like faces embedded in its fractal swirls. "Notice how much detail this shirt's got? I never could have seen it all in time to make a copy just from lookin' at it. The store-guy uvvied me the design. Reason he keeps the store windows covered is some folks will just eyeball one of his shirts and alla-make a half-ass knockoff of it. There was a gaaah right outside the store, matter of fact, who looked me over and made a copy of my new shirt, then turned around and sold it to a tourist. All smudged and blurry, though. Look over here on the sleeve, I just noticed this line o' little elephants. No way the pirated street copy picked that up."

"I think I'm too old for new ideas," sighed Stahn. "Don't want to buy, don't have to sell. What else did you see on Haight Street, Randy?"

"There was some folks in old-time metal armor with imipolex power hinges. Jumpin' around like silver jelly beans. I saw a guy givin' away jeweled Easter eggs, all diamonds and rubies, and when you took one, he'd make it disappear. April fool! Another fella was walking down the sidewalk poppin' out a concrete lawn dwarf every step he took. Skinned my knee on one of those suckers, and allaed a bunch of 'em back into air. Some hairfarmers made themselves a pizza ten feet across and didn't eat but a corner of it, then just left it on the sidewalk so you had to step around it. Wasn't nobody bothering to clean it up, and when I went to turn that one into air, one o' the hairfarmers yelled at me not to waste food. One gaaah was standin' around naked doin' his laundry in the middle of the street; he had a washin' machine hooked to a quantum dot battery and he was usin' his alla to feed the water into it. He was just lettin' the wastewater spill out on the ground. He shoulda alla-made it back into air, but I didn't feel up to hasslin' him. There was a peck of musicians playin' electric guitars hooked to batteries, and a bunch of women doing brain concerts on sheets of imipolex hangin' off the lamp-posts—right confusing, all the noise. One gaaah had a swarm of maybe a hundred dragonfly cameras buzzin' all over gettin' in everyone's face and he was mixing their video so you'd just about go crazy lookin' at the output—it was runnin' on an imipolex billboard he'd pasted to the wall. Lots o' cars and custom motorcycles. One of the choppers had a bathtub for the driver to sit in, and it wasn't just a tub, it was a merge love puddle. Can you imagine drivin' a hog while you're merged? Your eyeballs stickin' up on little stalks?" Randy laughed and shook his head. "I love this city. First place I ever felt normal. The craziest thing I saw in the Haight was two stoners taking turns zapping each other into air. And then recorporatin' the aired-out gaaah from his alla."

"Ow," said Babs. "I wouldn't do that for anything. Yoke said there's a real chance of not being able to come back."

"I hear there's been a lot of people getting 'aired out,' " said Wendy. "And not for fun. People trying to kill each other."

"Yeah, but remember that it hasn't been working," said Babs. "Seems like Om's got it set so that a dead person's alla starts beeping after a day. An alla is indestructible, and someone always finds it. And if it was an alla that killed you, your alla offers to bring you back."

"Like in *The Telltale Heart*," said Stahn. "That Poe viddy where the murdered man's heart under the floorboards is beating so loud that it shakes the room. So what else did you see on Haight Street, Randy?"

"Did I mention that it's crawlin' with moldies down there? It's a good thing they can't reproduce themselves but every six months. Even if the average moldie don't live but two years, that makes three times as many moldies every two years, less somethin' makes 'em cut back. Lord knows I'm the last one to say anything against moldies, but they could run us outta room! They don't hardly smell like nothin' anymore. I can tell you got that new stinkeater bug too, Ms. Mooney."

"Oh, call me Wendy," said Ma. "Yes, Cobb brought some over here before he left with Darla. He said since I'm a public figure, I should be an example. So I went ahead and infected myself with stinkeater. It's not an infection, really, it's more like a symbiosis. I benchmarked my computation rate before and after the stinkeater, and there's an eleven percent enhancement. So I'm telling all the moldies to do it. Stahn likes it and I do too."

"She's moanin', huh?" said Stahn, admiring his wife. "But I'm with you on what you said about too many moldies, Randy. We three were just fabbing about it. Too many people, too many moldies, too much *stuff.* I think the allas suck. Look out there right now. My moron neighbor Jones is up on his roof again. I bet he's planning a second tower for his house. I can't fucking believe it. And see the house right down the hill from him? Used to be a beautiful madrone tree there, and now Ms. Lin has a garage. For what? For her brand-new fucking electric-motor-retrofitted vintage 1956 Rolls-Royce Silver Shadow with twenty-four-karat-gold trim. A garage to protect her car that she made out of air and could replace in one second."

"Don't make yourself sick, Stahn," said Wendy. "Let's go out in our backyard and build the tree. Randy, we were thinking we'd make a redwood with some kind of tree house in it. And we figured out that if each of us alla-makes a section at the same time, the tree can be a hundred and sixty feet long from top branch to bottom root. Come on, we go out this way."

"Maybe it should be two hundred feet," said Stahn when they got outside. He was starting to get excited. "A monster tree. That'll show 'em ." Their yard was maybe fifty feet on a side.

"Let's call Saint," suggested Wendy. "He should be here for our little get-together. With five allas, the tree could be two hundred six feet and 1.69 inches. Call your brother, Babs, I don't want to always be the one to bother him."

Saint answered Babs's uvvy call right away. " 'Sup, sis?" He sounded cheerful and lively.

"I'm over at Ma and Da's with Randy," said Babs.

"Yaaar. Did you tell them yet?"

"There hasn't been a good moment. Da's all uptight about the neighbors. We're going to help him put up a giant redwood."

"Make a sequoia instead." Saint had a contrary streak.

"A big tree," said Babs. "I don't really care what kind, but now Da's fixated on redwood. Anyway, that's what right for this climate. If you were here, there'd be five of us and the tree could be two hundred feet tall instead of a hundred and sixty. What are yon doing anyway?"

When Saint had gotten his alla, he'd quit working at Meta West. Recently he and Phil and Randy had been talking about starting a business. But for now he'd been spending most of his time riding his bicycle and playing uvvy games with friends. And he had a new girlfriend.

"I made a bicycle that I can ride on the water," said Saint. He patched in a view of where he was: out on the bay, near the Golden Gate Bridge. He glanced up at the people-nests encrusting the underside of the bridge, then turned his attention back to the water. There were exceedingly many recreational watercraft around him. Everyone who'd ever wanted a sailboat or DIM board had one now. And you didn't need an expensive dock for your boat—when you finished using it, you just turned it back into air. Saint abruptly veered to avoid a collision. "This is too much fun to stop right now. And I'm supposed to meet Milla later. Whoah, here comes another boat. Just say hi for me. It's enough if Da's tree is a hundred and sixty feet. Tell him not to be so greedy. And to make it a banyan."

" 'Bye, Saint."

"Good luck with Randy and the rents."

"He doesn't want to come," Babs told the others. "He's out bicycling on the bay. And then he's going to see *Milla.*" She stressed the last word as bait for her mother.

"We haven't met Milla yet," complained Ma. "You children are so secretive."

"You two are so hard to talk to," said Babs.

"Let's make the redwood," said Stahn. "I'm stoked."

Babs found a redwood in her alla catalog, and scaled it up to 160 feet, including the big fan of roots at the bottom. She jiggled around four bright-line maximum alla cubes and readjusted the image until everything just fit lengthwise. There was still room to spare on the sides, so Babs enlarged the redwood some more, then lopped off the parts that stuck out. This gave the effect of a really big redwood that had been topped. The trunk was thick all the way up.

"Floatin'!" said Stahn when Babs uvvied everyone the pattern of the tree overlaid with the four alla cubes. But then he paused. "What if it falls over? Then we lose our house as well. We end up with nothing."

"We could alla-make a new house if it came to that," said Wendy. "I've been thinking of all sorts of improvements."

"I want a real house, not a realware house," insisted Stahn.

"But just think," said Wendy teasingly. "If it falls, maybe it'll reach clear across the street and crush the Joneses!"

"Yaaar," said Stahn. "Tree good, house bad."

"It's not going to fall," insisted Babs. "Like I said, Randy and I made a bunch of big palm trees from two pieces each. If two pieces work, so will four. Now, Da, you make the roots and the bottom of the trunk, Ma can make the next piece, Randy will do the piece above that, and I'm going to make the top. Oh, and we better wear earplugs."

They placed themselves in four different corners of the backyard, made themselves earplugs, and carefully aligned their alla control meshes.

"Hold on a minute," said Babs, and privately readjusted the design of her section. "Okay, now I'm set. On three. Let's count together."

"One, two—actualize!" said the four.

Ka-whooomp! The ground beneath their feet shuddered, filling up with the roots. Jones across the street shouted in surprise at the noise. Above them towered 120 feet of fluted trunk, garlanded with swaying branches whose needles shivered in the breeze. But then—

"It's falling!" screamed Stahn, streaking across the yard. "Run!"

From across the street Jones echoed Stahn's shriek. Frantically Babs stared upward, projecting her largest cubical alla control mesh, ready to convert the tumbling behemoth into air before it crushed her. The tree was so big that it was too late to run. But—

The tree wasn't falling.

"April fool," said Stahn, his long smile an icon of utter delight. "Gotcha."

"Phew," said Randy, with a loose grin. "What a lift."

"Zerk," said Wendy, poking Stahn. "We're not always this hard to be around, Randy."

"Hey, I'm havin' a good taaahm. But what are those holes up in the top?"

Stahn glanced up, worried. "Don't tell me there's something—"

"I put a room inside it," said Babs. "Just like in that book we read when I was little. I put a nice room with a door and three windows. And a deck."

"*The Little Fur Family,*" remembered Wendy. "How sweet."

"Is it strong enough, hollowed out like that?" wondered Stahn.

"Sure," said Babs. "Redwoods have hollow spots in them all the time."

"How do we get up there?" was Stahn's next question.

"Anemone boots and Spider-Man gloves," said Randy, quick as a flash. "Me and Babs found 'em when we wanted to climb our palm trees. I'll show you in the alla catalog. They used to be made by a company named

Modern Rocks out to Colorado. Guess they outta business now—like all the other folks with goodies in the alla catalogs."

Stahn alla-made himself a set of the bulbous yellow plastic boots and gloves. "Stuzzadelic! I never would have bought them."

"See, he's finally getting the picture," said Babs. "With an alla you get all the wavy stuff you'd never buy. And then you turn it back into air. Consumerism isn't wasteful anymore." She and Randy made themselves Spider-Man gloves and anemone boots as well. "I'll go first. Watch how I do it, Da." Babs stared at the first branch she wanted to get to, then spread the fingers of her right hand. Her Spider-Man glove shot out a thick, sticky rope of imipolex—a bit like a frog's tongue. The glove had a DIM linking it to Babs's uvvy, and it knew to shoot its tongue at whatever Babs was staring at. Now Babs relaxed her fingers. This gesture told the strand of imipolex to slowly contract, pulling her up. Meanwhile the toes of her anemone boots had split into a zillion pseudopods that walked their way along the bark like the legs of a millipede, preventing too much strain on Babs's arm, as well as ruling out any chance of her being yanked around uncontrollably. Babs smiled down from the first branch, securely anchored by her anemone boots. "Come on, Da, it's easy."

"I'm supposed to do this every time I want to visit my lookout?"

"You can figure out an easier way if you like. That's the fun of having an alla. It lets you try all sorts of new things, and if something doesn't work, you get rid of it."

"Or you pile it in your yard like the Joneses."

"Sooner or later they'll realize they don't have to hoard. Matter doesn't matter anymore."

Stahn shot up a tongue of imipolex with each hand, and gingerly hauled his way up to stand beside her. "This is easier than it looks. Thanks, Babs."

Now Randy climbed up to join them. Babs took off fast, closely followed by Randy, the two of them scampering up the tree like a pair of squirrels. *Splat* kick kick, *splat* kick kick. What fun! Babs could see Stahn far below them, creeping along. And Wendy? There she was, swooping around the tree like a sea gull. She'd unfurled her Happy Cloak into a huge set of wings. She reached the top before Babs and Randy.

"Oh, this is beautiful," she called down. "There's a cute, round room."

The trunk was about ten feet across up here. The room was carved right into the living heartwood of the tree, with two polished bucket seats, three little porthole windows, and an arched door. The widest part of the floor was maybe five feet across. A plump burl of the redwood bulged out to make a deck in front of the door, with four more seats carved into it. Once they were all up top, they tried out everything, and then Ma and Da sat on the deck, while Babs and Randy sat cozily in the little room.

"This view kicks ass!" exulted Stahn. "I can see the whole city and both bridges! I can even see the Farallon Islands!" He leaned over, chuckling with satisfaction. "Jones looks like a bewildered gopher. Should I give him the finger? Alla down a bucket of piss?"

"Don't goad him," said Wendy. "He might turn us all into air. That's been happening quite a bit, you know. I hear there's been too many killings for the Gimmie to even keep track of. And not everyone's been able to get recorporated."

Stahn winced at the thought. "You're right. I have to be nice to Jones. Maybe I could convince him to replace his tower with a tree. This is where it's at, no lie. Is it stuzzy in that room, Babs?"

"You want to trade places?"

"No no, the cozy nook should be for the lovers. Ma and I can try it when you're gone. Hey, Wendy, can you viz letting me bone you up here? Tarzan and Jane. But our feet would stick out of the door."

"You could alla-carve bigger rooms lower down in the tree," said Babs equably. She was accustomed to her father's gaucherie. Maybe that was why she was so comfortable with Randy. Babs patted Randy's hand, and he smiled at her. The redwood room had a nice, fresh fragrance. Tendrils of late afternoon fog were drifting by.

"We could live in a tree like this, Babs," murmured Randy. "Maybe we oughta put one up by your warehouse. Or once I get my consulting business goin' I can buy us some land down in the Santa Cruz Mountains and we can live in a tree out there."

"What kind of consulting do you want to do, Randy?" asked Wendy. Her hearing was preternaturally sharp.

"Nose much, Ma?" said Babs, implicitly daring her mother to ask the question that was really on her mind.

"And you're planning to live together? That's nice . . . " Wendy's voice trailed off, begging for more information.

"We're engaged," said Babs, finally springing her news. "We're going to have a double wedding with Yoke and Phil on the first of June."

Randy, May 1

To Randy's relief—and slight surprise—Babs's parents gave his marriage proposal their blessing. He settled in at Babs's, waiting for the big day and working on some projects with the others. It seemed important to try and do good things with the allas, all the more so because the world news was bad. Savage conventional wars had broken out in Africa, Central America, Quebec, and the Balkans. There was sporadic gang fighting in parts of the U.S. too, mostly near Boston, Dallas, Atlanta, and Los Angeles. Needless to say, there were almost no women doing it, and the moldies were staying pretty well out of the fray as well. It was just men fighting men. Everyone had all the food and shelter they wanted, so there was no logical reason to fight—but men were doing it anyway, using all the great new weapons they could alla up for themselves.

It turned out that Phil was right—the allas wouldn't undo the ordinary kinds of deaths. If someone shot you or blew you up, your alla wouldn't save you. The alla recorporation feature was indeed designed only to undo any killings that had been done by an alla itself. Even so, there were men who used the allas to make themselves weapons so they could beat and rape and torture and kill at will, growing more cruel and brutal every day. The killers were killing each other off, but still there seemed to be no shortage of them. And the innocent were dying as well. The only thing keeping the wars down was that the Metamartians' flying saucer kept appearing at the goriest battle scenes. First the saucer would call for peace, and then it would beam down rays to destroy everyone's weapons, and if the men still kept on fighting, the saucer would incinerate them. But the Metamartians couldn't be everywhere.

Babs was in a frantically creative mode, as if trying to prove it hadn't been a mistake to distribute the allas. In mid-April, Theodore helped her put on a show at the Asiz Gallery. Theodore was being a good sport about losing Babs, which surprised Randy, who kept expecting some Kentucky-style sneak attack from the guy: a stolen vehicle, a midnight beating, an arson fire, a tip-off to the Gimmie. But it never came. Instead Theodore got Babs gallery space and wrote a great little catalog for her. Randy was unable to comprehend such behavior.

Babs's show was called "Realware Worms," and it featured twenty of her worm-farms. Some were the ones she'd been making before she got the alla: mazes of plastic tubing filled with soil and a mixture of real and imipolex DIM worms. Just to play with the categories a little, Babs had also made some new versions of these, using alla-made realware biological worms in place of "wild" biological worms. In addition, she'd alla-made a half-dozen large transparent shapes filled solid with writhing DIM worms. There were cubes of plastic worms, some big doughnut shapes, and even a mounting, squiggly spiral like a moonshiner's "worm coil" condenser. That last one had been Randy's suggestion, he was proud to say. To fill out the show, Babs hung a lot of her lace on the walls and alla-made seven variations on her cartoonlike dune buggy, giving them hard "kandy kolors" that marched up the spectrum: red, orange, yellow, green, blue, indigo, violet. Babs put smiling worm logos on the car doors so they'd fit the show's theme, and parked the "worm buggies" in a cutely angled row on the sidewalk outside the Asiz.

The title of the show was a good idea, as everyone was still in the process of trying to assimilate what "Realware" might mean. There was a big crowd on opening night—the guests all decked out in freaky S.F. outfits like never before seen—but the sales were disastrously weak. The potential customers seemed to want to go home and make their own copies of Babs's works with their allas. In fact, one woman with a beehive hairdo and a skirt made of dangling transparent dildos stood out on the sidewalk staring really hard at one of the worm-buggies for half an hour and then—*whoosh*—used her alla to make her own version, using the same base-model Metamartian alla catalog dune buggy that Babs had used. The art on the knockoff worm buggy wasn't quite the same, for it came out of the dildo-skirted woman's head and not Babs's, but it seemed to suit her well enough, and maybe better. She hopped in her new car and drove off, with Randy running after her down the street shouting empty threats.

The situation with the lace was a bit different. The decorations of the worm-buggies were big and easy to mentally represent, but the lace simply had too much pattern, produced as it was by colonies of interacting DIM-based fabricants. No casual gallery-goer would be able to mentally specify the twists and turns of all the lace knots for his or her alla. Even so, Randy did catch a tipsy man in orange leather leaving the gallery wearing a mantilla of crude knockoff lace on his shoulders. Rather than being knotted, the copied lace's threads were simply fused at the crossings. And the overall pattern repeated itself every four inches, instead of subtly varying all along the mantilla's length.

The plastic worms were the least susceptible to copying, as it was their living behavior that made them art. Their flocking, their wriggling, their subtly oscillating hues—all of these were based on limpware DIM designs that Babs had invented for them with Randy's help. And there was no way to "see" these microscopic code designs just by looking at the worms. Yet everyone was in such a do-it-yourself frenzy with their allas that they seemed to overlook this fact.

The sole person to offer to purchase one of Babs's works was a sleek banker named Chock Fresser. Fresser wanted to acquire the show's centerpiece: a twelve-foot transparent pretzel filled with imipolex worms in a thousand different shades of blue and green; it was called "Wowo Worms."

But Fresser didn't want to take delivery on the physical item; he wanted Babs to uvvy him a copy of the software design so he could alla-make the work in situ at his house. "Too much trouble to ship it home," said Fresser. "Packing, unpacking—who needs it anymore? Give me the code and that way I can bring 'Wowo Worms' in and out of storage as needed."

The gallery owner, Kundry Asiz, was a good friend of Babs's from high school. When Babs suggested to her that they shouldn't sell the code to Fresser since money didn't matter anymore, Kundry pointed out that, yes, there was a sense in which money didn't matter anymore, but there were still several senses in which it did—first of all, it was crass human nature for people to give more attention and respect to art they had to pay for, and secondly, the rent on a space like the Asiz Gallery was something the alla couldn't finagle them out of.

So Babs agreed, and Fresser walked off with the complete code for the "Wowo Worms." And a week later, tacky little desktop copies of it were for sale in every gift shop on Fisherman's Wharf—with nary an attribution to Babs. Kundry put some heavy pressure on Fresser and got him to triple the original purchase price, but it wasn't a fully satisfying resolution.

"We gotta figure out a way to sell a design for onetime use only," said Randy. He and Babs were sitting on the ant-decorated couch in Babs's warehouse. Babs's brother Saint was there too. It was the first of May.

"Use a one-time encryption zip," said Saint. "I learned about that stuff when I was working for Meta West. You can zip your design and send the zipped version to the user with an unzipper that trashes itself after its first use. Like cheap pants. The first time you open the fly, the zipper sticks for good. You can publish the image of your work in the alla catalog, and when somebody orders it, they get a single zip of the design with its own unzipper. And of course the unzipper is tailored only to feed the information into an alla and not into any kind of a storage device."

"I get it," said Babs. "I could make an art catalog that's like a catalog used to be. There's just images of things, and you have to uvvy in some funds to take delivery on an item. And if you want another one, you have to pay again. That's a brilliant idea, Saint. I wish I'd known about that before."

"Live and learn, sis," said Saint. "Just think about the poor companies that had every one of their products put into the Metamartian alla catalog."

"Like Modern Rocks," said Randy. He liked his Spider-Man gloves and anemone boots so much that he'd looked into the fate of their manufacturer. "I found out they really did go down the tubes. The Metamartians didn't leave no holes. Whatever the aliens put in that catalog is there one hundred percent, the whole design coded up in nanotech blueprints.

Those Metamartians did their homework. Now, this trick of yours, Saint, is everyone gonna know about it? It would be good to spread it around, so's artists and inventors can get some kind of reward."

"Maybe I should *sell* my trick," said Saint. "Call it the One-Zip. If I can actually figure out the details. I'm not really that much of a programmer. But you two sure went for it. Yeah, I need someone to help me productize."

"Why is everyone always talking about buying and selling these days?" said Yoke impatiently. She'd just walked in. "You sound like a bunch of businessman numberskulls. Guys with calculator DIMs in their heads. Phil's the worst of all. Going on and on about selling his blimps. Money lags! What does anyone need xoxxin' money for anyway? And meanwhile people are killing each other for fun." Without waiting for a response, Yoke stalked across the room to study the pair of huge aquariums she'd installed. One contained a realware South Pacific reef with hard and soft corals. The biologicals were all alla-made realware: primarily coral polyps and the diatoms they fed upon. The other tank held Yoke's work-in-progress, a colony of miniaturized limpware polyps that were supposed to build an artificial reef. Yoke's polyps weren't doing so well today. When he'd gotten up this morning. Randy had noticed that Yoke's artificial reef had petered out into ugly little crumbly excrescences, not at all like the smooth, branching staghorn shapes she was shooting for.

"Xoxx it," said Yoke, staring into her tanks. "This is the only thing I'm able to try and control—and it's too hard. You have to help me tweak them some more, Randy."

"How's Phil's blimp doin'?" Randy asked Yoke.

"Oh, he's got it spread out on the roof," said Yoke, wandering over and alla-making herself a cup of coffee. "It's slowly getting better. The Phlyte Blimp. Can you hear the trademark? What is it about Phil and money all of a sudden, Randy?"

"Phil wants to make a mark on the world," said Randy. Looking into himself, Randy realized that he didn't share that ambition. He saw his role as a background guy, not a foreground guy. A consultant. Someone who helped people make connections and do things. He was happy to help Babs with her worms, Phil with his flying machines, Yoke with her reefs, and maybe Saint with his One-Zip realware alla code encryption. But he wasn't into power-driving. Hell, he was just happy to have a shot at a normal life. If only the world would let him. "For some people money's a way to keep score," he said mildly. "Practically all it's good for anymore."

"Don't forget real estate," said Babs. "Yoke and Phil need money if they ever want a place of their own. Not that I mind having you guys squatting on my wall and my roof. But you know, eventually—"

"We can leave anytime you want us to," said Yoke, getting prickly. "There's plenty of free land on the Moon. Or Mars. Or the asteroids. We'd be safer from the fighting anyway."

"I don't see you wantin' to go back into space," said Randy. "No more than I want to go in the first place. Earth's where it's at. And, look, with the allas we don't need to waste land on farms no more. That frees up a lot of cheap acreage. Or, hell, you can get an acre up on the side of some mountain any old where. With an alla you don't need power or plumbing or a place to shop. Everyone can be happy, everyone can have a nice place to live."

"So why do people keep killing each other?" wondered Babs. "Just for the rush? Thank God things are still calm in San Francisco."

"I hear things are getting really tense in Oakland," said Saint. "I'm starting to wonder if giving out the allas was such a good idea."

"If we ever get to talk to the Metamartians again, maybe we should ask them to get rid of the allas?" said Randy. "Hard to decide. Hey, did I tell you that my father's flying back down inside of Cobb? Comin' early for the wedding. He should get here today."

"I wish Darla had stayed," said Yoke, looking sad. "As soon as she talked to Whitey, she got all homesick and made Cobb fly her right up to the Moon. I think she wanted to make double sure that they didn't finish growing that new Darla clone to replace her. So, fine, now they're all together up there, but what good does that do me? I want my parents and my sister! They should be the ones coming back with Cobb, not Willy. Whitey says I should come get married on the Moon. He thinks it's getting too dangerous down here. But Phil's totally into having the wedding with his family and you guys. Xoxx it. A wedding's hard enough, so why in God's name are we doing two at once?"

"Don't look at me," said Randy. "It was you and Babs decided to make it a double. It was like you gals thought gettin' married to Phil and me was such a crazy stunt, why not push it right out to the edge. Like a viddy soap finale or somethin'."

"I know," sighed Yoke. "I can remember the mood, but I can't get myself back into it. Babs and I were so giggly that night. We'd released the allas to the public and it was going to be paradise. And now there's war everywhere. Even Phil and I had a big fight just a minute ago. Not that there's any comparison."

"Poor Yoke," said Babs. "Fight about what?"

"It's Phil's mother, Eve," said Yoke, frowning. "Maybe you already know about this, Babs. Eve got this idea that we shouldn't have the ceremonies out here in front of your warehouse like we'd been saying we'd do."

"Oh yeah," said Babs. "I know about this. I kind of agree with her."

"Well, thanks a lot for letting me know," snapped Yoke, her eyes flashing. "Five minutes ago Phil tells me that Eve and Wendy reserved us a ballroom at the Fairmont Hotel. Like we're sixth-graders in a school pageant. Or no, it's worse than that. It's like we're nobles celebrating while all over the world people are suffering. Especially women. I—I really unloaded on Phil. I told him I don't want to get married at all." Yoke's chin quivered and she began crying. "This is turning into a nightmare."

Babs gave Randy a look, and he got to his feet. "Hey, Saint, let's go upstairs and look at Phil's blimp. You too, Willa Jean."

"Yaaar," said Saint. Willa Jean strutted rapidly across the floor and jumped into Randy's arms.

Phil had cantilevered a kind of staircase of mini-trampolines out from the side of Babs's warehouse. You could climb to the roof by hopping from one elastic sheet to the next. And there was a fireman's pole for coming back down. Phil and Yoke had added three more rooms to their original alley-nest; each room was level with one of the layers of the trampolines.

"Feel like one o' them fish," Randy observed to Saint as they bounced upward.

"A salmon," agreed Saint. "Heading upstream to spawn. Hey, Phil, watcha doing? We're here to spawn all over everything."

"Hi, guys," said Phil, looking up from a big flat air bag lying on the roof. "I'm working on the Phlyte Blimp. Trying to. I can't think. They're fighting in Oakland. Look over across the bay, you can see the fires."

Sure enough, across the water smoke was streaming up from the city of Oakland. Yet high above the smoke it was a pleasant spring day with fluffy white clouds against the pale blue.

"I just checked the news," said Phil. "It started as a gang thing. And now it's turned racial. Everyone getting even for getting even for getting even. How long is it we've had the allas now?"

"Two months," said Randy. "You'd think people would have it together by now." Two months ago had been when he'd realized that he loved Babs. And in another month they'd be married. If only things would calm down. If only people would remember to be kind.

"Oh, shit," said Saint. "Look at Oakland now."

Someone had just done something to make one of Oakland's office buildings collapse. Maybe they'd alla-converted part of its foundation into air. The wind shifted toward them and Randy could smell a whiff of smoke, could hear a faint crackle of gunfire.

"Make them stop," prayed Randy, and just about then a flashing bright saucer appeared in the sky over Oakland. The Metamartians to the rescue, once again. There was a distant rumble; the saucer was talking to the men fighting. And now a series of rays darted down from it; it was said that when a saucer appeared at a battle scene, it would destroy everyone's alla-made weapons.

"The allas have to go," said Randy, really believing this for the first time. "It's not going to be worth it. Especially after the aliens leave."

"Let's fly to Oakland and help," said Phil. "We can use my blimp."

"Good idea," said Randy. "And while we're at it, maybe we can get close enough to the saucer to talk to the Metamartians."

Phil used the alla to instantly fill his Phlyte Blimp up with helium. The great balloon was covered with something like imipolex linguini that Phil called "Smart Hair." The blimp bobbed above the rooftop and a sudden breeze threatened to sweep it away. But then the plastic linguini began intensely beating, holding the unwieldy shape in place.

"It has passenger slings for us to sit on," said Phil, indicating a trio of loops that dangled from the blimp's underside.

"Have you actually tested it?" asked Saint.

"Sure," said Phil. "Well, not with three people. But if something goes wrong, we can always alla ourselves some hang-glider wings. Come on. Let's dart over to Oakland and make sure all the injured people have healer machines. We can be there in three or four minutes."

"I'm for it," said Randy. "Be nice to do something good for a change."

Once they were settled into the slings, the blimp's Smart Hair began rippling in steady waves. They slid through the air as smoothly as a pumpkin seed. Phil steered them toward the saucer, but before they got close to it, the bright disk darted away, moving too fast for the eye to follow. And then they were above the bloody streets of Oakland.

"Careful," said Saint. "Someone might shoot at us." But the saucer had temporarily disarmed everyone. The weaponless fighters were slinking away, leaving dozens of injured people on the streets and sidewalks. Phil landed the blimp, and the three boys moved among the injured, using their allas to make healer machines. Soon more rescue workers began to appear. And then some builders arrived, using allas to clear away the rubble and repair the shattered buildings.

"Looks like things are under control now," said Saint after a while.

"Let's go back," said Phil. "I have to tell Yoke I'm sorry."

"Shitfire," said Randy, checking the time. "My dad's about to come."

The ride back was a little slower, as a strong wind had started blowing from the ocean. But the blimp's Smart Hair kept them on a steady course. The boys were quiet, thinking of what they'd seen. Some people had been too far gone for the healer machines.

Back on the warehouse roof, Phil deflated his blimp and examined its skin, using his fuzzy pocketknife to tweak its little flaps. "I'm glad this worked," he said. "Those poor people."

"Your blimp is good, Phil," said Saint.

"I've been thinking," said Phil. "I don't actually need moldie-quality imipolex to make these things. Which is important, because I want to keep making them even if we get rid of the allas and imipolex is expensive again. I think regular production-quality piezoplastic would work if I used a simple enough algorithm. Your dad could help me with the code, Randy. How soon is he coming, anyway?"

"Could be any taaahm now." Randy peered up at the sky.

"Good," said Phil, patting his flattened blimp. "Okay, I'm going down to talk with Yoke." He jumped off the edge of the building and slid down the fire pole.

"After seeing Oaktown like that, I'm against the allas too," Saint told Randy. "I need to think of a career that doesn't depend on them."

"What about your water bicycles?"

"Good idea. Maybe your dad could help me with their DIM chips."

"He knows a lot," said Randy with a proud smile. "Shitfire, my father invented limpware engineering and the uvvy too. When I was growing up, I never realized I had such important relatives. I thought I was just a nobody from nowhere."

"Not anymore," said Saint, looking upward. "And, yaaar! Here he comes!"

A shiny moldie form was descending, riding on the sparkling column of an ion jet. It was Cobb with someone inside him. Randy tucked Willa Jean under his arm, and he and Saint slid down off the roof to stand by the patch of gravel Cobb was heading toward. Hearing the hollering, Babs, Phil, and Yoke came out of the warehouse. Randy noticed that Phil and Yoke were smiling and holding hands again.

Cobb plopped gently to the ground and split open, disgorging a gray-haired fifty-year-old man. The man looked happy to be out in the air. He made a little bow. "Hi, everyone, I'm Willy Taze." He sized up the five of them, then stepped forward and shook Randy's hand.

"My son," said the gray-haired man, looking Randy over. "We finally meet face-to-face. Sorry it wasn't sooner. This feels good. I was a fool to put it off. I was sorry to hear about your mother, she was gone before I got a chance to talk this over with her. Quite a woman. So you're getting married, eh? Marriage is the part I never did. I'm such a geek that I only managed one single squirt inside a woman my whole entire life. And you seized that unique opportunity to get born, Randy. My very best sperm cell. Good boy!"

"Thanks," said Randy, quite overwhelmed. "So you really my pa?"

"He's my grandson and you're my great-grandson," exulted Cobb. "High time you two met! For God's sake give him a hug, Willy. You won't catch anything."

So Randy and his father hugged. It felt good. Willy beamed at him, then turned to the others, talking a mile a minute, like a man who's been alone too long. Randy knew the feeling.

"Hello, Yoke, it's great to see you again," said Willy. "That's so wonderful that you got us the allas! What a change those things are making on the Moon! So far we loonies have been too smart to get into any wars with each other. Not like the stupid mudders."

"We were just over in Oakland givin' people healer machines," put in Randy. "Things was mighty screwed up."

"Up on the Moon, everyone's been busy making sublunar parks and ponds," said Willy. "You wouldn't recognize the place anymore. And the moldies are happily stockpiling megatons of imipolex. Your parents send their best, Yoke, and believe it or not, they're getting along fine. I think almost losing Darla shocked some sense into Whitey. Joke's flying down in a few days, and Corey Rhizome is coming with her. And this must be Phil Gottner?" Willy smiled and shook Phil's hand. "Randy told me a little about you on the uvvy." Willy turned his attention to the two others. "And these other two must be Sta-Hi's kids—I think it's Babs and Saint? I mean 'Stahn,' not 'Sta-Hi.' He's still clean and sober, right? Wavy. You wouldn't want to be at a wedding with the old Sta-Hi. Isn't this something? You're such beautiful young people, all of you. Especially Randy! And Babs! Imagine having Babs for my daughter-in-law! I have to admit that I'm thrilled."

"Hi, Willy," said Saint. "I'm glad to meet you. Phil and me were hoping you'd help us with some limpware engineering."

"Don't start pickin' his brain just yet," said Randy. "Let him go inside and get some food. He's been cooped up inside Cobb for a week."

"My son!" exclaimed Willy, hugging Randy again. "You look wonderful. This is more than I deserve! Yes, I'm going inside to rest."

"I'll be there in a minute," said Randy, looking down at Cobb, who'd let himself slump to the ground. "How you feelin', Great-grandfather Cobb?"

"I'm tired," said Cobb, puddled on the ground. "And I heard some really bad news just while I was landing. I think I'll lie out here in the sun for a while. If I alla up a bottle of quantum dots, will you pour them into me?"

"Shore."

Like most moldies now, Cobb had his alla embedded inside his flesh.

Without moving a muscle, he projected out a mesh and alla-made a shiny gray magnetic bottle of quantum dots. Randy held up the little bottle to the light, checking the meter.

"You want the full terawatt, Cobb?"

"You know it," said Cobb, growing a funnel up out of his chest. Randy poured the glittering dust of the quantum dots into the old man moldie. "Thanks," said Cobb. "That helps; but I've just about had it with this planet. People are so—did my stink-eater bug catch on at least?"

"It did," said Randy. "Big-time. People and moldies are gettin' along better all the taahm. It's just the men fighting each other that's ruining things. As for me personally—I got such a good thing goin' with Babs I can't hardly remember what I used to see in bein' a cheeseball. Leave Cobb alone, Willa Jean, run on inside." Randy pushed Willa Jean away from Cobb and toward the warehouse door. "Everyone's grateful to you, Cobb. But what's this about you bein' tired? We was expectin' you to run for mayor."

"No," said Cobb. "I'm ready to move further on. Politics should die. Politics used to be about dividing up scarce resources—and nothing's scarce anymore. With the allas here, politics is just about hatred and war. Want to know why I'm so bummed all of a sudden? Guess what I heard on my uvvy just as I touched down? People have started throwing kiloton bombs."

"Nukes?" asked Randy. "I thought—"

"Conventional explosives," said Cobb. "If you ask it to, an alla can make you a thousand ton cube of TNT. Some people just realized. Most of downtown Jerusalem's gone. And now I'm hearing"—Cobb sighed. "Baghdad too."

"We should block the allas from making weapons," said Randy.

"But what's a weapon?" said Cobb. "Gasoline is a weapon. Oxygen and hydrogen. Acid. Even a rock is a weapon if you drop it from high in the sky. I think we should tell the Metamartians to tell Om to take away the allas."

"I saw their saucer in the sky over Oakland earlier today," said Randy. "And then they darted away. I bet they were going to the Mideast. Jerusalem and Baghdad got flattened?"

"Yes," said Cobb.

"What should I do?"

"Live your life, however much of it's left for you. Marry Babs."

Yoke. June 1

"Hold still," said Joke, leaning forward to touch up Yoke's eye makeup. The twin sisters had always preferred using each other to using mirrors.

"There," said Joke. "Perfect." She leaned back and smiled. The two of them were in a bridal dressing room off the Fairmont Hotel's top-floor ballroom. It was almost time for the wedding. Yoke could hear music; Saint and some of his friends were brain-playing ancient flute motets on sheets of imipolex-with hints of heavy metal. "I'm glad we're doing this on Earth," said Joke. "It's so pretty down here. If only things don't keep getting worse. The heavy gravity is good for a ceremony. It makes everything seem solemn." Joke moved her arms in slow, marching motions. "Are you stoked?"

"You like Phil, don't you, Joke?"

"He's great. That blond hair and dark chin—yummy. And he looks at you like he's so in love. Emul and Berenice approve too." Thanks to some unfortunate wetware meddling, Joke had been born with two pushy robots' minds coded into the right hemisphere of her brain. It made her very knowledgeable, but her spatial perception was lousy. "They, um, did some research on him."

"Do I want to know?" asked Yoke.

"It's all good," said Joke. "Emul says Phil has a clean criminal record and he's exactly who he says he is. And Berenice says Phil's genome is not only mutation-free, but a very good fit for ours. I mean yours. So I wanted to tell you. Sorry."

"Oh, it doesn't matter," said Yoke. "I've abandoned any hope of privacy—at least for today. What a circus."

"And here comes the clown!" said Yoke. A hard-looking man was peeking in the dressing room door. Their father, Whitey Mydol. He had a Mohawk strip of hair that went down the back of his head and continued on into his shirt collar. And over the shirt he was wearing a tuxedo. "I'll go check on Ma," said Joke, and moved out of the way; the tiny dressing room was only big enough for two people.

"Clown is right," said Whitey, his rough face splitting in a surprisingly pleasant smile. "I'm walking funny. How many days did it take you to get used to this gravity, Yoke?"

"Three, four weeks. Hi, Pop. How do I look?"

"You look—oh, Yoke, you look like an angel. You remind me of Darla—back when. She says our twenty-fifth anniversary is coming up this month."

"Are you being nice to her, Pop?"

"What a question!" Whitey shifted uneasily, looking too big for the tiny, white-upholstered bride's room. "Don't worry about us, Yoke, things are better. I was bad, but I'm being good again. Anyway, it's me who should be asking you things. Like are you totally sure you want to marry Phil? I can get you out of it if you want." He cracked his scarred knuckles as if thinking about a fight.

"I'm doing this," said Yoke firmly. "Are you with me or not?"

"For sure." Whitey ran his hand back and forth over his head, fluffing his Mohawk. This was the first time Yoke had ever seen him wearing a shirt and suit coat, let alone a tuxedo. "I just thought it's the kind of thing a father's supposed to ask. Phil's a good man. And we've already paid for the room." He gave a grim chuckle. "Might as well do it, then, before some dook sets off a bomb. How do we know when to march up the aisle?"

"When the music changes." And then it did.

"Here Comes the Bride," said Whitey, holding out his arm.

In the little hallway, they found Babs and Stahn, coming out of their own dressing room. While Yoke's dress was a sleek sheath of silk with a tulle veil, Babs had gone "smart art"; her dress and hair were alive with slowly moving pearl DIM heads.

The Fairmont owners had alla-remodeled the top-floor hall-room with a gorgeous parquet wood floor and white silk-covered walls winking with little diamonds. There were dozens of floor-to-ceiling windows, all flung wide-open to let in the gentle June breeze. The sweetness of it caught in Yoke's throat. If only the world could stop its downward spiral. Five more cities had been blown up in the past four weeks.

The chairs were arranged so that the ballroom's aisle was double wide; that way Yoke, Whitey, Babs, and Stahn could walk up side by side, with nobody first and nobody second. Waiting up in front by the windows were Randy and Phil, standing on either side of—Cobb Anderson.

It had developed that none of the four betrothed had a close enough church affiliation to know of a particular minister to use. So Cobb had quickly picked up a Gimmie justice-of-the-peace license and offered to perform the ceremony himself. The old man moldie claimed he was tired, but he still loved to put himself at the center of things. Randy was thrilled to be getting married by his great-grandfather, and Babs didn't mind. As for Yoke and Phil, they too were glad to have Cobb supervise this religious ceremony-for had not each of the three seen the same Divine SUN?

Though it was a beautiful service, the time seemed to pass in funny spurts. Everything was crawling while they were walking up the aisle. This was the part Yoke had always visualized as a little girl thinking about weddings. Walking up the aisle in your bridal gown. It was almost as if she could feel her own eyes watching her. The man at the end of the aisle had always been vague, but now, today, he was clear. Dear Phil. Then things speeded up, and suddenly Yoke and Phil were saying "I will" and "I do." Time all but stopped for the ring part and the kiss. Phil had a brand-new ring for Yoke, which was good. Babs and Randy's vows happened in fast-forward; Yoke didn't hear a word of them. And then they were walking out in slow motion and it felt to Yoke like something she had done a hundred times before.

The waiters cleared the chairs away and set out big tables that they filled with alla-made food; Phil and Babs had made up the designs for the wedding feast. Darla was one of the first to hug Yoke, and then Whitey and Joke. And then Yoke hugged Randy and Babs.

"We're married," laughed Babs. "It's going to be so fun." But there was a shrill edge to her gaiety. Disaster was stalking them all.

Everyone was there. Yoke's bridesmaid was Joke, of course, and Babs's was her art-gallery friend Kundry Asiz. Saint was Phil's best man, and Corey Rhizome served as Randy's.

Randy and Corey had taken quite a liking to each other over the last couple of weeks. One thing they had in common was that they were both really into garage-style limpware engineering. Corey even helped Yoke to finally get her imipolex coral working. Yoke's new thing this week was growing her reefs in air instead of water; she'd started using DIM gnats for the polyps. In fact yesterday she'd grown a fabulous organic-looking headboard for her and Phil's bed. It was a struggle to keep on doing things, with the murders and battles and bombing getting worse every day. But love and art still mattered; yes, they mattered more than hate and war.

The older generation at the wedding party included Darla and Whitey, Stahn and Wendy, Randy's father Willy Taze, Phil's mother Eve, and even Phil's stepmother Willow. Phil's Uncle Rex was there too, as well as his grandmother Isolde and his great-aunt Hildegarde, who had the most astonishing face. They all thought Yoke was wonderful, and said they'd known she was perfect for Phil when they'd seen him talking to her at poor Kurt's funeral. Oh, and Randy's newfound aunt Della Taze had turned up from San Diego, mainly to see Willy. Della had brought her aunt along, seventy-nine-year-old Isle, a bit wobbly and sour, but Cobb Anderson's daughter nonetheless. Cobb was overwhelmed to see her.

Among the younger guests, Terri and Tre Dietz had come up from Santa Cruz with their kids Dolf and Wren, who were loving it. In honor of the happy day—and who knew how many more happy days there would be?—Randy and the Dietzes even made friends, with apologies and forgiveness all around. In fact little Wren was on the floor playing with Randy's plastic chicken Willa Jean. Aarbie Kidd hadn't been invited, but Theodore was there with a leather biker as his date. Derek and his dog Umberto had come with Kundry. There were plenty of others as well; in fact at the last minute, Yoke's friends Kandie and Cocole had even turned up from the Moon, they said they'd been wanting to visit Earth anyway, so why not now, before it was all blown up.

There were even a few moldies among the guests. Phil had asked Isis Snooks, who'd been such a help with his blimps, and Isis had brought along the flashy Thutmosis as her date. Wendy and Cobb each had a few moldie friends, and they were there too. Thanks to the stinkeater bug, mixing with moldies wasn't much of a problem anymore, so long as you had an open mind.

People were drinking champagne like there'd be no tomorrow, jabbering away like magpies, everyone jumping at every loud noise. In the last month, Dakar, Hamburg, Hong Kong, Belfast, Antwerp, and Paris had been hit by enormous bombs. Allas had repaired the buildings, but a lot of people had died. And just yesterday New York City had been bombed too. Everyone was on edge, waiting for the next thing to happen. And then it did.

"A flying saucer!" screamed Phil's mother, Eve. "Look out, Phil! Oh, what if they've come for you again?"

The saucer hanging outside the ballroom windows was a traditional metal disk with a dome in the middle. The Metamartians' ship.

"They can help us!" shouted Randy. "They can take away the allas!"

The frames and sashes of the windows quivered as if water were passing over them, and then the saucer had slid through the wall and into the ballroom. It rested there, cocked a bit toward one side, just fitting between floor and ceiling. A radial line appeared along the curve of the central dome, and then a pie-shaped sector of the curved metal slid open. Out came eight figures: the seven Metamartians from before, plus a new one, a gray little shape like a bald girl with big, almond-shaped eyes.

Yoke sniffed at the air—yes, there was the scent of old-fashioned moldies. The Metamartians hadn't yet caught the stinkeater bug.

"We are here to salute the nuptials," said Shimmer, holding up her hands and making soothing gestures. "Please remain calm, dear friends. We come in peace, seeking your aid. I am Shimmer from Metamars, and my companions are Ptah, Peg, Josef, Siss, Wubwub, Haresh. As many of you know, it is we and our god Om who have brought mankind and moldies the alla. And our gift has been mediated by these four whose marriages you celebrate today: Yoke, Phil, Randy, and Babs. We too have a blessed event to rejoice in: the birth of our sevenfold daughter Lova." The gray little Lova bent her mouth up into a U-shaped smile and bowed, making flowing gestures with her long-fingered hands.

"Skip the bullshit and take away the fucking allas!" yelled Willow. "They're ruining our world and you know it!"

"She's right," called Randy. "Tell Om to take the allas away!"

"Please, Om!" shouted Babs. "The allas are wrong for us. We aren't ready."

Lova bowed again.

"She's butt-ugly," said Yoke, all her tension rushing out into a sudden guffaw. "They're making fun of us."

"Careful," said Darla, coming up behind Yoke. "They're going to ask for something big. It's like in a fairy tale. The witches at the princess's wedding."

"You right, Darla," said Wubwub. "But what we after is no big thing: we need help gettin' outta here is all. We don't know which way to go toward two-dimensional time. And we got the notion one of you can help us. How 'bout it, Phil?"

Yoke threw her arms around Phil. "You leave him alone!"

"Wait!" said Phil, digging in his pocket. "Maybe it's this thing—" He pulled out his little black ball with the bright spots inside it. "Is this what you need, Wubwub? The fishbowl thing I got from Om? It's a star map, isn't it? Turn off the allas and use the star map to go."

"It's a map, but it ain't gonna help us none," said Wubwub, showing his crooked, yellow teeth in a long smile. "But let me see it anyhow."

"Throw it to him, Phil!" said Yoke. "Don't let him come near you!"

So Phil tossed his little ball, and Wubwub caught it. The Metamartians pressed forward to peer at it, and the beetle Josef actually crawled around upon it.

"Yes, Om already gave me one of these through my alla," said Shimmer shortly. "It's a star map, but it's of no use. It only shows your part of the cosmos. Your map shows your zone, and we have another map that shows our zone, the good part of the cosmos with two-dimensional time. But there's no master map that shows the interdimensional connection. We can't find the passage, and we can't understand Om's explanations of where it is."

There was an explosion somewhere outside, not too terribly distant. A few of the guests screamed.

"Turn off the allas right now!" cried Yoke. "Can't you see they're a disaster?"

"We can ask Om to do it," said Ptah quietly. "In fact Om can even disactualize all of the bombs and weapons that people's allas have made. Turn them back into air. All this can happen—provided that one of you will help us on our way. It's your ability to dream that we need, you see. Human dreaming is a rudimentary reaching out toward two-dimensional time. If one of you comes with us as we travel out across your galaxy, then we can watch this person repeatedly sleep and dream—and we'll be able to sniff our way out toward the fat part of time. We need a harbor pilot, in other words. A native guide. So how about it, Phil? You can bring Yoke if you like."

A sudden mesh of alla-control lines appeared around the seven Metamartians. It was Whitey, standing at Yoke's side, holding out his alla and trying to turn the aliens into air. But at the instant Whitey said "Actualize," each of the aliens hopped off to one side. Whitey accomplished nothing more than turning some air into air.

"Senseless violence," said Shimmer. "How typical. What's the matter with you men anyway? We've been trying to calm things down, but it seems to be hopeless. All we're asking today is that an Earthling accompany us as we move on. We want to take one of you who knows us a little bit. If we simply abduct some random human, they'll be too frightened to help us. And not everyone can dream in the right way. Phil's our first choice because his dreams are just right. Om's been looking through people's memories. Those mountains you always dream about, Phil—they point toward two-dimensional time."

"I can dream as well as Phil can," said Cobb, his voice loud and firm. "I dream about mountains all the time. Leave the young folks alone."

"The great old man," said Peg.

"He not human," said Siss.

"Yes, he is," said Shimmer, cocking her head as if listening to an inner voice. "In fact, Om says he'll be fine. She hadn't thought to look before, but her records show that Cobb's dreams are just as useful as Phil's."

"Moldies dream?" Darla whispered to Yoke. "I didn't know that."

"Of course we do," said Isis Snooks, overhearing. "What did you think we were? Machines? I'm glad Cobb is doing this. It'll get us some xoxxin' respect."

"Come aboard, Cobb," Ptah was saying. "We'll fly to the outer atmosphere and power up to just below the speed of light. Once we get enough readings, we'll chirp into personality waves and really be on our way. We'll show you how."

"If I come, will Om turn off the allas?" asked Cobb.

"Om is ready to do that," said Shimmer. "By now she has collected a complete enough set of human memories. She'll remember your race forever. She only hopes you don't feel you've been cheated once the allas are gone. But the constant killing and the explosions—"

"I suppose we're too primitive," said Babs sadly.

"It's not just that," said Josef. "It's that one-dimensional time isn't a good place for realware. Some of your bombings weren't even deliberate. Apparently people have started setting off bombs by accident in their dreams. The more that people worry about bombs, the more bombs there will be. Your human dreaming is a risky business. Although Metamartians don't dream, we've occasionally had runaway alla misuse, our own epidemics of mass hysteria. But for us a global disaster doesn't much matter—because we have so many strands of time. No, I'm afraid that at this stage of your culture, and with your uncontrolled dreaming, your single line of time is simply too fragile for the allas. You do well to want Om to take them away."

"Then it's a deal," said Cobb. "I'll come with you and dream the way toward two-dimensional time. And you'll ask Om to take away the allas."

The Metamartians were silent for a moment, communing with Om.

"Everyone sure they don't want no more alla?" called Wub-wub. There was another explosion outside, this time closer than before. "Om wants to know."

"No more alla!" screamed the crowd.

"Hurry up," cried Yoke. "Do it now! And have Om take away the alla-made weapons like Shimmer said she could."

"So be it," said Ptah.

Yoke felt a wriggling in the pouch at her waist. Her alla, and everyone else's, was gone. The air filled with a palpable sense of safety and ease. The people and moldies laughed and hugged each other.

"Lez go, boss," said Wubwub to Cobb. "Know what I'm sayin'?"

"Oh, Cobb," said Yoke, kissing the old man moldie.

"It's fine," said Cobb. "I've hung around Earth long enough."

"It would be easy for me to use your software to make a new one of you to live here," Willy told Cobb. "We have your software stored on an S-cube."

"Please don't do that," said Cobb. "I don't want anyone bringing me back to Earth again. I'm done here. I'll travel on with the Metamartians, but when this trip plays out, I want to finally make it into the SUN."

"He's right," said Yoke. "Cobb deserves his chance to go to Heaven."

"Good-bye, everyone," said Cobb. "And bless you, my children."

He strode up into the saucer with the Metamartians. The hotel wall wavered again, and the flashing disk of the saucer vanished into the heavens.

It was a perfect day. The newlyweds' eyes were soft, their kisses wet, their hearts free, the big world real.

AFTERWORD

I just finished rereading the four *Wares* novels for this omnibus edition. The books had been scanned from the old paperbacks, and I had to correct a number of typos that had crept in. Being a writer, I can't reread something of mine without seeing things to fix, so I made a few small tweaks as well—making the novels consistent from one to the next, and smoothing the flow. But don't worry, the old outrageous scenes are all here in their full rough vigor.

It took me about twenty years to write these novels, and it's an odd experience to fast-forward through them in a few days. Naturally, I ask myself what the books were in fact about. I see three main threads: consciousness, drugs, and eyeball kicks.

The consciousness thread explores what it takes for something to support a mind. *Software* (1982) suggests that your mind as a software pattern that could run on a robot body. *Wetware* (1988) points out that DNA is a tweakable program, so you can in fact grow a new meat body for your software to live in. *Freeware* (1997) proposes that aliens could travel as radio signals coding up the software for both their minds and their bodies. And in *Realware* (2000), the characters obtain a device which can create living beings from their descriptions.

The drug thread asks how the humans and other beings of the future will get high. What kinds of visions will they have, and what kinds of problems? As the inevitable consequence of getting older, my attitude towards drugs shifted a little over the course of writing the four *Wares*. In the second two volumes, the characters are having more problems with their drug use and by the end—incredibly—Sta-Hi himself gets sober. Even so, right up to the end of *Realware*, I remain devoted to breaking free of consensus reality, and to the dadaist humor and skewed dialog that emerges from the stoner mind-set.

The eyeball kicks thread is about depicting the gnarly, trippy scenes that might occur in a future where we're mashing together different notions of consciousness with a countercultural attitude. I put a lot of energy into certain set-piece scenes and iconic images—I think of the two moldies juggling each others' bodies as sets of balls, the birth of Manchile after a nine-day pregnancy, Randy Karl Tucker tripping on camote with his moldie girlfriend wrapped around his head, and, of course, the Little Kidders preparing to eat Sta-Hi Mooney's brain from his skull with cheap steel spoons.

⌇

How did I end up writing these strange novels?

At age sixty, in 1974, my father, Embry Cobb Rucker, had a heart attack. In order to replace his clogged coronary arteries, his surgeon turned to bypass surgery.

This operation was still quite new. They opened up Pop's whole chest, leaving a vertical scar at least a foot long. The drugs and the trauma had a bad effect on him. He had tortuous, freaky dreams that set him to crying out in his sleep.

Pop's brush with death seemed to change him. He grew a white beard. He'd show me the scar on his chest and run his finger along it like undoing a zipper. "This is where they opened me up," he'd say in a tight voice.

His sense that he was living on borrowed time made him unhappy with his lot, and less patient with my mother. He fell into an affair with another woman. My parents divorced in 1979—and they never spoke to each other again. Mom even had her wedding melted into a puddle of gold that she occasionally wore as a pendant. It was awful.

My wife and I were in Heidelberg on an academic grant at this time— among other things, I'd write an academic paper called, "Towards Robot Consciousness." Pop and his new woman friend came to visit us in the fall of 1979. It was a mournful, uncomfortable encounter. Pop was a mess—he was consumed with guilt about leaving Mom, and he was drinking more heavily than ever before. His girlfriend was stiff and brittle with us. She disapproved of me, as if I were unworthy of being Pop's son.

After a few long days, I put them on a train for Paris. They were planning to stay in a good hotel and live it up. Poor Pop. He'd done his duty all his life. Now Death was stalking him and he was trying to have fun. Seeing his train pull away, I felt as if my heart would break.

What to do? I started work on my third science fiction novel. I figured I'd write a transreal novel inspired by actual people I knew—but without overtly using myself as a character, as I'd done in my previous two novels *Spacetime Donuts* and *White Light*. I sensed that this move would open up the vibe.

One character, called Cobb Anderson, would be an old man modeled on my father in his current state. To some extent I could project myself into this character too. For all our disagreements over the years, Pop and I never were all that different. Another factor in my writing about Pop was that I was in some sense trying to inoculate myself against ending up like him—besotted, afraid of death, and on the run from my family.

The other character in my novel was a young guy called Sta-Hi Mooney, based on my wild and wacky friend Dennis Poague—a guy who used to turn up in Geneseo, New York, to visit his big brother Lee who was teaching there with me in the early 1970s. What I liked about Dennis was that he seemed to have no internal censor. He always said exactly what he was thinking. He was relatively uneducated, but he had a fanciful mind, and a hipster, motor-mouth style of speech. And, as with Cobb, there's something of me in Sta-Hi, too.

In the opening scene, Cobb is sitting on a beach in Florida drinking sherry, and he's approached by his double. At first I thought I was writing a time-travel novel, but then I hit upon the notion of treating the human mind as software. Cobb's double is a robot copy of his physical form, some other robots will extract Cobb's personality from his brain, and they'll run the extracted human software on the robot who looks like Cobb.

"Software." In 1979, this was a technical and little-known word—I'd picked it up from an article in the *Scientific American*. I decided to use it for the title of my book. I finished *Software* near the end of our stay in Heidelberg, in the summer of 1980, and I had no trouble selling it to Ace Books, who'd already published *White Light*.

My idea of copying a person onto a robot was a fresh concept in those days, and my book also drew some intensity from its father/son theme and from the colorful anarchism of my robot characters—the boppers.

I should mention that, although I knew all about the theory of computation from my studies of mathematical logic, I didn't know jack about real-world computers—we SF writers very often don't know the technical details of what we're talking about. In 1979, the only way to access a computer was to use a text terminal with its nasty, inscrutable protocols—or to feed a deck of punched programming cards to a giant machine in a basement.

An oddly anachronistic thing about *Software* is that, in those years, I couldn't imagine there being a really small computing device with the power of a human brain. So, instead of giving my Cobb-emulating robot a supercomputer that could fit inside this bopper's skull, I had the Cobb-robot's brain be a big supercooled clunker that follows the robot around in the back of a refrigerated van that's disguised as a Mr. Frostee truck. But that's okay. It makes the novel more fun. And, at a deeper level, the brain in the truck is nice concrete symbol for an organization which maintains complete control over its agents.

⌇

Philip K. Dick died of a stroke in the spring of 1982. By then he'd become one of my favorite authors, and I'd began thinking about him a lot. At this point, I was living as a freelance writer in, ironically enough, the conservative town of Lynchburg, Virginia.

Some writers and editors were organizing an annual literary award honoring the memory of Philip K. Dick—and in the fall of 1982, my Ace Book editor, Susan Allison, told me that my novel *Software* had been nominated. I felt like I had a good shot at the award, given that my SF has that something of the same off-kilter, subversive quality as Phil's. I began dreaming that my writing income might rise to a sustainable level.

And in March of 1983, I got the Philip K. Dick Award for *Software*. My wife Sylvia and I flew up to New York City for the awards ceremony. Earlier that evening we had dinner with Susan Allison, the editor David Hartwell, a writer friend of Phil's called Ray Faraday Nelson, and the well-known author Tom Disch—who was the one who'd initially proposed starting the award. Disch was a good guy, immensely hip and cultured.

Our whole party walked over to Times Square, where we saw *Bladerunner*, the brand-new movie based on Phil's novel, *Do Androids Dream of Electric Sheep*. On the way over, I talked to Ray Nelson.

I liked the *Bladerunner* movie a lot, particularly the first part, with the blimps bearing electronic billboards, the cop smoking pot while he interviewed the android, and the dark futuristic city with the neon lights glinting off pavements slick with rain. The last part of the movie seemed too violent, and inappropriately so, given that Phil's *Androids* novel had largely been about empathy and peace. But that's Hollywood.

"Phil would have loved it," Ray Nelson reassured me. Actually, I'd been wondering if Phil's worrying about the movie in progress was what drove him to his fatal stroke.

The award ceremony was in an artist's loft, with the hallways covered in reflective silver paint. One of the first people I ran into was my artist friend Barry Feldman from college. Incredibly, he was wearing a suit, and he looked like Chico Marx at the opera. He seemed just a bit envious of me getting an award—although Barry was a great painter, working all day long in his studio, he wasn't breaking into the gallery scene. On a sudden whim, I told Barry he could pose as me and enjoy the fame.

As I was such an outsider to the SF scene, nobody knew what I looked like, and the substitution worked for about half an hour. Barry stood by the door shaking hands and signing books, twinkling with delight. I stood across the room, drinking and hanging out with Sylvia, my friend Eddie Marritz, his wife Hanna, and the editor Gerard Vanderleun, who'd handled my non-fiction book *The Fourth Dimension* for Houghton-Mifflin. In the end the identities got sorted out, and I met the people I needed to meet—among them was Susan Protter, who'd end up being my literary agent for the years to come.

Later that evening I stood on the bar at one end of the silvery room and delivered a short speech that I'd composed on the plane up from Lynchburg.

> "If I say that Phil Dick is not really dead, then this is what I mean: He was such a powerful writer that his works exercise a sort of hypnotic force. Many of us have been Phil Dick for brief flashes, and these flashes will continue as long as there are readers. . . . I'd like to think that, on some level, Phil and I are just different instances of the same Platonic form—call it the gonzo-philosopher-SF-writer form, if you like. . . . If it is at all possible for a spirit to return from the dead, I would imagine that Phil would be the one to do it. Let's keep our eyes open tonight, he may show up."

At the end of 1985, I'd just finished writing *Mind Tools*, a popular non-fiction book about math, and I was stoked to write science fiction again. I always start missing SF before too long—the funky old-school grooves, the wild thought experiments, the idiosyncratic characters with their warped argot, the eternal pursuit of transcendent truth.

Ace had let *Software* go out of print, so now Susan Protter got me a deal with John Douglas at Avon Books to reissue *Software* along with a projected sequel to be called *Wetware*. Both would appear as mass-market paperbacks.

Odd as it now seems, it was only with *Wetware*—my thirteenth book— that I started writing on a computer. The previous dozen manuscripts were all typed, with much physical cutting and pasting. Sometimes, if I couldn't face typing up a fair copy of the marked-up and glued-together final draft, I'd hire a typist.

But with *Wetware* I was ready to change. I was still a freelance writer in Lynchburg, Virginia. Sylvia, the kids and I drove up to Charlottesville in November, 1985, and visited the only computer store in central Virginia. I ended up with what was known as a CP/M machine, made by Epson, with Peachtext word-processing software, and a daisy wheel printer. The system came with a Pac-Man-like computer game called *Mouse Trap* that the kids loved to play.

While I was gearing up for *Wetware*, I'd started what I thought was going to be a short story called "People That Melt," and I sent the story fragment to my cyberpunk friend William Gibson, hoping that he'd help me finish it and, not so incidentally, lend the growing luster of his name.

He said he was too busy to complete such a project, but he did write a couple of pages for me, and said I was free to fold them into my mix in any fashion I pleased. As I continued work on my "People That Melt" story, it got good to me, and it ended up as the first chapter of *Wetware*. As a tip of the hat, I put in a character named Max Yukawa who resembled my notion of Bill Gibson—a reclusive mastermind with a thin, strangely flexible head.

Once I got rolling, I wrote *Wetware* at white heat. I think I finished the first draft during a six-week period from February to March of 1986. I made a special effort to give the boppers' speech the bizarre Beat rhythms of Kerouac's writing—indeed, I'd sometimes look into Jack's great *Visions of Cody* for inspiration. *Wetware* was a gift from the muse—insane, mind-boggling, and, in my opinion, a cyberpunk masterpiece.

∽

A couple of years later, in 1989, *Wetware* would win me a second Philip K. Dick Award.

This award ceremony was at a smallish regional SF con in Tacoma, Washington. It wasn't like the artists' loft in New York at all. It was in a windowless hotel ballroom with a dinner of rubber ham and mashed potatoes.

I still wasn't making much money from my writing, and I'd started working two day jobs, teaching computer science and programming in Silicon Valley. I didn't have time to write as much as before, which was putting me into a depressed state of mind. Winning the award, I felt like some ruined Fitzgerald character lolling on a luxury liner in the rain—his inheritance has finally come through, but it's too late. He's a broken man.

In my acceptance speech, I talked about why I'd dedicated *Wetware* to Phil Dick, and why, in particular, I'd added a quote from Albert Camus about Sisyphus.

> "I see Sisyphus as the god of writers or, for that matter,
> artists in general. You labor for months and years, rolling

your thoughts and emotions into a great ball, inching it up to the mountain top. You let it go and—*wheee!* It's gone. Nobody notices. And then Sisyphus walks down the mountain to start again. Here's how Camus puts it in his essay, *The Myth of Sisyphus*: 'Sisyphus, proletarian of the gods, powerless and rebellious, knows the whole extent of his wretched condition: it is what he thinks of during his descent. The lucidity that as to constitute his torture at the same time crowns his victory. There is no fate that cannot be surmounted by scorn. One must imagine Sisyphus happy.' "

As so often happens to me, nobody knew what the fuck I was talking about. One of the fans invited me to come to his room and shoot up with ketamine, an offer which I declined. Outside the weather was pearly gray, with uniformed high-school marching bands practicing for something in the empty streets.

~

In 1995, I'd been laid off from my programming job, but I was still a computer science professor at San Jose State University, south of San Francisco. A year had gone by with no novel even started, and now it was time to get back on the One True Path. I decided to return to the world of *Software* and *Wetware*, and I began work on *Freeware*, which would eventually appear in 1997.

I sometimes write well when I don't feel particularly creative. On a given day, it can be good if I'm just doggedly trying to finish the next scene of another goddamn novel. If I feel like I'm crafting a masterwork, the language is more likely to get away from me. When nothing is at stake, I'm free to go wild with the effects and have my characters say brutally honest things—without losing control. I develop a deadpan, surreal tone that I think of as writing degree zero.

The meaning of "freeware" in my novel is that, throughout the universe, alien minds are traveling from world to world in the form of compressed information files—akin to the files you might download from the web. When these rays strike a sufficiently rich computational object, the object may wake up—and begin emulating the alien mind.

In *Freeware* there are indeed a lot of computationally dense objects on Earth—these are descendants of the *Software* boppers, whose minds now inhabit soft bodies made of gnarly, mold-infested piezoplastic. I really liked the idea of having flexible, slug-like robots that stink—as different as possible from the standard images of machine-men. The form of the moldies had a lot to do with the computer science research I'd been doing on chaos and on cellular automata.

My old character Sta-Hi is an ex-senator in *Freeware*—by now he calls himself Stahn. Due to various mishaps, Stahn's wife Wendy has her personality living in a piezoplastic ruff that she wears on her neck. And Stahn's drug and alcohol problems are seriously messing him up.

While I was writing *Freeware* in 1995, I was seeing a lot of my artist and cartoonist friend Paul Mavrides. Mavrides had created a number of images for a parodistic cult called the Church of the SubGenius, which has a not-quite-divinity called "Bob," always spelled with the quotes. The Church, which manages to get people to mail in donations, is a complex, interactive bit of dada art—or rather "bulldada," as they would have it.

More recently, Mavrides had taken to painting on black velvet. But he wasn't painting Elvis, the Virgin of Guadalupe, or dogs playing cards. He was painting the Kennedy assassination, the bodies at Jonestown, the Challenger explosion, the AIDS virus, and cockroaches.

Mavrides was a saturnine, puckish character, a little younger than me, and in some ways an inspiration for my character Corey Rhizome— although I hasten to add that Paul doesn't share most of Corey's bad traits. I thought of Paul as an old-school beatnik, with his finely honed sense of the absurd and his espresso-dark cynicism. I liked taking a day off and driving up to San Francisco to hang in his studio, often smoking pot, later going out with him for coffee or tapas on nearby Valencia Street. During those peaceful afternoons, if we were in the mood, I'd read Paul the latest chapter of my novel-in-progress while he painted. A writer reading new work to his artist pal—that felt like the way life should be.

☙

In January, 1997, I decided to write another *Ware* book, this one to be called *Realware*, with part of it set in the South Pacific island kingdom of Tonga, which my wife and I had recently visited. *Realware* continues along the thread I followed throughout the *Ware* series, that is, the process of expanding the range of things that we might regard as being conscious patterns of information. Ten years later, I'd push my expanding-consciousness thread yet another notch further in my pair of novels *Postsingular* and *Hylozoic*, in which ordinary, unprogrammed matter comes to life.

I structured *Realware* as a pair of love stories—I'd come to feel that it's a good idea to have romance at the heart of a novel. I also included a scene with my main character hugging his estranged father and seeing him off to something like Heaven. And old Cobb himself achieves an apotheosis as well. In writing these scenes, I felt as if I were partially laying to rest the specter of a painful argument I'd had with my father the last time I'd seen him, shortly before his death in 1994. One of the virtues of writing is that you get to revise your past.

I was happy with how *Realware* came out, I felt it had good tightness and focus. But by now I felt like I'd pushed the series as far as I could— although I do sometimes wonder what kinds of adventures Cobb had with the Metamartians in their flying saucer. I got the idea for the very last line of the *Ware Tetralogy* from Sylvia.

∽

One of my other recent writing projects has been an autobiography, with the working title *Nested Scrolls*, slated to appear from PS Publishing and from Forge Books in 2011. Much of the material in this afterword is in fact drawn from my memoir. So seek out *Nested Scrolls* if you want to know what else I've been doing for all these years. And for ongoing information, you can always check my blog, www.rudyrucker.com/blog.

I'm very happy to see my *Wares* in one volume like this, and to reach a new generation of readers. Enjoy the adventures—and seek the gnarl.

—26 April, 2010, Los Gatos

ABOUT THE AUTHOR

Rudy Rucker is a writer and a mathematician who worked for twenty years as a Silicon Valley computer science professor. He is regarded as a contemporary master of science-fiction, and received the Philip K. Dick award twice—for his novels *Software* and *Wetware*. His thirty published books include both novels and non-fiction books. He lives in Los Gatos, California. See his page **www.rudyrucker.com** for more information.